CHANNELING
WONDER

Series in Fairy-Tale Studies

General Editor
Donald Haase, Wayne State University

Advisory Editors
Cristina Bacchilega, University of Hawai'i, Mānoa

Stephen Benson, University of East Anglia

Nancy L. Canepa, Dartmouth College

Anne E. Duggan, Wayne State University

Pauline Greenhill, University of Winnipeg

Christine A. Jones, University of Utah

Janet Langlois, Wayne State University

Ulrich Marzolph, University of Göttingen

Carolina Fernández Rodríguez, University of Oviedo

Maria Tatar, Harvard University

Jack Zipes, University of Minnesota

A complete listing of the books in this series can be found
online at wsupress.wayne.edu

CHANNELING
WONDER

FAIRY TALES
ON
TELEVISION

Edited by Pauline Greenhill
and Jill Terry Rudy

WAYNE STATE UNIVERSITY PRESS

DETROIT

© 2014 by Wayne State University Press, Detroit, Michigan 48201.
All rights reserved. No part of this book may be reproduced without
formal permission. Manufactured in the United States of America.

18 17 16 15 14   5 4 3 2 1

Library of Congress Control Number: 2014936570
ISBN 978-0-8143-3922-0 (paperback);
ISBN 978-0-8143-3923-7 (e-book)

"Ten Minutes Ago" © Richard Rodgers and Oscar Hammerstein II
(and renewed by Williamson Music) used courtesy of Williamson Music (ASCAP).

Designed and Typeset by Bryce Schimanski
Composed in Scala

CONTENTS

PART II
MASCULINITIES AND/OR FEMININITIES

PART III
BEASTLY HUMANS

PREFACE AND ACKNOWLEDGMENTS

Just as in most difficult fairy-tale tasks, works like this don't happen without a lot of magical helpers. *Channeling Wonder* originated with Jill's suggestion to Pauline, at the American Folklore Society meeting in October 2011, that perhaps it was time for a book on fairy tales on TV. Pauline thanks Jill for working with her on the project. In turn, Jill thanks Pauline for taking it on and making it happen in an expeditious and wonderful way. Both thank Pauline's radical research assistant Marcie Fehr for suggesting this book's title: "Channeling Wonder," which makes her our fairy godmother and just goes to show that fairy godmothers can be young and fabulous as well as old and fabulous.

We appreciate the contributors for bearing with us during the process and for responding to our queries and suggestions with grace, equanimity, and speed. (They all clearly have seven-league boots!) The Wayne State University Press reviewers were both kind and rigorous. We also thank Don Haase and Annie Martin for their ongoing warm encouragement and Kristin Harpster, Jamie Jones, Sarah Murphy, Emily Nowak, and Kristina E. Stonehill for helping take the project through so many seemingly impossible tasks!

Pauline thanks the Research Committee of the University of Winnipeg (UW) for funding the development and preparation of *Channeling Wonder* and for a special publication grant. As always, UW research goddess Jennifer Cleary was in our corner. Dean of Arts Glenn Moulaison's very welcome support always includes some quality humor. The Social Sciences and Humanities Research Council of Canada's funding for "Fairy Tale Films: Exploring Ethnographic Perspectives" (2011–2016) (with co-applicants Steven Kohm, Catherine Tosenberger, and Sidneyeve Matrix and collaborators Cristina

Bacchilega and Jack Zipes) was indispensable. Though they were not directly funded by our grant, Cristina's and Jack's support for our work never faltered and never failed. And there are no better colleagues in the universe than the fabulous Women's and Gender Studies department gang at UW. Roewan Crowe, Angela Failler, Fiona Green, Michelle Owen, and Trish Salah, you know I owe you!

Jill thanks the College of Humanities at Brigham Young University and Dean John Rosenberg for a research leave early in this project and for sponsoring the Humanities Center, including the Romantic and Victorian Studies Group, to bring visiting scholars to campus and foster scholarship. She acknowledges especially the contributions of her English department colleagues. Cristina Bacchilega, additionally, has been a crucial early advocate and superb mentor. Exchanges with these scholars, and with our research assistants including Leah Claire Allen, Christa Baxter Drake, Marcie Fehr, Kirstian Lezubski, Kendra Magnus-Johnston, and Allison Norris, have enriched the perspectives behind the book.

Copyeditor Kelly Burch approached our manuscript with humor and discretion—and a remarkably light hand! Indexer Kristy Stewart separated the lentils from the ashes.

Like the heroes of fairy tales, our achievements really result from others' special qualities and talents, and because of them, we got what we wanted. We sincerely hope that our helpers, too, are rewarded for all they've done for us. Fairy-tale justice demands it!

CHANNELING
WONDER

INTRODUCTION

Channeling Wonder

Fairy Tales, Television, and Intermediality

Pauline Greenhill and Jill Terry Rudy

Television has long been a familiar vehicle for presenting fairy tales because it offers a medium in some ways ideal for the genre.[1] TV channels wonder when sounds and images literally float through the air and into television sets (and other devices) in homes, schools, and workplaces. Both more mundane and more wondrous than cinema, it shares these qualities with fairy tales. Even apparently realistic forms like the nightly news employ discourses of "once upon a time" and "happily ever after," for example, describing commoner Kate Middleton's marriage to heir to the British throne Prince William as a fairy tale, a Cinderella story, and so on (e.g., Lyall 2010). While viewers and critics may attend to individual TV shows, Raymond Williams asserts this is "at some distance from . . . the central television experience: the fact of flow" (1974, 95). Williams boldly admits that many of us sit there "hour after hour goggling at the box" because the intentional flow of television creates an experience that works as "the grabbing of attention in the early moments; the reiterated promise of exciting things to come, if we stay." This is why "watching television" aptly describes the experience, more so than tuning in for just one show or event (1974, 94–95). This flow, as Williams theorizes, involves variety becoming a unity. This book invites the contributors and readers to consider what happens when fairy tale, a narrative genre that revels in variation, joins the flow of television experience. Fairy tales hook viewers with their ability to grab attention and promise exciting things to come.

North American audiences might think first of the many Disney productions that have appeared on the small screen, including those originally produced for the cinema. But this volume's contributors demonstrate how into the twenty-first century and across the world, a wide range of fairy tales have made their way into televisual forms. These range from musicals like the Rodgers and Hammerstein *Cinderella*; to Jim Henson's anthology *The StoryTeller*; to short cartoons like the sardonic *Fractured Fairy Tales* that punctuated *Rocky and His Friends* and *The Bullwinkle Show*; to commercials like the Italian *Carosello* series; to children's shows like *Super Why!*; to made-for-TV movies like the American *Snow White: A Tale of Terror,* the French *Bluebeard,* or the British *Red Riding Trilogy*; to series like the Japanese anime *Revolutionary Girl Utena* and *Grimm Masterpiece Theatre [Grimm's Fairy Tale Classics]* and the live-action *I Want to Be Cinderella!, Train Man,* and *Rich Man, Poor Woman.* In addition, tales like "Hansel and Gretel," "Little Red Riding Hood," "Beauty and the Beast," "Snow White," and "Cinderella"—and/or their main characters, themes, and motifs—appear in long-arc serials like *Merlin, Buffy the Vampire Slayer,* and *Dollhouse* and on variety shows, dramas, situation comedies, and reality TV. The television experience means that "television must produce 'parts' that each week embody the whole while also finding, within such repetition, possibilities for novel and diverting variations" (Sconce 2004, 101). This requirement helps to explain why fairy tales remain ubiquitous on TV; they allow the needed variations but still resonate, given the narrative form's familiarity. It also explains the extensive, although not inclusive, range of this essay collection.

Given the fairy tale's potent malleability, it is no surprise that fairy tales, and fairy-tale references and allusions, mesh with television's structures, genres, and modes of presentation. As Kendra Magnus-Johnston's chapter discusses, television's sometimes fleeting and temporary aspect makes it impossible to fully document every use of fairy tales. Still, Kevin Paul Smith (based on Gérard Genette [1997]) posits eight possible ways fairy-tale intertexts can work in literature—and, we would add, on TV—authorized (explicit in the title); writerly (implicit in the title); incorporation (explicit in text); allusion (implicit in text); re-vision (giving an old tale a new spin); fabulation (creating a new tale); metafiction (discussing fairy tales); and architextual/chronotopic (in setting/environment; 2007, 10). Recently, audiences and reviewers alike have interpreted as fresh, offbeat, and risky the new televisual guises of tales that scholars have long studied as cultural texts resonating over centuries. Yet shows appearing since 2011, like *Once Upon a Time* and

Grimm, by no means innovate in bringing live-action fairy tales to television. Even 2012's *Beauty and the Beast* series is based, not on the Aarne-Thompson-Uther (ATU) tale type 425C[2] or the Disney film but on the 1980s–1990s drama series—more reason for the studies in this book, now.

We editors admit that the debuts in fall 2011 of *two* American fairy tale–themed shows on different channels with radically diverse plots and modes prompted us to ask sociologist Erving Goffman's perennial question: "What is it that's going on here?" His situational approach explains "the answer . . . is presumed by the way the individuals then proceed to get on with the affairs at hand" (1974, 8). The shows' convergence drew us and our contributors to get on with using our folklore, literary, film, and cultural studies training to reach toward understanding the relationship between media intersections, participatory behavior, and collective intelligence (see Jenkins 2006). Jessica Tiffin explains fairy tales' prodigious flexibility and multiple purposes: "The essential nonreality of fairy tale, together with its existence as a particularly coherent 'set of signs,' allows it to be playfully manipulated . . . as both structure and fiction. At the same time, play with form—ringing the changes on fairy tale—works particularly well because the form is familiar and highly recognizable" (2009, 20–21). Her ideas apply to the many modes in which fairy tales have appeared on television. They channel the fantastic, the magical, the dark, the dreamy, the wishful, and the wonderful in content and transmission.

Oral and literary fairy tales migrate into diverse media besides television; the cinema, visual arts, opera, ballet, theater, and games offer venues for their plots, themes, images, and characters. Contemporary fairy-tale rewritings and intertexts have garnered scholarly attention too ample to detail (at least from Bacchilega 1997 to Turner and Greenhill 2012). Fairy-tale films merit recent and continuing attention. Jack Zipes's (2011) history considers major figures like Georges Méliès and Walt Disney; analyzes the contribution of animation; studies cinematic tales, tale types, and fairy-tale novels; and shows the remarkable creativity displayed in Central and Eastern Europe. Dani Cavallaro (2011) links mainly European fairy tales and Japanese anime. Pauline Greenhill and Sidney Eve Matrix's edited collection (2010b) gathers work on hybridity, commodification, and feminisms, mainly in American films. Walter Rankin (2007) considers eight blockbuster horror/suspense films and their fairy-tale connections. Some of this work considers material originally presented on television without distinction from cinema.[3]

However, cultural studies scholars have long argued for the recognition of cinema and television as media with diverging sociocultural, political, and economic contexts, creators, audiences, and performance circumstances (see, e.g., Kaplan 1983; Petro 1986; Williams 2003; D'Acci 2004; Bignell 2013). This book distinguishes televised from other filmed fairy tales, seeking to better understand some intertextual and intermedial threads spun and cast by channeling wonder. We suggest that traditional modes of fairy tales and their transmission are to television as modernized modes of fairy tales and their transmission are to cinema. Film has a formal and professional mode of transmission and reception, and TV a more informal and local one.

Folklorists understand fairy tales as traditional narratives of wonder and magic, transmitted not only orally but also informally, locally, and face-to-face within and across communities and social groups (see, e.g., Ben-Amos 1971; Falassi 1980). Even fairy tales with known authors, like Hans Christian Andersen, Edith (Bland) Nesbit, Oscar Wilde, or Mary Louisa (Stewart) Molesworth, were spread primarily via books read in family homes, aloud, or in solitude. More recently, Europeans and North Americans may encounter these narratives in less personalized and often professionalized contexts: written in books they study at school and college or university, told by specialist storytellers from a stage, or indeed presented through various audiovisual media. The performance of fairy tales on television versus the cinema screen parallels this distinction.

Unlike fairy-tale films, traditional and televised fairy tales alike reach their audiences in familiar circumstances—often their own homes. As Donald Haase comments, "Relying on performances that are visually and aurally experienced, the televised fairy tale might seem to be a social event reminiscent of the oral tradition" (2000b, 513). Other recent modes for transmitting fairy tales, including cinema, can be received in more impersonal surroundings. As Tiffin notes, "The distance from the cozy oral storyteller in a small circle of listeners could not be greater" (2009, 179). We wouldn't take that argument too far, especially since many across the world no longer view films on cinematic screens but instead watch them on their own televisions and/or computers. And, as Haase also affirms, "The literary affinities of the televised fairy tale . . . are . . . evident. Not only does the televised fairy tale frequently draw on stories from the print tradition, it is also a scripted presentation that has none of the spontaneity or variability associated with traditional notions of oral storytelling. Similarly, viewers are clearly not engaged in a face-to-face, two-way social relationship with the narrator, performers, or creators" (2000b, 513). Yet television's differences from other cinematic forms circle around the fulcrum of its intimacy, just as fairy tales invoke simultaneously the broadest human concerns and the most familiar aspects of interpersonal relationships. Thus, in *Channeling Wonder*, we focus on how television channels the wonder of fairy tales, but we also attend to the increasing role of other mediated forms such as websites in the distribution, textualization, performance, and reception of traditional and literary tales on TV. We begin with a look at television studies and its interaction with folklore scholarship; we then turn to fairy tales as television texts and how the intersections of the two have, specifically and intermedially, channeled wonder.

Channeling: Television

Saying "TV is a hybrid monster, coevally subject to textuality, power, and science—all at once, but in contingent ways," Toby Miller (2010, 146) notes that TV studies' aims and practices consider "how television functions, who controls it, how it makes meaning, and what audiences do with the result" (2002, viii). Access, technology, and economics are significant in this interdisciplinary field, which ranges broadly across "monopoly capital, cultural imperialism, conditions of production, textual meaning, gendered aesthetic hierarchies, audience interpretation, and pleasure" (2002, 2). Yet art, aesthetics, and commerce need not conflict; as Tiffin writes, "The postmodern cultural environment . . . means that . . . self-consciousness, irony, and the pleasures of recognition are highly saleable commodities" (2009, 188).[4] Indeed, the commodification endemic to the production, broadcasting, and reception of most television need not negate the underlying and overriding necessity of storytelling and the enjoyment and instruction of its aesthetic forms and themes.[5] That process may be highlighted for North American viewers in the series *Carosello* (see Bacchilega and Rieder's chapter); its connections between commercial and narrative content don't follow the models with which we're familiar.

Zipes argued that folklorists "have revealed how television and film exploit folklore to evoke images of the attainment of happiness through consumption" (1984, 334) but criticized them for avoiding the implications for political economy. The specific intersections of pleasure, commodification, and tradition in various uses of fairy tales on television make avoiding their politicized implications somewhat difficult. Such powerful intersections, as Zipes argues, demand attention. Fairy-tale narratives, characters, images, and ideas well serve television's commercial aspects; like other adaptations and remakes, they ensure an audience that is at least partially engaged at the outset, and even their most provisional commitment facilitates the ongoing attention that leads to the ultimate desired result—selling goods and services via commercials (see, e.g., Flitterman 1983). Most contributors to *Channeling Wonder* deal with televised fairy tales' aesthetics, but the ideology is never far behind the art.

Though less universally stigmatized as low culture, television is still understood by some "as a technological and cultural 'problem' to be solved rather than a textual body to be engaged" (Sconce 2004, 94). Yet as Jeffrey Sconce argues:

> Television . . . has discovered that the cultivation of its story worlds (diegesis) is as crucial an element in its success as is storytelling. What television lacks in spectacle and narrative constraints, it makes up for in depth and duration of character relations, diegetic expansion and audience investment. A commercial series that succeeds in the US system ends up generating hundreds of hours of programming, allowing for an often quite sophisticated and complex elaboration of character and story world. Much of the transformation in television from an emphasis on plot mechanics to series architecture . . . has developed from this mutual insight by both producers and audiences. (Ibid., 95)

Many of the contributors offer excellent examples of series architecture's significance. *Once Upon a Time* (see Hay and Baxter's chapter) and *Grimm* (see Willsey's; the two compared in Schwabe's chapter), for example, follow upon their creators' previous successes with long-arc serials—in which individual episodes resolve, but an overall story is told through a season or longer—like *Lost* and *Buffy the Vampire Slayer*. Episodic telefilms in which viewers watch "a continuing group of characters perform a self-contained story" (Sconce 2004, 97) include miniseries like Nick Willing's *Tin Man* (2007; see Noone 2010; Smith 2010) and *Alice* (2009) or David Carson and Herbert Wise's *The 10th Kingdom* (2000; see De Vito and Tropea 2010). These shows fit a predetermined time period, but their episodic division means that they must hold audience attention over several days—indeed, serial presentation may actually increase interest. Miniseries can be longer than most films released to theaters without risking audience engagement, because their extended time allows for plot and character development well beyond the constraints of a shorter form.[8] As such, miniseries and long-arc serial television play with fairy tales' episodic plots and minimal character development.

"Genre is central to TV, as evidenced by, for example, the routine practices of classification undertaken by program guides. . . . Genres are about the interplay of repetition and difference, and their organization and interpretation by producers, audiences, and critics" (Miller 2010, 82). Not just abstract classifications based on specific features like music, title cues, and particular performers, creators, and producers (see Bignell 2013, 124–45), genres seek particular audiences (and, of course, particular sponsors)— "fluid guides" (Miller 2010, 83) rather than invariant forms. Thus, as Trudier Harris notes, "Fairy tales and legends shook hands with television to form unions for which we do not yet have names" (1995, 518). Though fairy tale has consistently been implicated in the "economy of genres" on television (see Bacchilega and Rieder 2010, 32), it is not a TV genre in itself but an apt part of television experience flow.

Some well-known examples of fairy-tale TV take the anthology format. Thus *Faerie Tale Theatre* and *The StoryTeller* (see Rudy's chapter) include a series of freestanding, discrete tales, often using a frame narrative like the latter's Storyteller (John Hurt), the fictive narrator. Similarly *Super Why!*, aimed at young children, has formulaic plots and recurring characters (see Brodie and McDavid's chapter). The fairy-tale serial, in the form of situation comedies like *Bewitched,* 1964–1972, *I Dream of Jeannie,* 1965–1970, and *The Charmings,* 1987–1988 (see Haase 2000b, 515, 517 and 2008, 950) made a relatively brief appearance on American television. However, into the 1990s came the cumulative narrative with individual characters or events as plot foci but "interwoven with long-term story lines that may or may not receive attention that week or even that season" (Sconce 2004, 98). The first *Beauty and the Beast* series (1987–1990) took this form, and among shows discussed here, *Grimm, Once Upon a Time,* and *Merlin* (see Nelson and Walton's chapter) obviously exemplify it. Such programs tend to offer a "'realist' aesthetic" and "increase connotations of 'quality'" (Sconce 2004, 99).

As *Channeling Wonder* demonstrates, TV fairy tales are directed at a wide age range. Specific shows, however, seek particular age groups. *Super Why!* (discussed in Brodie and McDavid's chapter) and *Grimms' Fairy Tale Classics* (Jorgensen and Warman's chapter) are for children, and the made-for-TV movies *Snow White: A Tale of Terror* (Wright's chapter), *Bluebeard* (Barzilai's chapter), and the *Red Riding Trilogy* (Greenhill and Kohm's chapter) and shows like *Grimm* (Willsey and Schwabe's chapter), *Dollhouse* (Jorgensen and Warman's and Tresca's chapters), *I Want to Be Cinderella!* (Barber's chapter), and *CSI, Lost Girl* and *Criminal Minds* (Tresca's chapter) are mainly for adults. *Train Man* and *Rich Man Poor Woman* (Barber's chapter), *Once Upon a Time* (Hay and Baxter's and Schwabe's chapters), and reality TV (Lee's chapter) are primarily adult interests but don't exclude younger audiences. *Revolutionary Girl Utena* (Lezubski's chapter), *Buffy the Vampire Slayer* and *Supernatural* (Tresca's chapter), and *Merlin* (Nelson and Walton's chapter) are aimed at adolescents but may interest some adults. Fairy-tale content can include a diverse audience, often involving them in different ways. Both the *Carosello* commercials and *Fractured Fairy Tales* discussed by Bacchilega and Rieder offer various levels of interpretation accessible to diverse spectators, as do *The Simpsons* (discussed by Tresca), *The StoryTeller* (Rudy), and the *Cinderella* musicals (Sawin).

Though TV programming's time-sensitive scheduling fictively involves all ages—at some points separately and at others simultaneously—it is at best a crude tool. The pattern of children's programming (see Hendershot 2002) in early morning and midafternoon (before and after school); women's during the day; adolescents' in late afternoon and early evening; and adult (male) later in the evening is undermined by TiVo and other DVRs as well as other means of time shifting. Further, not all women are home during the day and parents may also view children's programming (or whence Brodie and McDavid's autoethnographic chapter?). The TV audience is extensively a constructed and metaphorical entity. Where business sees consumers, government sees the public (or publics), mandating limits to sex, violence, and coarse language (Hartley 2002). The presumptive genders (see D'Acci 2002; Meehan 2002), classes (see Taub 2002), (hetero)sexualities (see Sara Jones 2002), and (white) race of viewers needs deconstruction (see Gillespie 2002; Ginsberg and Roth 2002; Valdivia 2002).

Much television audience research has criticized presumptions of a simple identity politics. The conjecture that viewers want to see only folks like themselves, and that they directly identify with and act on the actions they see, has been replaced with the idea of "interpretive communities" fostered particularly in online intermedia (see, e.g., Miller 2010, 110–44; Bignell 2013, 256–80). Nevertheless, people of color are rare in European and North American fairy tale–themed television, particular as primary characters. Exceptions include the African American *Cinderella* Rodgers and Hammerstein musical (1997; see Sawin's chapter; Barr 2000) and the mixed-race actors who play Guinevere on *Merlin* (see Nelson and Walton's chapter) and Catherine Chandler on the new *Beauty and the Beast*. But as Lee's chapter discusses, punishments for losers on reality TV shows can implicate racist and colonialist ideas; the "Bad Wife" must eat Moroccan food and belly dance. Queer sexualities and transgender are even rarer; though reflecting anime's frequent use of same-sex relationships between girls and the gender transformation, *Revolutionary Girl Utena* (see Lezubski's chapter) has both.[7]

Repudiation of TV as a lowbrow medium is passé in television studies. Indeed, made-for-television movies like Breillat's *Bluebeard* (see Barzilai's chapter) often rival or surpass films destined first for theaters, and many, like *Snow White: A Tale of Terror* (see Wright's chapter) and the *Red Riding Trilogy* (see Greenhill and Kohm's chapter) have theatrical release. But condescending attitudes characterize reactions to reality TV (see, e.g., Miller 2010, 160–62). Arguably like this newer TV genre, fairy tales in all their manifestations can hit the lowest common denominator but also become very arty—sometimes both at the same time (see Bacchilega and Rieder's chapter). Fairy tales share focus on transformations with much reality TV (see, e.g., Levine 2005), but play with reality can be crucial across genres (see Schwabe's chapter). Other genres may obscure their repetitive structures more than reality television does; however, a close examination can reveal a syntagmatic sequence even more invariable than that asserted by Vladimir Propp (1968) for fairy tales.[8]

Sconce argues, "The series to spawn the most involved audience communities . . . are those that orchestrate a strong and complex sense of community while also leaving a certain diegetic fringe available for textual elaboration . . . worlds that viewers gradually feel they inhabit along with the characters" (2004, 95). Hay and Baxter's chapter on *Once Upon a Time* and Nelson and Walton's on *Merlin* clearly demonstrate shows' and fans' creative engagement in intermediality to foster such a sense of community (also Jenkins 1991, 1992, 2006; Tosenberger 2008a, 2010). Fan ethnographies, and autoethnographies like Brodie and McDavid's, Sawin's, and Bacchilega and Rieder's chapters, often overlap, not only in content—using quotidian personal experience to investigate national and global structures (see Ellis and Bochner [1994] 2000; Ellis 2004)—but also in the position of the writer exploring experience firsthand.

While folklorists have been generally less than attentive to film,[9] they rarely consider television. Hitherto, many participated in the demonization of TV, joining work spotlighting "engineering and panic" (Miller 2002, 1)— the physical mode of production and the fear that the new medium would efface and/or supplant all other culture. Tom Burns's (1969) article mainly enumerates items of traditional culture noted in a single day of TV watching.

A JSTOR search in 2012 for "television" from all folklore journals yielded a surprising small 1,152 items. Adding "fairy tale OR folktale" cut the number down to 202, the oldest from 1954. The majority included little more than asides on the medium, and only four articles have "television" in their title. In 2003, Mikel J. Koven argued that a critical survey of folklore studies and popular film and television was necessary (176). He pointed out research on TV soap operas and *Märchen*/folktale[10] telling in (French) Newfoundland—finding "traditional narrative formations" in soaps' visual and textual structures (ibid., 178). Implicit in this argument is the error by folklorists and other students of literature (e.g., Buchan 1972; Lord 2000) who presume that structures found in oral texts are by definition (only) oral. Yet the Newfoundland research also participated in hand-wringing about "the loss of traditional performance styles . . . in keeping with the perception of the devolutionary influence of the mass media" (Koven 2003, 178).

Most folklorists have presumed that television has destroyed tradition and sometimes even reify it as folklore's archrival, as in K. M. Briggs: "Television is [folktales'] great enemy, though there have been others. The great necessity for the transmission of elaborate tales is leisure. A good many people have more leisure now than they ever had, but unfortunately it is swallowed up by television or Bingo, and the chain of tradition is in danger of being broken" (1968, 84).

This discourse echoes in the assertion of criminal intention that "television came to steal the time reserved for the folk narrator" (Virtanen 1986, 224). Dan Ben-Amos, in defining folklore as process, intones: "A song, a tale, or a riddle that is performed on television or appears in print ceases to be folklore because there is a change in its communicative context" (1971, 14). Linda Dégh and Andrew Vázsonyi's work on *Märchen* and legend in television advertising demonstrates greater nuance. Saying, "Magic is merchandise of prime necessity. Magic is in demand. People who travel by airplanes still cannot do without the magic carpet" (1979, 49), they link fairy tales' magical content with commerce: "Giants, dwarves, fairies, witches, mermaids, anthropomorphic objects, personified principles appear on the television screen to enlighten the viewer on the value of certain commodities, as often as the clowning of comedians, the horror of suspense dramas, even sports games, stop to allow room for an 'important message' from the sponsor" (ibid., 50). Though they contend, pessimistically, that television "terminated occasions for traditional storytelling," they continue that it "now helps the *Märchen* to survive on the basis of entirely new traditions" (ibid.,

56). One might surmise that commercials (see Bacchilega and Rieder's chapter) are forerunners to the concept that fairy tales are real that is so central to *Grimm* and *Once Upon a Time* (see Schwabe's chapter) as well as to the reality TV series Lee considers.

Folklore's death is regularly announced and prematurely mourned by those who think they arrived ten or twenty years too late to get genuine, unspoiled, authentic material (discussed, e.g., in Greenhill 1989). Yet Dégh notes, "Television from the early 1940s suddenly expanded the limits of common audience awareness still further. Through a relatively limited number of popular characters and through paraphernalia, tone, and style, the Grimm tales became generally known, reaching even those who otherwise never would have encountered them" (1979, 101). The familiarity not only of tales like "Cinderella" (see Barber's and Sawin's chapters), "Little Red Riding Hood" (see Greenhill and Kohm's chapter), "Sleeping Beauty" (see Jorgensen and Warman's chapter), and "Hansel and Gretel" (see Tresca's chapter) but also of the *idea* of fairy tales may be a reason behind their popularity on TV. Like sequels, films based on popular books like the Harry Potter, Narnia, or Lord of the Rings series, and remakes (from films and increasingly also TV), traditional fairy tales' familiarity serves television and vice versa.[11] Alan Dundes defends mass media, including TV, as productive rather than destructive: "If there is any validity to what has been termed the concept of 'postliterate man' (as opposed to preliterate or nonliterate man), referring to the idea that the information communicated by such mass media as radio, television, and movies depends upon the oral–aural circuit rather than upon writing or print, then it becomes even more obvious that oral tradition in so-called civilized societies has not been snuffed out by literacy" (1969, 15). We concur that television is more a continuation than a departure for fairy tales. As such, we explore in greater detail how we use the term "fairy tale" and how its re-mediation on television has been explored by TV studies.

Wonder: Fairy Tales and Intertextuality/Intermediality

Stith Thompson calls wonder tales or fairy tales "stories filled with incredible marvels" ([1946] 1977, 21). Folklorists distinguish myths and legends from folktales—which include fairy tales (Bascom 1965)—not by their forms but by "the *attitudes* of the community toward them." Myths seem "both sacred and true. . . . core narratives in larger ideological systems. Concerned with ultimate realities, they are often set outside of historical time . . . and frequently concern the actions of divine or semi-divine characters" (Oring 1986, 124). Legends "focus on a single episode . . . which is presented as miraculous, uncanny, bizarre, or sometimes embarrassing. The narration of a legend is, in a sense, the negotiation of the truth of these episodes." This genre, "set in historical time in the world as we know it today . . . often makes reference to real people and places" (ibid., 125). Folktales, in contrast, "are related and received as fiction or fantasy [and] appear in a variety of forms" (ibid., 126). Though fairy tales also come in literary forms, based primarily in an individual author's creativity, most folklorists (including the majority of this volume's contributors) understand fairy tales as *Märchen*: the "tales of magic" numbered 300–749 in the ATU classification (Uther 2004, I:174–396).

Literary tales, "written by an individual, usually identifiable author . . . [may] draw upon preexisting published material for some or all of their characters and plot . . . [but] put them together in a new way . . . [and] exist in only one version, fixed in print" (Harries 2008, 579). This distinction between oral folktales and literary fairy tales, however, is not uncontroversial. Oral fairy tales can come in written forms (such as the collections of the Grimm brothers), but written texts of various forms and genres make their way into oral narratives (see, e.g., Labrie 1997). And the two are rarely discrete in the popular imagination; Andersen's "The Little Mermaid" is generally seen as the same genre as the traditional "Little Red Riding Hood" (ATU 333). Yet distinguishing characteristics go beyond origins and transmission. Traditional wonder tales usually end happily; literary tales often do not. Most Euro–North Americans expect fairy tales' main protagonists to "live happily ever after." But in Andersen and Wilde, the conclusion can be sad or depressing. Contrast the Disney film's happy ending to Andersen's, which concludes with the title character transformed into sea-foam as she fails to marry the prince (see, e.g., Bendix 1993).[12]

Despite fairy tales' ubiquity, TV scholars rarely consider them. A JSTOR search in film studies of "television" plus "fairytale/fairy tale/folktale/folk tale" reveals a generally pejorative use, meaning untruth or implausible fiction. "A docudrama on John F. Kennedy, *Johnny We Hardly Knew Ye* (January 1977, NBC-TV), was termed a 'fairy tale' due to various inaccuracies and distortions" (Hoffer and Nelson 1978, 26). *Into the Woods,* a fairy-tale musical screened on TV is addressed in a casebook (Mankin et al. 1988). More recently, discussions of *Buffy the Vampire Slayer* (Wilcox 1999), *Animaniacs* (Dennis 2003), and reality dating shows (Tropiano 2009) reference fairy tales. None focuses specifically on the genre though authors mention its key features as show elements: fairy tale as adventure, the "fairy tale cum nightmare" (Schneider 2002), and fairy tales as romance, material success, and magic (Tibbetts 2001). They note recurring "Cinderella" motifs in the sitcom *The Nanny* (Brook 2000), fairy-tale structures in a Disney reality wedding show (Levine 2005), and expectations of happily ever after fostered, and foiled, by the series finales of *Seinfeld* and *The Sopranos* (Corrigan and Corrigan 2012).

Reviewers as culture critics mediate the encoding and decoding of television (Gray 2011). Stuart Elliott (2011) notes that fairy tales were "usually not a strong draw," predicting early cancellation for *Grimm* and *Once Upon a Time*. Despite his erroneous prediction, he sees fairy tales as necessary on TV because "the plots in this world—about the police, detectives, doctors, lawyers—have been told and retold again." Terrence Rafferty (2012) sees *Grimm* and *Once Upon a Time* as more generically apt than the recent films *Red Riding Hood* (2011) and *Beastly* (2011). He attributes this fit to television's seriality: "Maybe the succession of weekly episodes more closely approximates the regularity and one-thing-after-another quality of bedtime stories." To him, *Grimm* and *Once Upon a Time* convey a "neither-here-nor-there feeling" that seems to match "a chronic sense of unreality" that pervades "the developed world."

Vanessa Joosen's approach to fairy tales and contemporary retellings augments these cultural critics' observations. Joosen's discussion of a "horizon of expectation" identifies key features of wonder tales and points out specific changes over time that relate to the proximity between these stories and fantasy and reality. These traits include an indefinite sense of place and time, familiarity with the supernatural, flat characters, quick plot progression and optimistic endings, style marked by fixed formulas and repetitions, and linear telling by a third-person omniscient narrator with no distinguishing marks of identity (2011, 13). Retellings disrupt some or all elements of this horizon of expectation, usually by adding attention to reality. They may be set in a specific, more real place and time; develop boundaries between fantasy and reality; provide character backstory and psychological motivation; challenge happy endings; reduce plot focus in favor of characterization; eliminate repetition while retaining symbolic numbers; and incorporate first-person or other shifts in narration and chronological organization (ibid., 13–15). Televised fairy tales similarly effect such shifts while maintaining recognizable intertextual links with traditional tales. Television's seriality works especially well for establishing the horizon of expectation while keying on a fluid relationship of fantasy and reality.

Wonder invokes and responds to this fluid relationship, helping to illuminate fairy tale's persistence in, and even conscription of, new media. When folklorists defined the wonder tale as a canonical study object, they sought to rescue both orality and wonder from the march of literacy and rationality in the eighteenth century (Bendix 1997; Bauman and Briggs 2003; Conrad 2008). The politics of wonder (see Bacchilega 1997, 2013) and intermediality become key to channeling wonder. Bacchilega explores the relationship of magic and wonder in fairy tales' textual, intertextual, and ideological contexts, nuancing histories of the wonder tale by acknowledging both conservative and dynamic forces at play textually and contextually: "The tale of magic produces wonder precisely through its seductively concealed exploitation of the conflict between its *normative* function, which capitalizes on the comforts of consensus, and its *subversive* wonder, which magnifies the powers of transformation" (1997, 7).

Yet she notes a growing disenchantment with magic: "If generally the desired effect of this poetics of enchantment is the consumer's buying into magic, then, the contemporary call for disenchanting the fairy tale is directly related to a now-public dissatisfaction with its magic as trick" (2013, 5). The strong link between magic and advertising analyzed by Dégh and Vázsonyi (1979) and between television and commodification discussed in chapters by Hay and Baxter and Bacchilega and Rieder suggests televised tales are complicit in magic as trickery and still open to wonder in an era of convergence culture and commodification. "Actively contesting an impoverished poetics of magic, a renewed, though hardly cohesive, poetics and politics of wonder are at work in the contemporary cultural production and reception of fairy tales" (Bacchilega 2013, 6). The magic of televised tales may be a trick to sell products and even desirable life experiences; consider the reality dating shows Lee's chapter analyzes. Still, the variety of approaches to fairy tale on television, in both its production and reception, confirms the ongoing possibility of wonder as both an emotional state related to awe and marvel and an active possibility of pursuing curiosity and inquiry (Bacchilega 2013, 191). Brodie and McDavid's, Sawin's, and Bacchilega and Rieder's autoethnographies, along with references to fan communities in chapters by Hay and Baxter and Nelson and Walton, show viewers who wonder about and with the fairy tales they view on television.

Although folklorists define wonder tales using the imperative of orality, Bacchilega's approach to a poetics and politics of magic and wonder shows this to be only a starting place. Zipes affirms, "In the last forty or fifty years, folklorists, literary critics, historians, and scholars of folklore and fairy tales from many different countries have been more interested in the intersections between the oral and literary traditions than trying to privilege one over the other" (2012, 164). Greenhill and Matrix observe that the genre is "a shape-shifter and medium breaker" (2010a, 3). Here we suggest the fairy tale just might also be a medium *maker*. Spanning space and time, normative and transformative, changing as it replicates magic and wonder, fairy tale is an early and persistent mode for successive communicative technologies. This use value may accrue because humans crave stories and wonder. As Gordon Henry, Jr. observes, "Stories seem to transcend jurisdictions of nation, culture, time and text, irrespective of whether they are spoken, written, heard, smelled, filmed or performed. . . . Stories are intertextual, transcendent, evocative, and arguably efficacious" (2009, 18; see also Frank 2010). Intermediality recognizes the fairy tale's transcendent jurisdiction as an elemental story type.

Like many analytical terms, "intermediality" comes with a plethora of definitions and related possibilities: media, transmedial, multimedial, plurimedial (Wolf 2011, 4). Foregrounding the sense of relationship associated with "inter," we prefer "intermediality" to encourage attention to how the fairy tale engages semiotic modes and technological channels. Marina Grishakova and Marie-Laure Ryan state, "In a narrow sense, [intermediality] refers to the participation of more than one medium—or sensory channel—in a given work" (2010, 3). Ryan also advocates studying narrative across media because most narratology "directs us to the importance of narrative in mostly language-based practices" but attending across media "focuses on the embodiment . . . the particular semiotic substance and the technological mode of transmission of narrative" (2004, 1). Television, inherently intermedial, simultaneously involves sound and sight.

But traditional expression, including story, also is inherently intermedial. Barre Toelken asserts that folklore's medium is not its only message: "Folklorists deal with a particular and well-established species of learning and expression which uses culture-based interactive codes and formulas. It occurs with or without literacy" (1996, 47). While folklorists may prefer studying materials transmitted in face-to-face communication, they also acknowledge that people use new media to share stories and other traditional expressions (see Blank 2009, 2012). Because variation is key to tradition and more specifically to folklore's interactive codes and formulas, intertextuality has proven valuable to fairy-tale scholarship (Smith 2007; Greenhill and Matrix 2010a, 2010b; Joosen 2011). We offer intermediality as a corollary, not as an end in itself. Rather than simply spotting the fairy tale in each different medium or new technology, intermediality can offer a better understanding of what fairy tales do to clarify a human need for channeling wonder.

Tiffin (2009, 228) suggests a trend in fairy-tale film toward pastiche and irony. Recent Disney productions have aimed at pastiche, apparently refusing (while simultaneously affirming) the fairy-tale ethos that their earlier work enforced and reinforced (see, e.g., Bacchilega and Rieder 2010; Pershing and Gablehouse 2010). Yet a multitude of other recent films, especially from outside the United States and the Hollywood blockbuster machine, show various ways fairy tales can be successfully reworked and reinterpreted.[13] Arguably, as *Channeling Wonder* demonstrates, the rereading of fairy tales in their re-mediation on television has been even more extreme than in the cinema.

The example of television offers an understanding of how rapidly changing and adapting media systems incorporate both new and old materials and perspectives. As early as 2004, Lynn Spigel listed: "The demise of the three-network system in the United States, the increasing commercialization of public service/state-run systems, the rise of multichannel cable and global satellite delivery, multinational conglomerates, Internet convergence, changes in regulation policies and ownership rules, the advent of HDTV, technological changes in screen design, the innovation of digital televisions systems . . . and new forms of media competition" (2004, 2). Lezubski's chapter on the anime *Revolutionary Girl Utena* implicates how intermedial relations affect texts. With manga (comic book) preceding the anime television series and the feature film following, TV cannot be entirely divorced from the other media—all of which use fairy-tale themes and characters. In particular, a crucial intermedial relation has developed between television and the internet:

It is silly to see the Internet in opposition to television; each is one more way of sending and receiving the other. The fact is that television is becoming *more* popular, not less. It is here to stay, whether we like it or not. I suspect that we are witnessing a *transformation* of TV, rather than its demise. What started in most countries as a *broadcast, national* medium, dominated by the state, is being transformed into a *cable, satellite, Internet,* and *international* medium, dominated by commerce—but still called "television." (Miller 2010, 19)

Transformations and interactions between social media and other internet forms are present in Hay and Baxter's consideration of *Once Upon a Time* and Nelson and Walton's of *Merlin*. Fan involvement goes beyond commenting on the series; they can choose to play games based on the series, write fan fiction, and/or edit video interpretations. While commerce is certainly an aim in the networks' and producers' encouragement of these activities, they cannot entirely control how audiences will re/present the shows they see. The potential remains for resistant texts to damage the reputation, undermine the branding, and skew the intended audience of a TV show.

Haase notes the importance of television as a mode for disseminating fairy-tale films of all types, in particular acknowledging that "repeated televised broadcasts of Victor Fleming's 1939 feature film *The Wizard of Oz* became a popular tradition that helped to enrich the American experience of fairy tale" (2008, 948). Similarly, with respect to Jacques Demy's *Donkey Skin* (Peau d'âne, 1970), "While *Peau d'âne* will strike Americans as rather offbeat, to say the least—with elements of scatological humor, implied incest, wild anachronisms, and eye-popping visual design—it is a well-known and beloved fairy tale in France. Indeed, it is probably Demy's most familiar film among French audiences, due to its enormous appeal with children and repeated television showings over the years—not to mention its wickedly tongue-in-cheek approach to the enchanted fairy-tale genre" (Hill 2005–2006, 40). This film underlines Euro–North American television's bourgeois and often culturally circumscribed audiences. French exchange students in Pauline's fairy-tale film course affirmed to their shocked Canadian colleagues that, indeed, they had seen and enjoyed *Peau d'âne* as children. Most North Americans would exclude the film from childhood television fare because of its focus on the king's incestuous desire for his daughter. Similarly, television anime fare like *Revolutionary Girl Utena* (see Lezubski's chapter) is unlikely to ever make mainstream North American television screens or to be seen as child friendly, given its explorations of transgender, heterosex, and homosex.[14] Though Disney's *Mulan* (1998) includes a cross-dressing character, her chaste yet heterosexual alibi is retained throughout the film and there is no play with the idea of a female among a group of soldiers.[15] These issues of age, gender, beastliness, and commerce pattern the chapters in *Channeling Wonder*.

Overview

The chapters in "For and about Kids and Adults" underline how television's time segmentation, as well as its ideology, presumes specific age groups as audiences. Yet, as Brodie and McDavid's chapter indicates, even though *Super Why!* is directed at children, parents or other adult caregivers are rarely absent. The writers' autoethnographic focus upon their own positions as folklorists as well as parents organizes their examination of the benefits and drawbacks of using traditional culture in such contexts. Nelson and Walton address a show intended for young adults, considering how *Merlin* uses fairy-tale plots, tropes, and characters to offer lessons to the targeted age group. Yet the show also exploits various new-media platforms to extend its targeted demographic's participation. Tresca looks at how "Hansel and Gretel" is interpellated into individual episodes of an astonishing variety of TV genres. Though the story's historical context, in which underclass poverty and starvation lead parents to desperate acts, remains part of contemporary North America, these shows instead focus upon children's potential for independence and autonomy. Rudy's consideration of *The StoryTeller* shows how its intermedial complexities construct taleworlds and storyrealms that resonate for multiple audiences. Viewers are not constructed by age but instead as distinctive televisual interlocutors.

In "Masculinities and/or Femininities," the authors address modes for constructing and interpreting sex and gender. Sawin's autoethnography takes readers through her experience of the 1965 *Cinderella* musical as offering sometimes compliant, but also potentially feminist, views. Rather than dogmatically dismissing its focus upon princess culture, she playfully asks readers to consider whether fantasy may have value outside a literalist reading. Barber looks at how three Japanese television shows play with concepts of masculinity and femininity. She notes that increasingly, in changing economic contexts, appearance has become salient in conventional Japanese ideas about men, replacing former ideas about loyalty to employers and dedication to family. "Sleeping Beauty" gets attention in two quite disjunctive shows, the Japanese anime *Grimm's Fairy Tale Classics* and television auteur Joss Whedon's *Dollhouse*. Despite the unlikeliness of a protagonist who sleeps until she's rescued by a prince being seen as anything other than heteropatriarchal, Jorgensen and Warman locate feminist possibilities in the readings these shows offer. Lezubski turns to yet another Japanese anime series, exploring how *Revolutionary Girl Utena* directly offers uncoded transgressive sexes, sexualities, and genders. She juxtaposes these not only with the more compliant *Sailor Moon* series but also with real and fictive royalty and their travails in the Japanese press.

"Beastly Humans" works though shows that arguably operate on the edge—if not directly in the middle—of the horror genre. Greenhill and Kohm examine the British *Red Riding Trilogy* and its attention to the brutal and inhumane qualities of institutionally, economically, and socially powerful men. As in Charles Perrault's version of the fairy tale "Little Red Riding Hood," innocent victims rarely escape with their lives. *Grimm,* as discussed by Willsey, offers a somewhat more cheery perspective, despite its implicit homophone "grim." It presents the historical and diegetical Grimms as the enemies of evil "Wesen," while indicating that humans can be more brutal than these apparent beasts. Wright considers how *Snow White: A Tale of Terror* offers an unlikely sympathetic figure in the fairy tale's wicked stepmother. But again, the true beasts are human beings who, lacking help from others, cannot move beyond their personal tragedies. Breillat's *Bluebeard* gives Barzilai an opportunity to explore intriguing visual filmic references. She links them not only to artistic representations but also to the filmmaker's feminist intentions.

"Fairy Tales Are Real! Reality TV, Fairy-Tale Reality, Commerce, and Discourse" turns to issues that have long fascinated television scholars— the medium's links between art and economics. Lee's chapter begins the section with a nuanced consideration of how various reality shows employ fairy-tale themes and ideas. Even less obvious candidates, like house makeover shows, work through notions of renovation as a "fairy tale"—and are too often followed by unfortunate consequences that deconstruct the idea that after transformation, everyone will "live happily ever after." Schwabe explores the different modes through which fantasy and real worlds interact in two recent fairy-tale long-arc serials. Developing a typology of the links, she locates the historical roots of these forms in magic realist literature and film implicating the wonder tale. In contrast, Hay and Baxter consider the specific interactions between fairy tales and commodities seen in *Once Upon a Time* as a new development for Disney on television. They show how sympathetic backstories engage viewers with otherwise apparently unpromising characters like the evil queen, bringing a diverse and committed audience to the long-arc serial. Even more direct links with TV's profit-seeking purpose can be seen in Bacchilega and Rieder's autoethnographic work on the Italian *Carosello* commercial/show and the American *Fractured Fairy Tales.* Both transcend their uses of seriality, by addressing and sometimes lampooning their audiences' national and personal self-concepts and, paradoxically, avoiding fairy-tale commodity fetishism.

Channeling Wonder closes with Magnus-Johnston's elaboration of the joys (and mostly the sorrows) of working to construct a teleography that represents fairy tales on TV. As the teleography that follows shows, the fairy tale's ubiquitous presence in the medium, crossing genres, modes, and content styles, renders truly impossible anything like complete coverage but displays compelling possibilities. Now, we invite readers to go with the flow, sitting there with this book hour after hour, or to channel surf from chapter to chapter. Mostly, we encourage wonder with fairy tales on television.

Notes

1. Haase (2000b, 2008) offers the beginnings of a history of fairy tales on television. Unfortunately, a fuller account of the topic is beyond our scope.
2. The tale type index originated by Aarne, edited and updated by Thompson and then again by Uther (2004; discussed below) numbers traditional international folktales.
3. Tiffin examines *Snow White: A Tale of Terror* (see Wright's chapter; 2009, 204–6). Zipes (1997) considers the television creations of Jim Henson (see Rudy's chapter) and Shelley Duvall as alternatives to Disney. He mentions that Catherine Breillat's *Bluebeard* (2009) was made for French television (2011, 167–68). However, perhaps because, as Barzilai's chapter discusses, it lacks obvious textual markers—like an episodic structure friendly to commercial interruption—he explores this origin no further.
4. Tiffin refers to current film cultures, but her insight applies equally to television (see, e.g., Hay and Baxter's chapter).
5. Wilson writes of the aesthetic impulse not as a "move beyond practical need—beyond necessity" but as a "move to a deeper necessity, to the deeper human need to create order, beauty, and meaning out of chaos" (2006, 13).
6. *Alice,* at 240 minutes, and *Tin Man,* at 270, are at least twice the length of most longer cinematic features; *The 10th Kingdom,* at 417, is over three times that duration.
7. Presumptions that this absence reflects a lack of queer and trans in fairy tales are simply wrong (see, e.g., Turner and Greenhill 2012).
8. Some film scholars mistake paradigmatic and syntagmatic structures for the traditional folktales themselves, taking the form as its own manifestations (see, e.g., McLean 1998, 4). Just as a girl wearing a red hooded coat doesn't make a "Little Red Riding Hood" film (see, e.g., Kohm and Greenhill 2013), binary oppositions and helper figures do not make a television show myth or fairy tale. It would be difficult to find *any* television show entirely lacking in binary oppositions and helpers (see also Fell 1977; Harriss 2008). David Bordwell notes wryly, "For many critics, Propp has become the Aristotle of film narratology; yet his influence has come at the cost of serious misunderstandings" (1988, 5).

9. Exceptions include Sherman (e.g., 1998, 2005), Koven (e.g., 2003, 2007), and Sherman and Koven (2007).

10. As discussed below, *Märchen* is the German term for the wonder tale comprising the "Tales of Magic," numbers 300–749 in Uther's tale type index (2004).

11. The success of extremely repetitive reality TV shows like *What Not to Wear* indicates that reiterating structures are no drawback. Brodie and McDavid's chapter explores how *Super Why!* uses this familiarity to resonate with children. Indeed, it can be difficult to separate structure from content in most shows for the very young.

12. For more about distinctions between and among oral and literary fairy tales, see Zipes (2000) and Oring (1986).

13. Consider, for example, *Pan's Labyrinth* (2006) and *The Fall* (2006). See also Zipes, Greenhill, and Magnus-Johnston's forthcoming edited collection *Fairy Tale Films beyond Disney: International Perspectives.*

14. Series like *The Rose of Versailles* (1979–1980) incorporate cross-dressing, and *Kasimasi: Girl Meets Girl* (2006) brings transgender.

15. In contrast, traditional broadside ballads explore ideas around sexual attraction and sometimes also sexual relations between the cross-dressed woman and the men and women she encounters (see Greenhill 1995).

PART I

For and about
Kids and Adults

1

WHO'S GOT THE POWER?

Super Why!, Viewer Agency, and Traditional Narrative

Ian Brodie and Jodi McDavid

The children's program *Super Why!,* a coproduction of the Canadian Broadcasting Company (CBC) and the American Public Broadcasting System (PBS), incorporates a variety of genres: the child-as-adventurer common to educational programming like *Dora the Explorer* and *The Cat in the Hat Knows a Lot about That;* the superhero team; and traditional, folk, and public domain narrative. It introduces spelling, literacy, and vocabulary, alongside rudimentary answers to social problems as experienced by preschoolers. Working within a rigid structure, every episode entails the Super Readers, a team of four child superheroes, each with a lexicographical superpower, entering a book's pages to address a problem in the story that parallels a problem one of the heroes has in her or his daily life.

Alongside the Super Readers, viewers encounter a series of layered worlds: a television program opening in a real library, the protagonists' Storybrook Village,[1] reached through a bookshelf in that library, and the particular narrative that focuses each episode. Breaking the fourth wall, addressing viewers directly, endowing them with the name "Super You" and "the Power to Help," and asking for assistance in three tasks, the show turns viewers into an active story character.

We approach *Super Why!* from two different contexts. Our first encounter with the show came through our son, who had started watching it at age one alongside the slightly older children with whom he shared a sitter. It became a mainstay in our house largely due to the excitement he expressed when it came on and his irritation upon each episode's completion. We developed a grudging respect for the show when we saw its positive influence on his burgeoning alphabet and reading skills. This respect came despite our backgrounds. Neither of us is a particularly conservative folklorist by training or inclination. We are comfortable with the idea that there is no fixed text, that the motif and tale type indices should be read more as a history of the ongoing reimaginings of particular clusters of names, motifs, and plot points and less as a definitive listing of canonical tropes and that without dynamic retelling the tradition lies moribund. We concur with Pauline Greenhill and Sidney Eve Matrix that "the movement of traditional fairy tales to cinematic form may have enabled their commodification in capitalist socioeconomic structures, but filmed fairy tales are as much the genuine article as their telling in a bedtime story or an anthology" (2010a, 3), and we argue that this holds equally true for television.

Yet we remain "uncomfortable," to use a weak term, with how *Super Why!* presents traditional narratives. What follows comprises our efforts at articulating this discomfort and reconciling our ambiguous feelings both as parents and as folklorists. Without challenging the program's effectiveness in developing child viewers' reading skills, we address a series of interrelated questions. These concern the reworking of traditional texts to articulate both problems that need solving and easy solutions and the functionalist interpretation of fairy tales as a source for moral and social education. We explore these issues within the program's layered worlds and from its creators' perspectives.

"Fairy Tales" and Other Traditional Narratives in *Super Why!*

The idea of fairy tale resonates through *Super Why!*, explicitly with the description of Storybrook Village as "where all our fairy-tale friends live" and implicitly through the preponderance of *Märchen* used. In the sixty-five episodes produced for the initial order of *Super Why!* (to which we limit our discussion), virtually one third (twenty-one) are ATU tale types, all set in a typical Grimm/Perrault Northern European setting, save for an Arabian Nights location for "The Three Feathers" (1, 37; based on ATU 610). Sixteen have ATU types in the 300 to 749 classic range of "fairy tales" proper (Propp 1968, 18; Holbek 1989, 61). An additional six episodes revisit ATU tale types as "sequels," as pastiche, or as retold from a different character's perspective. The second largest category, literary fairy tales from the mid- to the late nineteenth century, includes six from Hans Christian Andersen, Carlo Collodi's *Pinocchio*, Lewis Carroll's *Alice in Wonderland*, and Clement Clarke Moore's "A Visit from St. Nicholas." Other traditional narratives outside the ATU system include three Japanese tales, one from Puerto Rico, and one from Australian Aboriginal mythology. Both "Aladdin" and "King Midas" have an episode, as do four Aesop fables and three nursery rhymes. Finally, five original stories were included in the first season: one on the Tooth Fairy (using some legendry material, see Wells 1991) and four genre exercises: haunted house stories, comic books, pirate stories, and, as an outlier, cookbooks.

While tales and sources vary, as we shall demonstrate, the program's very structure and purpose makes all conform. Protagonists need to either redress a wrong or recognize their behavior's limitations in order to overcome a problem, coinciding with one facing a Super Reader in their world. The reader enters stories, it is implied, as guidance for their actions.

Entering into Layered Worlds

Each episode's structure is rigid. The recurring and invariable elements contribute to the exigencies of conforming to a specific time requirement, the economics of recycling and repurposing animation and sound, and the pedagogical benefits repetitiveness has for developing reading (alphabet, spelling, basic grammar) and literacy (narrative competency) skills. Given the repetitiveness of most stories that children of this age tell (Sutton-Smith 1981, 2), such a tight structure offers great benefit for comprehension. And just as Vladimir Propp's morphology (1968) represents a fairy-tale grammar—articulating how a reader or viewer (culturally) recognizes a certain type of story and can not only predict its outcome but create new ones within that structure—this framework allows for recognition and potential experimentation for a child becoming aware of story possibilities.

Super Why! is structured as a series of movements away from the reality of viewers' quotidian worlds to an expressly fictional ontology (Young 1987, 14). With each step, narrative choices are increasingly limited while narrative freedoms are simultaneously opened. Within the story, the child—expressed through the Super Readers' endowing them with the name "Super You" and directly requesting their help—has a freedom and agency not granted them in the day to day.

To each episode, viewers bring their developing language and literacy skills, senses of story and narrative expectations, and concepts of how to act in social situations. (When he started watching television and *Super Why!* in particular, our son was just over a year old; none of these skills or senses was particularly developed.) Additionally, they may have an initial grasp on a corpus of genres, stories, and motifs in circulation through a variety of media in English-speaking North America. Finally, viewers might also bring both a general fluency with (children's) television conventions and prior experience with *Super Why!*'s episodic structure.

The program's figurative and literal framing device allows viewers license to recognize that what will unfold is beholden to rules and expectations different from daily life. Their actions will have no effect on the story, even when the narrative suggests that such interaction is possible. Viewers can only explore the presented world within the program producers' parameters as well as the TV's rectangular frame. The viewing room and context may lack the cinema's pageantry, and thus television's viewing rituals may pale in contrast to those of film going (McDavid and Brodie 2005, 12). Nevertheless, a performance occurs and one may therefore be temporarily transformed and/or transported. As Bengt Holbek notes, fairy tales are "signaled by opening and closing formulas emphasizing their distance in space and time" (1989, 42).

Each episode's prelude and introduction, along with its eventual closure, informs viewers that this shift is indeed happening. As we discuss below, after the credits, the camera swoops through a library/reading room before zooming into the bookcase. Character Whyatt's emergence behind the stacks and the opening up on to Storybrook Village effects the shift to the animated world. Paul Wells writes, "Animation may be seen as a self-enunciating medium, literally announcing its intrinsic difference from other visual forms and cinematic imperatives" (2003, 16). The stark contrast between the live-action library scene, however abbreviated, and Storybrook Village's animation does not simply announce difference from other cinematic imperatives but moves from the quotidian into the story's ontologically different world. We highlight this seemingly self-evident observation because *Super Why!*'s producers employ this distinction technique again when the Super Readers enter the book. In contrast to the immersive, three-dimensional animation style used for Storybrook Village, the book's world is rendered in computer-generated cutout animation that emphasizes the two-dimensional "paperiness" of the story as book, allowing for letters and words to appear within the diegetic space, while the Super Readers remain in their 3D animation style. However idyllic and fantastic Storybrook Village may appear, the Super Readers cannot use their powers within it. Holbek notes the use of "metafolkloristic utterances" (1989, 42) by storytellers to continually confirm the story's fictional universe, akin to the increasingly nonrealistic animation style.

The Super Readers

Storybrook Village is populated by characters from the world of fairy tales, albeit mainly from the Northwestern European canon, occupying buildings including Peter Peter Pumpkin Eater's house, Miss Muffett's Tea Café, and the Old Lady's Shoe (Out of the Blue 2007a). *Super Why!* is built around the adventures of four children who lead lives ostensibly similar to the implied viewer's (Kozloff 1992, 80–81) but who each have particular powers and qualities.

The "olive-skinned" ("*Super Why!*" 2007–2012) Whyatt Beanstalk, aka Super Why, younger brother of Jack from "Jack and the Beanstalk" (ATU 328A), dresses in a polo shirt with a long-sleeved T-shirt underneath, khakis, and brown loafers. When he transforms into Super Why, he wears a green body suit with purple briefs, a purple cape, a green face mask, and purple boots that allow him to fly. The ostensible leader of the Super Readers, he has Why Writer—a pen and highlighting tool, helping him with his "Power to Read."

Little Red Riding Hood (from ATU 333) lives with her grandmother. With her hair in pigtails, she wears a short skirt and matching top with a hood and gets around on skate-shoes. White-identified, she is physically active and involved in sports. When she transforms into Wonder Red she dons a purple tank top and shorts onesie, rollerblades, a red cape, and a red helmet with a purple stripe. From her Wonder Words basket she can provide rhyming words; she has "Word Power."

Although he is not bullied, Pig, youngest son of the brick-building pig from "The Three Little Pigs" (ATU 124), frequently finds himself in his two older brothers' shadow. He regularly wears a hard hat, a yellow T-shirt under overall shorts, and work boots, but when he becomes Alpha Pig he has safety glasses, a short-sleeved purple bodysuit, a tool belt, and a yellow cape. His off-white work boots become brown leather and his light yellow hardhat safety orange. In a wooden toolbox he keeps his Alphabet Tools, which bring his "Alphabet Power."

Princess Pea, daughter of the Princess on the Pea (from ATU 704), is African American and wears her hair down, along with a long purple dress and matching crown. In contrast to Red, she takes greater pleasure in delicate pastimes such as dress-up and tea parties. As Princess Presto her straightened hair is brought up under her silver tiara. She wears a light pink, star printed ball gown, and her cape gives the impression of fairy wings (with which she can fly). She has a Spelling Wand, and her "Spelling Power" spells the word for an object, making it materialize.

The Structure of Every Episode

The opening theme song ("Who's Got the Power?") plays over a montage of scenes from various episodes. The episode proper begins in a preschool's library or reading room. The camera pushes through to focus on a bookshelf with a small gap in the stacks. From behind the books a small boy—rendered in 3D animation—emerges. "Hi! So glad you're here. It's me, Whyatt!" Behind him a glowing question mark appears on what can now be discerned as an arched doorway. Whyatt presses the dot and the door opens. The camera pushes forward and follows Whyatt through to a promontory overlooking a verdant and pastoral animated landscape. Tented hardcover books tower in the distance. The foreground shows a pumpkin house, a shoe house, a teapot house, a castle on a cloud moored by a beanstalk, and several normal houses with splayed hardcovers for roofs. Flowers are open books. "Welcome to Storybrook Village, where all our fairy-tale friends live."

An alarm sounds (a ringtone version of the theme song) and Whyatt takes a small handheld computer from his pocket. The episode's new material is introduced; the computer indicates something he should investigate, usually a problem involving one of his friends. Typically, scenes show him walking to the site, passing by random characters in Storybrook Village (and thus the fairy-tale universe). Whyatt arrives and witnesses (or is sometimes the main actor within) a vignette ending with one of the four main characters unsure of how to act. (We discuss examples in the next section.) "This is a super big problem, and a super big problem needs us, the Super Readers! We need to call the rest of the Super Readers: call them with me! Say, 'Calling all Super Readers!'" Several children's voices, presumably in chorus with viewers, say, "Calling all Super Readers!" "To the Book Club!" "To the Book Club!"

The reused animation returns as the characters reassemble at the Book Club, introducing themselves as they arrive: "Whyatt here!" as he runs in; "P is for Pig!" as he rides up on a big wheeled tricycle; "Red Riding Hood rolling in!" as she glides past on her skate-shoes; and "Princess Pea at your service!" as she alights from a horseless carriage with button wheels. "And you," Whyatt says, pointing to the camera, "say your name." A pregnant pause, as Princess Pea waves hello and the other characters smile with recognition. "Great, we're all here! Together we will solve our problem. Let's go!" They move indoors and assemble at a conference table, pausing for Whyatt to insert his handheld device into a large monitor overlooking the table. They sit in their respective seats: Whyatt has a director's chair; Princess Pea a throne; Pig a wooden stool; and Red a rolling desk chair.

Whoever has the problem stands at a dais made from two dominos and presents the issue. Whyatt presides, unless the problem is his, when another takes his place. The problem is articulated into a question, and the chair identifies it as such ("Good question!" says Whyatt: "That's our question!" says Red.) "When we have a question," Whyatt says, "we look . . . in a book!" they say in chorus. "Which book should we look in?" asks Pig. Princess Pea moves to a bookshelf and twirls her wand: "Peas and Carrots / Carrots and Peas / Book come out / Please, please, please!" A book floats down from the shelves. "Let's read the title of this book," Whyatt says, and then he does so. He continues, "We know what to do: we need to jump into this book and find the answer to our question. First, we look for Super Letters and then put them in our Super Duper Computer. Super Duper Computer, how many Super Letters do we need?" He holds the handheld device up to the camera as it one by one draws in the blanks. "Wow! In this story we need [number] Super Letters, and then we'll get our Super Story Answer!"

"It's time to transform. Ready?" "Ready!" they all reply. "Put your arms in!" and, pointedly looking at the camera, "Put *your* arm in! Super Readers . . . to the rescue!" in chorus, and they introduce themselves in turn: "Alpha Pig, with Alphabet Power!" "Wonder Red, with Word Power!" "Princess Presto, with Spelling Power!" "Super Why, with the Power to Read! And Super You, with the Power to Help. Together we are . . . the Super Readers!"

"Why Flyers," Whyatt calls out, as four small planes swoop in, "we're ready to fly into this book." It opens, and the planes fly through the opening page and enter its world, rendered in a stylized paper-cut animation style. They land and leap out of the planes. The Princess says, "Presto! We are in the book [title]." The book's first few sentences and accompanying still drawings pop up. "Let's read," Whyatt says. He pulls out his Why Writer, which both highlights and writes. "Why Writer, highlight! Read with me." As he reads, the drawings begin to move and act out the sentences. Eventually, a problem, a question, emerges, explicitly paralleled with the problem from Storybrook Village. "And that, Super Readers, is why we are in this book," Whyatt explains.

The next twelve minutes—the episode's core—vary according to the story being interpreted. The Super Readers meet the protagonist. Invariably they must travel somewhere and procure or transform an object to meet a specific need. Whatever the particular test, two of the three non-Whyatt Super Readers are employed as helpers: Alpha Pig either builds or follows a trail of letters from A to Z; Princess Presto spells an object's name to make it appear; Wonder Red transforms one object into another that rhymes with it. At the successful completion of the first test, Whyatt tells viewers to "Remember to keep your eyes out for Super Letters." Glowing letters emerge, unseen by the characters but not viewers. "[Gasp!] You see Super Letters? Which letters did you find?" The chorus of children reads them, and Whyatt repeats them. "We need to put them in our Super Duper Computer!" The letters fly into the handheld, each landing in its respective blank. "[Number] more Super Letters, and then we'll get our Super Story Answer! Right on, Readers!" This sequence repeats, with little variation, at the successful completion of the second test.

Finally, the protagonist faces an impasse they cannot resolve because the story says it must be that way: "It says so in my story!" and the relevant sentence appears. "Super Why to the rescue! With the Power to Read, I can change the story and save the day!" Whyatt identifies a word to change and highlights it in the sentence. His Why Writer offers three alternatives, and viewers select one based on Whyatt's suggestions. When time allows, an incorrect word is chosen, and the scenario plays out until proven incorrect, before the right one is selected and proven. The protagonist's story reaches a resolution, the problem solved and how it was overcome recounted and clarified. The final Super Letters emerge. This time, when they land on their respective blanks, the screen goes blank, and Whyatt exclaims, "We found all of our Super Letters! Now we can get our Super Story Answer!"

The protagonist thanks the Super Readers, and they say their good-byes. "Why Flyers, back to the Book Club!" They fly out of the book, and as they hop from the planes they change back to their everyday identities. Whyatt again attaches the handheld to the large monitor: "Super Duper Computer, give us our Super Story Answer! Read the letters with me!" Whyatt reads the Super Letters one by one, in order, then reads the word or phrase. "Our Super Story Answer is [word or phrase]! But, *why*?" Its emergence as the solution to the story protagonist's problem is first recounted, followed by its provision as the original question's response—the problem within Storybrook Village. Armed with this answer, the character returns to the vignette and negotiates the difficulty. "Hip hip hooray! The Super Readers saved the day!" Whyatt exclaims. The four manifest in the village square, dancing to the closing song, which not only contains and repeats that line but also includes "We changed the story, we solved the problem, we worked together so hip hip hooray!" sung while clips of both stories' successful resolutions are shown. The closing credit sequence rolls.

Two Episodes in Detail

The story—framed to be entertaining and engaging to children—is predicated on teaching literacy and language skills. Each episode reformulates the chosen tale to hit three of four key areas—alphabet, spelling, phonics, and reading comprehension. The following two synopses demonstrate a typical episode's flow.

"Hansel and Gretel"
(1, 2; written by Angela C. Santomero, based on ATU 327A)

"Oh right: today we're having a picnic with my friends in the park. Come with me!" Red sees Peter Piper and runs to meet him. She takes one of his pickled peppers and eats it. "You can't just take one of my peppers, Red," he says and walks away. Red sees that he is mad. "What should I do if I want one of Peter Piper's peppers?"

The Super Readers enter "Hansel and Gretel," which begins "Hansel and Gretel found a gingerbread cookie house. A witch lived in the gingerbread cookie house. Hansel and Gretel ate the gingerbread and the witch got mad." "Oh look: the witch is mad at Hansel and Gretel." "Just like Peter Piper is mad at Red for eating his peppers! Peter Piper and the witch are both mad. We need to find that witch!"

Alpha Pig uses his magnifying glass to follow a trail of alphabet crumbs; at each fork he follows the next letter in sequence. The path leads to a stream they must cross. Princess Presto spells "raft" to make one appear. At the house, Hansel and Gretel won't stop eating the house, which upsets the witch, who closes herself inside. Hansel and Gretel are sad that they can't talk to her. "It's no use: it's our story. Look: 'The witch closes the door.'" Super Why changes the word "closes" to "opens." The witch emerges. Hansel and Gretel apologize; they affirm that the cookie house is so so yummy, but they realize they should have asked her first. The witch thanks them for the apology. An oven timer buzzes and she brings out small gingerbread houses baked especially for the children. They ask for one, and the witch thanks them for asking and gives them the cookies. Princess Presto spells "fix" to repair the house.

The Super Story Answer is revealed: "Ask first." "I get it: Hansel and Gretel needed to ask first. So my question is, 'What should I do if I want one of Peter Piper's peppers?' And the answer is, 'Ask first!' Oh, that's true! Okay, I know what to do now. Thanks Super Readers. C'mon!" Red finds Peter Piper sitting at the foot of a tree.

> "Peter, I'm sorry I took one of your peppers."
> "You are?"
> "Yes: those peppers belong to you. If I want one, I should ask first."
> "You know, I still have a few peppers left."
> "You do?" She reaches out, then halts. "Oops. If it's alright with you, may I have one?"
> "Well, since you asked, of course!"

Hip hip hooray.[2]

"Sleeping Beauty"
(1, 28; written by Claudia Silver, based on ATU 410)

"Oh no! Looks like Princess Pea has a problem. C'mon!" Peter Piper and Little Boy Blue are kicking a soccer ball around, and Whyatt joins in. Princess Pea wants to play tea party with the Three Little Pigs, but they want to play pirate instead. Having never played pirates herself, she is loath to join. "What should I do if I don't want to play something else?"

The Super Readers enter "Sleeping Beauty," which begins "Sleeping Beauty loved to sleep. The prince wanted her to go to his soccer party. Sleeping Beauty did not want to go. 'Soccer? I've never played soccer before. No thanks. I'd rather just sleep like I always do.'" "That's just like me! I'd rather have a tea party like I always do!" "Sleeping Beauty and Princess Pea both want to do the same things they always do. We need to see what Sleeping Beauty does about the prince's soccer party!"

In Sleeping Beauty's chambers, they cannot wake her. Alpha Pig uses his Alphabet Tools, building an "l" to turn on a lamp (which she shuts off by throwing her tiara), an "r" to turn on a radio (which she sleepwalks toward and shuts off), and finally a "d" to get her dog to wake her up. The Super Readers ask her about the soccer party. She reaffirms: "I've never played soccer before, so I don't want to go." Despite being shown demonstrations of the fun of skating and twirling, she remains unconvinced and returns to sleep. Super Why suggests getting her outside, but she merely falls asleep in a flower bed. To wake her again, Wonder Red tries a yell, then changes it to "bell," which wakes Sleeping Beauty. The soccer party is about to start; the Super Readers encourage her to go. "It does sound fun, but I only like to do one thing: sleep. It says so in my story. See? 'Sleeping Beauty loves to sleep.'" Super Why adds more words to the sentence, so that it says, "Sleeping Beauty likes to sleep and sing and run." "Wow! Running is fun, too. You know what? There are so many fun things to do; I just never tried them before." Sleeping Beauty goes to the party and thinks she may have fun playing soccer.

The Super Story Answer is revealed: "Try new things."

> "Because when Sleeping Beauty tried new things she learned there were lots of things she liked to do. So my question is, 'What do I do if I don't want to play something I've never played before?' And the answer is, *try new things*. I see. Maybe instead of playing tea party like I always do, I should try a new thing! Come with me!"

Princess Pea decides to try playing pirates, though she still loves tea parties. The eldest pig tells her that she makes an excellent pirate. Hip hip hooray.

Adapting the Stories

Even those with only the most cursory familiarity with the *Märchen* models for the above examples can note absences. In "Hansel and Gretel," gone are the father and stepmother, abandonment in the forest, separation of the children, Gretel's enforced housework, the witch's desire to eat the siblings, Hansel's deception in the fatness test, killing the witch, and the return home. Only the trail of breadcrumbs (which the Super Readers follow into the forest, not out) and the gingerbread house remain. In "Sleeping Beauty," one would be hard-pressed to argue for motif congruity between a woman being cursed to a hundred-year sleep (F 316.1) and sleep being something she really likes. The issues we raise with such use of fairy tales may seem highly reactionary—that tales are "corrupted" for television and educational broadcasting. As mentioned above, we do not decry creative uses of traditional texts, yet we remain wary of some of *Super Why!*'s variants and of its overall structure.

In each episode, the Super Readers enter a story as it appears in a book. The choice of a book makes sense representationally: it requires no additional character (such as a storyteller); the Super Readers enter on their own, emphasizing reading's independence; and it offers a diegetic landscape for the text. But presenting narrative as fixed and unidirectional with an (anonymous) author as ultimate authority starts to obscure the possibility of multiple variants. Jack Zipes suggested that a tale's published version "gave it more legitimacy and enduring value than an oral tale which disappeared soon after it was told" (1994, 74). Such reification, directed at such a young audience, seems to deny the pleasures of storytelling, both for audiences and, eventually, for tellers.

With Northern European tales so broadly represented, and the likelihood of children encountering other variants, our concern with the privileging of *Super Why!*'s version through its association with text might be assuaged. But when one extends beyond more commonly mediated tales, the issue of representation is brought into firmer contrast. In "Tiddalick the Frog" (1, 27; written by Shilla Dinsmore), the Super Readers discover Tiddalick, from Australian Aboriginal myth (Waterman type 2400 [1987]), as a frog who frolics in puddles after it rains, using up all the water, much to the chagrin of Kangaroo and Wallaby, who need it, respectively, to bathe and garden. They change his story from "jumps in" to "shares" water; the Super Story Answer is "Save water," which applies to the problem of Whyatt's mother being angry at him for running the tap. Gone are the themes of Tiddalick drinking all the water in the world, the proposed solution of making him laugh, the failed attempts before Eel stands straight on his head, and how by spewing out all the water he causes the great flood.[3]

In "Momotarō the Peach Boy" (1, 33; written by Betty Quan), Momotarō and his friends (a dog, a monkey, and a pheasant) will not stop arguing on their way to confront an ogre terrifying their village. When they cooperate by lifting a giant feather to tickle the ogre, he stops roaring and starts laughing—the change to the story suggested by Super You. The Super Story

Answer is "Work together," which helps Pig and his two brothers build their fort. It differs from the traditional version's attention to Momotarō's enormous appetite and size, his fierce intelligence, and his intense purpose and determination (Seki type 159 [1966]). His miraculous birth is presented in an aside, his triumphant return with the ogre's treasure elided, and the disagreements between him and his animal companions—the point of the story's invocation—a new invention.

This illustrates one discomfort we feel in our at times cross-purposed roles as both parents and folklorists. By choosing only a few non-European tales and removing significant aspects of their cultural specificity, *Super Why!* presents viewers with a text far removed from the plurality of versions originally performed. With "Hansel and Gretel" and "Sleeping Beauty" we are confident that our son—simply by living in North America—will be exposed to a range of versions and manifestations. He will have the opportunity, consciously or not, to locate the *Super Why!* version within his conception of the type and even come to appreciate the show's writers' creative use of traditional texts. But for less broadly disseminated tales, we fear that, when not given evidence to the contrary, the version becomes *the* type.

Even the European versions demonstrate how the desire to render a tale as the protagonists' opportunity to learn a valuable lesson can fundamentally alter what might otherwise be taken from that story. Thus, for example, in "The Magic Porridge Pot" (1, 31; written by Jennifer Hamburg, Andrea Maywhort, and Eric Salet, based on ATU 565 "The Magic Mill"), a girl has been given a magic porridge pot but does not listen to her father for the spell to make it stop. As a consequence, her whole village becomes overflowed until she stops to "Listen" (the Super Story Answer). In more traditional versions, only the rightful owner can stop the pot (or mill), and it overflows when used by someone else; in many instances, when the protagonist is a young girl, her parent misuses it, and the child has the power. Although the *Super Why!* narratives emphasize the emergence of self-empowerment, they often negate the possibility of the child being already empowered, sometimes present in traditional narratives.

Super You, with the Power to Help

Holbek's observed salient fairy-tale characteristics include both storytellers and audiences identifying with the protagonists, not only with respect to sex and gender (male and female storytelling repertoires differed) but also because the fairy-tale protagonists' sociocultural situation initially mirrored their own (1989, 42). This identification operates twofold in *Super Why!* In the first instance, the Super Readers are meant to be recognizably similar to the home viewer, albeit perhaps a few years older. As the PBS website parents' page states, "Each of these characters is re-imagined as an everyday kid, not unlike your child's own friends" (Out of the Blue 2007b, "Program Summary"). In the second instance, the story protagonists are, with a few exceptions, rendered as the same age. The narrative moves viewers through to a world, however fantastic, wherein their norms are validated (Holbek 1989, 42) or, more precisely for this instance, constructed and instructed.

This projection goes further, of course; with the deliberate breaking of the fourth wall, viewers do not simply project themselves on to the Super Readers, they are invited along. In her discussion of *Dora the Explorer*'s similar use of direct address, Erin Ryan notes how "the use of the word 'we' implies that the audience is just as much a part of the story as Dora and her animated friends. Preschool children may believe that they are an instrumental part of solving Dora's problems; a belief that has the potential to positively affect the self esteem and confidence of audience members" (2010, 60). The mode of representation makes Super You, the viewer, ultimately responsible for the story outcome. Along with facilitating the Super Readers' letter and word choices, viewers find the Super Letters required for the Super Story Answer. Viewers' ongoing integration with the Super Readers' actions reaffirms their empowerment. Again, *Dora the Explorer*'s cocreator Chris Gifford said, "To have a character act as an avatar for them, [preschool children] feel as if they are actively helping her every step of the way. That feeling of empowerment is so exciting to them" (qtd. in Ryan 2010, 66).

The flip side of this interactivity and agency is that it is purely a construct of the program creators. When children do not react to requests for interaction, the show nevertheless proceeds as if they had. To illustrate, one Sunday in June 2012, at age four, with his mother still asleep, our son asked to watch television, specifically requesting *Super Why!* The episode was "Momotarō the Peach Boy." When the Super Readers asked for his name, he gave it. When the word "arguing" was mentioned, he asked what it meant. When he saw the first Super Letters, he squealed. Once the ogre was defeated, he apparently lost interest and instead focused on the toys he was playing with throughout; but when the Super Story Answer was revealed, he repeated it and said "Work together. Hey, you and I work together when we play!" (We recognize how saccharine this reads.)

We started another: "The Gingerbread Boy." He watched some of the story but none of the preamble. Quite content to leave the room, he brought some toys to the kitchen. But he soon returned and, when the dangers of the gingerbread boy almost hurting himself by running too fast were stressed, he sat down on the couch to watch. When the last three Super Letters ("b e f") appeared, he said "Be careful" instead of reading them out. Whether he remembered or figured it out anew I couldn't tell and, when asked, he said he didn't know. (He wasn't in the room when the first were revealed and didn't appear to be paying attention when the next ones were.) With the Super Story Answer finally revealed, he asked what "Be careful" meant. In sum, he engaged with the show only to the extent that he wanted; he was comfortable with the notion that it would proceed without his input.

Lawrence Sipe notes the many predictable ways a child might respond to a story: working at understanding its narrative elements, comparing and contrasting it with other stories or their real life (like our son did with "Work together"), or subsequent creative reexpression (retelling, play performance, drawing a scene from it, and so forth). But "expressive performative engagement" (2002, 476) also occurs when reading, particularly during "interactive read-alouds." Sipe notes five: *dramatizing*, physically acting out elements within the story, such as roaring when a monster is described; *talking back*, addressing characters directly, such as telling Little Red Riding Hood to be careful because Grandmother is actually a wolf; *critiquing/controlling*, suggesting alternatives in plots, characters, or setting, such as that Little Red Riding Hood ought to have lied to the wolf about her basket's contents; *inserting oneself*, in presenting themself as additional characters in the story, interacting with protagonists, suggesting alternatives, sometimes through physical enactment; and finally *taking over*, where the listener uses story elements to create something wholly other from the original, usually as subversion or parody (477–79). Sipe suggests a continuum within this typology; in moving from dramatizing to taking over, one increasingly operates within a Bakhtinian carnivalesque mode.

All five modes are implied in *Super Why!*'s interactivity at one time or another, although "taking over" might be reserved for the few pastiche episodes, while "dramatizing" through physical movement is little more than making letters with one's fingers. On the other hand, "talking back," "critiquing/controlling," and "inserting oneself" form the core of viewers' activities. They are directly addressed and asked for responses and also help select words to insert into the story; the entire character of Super You wraps the interactivity into a singular premise. Where Sipe's model does not work is the very real difference between an interactive read-aloud and the television program. In the former, readers/narrators can adapt to the expressive performative engagements; in the latter, the homeostatic narrative is molded around a limited menu of expected and encouraged expressive performative engagements that need never actually occur.

Robert C. Allen notes how the eighteenth-century novel briefly gave rise to a "characterized fictional reader," directly addressed by the narrators of such books as Henry Fielding's *Tom Jones* and Laurence Stern's *Tristram Shandy* (1992, 86). Similarly, television often breaks the fourth wall and addresses viewers directly, most often in news, advertising, game shows, talk shows, and educational programming. Allen never goes so far as to suggest a "characterized fictional viewer"; his examples from fictional television never extend beyond noting an occasional look into the camera or asking a rhetorical question. However, by such techniques as naming the viewer, directly addressing them, and waiting for Super You's answers to posed questions, *Super Why!*'s creators have imbued them with a host of qualities that make them a character operating in the same ontological realm as the other Super Readers.

What is presented in the guise of a dynamic "storytelling event," replete with the reciprocal set of rights and responsibilities and the fluid identities of storyteller and story listener suggested by Robert Georges (1969), over time reveals a highly unidirectional and static narrative: We—the Super Readers including Super You—appear to enter and then change stories to uncover answers to common problems, but instead we grow to discover that indeed we have no control over the story and that the meaning we take from it—which may extend beyond this one version to the entire type—is a preconditioned, pat answer.

"Real-World" Problems

Story is an excellent vehicle for digesting and interpreting worldview. Elizabeth Tucker notes, "Within the tale's clear-cut limits, young narrators can express their developing views of the world around them" (1980, 19). The "narrated at" child is similarly encouraged to use story to explore worldview, however framed and limited that investigation might be. In each *Super Why!* episode, a character encounters a problem, resolved by looking in a book and flying into a story's world to get the Super Story Answer. This answer is never longer than sixteen letters, suggesting little room for nuance. In theory, the superheroes have "real-world" problems similar to those of children in contemporary times. The parents' website suggests, "In every episode, one of the friends encounters a problem with another Storybrook Village character (For instance, Jill from the Jack and Jill rhyme is not being nice). As in real life, the problems require preschool social skills to resolve" (Out of the Blue 2007b, "Program Summary"). Social relationships and societal rules are typical fodder for problems the Super Readers confront.

Super Why! approaches the audience squarely from the perspective of middle-class problems. The created presentation of congruity between viewer and Storybrook Village and Super Reader and fairy tale simultaneously makes assumptions about viewers and takes liberties with traditional narratives. The "typical" children's problems more accurately show points of contention between the adult's world and the child's. While *Super Why!* seems to attempt to assuage social anxieties, we would argue that it actually creates awareness of potential sources of social anxieties or suggests and instructs social mores. Political and social issues center many story lines, sometimes quite explicitly: in "Tiddalick the Frog" the Super Story Answer, "Save water," has little to do with the traditional narrative but much to do with contemporary concerns. In the revisited "Hansel and Gretel: A Healthy Adventure" (1, 46), the witch eats pieces of her sugar house and therefore lacks energy, with the Super Story Answer being "Healthy," in contrast to the initial telling when the children eat the witch's house without asking and learn to "Ask first."

The two Hansel and Gretel episodes have given us pause. Over time, a narrative initially illustrating starvation, want, and abandonment, transformed to a Victorian narrative about "stranger danger" and abduction fears[4] while maintaining some fanciful imagery about houses built of candy. The rich polyvalence of traditional narrative allowed multiple meanings, whereas viewers are directly instructed to take only one lesson from each *Super Why!* version. Within the *Super Why!* universe, the implied worldview is one of safety, the only real "danger" coming from the self.

Perhaps our questions can be better illustrated by issues the show does not address. For example, the writers have not confronted gender issues. The two main female characters form a complementary dyad of differing ways of exercising "girlhood": the princess and the tomboy. But taken separately they are stereotypes that reinforce that dichotomy (and are somewhat annoying).

Princess has tea parties; Red plays sports. Princess is afraid of not being dainty; Red gets in trouble when she is too headstrong. As Super Readers, Princess switches from a dress to a full gown, while Red transforms into a roller derby girl. Meanwhile, Pig's problems principally stem from being little and the youngest, while Whyatt's are based in large part on his impetuousness. We see missed opportunities for portraying other kinds of difference. Though the African American Princess Pea may dispel some concerns about racism, when Gwen Sharp looked for merchandise, the character's "blackness" appeared on a sliding scale. Dolls ranged from dark-skinned with black hair to a Caucasian pink with purple hair, leaving Sharp to comment, "The choices about what the Princess Presto doll should look like in doll form put PBS in the position of appearing to think that a mixed-race character needs to be whitened to sell" (2011).

Finally, by rendering only fairy tales featuring protagonists who are identifiably and perennially children, a principal theme that tales traditionally explored—the shift from childhood to adulthood—is necessarily cut off. Cinderella wants to go to the prince's dance party to dance—not to pursue upward mobility, escape penury and want, and create a family. The princess wants Rumpelstiltskin to spin straw into gold to make her house pretty for her tea party; she is not desperate because her father has presented her to a prince as capable of such a feat that she must perform on pain of death, albeit with a reward for success.

Perhaps preschool programming is neither the time nor the place for introducing such issues to children. *Super Why!*'s creators maintain that reading fundamentals, and only secondly social mores, are the show's core objectives. Angela Santomero states: "My series introduce and resolve challenges right away, providing conflict-resolution skills when they're needed most. I also work hard to create 'sticky' content so that when an episode ends, the main ideas are firmly rooted in viewers' minds. The focus needs to be on teaching children how to think, not what to think" (2010). Perhaps morality and social messages figure so extensively in *Super Why!* because it fills a niche that parents find missing from the children's television market. Indeed, in our broad experience with media directed toward children ages two to seven (an experience rooted in having a child with a rather voracious appetite for television with parents who screen heavily for content), we can safely say that few other shows venture into this terrain. Yet when "the answer" to a story is provided, the multiple differing meanings of traditional narrative move to the background. As Donald Haase states, "Fairy tales consist of chaotic symbolic codes that have become highly ambiguous and invite quite diverse responses" (1993, 235), but Storybrook Village enjoins one correct response, and certainly no "irresponsible reading" (ibid., 239). Should the *Super Why!* version be a young viewer's first exposure to a tale type, we can only speculate how she will interpret subsequent exposures.

Who HAS Got the Power?

When *Super Why!* first aired in September 2007, the *New York Times* wrote, "As a reading lesson, 'Super Why!' is brilliantly clever. As a lesson in literary interpretation, it fails miserably. In its effort to meet children where they are, to translate the great works of the ages into digestible bites that invite rather than challenge, 'Why!' perfectly reflects the attitudes of this age" (Stewart 2007). Although we would like to think our son's genetic inheritance helped, and we know that reading to him so he could always see the words on the page was a key contributor, there is little doubt in our minds that *Super Why!* is one of the reasons he has a remarkably advanced reading level. His alphabet and sounding out skills have been found surprising at his daycare, especially as he was never much for talking; he could practically read before he could talk. As an introduction to the world of traditional narrative, however, it stung. We found ourselves impelled (compelled?) to watch a show about fairy tales out of a sense of parental but not folkloristic duty. Sotto voce utterances of "That's not how that goes" or "Why would she do that?" or "That's not even a fairy tale" resonated through our living room, no doubt. Nevertheless, we have the *Super Why!* app for the iPad, a DVD, a storybook, an activity book, and even an Alpha Pig figure, not all purchased begrudgingly.

Super Why! is funded in part by grants from the US Department of Education's Ready to Learn initiative, which "supports the development of educational television and digital media targeted at preschool and early elementary school children and their families. Its general goal is to promote early learning and school readiness, with a particular interest in reaching low-income children" (US Department of Education 2011). In 2005, the mandate moved away from developing social skills to focus solely on literacy (Corporation for Public Broadcasting 2011, 8), and *Super Why!* has proven itself, albeit in studies funded by and presented through the Corporation for Public Broadcasting (ibid., 16). Using the reading of traditional tales as a backdrop, and transposing the quotidian problems of a preschooler to them as the foregrounded cause of narrative tension, is clearly one effective strategy for developing literacy skills.

Nevertheless, we worry about the cultural capital and cultural literacy lost with a boiled-down, fractured, or completely changed narrative that fails to tackle issues of, among others, sex and gender, race, and class. While arguably other popular culture forms of fairy tales are directed toward children in this age group, none explores tales so consistently and explicitly with an educational mandate. We hope that children will be exposed to other forms and grasp the possibilities of type and version, however inchoately. But how *Super Why!* will alter its understanding of what fairy tales *are* and *do* remains to be seen. Finally, what effect this will have on the common storehouse of narrative that operated as polyvalent cultural shorthand in our society is unclear. But the boy can read.

Notes

1. Not to be confused with *Once Upon a Time*'s Storybrooke, Maine, discussed in Hay and Baxter's and Schwabe's chapters.
2. Tresca's chapter discusses very different TV episodes based on "Hansel and Gretel," and Jorgensen and Warman's chapter discusses two other "Sleeping Beauty" shows.
3. A variant (Waterman type 2410) suggests that these events explain why the frog is moist, very small, and not mirthful.
4. Zipes suggests that the tale's central theme is not simply abandonment but its rationalization (1997, 59).

2

MERLIN AS INITIATION TALE

A Contemporary Fairy-Tale Manual for Adolescent Relationships

Emma Nelson and Ashley Walton

Among the histories of which they sang or talked, there was a famous one, concerning the bravery and virtues of KING ARTHUR, supposed to have been a British Prince in those old times. But, whether such a person really lived, or whether there were several persons whose histories came to be confused together under that one name, or whether all about him was invention, no one knows.

Charles Dickens, *A Child's History of England* (1852, 335)

n fall 2008, a family drama called *Merlin* premiered on the British Broadcasting Corporation (BBC), opening: "No young man, no matter how great, can know his destiny. He must live and learn. And so it will be for the young warlock arriving at the gates of Camelot" (1, 2).¹ The series title and introduction allude to the Merlin of myth, protector and seer to the legendary King Arthur. However, the unfolding story subverts expectations. According to series cocreator Johnny Capps, the BBC's Merlin (Colin Morgan) is "a geeky kind of teenager who is still struggling to find himself" (2 DVD special features), not a wise old wizard. *Merlin* deliberately deviates from historical versions to explore modern Westernized cultural concerns: Arthur (Bradley James) recast as an adolescent who needs help to achieve his destiny; Merlin reimagined as Arthur's servant, friend, and would-be peer, with the gift of magic in a society that brutally represses it; Morgana (Katie McGrath) as a sometimes compassionate witch struggling to find autonomy; and Guinevere (Angel Coulby) as an intelligent and resourceful servant. *Merlin*'s play with concepts of race, gender, class, and family—familiar subjects in young adult (YA) literature—in the context of a fantasized medieval-like setting focuses our chapter. We also demonstrate how the show's young adult audience, using social media, responds by interpreting the show's characters and their dilemmas.

Merlin reinvents Arthurian lore as an initiation tale and coming-of-age story. As the youthful characters struggle to mature in a fresh version of a familiar narrative, fairy-tale archetypes create dynamic new relationships and perspectives for contemporary audiences. Director James Hawes notes, "It's young kids in this extraordinary magical world, but that kids today could relate to" (1 DVD special features). Indeed, the opening episode shows the title character looking little different from an average Euro–North American kid; he wears a nondescript jacket and trousers—no medieval hose and tunic. Capps comments that the creators "saw [Arthur] as a modern-day Prince Harry," citing his "Prince Harry gaucheness" (1, 1 DVD commentary). Though American audiences may not connect hopes for redemption of the current British monarchy and Arthur's democratizing impulses, they may appreciate the show's lack of pantomime or high theater acting, which creates a naturalistic atmosphere. Its creators see *Merlin* as a "family show," but they deliberately look to "push" the limits of its original British Saturday night slot (ibid.).

Seeking a large-scale, epic appearance, Capps notes that the creators "wanted [*Merlin*] to look like a movie"; they used wide shots in order to give it a "cinematic quality" (ibid.). Yet their aim was not historical epic but instead fantasy. The presence of a gnomic dragon (voiced by John Hurt) who informs Merlin of his fate marks the genre. DVD commentaries allude to criticisms that *Merlin* has too many anachronistic elements, taking liberties with traditional Arthurian stories and ignoring historical facts by sprinkling medieval weapons, architecture, and scenery with contemporary speech and behaviors.[2] This is no accident; creators and directors note that a fantasy series like theirs offers more plot and character openings than a period piece might. Capps sees *Merlin* as combining "big epic, great comedy . . . big stories [and] big emotions." Their models are "action adventure movie standards" (ibid.) like *Raiders of the Lost Ark* (1981) or *The Bourne Ultimatum* (Greengrass 2007), so they "play games with the legend" as cocreator Julian Murphy says (1, 1 DVD commentary).

However, *Merlin*'s influences are eclectic. The film *Diva* (Beineix 1981) inspired a song that literally enchants the court in "The Dragon's Call" (1, 1); *The Terminator* (1984) was a model for the Black Knight in "Excalibur" (1, 9); *Seven Samurai* (1954) structures the plot of "The Moment of Truth" (1, 10); the TV series *Jeeves and Wooster* (1990–1993) with its ditzy aristocrat perpetually rescued by his savvy servant invokes Arthur and Merlin's relationship; the TV show and film *The Odd Couple* (1970–1975; Saks 1968) summons the quips between Merlin and his mentor Gaius (Richard Wilson; and even *Basic Instinct* (1992) models the femme fatale in "The Gates of Avalon" (1, 7).

Fairy-tale references include a two-part "Beauty and the Beast" (2, 5 and 6) episode, which little resembles the tale type (ATU 425C). Scenes wherein Merlin magically cleans Gaius's quarters recall "The Sorcerer's Apprentice" in Disney's *Fantasia* (1940). Murphy notes: "*Beauty and the Beast* and Jean Cocteau . . . were our inspirations; it was trying to get that fairy tale quality, that magical world quality" (1, 1 DVD commentary). *Merlin* plays with fairy-tale patterns—quests, impossible tasks, magical helpers, and so on—to render complex themes, characters, and ideas recognizable to adolescent viewers, layering the classic story with modern dialogue and gestures. Imbuing *Merlin* with contemporary elements while frequently ignoring historical accuracy allows the television series to forge characters' relationships in ways that would otherwise be impossible or seem disingenuous because of medieval hierarchies that marginalized servants, women, and children. The deliberately ahistorical presentation of an apparent period piece allowed creators considerable freedom.[3] Incorporating themes of class, gender, and family prominent in fairy-tale discourse as well as in YA literature, *Merlin* acknowledges the negative but historically accurate treatment of oppressed groups, but its characters often undermine patriarchal familial and sociocultural hierarchies. The son is wiser than the father; the servants more capable than their employers; commoners more noble than royalty; and women as well—often even better—versed in warcraft and witchery as men.

Arthurian stories have evolved over the centuries from Christian myth and political legend to contemporary versions that indicate their wide appeal and continued relevance. For example, the first written work seeking to validate the historicity of King Arthur is Geoffrey of Monmouth's *Historia Regum Britanniae* (1136), which was greatly influenced by Welsh monk Nennius's *Historia Brittonum* (828–30). These sources' authenticity is questionable, but they resulted in later adaptations, including operas such as Henry

Purcell's *King Arthur* (1691), Carl Goldmark's *Merlin* (1886), and Amadeu Vives's *Artús* (1895). Arthurian literature dates to the eleventh century, in Latin, French, Welsh, German, and other languages. Thomas Malory's *Le Morte d'Arthur* (1485), Alfred, Lord Tennyson's narrative poems *The Idylls of the King* (1856–1885), and T. H. White's *The Sword in the Stone* (1938) and *The Once and Future King* (1958) are the best known. Film and television versions include Walt Disney's animated *The Sword in the Stone* (1963), Joshua Logan's musical *Camelot* (1967), John Boorman's *Excalibur* (1981), and, more recently, Hallmark's television miniseries *Merlin* (1998) and Starz's *Camelot* miniseries (2011). Into the twenty-first century, the story shows no signs of losing appeal or momentum; Arthurian tales continue to appear in songs, comics, video games, board games, television series, and films (Lupack 2002, 1–3).

Arthurian narratives exemplify how "fairy tales blend easily into related kinds [of stories], like myths, legends, romances, realistic folk fables, and cautionary tales" (Sale 1979, 23). Camelot and the round table incorporate myth rooted in Christianity via spiritual, supernatural events, such as God's chosen one drawing the sword Excalibur from the stone, the Holy Grail, and Arthur and his knights as divinely inspired leaders. They use English, Welsh, Celtic, Irish, and Scottish legends of a powerful king or soldier. They integrate fantastical elements, magic, wonder, and moralizing that recall fairy-tale generic conventions. Arthurian tales reflect values and beliefs of past cultures, but retellings replicate and recreate contemporary knowledge: "Arthuriana is important because it is a study of our culture on many levels . . . to understand our society, our values, and our dreams" (Lupack 2002, 2). As a contemporary retelling, *Merlin* mirrors and speaks to its current audience.

While Arthuriana has developed and changed over the centuries, the BBC innovates in adapting it to an adolescent cast and audience. Replacing the older sorcerer Merlin with a peer to the young Arthur enables themes significantly different from those of children's and adults' versions. Focusing on relationships rather than historical fidelity, *Merlin*'s themes, ideas, actions, and characters evolve in ways that teens can apply to their own personal struggles.[4] However, the series is designed to appeal to a wider audience with positive messages and family values like courage, leadership, loyalty, and equality (Capps, 2 DVD special features), validating the claim that increased adolescent and adult interest in YA fiction is "indicative of the quality and enduring themes [it] addresses" (Grady 2011).

Arthur's family dynamic varies over time, but most often he is born after Uther rapes Igraine, his enemy Gorlois's wife. *Merlin* creators sanitize the tale, reinventing Ygraine as Uther's legal but barren wife who conceives Arthur by magic and thus dies. In thirteenth-century literature, Morgan(a) le Fay is the legitimate daughter of Igraine and her husband Gorlois—and is thus Arthur's half sister through their shared mother. However, *Merlin*'s Morgana is *Uther*'s (Anthony Head) *illegitimate* daughter from an extramarital affair, and Arthur his *legitimate* son and heir. Eliminating the rape from Arthur's origin narrative makes him the rightful heir of noble birth; injecting infidelity into Morgana's gives the initially likable and altruistic princess a justifiable cause for turning on her father. Yet lacking a single origin story, Arthuriana has at least two different forms: historical attempts to identify Arthur and folkloric versions relying on peasant tales and mythos (Higham 2002, 97). *Merlin*'s portrayal of adolescence combines the two. The story arc of the four young primary characters—Arthur, Guinevere (Gwen), Merlin, and Morgana—explains the development of their adult manifestations: Arthur as noble king, Guinevere as conflicted queen, Merlin as powerful wizard, and Morgana as destructive witch.[5] As they come of age together, reflecting the angst, anticipation, and longing for love and acceptance prevalent in contemporary YA fiction, their narratives parallel the fairy tale's historical use of initiating adolescents and helping them adapt to their future adult roles.[6]

Fairy tales similarly show characters verging on adulthood overcoming obstacles, finding romance, determining self-worth, discovering sexuality, and interacting with family: in "The Princess and the Frog" (ATU 440, "The Frog King or Iron Henry"; Uther 2004), the girl must "overcome her aversion to the frog, a phallic symbol repulsive at first but rewarding at last" (Falassi 1980, 40); in "Donkey Skin" (ATU 510B, "Peau d'âne")[7] the princess must leave her family, learn female duties, and marry a prince in order to find fulfillment (Falassi 1980, 46). "The sequence of fairy tales seems analogous to that of coming into the cultural world from a more innocent state" (ibid., 42). Of course, adolescence itself is a social construct, accommodating a transitional stage between childhood and adulthood that varies widely between cultures and eras. In Western societies, for instance, adolescence has shifted from a barely recognized transition to a phase "central to life, a period of preparation and self-definition" (Hine 2000, 11). *Merlin* explores the attributes British and North American cultures ascribe to teens, including rebellion against elders, innovation, and preoccupation with sex and peer relationships.[8]

Fiction author Shannon Hale, widely known for her YA fairy-tale adaptations,[9] argues that teens can "explore, learn, question, and play" through stories that present options and ideas specific to their life stage (2012). Contemporary YA fiction in general and fairy-tale adaptations in particular have evolved into complex retellings that resonate with adolescent—and, increasingly, adult[10]—audiences: "The more [fairy tales] are told, the more complex they become, [and] each new modern take draw[s] in a larger audience" (Babu 2012). YA fairy-tale adaptations illustrate common experiences and empower viewers to redefine themselves through significant socializing narratives.

Creator Capps claims that *Merlin* innovatively inverts traditional relationships between the characters to create new tensions (2 DVD special features). As they learn together, Arthur, Gwen, Merlin, and Morgana form bonds and ruin relationships in ways that appear to American audiences as typical of high school television dramas (see, e.g., Byers 2005). As in the latter form, teenagers are often as (if not more) intelligent and capable as their elders, undermining and upsetting traditional parental and other authority figures. *Merlin* explores didactic themes that complicate medieval social structures to reinforce current ideologies.

For example, Gwen and Morgana undercut conservative gendered ideology by voicing opinions, fighting alongside men or leading armies, and determining their own destinies, all while maintaining their conventionally defined femininity.[11] They complicate class, as servant Gwen becomes queen and royal. Morgana becomes an outcast, choosing independence over court life. With her mother dead and her father executed for witchcraft by King Uther, Gwen's friends become her kin, "reshaping families from the biological order to the social" (Warner 1994, 217). Morgana eventually turns against her family and friends, choosing to destroy them rather than continue her princess narrative. "Beneath the nursery veneer, or perhaps because of it, fairy tales are among our most powerful socializing narratives" (Orenstein 2002, 10). *Merlin* similarly offers audiences means to understand and redefine the self within and against social and cultural limitations.

Merlin Complicating Race/Gender

Fairy-tale images like the handsome prince and the innocent persecuted heroine can comprise adolescent codes for what it means to be male or female,[12] "maps for coping with personal anxieties, family conflicts, social frictions, and the myriad frustrations of everyday life" (Tatar 1999, xviii). Yet scholars disagree on whether that influence is positive or negative. For example, Andrea Dworkin believes traditional fairy tales reinforce patriarchal prescriptions of gender normativity and "values and consciousness printed on our minds as cultural absolutes long before we were in fact men and women" (1974, 32). Conversely, Alison Lurie argues, "These stories suggest a society in which women are as competent and active as men" (1970, 42). Whatever their influence, traditional fairy-tale characters' flat aspects make them potentially interpretable: "The fairy tale has no real interest in human subjectivity or psychological characterization of the individual. . . . Characters are rendered down to essentials, described in terms of one or two defining characteristics" (Tiffin 2009, 14). In contrast, contemporary fairy-tale versions tend to complicate gender and offer new perspectives on identities, often consciously avoiding reinforcing gender normativity.[13]

Merlin similarly creates complex individuals with whom teen viewers can identify as they build their own complicated relationships. Subplots of courtship and coming of age mingle with the well-known story: Arthur becomes responsible for the kingdom, and Merlin learns to use his magic in others' best interest. Morgana attempts to balance familial loyalty with individuality (before she exchanges the princess for the witch narrative), and Guinevere, the commoner turned princess, navigates romantic interactions. Their internal and external role exchanges make them multidimensional heroines rather than categorically simplistic princess or witch characters.

Traditional narratives usually portray Guinevere as fair, light-skinned royalty.[14] However, *Merlin* inverts expectations in casting Coulby, a mixed-race actress, in the role of Morgana's servant who becomes queen at the fourth season's conclusion.[15] *Merlin*'s Gwen might initially seem the oppressed Cinderella-type serving girl, but the show complicates her racial and gendered identity, since Gwen's femininity is quite unprincesslike. Gwen breaks from traditional female portrayals in Arthurian narratives through her resourcefulness and intelligence. Though she does her fair share of cleaning, helping her mistress, and fulfilling many aesthetic ideals of femininity, she also has a keen understanding of the blacksmith's trade and can handle a sword in combat, knowledge typically gendered male. In the series' second episode, Gwen tells Merlin how to properly put on a knight's armor and he asks, "Why are you so much better at this than me?" His question implies that as a man he should know more on the subject. Gwen replies, "I'm the blacksmith's daughter. I know pretty much everything there is to know about armor . . .

which is actually kind of sad." Instead of being proud of her knowledge, she initially suggests embarrassment and regret at her gender-atypical familiarity with warlike accoutrements. However, Merlin says, "No! It's brilliant!" and they exchange smiles. Merlin, who generally centers the show's perspective, sees Gwen's knowledge and intelligence as an asset, not a detraction. That she simultaneously inhabits traditionally male- and female-oriented spheres makes her a balanced and whole individual.[16]

Merlin's Morgana similarly complicates gender as the king's ward (she is revealed in season three to be his illegitimate daughter). Her lifestyle initially reflects the traditional fairy-tale princess rather than the sorceress and enemy to the kingdom found in most Arthurian stories. Morgana breaks fairy-tale expectations when she chooses to pursue her vendetta against King Uther and his son Arthur, yet she never simply becomes an archetypal, simplistically evil witch. On the contrary, she often exemplifies sympathy, love, and inner conflict. In traditional Arthuriana, Morgana is Arthur's, Merlin's, and Guinevere's antagonist. However, *Merlin*'s Morgana often, particularly in the first two seasons, shows them love and admiration. For example, in season two, one of Uther's many enemies kidnaps Gwen, who has stayed behind so that Morgana (their intended target) can escape, but Uther refuses to pay the ransom. Morgana convinces Arthur to rescue her, stating: "How could you be so heartless! Gwen is the most kind, loyal person that you will ever meet, and you would leave her at the mercy of those animals! Have you no shame? Do you think of no one but yourself?" (2, 4). This grief-stricken Morgana loves Gwen and wants to bring her back safely. Instead of painting Morgana as innately evil, *Merlin* complicates binary categories of good and evil.

By inverting conventional fairy tales that may socialize girls to become submissive and objectified, *Merlin* changes expectations of female characters and provides perhaps hitherto unfamiliar heroines: the serving girl with a voice; royals and servants who are friends; the dark-skinned girl as queen, not sidekick; and the stereotypical witches recast as young, beautiful, and multidimensional. The complexity of *Merlin*'s female characters can be attributed to the show's focus on an adolescent audience, as it provides scenarios in which teen characters determine how gender roles should be enacted and illustrates for their audience how girls/women can behave independently, regardless of perceived social expectations for females.

In addition to complicating female stereotypes, *Merlin* subverts expectations for flat male archetypes through Merlin and Arthur. Typically in Arthurian tales, Merlin is the sidekick to Arthur's capable hero. In *Merlin*,

Arthur is certainly still the athletic knight in shining armor, but he needs Merlin's magical help. Because of Uther's death sentence on anyone practicing or even associated with magic (except, of course, himself, when he finds it expedient), Merlin must assist Arthur secretly and subversively; the prince remains oblivious to the fact that his servant has rescued him time and time again. The main character is the skinny, physically uncoordinated, not stereotypically handsome, but gifted Merlin. He often clearly has greater power than the royal Arthur. For example, in the series' first episode, when the two meet for the second time, Merlin says to Arthur, "Look, I've told you you're an ass. I just didn't realize you were a royal one." After some banter, Arthur laughs and says, "I could take you apart with one blow." Merlin snaps, "I could take you apart with less than that."

Viewers see that although Arthur has greater strength, instantiating current hegemonic masculinity's insistence on male physical prowess (see, e.g., Iacuone 2005), Merlin has supremacy. He proceeds to humiliate the prince by using small magic spells to make him look clumsy. Not only is Arthur helpless in the situation, but he also fails to realize that Merlin is the one in control. Showing Merlin as a character with real power complicates his helper role, suggesting that, for men, physical strength and social standing are not the only advantages worth having. In fact, Merlin's role as the working-class hero prevailing through cleverness is prominent in fairy tales such as "Tom Thumb" (ATU 700, "Thumbling"), "Jack and the Beanstalk" (ATU 328A), and "The Race between Hare and Hedgehog" (ATU 275A). *Merlin* thus resists sociocultural limitations through characters who find their own strengths, passions, and skills rather than being boxed in by gender expectations. The skinny helpmate Merlin rescues the strong, handsome prince. The maid is the intellectual equal of the male characters. And the evil witch has more compassion than the king.

Merlin and Class

Many Arthurian stories engage characters from rigid class systems. Indeed, even in *Merlin,* commoner characters like Lancelot and G(a)waine cannot become knights, no matter how much valor and prowess they display, until the democratic Arthur dispenses with class. His father King Uther sees leadership, fealty, and servitude for both women and men as driven by class, not character. But unlike traditional Arthurian stories in which social distinctions determine characters' very different fates, peasants and kings can be friends and a serving girl can become a princess. Thus, in *Merlin*'s initiation tale, characters illustrate "strengths, human frailties, sufferings, and strong senses of humor . . . [helping viewers] understand that the human condition is tragic, comic, sad, and joyous, and shared by all of us" (Cope 1998, 8). By promoting a meritocracy geared toward a middle-class audience, *Merlin* bridges differences rather than focusing on social structures allegedly now absent in Europe and North America. However, the series still maintains bourgeois Euro–North American ideology like the "rags-to-riches" narrative, gearing it for YA audiences who may fantasize about fitting in among peers or becoming something other than what they are.

Merlin reinvents class in its Arthur and Guinevere story arc. Its Guinevere—initially a servant, not royalty—ultimately becomes queen. She and Arthur, two adolescents born into different life situations, find similarities and focus on mutual goals rather than attending to tradition or status quo. In "Queen of Hearts" (3, 10), Arthur's father Uther discovers his son's love for Gwen and forbids him to see her again. When Arthur asks why it matters, Uther responds, "The survival of Camelot depends on forging an alliance through your marriage. Your first duty is to Camelot." When Arthur refuses to give up Gwen and suggests he would rather relinquish his crown than be without her, Uther at first banishes her but then decides that the prince falling in love with "someone like *her*" is so unthinkable that the only possible explanation is magic. True to form, Uther orders Gwen to be burned at the stake. As usual, Merlin intervenes to rescue her. So, while the show displays the expectation that royal marriages be arranged for political purposes, Arthur chooses otherwise (unless he is enchanted). But *Merlin* also undermines its apparent medieval context because as a prince, Arthur would be unlikely to interact with his sister's servant, let alone fall in love with her and offer to give up his kingdom for her. The distinction between traditional and progressive characters is not merely generational; the elderly Gaius, Merlin's mentor, tends to side with the adolescents. In contrast, Arthur, Morgana, Merlin, and Gwen push against Uther; the king fails to relinquish old ideas as the adolescents work to redefine the future.

Both Gwen's independence and Arthur's refusal to accede to his father's demands suggest the significance of adolescent autonomy throughout the series—a predominantly Westernized notion of individuality in which people can aspire to be anything they choose without social class limitations. Arthur vows that when he is king he will abolish "ridiculous customs" of class separation to be with Gwen, dismissing traditional mores in favor of romanticized versions of love superseding class. Not coincidentally, this concept echoes the fairy-tale Cinderella—the serving girl becoming queen. By staging Gwen as socially inferior to Arthur and exploring their sexuality and individuation as a coming-of-age narrative, *Merlin* creates a rags-to-riches ideal according to which people may bond regardless of lineage or social status.

Merlin also questions class through the royal teenagers' interactions with their servants, which explores ethical principles. Arthur and Merlin and Morgana and Gwen create compelling cross-class friendships absent from tradition. For example, before Morgana turns on her friends and family, she repeatedly stands up for the servants and their rights as individuals. In "The Poisoned Chalice," Arthur, conflicted about seeking a cure to save Merlin because his father forbade him to risk his own life for a lowly servant, gets support from Morgana: "Sometimes you have to do what you think is right and damn the consequences." Arthur responds, "If I don't make it back, who will be the next king of Camelot? There's more than just my life at stake." Morgana says, "And what kind of king would Camelot want? One who would risk his life for that of a lowly servant, or one who does what his father tells him to?" (1, 4). For both, doing what they think is right and "damn the consequences" becomes a series thread, though results differ from episode to episode.

Themes of equality and friendship suggest that *Merlin* is a socializing narrative that targets YA viewers. Teaching leadership skills to young adults, Laura Oliver and Kae Reynolds implemented *Merlin* into their curriculum, suggesting, "Utilizing film and popular media . . . as a vehicle for social change can make learning more accessible" (2010, 123). They link how Arthur treats his servants with the messages his actions convey because "students can transport the characters' actions into present-day issues, reflect and discuss ethical concerns, and relate . . . principles to their own experiences" (ibid., 130). In "The Moment of Truth," Arthur and Merlin, with Morgana and Gwen, return to Merlin's mother's village to fight bandits who are terrorizing the peasants. As Merlin attempts to dress Arthur for battle, the prince brushes him off and helps his servant with his own armor instead and "demonstrates how serving is important to leading" (ibid., 127). Arthur serves Merlin in his role as a leader, yet he goes beyond merely hierarchical control, demonstrating affection and respect. When Arthur believes that they may not survive the battle, he offers his hand to Merlin, saying simply, "It has been an honor" (1, 10), showing equality, friendship, and open-mindedness.

Merlin further exchanges historicity for bourgeois perspectives on class when Merlin restores Arthur's self-confidence. After Uther's fourth-season death (4, 3), Arthur becomes king. Morgana takes Camelot by force, driving the residents from the kingdom, and Arthur feels that he has failed. To restore the new king's courage and confidence, Merlin lodges a sword into a stone. Spinning a tale about his master's lineage, Merlin explains that only the one true king can remove it: "You *are* special. You and you alone can draw out that sword" (4, 13). Merlin's ruse works to restore Arthur's faith. Both believe in something greater than themselves: Arthur has an altruistic desire to see Camelot succeed, and Merlin believes that only Arthur can lead them.

Arthur insists on equality with the selfish outlaws Tristan and Isolde—characters who historically predated and perhaps influenced Arthur and Guinevere's relationship. Repeatedly, Tristan questions Arthur's decision to rescue Merlin: "Can't say I've detected many kingly qualities so far" and "first you go back to rescue a servant and now you're getting your hands dirty. But why shouldn't you? You're just like everybody else. There's nothing special about you, is there?" (4, 13). Tristan's continual questioning of class and social status draws a sharp contrast between his own intolerance and Arthur's humility. Though Tristin claims that Arthur's interactions with Merlin are "unkingly," the series suggests that his democratic actions, influenced by Merlin's friendship, are quite the opposite. Ultimately, Tristan and Isolde choose to fight alongside Arthur and his small band of peasants in an attempt to regain Camelot because, says Tristan to Arthur, "You have shown that you fight for what is good and what is fair," to which Arthur responds, "We will stand together as equals" (4, 13). Blending legends to add Tristan and Isolde as teaching tools, and through Arthur's reliance on Merlin to regain faith in himself, *Merlin* creates a new narrative of class equality: mutually respectful interdependence between servants and royalty.

Consistently, Arthur, Morgana, Merlin, and Gwen determine their actions as individuals, not through socially prescribed notions. Merlin and Gwen both save Arthur repeatedly and provide him and Morgana with alternative perspectives. As in fairy tales, these perspectives are powerful socializing agents because they address young people's anxieties about acceptance, "allowing the projection of both grandiose wishes and an identification with the hero—a hero who often finds a magic object or person that transforms his or her life" (Jacobs 2011, 888). Transformation in *Merlin* comes from the servants: Merlin helps Arthur see beyond his own needs and arrogance, and Gwen's love makes him want to be a better person.

Merlin and Family

The series deals extensively with family relationships, indicating the impacts of domesticity on adolescent autonomy. Yet kin conflict ensues, as *Merlin*'s protagonists' closest relations are often their most dangerous enemies. Arthur in particular, in order to succeed, must distance himself from his tyrannical father Uther and his treacherous half sister Morgana. Dysfunctional fairy-tale families, notorious for jealousy, incest, abandonment, murder, and cannibalism, provide a compelling social setting for young adults coming to terms with themselves in relation to those around them. Fairy tales provide adolescent literature when children sever kin ties to ensure "true escape from family and the commencement of an autonomous existence" (Ewers 2003, 79).

Similarly, family connections, or lack thereof, validate *Merlin*'s royal characters' search for autonomy; Arthur attains independence only after Uther's death, and Morgana becomes free only when she chooses to leave home. Commoner characters, on the other hand, lack complicated ties: Merlin is raised by his uncle; Guinevere is orphaned early in the series; and Lancelot appears to have no family. Parentless children are central to fairy tales; adolescents dissolve parental family structures to "develop new models of world apprehension and new cultural rules" (Ewers 2003, 82). That Merlin, Gwen, Lancelot, and other orphan commoner characters act autonomously despite their lower-class status, on the one hand, and the power of Arthur and Morgana is constrained by nobility until they break from their father, on the other, suggests a pattern of initiation tales.

Parentless figures also imply ideals consistent with contemporary YA narratives that make mothers and/or fathers either a necessary evil or irrelevant to adolescent decision making. In *Merlin,* for example, Uther instantiates normativity's evils, tirelessly trying to uphold and/or reinstate class boundaries, gender roles and hierarchies, and parental authority, while his children question his actions and assumptions. Uther vehemently opposes magic and condemns to death anyone caught using it, while the teenagers recognize its potential value and Morgana and Merlin practice it. Uther also refuses to allow Gwaine and Lancelot to serve as knights because they lack noble lineage, despite Arthur's relentless begging for exceptions. Whereas Uther's viewpoints are unbending, Arthur, Merlin, Gwen, and Morgana accept each other despite differences in class and gender. Frequently in the series adults are blinded by prejudices and outdated perspectives.

Uther in particular serves as an adversary for Arthur and the younger generation as they define themselves as individuals. Although traditional stories of Arthur begin after his father has died, *Merlin* incorporates Uther into the day-to-day narrative, heightening the focus on the primary characters as adolescents who are coming of age. Although the king is usually overbearing and controlling, viewers occasionally see his humanity, as he portrays a strong and present father figure. Yet fairy-tale paradigms are reproduced in *Merlin*'s mother figures, absent for the majority of the tale. *Merlin*'s cast of mothers as either sacrificial icons or irrelevant is not unexpected. Although its creators have complicated the legends by developing unique character arcs for these women, they still fall into a category of mothers who are either entirely absent or one dimensional or whose competence "trains her child for her own obsolescence" (Greenhill and Brydon 2010, 130).

Entirely absent mothers include Gwen's, who is never mentioned, and Arthur's, who died in childbirth. These absences reenact the "classic and much-loved story of female wish-fulfillment, [in which] the heroine's mother no longer plays a part" (Warner 1994, 205). In "Snow White," for example, "through the death of the mother . . . the child actualizes her autonomous self and is also able to identify with the male prince" (Jacobs 2011, 878). Gwen thus exemplifies a fairy-tale princess who finds independence, love, and viewer empathy as a hurt and lonely victim of fate. For Igraine, Arthur's mother, *Merlin*'s creators' twist of traditional versions requires magic for her to conceive a child, after whose birth she dies. Gwen's mother's absence fosters her autonomy, but lacking a mother to rear and protect him, Arthur is forced to find his own path. In both cases, "it's the removal of the adult's protective presence that kick-starts the story, so the orphan can begin his 'triumphant rise'" (Just 2010). With or without parental influence, adolescents finding their strengths and making it on their own is a significant theme in both YA fiction and fairy tales.

Merlin's mother Hunith, in contrast to Gwen's and Arthur's, is introduced in the first episode of the series when she sends Merlin away to be raised by Gaius (1, 1). "Many contemporary YA novels seem to reflect genuine confusion over what the job of parent consists of, beyond keeping kids fed and safe" (Just 2010). Hunith, though alive and loving, is mainly irrelevant to Merlin's life, except when he must help her with village invaders (1, 10). Ultimately, Merlin unintentionally sacrifices her life to save Arthur's (1, 13). *Merlin*'s protagonists reflect contemporary YA fiction in which "dramatic conflict occurs not in a vacant lot but in the home, around the dining table"

(Just 2010). In response, Gwen, Merlin, Arthur, and, to a lesser extent, Morgana and Lancelot create their own relationships and develop a chosen family in place of their parental ones. For example, when Merlin returns to his home village, Ealdor, Arthur, Gwen, and Morgana follow, refusing to leave him and instead fighting by his side as he defends a village that is otherwise irrelevant to them (1, 10). Their desire to be there for each other, even for Arthur and Morgana in direct defiance of their father's wishes, illustrates them placing more value on their chosen family than their biological one. *Merlin*'s rich tapestry of domesticity within the context of magic and fantasy helps to make it relevant to its audiences.

Real Dilemmas

Like the best literature, including that for young adults, *Merlin* offers more than a simplistic series of good and evil characters. Merlin himself regularly makes mistakes and frequently faces real dilemmas in which no alternative appears viable. For example, in "The Beginning of the End" (1, 8) Merlin must choose between letting Uther's soldiers find and execute a young Druid boy or jeopardizing Arthur's fate by allowing the child, Mordred, to live. Those who know the Arthurian story, in which Mordred is ultimately responsible for Arthur's death, know which decision Merlin makes. That his actions often seek the immediate response over his ultimate fate (usually articulated by the dragon) suggests the tragic hero's fatal flaw. *Merlin*'s narrative explores dichotomies of right/wrong, good/evil, and its subtle didacticism complicates familiar motifs, characters, and situations.

To quantify *Merlin*'s impact as a training manual for adolescent audiences with respect to race, gender, class, and family would be impossible. Yet interactive games, viewer comments, and fan responses on social media like Facebook and YouTube indicate the show's success in creating a socializing narrative. For example, in July 2012 at the San Diego Comic-Con, *Merlin* producers announced a new Facebook game in which fans can choose a *Merlin* character avatar and extend their interactions with the characters beyond the show itself. Imre Jele, the game's creator, designed it to let audiences experience more of what they love about the show—bravery, heroism, and adventure—by reenacting their own versions of the stories (Osborne 2012). He sees *Merlin* as "a rich ecosystem where you have the toys, the collectible cards, books, of course the TV shows, the DVDs . . . [creating] a very engaged audience, and that audience is engaged all year round. . . . Not just . . . when the show is airing" (ibid.). Audience conscious, the platform has primarily free usage and requires no equipment other than a home computer. The Facebook game page has received more than 57,935 "likes" since its publication in May 2012 (Facebook 2012b),[17] and user comments, in a variety of languages, indicate that for fans, the game's popularity may approach that of the series.

Additionally, in January 2012, Shine TV asked on *Merlin*'s official Facebook page: "How has *Merlin* inspired you or changed your life?" The 461 responses show considerable impact. Xin Ying states: "Merlin [the show] is the one thing that changed my life. . . . Merlin does everything he feels it's right." Chaya Dieffenbaugher comments: "I really love this show, the cast members are my age, the plot has an exciting modern twist. Have you enchanted me? I'm hooked!" and Christabelle Tatti says, "Merlin [the show] has taught me a lot of great values in life. Too many that it would take a long long time for me to list them all down. Merlin [the show] is the best tv show ever because it is real and honest" (Facebook 2012a). Manifestly, for fans, the show creates meaning beyond just another story.

Merlin's presence on YouTube offers another example of effects on its YA audience. In December 2010, a nineteen-year-old UK YouTube member initiated a "Merlin Fan Questionnaire" and requested that fans post their favorite series clips (MagicalUnicorn22). Dozens responded with montages of *Merlin*'s swordfights, kisses, speeches, magic, fantastical beasts, and villains. A nonconclusive sampling of user profiles indicates that the majority of responders ranged from sixteen to twenty years old. The images also indicate that many fans view the series as a new, multidimensional story through which they can choose their own interpretations. For example, discussions of Arthur and Merlin's "bromance," or perceived sexual tension, indicate a culture that questions traditional relationships in terms of contemporary gender roles.[18] Many videos also include Freya, a magical girl who becomes romantically involved with Merlin, as their favorite princess character or love interest over the traditional Guinevere. The fans' focus on Freya suggests that moving away from traditional Arthuriana resonates with audiences who want Merlin to be humanized and who also empathize with Freya as a tragic character who deserved more than she received.

Response suggests that *Merlin* enables for fans "imaginative strategies to help them act on their hopes for themselves and cope with personal dilemmas" (Fisherkeller 1997, 487). Media such as television and social media like Facebook and YouTube offer adolescents resources for learning and companionship. The new media environment suggests the importance of shows like *Merlin* that take seriously their efforts to teach and empathize with young adults, both in and beyond the show, by creating and developing a fan community.

The story of King Arthur has seen many retellings over the centuries. The teen coming-of-age story in *Merlin* presents the legend/myth via widely recognized fairy-tale motifs. It raises issues that adolescents grapple with on a daily basis, and through its sometimes realistic, sometimes fantastical dilemmas, the series provides a model for answering present-day questions about friendship, romantic relationships, parental influence, societal expectations, and so forth. *Merlin*'s likable, relatable characters encourage viewers to identify with their experiences and imagine the possibilities of a kingdom that existed once upon a time through present-day concerns, giving adolescents the hope and ability to vicariously discover who they are, what they believe, and what they can accomplish. Consciously moving from the historicity of myths and legends that portray "the sacred, the miraculous, and the heroic," *Merlin* focuses on "fairy tales [that] are devoted to the mundane: the drama of domestic life, of children and courtship and coming of age" (Orenstein 2002, 8). The series plays with expectations of fairy-tale figures living mundane lives of domesticity but infuses them with fantastical elements that allow the characters to become greater than their positions suggest.

By appealing to viewers' sense of morality, justice, love, loss, and romance, *Merlin* expresses values and struggles relevant to contemporary young adults. The BBC's approval for a fifth season attests to its popularity and value. *Merlin*'s interactive paratexts, complex characters, and relevant themes resonate with audiences in a way that teaches and entertains, "holding that extra sense of magical or mystical significance despite their expression in a domesticated format" (Tiffin 2009, 11). The show draws viewers to the idea of something familiar. By season three's end, characters are stabilizing into their adult locations and vocations. Arthur knights a group of brave commoners and acknowledges his love for Guinevere; the characters know what viewers have long realized: Morgana is the bad seed. Merlin's secret remains, but prejudice against magic abates. As the series progresses, character arcs and story lines seem to push past the familiar tropes and plot expectations. However, the show's five seasons continually offer its audience a fresh perspective on myth, legend, and fairy tale alike, illuminating ideas essential to the coming-of-age experience in a discussion of race, gender, class, and family in contemporary society. Thus *Merlin* has engaged its adolescent audiences in ways few adaptations can match.

Notes

1. (Season, episode).

2. They rather sardonically comment on viewers' criticism that tomatoes were unavailable in medieval Europe for throwing at Merlin in the stocks, when the same audience members are apparently unconcerned that a fire-breathing dragon who alternately counsels Merlin and lays waste to villages would also presumably have been absent (1, 1; DVD commentary).

3. The same creative use of anachronism manifests in Breillat's *Bluebeard* (2009; see Barzilai's chapter).

4. "Part of the humanness of adolescence is the feeling of being alone . . . that no one really knows what it's like to be him or her" (Cope 1998, 8).

5. Similarly, as discussed in Hay and Baxter's chapter, *Once Upon a Time* offers back-stories to explain characteristics of its fairy-tale protagonists.

6. In the Tuscan *veglia*—evening rituals around the hearth during which family and friends shared traditional culture—fairy tales offered a "crucial socializing and stabilizing force . . . [in which] adolescents were shown through folktales, folk songs, and dance the conventional path to adulthood, courtship, and marriage" (Falassi 1980, xviii).

7. "Donkey Skin" is the story of a queen who "made her husband swear not to remarry unless he found a woman superior to her in beauty and goodness. Entrapped, the king eventually discovers that only his lovely daughter can fit the bill" (Tatar 1999, 104).

8. Literary agent Meredith Barnes argues that adolescent fiction is important because "every decision feels life-changing, and every choice in these books can seem life-or-death . . . it's the first time, and thus very powerful" (qtd. in Grady 2011).

9. Hale's novel-length fairy-tale adaptations include *The Goose Girl* (2003; ATU 533, "The Speaking Horsehead") and *Book of a Thousand Days* (2007; ATU 870, "The Princess Confined in the Mound").

10. Three thousand YA novels were published in 1997, jumping to 30,000 in 2009 with sales exceeding $3 billion, suggesting that adults are also purchasing adolescent fiction (Grady 2011).

11. This pattern characterizes another successful series, *Buffy the Vampire Slayer* (1997–2003; see Snowden 2010).

12. These ideas' literalization in reality TV is discussed in Lee's chapter.

13. See, for example, discussions of Angela Carter (e.g., Lau 2012), Jeanette Winterson (e.g., Orme 2012), and Dan Andreason, Ed McBain, and Bill Willingham (e.g., Friedenthal 2012).

14. *Gwenhwyfar* (Welsh) translates to "white enchantress" or "white fay" (see Bennett 1938).

15. In "The Sword in the Stone," the final episode of series 4, King Arthur crowns Gwen queen in a formal coronation ceremony.

16. Despite the princess molds abundant in classic fairy tales, some female characters successfully occupy both female- and male-gendered spheres. Peg Bearskin and her counterparts Mutsmag (ATU 327B, "The Brothers and the Ogre"/ATU 328, "The Boy Steals the Ogre's Treasure") and Kate Crackernuts (ATU 711, "The Beautiful and the Ugly Twinsisters") pass as "their desired female sex/gender, though they act

in nonstereotypical ways." Peg and Tatterhood (also ATU 711) initially "fail to pass initially as 'normal' women, but ultimately transform/transsex, and are then read not only as women, but as beautiful ones" (Greenhill, Best, and Anderson-Grégoire 2012, 201).

17. As of December 12, 2012.

18. A great deal of fan fiction develops (homo)sexual relationships suggested in literature, film, and TV (see, e.g., Tosenberger 2008a, 2008b).

3

Adapting "Hansel and Gretel" for Television

Don Tresca

> At the edge of a great forest, there once lived a poor wood-
> cutter with his wife and two children.
>
> Tatar 2004, 73

Thus begins one of the most cherished fairy tales in world literature. "Hansel and Gretel" (ATU 327A) is so well known by nearly every European and North American reader that the opening sentence alone instantly conjures images: a dark forest, a trail of breadcrumbs, a ginger-bread house, a cannibalistic witch, the gaping maw of an oven big enough for a human body, and two young siblings, abandoned by their parents, struggling to survive in a harsh and dangerous world. Although its origins may stretch as far back as the Great Famine in the fourteenth century (Opie and Opie 1974, 237),[1] the Grimms' version is familiar to most readers. The brothers were introduced to it by storyteller Dortchen Wild (Zipes 2006b, 197), who eventually became Wilhelm Grimm's wife (Peppard 1971, 113). Published in their 1812 collection *Kinder- und Hausmärchen*, "Hansel and Gretel" achieved worldwide popularity after Engelbert Humperdinck com-posed an opera based on it in 1893 (Zipes 2011, 195).

Film's advent in the late nineteenth century and television's growth in the mid-twentieth brought the tale to wider audiences. Typically, most such early versions were direct adaptations of the Grimms' story or the Humperdinck opera (Zipes 2011, 194). While some filmmakers and television producers used the characters in situations outside traditional fairy-tale settings (including Warner Brothers' 1954 Bugs Bunny cartoon "Bewitched Bunny" and a 1971 episode of the sitcom *Bewitched,* "Hansel and Gretel in Samanthaland"), such uses continued to homogenize the tale, making it more fit for children than adults. As early as the 1970s, filmmakers began experimenting extensively with the story lines and themes of "Hansel and Gretel" in more contemporary and more mature settings. Films such as Curtis Harrington's *Whoever Slew Auntie Roo?* (1972), Matthew Bright's *Freeway 2: Confessions of a Trick Baby* (1999), and Pil-Sung Yim's *Henjel gwa Gueretel* (2007) did much to bring a darker, more sinister edge. Clearly not meant for children, these works combined violence, horror, and sometimes extreme sexuality.

Like film, television sought to reclaim fairy tales for adult entertainment. Several programs in the 1990s and 2000s continued the dark tone of contemporary Hansel and Gretel–influenced films but also integrated some of the fairy tale's complex social themes into their story lines. Max Lüthi saw in "Hansel and Gretel" and other fairy tales focused on young children a strength and independence in the characters that he found missing from those with adolescents. These children

> are by no means helpless; many of them free themselves by their own ability and cunning. The fairy tale shows not only that children have need of care and protection, it also gives them the ingenuity to make their way and to save themselves. In contrast to the older, adolescent heroes in the fairy tale, Hansel and Gretel do not venture forth happily into the woods, but attempt to return home. Yet the child, no matter how much it depends on the care of grownups, is surer of himself than the adolescent, whose dependence on mental and spiritual help is reflected in the dependence of fairy-tale heroes on gifts from supernatural beings. (1970, 65–66)

In fact, in the Grimms' version of "Hansel and Gretel," the two receive help from a beautiful white bird that directs them to food at the witch's house and from a white duck that conveys them across the water. But ultimately, only the two children's own cunning and self-confidence save them. In this chapter I focus on eight television shows from the 1990s and 2000s: *CSI: Crime Scene Investigation, Criminal Minds, Sherlock, Dollhouse, Lost Girl, Supernatural, Buffy the Vampire Slayer,* and *The Simpsons.* They use the "Hansel and Gretel" tale to show how children, adolescents, and young adults of this era use (or fail to use) the inborn ingenuity and cunning Lüthi detailed to escape the evils that confront them in the modern world. No longer do children need fear cannibalistic witches in gingerbread houses; they now must deal with pedophiles, serial killers, and child abductors.[2] Like their fairy-tale counterparts, they often show considerable pluck and capability; but unlike Hansel and Gretel, these TV figures must in the end rely on adults to save them.

CSI: Crime Scene Investigation

"Gum Drops" (6, 5)[3]: The CSI team is called in to investigate a house containing several pools of blood but no bodies. The team determines that a family of four lived there; however, only three pools of blood are found. Although the rest of the team thinks that the youngest family member, Cassie (Mary Mouser), has also been murdered, the case's lead investigator, Nick Stokes (George Eads), is convinced the little girl is still alive. His obsession with finding her is fueled by his discovery of a piece of unwrapped chewing gum at various key locations. He becomes convinced that Cassie actually left it behind as a trail to lead the investigators to her, as Hansel and Gretel left breadcrumbs. Ultimately, Nick's intuition is confirmed when the gum trail leads him to the family's killers, the bodies, and finally Cassie herself, holding a final piece of gum in her hand.

In many ways both the most literal and the most realistic of the television episodes adapting "Hansel and Gretel" for a modern adult audience, "Gum Drops" is fundamentally the story of a family destroyed by the parental figures' internal corruption. In many traditional versions, the danger to the children comes from the mother (or stepmother, as she becomes in later revisions of the tale), who wishes to abandon them to the dangers of the forest in order to save herself from starvation. In "Gum Drops," the dangerous figure is instead the father, who places his family in jeopardy by cultivating an illegal marijuana-growing operation in their basement. In both cases, the relinquishing parent is ultimately destroyed as a punishment for her or his transgressions, as required under the code of fairy-tale "justice" (Lanham and Shimura 1967, 40). This parent is punished by death, as are the mother and brother in "Gum Drops," who are both complicit in the father's criminal actions.[4]

As in "Hansel and Gretel," the youngest child rescues herself through sheer ingenuity. Both stories document the child's/children's intelligence. Hansel successfully uses logic to make his way home by following a trail of dropped stones. Later, he attempts to repeat the act using breadcrumbs but is undone by natural forces: birds that eat these morsels. In "Gum Drops," Cassie's intelligence is related to the audience early on by her voiceover: "I knew all of my lines, and Hansel's too," suggesting simultaneously both her natural intelligence and her ability to take on both roles within the story.

Also both stories involve trickery. Gretel convinces Hansel to use a bone to hoodwink the witch into believing he is too scrawny to eat. The girl then tricks the witch into checking the oven, pushes her in, and burns her alive. Cassie fools her abductors by not swallowing the drugged candy she is given, spitting it out surreptitiously, and she secretly leaves the gum behind as a clue to lead searchers to her location—an idea she gleaned from her role as Gretel in her school play. Exposed to the harsh reality of the witch's cannibalistic plan, Gretel must use both her intelligence and her wiles to emerge victorious. Cassie does the same. Her abduction, witnessing her murdered family being dumped into the lake, and subsequent near death open her up to a mature realization of life's dark and hostile nature. These experiences take her childish trickery of hiding cough medicine in her shoe (which Nick discovers while searching through her house and later likens to "hiding green beans in your napkin") to the more complex ruse of dropping subtle clues and feigning drugged unconsciousness and later death.

Criminal Minds

"The Boogeyman" (2, 6): The FBI Behavioral Analysis Unit is summoned to a small Texas town to investigate the mysterious murder of two young boys in the woods. During the investigation, they focus initially on a creepy elderly man who lives in a supposedly haunted house on the woods' edge. However, they locate another victim (a girl), then find the elderly man dead of a heart attack. They refocus their investigation on the elementary school guidance counselor after discovering his fingerprints in the elderly man's house along with "souvenirs" of the previous murder victims. However, a report on a search of the counselor's residence leads one investigator to realize that the man is not the killer; it is instead his young son. Searching the woods—the boy has entered them with another potential victim—the agents find and subdue him right before he brutally murders again.

While never directly referencing "Hansel and Gretel," this episode uses many of its tropes and themes. Like it, the episode implicates children's fears of abandonment (Bettelheim 1976, 15; see also Joosen 2011, 123–214). Jeffrey (Cameron Monaghan), the youthful murderer, is physically abandoned by his mother and fears losing his father's attention because of the latter's relationships with other children for whom he serves as a guidance counselor. Both the literal abandonment and Jeffrey's fear trigger his impulse to kill. But just as Hansel and Gretel never blame their parents (Zipes 1997, 51), Jeffrey never faults his mother and father for the murders he commits, simply telling the lead agent, Jason Gideon (Mandy Patinkin), that he murdered the other children "because I wanted to."

The murder location likewise becomes crucial and ties the episode to "Hansel and Gretel." Jeffrey murders his victims in the woods because they represent the loss of security and civilized values (Heuscher 1974, 258). When he is there, Jeffrey becomes a ruthless killer, while his victims lose their sense of safety and trust in another child. There Jeffrey's anxieties—as well as those of the other children, in particular Tracy (Elle Fanning), his potential final victim—"are played out on a court devoid of adult intervention" (Willard 2002, 68). The child victims' access to comfort and safety is denied, and they are forced into a brutal and hostile environment without support, forced to fend for themselves. Tracy, like Gretel, summons an inner strength and fights back against the killer and, in doing so, demonstrates that she has the necessary skills to survive in "a once-fair world now marred" (Ware 2003, 51) by the taint of Jeffrey's evil.

Food consumption[5] in the old house in the woods also ties the story to the tale. Jeffrey's father delivers food to the elderly man who lives there; in eating it, the boy feels he is accepting a paternal gift. For Jeffrey, food becomes a replacement for the love he believes he has lost in his parents' "abandonment." Thus, his father serves as an unwitting accomplice in Jeffrey's murderous actions, just as the father's behavior in "Hansel and Gretel" ultimately leads to the witch's death when he leaves the siblings in the woods. While the father's deeds in the fairy tale lead to a positive result, allowing Hansel and Gretel to mature and develop their instincts as "survivors" in the "savage" world (Ware 2003, 50), Jeffrey's father's actions have the opposite result, feeding the boy while he engages in his brutally violent behavior. While the father is not directly guilty of the murders his son commits, symbolically he allows Jeffrey to become part of the "savage," violent world from which Hansel and Gretel in their tale must escape.

Although Jeffrey is a child, his extraordinary and seemingly insatiable appetite for cruelty and destruction marks him as a classic fairy-tale villain, whose sole purpose is to fill his victims' lives with misery and despair (Kokorski 2011, 147). Since his victims are children who do nothing to warrant being targeted by such brutality, the audience's revulsion and disgust are triggered against Jeffrey. However, unlike the original tale in which the villain is a cannibalistic witch, this episode ends with a surprise reveal. The murderer is himself but a child; consequently, the audience may be disoriented, unsure how to react to the fact that a child's innocence has been corrupted and transformed into monstrosity (Bacchilega 1997, 28).[6]

Sherlock

"The Reichenbach Fall" (2, 3): The evil James Moriarty (Andrew Scott) has hatched a deadly plot to discredit and destroy Sherlock Holmes (Benedict Cumberbatch). He kidnaps two children, a boy and a girl, and leaves clues behind referencing "Hansel and Gretel." Among the signs are a book of Grimms' fairy tales, an envelope containing breadcrumbs, a burnt gingerbread man, and a trail of footprints made with linseed oil, showing the children's path out of the bedroom but also that of the man who abducted them. Sherlock deduces from the trace of minerals, vegetation, and chemicals used in the manufacture of chocolate found in the man's footprints that the children have been taken to an abandoned candy factory on the outskirts of London. A message from Moriarty urges them to hurry because "they [i.e., the children] are dying." Sherlock and the police race to the factory and discover the children unconscious with a number of empty candy wrappers. Sherlock determines that the candy was laced with mercury. The more the children ate, the quicker they suffered the poison's effects. Fortunately, the authorities arrive in time, and the children are saved.

This *Sherlock* episode suggests the limits of children's ability to fight against the forces conspiring against them. Like the adolescent characters in fairy tales identified by Lüthi, these children must be saved by an outside "magical" source (1970, 66). However, proving life "is no fairy tale" (Heiner 2012, 10), Holmes solves the case through empirical deduction, not magic. However, Moriarty sets the scene to make strong deductive leaps look like magic—something fantastical and make-believe. He tries to convince the authorities and the public (through the media) that Holmes is a fraud and the main villain. Moriarty uses images from "Hansel and Gretel" because of its associations with child abduction and cannibalism. Rather than focusing on its positive lessons about children learning self-sufficiency, Moriarty specifically accentuates those aspects deemed negative by the tale's psychological critics: children's oral greed, their gluttonous nature that threatens the parents with starvation (Bettelheim 1976, 160–61; see also Joosen 2011). Moriarty correctly surmises that the children will be unable to resist the candy's temptation and hopes their greed will literally kill them (Heiner 2012, 8).

Here the kidnapped children's narrative serves as a "cautionary tale" (Bettelheim 1976, 27) of moral instruction designed to teach a specific lesson. Holmes needs to learn both humility (his conversation with reporter Kitty Reilly [Katherine Parkinson] is particularly revolting in its condescension and cruelty) and the consequences of celebrity status, particularly regarding the manner in which scandals can turn the public and media can turn against a celebrity. However, fairy tales present the world as a "fearful place," a domain of cannibalistic witches and big bad wolves that must be vanquished (Richards 1999, 833). Only severe and often violent action will transform the world. Unresolved conflict removes "anticipation of a better place" (Haase 2000a, 361). Modern tellings may replace the Grimm tales' overt violence by allowing the villain "a hasty getaway" (Richards 1999, 833).[7] This episode creates tension because the villain initially appears to be winning. Moriarty succeeds in turning the public and police against Holmes and forces him into a suicidal situation. Ultimately, although the case is solved and the children returned safely and relatively unharmed to their parents, the perception that the evil Moriarty has successfully beaten the good Holmes runs counter to fairy-tale fundamentals in which "the meritorious individual will win out in the end" (Bausinger 1987, 80).

Dollhouse

"Ghost" (1, 1): A young woman is abducted at gunpoint by criminals looking to extort money from her rich father. The show's main character, the "Doll"[8] Echo (Eliza Dushku), is implanted with the memories and personality of Eleanor Penn, an expert kidnapping negotiator instructed to ensure the girl's release. However, during the ransom exchange, Echo's personality loses control because she recognizes one kidnapper as the "Ghost," who kidnapped and brutally sexually assaulted her years before. Echo/Eleanor becomes determined to prevent the same thing happening to this new girl and becomes obsessed with finding and stopping the Ghost. She finds the kidnappers' lair and confronts them, turning the other criminals against the Ghost and tricking them into shooting each other. She escapes with the girl unharmed and delivers her to her father.

Dollhouse's story line is structured around fairy-tale conventions (see Jorgensen and Warman's chapter). Its "concerns with the articulation of a coherent self and the construction of consciousness" suits expression in fairy-tale form (St. Louis and Riggs 2010, 60). The episodes "Ghost" and "The Target" (discussed in detail below) specifically deal with these issues. They also present "Hansel and Gretel" tropes and imagery, including the endangered child, the monstrous ogre/witch, the dark and dangerous forest, the shelter of false security, the evil mother, and the benevolent father. In "Ghost," a male teacher, not the child's father, is responsible for her capture and imprisonment by the ogre/witch figure in the "savage place" (Ware 2003, 60) of the modern world. Eleanor/Echo knows that the Ghost is no cannibalistic witch but that he wishes to devour the child by possessing her sexually and then casually disposing of her. Thus, roles are reversed. The father figure becomes the evil force who imprisons the child, and the good mother(s)—both Eleanor/Echo and fellow Doll Sierra (Dichen Lachman), who arrives at the end as leader of a hostage extraction team—rescue the child from his clutches. To hunt the Ghost and save the child, Eleanor/Echo breaks free from her programming and goes rogue, which the Dollhouse views as negative; Dolls should not act without direct instructions from the establishment itself. From the first episode, then, the show establishes Echo as capable of independent thought and action and "emphasizes the dangers and difficulties of" that autonomy (St. Louis and Riggs 2010, 65). The Gretel characters of the abducted child and Eleanor link to Echo herself, who has been abandoned, imprisoned, and enslaved. Evil witch Adelle DeWitt (Olivia Williams), head of the Los Angeles chapter of the Dollhouse, presides over a candy-coated paradise where Dolls are used and abused for clients' entertainment and the owner and controller Rossum Corporation's enrichment.

"The Target" (1, 2): Echo is implanted with the personality of Jenny, a young outdoorswoman romantically involved with Richard Connell (Matt Keeslar), an avid hunter. After a brief sexual encounter, Richard announces to Echo that he is going to hunt her as prey "to find out if she deserves to live." She shelters in an abandoned ranger's station, where she drinks from a planted canteen filled with poisoned water, causing hallucinations of past personalities, including her original Caroline. Richard shoots Echo's handler/bodyguard Boyd (Harry Lennix) in the shoulder with an arrow as he tries to help Echo escape. Echo then has to help Boyd, reversing their roles. Confronted by Richard, Echo uses skills developed from previous personalities, to which the drugged water gives her access, to kill him.

In this episode, the Dollhouse abandons Echo in a dark forest in the hands of homicidal maniac Richard, who plans to hunt her for sport. Her reduction to a "hunted animal" (Pickard 2009, 8) aligns her with Hansel in a version that appeared in the 1823 edition of *Kinder- und Hausmärchen*. Hansel and Gretel choose to leave home to escape their abusive stepmother (the father is never mentioned). After traveling for a time, they come upon a great forest. Hansel wants to drink from a brook, but the stepmother (an evil fairy) has enchanted the waters to transform whoever drinks from them into an animal. Gretel hears the brook whisper its secret and tells Hansel not to drink. He acquiesces, and the two move deeper into the forest. After coming across two such enchanted brooks, Hansel can no longer control his thirst, drinks from a third, and transforms into a fawn. He and Gretel shelter in an abandoned cottage.

The king's hunting party passes through the forest, and Hansel demands to be let out to witness the festivities. Although Gretel is concerned for his safety, she lets him go. Hansel watches the hunters and evades them through his swift running but on the second day he is injured. He returns to the cottage, watched by a huntsman. The next day the king orders that the fawn be followed but not harmed. When he sees it enter the cottage, he approaches and views Gretel, becoming instantly smitten and asking her to be his bride. She agrees as long as Hansel can live in the castle with them. As a reward for his new bride, the king seeks out and punishes the evil fairy and has Hansel transformed back into a boy (Taylor 1985, 116–20).

Many of the images and tropes that appear in this version appear in "The Target": the human transformed into an animal—literal in the tale, symbolic in the episode; the enchanted/poisoned water; and the empty cottage/ranger station. However, Echo has no protective king/father to rescue her.[9] She must rely on her own ingenuity and skills. Like Hansel, Echo drinks the "cursed" water, and it transforms her. However, her alteration is the reverse of Hansel's. She begins as the fawn: docile, playful, innocent, Richard's perfect victim. However, the drugged water expands her mind, giving access to her power—her previous personalities' knowledge and skills. She gains "both the intelligence and moral accountability to harness the positive potential of a child's flexible worldview to an adult's sense of duty and accountability" (St. Louis and Riggs 2010, 72). She thus changes from the docile Hansel to the aggressive Gretel, taking control of the situation and gaining the upper hand, destroying Richard in the same manner as he had planned for her.

Lost Girl

"Mirror Mirror" (2, 4): Kenzi (Ksenia Solo), the heroine Bo's (Anna Silk) best friend, invokes the Russian hag Baba Yaga (Kate Lynch) to curse Bo's ex-lover Dyson (Kris Holden-Reid) for flaunting his newfound single status. Dyson becomes repellant to women to the point of violence, putting both his private and professional (as a police detective) lives at risk. Bo tries to invoke Baba Yaga to break the curse, but the witch instead attempts to drag her into her realm as payment. Kenzi steps forward and demands to go in her place. Once in Baba Yaga's realm, Kenzi discovers other young women, enslaved by the witch over the centuries for attempting to break her deadly curses. Kenzi tries to lead a revolt, but they are clearly too frightened. When the witch arrives, Kenzi finds out why. Each is forced to draw a marble from a bag; the witch cooks and eats the loser with the black marble. Bo discovers how to pass into Baba Yaga's realm uninvited. The witch immediately defeats her. Kenzi then confronts the witch, smashing the magic mirror she uses to communicate with the mortal realm and using the pieces to free the other women. The witch attacks her and nearly throws her into the oven. However, Baba Yaga's last remaining slave, a feral man who acts as "guard dog," breaks free from his chains and attacks the witch, throwing himself with her into the oven, which Kenzi then slams shut. The witch dead and the curse broken, Kenzi and Bo return to their world.

The Russian fairy tale of Baba Yaga has long been seen as an early forerunner of "Hansel and Gretel" (Haney 1999, 17). Like the cannibalistic witch who terrorizes Hansel and Gretel, Baba Yaga enslaves young women while fattening them up for a meal. She dwells in a magical hut on chicken legs, surrounded by a fence made from her victims' bleached bones. This disturbingly frightening barrier also serves as "a clear signal to anyone who would dare to pass through that they must be prepared for an initiatory underworld experience" (Strong 2001, 1). Kenzi's journey to Baba Yaga's realm represents a transforming moment for her. Many critics see personal transformation as essential to fairy tales' "mythic matrix" (Stephens 2000, 331); Jack Zipes calls it "perhaps the key theme of the fairy tale up to the present" (1992, xvi).

While most narratives require the protagonist to change, fairy tales often dramatically take them from average person to extraordinary hero (Bausinger 1987, 78–79). Kenzi, long dwelling in the more powerful Bo's and Dyson's shadows, in this episode establishes herself as a hero, fitting in among a company of much more powerful individuals. Her ordeal and defeat of an incredibly dangerous adversary mirrors Hansel and Gretel's journey. They progress from the domestic insecurity of their father and stepmother's home to a place of terror—the evil witch's gingerbread house—and then back again to a reconstituted house (Zipes 1997, 54), their arms full of treasure, symbolic of the psychological riches they have obtained.

The other essential fairy-tale element this episode explores is the need for vengeance and punishment for individuals who have transgressed against society, represented by the primary heroes. Kenzi's impetus for invoking Baba Yaga is revenge against Dyson on Bo's behalf. The evil witch's curse manifests what the viewer may also want. Bo, the primary heroine and, therefore, the character to whom the audience should be most loyal, suffers because of Dyson's action. The fairy-tale scenario offers a level of satisfaction against the man transgressing against Bo. Baba Yaga does to Dyson what viewers may wish they could,[10] pulling them further into the narrative and providing a sense of justice (Lanham and Shimura 1967, 40).

Supernatural

"Bedtime Stories" (3, 5): Elements of many popular fairy tales combine in an episode about young Callie (Tracy Spiridakos), traveling out-of-body to various locations and forcing people to act out scenes from her favorite fairy tales, including "Hansel and Gretel," "The Three Little Pigs," and "Red Riding Hood." Callie herself suffers in the living nightmare of a coma due to her evil stepmother poisoning her in a case of Münchausen by proxy. At every scene, she manifests as she appeared when she was first poisoned, a beautiful, dark-haired child. Demon-hunting brothers Sam (Jared Padalecki) and Dean (Jensen Ackles) Winchester initially believe the attacks are the work of demons. However, Sam quickly realizes that the problem is more mundane—a figure of fairy-tale horror. When Dean dismisses the notion as ridiculous: "I thought those things ended with everyone living happily ever after," Sam responds, "No, no, not the originals. See, the Grimm Brothers' stuff was kinda like the folklore of its day, filled with violence, sex, cannibalism. It got sanitized over the years, turned into Disney flicks and bedtime stories." Ultimately Sam and Dean uncover Callie's whereabouts (in a hospital bed, being treated by her father) and stop her rampage by getting her father to understand what happened to her.

The episode's overall theme concerns the aftereffects of child abuse both on the victims and the community. The small "Hansel and Gretel" segment accentuates the theme. A young couple (adults, not children), lost in the woods, come across a house. When they approach, they are greeted by a kindly looking elderly woman. They initially merely ask for directions, but the man becomes tempted by the smell of a pie cooling in a window, and the elderly woman asks them to come in and share it. Naturally the pie is poisoned, and both the man and woman succumb. The elderly woman slaughters the man with a kitchen knife while the woman screams. During this attack, the woman notices Callie standing nearby, watching. After escaping, she informs Sam about the girl and wonders how she got there.

Significantly, this segment is Callie's first appearance in the episode. Like "Snow White," the tale most closely associated with Callie herself, "Hansel and Gretel" concerns an evil stepmother's machinations to rid herself of her husband's children. Although the motivation differs (vanity and power in "Snow White" and survival in "Hansel and Gretel"), the result is identical. The children are taken to the woods and abandoned to fend for themselves. They ultimately meet evil witches who are manifestations of the evil stepmother, and both fall victim to her trickery. But the similarities end there. Snow White is freed from her sleeping curse through outside means, but Hansel and Gretel must rely on their own wits to escape the clutches of the witch and return home. Callie knows no one can free her from her endless sleep, from the pain of the abuse she suffered at her stepmother's hands. Life is no Disney fairy tale and, thus, she cannot free herself from the horror. Because Callie cannot take control, Hansel and Gretel's tale does not end in the traditional manner: *Supernatural*'s Gretel takes initiative and escapes by knocking unconscious and pushing the elderly woman into the oven; Hansel, not so lucky, is murdered before there is any chance to get away.

In this episode, unlike many others, the featured fairy tales maintain their folklore classification as fictions (see Bascom 1965). They are not really happening; they are instead the villain's scripts to punish those who will not acknowledge her pain and her stepmother's culpability. Callie engages in these dark behaviors to make her father accept his part in her condition. Like Hansel and Gretel, she seeks to take the matter into her own hands and save herself (through death). She wants her father to understand that he could have stopped the abuse and prevented her death if only he had paid proper attention to her care and protection. Parents must take responsibility for their actions, not rely on children to save themselves, as Hansel and Gretel do, from callous and cruel behavior (Tatar 2003, 7).

The episode reiterates this theme through its comparison of two differ-ent fairy-tale types: the dark Grimm tales and their sanitized Disney versions. Most North Americans know the latter sweet, innocent, adorable stories for children. In them, unpleasant events are temporary and easily fixed; girls are docile princesses and boys brave princes; and everyone lives happily ever after surrounded by loved ones in a beautiful, glittering castle. The villains—usually older women—are tastefully disposed of, their deaths never shown on-screen (Tosenberger 2010, 5.1). But many fairy tales are dark and bloody, "full of sex, violence, and cannibalism." "Bedtime Stories" instantiates this type, "a rescue operation, uncovering the 'real' fairy tale and liberating it from Disney oppression, and theoretically also recovering the 'true' voices of the 'original' tellers, usually figured as female" (ibid., 5.2).

That Callie is female reinforces fairy-tale gendering. While Dean dero-gates Sam's knowledge of fairy tales as "gay," Sam understands that their very goriness and sexual aspects render them appropriate for masculine interest (Tosenberger 2010, 5.9). And Callie understands it as well. Her appearance within the tales as they play out in "reality" calls attention to the juxtaposition of innocence and horror that fairy tales represent.

Buffy the Vampire Slayer

"Band Candy" (3, 6): The school principal requires Buffy (Sarah Michelle Gellar) and her friends Willow (Alyson Hannigan) and Xander (Nicholas Brendan) to sell candy bars for the school band to buy new uniforms. The candy has a strange effect on the adults who eat it. They become immature, acting like rowdy teenagers. Buffy intimidates the principal into revealing where the candy came from. She discovers the operation's mastermind is an old enemy, the wizard Ethan Rayne (Robin Sachs). Ethan tells Buffy that the candy "dulls" the adults' minds while the city's vampires collect tribute for a demon named Lurconis. Buffy and her friends' research uncovers that the demon eats babies and lives underground, probably in the city sewers. Rac-ing there, they interrupt the ceremony. Buffy's mentor Giles (Anthony Stewart Head) and mother Joyce (Kristine Sutherland) rescue the babies while Buffy fights the demon, finally killing him by igniting a fire with a loose gas pipe. The next day, the adults revert to normal, and Giles and Joyce share a rather awkward moment that indicates a sexual relationship occurred during their transformation.

"Gingerbread" (3, 11): The dead bodies of a boy and a girl are discovered with mystical symbols drawn on them. In response to the children's death, Buffy's mother Joyce organizes a parent's group called MOO (Mothers Opposed to the Occult) that seeks to remove all occult influences from their children's lives. MOO quickly becomes a totalitarian organization, instituting curfews and encouraging teenagers to report on each other's "inappropriate" behavior. Buffy confronts her mother on these issues, but Joyce refuses to back down. The audience learns (though Buffy does not) that Joyce is being visited by the spirits of the dead children, who demand revenge on the "bad girls" for their murders. While investigating the deaths with her friends, Buffy realizes that absolutely no information has been provided about the children, such as their real names and their parents'. Research reveals that every fifty years, the dead bodies of two nameless children are discovered. A demon assumes their guise to spread chaos, inciting a town to kill the "bad girls," innocents accused of witchcraft. The earliest record, from 1649, of a cleric in the Black Forest discovering the bodies of Hans and Greta Strauss, has inspired "Hansel and Gretel." A vigilante mob captures Buffy and her Wiccan friends Willow and Amy (Elizabeth Anne Allen) and ties them to wooden posts surrounded by occult books from Giles's research library. Joyce sets the book pile afire. Giles races to the site while working on an incantation he believes will cause the demon to reveal its true form, thus breaking the spell on the townspeople and allowing Buffy to kill it. Arriving at the "witch burning," he sees the children in the crowd and recites the incantation. The demon transforms. Buffy pulls from the ground the stake to which she is attached and impales the creature.

Both episodes deal with a major fairy-tale motif in "Hansel and Gretel": parental bad behavior or neglect leaves children—in these episodes, teenagers—isolated and vulnerable to monstrous forces beyond their control (Bridges 2009, 97). In "Band Candy" and "Gingerbread," as in "Hansel and Gretel," parental authority has been compromised through mystical means, which forces the children/teenagers to fend for themselves, make their own decisions without parental supervision, and define their own survival plans (Lüthi 1970, 65–66). Parental figures in all three narratives are more concerned with personal comfort or nebulous social issues than the welfare of their children. Some see this selfish attitude as a recent development and note that parents more and more frequently express concerns about their inability to control their children's behaviors (e.g., Ware 2003, 51).

"Gingerbread" in particular uses "Hansel and Gretel" to highlight children's/teens' vulnerability to the whims of adult hysteria and moral panic. The episode dramatizes the real-life struggles of children/teenagers isolated from their parents who reduce them to a social problem (such as drug abuse) rather than seeing them as individuals (Bridges 2009, 100–101). The most prominent example occurs when Willow's mother, Sheila Rosenberg (Jordan Baker), attempts an intervention against her daughter over her possible witchcraft involvement. Rather than offering true parent–child communication, counseling Willow on the personal and heartfelt reasons she feels the occult is dangerous, Sheila immediately depersonalizes the interaction, citing "a recent paper about the rise of mysticism among teenagers" (ibid., 99). Parents' isolation from offspring becomes so great that the community overreacts, attempting to destroy Buffy, Willow, and Amy rather than endeavoring to discover the true danger source, symbolized by the disguised demon (ibid., 101). Likewise, Hansel and Gretel's parents abandon the children in the woods rather than seeing their food shortage problem as the family's, not their own. In "Hansel and Gretel" and these episodes of *Buffy,* ultimately the children must solve the problem and save themselves and their families.

The Simpsons

"Treehouse of Horror XI: Scary Tales Can Come True" (12, 1): One segment from this episode features Bart (voiced by Nancy Cartwright) and Lisa (voiced by Yeardley Smith) Simpson as Hansel and Gretel, abandoned by their parents in the woods after Homer (voiced by Dan Castellaneta) loses his job as the village oaf. With the aid of Lisa's book of Grimms' fairy tales, the two children journey through the wilderness and meet various fairy-tale characters like the troll from "The Three Billy Goats Gruff," Goldilocks, and the Three Bears. Meanwhile, Marge (voiced by Julie Kavner), upset that Homer abandoned the children when they could have sold them, orders him into the forest to find them. The children shelter in a gingerbread house; Lisa warns Bart of the danger, but he is too busy eating candy to take heed. When the witch attacks, the children are saved by Homer's arrival as he eats through a wall of the house. The witch zaps him with a magic spell and transforms him into a half-chicken, half-fish creature with donkey ears and broomsticks for arms. When she tries to throw him in the oven, he overpowers her and tosses her in instead. The reunited family is saved from starvation thanks to Homer, whose chicken body can lay eggs to feed them all.

This segment serves as a satirical skewering and/or inversion of various fairy-tale conventions. The father is fully responsible for abandoning the children in the woods. In fact, the episode suggests that he has done this before, telling Bart and Lisa, "Say 'hi' to your other brother and sister" as the screen shows two skeletons resembling them. The abandonment is played for laughs, primarily because of the situation's unreality. Lisa's fairy-tale book tells her exactly what is going to happen; she is much better prepared for the task at hand than anyone else. The children are never in any real danger primarily because of the adult characters' idiocy. The episode plays with a variety of fairy tales. Bart and Lisa stumble into the home of the Three Bears and inadvertently lock Goldilocks (voiced by Nancy Cartwright) inside, preventing her usual escape and causing her gruesome death, suggesting both the traditional fairy tale's bloody brutality and that none of its rules apply here. Likewise, Homer's encounter with Rapunzel (voiced by Tresse MacNeille) causes him to rip her hair and scalp off when he attempts to climb the tower.

Marge's reaction to the children's abandonment suggests a changing of gender identification. Here, the father leaves the children and the mother protests, "What! You threw our precious babies into the woods?" However, in a further twist, Marge reverts to the traditional mother figure's evil intentions, "We could have sold them!" offering a fate potentially even worse than abandonment. The father becomes a heroic figure again, attempting to find the children, if for less than altruistic profit motives.

The dark elements typically associated with "Hansel and Gretel" (child abandonment, child murder, pedophilia, cannibalism) are satirized primarily because the program's audience knows that Bart and Lisa by no means fit the traditional molds of Hansel and Gretel. The Simpson kids are smarter than any adult, far too streetwise to be caught in a situation that offers any real peril. When danger arises, they use whatever means are at their disposal to save themselves, including sacrificing another child (Goldilocks). The adults (including the evil witch) are buffoonish and nonthreatening. This episode shows the dark and violent nature of the reality faced by the children in "Hansel and Gretel," simultaneously mocking that threat to Bart and Lisa themselves.

Child Power but Adult Rescue

If, as Zipes (2011, 193–223) argues, "Hansel and Gretel" is a story of adults "abusing and abandoning" children, the TV series I've discussed focus primarily on the kids' own ability to "make their way and . . . save themselves"

(Lüthi 1970, 65). Abandonment and abuse in these narratives sometimes appears as little more than a plot device to demonstrate the children's prodigious capabilities. With the exception of *Sherlock,* all the narratives ultimately require the apparent victims to demonstrate their intelligence, skill, cunning, and power. Yet these narratives of powerful children/adolescents/ young adults, presented in series aimed (though not exclusively) at adult audiences, also extensively mitigate their youthful protagonists' control over their world. While many of the shows demonstrate the self-sufficiency and ingenuity of children (such as Cassie in *CSI: Crime Scene Investigation,* Tracy in *Criminal Minds,* Kenzi in *Lost Girl,* Buffy and her friends in *Buffy the Vampire Slayer,* and Bart and Lisa in *The Simpsons*), these young people still rely on adults to help save them from the contemporary witches they encounter.

None of the Hansel and Gretel figures in these modern television shows alone saves him- or herself. Cassie, Tracy, Kenzi, Bart, and Lisa all survive their encounters due to their self-sufficiency but are ultimately rescued by adults (Nick Stokes, Jason Gideon, Bo, and Homer Simpson, respectively). Even Echo must rely on people who are almost all her elders—the Dollhouse organization employees who have uploaded the personalities into her head to allow her to achieve victory over the murderous Richard and the pedophilic and murderous Ghost. When these many characters, along with the children in *Sherlock* and Callie in *Supernatural,* cannot save themselves without direct intervention from other adult and/or magical figures, they prove Heidi Anne Heiner's contention that life "is no fairy tale" (2012, 8).

Speculating on the reasons for this apparent transformation in the final outcome of these versions of "Hansel and Gretel," it is particularly telling that the same pattern recurs across genres from cop shows that seek to explore realistic situations—*CSI: Crime Scene Investigation, Criminal Minds*—to a historical whodunit—*Sherlock*—to apocalyptic fantasies—*Dollhouse, Lost Girl, Supernatural, Buffy the Vampire Slayer*—to an animated family show— *The Simpsons.* While adults may be uncaring or actively iniquitous, child villains also appear in these current versions. What is absent from these shows is a polarization of older characters (negative) versus younger characters (positive); their episodes make at least some adults the children's friends and rescuers. Perhaps demonstrating the original Hansel and Gretel's self-sufficiency to current audiences would challenge not only contemporary ideas of the innocence of children but also the presumption that kids literally cannot survive without adult care and attention.

While no one would be foolish enough to suggest that the problems these shows raise—pedophilia, kidnapping, and murder—are simply fictitious, it is perhaps ironic that the problem faced by the Grimms' own Hansel and Gretel and their parents—the possibility of starvation and lack of economic self-sufficiency—is increasing in Europe and North America. With a growing underclass among those who once prospered and when the economic power of privileged children as consumers is paralleled by the increasingly precarious condition of those who are marginalized by their parents' and their own poverty, the original motivation for Hansel and Gretel's abandonment—hunger and famine—can only be presented in the context of the Simpsons' satire. Perhaps it is equally ironic that the solution to those problems, as well, lies with adults, not with the individual capacities of children.

Notes

1. A fourteenth-century manuscript about the Land of Cockayne describing a house made of confectionery (sweet baked goods and candy) supports this theory.
2. "Little Red Riding Hood" is often a vehicle for exploring pedophilia in films (see Greenhill and Kohm 2009).
3. Although "Gum Drops" uses chewing gum a girl drops as clues for the detective to follow, Northern Americans and Europeans may associate gumdrops with the gelatinous candy blobs often decorating holiday gingerbread houses.
4. Cassie is unaware of the true nature of his activities. She only knows that "Daddy's garden was supposed to be secret."
5. The only food Jeffrey does not consume is creamed spinach due to his milk allergy, a plot point that becomes significant to identify the boy as the killer. However, unpalatable or poisonous food in the home relates to fairy-tale images by recalling the morally poisonous act of gluttony that almost leads to Hansel and Gretel's undoing.
6. Ideas about the corruption of children, and about abused or abandoned children who grow up to become killers, also appear in several "Little Red Riding Hood"–themed crime films (see Kohm and Greenhill 2010).
7. A tale like "Red Riding Hood" can frighten and traumatize children if the wolf escapes, as in the Charles Perrault version, which lacks the Grimms' woodsman savior because "the threat of the wolf remains unresolved" (Richards 1999, 833).
8. In *Dollhouse*, "Dolls" are human beings who have had their memories and personalities removed, turning them into mindless automatons who can be implanted with artificially created ones or those of others.
9. Echo's protector, Boyd, serves as her father figure. Despite his best efforts, he cannot defend her against Richard. His status as a king (recalling the 1823 "Hansel and Gretel" version) becomes clear in the show's second season when he is revealed to be the Rossum Corporation's head.
10. Yet vengeance's uncontrollable nature allows for unintended consequences, causing Bo further pain and putting Kenzi in mortal danger in Baba Yaga's realm.

4

Intermediality and the Artistic Making
of *Jim Henson's The StoryTeller*

Jill Terry Rudy

S tories regularly appear at the same time and in the same space as the storytelling in *Jim Henson's The StoryTeller* (*JHTS*), a live-action/ puppet series. In the first episode, "Hans My Hedgehog" (ATU 441), viewers initially see the old Storyteller (John Hurt) seated by a fire, dressed in a patchwork cloak, saying, "Imagine, a cold night, and a dark night. A night like this one."[1] He begins reciting the story of a childless couple. But two minutes into the twenty-four–minute episode, viewers have seen the story action of Farmer (Eric Richard) and Farmer's Wife (Maggie Wilkinson) in their cottage and heard dialogue in the characters' voices. This stratagem is not too unusual for a televised tale; viewers regularly hear and see characters and their actions without a narrator. But for a series called *StoryTeller*, this move paradoxically suggests that showing the story will attract the viewers' attention as much as telling it. Indeed, as the shot pans out, viewers realize that this scene between the farmer and his wife has been enacted on a ceramic platter in the room where the Storyteller relates his tale. This move creates both confusion and curiosity. Indeed, in all the episodes, at unpredictable moments viewers see and hear the story and storytelling happening at the same time, in the same space.

The proximity of showing and telling in *JHTS* highlights the possibilities of television as a storytelling medium for fairy tales, especially through the production values of the Henson Company. In most television shows, either the story unfolds without a narrator or the narrator remains at a different time and space. Jack Zipes refers to this recurring juxtaposition in *JHTS* as a "perfectly timed estrangement effect," which, along with other camera and editing techniques, works to "surprise and alter if not expand the perspective of audiences" (2011, 221). Perhaps the Storyteller appears in the same spot where a story character just stood, or a story character walks across the floor in the Storyteller's room. This nearness of story and storytelling cannot happen through sight and sound together when one is hearing or reading rather than being shown a story.

In this chapter, I argue that it is important to analyze this estrangement effect in terms of specific modes of communication because the effect both confirms and expands the audience's perspective toward fairy tale and storytelling. Visually and audibly representing tales in the Henson Company way opens audiences to broader perspectives on narrative possibility. Similarly, fairy tale as a genre evokes and rewards such openness. The estrangement of fantastically juxtaposing the story and the telling paradoxically envisions the nearness of wonder with everyday life—a move associated with the fairy tale for centuries (Tiffin 2009; Joosen 2011). Ultimately, this deeper reality is reached by breaching narrative distance on-screen as the show brings showing and telling together through sounds, spoken words, and visual effects. So while *JHTS* honors the storyteller, it extends *telling* stories into the more mediated contemporary realm of *showing* stories. This Storyteller, indeed, is possessed by Jim Henson and his production company—a spell that is both cast and broken by the estrangement effect, which invites viewers to possess themselves, and lose themselves, in these stories.

To better understand what is going on here, in this study of *JHTS* I follow two of W. H. Auden's six reasons for textual analysis. One is to "convince others that they may have undervalued an author or a work" (1962, 8). The full effect of *JHTS* has been undervalued because its relation with viewing tales, rather than only hearing or reading them, has not been considered in detail.[2] Another reason is to "throw light upon the process of artistic Making" (ibid.). The artistry of *JHTS* is acknowledged by Zipes and Donald Haase, but the show has been only a brief example in their longer studies (Zipes 1997, 2011, 220–21; Haase 2008, 949–50). I attend to aspects of the "artistic Making" by studying three of the communicative modes used to achieve the estrangement effect of putting the story and storytelling in proximity. Sounds, spoken words, and visual images work together in viewing the show.

For literary-oriented teachers, the pedagogical benefit of this intermedial approach is to include viewing as an important element of language arts.[3] Within folklore and fairy-tale scholarship, expanding the oral–literate divide to include viewing is another significant pedagogical and critical benefit. Additionally, an intermedial approach that considers both semiotic modes and technological channels draws attention to the ongoing consequences of media conglomeration in a globalized web (Bacchilega 2013) and to the aesthetic and philosophical significance of fairy tales and storytelling as a transformative human activity.

Storytelling and Story Showing Fairy Tales on TV with Intermediality

Through television channels, storytelling can be *story showing,* particularly in *JHTS,* collapsing the distance between space and time while still foregrounding the storyteller's role. This proximity of space and time augments what happens with oral or print storytelling because in these communicative modes story must *precede* the storytelling.[4] *JHTS* exploits and plays with televisual possibilities that meld the separate spheres of story and storytelling into one on-screen. Certainly film can do this too, and the high production values of *JHTS* indicate ways that television may replicate cinema.[5] I discuss the artistic series making by briefly addressing the concepts of mimesis and diegesis, the showing and telling of stories, and the related concept of chronotope, Mikhail Bakhtin's acknowledgement of the "time space" expressed in literature (1981, 84). I mention poet and scholar Maureen McLane's extension of this concept to "retro–neo chronotope" (2008, 49) to explore how Henson's 1980s television show honors the fairy tale as ancient storytelling while simultaneously showing the genre as part of the culture industry.

Intermediality draws scholarly attention to communicative modes, technologies, and systems of distribution, an approach not used much in fairytale scholarship, where intertextuality receives more discussion (Benson 2003; Smith 2007; Joosen 2011). Still, intermediality "is the medial equivalent of intertextuality and it covers any kind of relation between different media. . . . In a narrow sense, it refers to the participation of more than one medium— or sensory channel—in a given work" (Grishakova and Ryan 2010, 3). Media combines technology, as in a channel of transmission, and art, as in semiotic material or form of expression: "Channel-type media [such as television] can also give rise to a distinct type of narrative that takes advantage of their distinct affordances" (ibid.). *JHTS*'s estrangement effect offers just such a "distinct type of narrative," exploiting the possibilities of estrangement and nearness afforded by television viewing.

At its simplest, *JHTS* is a televised anthology of fairy tales linked by a narrator and his canine audience/interlocutor (a puppet voiced by Brian Henson) and sharing central themes of fantasy and family, loss and death. The series started from a collaboration of Henson and his daughter Lisa, who had taken a degree in folklore and mythology from Harvard University. Their intention was to remain "true to the subtlety and metaphoric richness of ancient stories" (Muppet Wiki: The StoryTeller 2013). Because the series includes a whimsical, yet forthright, approach to storytelling, some endings are more somber than happily ever after as each episode portrays the complexity and richness of time-honored tales. Often a central character is lost to his or her nuclear family because of some unique trait: Hans (Ailsa Berk), born to human parents as a hedgehog, leaves his peers' mocking to seek his way in the world; Fearnot (ATU 326, "The Youth Who Wanted to Learn What Fear Is"), played by Reece Dinsdale, sets out to learn how to shiver; Sapsorrow (ATU 510B, "Peau d'Asne"), played by Alison Doody, must leave home to escape her incestuous father (Geoffrey Bayldon). The two episodes directed by Henson take loss to its ultimate extreme and treat death directly. In the eighth episode, "The Heartless Giant" (ATU 302, "The Ogre's [Devil's] Heart in the Egg"), the Giant (Frederick Warder) loses his heart and his life as revenge for his cruel deeds. With "The Soldier and Death" (ATU 330, "The Smith and the Devil" and ATU 332, "Godfather Death"), the Soldier (Bob Peck) outwits Death (Alistair Fullarton) so convincingly that the soldier can never die and is rejected both in hell and heaven. Juxtaposing the story and storytelling becomes a notable way of visually representing loss and death.

The medium focuses this approach: television makes this unlikely narrative unity happen when the story characters appear on-screen in the same scenes with the live-action Storyteller and the puppet Storyteller's dog and vice versa. This estrangement effect expands perspectives on stories because narration usually separates spaces and times; taleworlds are "inhabited by characters acting in their own space and time," and storyrealms are "a realm of discourse spoken by persons who inhabit another space and time" (Young 1987, viii). Yet, *JHTS* envisions ways that those different spaces and times can be bridged in whimsical and polished storytelling and story showing performance. The *JHTS* tales occupy simultaneously the spatiotemporal worlds of stories *and* storytelling.

This turns out to be a replication of the proximity of showing and telling inherent in the metafictional possibilities of the fairy tale and human imagination. Fairy tale is a form "which essentially relies on the marvelous for some aspect of its self-conscious function" (Tiffin 2009, 27). This marvelous self-consciousness seems historically intermedial: "The specific trends of literary fairy tale at various times in its history have in the twentieth and twenty-first centuries given way to a particularly wide range of contexts and media for adaptation" (ibid., 25). Even when listeners are told a tale, they may imagine then and there seeing the recited action even if that action is fictional and associated with a time long ago and a space far away. *JHTS* portrays for viewers what they may have imagined but now can actually see and hear.

Each new medium engaged by fairy tale, whether orality, literacy, dancing, illustrated anthology, theater, or cell phone, perpetuates some juxtaposition of this showing and telling, sometimes leaving less to the imagination by bringing more visual imagery, motion, and sound to the story's production. The possibility of curtailing imagination through film made J. R. R. Tolkien reluctant about such adaptations (Wood 2006, 292). Currently, however, folklorist Juliette Wood notes that audiences want "making of" the film segments on DVD so they can "simultaneously enter into the fantasy and understand how it is created" (ibid.). Paradoxically, as each new medium of storytelling increases layers of mediation between storyteller and listener, it also seems to multiply *and* in some ways reduce time and space distances. Collectors, printers, illustrators, translators, actors, directors, and producers bring their own spaces and times to the telling *and* showing of tales.

Telescoping space and time is what television and fairy tale both do particularly well. Television brings historical or contemporary events from around the corner or around the world into homes, computers, and mobile devices. Toby Miller relates that even before television actually worked scientists and culture critics projected its possibilities for bending the time–space continuum (Miller 2010). Richard Whittaker Hubbell wrote in his 1942 book *4000 Years of Television: The Story of Seeing at a Distance* that the emergence of television was "a story of time and space annihilated" (qtd. in Miller 2010, 4). Perhaps television is more time and space fulfilled because, like the fairy tale, its narrative brings times and spaces together rather than destroying them altogether. Similarly, a tale's long ago and far away is told, read, and viewed in the present and recalled and retold in the future.

Fields such as film studies, linguistics, and folkloristics have developed the concept of diegesis to address these medial and philosophical aspects of stories and storytelling. Diegesis and the related concept of chronotope name the closeness of story time and space and storytelling time and space that make up *JHTS*'s artistry. As Plato and Aristotle discuss, mimesis, or showing, was distinguished to some degree from diegesis, or telling. Yet, film scholar Andre Gaudreault allows that Plato also acknowledged a diegesis *through* mimesis "as the portrayal of action through representation on stage" (qtd. in Gunning 2009, xxi–xxii). Gaudreault then introduces the term "monstrator" as a corollary to narrator to indicate one who "shows a story, presents it to an audience" (ibid., xxii). In the case of *JHTS*, the Storyteller on the screen would be the narrator, and Jim Henson and the production team would be the monstrators. Fascinatingly, a television series focusing on the Storyteller highlights the whimsy and artistry of the monstrator—the one who shows the story, or the storyshower (an almost nonsensical word to read in English). The monstrator's artistry, in connection with the storyteller's veneration, suggests why attention is due to presenting fairy tales as *JHTS* does. The televisual medium does not cancel out the storyteller but brings story showing into the narrative performance as well.

The concept of chronotope encourages looking into the way a distinctive time–space continuum of fairy tale may encourage story to blend with storytelling, as in *JHTS*. Chronotope is Bakhtin's term for analyzing "the intrinsic connectedness of temporal and spatial relationships that are artistically expressed in literature" (1981, 84). The attitude toward the time–space continuum in *JHTS* becomes multidimensional. *JHTS* flaunts the constraints on time and space through juxtaposing the story world with the storytelling world. I call this unification of worlds created by combining tales and televisual technologies a "retro–neo chronotope," a neologism McLane coins to describe balladeering in the eighteenth and nineteenth centuries. Balladeers commandeered print to collect, preserve, and enjoy what they perceived to be ancient, oral, narrative songs (2008, 49). With different technology but similar impulse, the Henson production team utilizes late 1980s cutting-edge media and technologies to recreate and entertain with fairy tales.

I focus on the two episodes directed by Henson to better understand the show's artistic making. Overcoming the separation of narrative time and space becomes the playful possibility of intermedial storytelling and story showing performances on network television that unite sound, image, and motion. The unity of semiotic modes (viewing by seeing and hearing) establishes the proximity of showing and telling, as I will point out. Considering each mode separately portrays how the production team uses distinct and combined media to create the nearness. This highlights the series' artistry and helps us recognize how the estrangement effect unfolds. Looking at each mode separately also encourages viewers accustomed to analyzing print to attend more strategically to sounds, audible words, and visual images.

Sound and the Unity of Taleworld and Storyrealm

Sound helps unify the taleworld and storyrealm through ambient noise, the musical score composed by Rachel Portman, and an occasionally overt sharing between the two spatiotemporal worlds. Sound itself (a footstep, the toll of a bell, the hiss of a devil gnashing his teeth) may not draw too much attention in telling or viewing tales. An oral storyteller may voice effects such as moans, shrieks, and gasps; a musical score and ambient sound become a typical, almost overlooked, part of the narrative in film, radio, and television. Because it is easy to miss while viewing, it is important to recognize when and how ambient sound and music link the taleworld and storyrealm into one televised sphere. Audible words, as essential sounds in this *JHTS* narrative performance, will be discussed in more detail in the next section.

Film scholars have studied cinematic music focusing specifically on distinctions and possible confluences of the worlds of the story, the film, and viewers. Etienne Souriau used the term "diegesis" to "describe one of the seven levels of 'filmic reality' to which the spectator engages with film" (Winters 2010, 226). Gérard Genette applied it to narrative levels and to "the spatiotemporal universe to which the outer action of the telling refers" (qtd. in Bunia 2010, 681). Claudia Gorbman's configuration of diegesis and film music particularly applies to *JHTS*. Music heard in the story itself is diegetic in contrast to nondiegetic music, such as the score (1987). Similar to Katharine Young's demarcation of story space and time from storytelling space and time, Gorbman's conceptualization distinguishes between sounds made and heard in the story and those outside it. Diegetic music, such as a character whistling, in *JHTS* would be heard in the taleworld, while nondiegetic music, such as the musical score, is heard by viewers alone. Yet some sounds from the taleworld may be heard in the storyrealm as well, thus juxtaposing the two into one sphere for viewers. This linking highlights the "distinct type of narrative" afforded by television (Grishakova and Ryan 2010, 3).

While Gorbman's demarcation of diegetic and nondiegetic music is useful, not every occurrence of music or sound is so easily delimited (as *JHTS* flaunts). There has been much debate about neatly dividing the categories; music's nuances as part of the film's narrative space can be overlooked in applying the narratological terms too strictly (Winters 2010). One way to learn about the significance of ambient sound and musical scores as part of the narrative is simply to view with the volume turned down and then to review with the volume back up.

"The Heartless Giant" provides good examples of how ambient sounds and the musical score juxtapose the taleworld, the storyrealm, and the viewers' own spatiotemporal world using televisual technologies to create the storytelling performance's narrative space. Ambient sounds heard by story characters and viewers, and sometimes by the narrator as well, clearly are diegetic in Gorbman's terms and become subtly crucial to the *JHTS* storytelling and story showing performance. Protagonist Leo (Elliott Spiers), a young prince, is first seen walking across Storyteller's floor on his way to encounter something in the castle dungeon that somehow appears below the floor. Leo is about to leave the dark grate in the castle when he hears a chain rattle. This is a showing of the story, not a recitation by the Storyteller, that requires pertinent ambient sound. Leo asks the creature in the dungeon to shake its chains once if it is a giant, twice if it is not. He, and viewers, hears one rattle of the chains. Leo gets visibly excited and asks the giant to shake the chains once if he has a heart and twice if he has no heart. He, and the viewers, hears the sound of a chain rattling twice. Though the juxtaposition of taleworld and storyrealm is not featured, the scene also includes a soft oboe melody heard only by viewers that sets a serious yet not scary tone for this encounter between Leo and the Giant. While ambient sound unites the taleworld with the viewer's world, the musical score is nondiegetic in Gorbman's terms and still plays a role as part of the viewers' narrative space that prepares for an understanding of characters and actions in the story (Winters 2010).

Sound actually juxtaposes the taleworld and storyrealm early in "The Soldier and Death," creating a narrative improbability that occurs seemingly effortlessly through the episode's technological prowess. Like the other eight episodes, credit for the screenplay goes to accomplished writer and director Anthony Minghella. But this episode in many aspects, such as basic plot and characterization, resembles Arthur Ransome's *The Soldier and Death: A Russian Folk Tale* (1920). Yet Minghella adds the Soldier's whistle, which never appears in Ransome's version. Its sound becomes a recurring motif and link between the story and storytelling with the televised tale.

The episode opens with a discussion between Storyteller and Dog about biscuits and a sack on the floor, then viewers hear about a soldier returning from a very far-off war. We see the soldier share a biscuit with a Fiddling Beggar (Stuart Richman) and hear the soldier receive a blessing from the Beggar of a better whistle. This whistle seems meant for television in order to unite the tale with its telling. As the screen jump-cuts from the scene with the Soldier and Fiddling Beggar to the Storyteller's room, Soldier's whistle still can be heard at the same time viewers see the Storyteller commenting on its improvement. Sound collapses the spatiotemporal distance between the story of the Soldier returning home from war and the storytelling scene in the Storyteller's room. *JHTS* exploits the narrative capabilities of television to project sounds from one place and time into others; in this case, the sound of the returning soldier's whistle occurs during the storytelling recitation and becomes part of the viewers' experience of the story.

These uses of sound, including the musical score, create moments when viewers may become aware of time-and-space simultaneity between the story and the storytelling. Sound perhaps most subtly connects taleworlds and storyrealms because viewers take the ambient noise for granted and may not fully register the musical score's emotional effect on the complete storytelling performance. But surely the absence or misuse of ambient sound or an overly timid or dramatic musical score would detract from the wondrous moments that bring showing and telling into proximity. Again, watching a scene or an entire episode with the sound turned off would help to confirm this point. Television brings these significant sounds to the fairy tales' telling and showing and underscores their fantastic possibilities.

Hearing Words while Viewing and the *JHTS* Fairy-Tale Style

While sound is an important medium for establishing and confirming the unity of the taleworld and storyrealm in *JHTS,* audible words and dialogue become especially marked in replicating an archaic fairy-tale style through television's audio capabilities. The fairy tale's "narrative style is characterized by fixed formulas, repetitions, and symbolic numbers" (Joosen 2011, 13). The special sounds and combinations of words of *JHTS* make these stories a modern homage to olden time tales. A review of "Fearnot" mentioned this aspect: "Minghella, a British playwright and former literature professor . . . retains both the childlike wonder of the tale and its distinctive literary traditions, right down to a trip described as going to 'a pond, by a hedge, by a field, by a mill, by a town'" (O'Connor 1987). Spoken words matter very much in maintaining the retro–neo chronotope; they keep stories flowing without drastically changing the fairy-tale narrative style of fixed formulas, repetitions, and archaic words.

The opening of "The Heartless Giant" illustrates Minghella's masterful use of the fairy tale's spare style. Most episodes begin with Storyteller speaking to Dog and to the unseen television audience, often through the imperative voice. But after the opening credits, the Giant's story begins with the Storyteller saying, "Think of all kinds of unpleasant things. And add Giant to them. And that's what you get when a Giant has no heart. Such a Giant once terrorized a country." In print, these sentences parse out as spare statements, evoked by the Storyteller's intonation and pauses. The word "giant" stands out because it is repeated in almost every sentence, three times overall, and takes both an object and subject position grammatically. When watching the show, viewers hear the Storyteller's spoken words that incorporate the compact, repetitive fairy-tale style.

While individual words are important, the dialogue also contributes much to the *JHTS* artistry, to the unity of the taleworld and storyrealm, and to the retro element of the retro–neo chronotope. Like the darker-hued images in the series, to be discussed in the next section, the dialogue matches the narrative style and the backward turn of the retro–neo chronotope. Here, the repetition, the formulaic speech, and the vocabulary of long ago become key retro elements of the artful dialogue. A discussion about the location of the Giant's heart exemplifies an archaic fairy-tale speech style and also indicates, through the Storyteller's repetition of key words in the same scene, the proximity of taleworld and storyrealm. It not only includes a series of prepositional phrases similar to the list mentioned by reviewer O'Connor above but also uses unique vocabulary suggesting a long-ago time:

> Giant: I'll tell you exactly where it is. And, you still not be able
> [*sic*] to find it. Far away, so far you cannot fathom it, so high
> you cannot climb it, is a mountain. And in the mountain is
> a lake. And in the lake is an island, in the island is a church,
> in the church is a well, in the well is a duck, in the duck is
> an egg, and in the egg is my heart.

Leo: I see.

Giant: No. Not so easy, little thief. Aye. Not such a diddle and a doddle as you thought. No, your father tricked me once. And I shan't be tricked again.

The Giant is not stupid, as he is at pains to convey at the end of this exchange. He uses the predicate "fathom" not only to explain the distance of the heart's location but also to suggest Leo's cognitive incapability. He constructs a formulaic description of the heart's location that repeats the prepositional phrase and the "to be" verb and object seven times in what remains a rather succinct sentence. This cumulative repetition fits the fairy tale's narrative style, as do the words "diddle" and "doddle," which seem to have no contemporary meaning. The dialogue evokes an archaic fairy-tale style.

This scene also brings the taleworld and storyrealm into proximity through word repetition. While the camera shot focuses on Leo as he responds to the Giant's outburst about being tricked, viewers hear the Storyteller's voiceover repeat the location of the heart—in reverse order and only using the prepositional phrases: "An egg in a duck in a well in a church in an island in a lake in a mountain. Impossible." No images display these objects, at least at this point in the story; the camera remains fixed on Leo until another jump cut to the Storyteller's face. Here the words viewers hear so close to when they were spoken by the Giant seamlessly connect the storyrealm to the taleworld. Although the Storyteller proclaims the impossibility of hiding a heart, the fairy-tale narrative style and its chronotope imply that such a feat must be feasible. Audible words, and other sounds, create and perpetuate the *JHTS* storytelling performance's retro–neo chronotope. For all the series' pertinent sounds and images, the Minghella screenplay spoken by the Storyteller and the story characters still matters very much. The telling of tales need not be overwhelmed by their showing through viewing the televised story.

Visual Images and the Muted Color Scheme of a *JHTS* Retro–Neo Chronotope

While sound and words establish and confirm the unity of taleworld and storyrealm, certain objects' images and the series' overall look create the retro–neo chronotope of long ago and far away appearing before viewers' eyes just now. The show's visual imagery consistently portrays distant, medieval-like worlds through castles, forests, huts, and cottages. The *JHTS* visuals almost always tend toward darker hues with torchlight, firelight, or gray skies casting a shadow over both the taleworld and storyrealm that evokes circumstances removed from a neon or fluorescent twentieth century. The darker end of the color spectrum is yet another way of evoking the retro–neo chronotope; the occasional contrast of bright white or a vivid red also confirms the Henson Creature Shop's capacity to put earlier times in high relief through technology and production values. Costuming and props also confirm the retropredominance created by the show's newer technologies. Taleworld and storyrealm characters wear tunics, tights, cloaks, gowns, and crowns. People from the taleworld appear in the storyrealm on platters, wall paintings, the floor, Dog's water dish, and Storyteller's tankard. At least four objects in "The Soldier and Death" overtly link the taleworld and storyrealm by appearing in both—a biscuit, a sack, a deck of cards, and the magical glass the Soldier uses to see whether Death is at the head or foot of a dying person. This combination of objects and dark-hued imagery portray the stories' whimsy and fantasy, while the overall look makes fairy tales both realistic and artistic.

Visual images juxtapose taleworld and storyrealm in "The Soldier and Death" because viewers see the four objects that look exactly the same in both realms. Dog is very interested in the biscuit in the sack at the Storyteller's feet as the episode opens. Viewers see the sack and the Dog sniffing, but no biscuit at this point.[5] After the whistle scene, and another on the Storyteller's wall painting with a Dancing Beggar, the Storyteller shuffles a deck of cards with a match cut to the Card Trick Beggar's deck (Walter Sparrow). Another match cut after the Soldier's Devil returns and cures Soldier's Son (Gavin Knights) again makes links. One second the Soldier holds a (magical) glass goblet in the taleworld and the next, viewers see a glass in the Storyteller's hand in the storyrealm. The Storyteller does not tell viewers how he happens to be holding a glass that looks exactly like the one just seen with the Soldier. And, in the closing moments of the story, as the Storyteller recounts the Soldier's well-being despite his sad fate of never being able to die, the Dog receives the long-awaited biscuit. When the Storyteller tosses the sack down, however, a deeply red devil scurries out and across the room—to Dog's great surprise. Through images that appear so easily in both the taleworld and the storyrealm, viewers experience the storytelling performance as a fabulous unity across the time–space continuum of these two locations.

The taleworld and storyrealm's visual appearance in "The Soldier and Death" corresponds with the series' general look of muted color scheme and costuming and scenery that vaguely evoke an earlier medieval or Renaissance time. Comparing the sets and color scheme with another televised tale anthology, Shelley Duvall's *Faerie Tale Theatre* (1982–1987), confirms that the fairy tale invites specific chronotopic images, consistently evoking a spatiotemporal world of centuries ago. Both shows portray many characters in Renaissance or medieval type costumes: tunics, tights, gowns, and crowns. Both shows are set in castles of gray stone and cottages of stucco and wood. But true to its title, Duvall's creates a theatrical world of pastel colors and stylized sets. The scenes look constructed for a stage set rather than somewhere the characters could actually live. The Henson visuals, on the other hand, look like real buildings and forests even when occasionally stylized as a painting on a platter, wall, or tankard. They tend toward the darker hues and render the taleworld less theatrical and more ancient than the lighter, more colorful hues of Duvall's production. Each approach acknowledges the fantastic and otherworldly aspects of the fairy-tale chronotope. But *JHTS* purposefully mutes the spectrum to show and tell fairy tales as rich, substantive stories from a darker time and space with weighty themes of life and death.

For this reason, it may be fitting that the scene where Soldier captures Death in his sack vividly contrasts light and dark. The room is lighted at the center through a recessed alcove window, and Soldier's bed sheets and clothing are a bright white. The magical glass goblet reflects this light. Death has a pale, white face framed by his dark cloak, and when Soldier asks Death to identify his sack and commands him to "Get in it," the dark sack seems minimized as Soldier joyfully twirls it around his pale legs and light bedclothes and coverings. While not all of the episodes are shot with such extreme dark and light contrasts, none utilize pastels or bright colors. The series uses the ostentatious distance of absent or muted color to create and maintain a retro world, far away in space and time yet present through the show's technological creativity.

Showing and Telling Tales through Channels of Distribution

As a televised fairy-tale series, *JHTS* makes the juxtaposition of the taleworld and storyrealm particularly apparent by emphasizing the old and new time–space of the storytelling. The production team approached the tales through "a rare combination of ancient tradition and modern technological artistry" (Muppet Wiki: The StoryTeller). Ancient tradition together with modern technology forms a retro–neo chronotope indeed. Befitting the intention of sharing these stories' richness, *JHTS*'s initial series included lesser known European tales and aired them in prime-time network television.[7] To indicate the tales' ancient narrative sources, each episode's opening credits simply attributes the stories to "An Early German Folk Tale" or "An Early Celtic Folk Tale" and to Minghella's screenplay. The lack of overt referencing maintains the tale's indefinite spatiotemporal chronotope; these stories are associated with a national or cultural group only in their past,[8] while the credit to Minghella acknowledges a contemporary approach. The prominent display of "early" and "folk" establishes a retro mode. Yet, the moments when story characters appear on platters or wall paintings can only be produced through visual technologies. The retro–neo chronotope of *JHTS* is Janus faced, self-consciously bringing together contemporary technology and ancient craft in its storytelling performance.

This looking backward and forward, as in all tellings and showings, also historically locates the Storyteller's identity. By selecting a male storyteller and a dog as the scene for the storytelling, the production company elides the work of scholars and collectors since Straparola and Basile, who associate fairy tales with female storytellers and groups of listeners. The feminist fairy-tale revolution had started almost two decades before the series aired in the late 1980s (Haase 2004a; Joosen 2011). Crucial works by Karen Rowe (1986) and Marina Warner (1994) recovered the historical role of female tellers, the domestic work of women, and the spinning of tales. The Henson Company still elected to portray the storyteller as a lone man speaking to a dog.[9] This contrasts with Duvall's anthology; she introduces the stories, and they have no narrators.[10] The male narrator, while not an impossibility, suggests the tendency in some histories of the genre to remember the male collectors, while the female story-tellers remain harder to identify (Hearne 1997). Enshrining a male Storyteller goes somewhat against the grain of historical settings and those of the TV program; this aspect of *JHTS* deserves further study.

The fabulous production modes and media technologies of *JHTS* mimic, even enact, the intermedial proclivities and artistry of telling fairy tales by inviting viewers to occupy various worlds all at once—a deeper reality that includes the fantastic and wonderful appearing on our television and other screens. Since the episodes originally aired, further iterations of *JHTS* episodes have appeared. In the late 1990s, some episodes became available as a book and on VHS. The show has been distributed in Japan on laser disc, and in 2003 the series was released on DVD with a definitive edition released in 2006 (Muppet Wiki videography). A 2011 graphic novel published by

Archaia Comics carries the *JHTS* title and includes completely different tales with script and art from well-known figures, including one story adapted from an unproduced Minghella teleplay. These various distribution channels indicate the capacity of media technologies and systems to bend, or at least extend, a time–space continuum through new and familiar media alike.

They also suggest the necessity of creating and networking with media corporations and conglomerates to produce, broadcast, and distribute television programs. While the series received critical acclaim,[11] ratings for the four *JHTS* shows that aired as part of the *Jim Henson Hour* were abysmal—near the very bottom of the Nielson rankings.[12] Still, the Jim Henson Company and its affiliates have kept the series available to viewers through distribution arrangements in a variety of media. The successive technologies of video, DVD, the internet, and mobile devices preserve *JHTS* as an electronic tale collection. The appearance of *JHTS* in successive media again highlights the generic proclivity of tales to look backward and forward.[13]

Viewers born before the 1980s know well that television episodes initially were only available through seemingly random reruns and rebroadcasts, as exemplified by the three recurrences of Rodgers and Hammerstein's *Cinderella* (1957, 1965, 1997) discussed in Patricia Sawin's chapter. Now many television shows can be purchased in DVD boxed sets, by pay per view, or via online access. These technologies and distributive networks play with nearness by making select shows available that initially aired only at a very specific time and place. Contemporary shows, as discussed by Hay and Baxter's chapter, build such convergence of time and space into apps and internet platforms that keep shows online with updated content or commentary 24/7. While this expanding availability affects a proliferating number of series, few shows are as metafictional as *JHTS* in flaunting the capacity to bend the time–space continuum within their diegesis. Yet few local retailers carry the DVD collection, and it is not inexpensive to purchase from online stores. Issues of controlled access indicate that even in the Henson Company's imaginative realm, these fairy tales very much are part of the culture industry and globalized communication and technological networks (Bacchilega 2013).

Putting It All Together: Intermediality and the Showing and Telling of Tales

My favorite example of the unity of showing and telling fairy tales in *JHTS* pays tribute to the timing and proximity of word, image, and sound that creates, even as it unites, their worlds. We return to the scene of Soldier at cards with the devils. The devils literally bring some of the series' richest color. Their vivid red, sinewy bodies combine with their sharp features, and sharper tongues, to challenge Soldier as they play for his soul, his whistle, and his teeth. A dialogue exchange, enumerating in descending order of importance what Soldier stands to lose, emphasizes the whimsy of this potentially very frightening prospect. The scene proceeds without any voiceover until the business of card playing seems to require the Storyteller's contribution. It is he who announces that Soldier continues to win as we also see Soldier jauntily dealing the cards and hear the moans of the losing devils. Viewers' repeated comments on YouTube attest to a favorite dialogue exchange as Soldier continues to win at cards.[14] The words are witty and blunt. One devil asks, "Is he cheating?" And another replies, "Well, I am. And, I'm still losing." This is backed up by another devil, who says, "Me too." By this point, we have the playful oboe from the musical score, the sights of flashing cards and frustrated devils, and the commentary of the Storyteller, who tells us that the devils "cheated to high heaven and low hell to no avail."

Here is where proximity and intermediality combine to great effect as the Storyteller's voiceover announces, "And the devils got into the kind of a fume that only devils can get in." Upon hearing "fume," viewers notice a whiff of smoke coming from a devil's ear. The Storyteller says, "Fume, fume, fume," and we see not only a devil smoking a cigarette but other devils fuming smoke from their ears without any apparent source except their frustration at losing. Soldier even waves his hand to disperse the smoking fumes. This is showing and telling, taleworld and storyrealm, retro–neo chronotope, and the spare fairy-tale style of formula and repetition and symbolic number (there are three fumes, indeed) enacted for the television screen through words, images, and sounds.

Turning again to the Ransome translation of "The Soldier and Death" suggests how printed words can evoke sounds in a reader's imagination. The devils arrive in the palace at "Twelve o'clock sharp and there was a yelling, a shouting, a blowing of horns, a scraping of fiddles and every other kind of instrument, a noise of dancing, of running, of stamping, and the palace cram full of devils making themselves at home as if the place belonged to them" (1920, 17). In the Henson episode, no raucous music of horns, fiddles, and various other instruments mark the devils' arrival; instead there are the ambient sounds of the clock, dirt falling from the rafters, and the devils' flapping wings. After Soldier strikes the match and sees the devils crowded around him, the most dominant sound is his whistle—memorable from the scenes early in the episode, when it juxtaposed the taleworld and storyrealm. The Ransome dialogue, however, suggests a similar whimsy as the devils proclaim to the soldier, "What are you sitting there so glum for, smoking your pipe? There's smoke enough where we have been. Put your pipe in your pocket and play a round of cards with us" (1920, 18). Minghella's screenplay reverses the action, and the Soldier initiates the card game and asks what they will be playing for. While the book can state that eventually the devils wager their "sixty bushels of silver and forty of gold" and send one devil out of the room sixty separate times to carry back the silver and forty to carry back the gold, the screenplay collapses these lengthy repetitions into the call for the cart filled with forty barrels of gold. The printed story can evoke many sounds through its description of the devils' raucous entry; it can extend the plot time by repeating one action 100 times. So, the printed word can play with the taleworld's spatiotemporal continuum, but it cannot enact it or expressly envision it as does the Henson episode.

Comparing story versions leads again to an appreciation of the intermedial possibilities of the semiotic modes of sounds, words, and images, along with their institutional technologies and distribution systems. The storytelling performance itself, whatever the media, brings together the taleworld and storyrealm for the listener, reader, or viewer. This chapter asserts that *JHTS* is particularly self-aware about playing with and foregrounding such juxtapositions in a multimodal capacity unique to film and television abilities to unite sounds, words, images, and motion. The Soldier's improved whistle from the Card Trick Beggar is heard in the Storyteller's room; the death-predicting glass goblet appears in the Soldier's hand at his deathbed in one second and in the Storyteller's hand near his fireside in the next. Voiceovers and jump and match cut between the taleworld and Storyteller and Dog in the storyrealm juxtapose and exploit the retro–neo chronotope of the Henson series. The show utilizes television production and distribution technologies and the Henson whimsy and artistry to honor the ancient tales of earlier times and to keep them available, for a price, in our globalized webs of telling, showing, and viewing.

Notes

I acknowledge Sara Cleto and Kerry Kaleba for their proposal to study narrative framing in *Jim Henson's The StoryTeller*. I thank Jamie Horrocks,

Pauline Greenhill, Christa Baxter Drake, Rebecca Hay, Emma Nelson, and Mary Rice for attentive readings.

1. "Hans My Hedgehog" was broadcast on NBC on January 31, 1987. Other episodes aired intermittently, some as stand-alone shows and others on *The Jim Henson Hour*.
2. A special *Journal of American Folklore* issue (Ben-Amos 2010) foregrounds attention to an oral/literate debate to which Zipes responds (2012, 157–89).
3. Since 1996, viewing and visually representing have been included as language arts by the National Council of Teachers of English along with speaking, listening, reading, and writing.
4. The fairy tale's philosophical ramifications are as yet undervalued.
5. See also Barzilai's chapter.
6. The dialogue overtly references the retro element as the Storyteller and Dog banter about the biscuit needed for the story. Dog asks if it is an old story; Storyteller replies, "Ancient. Antique." Then Dog replies, "Oh, stale biscuits then. Ugh."
7. A second series of four episodes involving Greek myths aired in 1990.
8. B. Grantham Aldred states that these retellings "draw primarily, but not exclusively, on the Grimm brothers' *Kinder- und Hausmarchen* (*Children's and Household Tales*, 1812–1815)" (2008, 450). The Grimms project in its day also effected a retro–neo chronotope.
9. Viewers may be included in the skeptical canine's questions and observations.
10. As of January 25, 2013, YouTube videos are available with several Duvall introductions spliced together: www.youtube.com/watch?v=JLjtOJd54wE.
11. See www.imdb.com/title/tt0092383/awards.
12. See www.tv.com/shows/the-jim-henson-hour/forums/nielsen-ratings-63948-18826 19. My title deliberately echoes Kay Stone's "Things Walt Disney Never Told Us" (see also Sawin's chapter). Comparison of the Henson Company with Disney is another fascinating area for further research.
13. Intermediality has become crucial to television, as discussed in Nelson and Walton's and Hay and Baxter's chapters.
14. When I started this research, I watched full episodes on YouTube and read viewer comments. Now, a three-minute synopsis is available from the Henson Company with "Top Comments" included, which seem very similar to the comments attached to the earlier episodes I viewed online (www.youtube.com/watch?v=SAyNkZ-ZQ0k).

PART II

Masculinities and/or Femininities

THINGS WALT DISNEY DIDN'T TELL US (BUT AT WHICH RODGERS AND HAMMERSTEIN AT LEAST HINTED)

The 1965 Made-for-TV Musical of *Cinderella*

Patricia Sawin

Ten minutes ago I met you.
You looked up when I came through the door.
My head started reeling,
You gave me the feeling
The room had no ceiling or floor.
In the arms of my love I'm flying
Over mountain and meadow and glen,
And I like it so well
That for all I can tell
I may never come down again.
I may never come down to earth again.

I t's February 1965, and I'm headed home from fourth grade at Flatirons Elementary. Despite my bulky winter coat, I'm waltzing up the sidewalk, pausing for a fleeting arabesque at the ballet barre/railing where I cross a half-frozen stream, singing the unutterably romantic "Ten Minutes Ago" under my breath and imagining myself whirling in the arms of a handsome prince. Like tens of thousands of American children, on Tuesday, February 23, I had been allowed to stay up to watch a television special, Rodgers and

Hammerstein's made-for-TV musical *Cinderella,* with Lesley Ann Warren in the title role.[1] Like many young women of my generation, I was entranced, feeling that the production spoke especially to me, despite awkward elements evident even to an easily impressed nine-year-old.

It is hardly surprising that as a girl I was taken with this highly promoted production. Yet I still love it and was thrilled to discover a battered videotape in a thrift shop. Consultation with other women who have thought extensively about both fairy tales and feminism reveals that many my age retain a fondness for this classic. In this chapter I explore my continuing positive reaction to a fairy-tale version that appears to be what Jack Zipes dubs a "duplicate" (as distinct from a "revision"), a new rendition that "reproduce[s] a set pattern of ideas and images that reinforce a traditional way of seeing, believing, and behaving" (1994, 9).

I engage in this analysis primarily as autoethnography, "an approach to research and writing that seeks to describe and systematically analyze personal experience in order to understand cultural experience" (Ellis, Adams, and Bochner 2011). Autoethnography honors the second-wave feminist realization that "the personal is political": to comprehend power's subtle workings we must gain insight into our own experiences, compare them with others', and recognize them as culturally conditioned (see Napikoski n.d.b). Autoethnography also responds to the postmodern insistence that research questions are inevitably personally influenced and socially constituted (Ellis and Bochner [1994] 2000); differently situated thinkers generate different knowledges (Ellis, Adams, and Bochner 2011). Autoethnographically "plac[ing] personal experience within social and cultural contexts" leads researchers to "raise provocative questions about social agency and socio-cultural constraints" (Reed-Danahy 2009, 28). Many see the methodology as a crucial component of ethical research practice because it "treats research as a political, socially-just and socially-conscious act" (Ellis, Adams, and Bochner 2011). Autoethnographers may choose to reveal intimate or embarrassing details without asking another source to be so vulnerable (see Denzin 2006 and Poulos 2010).

As Donald Haase notes, "The tendency of scholarship to problematize the fairy tale's relation to gender construction and female subjectivity leads back to the question at the root of early feminist interest in the genre— namely, to what extent does the classic fairy tale engender the sociocultural behavior and attitudes of its female readers and listeners?" (2004b, 25). Although feminist fairy-tale scholarship has evolved substantially since its emergence in the 1970s and my introduction to it shortly thereafter, I begin with the early critical texts. Ultimately, however, I situate my analysis relative to current feminist interpretive positions in order to explicate my interpretation of this *Cinderella* and to suggest why some apparently "traditional" fairy-tale versions may encourage their audiences to question conservative gender roles as effectively as versions considered reflexive and critical.

From me as a nine-year-old dancer, fast-forward a couple of decades to the University of Texas, where Beverly Stoeltje introduced folklore graduate students to the feminist critique of folktales, epitomized by Kay Stone's "Things Walt Disney Never Told Us" (1975). What Disney hadn't told us, Stone—with Marcia Lieberman (1972) and Alison Lurie (1970, 1971)—argued, was that many traditional folktales feature plucky, resourceful, brave, even violent heroines, like Molly Whuppee, who saves her sisters by tricking a giant, and the familiar Gretel, who pushes the witch into the oven. Disney was not solely to blame. The "refined literary men who edited the first popular collections of fairy tales for children during the Victorian era," like Andrew Lang (Lurie 1971, 6) and Wilhelm Grimm, included stories in which boys could be "slovenly, unattractive, and lazy, [without] their success be[ing] affected" (Stone 1975, 44) but shared only tales in which girls were beautiful and compliant (or were punished if not). American children's storybooks mainly popularized tales narrating the travails of the "docile dozen" (ibid., 43). The only fairy tales American children knew taught that "heroes succeed because they act, not because they are. They are judged not by their appearance or inherent sweet nature but by their ability to overcome obstacles, even if these impediments are defects in their own characters. Heroines are not allowed any defects, nor are they required to develop, since they are already perfect. The only tests of most heroines require nothing beyond what they are born with: a beautiful face, tiny feet, or a pleasing temperament" (ibid.).

Disney raised to iconic status the "pretty, passive" heroines who "seem barely alive," consistently selecting stories that featured female villains, "strongly reinforcing the . . . stereotype of the innocent beauty victimized by the wicked villainess" (though Grimm tales equally feature male villains) and "remov[ing] most of the powerful fantasy of the *Märchen*" by situating the tales in a "cloying fantasy world filled with . . . pretty flowers and singing animals" (Stone 1975, 44). Lieberman argued, "The best-known stories . . . have affected masses of children in our culture. Cinderella, the Sleeping Beauty, and Snow White are mythic figures" (1972, 383–84).

Forty years later, a young person fascinated with fairy tales may choose from a much wider variety of versions, many with feminist impetus, including Robert Munsch's beloved story in which Princess Elizabeth, reduced to wearing a paper bag after a dragon attack, rescues Prince Ronald but dumps him when he criticizes her appearance as unprincesslike (1980) and Ethel Johnston Phelps's collection of folktales with intrepid heroines (1981). Literary retellings have also proliferated since the 1970s; among the most influential are Angela Carter's (1979) and Emma Donoghue's (1997) tales that turn good and bad upside down and explore iconic images as symbols for complex psychosexual dramas. Zipes argues, "Since 1980 there has been an inextricable, dialectical development of mutual influence of *all* writers of fairy tales and fairy-tale criticism that has led to innovative fairy-tale experiments in all cultural fields" (2009, 122).

Both feminist criticism of "traditional" fairy tales and folklorists' efforts to popularize tales with forceful heroines contribute to the fairy-tale heroine's positive reimagining. Still, the Disney enterprise remains an extremely influential and largely conservative purveyor of images, especially for young girls. Intriguingly, between *Sleeping Beauty* (1959) and *The Little Mermaid* (1989) Disney steered clear of fairy tales. But a return to the genre, celebrated as their animated features' renaissance ("Disney Renaissance" n.d.; Greydanus n.d.), also revived—with only cosmetic updates—the heroine obsessed with romantic love. Although curious Ariel the mermaid dares to defy her father, she literally gives up her voice for a chance to win Prince Eric's love, arguably going to even greater extremes to get her man than the early passive beauties Snow White, Sleeping Beauty, and Cinderella.

Disney (and subsequently Disney-owned Pixar) evidently recognized that their audience would welcome fairy-tale films in which the heroine has goals other than (or at least in addition to) marrying the prince: bookworm Belle in *Beauty and the Beast* (1991); peacemaker *Pocahontas* (1995); warrior *Mulan* (1998); Tiana in *The Princess and the Frog* (2009), who dreams of owning a New Orleans restaurant; and Rapunzel in *Tangled* (2010), who uses her hair as a weapon. At last in *Brave* (2012)—significantly, the first Disney feature partly directed by a woman, Brenda Chapman—Princess Merida bests her suitors in an archery contest so she can determine for herself who and whether she will marry, and the most important drama concerns her relationship with her mother.

Yet when offering active female role models, Disney gives with one hand and takes away with the other. The studio promoted their live-action/

animation *Enchanted* (2007) as an homage to and a self-parody of the classic Disney fairy-tale films, but, as Linda Pershing and Lisa Gablehouse argue, it ultimately "offers a conventional, patriarchal worldview as a remedy for the alienation of modern life" (2010, 145). Even more influentially, while developing the relatively active and capable recent heroines, Disney also heavily marketed the fairy-tale characters collectively as the "Disney Princesses," now the largest "global girls franchise" (Wloszczyna 2003; Arkoff 2009; Clapp-Intyre 2010; Orenstein 2011). This "princess–industrial complex" tempts girls with pink, bejeweled items carrying the message that a girl's goals are to be pretty and kind. Cinderella epitomizes this collective; Peggy Orenstein, advising mothers on how to help our young daughters resist the pervasive argument that only beauty and sexual attractiveness to men matter, titles her book *Cinderella Ate My Daughter* (2011).

I regularly show clips of the Disney *Cinderella* (1950) in class to promote discussion of gender roles in folktales and to spark students' childhood memories that may well be implicated in their early gender identity formation. I saw it at least once as a child. But Rodgers and Hammerstein's from 1965, not Disney's from 1950, was the Cinderella I remembered and loved and with whom I identified. Informal interviews with friends and colleagues suggest the same was true for many American middle-class girls of my generation. And that version, although unabashedly romantic, suggests to girls in promising, if not entirely overt, ways that there is more to the story than love as a reward for passivity and beauty.

There have actually been three televised productions of the Rodgers and Hammerstein *Cinderella:* in 1957, created for Julie Andrews; in 1965 with Warren; and in 1990 starring Brandy.[2] The last one, produced for *Walt Disney's Wonderful World of Color* Sunday night television program (1954–1992), is most familiar to younger viewers and is notable for its multiracial cast, with Whitney Houston as the godmother. In it are a white king (Victor Garber), a black queen (Whoopi Goldberg), and their Filipino son (Paolo Montalbán). As Marleen Barr argues, however, "Disney's 'Impossible'/Possible Race Relations Dream" promulgates an assimilationist discourse; "race itself is never an issue within the fantastic premise of this *Cinderella*" (2000, 187). There is one poignant moment "when Cinderella places her bare black foot inside the magically custom-made glass slipper" and "the audience sees that a black foot belongs inside the glass slipper, that a black woman is a rightful fairytale princess" (2000, 188). Still, in the attempt to appear racially correct, Disney reinforces the simplistic heterosexual love story.

The 1957 version is musical theater aficionados' favorite. CBS invited Rodgers and Hammerstein to create it for Andrews, capitalizing on the recent success of another "for-the-entire-family musical spectacular," Mary Martin's *Peter Pan* on NBC, and on Andrews's acclaim for *My Fair Lady* on Broadway (Mordden 1992, 179–80). "The broadcast . . . was seen by the largest audience in the history of the planet at the time: 107,000,000 people in the USA, representing 60 percent of the country's population" ("Rodgers and Hammerstein: Our Shows" n.d.). Although this version was broadcast live in color, the black-and-white kinescope recording was not deemed of sufficiently high quality for rebroadcast and only became available on DVD in 2004. In this elegant, modern, adult version, Andrews is clad in sleek white chiffon, and Hammerstein's book includes extensive conversation among the characters to establish believable motivation. Andrews's expressive voice is entrancing. As an adult I certainly understand this version's appeal yet fault the critics who prefer it for assuming that their (white, adult, male) perspective is the only standard of quality.

Rodgers was offered the opportunity to remount *Cinderella* in 1965. Hammerstein had died in 1960, and Rodgers retained the original songs but invited children's book author Joseph Schrank to create a new script. Recorded in color VHS, it was rebroadcast eight times through February 1974. Critics question Rodgers's motivation for the simpler, more medieval presentation that reviewers dubbed a "children's special" (Du Brow 1965, 18)[3] and one scholar reviles as "puerile and cliché-bound" (Mordden 1992, 185). Rodgers's liner notes to the cast album explain only, "Although Oscar and I had stayed relatively close to the legendary fairy tale, we had kidded the plot a bit. We should have known that *Cinderella* has been around far too long for any treatment other than the traditional one" (qtd. in Block 2003, 191). Zipes lambasts all fairy-tale musicals as "hollow entertainment" but singles out this *Cinderella* for denigration:

> A classic example of live-action trash is the Richard Rodgers and Oscar Hammerstein made-for-TV production of 1957. This film features a mousy Cinderella, who constantly looks at the prince with goggle eyes, and a prince, who stiffly rides a horse and wards off his parents who want him to marry some wealthy princess. . . . The plot is so artificial and contrived, and the songs so mushy and saccharine, that one wonders why such an adaptation has been reproduced two other times on television in 1965 and 1997. (2011, 181)

The 1965 *Cinderella* arguably sells the previously adult romance to younger girls. One folklorist lumped it with the Disney princess films and called *Brave* the first she was happy to let her daughter see (Rachelle Saltzman, personal communication 2012). However, Jill Rudy concurred with my impressions, "I think that somehow this version, and [that of] *Rocky and Bullwinkle Fractured Fairy Tales,* prevented me from ever thinking that there was only a Disney approach to tales" (personal communication 2012). Others I asked about their memories immediately mentioned, with a swoon in their voices, how *romantic* the show was (Hanna Griff, personal communication 2012; Francesca McCrossen, personal communication 2012), and one burst into song (Jean Freedman, personal communication 2012). Yet our responses to this version also suggest ways in which a complex genre like a musical may introduce counterhegemonic, subtly feminist messages on the heels (or glass slippers?) of the conservative heterosexual romance plot.

Joan Radner and Susan Lanser identified "coding" in women's and racial and sexual minorities' esthetic expressions, arguing, "In creations and performances of dominated cultures, one can often find covert expressions of ideas, beliefs, experiences, feelings, and attitudes that the dominant culture—and perhaps even the dominated group—would find disturbing or threatening if expressed in more overt forms" and "such coded messages may ultimately help to empower a community and hence to effect change" (1993, 4; Radner 2009). Rodgers, Hammerstein, and Schrank could scarcely be considered participants in a "dominated culture." Yet in telling the story through alternately heartfelt and sassy songs and "updating" the teleplay for the mid-1960s audience, they offered girls the chance to identify with salutary and powerful possibilities in the tale for which Disney did not allow. Precisely because girls were attracted by the romance plot, we were paying rapt attention when this *Cinderella* hinted at other options for her life and ours. Its impact on me and other girls my age derives in part from the properties of 1960s television, in part from the musical's generic qualities and Rodgers and Hammerstein's style and intention, and in part from American cultural perceptions of the fairy tale at that time.

In the mid-1960s viewers in the United States could watch local independent stations or, at the national level, only the "big three" commercial networks, ABC, NBC, and CBS, plus NET (National Educational Television, PBS's predecessor). Especially large audiences viewed "spectaculars," highly promoted by advertisers. The 1965 *Cinderella,* taped for rebroadcast, was shown roughly yearly throughout my late childhood and adolescence, in contrast to movies like the Disney *Cinderella,* which we only got to see once in a theater. Still, like the *Wizard of Oz* (1939), *Cinderella* retained an air of specialness, because it was not always shown on the same date. We anticipated that it would come around again but weren't quite sure when (Griff 2012). Now, via the magic of Netflix and YouTube, my daughter can call up TV shows, cartoons, and movies on demand, but then we paid more attention because we had limited access.

These television specials also brought performers that audience members had seen in movies or knew about as popular Broadway stars into their own living rooms. Queen Ginger Rogers and king Walter Pidgeon were billed as the stars of the 1965 *Cinderella,* "introducing" Stuart Damon as the prince and "newcomer" Warren as Cinderella. My parents' generation's favorites thus conferred royal/star status on "the ones to watch" for my generation (Purcelli 1965; Smith 1965). Further, "during 1965, teenage girls seemed to take over the airwaves: Patty Lane and her Scottish cousin Cathy as well as Gidget . . . joined screaming Beatlemaniacs, girl singers, and the *Shindig* dancers as America fell under the spell of teenage girl culture" (Luckett 1999, 95). In those days I avidly watched not only *The Patty Duke Show* (1963–1966) and *Gidget* (1965–1966) but also programs that now strike me as miserably sexist—*Gilligan's Island* (1964–1967), *The Man from U.N.C.L.E.* (1964–1968), and *Petticoat Junction* (1963–1970). Still, television was starting to recognize girls like me—white, middle class—as people with interesting stories and an active role in the world. I sensed that recognition. TV was for and about me.

The Broadway musical's generic features and Rodgers and Hammerstein's artistic and political goals also influence this *Cinderella*'s impact. This team usually situated musicals in the contemporary or recent United States (Wood 2009, 110) and emphasized clever, catchy, topical songs. The fairy-tale plot was a departure, and the songs seem anachronistic to *Cinderella* as a premodern story, yet they consequently make this "timeless" tale relevant to current situations. This effect is most marked in the 1965 version; the sets and costumes are "implacably medieval," the Prince talks about "slaying some dragons," and one stepsister "rub[s] some unicorn oil" on her creaky knee (Mordden 1992, 185). Crucially, songs in which characters express their feelings radically transform the fairy tale's taken-for-granted quality. As A. S. Byatt notes, "The genre provides a 'clear' narrative form that does not require devoting attention to character motivation. 'Readers know what a fairy tale princess does'" (paraphrased and qtd. in Barr 2000,

187). The contrast between characters who do what we know they are supposed to and songs in which they reveal their innermost feelings destabilizes our sense that we know all there is to know about this familiar story.

Notably, too, "Hammerstein was a passionate and very vocal critic of racism in any form ([recall] 'You've Got to Be Carefully Taught' in *South Pacific*)" (Miller 2007, 64), and both Rodgers and Hammerstein created "stage works [that] address issues of racism and culture clash" and "were known to be very supportive of various social issues outside the theater" (Wood 2009, 114). Rodgers's "protesting of the House Un-American Activities Committee caused the FBI to open a file on him" (ibid.). In Laurey in *Oklahoma!*, Anna in *The King and I,* Ensign Nellie Forbush in *South Pacific,* and Maria in *The Sound of Music,* Rodgers and Hammerstein portrayed adventurous women who circumvented limiting gender roles. Admittedly, the need for commercial success often mutes their approach to controversial issues. My mother introduced me to social criticism of literature the night I came home crying from a school production of *South Pacific* and she explained that Rodgers and Hammerstein found it more expedient to let Lieutenant Cable die than to ask audiences to accept his interracial marriage with Liat. Still, they at least broach issues and evoke strong emotions.

The late 1960s and early 1970s also mark what has been dubbed a "fairy-tale renaissance," in which both scholars and literary authors flocked back to the form after a substantial hiatus (Zipes [1988] 2002; Joosen 2011).[4] In Europe the fairy tale shed its association with National Socialism, and in the United States "the rise of fairy tales and retellings . . . became part of a widespread reaction against what leftist critics considered the individualistic, rationalistic, and capitalist ailments of the twentieth century" (Joosen 2011, 4). Adults who had advocated realistic books for children reevaluated imagination's potential and no longer associated fairy tales purely with "fancy and illusion" (ibid.). Renewed interest in fairy tales may have reflected a "longing for the simpler life of earlier times, in reaction to the tides that characterized the 1960s" (McGlathery 1991, ix). Like Lerner and Loewe's Broadway hit *Camelot* (1960–1963), Rodgers and Hammerstein's *Cinderella* associates fairy-tale/legend themes with the period's hopeful, reformist message. As a child who learned to read with the realistic and banal *Dick and Jane* books (Gray et al., 1930–1970) but subsequently devoured Andrew Lang's *Fairy Books* (1889–1910), I can attest to rediscovered fantasy stories' appeal for that cohort of children.

The 1965 *Cinderella*'s key songs convey subtle messages in counterpoint to the story's dominant themes, a marked contrast with the Disney *Cinderella*'s consistency. One delight of all three Rodgers and Hammerstein productions is the self-confident, outspoken queen and her interactions with the king and prince. In Disney the prince has only a completely ridiculous, comical father, and in the Grimms the father's only role is "to sponsor a three-day festival . . . so that his son could choose a bride" (Zipes 1987, 87). In Perrault the king's son gives the ball himself, and his father shows up to "tell the queen softly that it was a long time since he had seen so beautiful and lovely a creature," implying her silent presence (Lang 1889). In the 1965 Rodgers and Hammerstein, the king and queen have a mature, balanced relationship that could serve as a model for their son's relationship with his future wife. (The 1957 version debased their example with more comedic business between the king and queen—her helping him get his formal breeches over his pot belly and his humoring her immoderate fondness for festivals and dancing.)

When the king and queen discuss marriage with their son and later watch him at the ball, they reveal that they fell in love young and still love each other. The king begins, "When I was his age," and the queen completes his sentence, "you had the remarkably good sense to fall in love with me." And the look on the prince's face as he dances with Cinderella reminds the king "of the first time I danced with you, my dear." They deal with their adult son in constructive and respectful ways. When the king insists that the prince must settle down, marry, and produce an heir, the prince responds, "I would really rather wait until I fall in love." The king abruptly exclaims, "Love? But we cannot leave a matter of such importance to chance!" while the queen defuses the situation by suggesting, "It's possible that love may follow," perhaps alluding to her own experience. The ballroom scene reinforces the parents' caring for each other. When the king asks the queen to dance, she responds, "I was wondering when you were ever going to ask me, Your Majesty," and they take the floor a bit stiffly but obviously enjoying the dancing and each other. The audience further appreciates the little joke in which the actress's and character's identities meld, since we know what a celebrated dancer the young Ginger Rogers was (and, since 1982, have seen her as a feminist icon, the person who "did everything Fred Astaire did, backwards . . . and in high heels").[5]

The prince, like his parents, is much more fully human than the prince in Perrault and in Disney, where he is a complete cipher—a stiff and almost faceless Ken doll. In the Grimms, he at least actively searches for the mysterious girl, insists on marrying only her, and even borrows an axe to chop down the tree and dovecote in which he thinks she is hiding. As Max Lüthi argues, the traditional folktale tends to have flat characters who do not learn, change, evolve, or age (1982, 11–23), but the nameless prince in "duplicate" "Cinderella" versions is the flattest of the lot. Even Zipes interrupts his diatribe against the Rodgers and Hammerstein *Cinderella to* concede, "The major shift in emphasis regards the prince. Almost all the post-1950 films to the present seek to develop a prince who is much more democratic and aware of his sentiments for Cinderella, whom he meets accidentally" (2011, 181). In this respect the musical *Cinderella* prefigures the post-1970 revisionist fairy tales in which "psychological development takes prime place" (Joosen 2011, 14). In 1957, the prince tells Cinderella to call him Christopher; in 1965 that detail is missing, but he still has (as the humorous song "The Prince Is Having a Ball" emphasizes) twelve names. And just before Cinderella appears at the ball, he laments that the assembled "fair young maidens" seem like "contenders for a prize—and I am that prize," revealing a startling degree of self-awareness.

Crucially, the 1965 version begins with added scenes in which Prince Christopher returns home after a year of successfully "fighting dragons and rescuing princesses" but unsuccessfully "looking for [his] true love" and stops at Cinderella's cottage seeking a drink of water. The prince's servant makes much of the fact that Cinderella's "kindness overcomes her fear" as she offers him a dipper of cool water despite her stepmother's injunction not to open the door. This scene shows the prince as gentle to a frightened young woman and gracious to Cinderella even when she appears poor and ragged. His subsequent conversation with his parents about the ball likewise reveals him as a kind, respectful, and thoughtful person who might indeed make a good husband and is not desirable just because of his wealth and power. Furthermore, he acknowledges Cinderella's kindness and generosity before he is struck (at the ball) by her beauty.

This prior meeting provides a delightful frisson in the ballroom scene. When the prince asks, "Have we met before," suggesting that her voice is familiar, Cinderella answers with words from the godmother's song, "It's possible. Tonight anything is possible." It also anticipates this version's slipper scene when Cinderella, with a little urging from her godmother, again offers the prince a drink of water, giving her some control over refreshing his memory. His characteristic "Thank you most kindly" and her characteristic

"You are most kindly welcome" lead him to remark, "We've spoken these words before, not only here but in a moonlit garden" and so to recognize her even before she tries on the glass slipper. Additionally, the prince displays wonderful deadpan humor in his enforcedly polite interactions with the stepmother and stepsisters, not a bad quality in a partner. And in retrospect, viewers can appreciate the delicious irony that Damon, who played the prince, enjoyed a three-decade run as Dr. Alan Quartermain on *General Hospital,* beginning in 1977 (McCrossen, personal communication 2012; "Stuart Damon" n.d.). He *was* (later) a soap opera heartthrob, albeit one whose desperate and unsavory behavior included affairs and drug addiction.

Warren was only eighteen when her *Cinderella* was taped. Trained as a ballerina, she is so slender that I now almost see her as promoting an unrealistic and unhealthy ideal of women's weight and shape. Compared to Andrews's brisk British self-confidence, Warren comes across as heartbreakingly vulnerable, especially when she arrives home after the ball and realizes she has no hope of seeing the prince again. She reacts to the prince's and her godmother's kindnesses with a mixture of delighted incredulity and sincere gratitude. She scarcely believes that the pumpkin has turned into a coach or that the prince has declared his love for her, but she does not act as if she doesn't ultimately deserve these dreams to come true. This Cinderella's amazement and gratitude were central to my identifying with her—if those things had happened to me, I liked to think that's how I would have reacted. Further, she was clearly American, a real person (not like the cartoon Disney Cinderella), and a brunette. In the era when television commercials for Clairol hair dye repeatedly asked, "Is it true . . . blondes have more fun?" (Undercover Blonde 2007), it was thrilling that a brown-haired girl like us could be the princess (Griff 2012).

The song Cinderella sings while her stepsisters prepare for the ball, "All Alone in My Own Little Corner," is wildly anachronistic and improbable. Superficially, it reinforces her timidity; she begins, "I'm as mild and as meek as a mouse. When I hear a command, I obey." When faced with danger in her fantasy she concludes that she is "glad to be back in my own little corner, all alone in my own little chair." And yet she proceeds to declare, "There is a place in my house, where no one can stand in my way" and "on the wings of my fancy I can fly anywhere and be whatever I want to be." In a song written fifty-five years ago Cinderella is not dreaming of a successful career in business, medicine, aeronautics, or government. One wonders why an already overworked and underappreciated young woman would want to become a milkmaid or a "slave in Calcutta." The appeal of being a "Norwegian princess" or an heiress who "has her silk made by her own flock of silkworms in Japan" is more obvious. Her most incongruous fantasies involve being a huntress in Africa who encounters a lioness or "a girl men go mad for" who feels that "love's a game I can play." Dishearteningly, Rodgers and Hammerstein's vision of women's liberation for Cinderella involves colonialist exploitation and using sexuality to manipulate men, but at least she dreams about independent adventures, many specifically "modern," with no hint of settling down or obeying a man, let alone marrying a prince.

Still, this Cinderella's fondest wish *is* to go to the ball and meet the prince again. Both Rodgers and Hammerstein and Disney draw primarily on the Perrault *Cinderella,* which thoroughly camouflages the link between the magical helper and the girl's dead mother. In the Grimms' version, a tree grows on the mother's grave from which birds throw down Cinderella's magical clothing, and the Russian "Wassilissa" is protected by a magic doll her mother bequeathed her (Von Franz [1972] 1982). These mothers are still powerful and promote their daughters' success (Panttaja 1993). A godparent traditionally promised to stand in place of a deceased parent and to ensure a child's spiritual and even physical well-being; Rodgers and Hammerstein's godmother is not Disney's silly, scatterbrained wielder of "bibbidi-bobbidi-boo" but a smart, serious woman who understands her own power and her goddaughter's psychology. In the Andrews version, Cinderella herself thinks up the magical substitutions (pumpkin and mice for coach and horses) and can almost be credited with turning her godmother, who comes calling in a conventional way, into a *fairy* godmother through the force of her wishing.

I'm sorry that Rodgers and Hammerstein chose to give Warren's Cinderella less initiative and to have her fairy godmother dress like and arrive magically via the same optical effect as Glinda the Good Witch in *The Wizard of Oz.* Yet allowing Cinderella less credit for the shift from "Impossible" to "It's Possible" also opens up potential song referents.

> But the world is full of zanies and fools,
> who don't believe in sensible rules,
> and won't believe what sensible people say.
> And because these daft and dewy-eyed dopes
> keep building up impossible hopes,
> impossible things are happening every day.

The two women sang those words a few years after the Civil Rights Act, which "outlawed the unequal application of voter registration requirements and discrimination in public facilities, in government, and in employment" (Napikoski n.d.a); the publication of Betty Friedan's *The Feminine Mystique* (1963); and the judgment in *Griswold v. Connecticut*, which established the right to privacy and contraception—a heady time, when it was easy to imagine all kinds of entrenched prejudice and restriction suddenly swept away. Celeste Holm, who played the godmother, had a reputation then, reinforced since, as a woman willing to buck convention in her private life—in her seventies she married a man forty years her junior—and as a character actress who played the gal who didn't get the guy but didn't care (Gates 2012). She struck me as gutsy, a woman who would have been called a "broad" in 1940s "old movies." Hannah Griff (personal communication 2012) recalls thinking of the godmother as "a sweeter Endora from *Bewitched*" (1964–1972), likening her to Agnes Moorehead's witch, mother to main character Samantha, who loved using her power to disrupt humans' boring, conventional lives.

Cinderella and the prince's meeting at the ball unfolds in two equally memorable songs. "Ten Minutes Ago" is a paean to love at first sight (although audience and Cinderella know it isn't really first sight) and is gorgeous but utterly conventional in persuading young women to follow their first impressions rather than determine if their love interest would actually make a good partner. At least both Cinderella and the prince admit sudden attraction's destabilizing effects. Not yet ready to say, "I love you," they share the sense that they've been sent reeling.

In contrast, "Do I Love You Because You're Beautiful (or Are You Beautiful, Because I Love You)?" astutely critiques love at first sight, acknowledging how people project their own fantasy: "Are you the sweet invention of a lover's dream or are you really as wonderful as you seem?" These lovers wisely raise doubts about their mutual infatuation. The prince subsequently reprises the song as a conversation with his parents, who urge him to consider that the woman he seeks may not be real. The king suggests, "She may be bewitched," and the prince replies, "She has certainly bewitched me, and I must find her." This conventional enough characterization of love anticipates Elisabeth Panttaja's argument that Cinderella is not so much the worthy mate for the prince as the possessor of the most powerful magic, a dress that bewitches and controls him (1993). Ironically, Warren's ball gown with the huge ermine collar was so heavy it caused nerve damage in her arms.

Still, the couple's tendency to question their own projective fantasies bodes well for their relationship and for their love as a model for others'.

As Cinderella and the prince dance off into the moonlit garden, the stepsisters—played by established comic actresses Pat Carroll (who later supplied the voice for the sea witch Ursula in Disney's *The Little Mermaid*) and Barbara Ruick—sing their complaint. They come off as poignant where their Disney counterparts are selfish. Their mother pushes them to compete for the prince despite likely disqualifying flaws—one bats her eyes constantly and one has a creaky knee—and insists they practice not doing things they really cannot help. Awkward and lacking basic self-awareness, they represent the sad fate of women prevented from accepting themselves as they are.

In thus treating the stepsisters, Rodgers and Hammerstein steer between Perrault, whose Cinderella is so forgiving that she weds the sisters to noblemen, and the Grimms, in which the stepsisters mutilate their own feet to fit into the slipper and have their eyes pecked out by the birds who befriend Cinderella. They give us reason to ponder the damage women do to themselves and each other by competing for men. The sisters' song "Why Would a Fellow Want a Girl Like Her?" perfectly captures the frustration and bitterness of women who know they will be overlooked in a world where the ultimate judgment of one's worthiness lies in being selected as a romantic partner by a man. Their honesty—if only to each other—can be alarming: "She's a frothy little bubble/With a flimsy sort of charm/And with very little trouble/I could break her little arm!" But viewers may sympathize with the sisters as they sing, "Why can't a fellow ever once prefer/A solid girl like me/ . . . A usual girl like me/ . . . A girl who's merely me?" As someone who already knew by age nine that I was neither the prettiest nor the most popular girl in my class, I think I loved this *Cinderella* because it let me identify with both Cinderella and the stepsisters, validating simultaneously my romantic dreams and my suspicions of them. I quoted the sisters' song to a colleague to explain why I wanted to write this chapter—and she started singing along; the song had spoken to her, too (Freedman, personal communication 2012).

Watching Rodgers and Hammerstein's *Cinderella* did not turn me into a feminist. I credit my mother and my graduate school professors with that transformation. And indeed, I recognize in retrospect how often I have played out a destructive Cinderella fantasy, being attracted to a man because I imagined that an alliance with him would magically confer a desirable role, not because he really cared for me. Still, in watching this delightful, if at times clunky, musical as a young person I was exposed to a variety of messages that girls (and boys) still desperately need to hear: watch out for the tendency to project your own image of perfection onto another person; look for a kind and respectful partner who listens to you; like yourself for who you really are; resist those who demand that you compete for love; accept powerful women's help; and if your Prince (or Princess) Charming does come along, don't hesitate to give him or her a little help in recognizing you. It took me many years to fully absorb these lessons. But I was at least open to hearing these first of many necessary repetitions because they were wrapped in an appealing fantasy; sung in catchy, memorable phrases to lilting tunes; and conveyed by a medium that had started to target girls like me as an audience and to tell us that we mattered.

One could also articulate a devastating critique of the Warren *Cinderella* as primarily a "duplicate" that naturalizes heterosexual romance as the reward for a woman's beauty and self-sacrificing sweetness. My dedication to my alternative reading draws equally on my remembered experience as a girl and my preference for one of two dominant strands of feminist fairy-tale scholarship. The volume and variety of such criticism produced over the past forty years have added tremendously to a nuanced understanding of the tales and their history, production, and effect. Yet feminists tend to divide into two camps: a glass-half-empty crew who see sexist indoctrination in all but the most explicitly revisionist texts and a glass-half-full crew who regard the magic tale as inherently hopeful and document a range of actual responses not necessarily constrained by the words on the page or images on the screen. Since the days when I climbed back into bed on lazy Saturday mornings, immersing myself in another of Lang's *Fairy Books,* my at first unexamined affection for the tales has inclined me toward the positive camp. What persuades me to affirm my membership with this autoethnographic chapter is feminists' increasing reliance on reader response theory and a philosophical or ethnographic appreciation of the complex ways in which readers and tellers interact with, learn from, and discover new messages in these perennially popular tales.

Lieberman (1972) sets the tone for the negative camp, depicting Lurie's (1970) promotion of lesser known tales with strong female characters as naïve and insisting on the power of the most highly publicized and widely spread versions. Zipes's historical analyses of how Perrault and the Grimms shaped their versions to "set standards for civilization" and to "socialize" obedient bourgeois children (1983a) further bolster the assumption that readers inevitably internalize the messages that critics identify in various tale versions. This assumption silently informs most analyses that treat text alone, most prominently commentary on fairy-tale versions whose creators aim at revision or parody that critics judge insufficient. I do not exactly disagree, for example, with Pershing and Gablehouse's claim that *Enchanted* "discards its metacommentary and is absorbed into the story line it supposedly parodies" (2010, 143) nor with Barr's observations on the way the 1990, Brandy, *Cinderella* misses the opportunity to offer a more explicit critique of naturalized race and class differences (2000). Feminists must call out those who claim to mount a self-critique of destructive gender, race, and class models but fail to deliver. I wonder, however, if all viewers have such stringent expectations. Once a version begins to destabilize comfortable assumptions, how can scholars know to what extent viewers are steered back into conventional thinking and to what extent they continue with their own critique unless we ask?

Consider, for example, *Ever After: A Cinderella Story,* starring Drew Barrymore (1998), which offers a legend frame tale in which Cinderella's great-great-great granddaughter calls the Grimm brothers to her castle and "sets the record straight" about her foremother's exploits (including knocking the prince off a horse with a well-aimed apple and lecturing him about how to treat his people better). Cathy Lynn Preston discussed the film with high school and college students and reports that they sometimes argued disapprovingly that it still focused on getting the prince—the implied but unstated injunction of heterosexuality—but just as frequently noted Cinderella's "mastery of language" and "cunning wit" (2004, 202). And I recall realizing with a jolt as the credits rolled that the woman narrator had just completely recast the story, wresting control from the men too often credited for fairy tales (see Rudy's chapter). Christy Williams, however, insists, "*Ever After* assumes a feminist stance but offers a mass-mediated idea of feminism where individual women can be strong and achieve equality through personal actions that do not, however, challenge or change the underlying patriarchal structure of society. . . . The problems identified by second-wave feminism are simplified, emptied of their radical critiques or systemic gender inequality, and marketed to young women" (2010, 101).

Each generation of feminist scholars must articulate its own evolving critique, but I regret that Williams discounts Preston's thoughtful report of viewer response. Cristina Bacchilega articulates sophisticated analyses of what Teresa de Lauretis calls "technologies of gender," noting, for example, that "the wonder child [in a story like 'Snow White'] . . . is the product of desires which are simply but artfully made to appear 'natural'" (1993, 2) and that "the artful naturalizing of [the innocent persecuted] heroine's initiation process (from being a child to being with child) conceals the narrative prescription of her dependence on patriarchy and heterosexuality as well as the proscription of her independence" (1993, 3; see De Lauretis 1987). Still, analyses thus framed do not allow other readers and viewers to develop their own ways of seeing through the naturalizing strategies or simply to interpret a tale differently based on their own experience.

The more hopeful fairy-tale analysts, by contrast, tend to pin their hopes on readers' and viewers' interpretive capacities, celebrating especially the potential of multigeneric or even mildly revisionist texts engaged, explicitly or implicitly, in dialogue with some presumed earlier version (Joosen 2011). Lurie is no more specific than her critic Lieberman in explaining *how* fairy tales that "suggest a society in which women are as competent and active as men, at every age and in every class" will "prepare children for women's liberation" (1970, 42). But she advocates that parents who want to prepare their children for such liberation "had better buy at least one collection of fairy tales," presumably one featuring the stories with intrepid heroines and powerful female helpers and hinderers she describes. She sees it as within parents' power to provide their children with an alternative to Disney. Even Lüthi, setting out simply to define the genre, takes a functionalist approach, arguing, "The folktale envisions and depicts a world that unfolds before us as the antitype of the uncertain, confusing, unclear, and threatening world of reality" (1982, 85) on the grounds of a crucial but complex "need of the human soul" not provided by other, simpler genres (1982, 83). Freudian and Jungian theorists take as axiomatic that readers will be able to unravel fairy tales' deep symbolic meanings and benefit by understanding their application to their own lives, at least subconsciously (see Bettelheim 1976; Von Franz [1972] 1982).

Zipes, in keeping with his Marxist perspective but in counterpoint to his precise historical interpretations, offers categorical insistence that fairy tales are inherently a source of resistance to social inequality and injustice: "The tales seek to . . . evoke profound feelings of awe and respect for life as a miraculous process, which can be altered and changed to compensate for the lack of power, wealth, and pleasure that most people experience. . . . Those who are naïve and simple are able to succeed . . . because they have not been spoiled by conventionalism, power, or rationalism" (2011, 22).

Some folklorists take Zipes's (1983b, [1983a] 1991) explanation of the ways Perrault, the Grimms, and others *shaped* their versions as evidence that the true/original/"folk" wonder tales had offered liberating messages while the collected/doctored ones had been corrupted. Zipes himself draws little distinction between pre–eighteenth-century oral tales, tales presented as collected by early folklore scholars, tales avowedly recast (or outright written) by literary authors in the eighteenth and nineteenth centuries, modern wonder tale–like stories like *The Wizard of Oz* (Baum 1900), and contemporary critically informed or parodic rewritings.

The hopeful contemporary critics (my kindred spirits) build on this fluid confidence that listeners will respond to fairy tales in complex ways, conditioned by their awareness of any text as one selective version always in dialogue with multiple other instantiations. This approach is clearly informed by feminist work on women's romance novel reading, which emphasizes ethnography (asking readers what they value in and get out of these works before disparaging them as antifeminist trash) and reader response theory (Radway 1984). Folklorists Clover Williams and Jean Freedman, in their study of romance readers, cite both "pioneer of reader response theory" (1995, 136) Louise Rosenblatt—who argues, "A literary experience gains its significance and force from the way in which the stimuli present in the literary work interact with the mind and emotions of a particular reader" (1938, 35)—and feminist poet Adrienne Rich—who insists, "Re-vision—the act of looking back, of seeing with fresh eyes, or entering an old text from a new critical direction—is for us more than a chapter in cultural history: it is an act of survival. . . . A radical critique of literature, feminist in its impulse, would take the work first of all as a clue to how we live . . . and how we can begin to see—and therefore live—afresh" (1972, 18). Further, Williams and Freedman point out that romance novel readers (and, I would argue by extension, fairy-tale readers and viewers) are so familiar with the genre's regularities that they are exquisitely attuned to any variation and to its creative and expressive potential (1995, 138).

Those fairy-tale scholars who have actually asked women about these stories' influence, like Preston, discussed above, document "more oblique and complex responses to the tales that supposedly govern our lives" (Harries 2004, 101). As Elizabeth Wanning Harries argues, drawing upon Kate Bernheimer (1998), "Though many writers testify to the power certain patterns and roles continue to have, others show that fairy tales have symbolic resonances that work against, or even contradict, the dominant models" (2004, 101). And crucially, in any work that involves "open dialogue" with some supposed original—in any story "written intentionally so that readers recognize the original setting, the characters and the plot pattern" (Nikolajeva 1996, 155)—the current text's events are "consciously played off against some common notion of the shape and content of an 'original' text, and [the authors] might hence assume that the audience will be in a position to weigh one off against the other," such that "the story will tend to be situated not in the focused text but in the process of interaction between the texts" (Stephens 1992, 88). Thus even as lighthearted a work as the Rodgers and Hammerstein *Cinderella* practices what Linda Hutcheon calls "repetition with critical distance" (1985, 8), inevitably to some extent disrupting the reader's or viewer's expectations.

Folklorist and storyteller Stone's evolving work has also significantly influenced my thinking about how individuals glean messages from fairy tales. She repeatedly analyzes her abiding fascination with the Grimms' "Frau Trude," in which a curious and disobedient girl is turned into a log and thrown onto the fire. At first, Stone interpreted the burning as destruction and punishment. "Her story enraged me because it seemed to be viciously and precisely aimed right at me" (1993, 291). Other possibilities emerged, however, when she retold the story and found herself focusing on the idea that the girl had "burned brightly" and on Frau Trude's words: "I have been waiting for you for a long time now and have longed for you" (1993, 293). In Stone's version, the burning log/girl throws off sparks that Mistress Trudy turns into a bird. The bird/girl listens to Mistress Trudy's stories, effectively apprenticing to the wise woman and expert storyteller, and then reveals her own skill by starting to retell her own story (ibid., 296). Stone ultimately sees this tale as part of her "deep interest in resourcefulness and transformation" (2004, 127). And Kay Turner offers a "transgressive," queer interpretation in which the girl, persistently "intrigued" by the forbidden, anomalous witch, finally encounters the woman who has been waiting and longing for her, and they create a life together, "unopposed, consummated but not consumed" (2012, 257, 269). How might readers imagine "Cinderella," that most familiar and most varied of the magic tales, if given a bit of encouragement?

And I argue that Rodgers and Hammerstein did give receptive viewers that encouragement, creating with their touches of parody and anachronism what Julia Kristeva calls an "ambivalent" text that "uses[s] another's work, giving it a new meaning while retaining the meaning it already had" (1980, 73). They allowed me to have my cake and eat it too, swooning over love at first sight while envisioning a liberated life in which the brown-haired girl gets to be happy, finds a caring partner, and follows her dreams to further

FIGURE 5.1 The author's daughter, age five, Halloween 2009.

adventures. Because they and I knew "what a fairy-tale princess does," their modest, sometimes silly deviations from the traditional script helped me recognize that I could enjoy the magic without sacrificing my real aspirations for independence and accomplishment. If our image of the girl with the fairy godmother comes from Lesley Ann Warren in 1965, maybe it's not such a bad thing to want (occasionally) to be Cinderella (Figure 5.1).

Notes

1. See Barber's and Lee's chapters for readings of very different live-action televised Cinderellas.
2. My history of the three shows draws on Mordden (1992), Block (2003), Wood (2009), and "Cinderella (Musical)."
3. Jacqueline Solis, subject librarian for folklore at the University of North Carolina, Chapel Hill, discovered these contemporary reviews and pointed me to other crucial sources.
4. The hiatus was scarcely absolute, since more than 130 Cinderella films were made during the twentieth century (Zipes 2011, 174), including the 1950 Disney version.
5. The line evidently originated in a 1982 "Frank and Ernest" cartoon by Bob Thraves, although it was popularized by Texas governor Ann Richards and many others (see "Ginger Rogers" n.d.).

6

"APPEARANCE DOES NOT MAKE THE MAN"

Masculinities in Japanese Television Retellings of "Cinderella"

Christie Barber

During the Meiji period (1868–1912), after Japan ended a long period of national isolation and reopened to international trade, the works of the Grimm brothers and Hans Christian Andersen, among others, were eagerly translated for Japanese readers. Often, the translated fairy tales targeted young readers and were seen to have an educational purpose. They were usually adapted to suit the new Japanese readership and context (Nakamura 2001, 106). Later, fairy tales again rapidly entered Japan after wartime bans on American material were lifted. In the 1950s, Disney films such as *Snow White and the Seven Dwarfs* (1937) and *Cinderella* (1950) were released in Japanese cinemas in quick succession. They exposed audiences to American fairy-tale adaptations and inspired Japanese animators such as Tezuka Osamu[1] (Yoshimi 2001, 169–70; Ellis 2008a, 513). The 1987 animated series *Grimm Masterpiece Theatre* (Gurimu meisaku gekijō) further established the popularity of fairy tales in Japan (Ellis 2008a, 513; see Jorgensen and Warman's chapter). Works that retell fairy tales, or at the very least use their motifs and structure, continue to be produced today (see Lezubski's chapter).

This chapter aims to explore how fairy tales have been reinterpreted in recent Japanese television drama, with specific reference to "Cinderella" (ATU 510A). There have been many "Cinderella" versions, in a range of languages over hundreds of years (Dundes [1982] 1988, vii; Zipes 2011, 172). Fay Beauchamp traces the tale's origins, the story "Yexian" from around 850CE, to an area that is now the border of China and Vietnam; she argues for renaming it the "Yexian/Cinderella story" (2010, 449). Tran Quynh Ngoc Bui's analysis of works from Vietnam and Southeast Asia uses the term "innocent persecuted heroine tale" (see Bacchilega 1993) to recognize both shared structure and motifs but also culturally specific functions and meanings from different times and places (Bui 2009, 37). In Japan, several folktales, each with many regional versions, have been described as "Cinderella" analogs, such as "Komebuku Awabuku" (or "Nukabuku Komebuku"), "The Bowl Bearer" ("Hachikazuki"), and "The Old Woman Skin" ("Ubakawa"; Seki 1966; Mulhern 1985; Mayer 1986; Reider 2011). In each, a girl mistreated by her stepmother transcends her position to meet a suitor, and they are happily married.

Charles Perrault's "Cinderella, or The Glass Slipper" (1697) and the Grimms' "Aschenputtel" (1812) have strongly influenced recent Western retellings (Zipes 2011, 172–74). In Japan, "The Strange Fate of Cinderella" (Shinderera no kien) appeared in an 1887 collection translated by Suga Ryō hō and titled *Ancient Western Fairy Tales* (Seiyō koji shinsen sōwa; Nakamura 2001, 105). Perrault's text was published in Japanese in 1950 and titled "Haidarake Hime" (literally "The Princess Covered with Ashes"). However, just as Disney fairy-tale retellings dominate in the West (Zipes 1995, 21), the Disney animated *Cinderella,* released in Japan in 1952, is probably the most familiar version to the Japanese. Shunya Yoshimi writes, "All of Disney's films, even the ones made before and during the war, were shown within just a few years during the 1950s. Because of this compressed time frame, the cultural influence of Disney on children and their parents was overwhelming" (2001, 170). I see the Disney "Cinderella" as the "pre-text"—the key, but certainly not the only, source from which a retelling develops—of many contemporary Japanese versions.

In this chapter I focus on three works: *I Want to Be Cinderella!* (Shinderera ni naritai!, 2006, directed by Takezono Hajime), *Train Man* (Densha otoko, 2005, directed by Takeuchi Hideki, Nishiura Masaki, and Kobayashi Kazuhiro), and *Rich Man, Poor Woman* (Ricchi man, pua uūman, 2012, directed by Nishiura Masaki and Tanaka Ryō). In different ways, each adopts *Cinderella* as a frame to explore tensions in how masculine gender identities are deemed desirable or otherwise in contemporary Japanese society. My interest lies in how the fairy tale and its retelling work to illuminate actual world structures and experiences (Bacchilega 1997, 3–4; Stephens 2011a, vi).

My analysis of "Cinderella" reworkings begins with what I call the "Cinderella script." The term "script" refers to a stereotypical sequence of "causally and chronologically" related (Herman 1997, 1048) actions or events that function in narratives as cues to activate expectations (Stephens 2011b, 14). Scripts require readers or viewers to draw on what they already know in order to interpret the text but can also be modified to generate new sequences. Narrative thus blends prestored knowledge with emergent information that conforms to, or challenges, readers' or viewers' expectations, triggering affective responses (Herman 1997, 1048; Tsukioka and Stephens 2003, 186; Stephens 2011b, 15; Trites 2012, 68, 72).

The "Cinderella" script synthesizes tale retellings and key motifs and flows as follows: first, the protagonist, of low social position, is mistreated and endures *hardship* in the form of menial tasks. Second, the protagonist *transcends* his or her social position, usually with a helper's intervention, using disguise and/or metamorphosis, and meets a romantic interest. Third, the protagonist is chosen for a *romantic union,* based on *recognition* of his or her true identity. The basis for this choice, and his or her true identity, often illuminate the ideologies driving the text.

Each work I examine evokes the "Cinderella" script through homologies in structure and motif, drawing on this fairy tale to interrogate concepts about ideal masculinity in contemporary Japan. All three resignify Cinderella, or Cinderella's male love interest, in forms of nonnormative and/or disapprobated masculinity, and each work illuminates the values and standards by which masculinities are accepted or rejected. Notably, while the three works rarely challenge conventional gender relations, they advocate accepting nonhegemonic masculinities on some level.

The hegemonic model of masculinity in Japan is the "salaryman" (*sarariiman*), the heterosexual, middle-class corporate/office worker (Dasgupta 2000, 192–93; 2003, 118; 2005, 168–69; Ishii-Kuntz 2003, 199; Roberson and Suzuki 2003, 3, 6–8). R. W. Connell defines hegemonic masculinity as the dominant and "most honoured and desired" (2000, 10–11) form; Michael S. Kimmel (2001, 272) says it is "a man *in* power, a man *with* power, and a man *of* power." The salaryman model of masculinity developed out of government efforts in the Meiji period (1868–1912) to modernize Japan, which involved building an efficient, skilled male workforce. The model became firmly established after WWII, when the state again built a male workforce that drove Japan's recovery and later international economic dominance (Dasgupta 2003, 120–23; Roberson and Suzuki 2003, 6–8). In return for "loyalty, diligence, dedication, self-sacrifice, hard work" (Dasgupta 2000, 193) in the company, the male worker would be rewarded with job security, continued promotion, and a like-minded community of colleagues.

However, as Connell (2005, 78) writes, "Even the *sarariiman* is vulnerable." Instability in the Japanese economy from the 1990s also led to wavering in the model's hegemony, destabilizing its basis in work; unemployment and poor job security undermine the salaryman's financial and social dominance. Other, simultaneous social and economic changes further undermined the model, including increased female labor force participation, the enactment of new gender equity and childcare leave laws, and increased advocacy (by the government and other groups) of men's involvement in such areas as housework and childrearing (Dasgupta 2000, 199; 2003, 130–31; 2005, 180; Ishii-Kuntz 2003, 199–201; Roberson and Suzuki 2003, 9–11; Taga 2005, 155–57). However, James E. Roberson and Nobue Suzuki (2003, 8) note, "Men are still commonly expected to want and to be able to become the official heads, primary providers and strong centres of heterosexual families." Romit Dasgupta (2005) also states that the hegemonic model remains "firmly entrenched" (168) and that "pressures to conform to hegemonic gender ideologies are still very real" (181).

Yet the salaryman model is incompatible with the actual experiences of some Japanese men, who struggle to secure long-term, stable, full-time work (and the related ability to support a family), the basis of salaryman hegemony (Slater and Galbraith 2011, para 16–18). David H. Slater and Patrick W. Galbraith identify another idealized model, "market masculinity," achieved through consuming various products and practices to attract others. But just like salaryman masculinity, this model, with its focus on physical attractiveness, may be unattainable (ibid., para 28–29). A Japanese term readily associated with this commodified masculinity is *ikemen* (literally "cool man," from *iketeru* [cool, stylish] and the English *men*).[2] *Ikemen* describes a physically attractive, fashionable man, who usually employs hair removal and hair coloring, among other cosmetics, in an effort to achieve physical attractiveness. Thus, alongside conventional schemas that describe men as strong, tough, aggressive, competitive, responsible, reliable, independent, and successful (Itō 1996, 88, 99; Ishii-Kuntz 2003, 198), the market masculinity model also requires men to cultivate an attractive exterior through beauty practices and fashion.

Considering the changing expectations for men regarding career, relationships, and parenting, Gordon Mathews (2003, 117) argues, "Japanese men today may face double pressure from work and home, pressure that their fathers did not face; and this may make being a man in Japan today more difficult than it was in the recent past." Each work I analyze engages with these stressors.

An "Average" Cinderella: *I Want to Be Cinderella!*

In the 2006 made-for-television film *I Want to Be Cinderella!* (Shinderera ni naritai!), direct reference in the title establishes a clear homology with the fairy tale. However, the Cinderella character is male. Through gender role reversal, the film offers the potential to challenge or reject the cultural presuppositions forming the "Cinderella" script, thus offering viewers another way to understand the world (Lee 2011, 136; Stephens 2011b, 13, 14).

The characterization of the protagonist, Kuramochi Bon (Sano Yasuomi), a fast food restaurant cleaner, establishes the homology with the "Cinderella" script's first motif. Other employees at the restaurant, led by Narumizaka Ken (Ōkura Tadayoshi), tease and shun Bon. Known as the "legendary man" (*densetsu no otoko*), Narumizaka has the privilege of serving customers at the counter, and his popularity among female patrons has led to a significant increase in sales, according him his celebrated status. Bon is perceived to be ugly—because he does not conform to Narumizaka's standard—and a large facial mole works as this label's key metonym. Flashbacks reveal that since childhood, Bon has been repeatedly called "ugly," "hideous," and "gross." The Chinese character used in Bon's name, which means "normal" or "average" and can have the additional negative connotation of "mediocre," reinforces the status gap between the central male characters. Even Bon's mother's strongest advice—that "appearance does not make the man"—cannot prevent him from desperately wishing to look like Narumizaka.

The film evokes the "Cinderella" script's second motif when Bon, on his way home from work, is run over by a stranger on a bicycle, and when he awakes, he finds himself in what appears to be a doctor's office. The stranger constitutes a homology with the fairy godmother in Perrault's "Cinderella," as he offers Bon a "cosmetic surgery drink" that will turn him into whoever he wants to become. The stranger warns Bon that there are only three bottles, each lasting for twenty-four hours, but assures him the potion will work if he has "imagination and belief." Emphasizing Bon's part in the potion's efficacy affirms that self-perception and self-belief play a vital role in constituting subjectivity. This idea echoes Laura Miller's assertion that while the romantic fantasy remains a key element of its appeal, "the meaning of

Cinderella has morphed into a strong message of self-transformation and individual achievement in the Japanese setting" (2008, 393). After drinking the potion, which in fact has no physical effect, Bon sees himself in the mirror as Narumizaka (as do the viewers). When Bon is transferred to a new store in the restaurant chain, the confidence he has gained through the potion enables him to serve customers for the first time, socialize after work with his new colleagues (who praise Bon for his confidence and charm), and go on a date with Saki (Ōwada Miho), a girl he meets at the restaurant.

The third motif appears at the film's close, when Saki—the daughter of the fast food company president—arrives at Bon's workplace to collect the "legendary man" so that her father can meet him (and presumably make him heir to the company as well as her romantic partner). Much to the other employees' surprise, Saki asks for Bon, who achieves accurate self-perception when Saki shows him photographs of their date, and he sees his appearance has not changed. This reinterpretation of the "Cinderella" script works to question the basis on which men are perceived to be acceptable or desirable: Saki chooses Bon based on his attributes of sincerity and other-regardingness, not on his status or physical attractiveness.

Moreover, the transformative potential of the configuration of the "Cinderella" script in *I Want to Be Cinderella!* comes through its focus on the social acceptance of a nonnormative form of masculinity. Saki prefers Bon even though he fails to meet conventional notions of the ideal *ikemen*. Narrative strategy affirms Bon's nonnormative masculinity by aligning viewer perspective with him and placing him in contrast to Narumizaka's arrogant, selfish, idealized masculinity. Bon's other-regarding, self-aware, authentic self, as opposed to the superficial, illusory "legendary man" Narumizaka, is deemed desirable. When Bon's belief that outer beauty makes him attractive is shown to be false, the film highlights the constructed nature of preferred and ideal forms of masculinity, encouraging viewers to question the standards for accepting or rejecting others.

The film depicts a range of nonnormative masculinities alongside Bon's as a comment on the ways in which the salaryman model is changing in contemporary Japan. The portrayals come via Bon's co-workers at the restaurant to which he is transferred, who are regarded, and see themselves, as losers: one works at the restaurant, as he has no other employment options; another lost his corporate job after restructuring and is separated from his wife and child; and the restaurant's manager is a reject from the head office. These depictions reflect actual world experiences,

wherein the salaryman model is unattainable or becoming further separated from men's lived realities.

That the Cinderella and fairy godmother characters are male and that
Saki chooses Bon reverse gender roles as represented by Perrault and the
Grimm brothers. But male Cinderellas are not especially unusual. For
example, in the Japanese folktale "Haibō" ("Ash Boy") or "Haibō Tarō" ("Ash
Tarō»),[3] a young man mistreated by his stepmother goes to work as a servant
to a wealthy man. He transcends his low position through disguise and/or
metamorphosis, his employer's daughter falls in love with him, and they are
happily married. The ash lad (*Askeladden*) is also a common figure in Norwegian folktales. "Cinderella" retellings sometimes have male primary characters, including the films *Cinderfella* (1960) and *The Secret of My Succe$s*
(1987) and the picture book *Prince Cinders* (Cole 1987). Ming-Hsun Lin
(2010, 92–96) argues that Harry Potter is a Cinderella figure transgendered
to male who is submitted to mistreatment by his relatives, rescued by others from his hardship, and, through self-sacrifice and the aid of the virtues
inherited from his mother, is able to defeat evil.

Although *I Want to Be Cinderella!* explores attitudes toward nonnormative
masculinities in Japan, it does little to challenge conservative ideas of gender
relations. Saki's characterization as an other-regarding young woman who
also takes the initiative in the relationship may appeal to female viewers, but
the role reversal is homologous with the shoe test performed by the prince
in well-known "Cinderella" versions. In being chosen by Saki, Bon submits
himself to her determination of his fate or, rather, to her father's—the one
who requests a meeting with the "legendary man." The film replicates the
positioning of one party in the relationship as a passive object of desire. Thus
the limits placed on Bon's agency undermine the message Saki's empowerment conveys about gender inequality; ultimately their relationship reinforces
unequal and oppositional relations between genders (cf. McCallum 2002, 131;
Joosen 2011, 89–92). Further, synthesizing some of the most prominent and
valued traits of the hero and heroine in fairy-tale retellings (Joosen 2011, 77),
Saki is physically attractive, virtuous, powerful, and wealthy. She is portrayed
as a much desired and gratefully accepted reward for Bon. This image not
only undermines the film's message that physical attractiveness and status are
overvalued criteria for judging others but also reinforces the idea that while
physical beauty may not be important in men, it is in women (ibid., 75).

This work reproduces the resolution of "Cinderella," in which heterosexual romance is the ultimate reward. As John Stephens and Robyn McCallum

state, retellings are shaped by "the implicit and usually invisible ideologies, systems, and assumptions which operate globally in a society to order knowledge and experience." Retold stories often uphold accepted values, behavior, and social structures (1998, 3–4). The affirmation of romance in *I Want to Be Cinderella!* conveys shared assumptions about accepted behavior in contemporary Japan: heterosexual coupling is the expected life course, and failure to follow this path indicates a failure to fulfill adult social responsibilities (Miller 2006, 157). While Bon may challenge conventional conceptions of masculinity, the narrative simultaneously reinforces established ideas about gender relations and life course in Japan.

An *Otaku* Cinderella: *Train Man*

The 2005 television drama series *Train Man* (*Densha otoko*)[4] both reinforces and challenges the fairy-tale pre-text. Cinderella in this retelling is the "Train Man," Yamada Tsuyoshi (Itō Atsushi), a recruitment agency employee[5] who meets the female protagonist, Aoyama Saori (Itō Misaki) when he saves her from an abusive drunk on the train. Yamada gets his nickname from members of an online forum for single men, where he posts about the event. Yamada's characterization as *otaku* establishes the homology with the "Cinderella" script's protagonist. The term "is now mostly used both playfully and pejoratively to denote ardent collectors of manga, anime and computer technologies" (Freedman 2009, para 9). Thomas Lamarre's translation of *otaku* suggests the source of the term's negative connotations: "the young male cult fan obsessed with manga, anime, games and/or computer technologies to the exclusion of all other social relations" (2007, 12). The first episode's opening scenes present a montage of *otaku* images: character figurines, cameras, computers and games, and shops and maid cafes[6] in the famous Tokyo electronics district of Akihabara. After this sequence, the camera zooms into the rooftop of a building in Akihabara, where Yamada stands, crying. He is thus doubly positioned in nonnormative masculinity from the start—not only his *otaku* identity but also his transgression of established masculinity schema by weeping.

The "Cinderella" script's first key motif manifests when his family, work colleagues, and even strangers belittle and reject Yamada because he fails to dress and interact in ways that meet social expectations. Depiction of his home clarifies Yamada's social position; he lives with his family above their bicycle shop. His situation contrasts with Saori's, whose sprawling, luxurious home, which she shares with her mother and younger brother, demonstrates her family's wealth.

Yamada's transformation, both in appearance and character, constitutes the second "Cinderella" script motif. His change involves a personal make-over and overcoming a range of setbacks in order to win Saori's affections.[7] The process begins when Saori sends Yamada two Hermes brand cups and saucers (the online forum thus refers to her as Hermes) as a thank you gift. Overcome by fear about how he should respond, Yamada consults the forum for advice. When he explains his apprehension that Saori will reject him once she learns he is *otaku*, the forum members commence the "Train Man Makeover Project," providing detailed advice and instructions on how he can change to win her.

Yamada heads to Tokyo's trendy Shibuya district and has a haircut, buys designer clothes, and replaces his glasses with contact lenses. The Shibuya makeover is completed to the tune of Roy Orbison's 1964 "Pretty Woman," alluding to the 1990 film that took its title from the song and included the original on its soundtrack. *Pretty Woman* is, of course, a "Cinderella" version and *Train Man* specifically replicates the motif of transformation through consumption found in it (see, e.g., Radner 2011, especially 26–41). Just as shopping transforms the prostitute Vivian's (Julia Roberts) identity, Yamada's makeover results from the consumption of various goods and beauty prac-tices. In one *Pretty Woman* scene, Vivian's fairy godmothers take the form of her love interest Edward (Richard Gere), who gives her his credit card and influence, the hotel's concierge, and numerous ingratiating shop assistants (Zipes 2011, 189). Yamada's helpers are the online forum members—in both the film version and the television drama the sequence is overlaid with their instructions and advice (Napier 2011, 160).

As part of the transformation in the second "Cinderella" script motif, Yamada also undergoes a journey of self-development. The pivotal stage comes when he decides to relinquish his *otaku* self. Even though he has already undergone his Shibuya makeover, he discards boxes full of character figurines, sells his games, and gets a ceremony from his *otaku* friends to formally declare he no longer belongs to their community. However, he soon realizes he cannot stop being *otaku,* and aiming to be honest, shows Saori that self—wearing glasses, jeans hitched up high over a tucked-in checked shirt, and a bandana on his head—confessing that he can live no other way. Saori unreservedly accepts him, and their relationship deepens as a result.

Saori's recognition and acceptance of Yamada's *otaku* self constitutes the third "Cinderella" script motif. The focus on the standards by which Yamada and others perceive and accept him illuminates the superficial and often problematic ways in which an individual is deemed desirable in society. By presenting a nonnormative masculinity as self-aware, other-regarding, authentic, and, ultimately, desirable, *Train Man* rejects the cultural presupposition that outer appearance is the primary—if not the sole—determinant of the individual's integration into the social world. Like Bon in *I Want to Be Cinderella!*, Yamada is accepted, at least to a certain degree, by others, despite his nonnormative identity as *otaku*. Yamada's decision to retain (to some extent) and share what places him outside the norm—his authentic self as *otaku*—after initial efforts to transform and hide it from Saori, enables him to achieve subjective agency. Yamada's resistance to social expectations, based on his moral integrity, enables self-constitution, develops his self-awareness, and establishes a significant social commitment to Saori.

Along with Yamada, the narrative affirms other forms of nonnormative masculinity. By positioning viewers to empathize with the alternatives, it questions the bases upon which forms of masculinity are deemed desirable or admired. Along with his closest *otaku* friends, Matsunaga (Gekidan Hitori) and Kawamoto (Sugawara Eiji), several members of the online forum in which Yamada posts also fail in some way to fulfill social expectations. They include an unmarried, chubby baseball fan, a *hikikomori* (shut-in; see Zielenziger 2006), a student who failed his university entrance exams, and a lonely man who separated from his wife after losing his job. This online community of others (which also includes some female members) eagerly and generously support Yamada, and his efforts to overcome adversity encourage at least some of them to make positive changes in their own lives.

The forum members further function to create the framework of Yamada's masculinity. They not only instruct him on how to transform, but when he progresses through each stage, their judgments of his success (or otherwise) define where that sequence places him as a man. The members constantly praise and promote courage and perseverance; they gauge Yamada's development and masculinity by his ability to display these qualities. On more than one occasion, Yamada says he cannot tell Saori that he likes her because he lacks the courage, and the forum members say, "Do you call yourself a man? Tell her!"; "Show some courage, and move on to the next stage!"; "Are you a Japanese man? Did you forget your Japanese spirit?"

When Yamada tells the forum that he and Saori have realized their mutual affection for each other, they respond with such comments as, "This is the result of hard work"; "What brought this about was Train Man's courage." Upon hearing that Saori no longer wants to see him after he lied about attending the comic book fair, they post, "If you give up now, you will revert back to your old self. You've gotten back up on your feet so many times"; "Don't give up so easily"; "Why don't you try to become a better man?" To encourage his own efforts to win her back, Yamada posts various signs around his room, which echo the comments of the forum: "Be assertive like a man"; "Be confident"; "Sexy!"; "Dandy!"; "Relax"; "Don't panic." The comments and signs outline the schema of being male in contemporary Japan. Yamada's masculinity takes a negotiated form, defined not just by his *otaku* status but also through the forum's instructions and expectations.

The series presents a constant contrast between Yamada's nonnormative masculinity and other forms. Yamada's boss at the recruitment agency at which he works, Kuroki (Satō Jirō), represents the hegemonic model of the salaryman. Middle aged and always dressed in a suit, he constantly berates Yamada's work performance. This treatment places Yamada firmly at the bottom of the workplace hierarchy. This relationship reverses, however, with another employee at the agency, Oikawa (Maekawa Yasuyuki), who represents the *ikemen* or "market" model of masculinity. Attractive, athletic, and trendy, his social superiority is expressed through his confident, suave manner of speaking. The series playfully conveys his dominance through his taste for expensive European suits; his easy rejection of women chasing him (calling them "annoying" and "ugly"); and his experience of living in Hawaii, which means he not only knows how to surf but also can use English. Kuroki fawns over Oikawa and imitates him, even repeating his sentences. Yamada and Kuroki, at their divergent locations in the corporate hierarchy, feel they can only dream of achieving Oikawa's ideal.

Oikawa expresses "a shift in Japanese canons of taste for young heterosexual men" in which "young men these days are increasingly concerned with their status as objects of aesthetic and sexual appraisal" (Miller 2006, 126). Miller highlights the interconnected forces influencing men's tastes and behaviors: consumption (of various products to alter appearance) as a means for constructing masculine subjectivity; a rejection of the hegemonic masculinity model, embodied by men of older generations; and a response to female desire (2006, 127). Oikawa's interest in brand-name fashion, styled hair, and trim, muscular, seemingly hairless physique signify him as cool and desirable (from both men's and women's perspectives) and express the way the consumption of beauty practices, cosmetics, and clothing works to define his masculinity. The depictions also suggest a rejection of the hegemonic model; the middle-aged salaryman Kuroki is weak, insecure, and dowdy in comparison to the confident, trendy Oikawa.

The interplay of these masculinities conveys the tensions arising from the changing nature of ideas and expectations about being male in contemporary Japan. As mentioned earlier, economic and social changes make meeting the hegemonic salaryman model difficult, and other forms of masculinity have emerged. However, just like the salaryman, the newer model of "market masculinity" may be unattainable or incompatible with men's lives. Yet an inability to meet either ideal may be deemed failure to progress as expected through the conventional life course as well as defeat as a man (Slater and Galbraith 2011, para 28–29).

Yamada cannot fully conform to either the salaryman or the *ikemen* model. His narration of his encounter with the drunk on the train clarifies his own perception of himself. When a young salaryman aids him and restrains the drunken man, Yamada comments, "The salaryman was so cool. . . . I was so uncool." Saori's friends Kaho (Satō Eriko) and Yūko (Sudō Risa) describe Yamada, posttransformation, as equally incompatible with the *ikemen* ideal; he is "in the middle of the lowest rank" and "totally NG,[8] honest but 120 percent the type who will end up as a friend, kind but lacks presence, faithful but a wash out, not bad looking but totally forgettable."

Yamada's transformation into a designer brand–wearing *otaku* who works full time at a recruitment agency thus seems to be a negotiation of masculinities that is not without contradiction. While refusing to discard his *otaku* interests and hobbies, he subscribes to the *ikemen* model's commodified masculinity; his efforts to alter his appearance are not necessarily aimed at rejecting the salaryman model (as may be the case for Oikawa) but instead at hiding his *otaku* appearance. As Freedman notes, "A main theme of *Train Man* is that it is okay to be an *otaku* so long as you do not look or act like one in public" (2009, para 36). Yamada's negotiated masculinity seems to be the product of the changing social and economic conditions Slater and Galbraith analyze, in which no one form of masculinity is fully legitimized or rejected.

Train Man's resolution reproduces that of "Cinderella" because it affirms heterosexual coupling as the ultimate goal. Yamada's transformation and subsequent union with Saori brings him happiness and acceptance as well as praise and admiration. Heterosexual romance is valorized as the reward for Yamada's courage, perseverance, moral integrity, and altruism. Thus, Yamada's alternative model of masculinity is incorporated into the dominant ideology of gender relations, and *Train Man* affirms conformity to conventional Japanese expectations about gender relations and life course (Freedman 2009, para 2–3, 43).

Indeed, *Train Man*'s heteronormative love story is made clear in the first episode of the series; Yamada, in Akihabara, and Saori, at a party on a boat, stand looking up at the sky, both watching the same fireworks display celebrating the festival of Tanabata. According to a Japanese folktale, Tanabata marks the only day of the year when Orihime (a princess who weaves the clothes of the deities) and Hikoboshi (a cow herder) can meet. The two fall so deeply in love that they neglect their duties, and Orihime's father separates them, only allowing them to meet once a year. The implication is that elegant, sophisticated Saori is Orihime, and Yamada, separated from Saori not just by their physical locations but also by his *otaku* appearance, is Hikoboshi. The series thus incorporates a version of "The Man on a Quest for His Lost Wife" (ATU 400)[9] as pre-text. Evoking this folktale through allusions as well as the protagonists' characteristics conveys established ideas about gender patterns and relations, leading viewers to expect from the beginning that Saori and Yamada's relationship will end in a romantic union. Simultaneously, *Train Man* adapts the Tanabata folktale to a new format and gives it contemporary significance (Stephens and McCallum 1998, 4; Lee 2009, 142; Stephens 2011b, 14). The interaction between the "Cinderella" script, Tanabata folktales, and *Train Man* "results in an integrated glocal product that is significant both globally and locally" (Gutierrez 2013, 21).

Ultimately, two key messages may be gained from *Train Man*. First, although it offers another example of Japanese television drama supporting nonnormative masculinities,[10] conventional ideas and expectations relating to gender relations and life course in contemporary Japanese society remain pervasive and strong, showing that the pressure on individuals to conform is difficult to resist. Second, although both Yamada and Saori choose each other based on more than just external appearance, physical beauty remains a key factor in his acceptance or rejection by others.

A Capable Prince: *Rich Man, Poor Woman*

The final series I discuss, the 2012 television drama *Rich Man, Poor Woman* (Ricchi man pua ūman), differs from the previous two examples in making the Cinderella character, Natsui Makoto (Ishihara Satomi) female. However, like *I Want to Be Cinderella!* and *Train Man,* this series illustrates the trend on Japanese television to support nonhegemonic masculinities. Makoto's prince, Hyūga Tōru (Oguri Shun), does not conform to the hegemonic salaryman model.

Advertisements before the show was broadcast describe it as "a real-life Cinderella story that any woman can long for, about an IT company president and a woman struggling to start a career!" Both this ad and the series title establish Makoto's lower social position and thereby introduce the "Cinderella" script's first motif. As a twenty-three-year-old woman from a small town in Kōchi, southern Japan, in her fourth year at prestigious Tokyo University, her initial hardship comes from the burdens of that final year. Along with assignments and part-time work, Makoto is trapped in the rigid and demanding graduate job-hunting system (*shūshoku katsudō*), wherein students apply for dozens of positions and attend many recruitment workshops and interviews. Despite her credentials, effort, and passion, Makoto, yet to receive a job offer, considers herself a failure. Allusion to the "Cinderella" script comes through the focus on Makoto's shoes during her job hunting; her black high heels have been scuffed to a dull, dirty gray as a symbol of her early hardship.

The first scene featuring Makoto and Hyūga further confirms the difference in their social positions; in episode 1, he zips past her on his motorbike as she walks near his office building, causing her to stumble. He dismounts, enters the building, and rises above Makoto in the glass elevator to his office, as she walks glumly away. Hyūga Tōru instantiates a nonnormative form of masculinity through his educational background; he left school after junior high—a rare occurrence in Japan.[11] Before establishing his company, Hyūga actively rejected the salaryman model; he was a *freeter* (a young person who subsists on part-time work).

However, despite his comparatively limited education, Hyūga's current status and wealth place him well above Makoto socially; at twenty-nine, he is a multimillionaire and founder and president of Next Innovation, a company that specializes in cellphone and online games. Hyūga's rejection of the salaryman model continues in his everyday life. His usual working attire, a T-shirt, casual loose-fitting pants, and sandals, would rarely be acceptable in any regular Japanese organization of similar standing and wealth. He wears suits only when attending formal meetings or press conferences.

He recognizes that he does not conform to conventional expectations of masculinity, describing himself as a computer *otaku* (*pasokon otaku*). His behavior early in the series emphasizes his separation from his social world; he is thoroughly self-regarding, sullen, and insensitive. His self-understanding as a misfit is somewhat related to his relationship with his mother, Sawaki Chihiro (Manda Hisako), who abandoned him when he was six years old. Hyūga's obsessive search for Chihiro took him to Makoto's hometown five years earlier, where he met the girl for the first time. It also becomes the driving force for his latest business venture to create a database of the entire Japanese population's personal information. Thus Hyūga, like Makoto, struggles to understand where he belongs in society—a somewhat different position from those held by the princesses Saki in *I Want to Be Cinderella!* and Saori in *Train Man,* who both sit comfortably in their social worlds.

The "Cinderella" script's first motif appears again when Makoto attends the recruitment seminar for Next Innovation. When Hyūga discovers that she has received no job offers despite being a student of Japan's best university, he belittles her before an auditorium of other jobseekers: "She is the Japanese education system's failure, or perhaps I should say, victim. Although she has studied as instructed, unfortunately she has turned out to be a redundant person." Hyūga's treatment of Makoto in this scene not only builds homologies with the protagonist's mistreatment in the "Cinderella" script[12] but also conveys one of the key criticisms the series makes about contemporary Japanese society. Makoto, trying to leave, stumbles and loses one of her new shoes. She does not repeat the passivity of many other "Cinderella" protagonists, however, for she picks up her own shoe, puts it back on, and turns around to rebuke Hyūga, telling him his way of judging people is superficial and likely mistaken.

Makoto transcends her position, following the second script motif, when Hyūga, impressed by her assertiveness and courage, asks for her name. She gives the name Sawaki Chihiro—living in the same small town, she and Hyūga's mother were acquaintances—knowing the effect it will have on him. In a sense, the man's (absent) mother becomes Makoto's helper (fairy godmother); as a result, she gets a contract position at Next Innovation. Subsequently, Hyūga directs Makoto's exterior transformation himself, as he takes her shopping for clothes to replace her drab gray job-hunting suit. In a scene again evoking the *Pretty Woman* scene discussed above, Makoto tries on outfits as Hyūga, waiting outside the fitting room, offers his approval or rejection. The allusion to "Cinderella" continues; Makoto's transformed appearance after the shopping makeover is revealed from the feet—where patent nude stilettos replace her black heels—upward.

The plot moves toward recognition of Makoto's true identity, following the "Cinderella" script's third motif, when she confesses to Hyūga that she falsified her name, using what he told her in their initial meeting in her hometown, which he had forgotten. He fires her, but she is later reemployed and their romantic interest in each other develops. However, before the third motif's union is achieved, the series replays its earlier stages, this time with Hyūga taking a Cinderella-like role. He is left destitute when his business partner and closest friend, Asahina (Iura Arata), engineers the company's collapse. This time, Makoto acts as Hyūga's helper, working with him to establish a new company and find new clients. In a reversal of Hyūga's direction of Makoto's transformation, she teaches him how to interact with clients. A scene evoking *My Fair Lady* (1964) has Makoto introducing, and Hyūga repeating, various polite expressions. She also coaches his responses to various business scenarios. Their relationship enables thoroughly intersubjective development, as both protagonists face hardship and undergo a transformation process that results in self-improvement, ensuring that both are active participants in their relationship.

Jack Zipes (2011, 189) asks, "Can a Cinderella girl act any differently in a socio-economic system that lays traps for her in every game situation? Can a filmmaker depict other valid possibilities other than complicity?" *Rich Man Poor Woman* offers a mixed response. Makoto rejects passivity and submission when, after leaving Hyūga to build his new company himself, she accepts a job in Brazil, based partly on her belief that he is not romantically interested in her but also on her desire to become independent and make a contribution to society. She judges her own individual success by her ability to find a career and do something useful, and these criteria also guide her judgment of Hyūga as a romantic partner, posttransformation. Makoto tells her friend that she is in love with him because he is "just too cool [i.e., good looking] and he can do his job so much better than before," to which her friend replies, "A capable man is the best, right?"

Hyūga also encourages Makoto to become independent and achieve her professional goals, delaying the romantic union that closes the "Cinderella" script. The characters' values and attitudes here illuminate actual world structures and experiences related to career and relationships in contemporary Japan. Physical appearance, status, and personality remain important, but independence (for both women and men) and an ability to meaningfully contribute to society also become criteria for judging others. When Makoto returns from Brazil she and Hyūga begin a romantic relationship, so the series eventually incorporates them into the dominant ideology of gender relations. However, compared to Bon and Saki and Yamada and Saori, Hyūga and Makoto have comparatively more opportunity—given to them by society, and each other—to pursue life courses beyond established social expectations.

Cinderella Televised Masculinities

Joosen argues that feminist Marcia Lieberman (1972) "stresses that 'millions of *women*' have formed their (limited) self-concepts on the basis of their favorite fairy tales and that the tales 'have been made the repositories of the dreams, hopes, and fantasies of generations of girls.'. . . The question of whether the tales have also contributed to the development of limited gender constructs for boys is not sufficiently addressed" (2011, 89). In analyzing Japanese retellings of the "Cinderella" script, I have addressed how this fairy tale has recently been developed to interrogate conceptions of masculinity in contemporary Japanese society. *I Want to Be Cinderella!, Train Man,* and *Rich Man, Poor Woman* rework the "Cinderella" script in ways that both reinforce and challenge conventional ideas about gender roles and relations.

While *I Want to Be Cinderella!* is a two-hour television movie, *Train Man* and *Rich Man, Poor Woman* each had eleven regular episodes that were broadcast weekly,[13] and as is common practice with live-action television series made in Japan, ran for only one season. This system of limiting TV drama episodes and seasons enables networks to capitalize on actors at the peak of their popularity. The inclusion of celebrities from other areas of popular media, especially the music industry, ensures viewership in what can be a fickle entertainment market. However, despite running for only a limited period, the works analyzed here reflect a broader trend across many forms of Japanese popular media to offer more diverse conceptualizations of gender identities and relations.

Further, though each work maintains heterosexual coupling as an expected goal of a conventional life course, they analyze social practice, values, and beliefs in relation to various forms of masculinity, asking the viewer to develop different ways of defining and judging themselves and others. Kimmel writes, "We come to know what it means to be a man in our culture by setting our definitions in opposition to a set of 'others'" (2001, 267); the nonnormative masculinities in each work oppose and open up potential challenges to the hegemonic model. Further, the affirmation of disapproved or nonnormative forms of masculinity, negotiated actively and flexibly by the character, highlights for viewers alternatives to the norm and possibilities for subjective agency in constructing gender.

Within the "Cinderella" script's framework, each show engages with both the salaryman and the *ikemen* models of masculinity, with the male protagonists struggling to define themselves in their context. The *ikemen* figure, focusing on appearance, offers an effective way of engaging the "Cinderella" script and giving it contemporary significance, even if only as a means to reconfigure it. The *ikemen* is portrayed as privileged and desired, and in *I Want to Be Cinderella!* and *Train Man* in particular, is at least initially depicted as the ideal form of masculinity. This model is not limited to television drama—it appears widely across many modes of Japanese popular media, highlighting the sexualization and commodification of men's bodies (Miller 2006, 126–28) and reflecting the values and tastes of contemporary Japanese society.

However, depicting gender construction as a process of negotiation affirms the argument that even when new models of masculinity emerge as a result of changes in society, they may not be achievable or desirable for all men. The male protagonists in the works analyzed struggle with the expectations associated with both the salaryman and *ikemen* models, and their efforts to understand and define their subjectivity in this context result in some form of compromise that blurs the boundaries and highlights the diverse forms masculinity can take.

Simultaneously, while acknowledging the *ikemen*'s limitations and problems, this model's emergence as a rejection of the salaryman should also be recognized. All three works suggest that what it means to be male is changing—based not just on economic and social conditions but also on men's own desires and goals. In rejecting the salaryman model, they articulate the equality-oriented change occurring (albeit slowly) in the actual lives of men and women in Japan. The *ikemen*'s challenge to conventional ideas about masculinity, and to established understandings of masculinity and femininity as oppositional concepts, could open up the possibility for more widespread change.[14]

As social, political, and economic conditions in Japan continue to change, popular media participate in the reconfiguration of conventional gender norms, affirming diverse forms and allowing subordinated individuals to assert their agency. Yet as the television dramas I analyzed show, these portrayals may be set within various constraints that reduce their positive effects. The limitations placed even on fictional characters suggest that there is still work to be done in moving popular media beyond the constraints of traditional conceptions of gender roles and relations in Japan.

Notes

1. Japanese names will follow the conventional format of surname, then first name.
2. The use of *men* in *ikemen* (as opposed to *man* in *sarariiman*) likely derives from *menzu* (men's), which usually refers to products, clothing, services, and practices targeting younger men seen in magazines, product labels, and retail locations— services for men in hair and beauty salons and department store sections with men's clothing and accessories. The same term would not be used for older men; for example, the department store section with clothing for them would be called *shinshifuku* (literally "gentlemen's clothes").
3. Tarō is a common Japanese male given name.
4. The *Train Man* story takes many forms: book, film, television series, stage play, and multiple manga versions.
5. Two 1980s updated "Cinderella" films similarly locate their action in the corporate world, both set in New York. *Working Girl* (1988) makes the main character female, but *The Secret of My Succe$s* has a young man seeking his fortune in the city (see Labrie 1997).
6. In maid cafes, staff dress in costumes (for female maids, often a short black dress overlaid with a white pinafore) and serve customers. Patrons visit not just because of the staff's visual appeal but also to engage in conversation with them in a comfortable environment.
7. Reality TV makeovers as "Cinderella" scripts are discussed in Lee's chapter.
8. NG in Japanese stands for "no good."
9. Japanese versions include "The Wife from the Sky World" (Mayer 1986, 25) and "Wife from the Upper World" (Seki 1966, 79).
10. Similarly, in her chapter, Lezubski discusses how nonnormative femininities are explored in the anime TV series *Revolutionary Girl Utena*.
11. Approximately 94 percent of Japanese students continue on from junior high to complete the noncompulsory three years of senior high school (Statistics Bureau Japan 2013).
12. It perhaps even better reflects the frequent mistreatment of Peau d'Ane by the prince or king in the related tale type (ATU 510B).
13. *Train Man* also had two special episodes that were broadcast two weeks and one year, respectively, after the regular series ended.
14. One example of change is the Japanese government initiative titled "The Ikumen Project" (*ikumen*, adapting *ikemen*, combines the Chinese character meaning "to raise (a child)" and the English "men"), which, as part of newly introduced laws related to childcare, encourages men to be more involved in parenting.

7

MOLDING MESSAGES

Analyzing the Reworking of "Sleeping Beauty" in *Grimm's Fairy Tale Classics* and *Dollhouse*

Jeana Jorgensen and Brittany Warman

The story of "Sleeping Beauty" (ATU 410) is one of the most consistently captivating fairy tales. It tells of a cursed princess dreaming in a tower, waiting patiently for her prince to rescue her. Those who recreate the tale for contemporary audiences spin the story anew, reconstructing again and again what it means both to sleep and to awaken. This chapter analyzes two modern television versions of the tale, one for children and one for adults, comparing their incorporation of feminist messages and parallel ideas about shaping narratives and shaping lives. The children's cartoon *Grimm's Fairy Tale Classics* (also called *Grimm Masterpiece Theatre*) and the adult program *Dollhouse* each remold the story to advance very specific rereadings of the tale.

Familiar all over the world, ATU 410 has become a Western cultural touchstone that is freely referenced by various media. Of several different versions, the best known have long been the French text by Charles Perrault and the German text by the Brothers Grimm. Disney drew on both for the beloved film *Sleeping Beauty* (1959), further cementing them as the standard versions in Western imagination. Both *Grimm's Fairy Tale Classics* and *Dollhouse* use the Grimm version as the starting point for their "Briar Rose" episodes.

The Grimms' first version of their folktale collection, *Children's and Household Tales* (1812) incorporated "Little Briar Rose" (Grimm 1998). The brothers debated including it, worrying that its antecedents, particularly Perrault's "The Sleeping Beauty in the Wood," were too well known for a collection that claimed to be purely German but ultimately decided to keep it due to its connections with the Germanic Norse story of Brynhild (Heiner 2010). Their title, however, seems to deliberately distance the tale from Perrault's by foregoing any mention of a "sleeping beauty." The Grimms continued to edit their version: the 1819 edition included some "modest stylistic changes" (Ashliman 2005), and by 1857 the story had been extensively expanded to contain more description and dialogue (Grimm 2001).

In the Grimms' story, a king and queen who have longed for years for a child are finally blessed with a daughter. They invite everyone to the palace for a feast in her honor and take special pains to invite the kingdom's wise women. However, because they only have twelve golden plates and there are thirteen wise women, they must exclude one. On the day of the feast, while the twelve invited wise women bless the child with magical gifts like beauty and virtue, the thirteenth suddenly enters the hall and curses the princess to die when she pricks her finger on a spindle in her fifteenth year. The twelfth wise woman, who had not yet given a magical gift to the child, could not undo the evil spell but she could change it: instead of dying with the prick of the spindle, she declares that the princess will sleep for one hundred years. Though the king orders all the spindles in the kingdom burned, the princess finds one on her fifteenth birthday and pricks her finger, which causes her to fall into a deep sleep along with all the rest of the people in the palace. An enormous briar hedge grows up around the structure and outsiders begin telling stories about the cursed princess inside. Many young men attempt to brave the briar hedge but all fail and die miserably. After one hundred years, the destined prince is allowed inside and awakens the sleeping princess with a kiss. The entire palace wakes up with her and she and the prince marry (Grimm 2001).

Reworkings of "Sleeping Beauty" have been quite abundant. Popular writers of the nineteenth century such as Christina Rossetti[1] and George MacDonald[2] were inspired by the tale. Numerous retellings in contemporary literature include Jane Yolen's *Briar Rose* (1992), which places the story in the context of the Holocaust, and Anna Sheehan's *A Long, Long Sleep* (2011), a science fiction novel in which the world changes dramatically during the protagonist's century-long stasis. Disney's is only one of several film versions and the tale's popularity has also spread to television, as in the *Castle* episode, "Once Upon a Crime" (2012).

Many contemporary revisions of "Sleeping Beauty" as well as other fairy tales address feminist concerns. Feminism is no monolithic category. Nicole Kousaleos points out that commonalities across multiple feminisms include the notions "that gender is a fundamental organizing category of experience; sexual inequality is a cultural construct; and male perspectives have dominated fields of knowledge, shaping paradigms and methods" (1999, 19). However, the degrees to which gender identity, anatomical sex, sexuality, and the relationship of these categories to the body and mind are constructed as fixed versus fluid differ. Kousaleos broadly divides the schools of thought into equality feminism (assuming that men and women are basically the same) and difference feminism (assuming that men and women are fundamentally different; ibid., 20–22). Elizabeth Grosz reads these relations in terms of the body; some feminist scholars view women's bodies as the source of both their oppression and their unique embodied knowledge; others see the body as precultural and thus are more interested in social constructionism as the cause of women's oppression; yet others take a stance on sexual difference or offer a more complex intertwining of body and mind, nature and nurture that foregrounds the lived body within a cultural context (1994, 15–19).

In feminist revisions as well as feminist scholarship on cultural texts, a distinction between political and theoretical feminisms is useful, though the two are rarely completely separate. Political feminist works attend to women's issues on an activist or consciousness-raising level, while theoretical feminist studies critique misogyny and patriarchal systems beyond merely drawing attention to their existence (Jorgensen 2010, 54–60). Thus in our analysis, feminist messages within a text can be mainly political—on the level of the plot addressing inequalities between men and women and revising sexist story lines—or more theoretical—exploring interconnections between body, mind, and gender oppression in a complex fashion. We do not intend to create a hierarchical relationship between political and theoretical feminisms; instead we point out different levels of engagement with gender dynamics that occur in expressive culture.

With their very different perspectives on the frequently gendered meanings of enchanted sleep and rescue, the "Briar Rose" episodes of *Grimm's Fairy Tale Classics* and *Dollhouse* defamiliarize the tale, "thus opening up the possibility of a shift in perspective that encourages the audience to reflect anew on these stories that have ossified as part of the bedrock of cultural narratives" (Greenhill and Matrix 2010a, 12). These television renderings question the stereotypical passive sleeping princess and assumptions about the allocation of gender and power within narrative. While both shows deal broadly with the problem of "the woman who withdraws from the social order" through sleep (Fay 2008, 273), their divergent resolutions offer new solutions for considering the broader ways in which both society and narrative mold acceptable identities for young people.

The "Briar Rose" Episode of *Grimm's Fairy Tale Classics*

The English-language *Grimm's Fairy Tale Classics* was originally an animated Japanese series called *Gurimu meisaku gekijō* (Grimm Masterpiece Theater; 1987–1989). Developed and produced by Nippon Animation in the late 1980s (Clements and McCarthy 2006), the show proved quite popular in Japan (Ellis 2008a). European fairy tales' influence on Japanese animation, called "anime," is well documented,[3] and several programs have drawn on the "Sleeping Beauty" story. Bill Ellis believes that *Gurimu meisaku gekijō's* success in Japan sparked the real beginning of the numerous references to Western fairy tales in anime (2008b)[4] and he writes extensively on ATU 410 connections in the very popular manga (comic) and later anime series *Cardcaptor Sakura* (Ellis 2008b). This series, by the collective of artists/authors known as CLAMP,[5] features an episode in which the characters perform a "Sleeping Beauty" play. However, the tale can also offer a way of understanding the series as a whole. Ellis (2008a) also notes many references to "Sleeping Beauty" in the equally well-known series *Sailor Moon* and argues that the popularity of "Sleeping Beauty" allusions in particular may be because of the tale's similarity to a particular Japanese folktale.[6]

In North America, *Gurimu meisaku gekijō* was broadcast by the children's television station Nickelodeon as *Grimm's Fairy Tale Classics* from 1989 to 1995 (Haase 2008, 949). This show "introduced many viewers [in North America] to anime"—a very particular style—in much the same way that the original series "popularized" Western fairy tales with Japanese audiences (Ellis 2008b, 513). Donald Haase contends, "Western classics originally adapted for Japanese television audiences [were] transmitted back to Western audiences in a Japanese art form, through the lens of Japanese culture, and in a format adapted for television" (2008, 949). "Briar Rose" is a particularly potent example of the fascinating reshaping that resulted.[7]

While it is difficult to verify whether the creators had a particular intention, the "Briar Rose" episode of *Grimm's Fairy Tale Classics* seems to alter the story specifically in order to advance a more feminist message (in the political sense, as discussed above). Fairy tales are frequently perceived as women's domain and "connected with women's issues" (Crowley and Pennington 2010, 298), and the popularity of contemporary feminist revisions is undeniable. Heroines who appear too passive in well-known versions, such as Sleeping Beauty and Snow White, are popular for feminist reimagining. Postmodern fairy-tale revisions frequently "expose . . . the fairy tale's complicity with 'exhausted' narrative and gender ideologies" (Bacchilega 1997, 24) and this often requires significant rewriting. This episode presents a different kind of story than those retellings, one that subtly advances particular contemporary ideas about women.

The feminist leanings of "Briar Rose" are presented early on with the appearance of the wise women, called "witch sisters," who are invited to the princess's feast. These women live all together in a castle. The entire kingdom fears their magical powers and ability to transform themselves into monsters, shown in the episode's early minutes. These self-sufficient, powerful characters are clearly visually coded as frightening witches— older women in black wearing items like capes and skull-shaped earrings. But, with the exception of the uninvited sister, they are also good-natured and kind women, eager to bless the princess. When the first comes forward to present her magical gift, she addresses it "to the princess [who] will someday rule this kingdom,"[8] a loaded statement that seems to indicate that the wise women believe the princess does not need a male counterpart to rule with her. Furthermore, when the twelfth witch must counter the thirteenth's curse, her strong, clear voice remarks, "I will save the fair princess." The prince usually gets credit for saving the princess, not the twelfth wise woman, whose spell prevents the princess's death. This version gives appropriate credit by having the witch acknowledge her own role as the princess's true savior.

Later, when viewers are first introduced to Briar Rose (voiced by Rachel Lillis) as a teenager, she is shown to be lovely and accomplished but also sad and isolated. Her father has forbidden her from ever leaving the castle in order to keep her safe, and the princess dreams only of freedom. Musing to herself while walking through her rose garden, she remarks, "Beautiful rose, I have your name but not the freedom you have to grow up in open spaces." Also a dedicated musician, she uses her art as a distraction from the rest of her world. Despite the limitations on her freedom, Briar Rose is far more developed as a person than she is in older versions. She has hopes and dreams, skills and interests, and ideas of her own about what her life should be like.[9]

After Briar Rose pricks her finger and she and the entire palace fall into their enchanted sleep, viewers see her would-be rescuers' actions. The pointed look at their failures is revealing. The village men attack the briar hedge with tools and fire but none can get through. Instead of dying as in the Grimm text, many are caught in the sleeping spell themselves. Angry, rough, powerful-looking men come as well, one stating, "The beautiful princess will be mine, all mine," but they too fail. The princess is not to be won and claimed: the person to break the spell must be her true partner, not her owner. He is revealed as an adventurous and brave but also kind prince who has dreamed of the castle all his life. He and Briar Rose are already deeply and meaningfully connected through their dreams of each other. The prince understands the princess in the way a true partner must; he is the one who is able to "hear [her] song." The castle gates open immediately for him and he finds Briar Rose asleep in her tower. He thinks that a kiss might awaken her, but the rose thorns surrounding her prick him before he can get close enough. Even though he is the right prince, this version does not allow the famous, nonconsensual kiss.[10] He and Briar Rose only kiss at the very end of the episode, when she is awake and willing, a rewriting that emphasizes their status as partners and Briar Rose's autonomy.

Vanessa Joosen's work on fairy-tale criticism's influences on fairy-tale retellings applies to the shaping of the *Grimm's Fairy Tale Classics'* "Briar Rose" episode. Bruno Bettelheim's popular *The Uses of Enchantment* "was without a doubt the most prominent psychoanalytic study of fairy tales in the 1970s" (2011, 123). The *Grimm's Fairy Tale Classics'* creators may have known Bettelheim's primary thesis that "fairy tales have a therapeutic effect on children" and are therefore necessary to their development—"the fairy tale liberates the child's subconscious so that he or she can work through conflicts and experiences which would otherwise be repressed and perhaps cause psychological disturbances" (Zipes 2002a, 182). Despite his insistence that fairy tales must be presented in their "original forms, which Bettelheim usually equates with the Grimms' versions of 1857" (Joosen 2011, 125), and the fact that many fairy-tale scholars now discredit the majority of his findings,[11] his ideas had a lasting impact on retellings, particularly in the 1970s and 1980s.

Bettelheim (1976) understands "Sleeping Beauty" as a tale about the journey of growing up. Indeed, in the *Grimm's Fairy Tale Classics* episode, the young princess's maturation seems to dominate the narrative. Before her magical sleep, she acts not unlike a privileged Euro–North American teenager: she is listless, is bored with her life, and longs for freedom. She shows no interest in other people or even events like her birthday, and her father muses to the queen that it is "as though she were a stranger." This "sleep" period in her life, Bettelheim argues, is both typical of adolescence and absolutely necessary for development.[12] He states that parents must accept these changes, despite their desire to keep their children young (1976, 230–23), which the queen specifically reminds the king in the episode. While Briar Rose experiences the enchanted sleep, her passive state actually begins long before in this nonmagical, "more realistic" (Joosen 2011, 158) narrative. Bettelheim also sees an inherent narcissism in the sleep of adolescence, a theme picked up in the television episode as well. Princess Briar Rose is initially quite self-centered— she is too caught up in her own tumultuous feelings, which causes her to experience "the isolation of narcissism" (Bettelheim 1976, 234).

The princess can only awaken and end this period of life when she is mature sexually and ready for the next phase. The fact that the rose thorns initially injure the prince rather than allow him to kiss the sleeping princess awake seems to directly undercut Bettelheim's insistence that the awakening is sexual in nature (Bettelheim 1976). But he believes that the princess awakens also to a union of "minds and souls" (ibid., 232). The episode prioritizes this aspect of the awakening. This choice strengthens the retelling's feminist qualities; the connection between the prince and the princess is no longer purely sexual but cerebral as well, which Bettelheim saw as essential to all mature, and therefore good, fairy-tale unions.

Despite the positive steps "Briar Rose" takes toward presenting a feminist reimagining of "Sleeping Beauty," it falls short, particularly with the characters of the evil thirteenth witch and Briar Rose's mother. The thirteenth witch is initially shown to be both powerful and confident in her abilities. She can make herself bigger than the entire castle, for example, and the twelfth witch even says that the thirteenth is stronger than she. Yet when the spell is broken and she has lost, the tale dispenses with her rather quickly, saying only that "the evil witch was sent away and was never heard from again." This seems an inappropriate and dismissive ending for such a powerful woman; the Grimm version makes no mention at all about what happens to her.

The queen likewise seems to be denied her proper due throughout the episode. The narrator states at the very beginning that "there was once a great king whose wish for a child was granted" and makes no mention whatsoever of the queen. Her role in the story is brief and she spends a great deal of it crying and lamenting her daughter's fate. Even the princess's personality has arguably less feminist aspects. Though she is independent minded, her thoughts return frequently to the idea that someone must rescue her. She never thinks of rescuing herself, only that someday someone else will give her the freedom she so craves. But her desire for rescue is necessary to the story because it means the princess thinks often of her prince. The teenagers thus establish their cerebral connection before they even meet— but the princess's passivity in this area breaks with the overall messages of feminism that the episode presents.

The "Briar Rose" episode of *Grimm's Fairy Tale Classics* subtly remolds the Grimm narrative, offering a more contemporary and feminist depiction of and for young girls. While it qualifies more as a political feminist revision than a theoretical feminist deconstruction of the tale's power dynamics, it largely advances less passive and male-dependent role models while still faithfully adapting a well-known and popular story.

The "Briar Rose" Episode of *Dollhouse*

The adult thriller series *Dollhouse,* while it contains fairy-tale elements, focuses on futuristic and technological themes (see also Tresca's chapter). The show's premise features brain technology that allows people referred to as "Dolls" or "Actives" to have their personalities wiped and replaced with those of others. These individuals are then rented out by the secretive corporation Rossum to, for instance, fulfill fantasies and solve crimes. The show's creator, Joss Whedon, is known for his strong female characters (Snowden 2010), witty dialogue, and innovative approaches to themes such as the apocalypse (Vinci 2011), heroism, and morality. However, while audiences celebrate many of Whedon's works, such as *Buffy the Vampire Slayer* and *Firefly,* as containing feminist messages and compelling world building, *Dollhouse* inspired ambivalent and even negative responses. As Catherine Coker notes, "*Dollhouse* has become Joss Whedon's most controversial work yet, with many fans, viewers, and critics troubled by the images and aspects of human trafficking and prostitution depicted on the show" (2010, 226). The show's treatment of complex and disturbing ethical questions in a fairy-tale mode exemplifies how "sexual and moral ambiguity remains a standard feature of fairy tale films for adults" (Greenhill and Matrix 2010a, 9). Like these films, *Dollhouse* works by foregrounding ambiguity, and yet its episodic structure, unique to TV, allows depth and complexity to be expanded upon and explored over time.

The show's reworking of ATU 410 in its "Briar Rose" episode (1, 11)[13] contains a scene in which the main Doll character, Echo (Eliza Dushku), reads the fairy tale to a group of children in a foster care home. The tale particularly resonates for one girl with a history of abuse, since she blames herself, as she does the fairy tale's protagonist, for not escaping on her own. Simultaneously, the plot of "Sleeping Beauty" is mirrored in the episode's overall structure; FBI agent Paul Ballard (Tahmoh Penikett) searching for Echo (or rather, for her body's original identity, Caroline) is portrayed as a valiant prince overcoming the castle's defenses to rescue the princess. In this episode, and in *Dollhouse* overall, sleep is at once therapeutic and annihilating, inviting an analysis of the series' incorporation of "Sleeping Beauty" as a comment on how both people and fairy tales can be shaped and exploited in multiple ways. The three main intertextual uses of fairy tales we discuss include the episode's retelling of the text of a version of "Sleeping Beauty," the positioning of Ballard as a prince–rescuer to Caroline/Echo's innocent persecuted heroine (see Bacchilega 1993), and the very notion of fairy tales as therapeutic. This discussion focuses on the first season of *Dollhouse,* because it contains the "Briar Rose" episode and because its fairy-tale metaphors are more pronounced.[14] The version of "Sleeping Beauty" that Echo, programmed to perform a charitable engagement that day, reads in the children's home is a pared-down picture-book version of the Grimms' tale. Echo has been sent specifically to help a girl named Susan (Hannah Leigh). Echo's personality imprint is an adult version of Susan, should she in growing up address her childhood sexual abuse in a healthy way. The episode shows Echo reading the end of "Sleeping Beauty" to the children, most of whom appear spellbound: "As soon as the prince kissed her, the spell was broken and Briar Rose opened her eyes. And as she looked at the face of the handsome young prince, the whole kingdom began to magically awaken all around them. The cooks in the kitchen and the boys in the yard, all rubbed their eyes and looked around them." Susan interrupts: "This is crap." In the ensuing discussion, she blames the tale's title character (and, it is implied, herself) for not having better common sense than to stay away from spindles, run away, or otherwise save herself from her fate.

Echo later talks privately to Susan about the fairy tale, suggesting that the child should not blame the protagonist for her fate. The conversation also includes references to the sexual abuse they both suffered while young and the feelings of complicity with which they struggle. Echo says, "You couldn't have gotten away. He was bigger, and stronger, and older. . . . It's okay to get rescued by someone else if you're young or small or you just can't do it yourself." Echo tells Susan to reread the story but think of herself as the prince, who "shows up at the last minute, takes all the credit. That means Briar Rose was trapped all that time, sleeping. And dreaming, of getting out. The prince was her dream. She made him. She made him fight to get her out." This reimagining of female agency within the tale parallels the feminist search for coded women's voices within traditional fairy tales (Rowe 1986).

"Sleeping Beauty" is also incorporated in the roles that main characters play, not just within "Briar Rose" but throughout the series. Thus "Briar Rose," as the penultimate episode in season 1, inter-refers to other fairy tales and fairy-tale characters throughout the first season, in particular those of Echo and Ballard. Echo is positioned as an innocent persecuted heroine as early as the show's first episode, "Ghost" (see Tresca's chapter), in which Echo's client watches her leave around five a.m. after a weekend of partying. His friend asks,

> "Dude, where's your friend?"
> "It's time for her to go. Had to get to her carriage before it
>   turned into a pumpkin."
> "What?"
> "Stroke of midnight."
> "Midnight?"
> "End of the ball."
> "Dude, it's like . . . it's like five."

Cinderella is an obvious example of an innocent persecuted heroine, though the exchange here highlights the temporal nature of her enchantment.

In "The Target" (1, 2) the man who rents Echo for an engagement turns out to be a psychopath who enjoys killing women for sport (see Tresca's chapter). After he creates a scenario in which Echo becomes his prey, he refers to himself as the "big bad wolf." Further, in the eighth episode, Ballard dreams he is kissing Echo, but she goes still and dead. Her pale, waxy skin contrasts against the bright red of her lipstick and her dark hair, visually suggesting a Snow White or Sleeping Beauty in reverse, as though Ballard's kiss has killed rather than revived her. Even though Echo is established as a strong character in her other interactions during the show, through these intertextual references she is shown to be in need of rescue.

Leading up to the events in "Briar Rose" when Ballard finally manages to storm the impenetrable castle of the Dollhouse, he, too, is framed with fairy-tale references. In "The Target," some of Ballard's colleagues mock him by saying, "A couple kids found a house in the woods all made of candy and gingerbread. We thought that might be up your alley." When in "Man on the Street" (1, 6), Ballard finally manages to locate and interrogate a Dollhouse client (a task that takes him many episodes, as the organization has enough high-ranking allies to help it cover its trail), the client rhetorically turns the tables on Ballard. The client redirects the conversation to Ballard's fantasy about rescuing Caroline (the real name of Echo's Doll body), saying, "But then the brave little FBI agent whisked her away from the cash-wielding losers and restored her true identity—and she fell in love with him." These references to "Hansel and Gretel" (ATU 327A) and "The Brave Little Tailor" (ATU 1640) from the Grimms' collection establish Ballard as a hero and rescuer.

In "Briar Rose," at the end of the scene in which Echo reads the fairy tale to Susan, viewers are shown the prince's illustration in the fairy-tale book; immediately, the camera cuts to Ballard, strengthening the implication that he is the prince figure. However, as the events in "Briar Rose" reveal, Ballard misjudges the situation: Caroline/Echo is not in need of rescue in the sense that Ballard thought, nor is he the hero he imagined himself to be. His helper in breaking into the Dollhouse is Alpha (Alan Tudyk), one of the show's villains, and Dollhouse security apprehends Ballard while Alpha steals away Echo. Ballard's embodiment of the rescuer role turns out to be misguided and misdirected. Part of the problem is that he is locked in his internal fantasy, his facile interpretation of the scenario that positioned him as the prince: "He could not understand that the Sleeping Beauty was awake and thinking, feeling pain and solving problems, because he was so sure of her being asleep" (Deritter 2010, 196). Indeed, after Alpha kidnaps Echo in "Briar Rose," she rescues herself in the following episode, demonstrating that both the characterizations of Echo as helpless heroine and Ballard as prince–rescuer are stereotypes that were meant to be broken.

The first season's main antagonist, Alpha (a Doll whose imprinted personalities have all merged with his original serial killer personality, thus making him extremely unstable and dangerous), also fits within a fairy-tale role in "Briar Rose." The only references to him prior to that episode were verbal, not visual, and they obviously position him as villain. In "Briar Rose," once he apprehends Echo and imprints her with a personality that recognizes and adores him, they kiss and he tells her, "I told you I'd come rescue you." She responds, "My prince." This positioning maintains Echo as the heroine in need of rescue, while viewers see that in Alpha's twisted fantasy, he is the hero rather than (as in reality) a killer who enjoys cutting up women. By setting up and then destroying fairy-tale expectations about the *Dollhouse* characters, the show uses fairy-tale intertexts in a more complicated fashion than simple retellings.

The other significant fairy-tale intertext in *Dollhouse* does not involve a specific tale but rather discourse about fairy tales in general. "Briar Rose" (and indeed, much of the scholarship on it) takes for granted the Bettelheim notion that fairy tales can and should be used therapeutically. As folklore scholars know, fairy tales are not universal or timeless; instead, their meanings and uses are socially determined. Jack Zipes writes, "The fairy tales we have come to revere as classical are not ageless, universal, and beautiful in and of themselves, and they are not the best therapy in the world for children" (2006a, 11). Indeed, fairy tales serve many functions, including the indoctrination of children with appropriate values coated in a film of appealing magic. For example, starting with the French court in the 1690s, "fairy tales were cultivated to ensure that young people would be properly groomed for their social functions" (ibid., 30).

There is nothing inherently therapeutic about fairy tales, but due to the popularity of Bettelheim's ideas, as discussed above, many North Americans uncritically believe that one of these stories' main purposes is to aid children in processing their issues. Bettelheim proclaims, "While it entertains the child, the fairy tale enlightens him about himself, and fosters his personality development. It offers meaning on so many different levels, and enriches the child's existence in so many ways, that no book can do justice to the multitude of contributions such tales make to the child's life" (1976, 12). This idea has been absorbed into the premise of "Briar Rose" that Echo's reading the tale to Susan will prompt the girl to evaluate and resolve her problems. Part of the evidence for this connection is that it is unclear whether Echo has been programmed to read "Sleeping Beauty" to Susan and the other children or makes that choice herself.[15] Either way, the naturalness of reading fairy tales to troubled children goes unquestioned.

However, just as the character roles trouble normative fairy-tale images, so too does the therapeutic reading of a fairy tale in the episode deepen the ways in which such narratives are made meaningful. Unlike the *Grimm's Fairy Tale Classics* episode's reaffirmation of Bettelheim's equation of sleep with steady maturation, the *Dollhouse* episode questions whether sleep provides a direct therapeutic parallel. Here, we disagree with Valerie Estelle Frankel's Bettelheim-inflected interpretation of Briar Rose's enchanted sleep: "When she has finished developing, the thorns part, the princess wakes, the prince is waiting" (2010, 69). Frankel writes, further, that if "little Susan is another Sleeping Beauty, trapped in the horrors of her abuse and unable to escape, Echo is her reflected self. . . . As they read the fairytale together, Echo is rousing from her enchanted sleep and gaining self-awareness, but she is still as exploited as her young charge" (ibid., 68). Associating development into maturity with the situations that trap Echo and Susan—slumbering until they are rescued—is ignorant at best and condoning abuse at worst. A Bettelheim-inspired interpretation of the tale (sleep as innocent growth) is manifestly incompatible with a reading of abused (and enslaved, in Echo's case) characters as sleeping (sleep as processing the horrors of childhood sexuality, so far from innocence). This comparison is especially fraught since the characters experience molestation at night,[16] leaving them most vulnerable during sleep, a time that (according to Bettelheim) protects the girls as they evolve into their mature selves.

Instead, we argue that *Dollhouse* uses the generally accepted idea that fairy tales can be therapeutic but does so critically. The fairy tale only "works" for Susan when she revises it so that she can emotionally relate to it as an active rather than passive character.[17] She says (viewers cannot see the book's text, so we do not know if she is reading or making up her own version), "The prince said, 'I will not let this stop me. I'm as strong as any spell. I'm as strong as any thorns. I won't let anything stop me from reaching her and saving her. I will go and rescue the Sleeping Beauty.'" Though Susan never appears again, she sounds convinced; it appears that she will be capable of working through her childhood abuse by revising the fairy tale. Simply expecting fairy tales to guide children through difficult times, then, is portrayed as unrealistic and overly simplistic. In fact, when Echo first reads the tale to the children, Susan's initial retort of "This is crap" becomes a full-fledged tantrum in which she screams and tears pages from the book. In contrast, Ballard's naïve acceptance of (and desire for) his fairy-tale role as rescuer is subverted by the episode's plot. He ends up being used by Alpha, not even able to rescue himself. Being mature enough to know when to accept and when to revise fairy tales is, thus, one of the show's more sophisticated points about the uses of enchantment.

The show's feminist content is, like its use of fairy tales, complicated and at times ambiguous. Certain patterns of sexist and misogynist behavior are explicitly critiqued within the show, thus placing it within a political feminist framework. Ballard is "revealed to be living out a homogenised heroic narrative that can be traced back to a patriarchal fairy tale" (Vinci 2011, 240). His narrow interpretation of events not only fails him but also shows how he is entrenched within the same destructive ideologies as those he fights and those he seeks to rescue. "Whedon's own radical feminist credo [posits]: it is the Man within society who programs women, and by doing so, sets them up to succeed or fail" (Coker 2010, 236). Similarly, in some fairy tales, only those heroines who follow their social programming to be dutiful and self-negating get ahead (Stone 1985). And, "The feminist ethos of *Dollhouse* is a thorough explication of what makes society an enemy of women, and how women can fight society and hopefully make it better. . . . Whedon has made it clear that he believes women's rights are an ongoing issue" (Coker 2010, 237).

However, foregrounding women's rights by depicting their objectification and violence against them in order to critique these processes is a slippery slope. Teresa de Lauretis's phrase "story demands sadism" (qtd. in Bacchilega 1993, 4) is certainly apt here. All the Dolls, and especially Echo, undergo constant physical and emotional violence: "Sometimes she's just generally beaten up, but a surprising number of the episodes involve her getting directly punched, in the face, by a man . . . it indicates a generally pervasive, less spoken male fantasy—the desire to perform harm, with one's own two hands, on a woman who is stronger" (Simons 2011, n.p.). This pattern certainly fits within the degradation that innocent persecuted heroines must face: "Undergoing humiliation therefore becomes the common experience for fairy tale princesses . . . fairy tale heroines are expected to accept willingly, or even be grateful for, these degradations" (Lin 2010, 85).

Although one could view Echo's subjugation as appropriate based on the evidence that she fulfills the innocent persecuted heroine role, it is still disturbing to see how "Echo is the ultimate male fantasy—she is a woman that literally anything can be done to for the right amount of money, with those actions then simply erased afterward" (Simons 2011, n.p.).[18] While *Dollhouse* presents and critiques misogyny, fulfilling the political feminist directive, the show also questions the inevitability of gendered power dynamics in a subtle and at times ambiguous way, engaging with theoretical feminism but perhaps not explicitly enough condemning sexism. Thus, from a feminist perspective, *Dollhouse*'s engagement with women's issues remains problematic.

Overall, the use of fairy tales in *Dollhouse* as text (with the reading of "Briar Rose" aloud), context (the framing of the Dollhouse itself as an enchanted castle full of sleepers), and subtext (the incorporation of the idea of fairy tales as therapeutic) is perfectly appropriate. "The Dollhouse can . . . be viewed as a microcosm for society itself. As children, we are programmed with gender expectations, sexual mores, and the thousands of other bits of cultural coding that we take for granted every day" (Coker 2010, 228). Fairy tales are undoubtedly part of this process, and thus with its many intertextual references, *Dollhouse* both implicitly and explicitly acknowledges the role of fairy tales among other expressive forms as an aspect of our cultural programming.

Dreaming Gender

Both the children's anime *Grimm's Fairy Tale Classics* and the adult program *Dollhouse* address the impact of social messages on and for the characters therein and thereby, implicitly, also the audiences. While gender roles and sexuality are major and obvious themes, the overall role of identity—whose identity and how it is shaped—is also implicated. The fairy-tale tropes that both shows integrate and alter in subtle but significant ways demonstrate that identity is a contested and constructed process, constrained and compelled by multiple forces. The notion of an internal, essential self (which may resist, fall victim to, or be created through the execution of social messages) is explored in both shows, as seen in the treatment of classic ATU 410 motifs such as the curse and the rescue as well as more general notions of power and control.

In both programs, the curse highlights how little control individuals have over the shaping of their identities. In *Dollhouse,* all the Dolls are "sleeping" in some sense of the word.[19] What precipitates the long sleep in both fairy-tale intertext and TV show is a curse. "No one 'volunteers' for the Dollhouse without having experienced some sort of 'curse,' usually trauma" (Palma 2012, 91). Echo's trauma results from her boyfriend's death and evading Rossum's corporate forces; other Dolls struggle with posttraumatic stress disorder and grief. The choice to "sleep" away trauma or grief is never free or unconstrained, for the Dollhouse's head, Adelle DeWitt (Olivia Williams), dangles bait "in front of desperate people she saw as perfect fits for the Dollhouse" (Anderson 2010, 163).[20]

In *Grimm's Fairy Tale Classics,* by contrast, the unavoidable curse is merely that of growing up, something everyone must experience (a fact that makes it no less unpleasant) in their journey toward becoming themselves. Though Briar Rose has no control over her fate in experiencing the curse, the twelfth witch's action ensures that the sleeping spell is not the end of life but rather a pause before awakening to new life. Even though Briar Rose, like all teenagers, must still remain "cursed," the twelfth witch plays a role of unexpected power, enforcing the idea that destinies can be changed.

Additionally, both shows deal with notions of rescuing or saving. While in *Grimm's Fairy Tale Classics,* the dream connection of the prince and princess highlights their ideal partnership, *Dollhouse*'s multiple, often failed, rescue attempts reveal that "the only person who can really save Briar Rose is herself" (Palma 2012, 90). Thus, "rescue is a gift one can only give to one's self" (Ellis 2011, 48). Both Echo and her original personality, Caroline, experience a strong need to save people, up to and including saving the world.[21] One reason Echo must save or rescue herself is that she *is* multiple selves; one of the show's plot arcs concerns her relation to the core self or soul of sleeping Caroline's body. Even when she experiences a composite event like Alpha's, she does not go insane. Instead, Echo's ability to integrate myriad identities is a literalization of her saving herself. Thus, any external attempt to save her (like Ballard's or Alpha's) will fail. Approaching rescue from a different angle, the *Grimm's Fairy Tale Classics* episode emphasizes that only the prince can rescue Briar Rose because theirs is a union of equals: a partnership, not a property exchange. Other men who try to rescue Briar Rose fail utterly because their attempts reflect their desire to possess the princess.

Both shows also emphasize the power of women in the rescue scenario. While the twelfth witch in *Grimm's Fairy Tale Classics* boldly proclaims, "I will save the fair princess," Susan in the *Dollhouse* episode imagines herself as the prince: "I'm as strong as any spell. I'm as strong as any thorns. I won't let anything stop me from reaching her and saving her. I will go and rescue the Sleeping Beauty." These congruent statements of agency, as performative acts, narratively demonstrate that women can take control of their situations and help other women—and sometimes also themselves.

Another intriguing overlap between the two ATU 410 television texts also concerns rescue. After the disastrous (but perhaps not surprising) attempt to read the fairy tale aloud, Echo tells Susan, "Briar Rose was trapped all that time, sleeping. And dreaming, of getting out. The prince was her dream. She made him. She made him fight to get her out." She could have been describing the *Grimm's Fairy Tale Classics* version of "Briar Rose" in which the heroine really *does* dream the prince and lead him to her. The latter rendition makes explicit what must be verbally unpacked in *Dollhouse*: the princess of ATU 410, for all her apparent passivity, manages to actively shape her life even under the curse's duress.

This chapter is less concerned with investigating these revisions' success than interpreting their meanings. With Pauline Greenhill and Sidney Eve Matrix, "Our question is not how successfully a film translates the tale into a new medium, but, instead, what new and old meanings and uses the filmed version brings to audiences and sociocultural contexts" (2010a, 3). A superficial glance at the ATU 410 retelling in the *Grimm's Fairy Tale Classics* series might lead to dismissing it as an overly sentimental and even antifeminist version that does not significantly rewrite the Grimms' tale. Similarly, a first look at the relationship between ATU 410 and *Dollhouse* might make it appear too fragmented and dark to fully access the fairy tale's meaning. We contend, instead, that both adaptations offer highly effective uses of "Sleeping Beauty" that foreground messages about gender, identity, and society in artistic and unexpected ways.

Notes

1. See Rossetti's poem "The Prince's Progress" (2001).
2. MacDonald's story "The Light Princess" is, in many ways, a parody of the "Sleeping Beauty" tale (1999).
3. See, for example, Ellis (2008a, 2008b), Cavallaro (2010, 2011), and Lezubski's chapter on *Revolutionary Girl Utena*.
4. For example, the *Dragon Ball* series led to the creation of the film *Dragon Ball: Sleeping Beauty in the Magic Castle* in 1987 (Clements and McCarthy 2006, 161). Additionally, Kihachiro Kawamoto Film Works in 1990 produced an entire "Sleeping Beauty" film that Jonathan Clements and Helen McCarthy describe as "a sinister retelling of the fairy tale that highlights its Freudian subtexts" (ibid., 335).
5. The connected series *Tsubasa: RESERVoir CHRoNiCLE* (2005), also by CLAMP, features the Sakura character and uses "Sleeping Beauty," albeit differently.
6. Ellis outlines similarities between "Sleeping Beauty" and a version of ATU 185, "Stories about Forecasting Fortune," and notes that no true Japanese version of ATU 410 has been found (2008b, 253).
7. Due to limitations with the Japanese language, we examine only the English-language translation. We recognize recent fairy-tale scholarship focusing on issues of native and outsider values (Kuwada 2009) and on a text's reception and positioning based on how its paratextual and contextual cues are mediated in translation (Bianchi and Nannoni 2011).

8. Unless otherwise indicated, all quotations in this section are from "Briar Rose," episode 18 of *Grimm's Fairy Tale Classics*.

9. Joosen offers a discussion of the ways contemporary fairy-tale retellings frequently add character depth (2011, 14).

10. It was not until the Grimms' version that the famous kiss to awaken Sleeping Beauty was added (Rodriguez 2002, 52). Many older versions, particularly Perrault's "The Sleeping Beauty in the Wood" and Giambattista Basile's "Sun, Moon, and Talia," have the prince doing far more than stealing a kiss. Though rape of the sleeping girl is a prominent feature it does not awaken the princess (Basile 2001; Perrault 2001b).

11. See, for example, Zipes (2002a, 179–205) and Joosen (2011, 184–212).

12. This ethnocentric and classist characterization of adolescence fails to recognize how youth and maturity are coded differently across cultures. Zipes notes that Bettelheim's "book is largely male-oriented and fails to make careful distinctions between the sexes, ages, ethnicity, and class backgrounds of children" (2002a, 189). Alan Dundes discusses how Bettelheim plagiarized portions of his book and possibly even abused some of his young wards (1991). The discerning reader regards Bettelheim's writings and representations skeptically.

13. (Series, episode).

14. However, a notable fairy-tale intertext appears in the second season, when the phrases "I'm your white knight" and "I'm your beautiful damsel" are the call-and-response dynamic of other characters.

15. This is also a more general problem with Dolls, as Echo is not the only one to creatively interpret her programming on a given assignment.

16. Her handler molests/rapes Doll Sierra (Dichen Lachman) within the Dollhouse at night.

17. This is, of course, precisely the opposite of Bettelheim's method of reading fairy tales, as he was obsessed with the "original version" (usually a Grimms' variant) and his interpretations relied on the exact phrasing of the translation he used. As Dundes observes, "Bettelheim's lack of familiarity with conventional folkloristics leads him to make a number of erroneous statements" (1991, 76), among which we would include the mistaken (from a folklorist's perspective) fidelity to a single version.

18. Simons continues: "The show perpetrates the worst kinds of violence on its female characters. Over the course of the two seasons on-air, Echo is repeatedly used for intercourse and made to pretend she enjoys it, one woman is removed from Doll status because of a physical deformity, another female is steadily and terrifyingly raped by her male handler—and even the term 'handler' suggests a male role intended to actively control" (2011, n.p.).

19. Throughout the show, the Dolls are programmed to wake up after an engagement and say, "Have I been asleep?" Further, when Alpha during "Briar Rose" adjusts the chemicals in the air being piped into the Dolls' sleeping pods he mutters to himself, "Stay asleep." During "Haunted" (1, 10), Topher (Fran Kranz) programs the Doll Sierra to embody his best buddy (someone who loves computer games, potato chips, and laser tag) to keep him company on what would be an otherwise solitary birthday, and she asks him why they can't play with "the sleepies."

20. Anderson comments, "These were people who were tired of telling their own stories, who couldn't handle living with situations brought about by or despite their choices, and chose instead to put themselves into the story of Sleeping Beauty. But here the

princess deliberately pricked her finger, because life in the castle was just too much" (2010, 163). This interpretation suggests Echo as a telling counterpart to the princess in *Grimm's Fairy Tale Classics* who certainly appeared unhappy with her situation, but not to the point of muting her pain by choosing the sleeping death.

21. Caroline, before her capture by Rossum and coercion into signing away her body, was trying to uncover and expose unethical animal testing in Rossum's labs. Whatever residue remained of Caroline's personality influenced Echo to also become a savior figure, constantly trying to rescue her friends when they were in trouble (see Espenson 2010).

8

THE POWER TO REVOLUTIONIZE THE WORLD, OR ABSOLUTE GENDER APOCALYPSE?

Queering the New Fairy-Tale Feminine
in *Revolutionary Girl Utena*

Kirstian Lezubski

J apanese animation, or anime, has often collided or, to paraphrase Dani Cavallaro, colluded with the fairy tale (2011, 1; see also Jorgensen and Warman's chapter). From Hata Masami's[1] 1971 *Andersen Stories* to Dezaki Osamu's 2005–2006 *The Snow Queen*, anime has often turned to fairy-tale themes, symbols, and characters (Cavallaro 2010, 64–65). The two forms are well suited for each other. Anime's potential to engage and challenge contemporary issues of its moment and time (Napier 2001, 4) mirrors fairy tales' capacity to subvert and destabilize, as much as to establish and propagate, current ideologies, for example around gender issues (see Zipes [1983a] 1991; Haase 2004a). Thus, modern television anime series with fairy-tale elements present a unique opportunity to examine how gender ideologies are secured, subverted, and shifted in response to contemporary issues, both narratively and cinematographically.[2]

This chapter examines how the female gender category and the master narrative of heteronormative love are reproduced and how that reproduction is queered through fairy tale in the 1990s *shōjo*, or girls', TV anime productions *Sailor Moon* and *Revolutionary Girl Utena*.[3] *Sailor Moon* met with sweeping success when it aired from 1992 until 1997 and has been credited with revitalizing the magical girl genre by casting girls as action heroes (Grigsby 1998, 60, 68; Gravett 2004, 78). However, at the narrative's heart is a fairy-tale plot about a destined prince and princess whose love saves the world. This figure of the fairy-tale princess, representing such idealized feminine characteristics as "patience, virtue, inherent beauty and magic" (Ashliman 2008, 771) and submission, dependence, and self-sacrifice (Kuykendal and Sturm 2007, 39) has important reverberations in contemporary Japanese media as well as traditional norms for feminine behavior. While some have identified a new feminine gender category in 1990s Japan (see Stefánsson 1998; Choo 2008), the princess's presence in media productions of this decade suggests instead a reiteration of the heteronormative binary gender system in which the figures of the prince and princess have come to represent static and "oversimplified gender role stereotype[s]" (Kuykendal and Sturm 2007, 39).

However, as popular as *Sailor Moon* was at the time, other media products, like fan-made comics and pornography, began to question its master narrative of heteronormativity (see Grigsby 1998; Kinsella 1998). These responses originated from the industry's margins, not from the Saturday prime-time slot that *Sailor Moon* left behind. But not too far from that prime-time spot, playing Wednesdays at 6:30 p.m.,[4] was a series produced by one of the *Sailor Moon* directors. While it never reached the same popularity, the 1997 *Revolutionary Girl Utena* (*RGU*) was as critical a response as any mainstream anime could be. Opposing *Sailor Moon*'s narrative of heterosexual love, *RGU* destabilizes the gender categories that its predecessor reproduces by constructing its prince and princess as transgender figures capable of revolutionizing the "schematic notions" (Zipes 2011, 19) of fairy-tale gender. In doing so, the series refigures fairy-tale gender into queer spaces of individual and societal transformation, encoded in the show as "revolution," rather than static representations of heteronormativity, encoded as "apocalypse." *RGU* suggests that the master narrative of binary gender is stagnant and limiting and opens a space where the "'unliveable' and 'uninhabitable'" (Butler 1993, 3) fairy tale of heteronormativity can be queered.

RGU through Fairy-Tale and Transgender Theory

Often described as the quintessential postmodern fairy tale,[5] *RGU* has been the subject of much study. At least seven articles on or referencing it have appeared in the journal *Mechademia* since its inception in 2006[6]; Emily Hurford published an MA thesis involving queer readings of the *RGU* manga (comic book) in 2009; and *Empty Movement,* the internet's largest English-language *RGU* fan site, has a special section dedicated to fan-written analyses. This growing wealth of scholarly and fan work testifies to the recognition of *RGU* and anime in general as "an art form of widely acclaimed autonomous calibre" (Cavallaro 2011, 1) that is capable of engaging serious social issues of its time.

Like Cristina Bacchilega's seminal (and contemporaneous) *Postmodern Fairy Tales, RGU* is mainly concerned with genre as "a powerful discourse which produces representations of gender" (1997, 9–10). Bacchilega focuses on revisionist tales by Western authors, but *RGU,* though neither Western nor a revision but an original story using fairy-tale elements, fits well into her description. For her, postmodern fairy tales "question and remake the classic fairy tale's production of gender [and] . . . . expose the fairy tale's complicity with the 'exhausted' forms and ideologies of traditional Western narrative . . . in order to question and recreate the rules of narrative production, especially as such rules contribute to naturalizing subjectivity and gender . . . [and] replace or relocate the fairy tale to multiply its performance potential and denaturalize its institutionalized power" (1997, 23). *RGU* manages to do all these things at once, which Bacchilega suggests Western revisionist tales do not (ibid.). Examining postmodern fairy tales outside the West, then, may reveal new nuances.

Transgender studies have also faced concerns about Eurocentrism. While the creators of *RGU* may not have foreseen it, the series' presentation of transgressive gender—as well as this chapter—responds to Helen Hok-Sze Leung's call for research and recognition of transgender subjectivities and representations outside Europe and North America. According to Leung, transnational research would keep the field of transgender studies from "reifying into an exclusionary narrative that is rooted only in the experiences" of the West (2006, 686). As an example, Hurford argues that *RGU* can present a challenge to the heteronormative expectations of American audiences (2009, 17). Yet divorcing anime and manga from its cultural moment does little to help identify either heteronormativity or queer responses to it in modern Japan, and while male homosexuality has been well documented and studied (see Leupp 1995; Pflugfelder 1999; McLelland 2000), lesbian and transgender subjectivities remained to some degree invisible in Japanese society and Western academic work of the 1990s (McLelland 2000, 10; Chalmers 2002, 2).

Using Western transgender theory to address Japanese subjectivities may, of course, fall into the trap that Leung warns against. Aware of the problems of applying inappropriately culture-based theory, Hurford draws on Mark J. McLelland's work on male homosexuality in Japan to argue that Foucauldian gender theory does not apply, as historically same-sex interactions were understood as social, rather than identity-making, acts (2009, 13). However, McLelland notes, "Japan . . . has not, *until very recently*, entertained the notion that 'sexuality' connotes an 'identity'" (2000, 2, emphasis added). Both McLelland (2000, 25) and Hurford (2009, 11) recognize the push toward Westernization in the Meiji era of Japanese history (1868–1912) as the moment when Western concepts of sexuality were imported, which aligns with the date of 1870 that Michel Foucault gives for the conception of modern discourses of homosexuality (1980, 43). This is not to say that Western gender ideologies transformed Japan but rather that "the very notion of the sexual as a distinct realm of human consciousness and experience was being constituted simultaneously in different societies" (McLelland 2005, 3). These emerging parallels between discourses of gender identity in the West and in Japan suggest that the gendering of modern Japanese subjectivities has indeed become an issue that can be addressed through Western gender theory.

Shōjo, the Culture Industry, and the Ryōsai Kenbo

Japanese manga and anime business forms a culture industry (Grigsby 1999, 183), as *Sailor Moon* exemplifies. Between the beginning of the series in 1992 and its end in 1997, Bandai sold US$1.5 billion worth of branded merchandise (Grigsby 1998, 60). This success belies the period known as "the lost decade"—when the Japanese bubble economy burst, due in part to a rise in surplus savings, a lack of conspicuous consumption, and the resulting deflation (see Tabuchi 2009; Fukao 2010). Yet even as the economy crashed down around them, young Japanese girls and their parents flocked in droves to buy Sailor Moon dolls, jewelry, and dress-up kits that would transform children into the series' eponymous Moon Princess. The franchise even outlasted the lost decade, with a new anime adaptation announced for 2013 ("Sailor Moon" 2012). That new *Sailor Moon* products continue to be pumped into the market while discussions of *RGU* merchandise are relegated to dusty corners of the internet attests to *Sailor Moon*'s normativity and its function in the cultural industry.

FIGURE 8.1 Tenjō Utena, left, as the prince, and Himemiya Anthy, right, as the Rose Bride. *RGU*, "Their Eternal Apocalypse," episode 25.

Though queer subjectivities were gaining visibility in 1990s Japan (McLelland 2005, 212), *Sailor Moon*'s emphasis on the destined heteronormative love of the fairy-tale prince and princess participates in a culture industry that reinforces traditional gender norms "cyclically as rigid invariants" (Horkheimer and Adorno 2002, 98). However, as Jack Zipes argues, "Though the traditional fairy tale has been greatly commodified . . . new forms of fairy tales and storytelling have not been proscribed or prevented from emerging. Nor are we as subjects bound to be homogenized, our identities totally determined as types of commodities" (1997, 9). *RGU* resists the homogenizing tendency of modern fairy-tale gender as seen in *Sailor Moon* and thus calls attention to the cyclical resurgences of these gendered norms.

RGU isn't one single work but includes the 1996 manga series by Saito Chiho, the 1997 thirty-nine-episode television series directed by Ikuhara Kunihiko, the 1999 theatrical animated film and the accompanying manga volume, various stage productions, and one video game.[7] In this chapter I focus primarily on the anime TV series. The narrative is multilayered and complex, heavily symbolic, and at times patently absurd—for example, the series' battles take place atop a floating arena underneath a rotating, upside-down castle, all explained as a "trick of the light" ("The Rose Bride," episode 1). To summarize: *RGU* is about princes and princesses. The main characters, Tenjō Utena (voiced by Kawakami Tomoko) and Himemiya Anthy (voiced by Fuchizaki Yuriko; see Figure 8.1), fourteen-year-old girls, attend Ōtori Academy and work through their adolescences as they search for their princes. Utena is introduced through a literal fairy tale: once upon a time, a young princess who had fallen into despair met a traveling prince, who gifted her with a ring to lead them together again in the future. However, as the prince rode away on his white horse, the princess realized that she admired him so much that she decided to become a prince instead of a princess ("The Rose Bride," episode 1).[2] Within the show's first minutes, Utena's decision to grow up a prince queers the heteronormative figures of the prince and princess.

Other than its trans-prince, though, *RGU* abides by many *shōjo* themes. The term *shōjo* means young women—a demographic rather than a genre—but in this context refers to stories that emphasize the heroine's psychological growth through love and interpersonal relationships (Thorn 2001), which are often homosocial and occasionally romantic. This emphasis on same-sex relationships can be traced to the same period of Westernization that saw the rise of gendered identities in Japan (Thorn 2001; Dollase 2003, 725–26). At this time *shōjo* publications became a distinct entity, as "children's magazines began to be segregated, as was the education system itself, along gender lines" (Thorn 2001). Simultaneously, Western texts such as *Little Women* were translated into Japanese with the intention of educating girls into the typical feminine ideology of the time, the *ryōsai kenbo,* or "good wife, wise mother" (Dollase 2003, 725–26, 736; see also Gössmann et al. 2004, 183). But though these early texts were meant to teach them how to grow up to be proper women, Japanese girls often interpreted them as escapist experiences, in which they could ignore "social expectations" (Honda Masuko qtd. in Dollase 2003, 730), which can be inferred from the contents: men are nearly invisible, and female homosocial and homoerotic relationships are at the forefront (ibid., 744). As such, stories provided a site for covert resistance to the *ryōsai kenbo* dogma, allowing Japanese girls to explore alternate modes of femininity, including same-sex relationships.

However, this resistance could occur only within girls' narratives, not in society at large. Hiromi Tsuchiya Dollase's study of the early *shōjo* text *Hanamonogatari* shows that "the realistic issue of marriage intrudes upon [girlhood]. . . . In reality, same sex love was never prioritized over hetero-sexual love in society. . . . [Girls] understood their destiny, accepting their social roles as mothers and wives" (2003, 746). Her claim, then, that same-sex love was socially acceptable in Japan until the 1920s (ibid., 744) is only partially true. While, historically, male homosexual practices were widely accepted (McLelland 2000, 20), lesbian relationships were construed as play and practice and limited to girls' school days before marriage (Dollase 2003, 744, 746). Thus, while early *shōjo* texts may have provided girls with a site for subversion, in reality they were normatively limited to becoming *ryōsai kenbo,* good wives and mothers.

This ideal of female normativity continues to crop up in the Japanese psyche during periods of social reform and discord. A history of gender in modern Japan notes that the Second World War saw a "revived version" of the *ryōsai kenbo* ideology, which again resurfaced in media of the 1980s and 1990s, the period leading up to the lost decade (Gössmann et al. 2004, 183, 211–12). The constructed nature of the ideology becomes clear, as its revival failed to match the reality. During World War II, traditional female gender categories were thrown into conflict with the war effort, while in 1990—just before the *Sailor Moon* manga hit shelves—women were already making up at least 40 percent of the paid work force (Havens 1975, 914; Foreign Press Center Japan 2007, 192). Though television had begun to present a diverse range of female experience by the 1990s, the underlying concern was often with a domesticized femininity (Gössmann et al. 2004, 211–12), and popular *shōjo* texts of this time also focused on reconstituting their girl characters into the *ryōsai kenbo* paradigm (see Choo 2008).

Sailor Moon, the Princess, and the New Feminine of 1990s Japan

Sailor Moon itself can be read as a popular culture reiteration of the *ryōsai kenbo* ideology, updated for the end of the twentieth century. Like *RGU,* the story is wrapped up in fairy tale: Tsukino Usagi (voiced by Mitsuishi Kotono), an ordinary fourteen-year-old girl, meets a talking cat that gifts her with a magical brooch that can transform her into Sailor Moon, the pretty soldier of love and peace. Usagi befriends other pretty soldiers as well as Tuxedo Mask (voiced by Furuya Tōru), a dashing gentleman in a full tuxedo and cape with whom she falls in love, who all help her on her mission to fight evil and find the lost Princess of the Moon.

But all semblance of ordinariness is shot when Usagi herself is revealed as the princess. As the fairy tale goes, once upon a time[9] Princess Serenity of the Moon Kingdom and Prince Endymion of Earth were destroyed in an epic battle of good versus evil. Reincarnated on Earth in the 1990s, Serenity and Endymion (Tuxedo Mask) must be reconciled in the present, or the entire world will be at stake. Henceforth the narrative shifts from an emphasis on friendship to hammering home the eternal, heteronormative love of the prince and princess that saves the day.[10] Not all relationships in *Sailor Moon* are defined by heteronormativity; two villains from the first season are gay, Sailor Neptune and Uranus (voiced respectively by Katsuki Masako and Ogata Megumi) are in a lesbian relationship, and in the last season, Seiya (voiced by Niiyama Shiho), who passes as male but is revealed to be female when he transforms into Sailor Star Fighter, tries to woo Usagi in Tuxedo Mask's absence. This attempt fails, though, after Seiya's female sex is revealed and Tuxedo Mask returns. In the end, *Sailor Moon*'s queer relationships all pale in comparison to the destined love of Princess Serenity and Prince Endymion.

Not only is the heterosexual relationship idealized over others, but Princess Serenity's adherence to traditional gender norms is actually constructed as saving the universe. In the second season, Usagi learns she is destined to become Neo-Queen Serenity of the thirtieth century. With her husband King Endymion, she bears one princess named Chibi-Usa (a diminutive of Usagi; voiced by Araki Kae), who in the fourth season begins a relationship with a boy who appears to her as a winged horse. That Chibi-Usa wants to be "a real lady like mom" ("Waizuman no Mashu," 2, 37), even falling in love with a fairy-tale figure, suggests that Usagi's daughter is more than just the de facto heir to Neo-Queen Serenity's throne. She deliberately replicates the signifiers of what it means to be a fairy-tale princess, discernible through the differences between Usagi and Neo-Queen Serenity, the latter more beautiful, graceful, soft-spoken, and well mannered.[11] But another important quality of the fairy-tale princess is the reproduction of the kingdom: she is "both the source of life and the source of rule," birthing more fairy-tale princesses who will grow up to reproduce the fairy tale again (Do Rozario 2004, 51). Rebecca-Anne Do Rozario's comment refers to Disney princess films, but the message also applies to *Sailor Moon*'s mainstream Disneyfied ideas: to be a princess means to be a heteronormative female who marries a prince, becomes a queen, and bears other princes and princesses.

This connection of the princess figure to heteronormative gender expectations for females also occurs in contemporaneous Japanese media productions outside of anime and had serious real-world repercussions for women of the time. In 1992–1993, the Japanese media was engrossed with the story of "'two princes' and their 'Cinderellas'" (Stefánsson 1998, 155)—the engagements of imperial crown Prince Naruhito to Owada Masako and people's prince of sumo Takanohana to Miyazawa Rie. Halldór Stefánsson argues that Owada and Miyazawa, career women respectively raised outside Japan and born half-Japanese, were seen as "a whole variety of 'new' female . . . oblivious to the proper order of things in the relations between the sexes, or to their 'destiny' to become housewives and mothers" (1998, 160). Miyazawa's relationship ended in dissolution, for reasons that may have included her refusal to give up her career. In contrast, Owada, crowned an official princess after her marriage to Prince Naruhito, is objectified even in Stefánsson's final paragraphs, when he writes that Naruhito "gained" a wife who "gave him privileged access" to a new world of international politics (1998, 157, 163–64).

Kukhee Choo notes the reconfiguration of gender norms in manga of the same period. Choo argues that, while *shōjo* of the 1960s and 1970s was subversive, 1990s *shōjo* saw "a shift towards a more domestic portrayal of femininity that seems to suggest a new formation of gender relationships" (2008, 276). Choo seems to use "new" to mean "recent," not "novel," suggesting that this gendered relationship actually returns to a traditional fairy tale as espoused in the relationship between prince and princess. She writes, "In order for [1990s *shōjo*] females to assert their status proportionate to all the Prince Charmings, they may be reverting back to the most traditional and most conservative—the 'ultra' domestic and nurturing—'mother' figure" (2008, 281, 290).

For Stefánsson, the new feminine similarly leads to a "new form of marginalization" that prejudices against the independence of 1990s Japanese women like Miyazawa (1998, 156). The ubiquitous princess figure offers another example: in 1993 the Japanese press—maybe taking a page from the British coverage of Princess Diana and Prince Charles's separation (Talmadge 2011)—unleashed an unprecedented and unprovoked attack against Empress Michiko, accusing her of bullying court staff, recklessly damaging the palace grounds to suit her own whims, and generally being "domineering, extravagant and thoughtless" (Sanger 1993). The fact that Empress Michiko is described elsewhere as soft-spoken, bland, and a master of the arts—"traits befitting the traditional role of Empress" (Lee 2000, 81)—suggests that the press's main annoyance was a suspected transgression against what royal women are supposed to represent: submissive, compliant, and selfless femininity.

Compared to the popular media's anxieties over real-life royal women, *Sailor Moon*'s Princess Serenity compliantly reproduces the culture industry's fairy tale of the normative and proper princess who marries a prince and bears a princely lineage, all the while remaining properly feminized. This new feminine that Stefánsson and Choo see emerging in the Japanese media of the 1990s actually reiterates traditional gendered relationships in which female subjectivity is fulfilled through marriage and motherhood and by submission to the patriarchal system of Japanese gender norms. Running counter to Japanese women's independence in the 1990s, the ideology is not a modern invention but a repetition of an old idea of feminine norms: the culture industry's cyclically emerging fairy tale of the prince and princess—the unlivable fairy tale of heteronormative love that saves the day.

Ikuhara and the Uninhabitable Fairy Tale: From *Sailor Moon* to *RGU*

However, Japanese women were not the only individuals affected by the normative fairy tale of the prince and princess. This narrative influenced tale-tellers as well, and *Sailor Moon* and *RGU* are both connected to one such storyteller, director Ikuhara Kunihiko. Two years after the media's obsessions with Owada, Rie, and Michiko and four years after beginning work on *Sailor Moon*, Ikuhara left the series, citing lack of creative control, and turned to *RGU*. According to the *RGU* director's commentary, he intended the series to be something else, something different from *Sailor Moon* ("The One," episode 37). In response to a question about female homoerotic relationships in *Sailor Moon* and *RGU*, he said, "I've tried to kill off Tuxedo Mask. . . . But no matter how many times I tried to kill him, he gets resurrected. . . . If I have a guy in the show, the love relationship gets to have a bigger role. . . . I thought it would be a loss if that would be the big motif just because a girl was the main character. I think there could be more shows with other motives than that" (Empty Movement 2000). Unlike *Sailor Moon*'s master narrative of heteronormative binary gender, *RGU* was meant to "change the world" (*RGU*, "The One," episode 37, director's commentary).

Beginning in 1997, the same year *Sailor Moon* ended its television reign, *RGU* reintroduced the figures of the prince and princess but did not simply reproduce them. Rather, *RGU*'s fairy-tale figures are a postmodern repetition with a difference (Taylor and Winquist 2001, 339). Responding to a question about the show's "prince and princess perspectives," Ikuhara says, "The story's opening itself feels a little old, doesn't it? (That was deliberate, by the way.) With a prince and stuff. Then we turn it around; it's only a fable—because what we want to express is 'revolutionary girls.' Because this is a story about becoming free of something that rules you" (Ikuhara 2011b, 17). The series not only deconstructs fairy-tale genders through Utena and Anthy, who I argue are a trans-prince and a trans-princess, but it also suggests that *without* such a transformation in the way gendered subjectivities are understood, the world is doomed to an apocalyptic end.

I use the "trans" modifier here to symbolize the transgressive and transformative possibilities of nonconforming gender identities. Susan Stryker outlines "transgender" as an umbrella term encompassing "individuals who were marginalized or oppressed due to their difference from social norms of gendered embodiment." Transgender theory thus has connotations of "changing sex," not just through surgical or material means but also through critical confrontations of gender discourses (2006, 4). Eva Hayward, considering differences between the prefixes "trans-" (as in transgender, transform) and "re-" (as in return, renew), asks, is transgender "transformation also re-generative?" (2008, 251). Extending her question to *RGU,* can transformation be revolutionary? Moreover, without transformation, are Japanese girls of the 1990s lost, destined only to repetition, as the old adage about history goes? Through its trans-prince and trans-princess, *RGU,* concerned with revolutionizing the cyclical repetition of fairy-tale gender in modern Japanese society, provides a timely answer.

Utena as Trans-Prince

Unlike *Sailor Moon*'s cisgender (normatively gendered) prince, *RGU*'s Tenjō Utena is a trans-prince, a fairy-tale figure in the process of regenerative transformation of gendered embodiment. Utena enacts on her body a yearning to become the prince of her childhood memories. She dresses in a version of the male school uniform, plays basketball with the boys, and fences; however, Utena denies that she acts "like a guy" and insists that she is both a girl *and* a prince ("The Rose Bride," episode 1). This doesn't need to be a

FIGURE 8.2 Utena defeats Tōga in the standard female student uniform. *RGU*, "For Friendship's Sake, Perhaps," episode 12.

contradiction: "Utena wishes to become a prince, which . . . is not exactly the same as being a boy" (Kotani 2006, 163). Some characters are less inclined to accept this view and see Utena as a tomboy waiting to find the right guy. Tōga (voiced by Koyasu Takehito), the first arc's antagonist, and Akio (voiced by Kosugi Jūrōta), the final arc's antagonist, both attempt to become her prince by constructing her as their princess in order to recuperate her into the dominant fairy tale of binary gender.

However, despite the attention that she receives from young men, Utena consistently reasserts her dual identity as a female prince. The plot begins with Utena chivalrously challenging Saionji (voiced by Kusao Takeshi), a peer who has dishonored her friend, to a duel. In winning, Utena also wins the hand of the Rose Bride, the series' princess Himemiya Anthy (*hime*, princess, is the first character of her surname). The student council members duel to make the Rose Bride their own in order to attain "the power to revolutionize the world" ("The Rose Bride").[12] From this point on, when Utena duels she transforms to wear the regal garb of a prince. Her epaulettes and sword complement her red and black outfit, subtly referencing the character design of Prince Endymion, but Utena's outfit unabashedly emphasizes her feminine figure with shorts and a jacket cinched at the waist.

While *Sailor Moon*'s prince and princess never truly question their relationship (Tuxedo Mask is often forced by their enemies to separate from Usagi, but he never doubts their chemistry), Utena and Anthy's relationship is more complex. Despite Utena's desire to become prince to a princess, she is initially less interested in dueling for the Rose Bride than in becoming her friend ("For Whom the Rose Smiles," episode 2). When Saionji returns for Anthy, Utena plans to lose—until he chauvinistically claims that the Rose Bride belongs to him. Having invoked Utena's princely sense of honor, Saionji is defeated once more, and from this point on Utena duels to give Anthy a sense of normalcy in their budding relationship and to free her from having to play the Rose Bride.

The tension between normalcy and Utena's princeliness is played up when, in episode 12, titled "For Friendship's Sake, Perhaps," Utena finally loses Anthy to the president of the student council, Tōga. In her sorrow, she turns her ideas of normality on herself and dons for the first and only time the female student uniform. However, upon realizing that a princess is essential to her identity as a prince, Utena, in a tattered blouse and skirt (see Figure 8.2), challenges and defeats Tōga. Utena's victory while dressed in the female uniform juxtaposes the inherent nature of her identity as prince against the façade of Tōga's princely male student uniform, complicating the idea that only men are princes, and women, princesses. Simultaneously feminine and noble, Utena proves that her princeliness relates less to her public gender performance—tomboy, feminine, or otherwise—than to her own intrinsic identity. Transgressing traditional norms of femininity, she simultaneously exists as prince and woman: a trans-prince.

Anthy as Trans-Princess

But if "For Friendship's Sake, Perhaps" positions Utena as the narrative's transgressive prince, it also proves that Anthy is no standard princess. Up to this point Anthy has appeared submissive and passive, shy and demure, domesticized and obedient to a fault. When Utena has transformed into her princely regalia, Anthy has magically donned a princess costume, tiara and all. During most of the dueling matches she has remained passively at the sidelines, and in this episode she stands back and silently watches

Utena battle Tōga. However, this duel differs not only in Utena's choice of the female student uniform but also because, for the first time, the narrative presents Anthy's private thoughts. Despite the small smile that she often wears around Utena, in her monologue Anthy drops her typical polite Japanese grammar and speaks plainly and coldly about how Utena is about to die under Tōga's sword.

This eerie moment foreshadows a larger narrative shift from presenting Anthy as the deferential and demure princess to instead making her a powerfully subversive woman who is machinating the dueling game and all those who participate in it, including Utena, on the behalf of her older brother, Akio. While this portrayal reaches its epitome in the narrative's last arc, a close look at the early episodes reveals it has been a subtle part of Anthy's character all along. For example, at the end of "The Rose Bride," Anthy makes a cunningly cruel comment to Saionji when she switches from addressing him as "master" to "schoolmate," reflecting his loss of the duel and of his power over her. This remark and others like it sway Saionji to challenge Utena to a second duel, which he loses. Less obvious but more unnerving is a second episode scene in which, in response to Utena's question about why she participates in the dueling game, Anthy replies subversively, "Why do you always dress like a boy, Miss Utena?" Utena's responds, "I like to," to which Anthy quickly adds, "That's my answer." Coming at the series' beginning, Anthy's peculiar answer could be overlooked or dismissed as internalized abuse, especially as the episodes progress to show her bullied and beaten by classmates and sexually abused by her brother.[13] However, none of these events occur without forwarding the plot, which are almost completely controlled by Anthy and Akio, complicating Anthy's comment that she participates because she enjoys it.

Akio and Anthy's relationship is *RGU*'s most complex, especially when it begins to involve Utena. While Akio initially performs the role of the kindly elder brother, the series slowly reveals that he is the chauvinistic and manipulative mastermind behind the dueling game. For most of the series he works his power through Anthy, but in the narrative's last arc he goes after Utena. Knowing that she dreams of finding her prince, he courts and romances her as only a prince could do, even riding in on a white horse to sweep her off her feet ("The Love," episode 35). Sensing something that reminds her of the prince from her dreams,[14] Utena falls in love with Akio and eventually has sex with him, presumably her first time ("The Prince," episode 33).

FIGURE 8.3 Akio and Anthy's fairy tale, in which the witch reveals herself as the prince's sister. *RGU*, "The Rose Crest," episode 34.

As Utena struggles to define herself as Akio's princess, she begins to question her dream of being a prince and thus her relationship with Anthy. Akio uses this uncertainty to manipulate Anthy when, in the episode following his and Utena's tryst, he tells her as she dresses after their own encounter, "I discovered a comet earlier. It's new. A star no one else knows about yet. But I won't tell anyone else about it. I won't even name it. It's amazing. . . . The feeling of discovering a new star. You feel as though doing that makes it your property" ("The Rose Crest," episode 34). The new star is Utena, Anthy's prince turned Akio's princess, but while he waits for her to respond, she silently and emotionlessly dresses, arranges her hair and glasses, and bids him good night. Frustrated by her indifference, Akio asks, "Must you still torture me?!" The subsequent shot reveals Anthy's lips as they slowly press into a thin smile.

Despite this tension, Anthy continues to act at Akio's behest, even manipulating Utena. Anthy's comment, thirty-two episodes before, is important to remember; she engages in this behavior because she herself enjoys it. As much as she plays the fairy-tale princess, she also enjoys playing the manipulative and malicious fairy-tale witch. In children's films, women who choose to transgress femininity's norms are marked with terms such as "the witch and the evil woman who lures, controls and conspires" (Mallan 2000, 26–28; see also Kuykendal and Sturm 2007, 39). But Anthy seems to perform both normative femininity when she submits to her various princes, including Akio and Utena, and witch like behavior when she emotionally manipulates them. Moreover, Utena's fairy tale about finding her prince is supplemented late in the series with Anthy's: one day, the Rose Prince—the savior of princesses everywhere—met an old lady who told him that a witch was planning to steal the light from the world. The gallant prince rode to the witch's castle to defeat her but upon his arrival was trapped by the old woman, who revealed herself to be both the witch and his younger sister (see Figure 8.3), for the Prince could never make his sister into a princess, and "a girl who cannot become a princess is doomed to become a witch!" ("The Rose Crest," episode 34). This scene's animation flashes between dissonant shots of a smiling Anthy when the title "witch" is proclaimed and shots of Akio's distant stare when the Rose Prince's name is mentioned. Though the princesses and witches of fairy tales offer mutually exclusive "simplistic and familiar binaries" of good/evil and young/old (Mallan 2000, 28) and, in this case, conforming versus nonconforming femininity, Anthy nonetheless manages to straddle and subvert both, becoming a trans-princess.

The Revolving Apocalypse

While Utena's and Anthy's identities as trans-prince and trans-princess may be transgressive in some ways, in others they are absolutely normative. Utena plays the prince's role to the hilt, while Anthy successfully embodies the deferential princess and the threatening witch, all stereotypical gendered positions. While this can be read as a failed feminist fairy tale with "straightforward reversal of gender roles and the substitution of strong female characters for more passive female characters" (Kuykendal and Sturm 2007, 40), critic Mari Kotani argues that through its girl prince in pink and its "just a bit too obedient" princess, *RGU* mocks the master narrative of heteronormativity: "[*RGU*] makes fun of the heroic heterosexuality and monogamy of traditional fairy tales such as Sleeping Beauty, Snow White, or Cinderella. Ultimately, from episode to episode, it is this queer couple that survives the series of duels—the mock prince and slave princess" (Kotani 2006, 16). Yet at the same time the latter reading fails to consider the anime series' conclusion; tragically, Utena does not technically survive the final duel. Utena's princely cross-dressing, while a queer act in and of itself, does not lead to a queer revolution of the *RGU* world, as her performance does not challenge the normative fairy tale as a whole. After all, she still requires a damsel in distress and thus constructs Anthy as one in order to define herself. This draws into question the possibility of revolution in a highly gendered fairy-tale world where "girls shouldn't brandish swords" ("End of the World," episode 38), as Akio chastises Utena before their final duel. He promises Utena that if she were to accept her position as a typical princess, "We'll be happy. Eternity will be ours and we shall love each other forever. And together, as prince and princess, we'll live in the castle forever and ever," perpetuating the heteronormative fairy tale seen in *Sailor Moon* and the Japanese media.

Such a conclusion, though, goes against Utena's own identity as prince. She rejects Akio's deal, and when he asks her if she understands the implications of her actions, she replies, "I'm going to be a prince!" The fairy-tale castle hovering just out of reach begins to crumble as Utena's decision to free Anthy "destabilizes" their world (Perper and Cornog 2006, 184). Yet the castle falling down around them is just an illusion, a "trick of the light" created by Akio's projector[15]; destroying it does not obliterate the hegemonic heteronormative narratives that Utena, Anthy, and even Akio are forced to enact. To return to Hayward's examination of the power behind trans- and re-, while Utena's gendered identity as prince may indeed be transgressive, is it *transformative*? Is it *revolutionary*? Or is she, like the Japanese media's return to the new feminine, simply the culture industry's reproduction of the fairy-tale gender binaries of old? An examination of *RGU*'s tropes of revolution and apocalypse suggests that Utena's insistence on her transgender identity is, in fact, capable of changing the world.

Despite Utena's desire to "be a noble prince who saves princesses" ("The Rose Bride," episode 1) and her attempt to revolutionize the world, her fairy tale ends in destruction; she lies defeated, abandoned in the crumbling dueling arena after losing the final battle with Akio, and her last words are "Forgive me, Himemiya . . . for pretending to be a prince . . . forgive me!" ("Someday, Together, We'll Shine," episode 39). Utena's apology is tragically ironic, as her death has come at Anthy's own hand; she stabs Utena in the back at Akio's behest. Anthy herself participates in the heteronormative fairy-tale system when she tells Utena, "You can never be my prince. Because you're a girl." Her participation is also tragic, though; the trauma of internalizing the heteronormative princess narrative is literalized upon her body; a

FIGURE 8.4 Anthy is stabbed by a million swords whispering "witch." *RGU*, "Someday, Together, We'll Shine," episode 39.

million swords stab her (see Figure 8.4), whispering "witch." Understanding that this final affront against Anthy's femininity originates in the very fairy-tale narrative of heteronormative female gender that Utena herself forced upon Anthy in defining her as her princess, Utena raises herself to her feet to save Anthy, sacrificing herself in the process.

After Utena's death, it seems that life as usual continues. Anthy and Akio meet to discuss their future plans and seem relatively unaffected. Planning on restarting the dueling game in order to, maybe this time, gain the power to revolutionize the world for himself, Akio tells Anthy, "So little time has passed since it happened, but they're all forgetting that she even existed. As I thought, she caused no revolution to occur." Akio's comment clarifies that he did not expect Utena to change the world, but it's worth considering another meaning of "revolution": to revolve. Utena's failure to change the world causes the narrative to loop back on itself. *RGU*'s narrative "operates recursively; it has been told, and retold, several times and in multiple formats, forming an intricate, self-referential complex of stories" (Hurford

2009, 20; see also Perper and Cornog 2006). Unlike many anime series that are only based on their original manga counterparts, the *RGU* manga, anime, and film serve as intersecting cycles of the same narrative. The anime even hints at the number of times the narrative has revolved—37,191 ("Gracefully Cruel," episode 11)—always ending in failure and the subsequent resurrection of the dueling game. The trope of revolution in *RGU* signifies not only change but also deadly repetition, in which Utena and others are sacrificed for the power to revolutionize the world.

This repetition is metatextually inscribed as apocalyptic through the repeated use of particular scenes and music. Like Usagi's transformation into Sailor Moon, one trope of *RGU* is the repetitive scene that plays whenever Utena transforms into the prince costume. *Sailor Moon*'s transformation scenes, repeated nearly every episode, take approximately forty-five seconds to occur; *RGU*'s take more than two minutes, which is extremely long by any standard, especially considering episodes are generally only twenty minutes long. The reuse of the animation in these transformation sequences doesn't just signal budget constraints; reinforcing *RGU*'s theme of repetition in conjunction with revolution, for two minutes the viewer circles Utena as she climbs a spiral staircase (see Figure 8.5). Furthermore, the music that plays during this scene connects the trope of repetition to apocalypse. Though "the power to revolutionize the world" is the series' catchphrase (like *Sailor Moon*'s "in the name of the moon, I'll punish you!"), heard just as often is the transformation sequence song chorus, "The Absolute Destiny: Apocalypse" (*zettai unmei mokushiroku*). The word for "apocalypse," *mokushiroku*, is deconstructed in the song's final phrases, which can be romanized as *mokushi kushimo shimoku kumoshi moshiku shikumo*. With *mokushiroku* being disassembled then rearranged ad infinitum, apocalypse literally connects to the repetition inherent in the *RGU* universe. Repetition itself becomes an apocalyptic event, constantly recurring metatextually in the show's structure as well as within its narrative.

That the transformation scene presents Utena's change into the prince at the same moment that this deconstruction of the word "apocalypse" occurs may suggest that, in fact, Utena's aspirations to princehood are apocalyptic. Because her attempts to escape the world of binary gender end in her own death and the subsequent reiteration of the fairy tale—Anthy must once again play the Rose Bride to whatever prince comes her way—*RGU* would appear to denounce any attempt to move outside of the fairy tale. This potential conclusion is driven home in a scene in the last episode in which

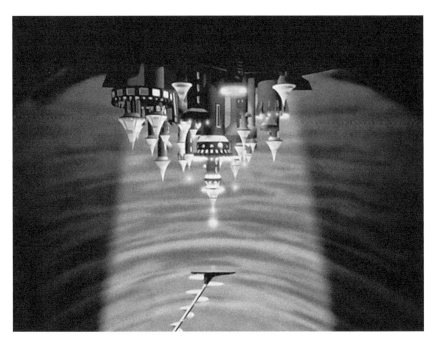

FIGURE 8.5 The spiral staircase that Utena climbs leads to the dueling arena under a rotating, upside-down castle. *RGU*, "The Rose Bride," episode 1.

Utena, lying defeated, suddenly envisions a slowly rotating merry-go-round, upon which her beloved childhood prince rides. In an agonizing moment of introspection, the prince of Utena's memory tells her that she has failed to secure the power to revolutionize the world and to save her princess from her awful fate, all because she is a girl ("Someday," episode 39). But just when he abandons his mount on the merry-go-round to present Utena with one last kiss, Utena, despite her mortal wound and mournful tears, abandons her past. Instead of playing his princess, she once again embodies the prince, suddenly pushing herself to her feet and stumbling forward to perish in an attempt to save Anthy.

Like the rotating merry-go-round, it seems that Utena's death has not changed *RGU*'s narrative trajectory—that, as Akio asserts, no revolution has occurred. But by the end of Akio and Anthy's last exchange, it becomes clear that someone has indeed transformed: Anthy herself. While Akio plans to restart the dueling games and therefore another reiteration of the narrative, Anthy—for the first time in 37,191 iterations—refuses. She abandons her brother and, asserting that Utena has not died but instead has merely left the fairy-tale world, enters the real world outside in order to search for her. The fairy tales end here, as do Anthy's identity as witch/princess and Aiko's dueling game and the search for the power to revolutionize the world, because a revolution has *already* occurred. Utena changes the world through her insistence on her queer identity as a trans-prince and provides Anthy with a space in which the categories of prince and princess have been deconstructed and thus no longer matter. In the final scenes, Anthy, dressed for the first time in a uniform of her own choosing (like Utena before her), steps across the boundaries of Ōtori Academy and addresses Utena without any honorifics; they are equals in the real world, not stagnant, rigid reiterations of the prince and princess of fairy tales.

Revolutionizing the Fairy Tale

In the end, *RGU* proposes that what has been revolutionized is the conventional fairy tale's binary gender system of prince and princess and the master narrative of heteronormativity. While Utena's attempt to become a prince ends in her demise, her insistence on her transgender identity opens up a space for Anthy to question the rules governing her own performance as princess and to abandon the repeated master narrative of heteronormative love. Moreover, the trans-couple escapes into a new world from Ōtori Academy, with its rigid and strict imposition of gender norms. Here *RGU* may offer a critical response to both same-sex relationships in earlier *shōjo* texts—that they must end when school does—and the repeated rise of the new feminine in contemporaneous Japanese culture and society. Remarkably, repetition of the fairy tale of binary gender and heteronormative love is apocalyptic in not only *RGU* but also *Sailor Moon;* the prince's and princess's reincarnation as destined lovers brings catastrophic events down upon them. Presumably, were Usagi and Tuxedo Mask free to choose whatever gender identities or performances, and whatever partner, they preferred—as Utena does throughout *RGU* and Anthy does by its end—the many fairy-tale apocalypses of *Sailor Moon* might have been averted.

While it has never reached the same popularity as *Sailor Moon, RGU* has nonetheless continued to present to fans and audiences alike a challenging critique of the Japanese culture industry through its analysis of contemporaneous issues such as the revival of the *ryōsai kenbo* ideology and the new feminine in 1990s Japan. By appropriating and revolutionizing the figures of the prince and princess, *RGU* suggests that the repeated rise of the fairy tale of binary gender is itself an apocalyptic event that must be changed. What's more, like *Sailor Moon,* the *RGU* series is currently seeing a revival, not only through remastered rereleases but also with increasing scholarly attention. I can only hope this means that, from 1997 to now and from this point on, a revolution is occurring in the real world outside of Ōtori Academy and in the stagnant fairy tales of binary gender and heteronormativity, as well.

Notes

1. In the Japanese style of surname first, given name second.
2. Thomas Lamarre distinguishes between full film and limited TV animation, which drastically decreases the number of drawings used to produce animation and thus "rel[ies] on other effects to impart a sense of movement" (2009, 19). Lamarre's theory explains why the fairy tale is so useful to television animation; the themes and archetypes provide budget- and time-constrained tales with a familiar sense of narrative movement.
3. *Bishōjo senshi sērā mūn* and *Shōjo kakumei Utena* in Japanese; see also Barber's chapter on gendering in live-action Japanese fairy-tale TV.
4. See www.tvdrama-db.com/drama_info/p/id-31974.
5. *Animerica,* a defunct US anime magazine, once called *RGU* "the stuff of a great postmodern fairy tale" (qtd. in "Utena," n.d.); fans often repeat this claim.
6. See Kotani (2006); Perper and Cornog (2006); Allison (2007); Benzon (2007); Rauch and Wilson (2007); Toku (2007); Ogg (2010).
7. For manga, see Saito (2001–2004, 2004). For musicals, see Ikuhara's personal websites www.jrt.co.jp/yos/ikuniweb/chronicle/utena/corostop.html and www.jrt.co.jp/yos/ikuniweb/menu/ikuniworks/films2.htm. For the video game, see Amazon.co.jp, www.amazon.co.jp/dp/B000069T95.
8. I use female pronouns to refer to Utena, as she insists that she can simultaneously be a woman and a prince and that the two are not mutually exclusive.
9. While the anime describes the Moon Kingdom as "like a fairy tale" ("*Umino no kesshin*," 1, 32), in the manga it is introduced with *ōmukashi ni* (a long long time ago; Takeuchi 1992, 107), which recalls the *mukashi mukashi* (once upon a time) beginning of *RGU* ("The Rose Bride"; see also Eubanks 2008). All translations from *Sailor Moon* are my own; translations from *RGU* are by Neil Nadelman.
10. Masami Toku disagrees: "Originally, the theme of shojo manga was women falling in love with men, but . . . things like friendship between women can be more important than love, as in *Bishojo Senshi Sailor Moon* . . . and [*RGU*]" (2007, 32). However, in the chronological future of *Sailor Moon,* Usagi is defined as a wife, mother, and queen, prioritizing heteronormative love over girls' friendship.
11. She is also in a deep magical sleep. *Sailor Moon* often recalls "Sleeping Beauty" (ATU 410; see Jorgensen and Warman's chapter); in an earlier episode, after reading that tale, Usagi falls into a deep sleep from which only Tuxedo Mask's kiss can awaken her ("Mezame yo," 2, 22).
12. What it means to "revolutionize the world" remains vague, but Ikuhara's commentary for the last episode indicates that, "revolution means gaining 'the power to

imagine the future.'. . . The princess bids farewell to the prince. No—she wasn't the princess any longer" (2011a, 11).

13. It is never quite clear if Anthy is raped or silently acquiescing, but the encounters are always initiated, sometimes violently, by Akio.

14. Akio is eventually revealed to be the prince that Utena met as a child, who has become jaded, devious, and distorted over time.

15. In the end, Akio reveals that he set up the dueling arena, projecting the floating castle overhead. His "eternal" fairy-tale castle is his own artificial construct.

PART III

Beastly Humans

9

CRIMINAL BEASTS AND SWAN GIRLS

The *Red Riding Trilogy* and Little Red Riding Hood on Television

Pauline Greenhill and Steven Kohm

The American comedy/crime drama *Castle* episode "Once Upon a Crime" opens with a woman in a Red Riding Hood costume running along a path through a wood (4, 17).[1] She turns, she screams. The scene changes, and writer Rick Castle (Nathan Fillion) and police detective Kate Beckett (Stana Katic) exchange their usual quips over the claw-marked, red-caped body in Central Park. On Halloween evening, 2011, dance professional Derek Hough and celebrity Ricki Lake present a "Little Red Riding Hood"–themed paso doble on the American version of the competitive reality show *Dancing with the Stars*. The paso dramatizes a bullfight, and it inevitably results in the Red/Ricki/bull succumbing to the wolf/Derek/bullfighter. The ubiquity of the story that Jacob and Wilhelm Grimm and Charles Perrault called "Little Red Cap" (ATU 333) on British and North American English-language television comprises made-for-TV feature-length movies like *Red: Werewolf Hunter* (2010) and episodes of series including *Popeye the Sailor* (1960), *Faerie Tale Theatre* (1983), and *Johnny Bravo* (2000). Mentions are too frequent to enumerate but include the season 4 final episode of *True Blood* with baby vampire Jessica dressing as Red.[2] In *Buffy the Vampire Slayer*, "Fear Itself" (4, 4), Buffy costumes as Red to attend a frat house Halloween party. Her choice hearkens back to "Halloween" (2, 6) in which trick-or-treaters became their cursed outfits' characters. Buffy, in a princess gown, became the stereotypical helpless, fainting fairy-tale ingénue. In the later episode, recognizing Red as anything but a wimpy princess, when asked what's in her basket, Buffy replies, "Weapons." Mentions in specials like *Rudolph's Shiny New Year* (1976) and *Once Upon a Brothers Grimm* (1977), in sitcoms like *Make Room for Daddy* (1958), and in variety programs like *The Rosemary Clooney Show* (1957) demonstrate the tale's lack of genre limitations.[3]

Most TV Reds proffer fantasy figures. Even those productions in which "Little Red Riding Hood" (henceforth Red [character] or LRRH [tale]) centers a narrative about crime tend to give decidedly lighthearted interpretations. For example, in *The Dangerous Christmas of Red Riding Hood* (1965), the wolf (Cyril Ritchard) opposes his wrongful incarceration while Liza Minnelli (as Red), Vic Damone (as the woodsman), and the rock group Eric Burdon and the Animals sing and/or dance; and in *The Trial of Red Riding Hood: A Fantasy on Ice!* (1992), Canadian Olympic silver medal skater Elizabeth Manley as Red faces trial for allegedly killing the missing wolf, played by Canadian sitcom star Alan Thicke.

In stark contrast, the brutal realism of this chapter's subject, the *Red Riding Trilogy,* appears unmatched in other Red-themed made-for-TV works. Its three 2009 films, *In the Year of Our Lord 1974* (directed by Julian Jarrold), *In the Year of Our Lord 1980* (directed by James Marsh), and *In the Year of Our Lord 1983* (directed by Anand Tucker), first aired on British television in March 2009 and were based on three novels from David Peace's *Red Riding Quartet: Nineteen Seventy-Four* (1999), *Nineteen Eighty* (2001), and *Nineteen Eighty-Three* (2002).[4] For horror combined with harsh cynicism, the *Red Riding Trilogy* (henceforth *RRT* or *Trilogy*) may be peerless.

A postmodern film noir (see, e.g., Barretta 2008), *RRT* uses the traditional LRRH narrative as a source for plot elements (girls venturing into everyday/dangerous places), visual images (the innocent red-coated girl), and metaphors (the wolf as predator linking to human sexuality). Originally made for television, the *Trilogy* was released theatrically in the United States and on DVD in Britain and North America.[5] *RRT* thus joins a myriad of LRRH feature-length films that range from fairly direct interpretations of traditional versions of the tale to highly inventive contemplations of its underlying symbolism (see Zipes 2011, 134–57). Several explore issues relating to crime and justice (see, e.g., Kohm and Greenhill 2010, 2011).

Where most other television shows make LRRH a touchstone for audience recognition and narrative structuring, in *RRT* the tale in addition serves to foreshadow often disturbing criminal and ecological actions and outcomes. Thus, in this chapter, we explore the *Trilogy* as *popular criminology*, an accessible discourse found in mass-mediated texts, often paralleling or contesting academic criminology, exploring issues pertaining to crime and justice (Rafter 2006, 2007). The subjects the three films address include violence, pedophilia, and serial killing, and police, governmental, and corporate corruption and brutality. But we also understand *RRT* as popular *green* criminology, describing the branch of popular criminology dealing with environmental harms; issues of space, place, and nature; and the oppression of human and nonhuman animals by people and institutions (see Kohm and Greenhill 2013).

"Popular criminology," found in vernacular, mediated forms like television and cinema, "differs from academic criminology in that it does not pretend to empirical accuracy or theoretical validity. But in scope, it covers as much territory—possibly more. . . . Popular criminology's audience is bigger . . . and its social significance is greater" (Rafter 2007, 415). Academic and popular criminology "should not be conceived as opposites, one concerned with reason and the other emotion. . . . Such misleading polarities reinforce the familiar false hierarchy in which scientific knowing is deemed superior" (ibid.). Popular criminology attends and appeals to its audience's hearts as well as its minds. Thus we use popular and green criminology to better appreciate how LRRH and *RRT* implicate the philosophical, moral, and emotional dimensions of relationships between crime and the environment. The *Trilogy* refers to the traditional tale in order to engage and sometimes shock audiences into reflecting on how social and environmental corruption can insidiously become part of everyday life and how individual actions bolster institutional vice.

RRT in particular instantiates Piers Beirne and Nigel South's definition that "at its most abstract level, green criminology refers to the study of those harms against humanity, against the environment (including space) and against nonhuman animals committed both by powerful institutions (e.g., governments, transnational corporations, military apparatuses) and also by ordinary people" (2007, xiii). The *Trilogy* likewise relates to environmental justice in linking "human oppression with environmental harms and [seeing] environmental oppression as connected to other forms of oppression" (Brisman 2008, 728). The films' representations of crime simultaneously (re)create, reflect, and query ideas about what constitutes criminality and what should be the appropriate responses to it from society in general and the criminal justice system in particular. As popular green criminology, the

Trilogy explores humans' relationships with each other and with their environment as social structural as well as individual acts. How the characters treat one another in these films parallels and/or implicates their relationships to nonhuman animals and the environment. To develop these links, we combine perspectives from ecocriticism, film studies, television studies, and criminal justice studies, as well as fairy-tale studies, to show how *RRT* elaborates and explicates green criminology.

Greg Garrard calls ecocriticism "an avowedly political mode of analysis" (2004, 3). He recognizes the centrality of popular cultural forms, noting, "As ecocritics seek to offer a truly transformative discourse, enabling us to analyse and criticise the world in which we live, attention is increasingly given to the broad range of cultural processes and products in which, and through which, the complex negotiations of nature and culture take place" (ibid., 4). Begun in literary studies (e.g., Kerridge and Sammells 1998), ecocriticism has increasingly been applied to crime (e.g., Ruggiero 2002) and the cinema (e.g., Willoquet-Maricondi 2010). As understood by Lawrence Buell, ecocriticism's analytical mode "unsettles received assumptions about the boundaries of nature writing and environmental representation generally; it provides a striking instance of the hermeneutics of empathy and suspicion as they are pitted against each other, and the potentially high stakes at issue in that conflict; and it reopens fundamental questions about both the cultural significance and the ethics of metaphor" (1998, 640). *RRT* raises and/or problematizes most of these issues, as we detail here.

Film studies enjoins attention to its subject's multimedia aspect; cinema should not be discussed in terms of narrative only (see, e.g., Grieveson and Wasson 2008). Thus, Allison Young argues that attention to "affective" and cinematographic dimensions allows a more nuanced appreciation of the representation of crime and justice (2008, 2010). Too often, criminological popular culture studies offer little more than quantitative exercises, counting instances of crimes or summarizing and categorizing stories (see, e.g., Allen, Livingstone, and Reiner 1997). Instead, Young urges that film analysis extend to elements like music, cinematography, and editing that influence viewers' moods and feelings. TV studies similarly explores the mediated complexity of texts but also draws on that medium's specific cultural, social, economic, and political contexts, attending to its institutions and audiences as well as to its contents (see, e.g., Miller 2010).

RRT breaks with traditional genre conventions, demonstrating a postmodern aesthetic. Film historian Drew Todd traces postmodern crime films' emergence in the 1990s, signaling "a rejection of linear storytelling, of expectations of genre conventions, and of easy distinctions between right and wrong" (2006, 51). Such films align with Rafter's identification of an alternative, critical crime film tradition rejecting one-dimensional "good guys" and happy Hollywood endings, showing evil regularly triumphing over good, and refusing a closing restoration of a moral order. Hallmarks of postmodern filmmaking include "playfulness . . . , multiple points of view . . . , concern with identity and identity politics . . . , irreverence (including a refusal to take themselves too seriously), eclecticism, and self-reflexivity" (Todd 2006, 53–54), offering audiences entertaining vehicles through which to question traditional notions of justice and criminal etiology.

Fairy Tales and "Little Red Riding Hood"

But why choose a fairy tale, and ATU 333 in particular, as a model or source for such crime films? Perhaps in part because the story is a well-known, international traditional tale; Hans-Jörg Uther's index notes versions from some forty ethnolinguistic groups (2004, 225). Traditional narratives in general allow for multiple, open meanings and have long enabled discourse on recurring sociocultural problems (see, e.g., Zipes 2012). Even a story as familiar at LRRH varies significantly. Most North Americans know the Grimms' version in which Little Red Cap, bringing a food basket to her grandmother, meets a wolf in the forest. He asks where she is going and then precedes her to the house, where he swallows Grandmother. When Red arrives, the wolf has installed himself in Grandmother's bed, in her clothes. Red comments, in a formulaic series, what big ears, hands, and mouth the grandmother/wolf has, and he eats her too. A passing woodsman shoots the wolf and rescues both Red and her grandmother. They place stones in the wolf's belly so that when he tries to escape he dies (Zipes 2002b, 93–96). Two other European forms of this narrative, distinguishable mainly by their endings, offer different possibilities. In the text published by Charles Perrault in 1697, no savior delivers Red and her granny. The moral is "Children, especially attractive, well bred young ladies, should never talk to strangers, for if they should do so, they may well provide dinner for a wolf. I say 'wolf,' but there are various kinds of wolves. There are also those who are charming, quiet, polite, unassuming, complacent, and sweet, who pursue young women at home and in the streets. And unfortunately, it is these gentle wolves who are the most dangerous ones of all" (Ashliman 1996–2012). A third ending, found in oral French versions, involves Red's self-rescue, with female help-ers. She recognizes that the wolf is not her grandmother but goes along with his plot, removing her clothes and getting into bed. Then she tells the wolf she must go outside to relieve herself. Suspicious, he attaches a string to her leg, but she unties it. When he discovers her ruse, the wolf runs after her. Sometimes she simply arrives safely home before her pursuer, or she may come to a river. Washerwomen on the other bank throw sheets across and pull Red to safety. They offer to do the same for the wolf but let go when he is in the middle of the stream, and he drowns.[6]

Whatever its form, the underlying structure of LRRH incorporates nur-turers and aggressors, victims and rescuers. In many recent retellings, some-times simultaneously, individual characters take both sides of these semiotic oppositions (Ghesquiere 2006). The same doubling and overlapping of fig-ures forms an essential element of LRRH crime films—works that manifest the plot and/or central images of ATU 333 and relate them to some aspect of law breaking and/or criminality. These semiotic transformations are fun-damental to understanding *RRT*. References go beyond a child in a red coat or a walk in the woods; LRRH films like the *Trilogy* bend and even invert the tale's plot structures and characters. Seldom unidimensional, both vic-tims and villains confront dangers—not only lurking in the woods but also closer to home. More complex and ambivalent than some traditional ATU 333 narratives, LRRH crime films question simple remedies to the problem of wolfish violence, which run the gamut from vigilantism to redemption. Particularly since the 1990s, this narrative structure and imagery has offered European and North American filmmakers and viewers a critical metaphori-cal tool, a malleable cultural referent to engage—often critically—with crime and criminal justice, a refraction of discord and anxiety in local and broader contexts.

Academics across the disciplines have read LRRH using an assortment of theoretical lenses.[7] Sometimes her stereotypically feminine characteristics seem overdetermined: "Little Red Riding Hood makes her little detour, does what women should never do, travels through her own forest. She allows herself the forbidden . . . and pays dearly for it" (Cixous 1981, 43). Alterna-tively, she can be understood as "cross-gendered in her narrative position: she plays principal boy, 'plunges' into the wood, 'plucks' flowers, makes things happen" (Attwood 1999, 100). A historical materialist/social realist perspective suggests that the tale's seventeenth-century audience would have been concerned with hunger and the active dangers of the outside world

(Darnton 1984). Symbolic analysis sees LRRH as a counterpart to an occupational and sexual rite of passage for young women (Verdier 1980). Probably the best-known psychological interpretation argues for child ambivalence and Oedipal conflicts in puberty and sexuality as its subject (Bettelheim 1976, 166–83). ATU 333 has even been seen as a mythic ritual narrative of the sun's daily progress (the wolf is night to Red's sun, daily delivered from his belly); alternatively Red is spring, reborn from the wolf of winter.[8] But the majority of sociocultural and literary readings argue that ATU 333 implicates sexuality and particularly rape (see, e.g., Brownmiller 1975; Garber 1992; Velay-Vallantin 1998).

LRRH's ecological implications have not been thoroughly explored, though we are not the first to do so. Michelle Scalise Sugiyama argues that the story "is rooted in the adaptive problem of predator avoidance . . . [since] big ears, big teeth, long nails, and hairiness are not characteristics reliably associated with seducers, rapists, or other criminals, whereas they are reliably associated with wolves" (2004, 121). Presuming an almost entirely literal materialist interpretation that few who study folktales would find convincing,[9] she admits "that the use of anthropomorphism invests the tale with a secondary, highly adaptive and—not coincidentally, I think—very popular message: strangers can be dangerous" (ibid.). We concur that LRRH explores the dangerous and potentially deadly cultural relations between settled (urban, village) and wild (woods, park) locations, and between nonhuman animals (wolf) and humans (Red, her grandmother, and the woodsman; see, e.g., Jones 1987; Douglas 1995; Orenstein 2002; Nelson 2008). Thus, ecocritical and green criminological implications become fundamental.

The *Red Riding Trilogy*

LRRH and *RRT* underline that "green crimes, like other crimes, are social constructions influenced by social locations and power relations in society" (Lynch and Stretsky 2003, 218); "the poor and the disadvantaged . . . suffer disproportionately from . . . environmental inequalities" (White 2008, 16). Institutions and individuals alike fail to include human implications in their search for revenue. When profit becomes the paramount aim—too often the *sole* aim—personal devastation follows for those who lack power in the capitalist system, and the environment can suffer irreparable harm. In *RRT,* environmental depredation parallels moral degradation:

[*RRT*'s films] paint a compelling picture of time and place, and retain much of their source's hellish intensity. . . . The superb design, filming and acting drip with gray-brown authenticity, showing 1970s/80s decay, depression and desperation in Northern England's rapidly postindustrialising pit villages, rotten boroughs and collapsing communities breeding the solipsistic barbarism neoliberalism would soon legitimize in this sceptic isle. . . . Recurring th[r]oughout unremitting menace and brutality are seedy property developers, vengeance-seeking rent-boys, creepily ubiquitous priests, paedophile rings, and disintegrating detectives trying belatedly to do the right thing surrounded by unredeemable . . . [West Yorkshire] Constabulary colleagues. The latter's endemic corruption extends beyond collusion and parasitism to running vice and pornography operations as well as enforcing for local Big Money, underlining their thorough integration into "polite" society and establishment hierarchies. (Jennings 2009, 19)

Reviewer Tom Jennings's above evaluation of *RRT* suggests that few cultural texts may better exemplify Buell's ecocritical "hermeneutics of empathy and suspicion" (1998, 640). But *RRT*'s context and its content encourage viewers to share its conviction that few adults are innocent and no one can remain a bystander. For those who saw it on British television and/or on DVD, the *Trilogy*'s primary viewing location on TV screens literally brings the story home. Though commonly associated in the neoliberal bourgeois mind with safety and stability, home in *RRT* is a dangerous location: murder, rape, and pedophilia are planned and perpetrated there. Similarly Grandmother's house in *LRRH*—not the woods against which her mother warns her—is where Red is most in danger. Middle-class viewers of *RRT* may come to doubt their understanding of home as haven, of police as friends, and of capitalists as benign. Watching torture scenes is unsettling in a movie theater, but the viewer can return home afterward. *RRT*'s television screening places these actions both figuratively and literally within the home.

RRT shows how the filmed representation of pedophilia (see Kohm and Greenhill 2011) culturally implicates specific uses of spaces (for commercial development or by children who play in and around abandoned cars, machinery, and other garbage in the absence of recreational areas). It also links crimes against ecology (mutilation of swans) and noncriminalized environmental devastation (nuclear power plants, urban decay, suburban development) with crimes against marginalized peoples and children as well as criminal justice system problems (including issues around treatment of suspects and offenders as well as governmental and police corruption). The connections emerge in the repeated boast by corrupt police, developers, and their cronies, "This is the North [i.e., Yorkshire, Northern England], where we do what we want." The three films, like Peace's novels from which they are adapted, are "very loosely based around the scandal surrounding the disgraced property developer John Poulson, and . . . more closely based around the infamous miscarriage of justice suffered by Stefan Kiszko and the hunt for the Yorkshire Ripper" (Howkins 2010).[10] Given the subject matter, the view of humanity is hardly positive. As one reviewer succinctly put it, "The police are routinely corrupt, journalists are venal and co-optable, and the wealthy are vampiric exploiters" (Fisher 2009).

But it is not entirely the films' subject matter that makes them so unsettling; their style also aims to trouble viewers. *RRT* is a disorienting fusion of postmodernism and film noir, and in it,

> things *just don't add up—they don't fit together.* It's a Gnostic terrain. The Gnostics believed that the world was made of a corrupt matter characterized by heavy weight and impenetrable opacity: a murky, muddy mire in which fallen angels—one of the persistent images in the *Red Riding* books and films—are trapped. The *Red Riding* world is one in which, as [screenwriter] Tony Grisoni puts it, "narratives disappear into the dark" (almost every scene in *1983* features an artificial light source feebly struggling against an overwhelming gloom). Light only brings more shadows; revelations only lead to more mysteries. We see much of the action only partially, from behind characters' heads or at oblique angles. (Fisher 2009)

Critics have compared *RRT* to postmodern/surrealistic films that explore the twisted underbelly of seemingly ordinary (sub)urban life (Cookson 2010). "Like David Lynch's *Mulholland Drive,* [*RRT*] creates a sense that satanic forces are at work just below the surface" (Howkins 2010). As with other postmodern crime films, nothing in *RRT*'s bleak world is as it seems. Facts are easily manipulated or fabricated outright. Perception itself is problematized through narrative and cinematography; viewers literally cannot see clearly a distinct truth. The only character who understands with any veracity is a psychic, but her knowledge is dismissed and ignored by the police and contradicted by doctored forensic reports. Intense close-ups, out-of-focus tracking shots, characters partly blocked by or framed through objects, and images obscured/reflected/refracted by glass create a claustrophobic and paranoid mood. Though postmodern films often eschew association with a specific genre, in mood and subject matter *RRT* embodies a contemporary noir aesthetic.

Marianna Valverde enumerates typical film noir signs: "night-time settings in which even the main actors' faces are left in the dark; relentless pared-down dialogue, through which very few facts and almost no feelings are conveyed, leaving the spectator grasping for meaning, any meaning; anonymous and ugly 'mean streets'; and, last but not least, a constant procession of glasses of whisky and cigarettes" (2006, 93). The *Trilogy* indeed makes liberal use of murky, smoke-filled interiors where characters smoke and drink and gloomy rain-soaked exteriors that provide no escape. The literal darkness evokes the pall of menace and depravity hanging over the region. Politicians, police, and hard-boiled journalists grapple with sordid evidence of child abuse, corruption, exploitation of women, and murder yet only seem intent on further obscuring the truth, never revealing it to the bright daylight. Noir tendencies and postmodern framing work together to amplify *RRT*'s perspective that the authorities cannot be trusted and anyone can become a victim.

In classic noir style, truth's only champions are outsiders. In *1974,* it's the young cocky newspaper reporter, returning home after a failed stint down South with a chip on his shoulder; in *1980,* the honest cop, brought in from Manchester to probe police failures in the Yorkshire Ripper investigation; and in *1983,* the grotesque defense lawyer, lacking ambition and blinded to his own family ties to the abuse, and the remorseful cop, who has a change of heart after years of participating in cover-up and graft. Like other noir protagonists, they take no pleasure in pursuing justice but drown out the task with whisky, cigarettes, and emotionless sex. Corrupted or easily corruptible, these men themselves fall prey to their adversaries' petty vices. Audiences can be excused for feeling ambivalent about their sometimes grim fates.

Reviewers concur that the narrative is puzzling, even obscure. "*Red Riding* is not just hard to follow—it believes in a culture and a narrative where things no longer click together. You never know the whole story or the larger purposes because the world is no longer run on those pious timetables" (Thomson 2010, 33). The visuals underscore the gritty and difficult content: "*1974* is shot on Super16, *1980* is shot on 35mm, and *1983* is shot on top-end digital video. The three films use light versus darkness as a running theme. . . . *1974* is rich in discretely presented period detail, making effective use of brutalist architecture and orange streetlights. Britain is shown in the moment at which post-war austerity is giving way to post-industrial decay. The world created is at once the early 1970's [*sic*] and, at the same time, a kind of satanic dark age" (Howkins 2010). Lighting in particular links the metaphor of clarity and obscurity with plot elements.

As we detail below, crucial for our understanding of *RRT* as popular green criminology is the linkage of institutional and economic power and hegemony with criminal acts against people, nonhuman animals, and the environment. Working-class folks in *RRT* are victims, underdogs, and thus Reds, but the bourgeois and petty bourgeois police, politicians, religious functionaries, and entrepreneurs alike, as well as middle-/upper-class lawyers, are wolves, predators who share moral and criminal failings. Police officers, lawyers, and journalists can be ambivalent woodsmen, but their flaws too often ultimately transform them into Reds or wolves. And yet the context remains realistic: "We are in West Yorkshire, where vestiges of modern life—places called Leeds and Hunslet, cars, highways, telephones, and television—do not prevent the feeling that we are in the Dark Ages, when hovels cling to the moors, where gypsy camps are set on fire, with the people passing hazardous lives in dread" (Thomson 2010, 32). Land development sites are locations for criminal behavior, from the burning of the camp to displace squatters and make way for bulldozers, to the discovery of the murdered, mutilated body of ten-year-old Clare Kemplay, whose disappearance focuses the first film.

In the Year of Our Lord 1974

Beginning with *1974, RRT* connects social structural issues with violence against marginalized peoples and animals and with destruction of habitations and habitat. As television studies scholars Amy Holdsworth and Barbara Sadler describe the series' debut:

> On March 5, 2009, amid a frenzy of publicity, [Britain's] Channel Four broadcast the first episode of a controversial three-part drama based on David Peace's *Red Riding* quartet. This was a violent and bleak story of police brutality and corruption set in West Yorkshire in the 1970s and '80s. Each episode of the drama repeated the

menacing toast/warning "this is the north—where we do what we want" and the sense of this mythical 'north' as a lawless, noirish, fantastical space is highlighted in the opening moments of the first part of the series ('1974'). . . . The dreamy quality of the opening episode is emphasized throughout by the smoke-filled haze of the newspaper and police office interiors, the grainy muted color palette and the rain-soaked twilight of the road that leads the ambitious Eddie (Andrew Garfield) back to this nightmarish world and does not allow him to escape; the north of *Red Riding* is elsewhere in time and space. . . . reproducing a familiar repertoire of images and mythologies, where the north is grim and the sun only shines "down south." (2010, 138)

1974 opens with journalist Eddie Dunford returning to his native Yorkshire from an unsuccessful career in London. His voiceover comments, "A little girl goes missing. The pack salivates. If it bleeds, it leads, right?" The viewer might initially surmise that he's referring to journalists as wolves, but later two characters implicate "the Wolf" in criminal acts. Red characters pervade the narrative. When young Clare Kemplay goes missing, she wears a red anorak (and flashes of a red-coated girl recur in this episode and *1983*).[11] Her mutilated body is discovered on the construction site of sleazy entrepreneur John Dawson (Sean Bean). Dunford describes Dawson's activities as "substandard housing, dodgy property trusts, backhanders to the local council." Paula Garland (Rebecca Hall), the mother of Jeanette Garland (missing for two years), wears a red hooded sweater when Eddie first visits her and during many of their meetings. She has been exploited by Dawson, who she says, "fucks who he wants to fuck. He takes what he wants," and whom she has known "all my life." Dunford's reporter friend Barry Gannon (Anthony Flanagan), also more Red than woodsman, has already unearthed evidence of corruption and conspiracy. Dawson has him brutally murdered. The mentally challenged Michael Myshkin (Daniel Mays), jailed for Clare's murder, is another Red, victim of the police and the legal system alike. At his arraignment he denies being the killer, saying, "It was the Wolf. Under those beautiful carpets."

Possible candidates for the woodsman role in *RRT* tend to be outsiders to their profession and ridiculed by their colleagues. Dunford refuses to follow his editor's instructions to tread carefully, declines to accept bribes, and eventually believes Gannon's claims about police complicity and conspiracy.

Dawson asserts that there's a wolf in the reporter, calling him "like me. We both like to fuck and make a buck and we're not right choosy how." Initially, perhaps, Dunford sees the child disappearances and murders as a way to make his name, but he begins to genuinely care about Paula Garland and he sees how Jeanette's disappearance has destroyed her. Rather than turning a blind eye to the corruption, Dunford wants to end it. Garland understands his self-image as the ATU 333 woodsman, saying, "You just want to rescue me. Well you're not the first. And do you think you'll be the last?"

In a repeated metaphor that recurs in *1983*, both Myshkin and Dawson's wife Marjory (Cathryn Bradshaw) allude to what's hidden "under the beautiful carpets." This trope suggests the evil in Dawson's house and underground and invokes all kinds of secrets swept under the proverbial rug. In a nod to Lynch's surrealism, secret horrors lurk just below the surface of "Shangri-La," Dawson's ironically named modernist/monstrous estate, about which Gannon quips, "All great buildings resemble crimes." "Shangri-La," constructed to resemble a swan, links Dawson to his abuse of animals, children, and women. But even from its opening scenes, *1974* hints that Dunford may be more Red than woodsman. As he prepares for his meeting with Detective Chief Superintendent Bill "Badger" Molloy (Warren Clarke), Gannon comments, "Into the lion's den you go." In the end, Dunford is neither wolf nor woodsman; he's Perrault's Red, dying at the story's close.

Images of war and genocide—perhaps the most destructive crimes against humanity and environment—pervade *RRT* but find their clearest expression in *1974*. Dawson frames a personal war in terms that recall Nazi plans for racial and social purity. In his luxury sedan, he drives Dunford through the postindustrial working-class ruins of Yorkshire, a landscape invoking the bombed-out remnants of British and European cities laid to waste in World War II. But as Dawson states, his England in the 1970s battles internal enemies: "This nation's in fucking chaos. . . . The country's at war, Mr. Dunford. . . . Your paddies, your wogs, your niggers, your fucking gypos, the poofs, the perverts, even the bloody women. They're all out to get what they can get. I tell you, soon there'll be naught left for us lot. Time to turn the tide." Indeed, Dawson perpetuates cultural genocide on Romani squatters, burning their camp to the ground to pave the way for his shopping mall development. Not only do images of the Romani encampment's displaced people and smoking ruins haunt *1974*'s protagonist's dreams, but they also evoke war and twentieth-century genocide. For Dunford, "it was like Vietnam or something."

Underlining the military metaphor, a corrupt police force maltreats Dunford with increasing intensity, culminating in horrific scenes in a claustrophobic concrete dungeon that the officers call "the belly." Mimicking torture from wartimes past and present, stripped naked, deprived of sleep, hosed down with cold water, the reporter endures physical and psychological suffering. Gannon's warning about "death squads" becomes prophetic. Paraphrasing Edmund Burke's famous quotation, often summoned in conjunction with the Holocaust, he warns Dunford, "The Devil triumphs when good men do naught." However, in *RRT*'s noir world, evil triumphs *despite* the best work of (mostly) good men.[12]

RRT's nightmarish war imagery gains force from the films' sensory properties. Scenes of epic violence are punctuated by transitions to pastoral images and sounds, often represented by birds. Following Dunford's torture, two cops throw him from a moving police van onto the moor. One declares: "This is the North. Where we do what we want." The scene shifts to Maurice ("Owl") Jobson (David Morrissey) burning a bag of evidence of political and police corruption, framed by the image of his boss Molloy looking on from his office window. Another scene shift returns to Dunford, slowly regaining consciousness by the highway, the peaceful sound of chirping birds contrasting with the horrors of his confinement and torture. A potent symbol of freedom, birds are often invoked in popular cultural representations of prisons and prisoners. Songbirds' calls painfully remind the incarcerated of their loss of liberty. In *RRT,* the juxtaposition of birdsongs against scenes of violence throws the latter into sharper focus. As Paula Garland walks, trance-like, followed by Dunford, toward Dawson's house, birdsongs begin just as "Shangri-La" comes into view. They remind viewers that Garland is a prisoner of this man who has mutilated her psychologically throughout her life, just as he mutilates swans physically.

On one level, the swan's mutilation and the Romani camp burning are individual acts by Dawson, an immoral/amoral/evil entrepreneur (with a stuffed swan suspended over his bed). Yet narrative and visuals alike link his actions directly to the police and indirectly to the environmental and social degradation that brutalizes people but also engenders social and ecological destruction. Joining violence against humans to violence against animals is fairly conventional (see, e.g., Agnew 1998; Fish 2008); but making a further tie to more systemic forms of violence against ecology is less so, despite Piers Beirne's assertion that "in countless ways human–animal relationships have traditionally been an inextricable part of humans' domination of one another, of the environmental and of nature" (2007, 73–74). Thus, Dawson's murderous pedophilia—which he terms a "private weakness. Fucking hell, I'm no angel"—invokes his extreme cruelty to animals, his callous disregard for human beings, and his corrupt co-opting of politicians and police who, in the name of profit, run prostitutes and distribute pornography. Dawson and his consortium boasting, "This is the North, where we do what we want," have an equal disregard for children, animals, women, the mentally and physically handicapped, marginalized ethnic groups, and the environment.

In the Year of Our Lord 1980

At the close of 1974, Dunford has killed John Dawson and some of his associates, but he is no woodsman; his action fails to end the crimes. 1980 opens with actual footage from coverage of the Yorkshire Ripper killings, which seamlessly merges into the fiction, another hallmark of postmodern filmmaking. Potential woodsman Assistant Chief Constable Peter Hunter (Paddy Considine) does not mind becoming a pariah in leading an investigation into the so far unsuccessful Yorkshire Ripper pursuit. His name, echoing a possible occupation of the LRRH woodsman, also marks his job uncovering what has been hidden—but he also has secrets to obscure. He has had an affair with subordinate officer, Detective Helen Marshall (Maxine Peake), who as a result has an abortion. Hunter seems wolflike in his exploitation of Marshall.

But though the Ripper comments of his victims, "They're all in my brain, reminding me of the beast that I am," alluding to wolfishness, 1980 has fewer direct allusions to ATU 333 than the other two films. In particular, it lacks red-coated women or girls. But because of its association with 1974 and 1983, we see it as exploring the position and actions of a potential woodsman in Hunter. 1980 also holds significant implications for green criminology, particularly in a crucial scene where Hunter visits the village of Fitzwilliam, home of a missing girl, in an unsuccessful search for the ironically named Reverend Martin Laws (Peter Mullan). A sense of foreboding, inscribed on the landscape of dreary row houses in the shadow of the iconic nuclear reactor's cooling towers, hints at lurking danger. The area initially appears void of humanity, save the odd child darting through muddy puddles while open fires burn in the background. Scrutinizing the dismal landscape as the ominous musical score builds toward a crescendo, Hunter is surprised by a group of children wearing crudely fashioned masks resembling animals. They surround him, firing toy pistols in an apparent cops and robbers game. Hunter is visibly shaken by the spectacle, which foreshadows his own impending containment and murder by corrupt officers of the West Yorkshire force with animal nicknames like "Owl" and "Badger." An out-of-focus camera captures Hunter backing away and then quickly cuts to his silhouette running toward his car.

Throughout *1980*, Hunter's sense of enclosure and embattlement is underlined in tight shots with characters and scenes contained, reflected in mirrors or glass, viewed through other objects (like the safety grate of the hotel elevator that literally encages him), or partially obscured. His perspective is rendered in extreme close-ups and even upside-down views. Though he sees the disconnect between the murder of Clare Strachan (Kelly Freemantle) and the Ripper killings, his place as Red rather than woodman is confirmed by his own multiple victimization. Predictably, given the interchanges between roles that characterize contemporary interpretations of LRRH, he loses his job, his house is torched, and, eventually, the conspirators murder him.

1980 primarily concerns the Ripper investigation and eventual, accidental resolution when a cop happens upon one of the murderer's crimes. Its characters, like those of the other two films, beg comparison with the traditional tale's Red, wolf, and woodsman. And though the story primarily follows police incompetence and corruption, those actions are implicitly linked with the ecology of urban spaces where even children mimic the violence they encounter in these devastated landscapes, mirrored in all-too-real police brutality. The film also calls on the specific location of Yorkshire, the North, where evil predominates and its individual and institutional perpetrators do what they want.

In the Year of Our Lord 1983

Unlike the works on which it is based, *1983* offers in conclusion a woodsman-like rescue. Indeed, not one but two woodsmen emerge. Lawyer John Piggott (Mark Addy) enters the film visiting his dead mother's semidetached house in run-down Fitzwilliam. Despite his multiply reiterated working-class connections, even he needs extensive persuasion before seeking an appeal of the murder verdict against his mother's neighbor's son, Myshkin, who claims, "It was the Wolf," not he, who killed Clare Kemplay. His case is strengthened by the fact that young Hazel Atkins (Tamsin Mitchell) has disappeared under similar circumstances, despite Myshkin's incarceration. Mainly wolf in *1974* and *1980,* in *1983* Detective Superintendent Jobson (the "Owl") turns woods-man. He has ambivalently occupied this position throughout; for example, a flashback reveals that he tipped off Eddie Dunford about the burning of the gypsy camp. His action is glossed by his superior Harold Angus (Jim Carter) as "you and your fucking conscience, Maurice. . . . Now fuck off and retire quietly." Genuinely remorseful for setting up Myshkin, and completely disil-lusioned with the cover-ups and corruption, he truly wants to find Hazel. He goes far beyond his colleagues' ethos, taking seriously insights from psychic Mandy Wymer (Saskia Reeves), with whom he develops a sexual relation-ship. During a séance, she explains, "It's happened before, three times. It's happening again now. Under the grass that grows beneath the stones and cracks. Beneath those beautiful carpets. Underground. The Rat and the Wolf are here. And the Pig. There's a swan too. The swan is dead." Rat, Pig, and Wolf reference specific members of a pedophile ring; the swan represents their young victim. Myshkin echoes Marjory Dawson's repeated words in *1974,* "The Wolf does [i.e., performs services] for John."

In *1983,* as in the other films, "on retrouve chaque jour un univers fami-lier: personnages monstrueux, collines cernées de crachin, petites banlieues déglinguées" ([every day we find a familiar universe of monstrous characters, drizzle-ringed hills, small dilapidated suburbs] Gombeaud 2009, 42). The physical setting appears simultaneously familiar and foreboding. Fitzwil-liam, dominated by six nuclear reactor cooling towers, has a derelict play-ground covered in junk; wrecked cars are dumped in what might otherwise be green space. Its working-class residents live in monotonous brick row houses or semidetached dwellings, their vast socioeconomic differences from their wealthy counterparts graphically represented by "Shangri-La" and the lavish home of Myshkin's upper-class accented lawyer, Clive McGuiness (Hilton McRae). Dawson's house is built to resemble a swan because, as Molloy says, "John loves swans." Dawson agrees: "They're beautiful crea-tures." But he appreciates swans, as he does humans and indeed the land and environment, only when he can manipulate them to his own purposes. Like his attitude toward the children and women he abuses, the "Pikeys" he displaces, and the police, politicians, and land he controls, his only use for swans is to satisfy his own corrupt and murderous desires.

Jobson has known of Laws's guilt from the beginning. *1983*'s nuanced exploration of animal characters includes the wolf–priest who masquerades as both helper and victim. When (in a flashback) the police pick him up for questioning about Clare Kemplay's disappearance and begin to torture him, he tells them to speak to Dawson. Later he appears as the pedophile ring's leader/recruiter. Metaphorical allusions link the co-conspirators' filthy, greedy, predatory behavior to culturally debased nonhuman animals, simultaneously constructing their victims as beautiful, defenseless, and innocent. The ecological moral is further driven by the fact that the crimes take place in a region literally ripped apart by more than a century of resource extraction and exploitation of the working classes. Many have perished from exposure to coal dust (including the wrongly convicted Myshkin's father) after toiling away below the grass, the "beautiful carpets."

BJ (Robert Sheehan), a rent boy who appears in all the films, plays a central role in *1983*. Another victim, a Red who also attempts to be a woodsman, he cannot bring himself to kill the Wolf, pedophile and killer Reverend Laws, as he intended. Jobson does so, cementing his own woodsman/rescuer status. In a move that diverts from the novel, eventually Jobson and Piggott save Hazel Atkins.[13] BJ's voiceover summarizes, beginning "Here is one who got away and lived to tell the tale." The film closes with flashbacks to happy childhood scenes with his mother at the amusement park at Blackpool, the tower momentarily visible. As the beach view cuts to black, the voiceover concludes, "One, two, three, four, five, six, seven. All good children go to heaven." The religious nursery rhyme and the working-class holiday resort underscore the irony of a society with institutions controlled by men whose relation to children and religion is entirely instrumental and self-serving. Though BJ escapes in the end, as Hazel does, their futures seem bleakly uncertain given all they have endured.

Popular Green Criminology and Fairy-Tale Television

Filled with criminal beasts, many of whom occupy positions in the police, political, and justice systems, *RRT*'s green criminology seems far from the usual lighthearted television fairy-tale fare. It better reflects the broad canon of pedophile crime films, reprising some of the themes and plots of films from the 1980s and 1990s (see Kohm and Greenhill 2011): underground pedophile rings operating in our midst; children secreted away into an abandoned mine shaft where powerful men (led by a pedophile priest) ritually abuse them; a public horrified but powerless. However, the *Trilogy* also challenges orthodoxies about violence and its relationship to the social and physical environment.

Like the independent fictional film *The Woodsman* (2004), *RRT* suggests that sexual abuse of children may be widely perpetrated at the hands of otherwise upright members of society. Moreover, reminiscent of postmodern documentary films like *Capturing the Freidmans* (2003), the trilogy disrupts simple notions of the discoverability of truth (see Greenhill and Kohm 2013), particularly in cases of child sexual abuse when the authorities are as much implicated as the rest of society. Indeed, *RRT* uses narrative and cinematic devices to argue that the truth is at times almost impossible to perceive by traditional means of investigation or observation. And in the tradition of the bleakest film noir, those who seek the truth in the *Trilogy* are generally doomed to an ugly fate, often before they can even understand the nature of their quest. In short, this series bears little resemblance to conventional television depictions of LRRH, even those that concern crime.

Further, some academic green criminology (see, e.g., Agnew 1998) constructs white, prosperous, middle-class North Americans as the most enlightened of any group on issues of criminalized ecological issues like animal abuse. Yet the worst offenders in ecological destruction globally are not the poverty-stricken residents of the global South, or the underclasses of the North, whose lack of consumer potential often makes them recyclers and minimal users of energy, for example. Some green criminology fails to recognize how often the most ecologically destructive actions like some forms of resource extraction are not criminalized while illegal actions like dumpster diving and pedicab driving actually benefit the ecology by reducing waste destined for landfills and reducing greenhouse gases.[14] *RRT*'s popular green criminology is politically, economically, and socially astute in locating the worse environmental destruction and interpersonal violence not in traditionally criminalized populations like the Romani but in capitalist entrepreneurs and their institutionally powerful supporters. It does so in particular by unsettling conventional ideas of who should be a Red/victim/underdog, who a wolf/exploiter, and who a woodsman/rescuer, reversing some academic green criminology's identification of the poor and social elite as metaphorical wolves and woodsmen, respectively.

RRT provides a rich example of popular green criminology in the way it implicates issues of class conflict, environmental (in)justice, and crimes against ecology, culture, and humanity. The series allows audiences to ponder profound questions of morality, ethics, and responsibility. Environmental devastation engenders exploiters as much as victims. Though individuals may be held responsible for specific acts, often they are innocent bystanders.

Even for those implicated in the criminal acts, when one perpetrator is removed, another takes his place. The best a victim—like BJ or Hazel—can hope for is to survive. But with the exception of Perrault's version and its cognates, the LRRH narrative structurally offers hope of rescue, either by an external woodsman or by Red herself and thus *RRT*'s conclusion is not entirely pessimistic.

Understood as popular criminology, the series offers audiences a popular cultural space in which to consider complex and disruptive views about social, ecological, and criminal justice. The repeated boast "This is the North, where we do what we want" becomes an ironic commentary on individual and systemic cruelty. Some indeed do what they want, and they do it regardless of the implications for those less powerful. The system encourages some and destroys others. Hegemonic masculinity is rewarded. Any other position is marginalized at best, brutalized at worst, including women (the Ripper's victims); children (victims of the Wolf's pedophile ring); and young, ethnic, racialized, mentally challenged men (scapegoats for actual perpetrators but also themselves victims of actual perpetrators). Thus, *RRT* can be read alongside critical academic criminological discourses that call for a radical reshaping of the societal conditions that produce harms and allow the powerful to exploit the poor with impunity. Though its origins as a made-for-British-television series might lead some to dismiss its lessons, the *Trilogy* holds transgressive and potentially transformative potential as a radical popular cultural call to action for environmental and social justice. It demonstrates that studies of fairy tales and fairy-tale media can implicate issues of crucial importance to humans and to the planet.

Notes

We gratefully acknowledge funding from the Social Sciences and Humanities Research Council of Canada, Standard Research Grant, "Fairy Tale Films: Exploring Ethnographic Perspectives" (principal investigator, Pauline Greenhill; coapplicants, Steven Kohm, Sidneyeve Matrix, and Cat Tosenberger; collaborators, Cristina Bacchilega and Jack Zipes). We also thank Jill Rudy for helping us to clarify our work.

1. (Season, episode).
2. Thanks to Meagen Chorney for bringing this to our attention.
3. We thank Kendra Magnus-Johnston for locating most of these examples.

4. These novels "probe the dark recesses of contemporary British history in novels overlapping the period (1970s–1980s) when the Yorkshire Ripper was being hunted. Peace's novels are grim, intense meditations on personal despair and official depravity. Legitimate police procedure is displaced by the abuse of power, and . . . virtually every investigative mechanism is tainted by brutality, dishonesty and the self-serving exercise of official authority" (Horsley 2010, 36).
5. See Barzilai's and Wright's chapters for other made-for-TV films subsequently released to cinemas.
6. See Verdier (1980, 31–56). Kaplan's short film *Little Red Riding Hood* (1997) follows this structure, minus female helpers.
7. See texts and analyses in Zipes (1983b) and Dundes (1989). Theoretical perspectives are critiqued in Vaz da Silva (2002, 113–62).
8. See Douglas (1995, 1–7). Nazis interpreted "Red Riding Hood as the symbol of the German folk, plagued by the wolf: the Jews. The Huntsman who rescued Red Riding Hood could not be anyone else, of course, but Adolf Hitler" (Dégh 1979, 95).
9. She comments, "The fact that, although sexual interpretations of the story assume that its warning is aimed at pubescent girls, the story appeals strongly to boys as well. This suggests that, on the universal level, the story simulates a facet of human experience that is common to both sexes" (Sugiyama 2004, 123). The presumption that only women and girls experience sexual exploitation and abuse is, of course, utterly false and is debunked in *RRT*.
10. On Poulson, see Doig (1996, 42–45); on Kiszko, see Fennell (1994, 59–60); on Peter Sutcliffe, the Yorkshire Ripper, see Jenkins (1988).
11. Girls and women wearing red jackets, coats, sweaters, and hoodies make LRRH references in many films (see Greenhill and Kohm 2009).
12. Rarely do women represent any other location but that of a victim.
13. Thus, *1983* follows the Grimms' version of ATU 333, in which the woodsman rescues Red, not the Perrault version, which ends with her consumption by the wolf.
14. See criticism of this perspective by Brisman (e.g., 2010).

10

Grimm and the Brothers Grimm

Kristiana Willsey

"The wolf thought to himself, what a tender young creature. What a nice plump mouthful."

The Brothers Grimm, 1812

These words appear superimposed against a backdrop of shadowy trees, illuminated by shafts of light. As the light dies and the forest darkens, the epigraph fades to black and the camera cuts to the first scene of NBC's "fairy-tale procedural" *Grimm*: a sorority girl in a red hoodie setting out for a jog in the woods. As she inserts her earbuds, the ominous strokes of the cello scoring the scene give way to the Eurythmics's "Sweet Dreams (Are Made of This)." The musical and textual cues lend a moment of dramatic irony to the scene, before the nondiegetic music is replaced by the pumping synthesizers of the eighties anthem, drawing the audience into the narrative. The camera lingers on a cherubic Hummel figurine (a porcelain collectible made in Germany) perched improbably on a fallen log. The girl stops to pick up the statue, a blond child in a kerchief, and looks at it in puzzlement for a moment before a hairy, snarling figure flashes across the screen and (off camera) tears her apart.

From the first moment on-screen, *Grimm* makes explicit that the show's source text is the *Kinder- und Hausmärchen*. The world-famous collection of folktales gathered by Jacob and Wilhelm Grimm (first edition 1812) is the canonical literary document the series takes as its starting point. But the old, familiar fairy tales are not the show's object. Like the Hummel figurine, they are the bait, the charming German object of art, a nostalgic relic of the Romantic era frozen in place. NBC's tagline promises, "Remember the fairy tales your parents used to tell you before bedtime? Well, those weren't stories, they were warnings." Come for the fairy tales, but stay for the monsters.

Grimm's format could be characterized as "monster of the week"—each episode features some new species of fairy-tale creature and the fallout of those creatures' interactions with an unsuspecting human world. Show cocreators/writers/executive producers David Greenwalt and Jim Kouf are on familiar ground with this narrative conceit, previously being involved with heavy hitters like *The X-Files, Buffy the Vampire Slayer,* and *Angel.*

The show centers on Nick Burkhardt (David Giuntoli), a police detective in modern-day Portland, who discovers he is a "Grimm," a descendant of the German scholars, and as such has inherited their magical ability to see behind the disguises of supernatural beings, or Wesen, in the show's jargon.[1] Nick explains, "Apparently my ancestors from Germany, the Grimms, who I guess I'm related to on my mother's side, had this same ability . . . that's what I can see—what the Grimms can see" ("Woman in Black," 1, 22).[2] Wesen operate in a society parallel to humanity, with its own politics, laws, customs, and rivalries. Traditionally Grimms have been their enemies, but through his friendship with the vegetarian reformed werewolf-turned-sidekick Monroe (Silas Weir Mitchell), Nick comes to occupy a more ambiguous place between the human and supernatural worlds.

Nick's status as liminal figure, negotiating between Wesen and human systems, has a textual equivalent in the epigraphs that open each episode. A framing device that transitions viewers from familiar tale to *Grimm* twist, the epigraph, too, negotiates between known and unknown. The quotations offer authority and stability, only to destabilize that authority and replace it with the "true story." Essentially, *Grimm*'s pointed use of literary quotations works in two directions: outwardly, to authorize its revisionist fantasies in the real world, and inwardly, to critique these texts' accuracy within the fictional show. The positions of history and fantasy are reversed, with textual worlds made distant and the televisual world immediate—a familiar move in fictional alternate history that calls real events and historical figures into question. The genre's appeal lies in a potent alchemy of recognition and alienation (see Hutcheon 1988; Rosenfeld 2002). The viewer, by recognizing the quotation—or the generic conventions it evokes—is granted a degree of insider knowledge. Familiar fairy tales become intriguingly unfamiliar, as they draw out violent and sexual subtexts.

Grimm's means of accomplishing this reversal is striking, in that it invokes a close relationship with its literary antecedents. In addition to the show's opening epigraphs and its clear line of descent from the nineteenth-century scholars, library research often plays a key role. However, *Grimm*'s construction of fairy-tale lore relies on a slippery and selective reading of the Grimms' canon. The increasingly narrow set of narratives, themes, and authors that have come to define the genre demonstrates what Susan Stewart (1991) called "artifactualization": the circular, reductive gathering and editing of texts according to a specific, subjective notion of what constitutes an authentic fairy tale. By striving to reinvest gothic horror into the too often Disneyfied landscape of fairy-tale adaptations, Kouf and Greenwalt participate in a purification project that reifies a persistent Romantic narrative about authenticity, which, I will show, has telling parallels to the purifying editorial practices undertaken by the Grimms themselves. However, while the brothers imagined their tales as the diminished descendants of a mythic golden age of oral literature, twenty-first-century adaptations—and *Grimm* specifically—often reconstruct fairy tales' origins in the psyche's dark recesses, imagining the first fairy tales as the expression of raw, primal urges.

In this chapter I demonstrate that *Grimm* draws considerable narrative momentum and rhetorical force from the tension between its literary sources and the reimagined fairy tales on-screen. But that tension is artificially heightened by an opaque use of quotation that simultaneously *creates* and *critiques* that preexisting authoritative discourse. Thus *Grimm*'s genre invocation/construction contributes to fairy tales' artifactualization, encouraging an overly simplified, Romantic reading of literary source material to offer an allegedly authentic alternative—the television show's gritty realism. Finally, I consider *Grimm* within the current vogue for dark fairy tales. Though some interpreters deem these violent and sexual adaptations as more authentic, I argue that "authenticity" is a problematic term that naturalizes and obscures the very contemporary need these retold stories fulfill. The current demand for "dark" fairy tales is consistent with a prevailing (neoliberal) cultural narrative in which (honest) savagery has been papered over by (self-deceiving and painstakingly performed) civilization.

Destabilized Textual Authority in *Grimm*

Grimm is certainly one of the most conspicuously literary television series in prime time. In an interview, Greenwalt says in response to a question on the fairy-tale source material, "Well I can tell you the tremendous amount of books that we've read and have on our shelves. But that would be showing off" (Greenwalt and Kouf 2011b). The resolution of each episode frequently relies on textual research.[3] Whenever Nick cannot explain some new element of his expanding reality, he visits an old trailer left to him by his aunt, where he goes through old books in arcane languages from his predecessor Grimms. While scholars like Maria Tatar (2003, 39–57), Susan Eberly (1988), and Eugen Weber (1981) might propose connections between fictional tales and the real-world conditions that produced them (see also Schwabe's chapter) by conducting research and assembling evidence that stories of incest, infanticide, and famine were more factual than fantastic, Nick has very little interpretive work to do. A quick search through his ancestors' journals never fails to turn up the creature in question's identifying features, cultural background, and vulnerabilities; for instance, "Hexenbiest: a witch-like creature that somewhat resembles a demon or a goblin. They work at the behest of royalty and are identifiable by a dark birthmark under their tongues" ("BeeWare," 1, 3).

The implication is that the historical Grimms couched their exploits as fiction, much as modern-day Nick falsifies his official police reports to hide his true abilities. The Grimms' fairy tales known and loved by audiences are reframed as both more true (than they appear in the nondiegetic world) and more false (being no longer simply fiction, but literary deceptions):

> Kouf: The Grimm books that [Nick] has are the original stories that were handed down from the Grimm brothers and passed on and added to by generations of Grimms. So [they're] more like profiles, criminal behavior and creatures. So that's what he's got. He's got ancient books to refer—to reference.
>
> Greenwalt: So that's the research material. But . . . the Grimm fairytales, that book does exist in the world of our show. That could be on a shelf somewhere. But what he's using is very specific profiling source material that's been handed down to him through his family. (Greenwalt and Kouf 2011b)

As Nick's peers are invested in keeping secrets from the nonmagical world, the show simultaneously fictionalizes the Grimm brothers and historicizes their literary productions, neatly recasting all previous iterations of the Grimms' fairy tales, including the *Kinder- und Hausmärchen,* as corrupted, diluted, or willfully redacted. The Brothers Grimm the show's audience may be familiar with are a cover story, a fabrication, and the Grimms they come to know through the show's repurposed history are the reality. *Grimm*'s writers accomplish this by destabilizing the authority of the very texts they use to validate their own contributions.

The epigraphs that open each *Grimm* episode explicitly position the show within an authoritative discourse, assuring viewers that the show's writers have done their homework and are thus entitled to contribute to the genre. The notion of the Grimms' folktales as coded allusions to historical events is more than a jumping-off point; the relationship between the contemporary television series and the nineteenth-century folklorists is revisited consistently throughout the series. For the show's audience, a quotation from the Grimms anchors the fictional story in a real-world literary history. It traces a line of descent from a centuries-old document with worldwide name recognition and trades on its cumulative authority. The epigraph, as literary theorist Gérard Genette notes, frames and clarifies the relationship between two separate texts. Its "most direct function is one of commentating, sometimes authoritatively, and thus of elucidating and thereby justifying not the text but the *title*" (1997, 156, emphasis in original). *Grimm* is a compelling title not least because it resonates with its English synonym; calling a show "Straparola" or "Jacobs,"[4] for example, wouldn't look nearly as forbidding carved out of stone and spattered with dark blood. The opening quotation and its attribution—*The Brothers Grimm, 1812*—validates the show's title and offers some return for the cultural caché *Grimm* receives by trading on its famous predecessors.

After all, "this use of the epigraph as a justificatory appendage of the title is almost a must when the title itself consists of a borrowing, an allusion, or a parodic distortion" (Genette 1997, 157). "Distortion" is an apt term for the selective reenvisioning of the Grimms in the NBC series. The Grimms from whom Nick has inherited his supernatural abilities are not the nineteenth-century scholars and linguists whose collections of German folktales and legends found an initially unexpected popular audience. The show takes a cue from Terry Gilliam's 2005 film, *The Brothers Grimm,* in recasting Jacob and Wilhelm as nineteenth-century vigilantes, monster hunters, and mercenaries who do not merely document the German people's oral literature but also access a secret history (see Magnus-Johnston 2013). The *Kinder- und Hausmärchen* becomes a codebook or a palimpsest making obscure or overlooked allusions to diegetical events: WWII, for instance, takes on startling new meaning when Hitler is revealed to be a Wesen ("Three Coins in a Fuchsbau," 1, 13).[5] The Grimms' textual authority is introduced only in order to be overwritten.

Repurposing the Grimms

Because *Grimm* needs to move beyond its source material to be a worthy and watchable adaptation, its writers cannot simply rest on the authority of the texts they quote. Rather, the opening quotations act chiefly as a foil against which the show's events work, conjuring images to "distort," to use Genette's term. In theory, Kouf and Greenwalt are rediscovering their source material's grim(m) potential—"the child molester as a Big Bad Wolf"—which some previous fairy-tale iterations have softened and sanitized for young audiences (Greenwalt qtd. in Long 2012). However, the quotations chosen more often emphasize the tale's Romantic, storybook inflections, the better to act as backdrop for the violence and brutality of the contemporary crime procedural format (a genre depicting the realistic—in theory—detection and pursuit of lawbreakers).

The textual reference of "Organ Grinder" (1, 10) is easily identified with "Hansel and Gretel": "We shall see the crumbs of bread . . . and they will show us our way home again." The story is among the best-known and most re-mediated of the Grimms' canon; "leaving breadcrumbs" has even become an idiomatic expression for making a trail to follow (see Tresca's chapter). *Grimm* isolates this iconic image through the epigraph, but while the Grimms' tale is hardly tame, dealing with child abandonment, cannibalism, and murder, the first three minutes of "Organ Grinder" racks up a body count. Set against graphic shots of one fresh corpse being heaved into a fiery pit and a second body drifting down a river as crows peck the blank eyes out of its bloodless face, the Grimm's quotation comes off as rather formal, disengaged from reality. The young people in the opening scenes did not find "[their] way home again," and the graceful presentation—a white font against dark trees, the letters' edges somewhat uneven, as if produced by a woodcut press—appears to come from a different time.

The *Grimm* version's horror and sadism relies, to a certain extent, on its contrast to the epigraph's formality and Romanticism: the discrepancy between the literary Grimms' cover story and the diegetical true story. Upon resolving the case and dispatching the villain, Nick hides evidence from his human partner that the organ-harvesting ring was supernatural—presumably falsifying his police reports just as his German ancestors fictionalized their tales. He frequently destroys inconvenient proof of the supernatural world, upholding the official story while he encounters more ways that familiar fairy tales are stranger and more brutal than the lead-in quotations describe. Juxtaposed against the police procedural genre's gritty urbanism, bloody crime scenes, and autopsy reports, the epigraph's poetic nineteenth-century language comes across as rather quaint—certainly watered down compared to the gruesome stories playing out on screen.

"Happily Ever Aftermath" (1, 20) plays by the same rules, opening, "And they all lived happily ever after." The ubiquitous, saccharine closing formula stands in stark counterpoint to the episode's actual conclusion: the beautiful Cinderella figure is in fact a shrieking bat hybrid who ends up murdering her entire stepfamily before being dispatched by her nonfairy godfather. The quotation and its burden of associations underscore the contrast between the "traditional" tale and the "dark" twist, with the literary text as foil for the tragic and bloody immediacy of the fictional show. Yet the phrase "happily ever after" does not belong to the Grimms, and the end of the 1819 version of "Aschenputtel" focuses not on enduring love but rather on retribution: "Afterwards, as [the stepsisters] came out of the church, the older one was on the left side, and the younger one on the right side, and then the pigeons pecked out the other eye from each of them. And thus, for their wicked-ness and falsehood, they were punished with blindness as long as they lived" (Ashliman 1996–2012). While "once upon a time" and "and they lived hap-pily ever after" have become the iconic fairy tale's predictable bookends, the narratives the Grimms collected were considerably more diverse in tone and less regimented in format than these formulas.

The familiar opening and closing formulas became associated with the Grimms through Edgar Taylor's first English translation (Schacker 2005). That the Grimms have become identified with these very English idioms is a testament to their centrality in popular conceptions of fairy tales. In another fictional representation of the brothers, the movie *Ever After: A Cinderella Story* (1998), Jacob and Wilhelm meet an aged member of French royalty, who has summoned them to her bedside to correct their version of "The Little Cinder Girl." As she begins her narration of the "true" story, she asks, "Now then, what is that phrase you use? Oh yes. Once upon a time" (see Stephens and McCallum 2002; Preston 2004; Williams 2010). *Grimm*'s writers play with a stacked deck; they benefit from treating textual references as simultaneously authoritative and archaic but rely on a reductive and selec-tive reading of the Grimms' canon.

The Grimms' unchallenged popular appeal over other fairy-tale writers and collectors is demonstrable; within the show's world, "Grimm" is not simply a name but rather a title or profession. All previous and subsequent monster hunters/scholars are "Grimms," because for American popular audiences, the Grimms are the (bloody, beating) heart of the fairy-tale genre, independent of geography or time period. Regardless of whether a version is the product of seventeenth-century French salons, Romantic German nationalism, English oral tradition, or Japanese legend, if it's a fairy tale, it belongs to the Grimms—or in this case, to *Grimm*. As Kouf states, "We're saying that the Grimms were the profile[r]s in their territory at their particular time. But anybody who told fairytales actually had the ability to see these characters. So they're kind of related to the Grimms. So we will draw on fairytales from all over the world" (Greenwalt and Kouf 2011b). Greenwalt adds, "They're a rare thing, but there are other Grimms in the world, all of whom are descended from the Brothers Grimm" (Greenwalt and Kouf 2012). The title "Grimm" extends back in time to earlier collectors, whose contributions to the library are written in Spanish, Japanese, and even Latin.

By this logic, there is every reason to draw equally on folklore from a variety of literary and oral traditions around the world—they are all (literally) kin. While *Grimm* opens with the quotation from *Kinder- und Hausmärchen* (1812) to lean on the authority of the historical Brothers Grimm, after that first attributed epigraph, the opening quotations have no specific author, collection, or edition. And they are not necessarily drawn from the Grimms. "Bears Will Be Bears" (1, 2) opens with a line from "The Story of the Three Bears," an English oral traditional folktale adapted by the poet Robert Southey (Tatar 2002, 245). "Lonelyhearts" (1, 4) takes a fragment of Perrault's 1697 "Bluebeard" as its epigraph, while "Last Grimm Standing" (1, 12) references Aesop's "The Slave and the Lion," and "Tarantella" (1, 11) adopts a line from "The Goblin Spider," a Japanese folktale translated by Lafcadio Hearn (Hearn 1931; Tatar 2002, 151). Kouf and Greenwalt know that the Grimms are not the only fairy-tale authors/collectors:

> Greenwalt: Eventually we're going to [be] drawing on fairy
>   tales from all over the place, all over the world.
> Kouf: Goldilocks is not a Grimm.
> Greenwalt: Neither are the Big Bad Wolf and three pigs.
>   (Greenwalt and Kouf 2011a)

Tales from various regions and eras appear in *Grimm,* but none beyond the first is explicitly identified or credited. This lack might be considered a misleading attempt to stretch the Grimms' cultural authority and name recognition over less familiar authors/collectors. Perhaps viewers with only a casual acquaintance with folklore could assume that subsequent opening quotations are drawn from the same source as the first. However, within *Grimm*'s mythology, all folktale and fairy-tale collectors are "Grimms" (profilers of monsters and defenders of humans against Wesen), thus all fairy tales are, by extension, fair game.[6] The Grimms have taken over the landscape of twenty-first-century fairy tales; they are the world's most recognizable and misunderstood folklorists.

This creative, inclusive use of multiple fairy-tale traditions becomes rather more fraught when the (still unattributed) epigraphs draw on nonfolkloric sources: "Of Mouse and Man" (1, 9) makes use of a (slight misquotation)[7] of John Steinbeck's 1962 Nobel Prize acceptance speech (not the novella referenced by the title). "BeeWare" opens with a line of dialogue from the 1955 Joan Crawford film *Queen Bee*, perhaps because the quotation was more fitting, and had a better fairy-tale ring, than anything they could find in the Grimms' tale of the same name. According to NBC.com's "Grimm Guide," "Leave It to Beavers" (1, 19; a title obviously alluding to the 1950–1960s sitcom) is inspired by "Three Billy Goats Gruff," a Norwegian tale collected by Peter Christen Abjørnsen and Jørgen Møe (1970). However, the text ("'Wait!' the troll said, jumping in front of him. 'This is my toll bridge. You have to pay a penny to go across'") does not appear in any translation of that tale. In fact, a troll that demands money, not blood, would disqualify this story from its ATU tale type, 122F, "Wait till I Am Fat Enough." The quotation may come from the children's picture book *The Toll Bridge Troll* (Wolff [1995] 2000). The premise of *Grimm* is that familiar fairy tales will be re-mediated and reinvested with new meaning by the show's police procedural format. The opening epigraphs act as touchstones to the earlier text. However, *Grimm* instead uses quotation to suggest a stylistic fairy tale–ness that relies on a slippery and self-serving construction of the genre as Romantic, Grimm dominated (if not Grimm exclusive), and marked by elevated, poetic phrasing.

A literary epigraph, borrowed from an older and more distinguished genre than television, lends weight to the story that follows. Russian linguist and literary theorist Mikhail Bakhtin calls this "authoritative discourse"; "it binds participants independently of its power of persuasion; it is both distant and high, an already acknowledged authority—what he calls a prior discourse" (Young 1993, 119). Such discourse is rhetorically compelling rather than internally persuasive—the manner of expression matters more than the meaning, hence *Grimm*'s slippery attributions. What is vital is the mood those words strike, their allusion to an earlier time and place, to the Grimm scholars, to the mystery yet to unfold.

Quotation marks typically indicate that the fragment of text has been taken, word for word, from a specific document. Quotations without attributions, with no reference to edition, collection, or translation, have other purposes. In "The Thing with Feathers" (1, 16)[8] the quoted text reads, "Sing, my precious little golden bird, sing! I have hung my golden slipper around your neck." This line appears in slightly more elaborated form in "The Nightingale," a literary fairy tale by Hans Christian Andersen: "You little precious golden bird, sing, pray, sing! I have given you gold and costly presents; I have even hung my golden slipper round your neck." However, the *Grimm* episode's plot has more in common with Aesop's "The Goose That Laid the Golden Eggs." A species of Wesen known as a *Seltenvogel* (rare bird) is trapped in an abusive relationship with a catlike creature known as a *Klaustreich,* who imprisons and force-feeds her to cultivate the precious golden egg forming in her throat. Beyond the superficial ("golden slipper" being reminiscent of "golden egg"), neither Andersen nor Aesop is especially thematically applicable to this episode. Andersen focuses on the shallowness and futility of wealth and station compared to the purer promises of nature and friendship; and since *Seltenvogel* apparently produce only one golden egg in their lifetime, the villain's mercenary motives aren't foolish ("killing the goose that lays the golden eggs").

Fortunately, this doesn't matter. While few viewers could identify the recontextualized Andersen quotation, the phrasing's formality and the antiquated term "golden slipper" mark the epigraph as coming from a fairy tale. From the fairy-tale allusion, the episode derives an elevated literary tone that it subsequently draws power from destabilizing. *Grimm*'s writers have no need to specifically attribute their epigraphs, because what these borrowings accomplish is not the kind of mutual transformation that comes of bringing two disparate but familiar texts into conversation. Rather, it's about establishing the genre expectations in order to undercut them. The difficulty is that the genre being invoked is also being constructed.

Artifactualization in *Grimm* and the Grimms

The simultaneous construction and naturalization of a genre, the better to establish the parameters for an authentic text, is something *Grimm* and the Grimms have in common. Poet and literary theorist Stewart calls this practice of culturally informed editorializing "artifactualization," noting, "there is no natural form here, but a set of documents shaped by the expectations that led to their artifactualization in the first place" (1991, 106). As Regina Bendix (1997), Charles Briggs (1993), and Tatar (2003) point out, for the Grimms, authenticity did not result from accurate transcription; it was as ephemeral and ineffable as the material itself and the unconsciousness with which it was spoken. Although in their first edition preface the brothers claim, "No details have been added or embellished or changed," they altered the tales significantly over the next seven editions. They explained such revisions not as interference with the original text but as a restoration of it (Grimms qtd. in Tatar 2003, 258). As Tatar puts it, "They no longer insisted on fidelity to the letter (as it were) of the tales they had heard, but on fidelity to their spirit" (ibid., 252). With each successive *KHM* edition, the Grimms sought and refined a specific notion of "the fairy tale," altered the texts they encountered to suit it, excluded what did not fit, and sincerely believed that the changes they made restored the German people's true spirit, "the essence of these stories," which despite regional and historical variation "still preserve a stable core" (qtd. in Tatar 2003, 256).

Describing the Grimms' editorializing as "purification," folklorists Richard Bauman and Charles Briggs marvel, "The brilliance of the Grimms' combination of textual ideology and metadiscursive practices is that it is the very interventions into the narrative that help create the illusion of fidelity! . . . The texts reproduced the features of a relatively homogenous genre that the Grimms had themselves created" (2003, 214). In publication, the tales were anonymized,[9] stripped of their performative context, and made uniform in style, and variants from different tellers were combined. *Grimm*'s fairy-tale references are subjected to a comparable process: anonymized and decontextualized, selected for aesthetic reasons rather than deeper significance, and shortened, simplified, combined, and supplemented by non–fairy-tale texts. Bauman and Briggs's "illusion of fidelity," achieved by the deindividualization and homogenization of references, aptly describes the effect *Grimm* achieves by flattening its source material's hybridity.

The key difference is that, according to the *Grimm* mythology, the generically bound fairy tales the epigraphs reference are already untrustworthy— they have been revised, not to restore them as the historical Grimms would have it but instead to conceal the Wesen world from their human readership. This "illusion of fidelity" is authority invoked in order to be denied. For the Grimms, narrative hybridity—mingling oral and literary versions, German stories with French—was corruption to be identified and removed.[10] *Grimm* renders fairy-tale hybridity invisible by the fictional conceit that all fairy-tale authors are Grimms. By constructing an image of the traditional fairy tale in order to explode it, *Grimm* cannot help but participate in the genre's ongoing artifactualization.

German Romantic nationalism, as embodied by the Grimms, took a remote, imagined prehistory when fairy tales were born to contextualize and make meaningful the onset of nineteenth-century modernity. *Grimm*'s quaintly formal and literary epigraphs perform similar labor, "plac[ing] such 'specimens,' characterized by fragmentation and exoticism, against the contemporary and so us[ing] them to establish the parameters of the present" (Stewart 1991, 103). As well-worn stories are mediated, re-mediated, and intermediated, any fairy tale that does not meet the allegedly authentic standards meets resistance.[11] A fairy tale begins with "once upon a time" and ends with "happily ever after." Its central character, a passive princess, an "innocent persecuted heroine," almost certainly has blonde hair and eventually gets married (Bacchilega 1993). While this oversimplified definition hardly describes all of the fairy tales told and retold on page and screen in the past century (see, e.g., Greenhill and Matrix 2010b; Zipes 2011), it is virtually impossible to tell a fairy tale without in some way responding to (whether affirming, contesting, parodying, or exploding) this inescapable trope. The process of artifactualization is ongoing, and it remains most successful when its work is least visible.

Artifactualization is responsible for the overuse of what Greenwalt calls the usual suspects; in self-perpetuating fashion, the best-known fairy tales are adapted anew; through constant re-mediation they remain well known (Greenwalt and Kouf 2011b). When the alleged "discovery" in Regensburg, Germany of 500 fairy tales collected by Franz Xaver von Schönwerth (an obscure Grimms' contemporary)[12] became a trending topic on Twitter, journalists jibed that perhaps now Hollywood would have more material to work with. One suggested, "At the current rate with which the studios are racing to reformulate the fairy tales of Charles Perrault, the Brothers Grimm, and other writers and collectors into modish, mostly live-action films, they will exhaust the familiar canon in two years tops" (Fuller 2012). Graham Fuller sardonically expressed hope that future audiences could look forward to something more original than multiple treatments of Snow White.

But the presumption that the dozen or so fairy tales incessantly told and retold on page and screen are the only ones in existence is an illusion, arising because the genre has become defined by a very small number of tales, repetitively re-mediated with increasingly rigid frameworks. With arti-factualization, however, the social and political mechanisms that produce the notion of authenticity become naturalized. Such a reduction of texts, framed as "survival of the fittest" (Mustich 2011) or a distillation of the genre, sug-gests that the tales that persist are, as Greenwalt says, "the ones that are really iconic [that] have been handed down you know, the ones that have lasting emotional [resonance that] have been obviously handed down [over] the years" (Greenwalt and Kouf 2011b). Ironically not unlike the historical Grimm brothers, *Grimm*'s writers locate authenticity in a stable emotional core, to which generations of audiences have intuitively responded.

Origin Stories and "Authenticity"

Just as the Brothers Grimm themselves edited the oral narratives they col-lected to better reflect what they understood as the authentic folk voice, *Grimm* invokes a particular fairy-tale image as the backdrop for its own brand of realism. As *Grimm* overwrites its literary source material's textual author-ity with the emotionally inflected visual stories on-screen, the series also constructs an origin story against which the epigraphs play. Within *Grimm*'s fantastic world, the existence of books written in a variety of languages, describing similarly improbable creatures and scenarios, offers incontro-vertible proof that familiar fairy tales share a common origin. Within the show frame, the entire repository of the world's folklore can be attributed to a single extended family who could see the magical world running parallel to humanity and who described that secret world indirectly, metaphorically, or fictionally. Encounters with Hexenbiests and Blutbads are fact filtered through literature.

In folkloristics, the imagined existence of a single story that explains all others is the province of "the Finnish historic–geographic method [which] sought to work backwards through the unfortunate changes (or . . . the mis-takes and errors) in order to find the pure unadulterated original ur-form" (Dundes 1969, 9). From this perspective, collecting and comparing a tale type's multiple variants were not merely a means to understand how social and historical context shaped that story to reflect its narrators' values and beliefs. The method had loftier ambitions—to recover a single, immaculate original.

Kouf and Greenwalt begin with the premise that fairy-tale truth origi-nates in the existence of the Wesen world; Dundes's layers of "unfortunate changes . . . mistakes and errors" are the fictional, literary versions that are actually coded or falsified accounts. However, the show links this idea to the mythology of a move from savagery to civilization and humanity's primal, animalistic nature waiting to be discovered, like the dark subtext simmering beneath a familiar fairy tale's surface. For *Grimm,* this darkness can be found in the psyche; Nick and his extended family see beyond the performance of politeness and civility that mask more bestial natures. In the pilot, Nick looks at wealthy, well-groomed Adalind Schade (Claire Coffee) and sees the witch beneath. In the story *Grimm* tells, civilization is only an act, deliberately obscuring something darker, older, and truer:

> Kouf: What we think is a child molester is actually a big bad
> wolf and we see that morph out as they become emotion-
> ally aroused. So that's how you—our main character, the
> Grimm, can see these characters beneath the humans.[13]
> Greenwalt: I think it's really hard to explain what the heck is
> going on in the world and the idea that there's actually crea-
> tures living among us who express the very strange emo-
> tions and impulses that we all have inside us (Greenwalt
> and Kouf 2011b)

Tellingly, Greenwalt invites audiences to sympathize with the Wesen, who must hide the animalistic urges that "we all have inside us." Just as fairy tales' "emotional resonance" is responsible for their persistence over the generations, the Wesen's "emotional arousal" (called "woge") betrays their fundamental inhumanity. But in their monstrousness they become most human and relatable. Greenwalt reflects, "Monroe is the most human of all the characters, because he's the one most fighting his demons and stuff inside" (Greenwalt and Kouf 2011a).

Though they draw on the familiar narrative of ascent from savagery and civilization, Kouf and Greenwalt are as concerned about the fallout of embracing progress, modernity, and civilization as were the nineteenth-century Grimms. This apprehension is most clearly articulated by "Big Feet" (1, 21) in which a Wildermann visits a therapist who prescribes a medical implant to permanently suppress his Wesen form. The device backfires, leaving him instead unable to control his violent outbursts. The message seems to be that humans need not embrace their innate brutality (presumably they should, like Monroe, keep it in check with Pilates and veganism), but they must understand and accept it. The savagery that lingers beneath the performance of civility is the emotional core that keeps society honest. It's a striking reflection of how attitudes toward progress have changed. For the Grimms, authenticity and truth were located in an ever receding mythic past when language was richer and more poetic than their own moment on modernity's cusp. For *Grimm,* authenticity and truth are preverbal and emotional, located intimately in the body; humanity's savage, premodern past was never left behind, only masked.

Making Old Fairy Tales New, Making New Fairy Tales Old

When interviewer Emma Mustich (2011) asked fairy-tale scholar and translator Jack Zipes, "Are 'dark' fairy tales more authentic?" the question was timely. *Grimm* is only one contribution to a much reported trend in realistic fairy tales.[14] At the beginning of the fall 2011 American TV season, two fairy tale–centered television shows premiered, *Grimm* and *Once Upon a Time.* Contrary to predictions that pitted the two against each other ("Once Upon a Time versus Grimm: Will Either Fairy Tale Series Live Happily Ever After?" [Cohn 2011]), despite mediocre reviews, both shows survived their first season with a stable fan base and were renewed for a second season (see Hay and Baxter's and Schwabe's chapters). In 2012, two major Hollywood adaptations of "Snow White" were released: *Mirror, Mirror,* which took a respectable third place in the box office its first weekend, and *Snow White and the Huntsman,* which exceeded expectations and took in 56.3 million at the box office its opening weekend (Young 2012). In 2013 *Hansel and Gretel: Witch Hunters* and *Jack the Giant Slayer,* among others, joined them. These stories adhere to a distinct pattern, as one reviewer commented: "There's one thing that today's fairy tale revivals want you to think: *These aren't the sanitized fairy tales of the Disney Princesses. These are the same stories for grown-ups.* In that respect, they could be seen as returning to their roots as folktales shared by adults that often (and somewhat gleefully) included sex or any amount of shameless, tasteless violence and grisly death in order to maintain the audience's attention" (McMillan 2012, emphasis in original).

The rhetoric of new adaptations of fairy tales marketed (convincingly or not) as older, darker, and more authentic again bears some relationship to nineteenth-century scholars' quest for an immaculate original. But rather than seeing the imagined ur-text as the poetic product of an idyllic premodern past, it conceives of the original story as harder and more savage (see Wright's chapter). Fittingly, Greenwalt (in Greenwalt and Kouf 2011c) cites

Bruno Bettelheim (1976), who argued that fairy tales' violent and sexual themes help children come to terms with their fears in safe, symbolic ways.[15] Like him, *Grimm*'s writers believe that audiences respond emotionally and intuitively to the "original" stories (for Bettelheim, the *KHM* 1857, seventh edition), "spontaneously grasping the deeper meaning of the tales on an unconscious level" (Joosen 2011, 125). *Grimm* is a narrative vehicle for the writers' conceit that fairy tales' dark roots resonate with the dark recesses of the human psyche.

Scholars of popular and vernacular culture (including Bendix 1997; Handler and Linnekin 1984; Stewart 1991; Lindholm 2008) strive to eliminate an (uncritical) obsession with authenticity from academic conversation. They argue that the word is an illusion of the very processes that created it in order to have something to save: "'Authentic' means original, genuine, or unaltered, but the semantic domain the term invokes has grown so broad and elusive that one is tempted to place it in the catalog of 'plastic words' devised by language scholar Uwe Porksen—words that have come to mean so much that they really mean very little while nonetheless signaling importance and power" (Bendix 1992, 104). The much discussed rise of dark fairy tales cannot be a return to more authentic forms, since such purification projects are (at best) futile and (at worst) bad faith; there is no ur-text, and efforts to recover it say more about those who seek it than about any objectively discoverable fairy-tale aura. The question is not, therefore, whether dark fairy tales are more authentic. What is significant, in this fairy tale–saturated market, is that "authentic" remains a highly charged and marketable word, invested, ex post facto, in the violence and sexuality of the source material.

Grimm's writers rely on the aura of the elusive "original" story to validate their revisions:

> Greenwalt: It's dark. I mean the actual tales themselves . . .
> Kouf: Are gruesome.
> Greenwalt: Are really gruesome. And we're not going quite
> that gruesome as the original tales are. But it is definitely,
> you know, it's definitely showing a dark underbelly of life,
> you know, leavened with humor and action. (Greenwalt and
> Kouf 2011b)

It's difficult to tell whether "the original tales" Greenwalt refers to are the Grimms, the "Grimms,"[16] or an imagined pre-Grimm oral text reflecting the dark recesses of the human psyche. Elsewhere, though, Greenwalt invokes the appeal of the "original story" to justify their inclusive hodgepodge of fairy-tale source texts: "We actually try to tell [*Grimm*] from inside the stories as opposed to understanding . . . academic things from outside the stories because that doesn't really help us with *the essential cores* of the stories" (Greenwalt and Kouf 2011b, emphasis added). Previous interpretations, academic research, and social and political contexts are discarded as something "outside the stories." Focusing on the "emotional resonance" that accounts for these narrative forms' persistence, the creators fall back on the same purifying rhetoric that drove the nineteenth-century Grimms. Kouf and Greenwalt being storytellers, not scholars, their redactive practices are less problematic in current scholarship than are the Grimms'. Yet, much interpretive work on the brothers' editorial practices focuses on their liminal status as storytellers and scholars (Ellis 1985; Zipes 2002).

Reviews and popular critiques congratulate contemporary fairy-tale retellings for restoring the stories. For example, "The reverse-sanitization of the fairy tale is a return to the origins of stories . . . they're embracing a concept of the fairy tale that predates even the Grimm Brothers—a trend appropriate enough for the oldest stories of all" (Meslow 2012). Of course, the Grimms' tales are replete with references to cannibalism, infanticide, bodily mutilation, and a rather prosaic attitude about mortality that feels harsh to today's readers. Tatar argues that the stories expressed the daily realities of the lower classes: "As shocking as the deeds of Hansel and Gretel's parents may seem to us . . . they may have tallied with the cruel social realities faced by readers and listeners of earlier generations" (2003, 50). But framing new versions as restorations and returns, stripping away the falsified layers that accrued in the intervening centuries, reveals more of its contemporary tellers than of the prehistory it imaginatively constructs. As Tatar points out, aspects of the stories that appear thrillingly "dark" to modern audiences may have been very believable for nineteenth-century readers—"darkness," like authenticity, is subjective (see Tresca's chapter).

The old version of authenticity is seeing a changing of the guard; *Grimm*'s pilot's opening scene playfully uses the Hummel figurine as a stand-in for the Romantic fairy tales the television series will tear apart. All of the associations for the term "fairy tale" are foregrounded: they are old-fashioned, German, safe, childlike, and, most significantly, a static, bounded object. The porcelain doll stands in for an idealized past that retreats into the distance as one approaches it. However, rather than seeking, as did the

Grimms, to restore the lost glory of an imagined premodern German oral literature, *Grimm* promises to peel back suffocating layers of screen and literary versions—the brothers included—to get at something older, darker, and more primal. Nick Burkhardt's unique ability is that he can see past performances of civilized behavior and recognize that the world is full of people only one emotional arousal away from becoming literal monsters. The show draws a coherent narrative arc from a primeval past of magic and monsters to a refined modern-day world that tries to deny its nature. The underlying mythology of *Grimm* and its cohort of dark fairy tales is a very modern story in which the Freudian return of the repressed is likened to the reemergence of authentic narratives, gesturing backward to an elusive image of humankind's primal, emotional, savage past that is always just out of reach.

Notes

1. Pronounced with a short "e" and an unvoiced "s," unlike the German. Modified German is *Grimm*'s specialized and secretive discourse. The show's werewolf, for instance, is *Blutbad* (bloodbath)—more appropriate to a situation or an event than a being, but the syllable *bad* permits a homophonic resonance with the "Big Bad Wolf."

2. (Season, episode).

3. Fairy tales as key to solving crimes is a recurrent film trope (see, e.g., Greenhill and Kohm 2011).

4. Giovanni Francesco Straparola, a Renaissance era Italian writer and fairy-tale collector, and Joseph Jacobs, a nineteenth-century folklorist and historian, both edited fairy-tale volumes somewhat comparable to the Grimms' but far less popularly known.

5. The Brothers Grimm were notorious favorites of the Third Reich, which deemed their tales the ideal vehicles for inculcating nationalism and teaching traditional German values (see Kamenetsky 1972, 1977, 1984). It's an interesting exercise to imagine Hitler as a villainous supernatural monster, being hunted by the same family of Grimms whose grandfathers' studies of folklore he (mis)uses to support his regime.

6. As Brodie and McDavid's chapter discusses, a similar homogenizing process takes place in *Super Why!*

7. *Grimm*'s quotation is "I am impelled not to squeak like a grateful and frightened mouse, but to roar," substituting "frightened" for Steinbeck's "apologetic."

8. This may be an allusion to Emily Dickinson's poem 314: "Hope is the thing with feathers— / That perches in the soul—" (1990, 5).

9. The notable exception was Hessian storyteller Dorothea Viehmann, the Grimms' ideal folk narrator, whose portrait they used as the *KHM* frontispiece.

10. Bauman and Briggs point out that the Grimms' editing actually naturalized this hybridity, as they incorporated proverbs, parallelism, and repetition, crafting literary texts with oral markers to cultivate an "aura of traditionality and authenticity" (2003, 210).

11. For analysis of the fairy-tale concept's solidification through the twentieth- and twenty-first centuries and Disney's role therein, see, e.g., Bell, Haas, and Sells (1995) and Zipes (1994, 1997).

12. The much hyped Schönwerth tales were not so much discovered as remembered. As Tatar remarked drily, "How astonishing . . . to discover that many of those 'five hundred new tales' are already in print and on the shelves at [university libraries]" (2012).

13. See Greenhill and Kohm (2009) on "Little Red Riding Hood" pedophilia films.

14. Whether or not fairy tales truly are enjoying an unusually successful moment is questionable; they are in vogue more often than not. The trend might be the invention of studio marketing more than objective fact.

15. Despite Bettelheim's continuing substantial popular readership, his methods and scholarship are questionable. As here, his influence is best seen in fairy-tale adaptations and revisions (see Joosen 2011, 123–26).

16. Elsewhere in the interview, Kouf refers to Nick's library—the detailed scientific drawings and descriptions of the Wesen world, not the diegetic Grimms: "The Grimm books that [Nick] has are the *original stories* that were handed down from the Grimm brothers" (2011, emphasis added).

11

A DARK STORY RETOLD

Adaptation, Representation, and Design in *Snow White: A Tale of Terror*

Andrea Wright

Well-known cinematic and televisual translations of popular fairy tales, particularly those from the Disney Studios, do not fully indicate their oral and literary predecessors' sometimes dark and unsettling nature. Yet despite the misconception that the screen fairy tale best suits a younger audience, the genre has provided some filmmakers with the opportunity to explore and experiment with mature themes, representations, and aesthetics. Michael Cohn's 1997 retelling of "Snow White" (ATU 709) as a "tale of terror," visually and thematically recapturing and enhancing the Grimm story's sinister nature, provides a significant example. Made for television, *Snow White: A Tale of Terror* (henceforth *SWTT*) offers a creative, adult-oriented retelling that Jessica Tiffin calls "in many ways a deliberately nasty piece of cinema" (2009, 204).

The screen version explores areas commonly associated with the written fairy tale, such as gender representations and social and contextual influences. The fascinating representations in this film include performances of masculinity and femininity, especially Sigourney Weaver's vibrant stepmother, Lady Claudia. A woman in the role of persecutor or possessor of malevolent powers often fascinates filmmakers. On a fundamental level, it is perhaps the destruction of women's image as protectors and nurturers that is so disturbing and yet intriguing about these characters. The screen fairy tale also invites consideration and assessment of filmic and aesthetic qualities. As Jack Zipes notes, using Robert Stam's approach, film adaptation can be understood in terms of "the artistic and technical mode employed by the filmmaker to change and re-create a known or popular text" (2011, 10). The process of adaptation and the ways that filmmakers translate stories from text to screen generates varied and stimulating productions that reference written sources but also reveal inspiration garnered from a range of cultural influences. In this film, gender representation, in conjunction with a visual style that combines historical, romantic, fairy-tale, and Gothic tropes, generates a truly dark and nightmarish fantasy. This chapter explores adaptation, aesthetics, and representation in Cohn's film and how they interrelate to create an eerie screen fairy tale. I argue, with particular reference to the representation of women, that the movie is innovative and unconventional, especially when compared to other "Snow White" adaptations and when read in relation to critical approaches to the story.

The title sequence of *SWTT* claims it is the Brothers Grimm's version. Indeed, one alternative title was *The Grimm Brothers' Snow White* (Stephens and McCallum 2002). The white Gothic-style text is displayed over a frame filled with blood. This intertitle, a peritext, influences and guides viewer expectations (Genette 1997, 1–5). Gérard Genette argues that every text has accompanying devices that mediate it for readers, which he calls paratexts. Of these, peritexts exist inside the work (e.g., chapter headings, intertitles) and epitexts (e.g., DVD sleeve blurbs, interviews) outside it. In this instance, the peritext immediately suggests this adaptation is more authentic, or at least more in touch with the Grimms' story, than others, particularly the culturally dominant Disney version.

In an interview that preceded the film's release, producer Tom Engleman recalled, "It was four years ago and I was reading the Grimm tale to my young niece. And as I was reading, I felt this sudden rush of discovery. Here was an untouched—at least by filmmakers—malevolent rollercoaster ride dealing with a young girl surviving a tough ordeal and emerging from it a strong and determined woman" (Jones 1997a, 25). Engleman's astonishment that, in his opinion, no existing adaptation captured the Grimm tale's essence indicates that with multiple versions available, the source text is often distant from public consciousness. Kamilla Elliott's comments on the broader literature/film debate connect pertinently with the fairy tale: "The adaptation is a composite of textual and filmic signs merging an audience consciousness together with other cultural narratives and often leads to confusion as to which is the novel and which is film" (2003, 157). In revisiting the source material and reconnecting with it, filmmakers can proclaim a renewed sense of fidelity to a text that has been adapted many times.

M. Thomas Inge argues, "Disney stands in relation to the twentieth century as the Brothers Grimm did to the nineteenth century" (2004, 140). Both produced popular versions that became definitive of their form, and both were retellers and reshapers. The Grimms collected, collated, edited, and reworked folktales for publication, and in doing so, somewhat controversially, put their own stamp on them (see Zipes 2002b). In adapting "Snow White," Disney edited and deleted aspects of the Grimm story, making it suitable for younger audiences and, arguably, following his ideological biases. Inge points out that the film was also indebted to the then relatively short history of film and not simply to the fairy tale.

Records indicate that popular film and entertainment personalities influenced Disney's animators' design and character decisions. Laurel and Hardy, Charlie Chaplin, Will Rogers, Harry Langdon, and W. C. Fields reportedly inspired the dwarves' creators. Early 1930s horror films such as *Dracula* (1931) and *Dr. Jekyll and Mr. Hyde* (1931) provided ideas for the sets and atmosphere (Inge 2004, 139). Disney also drew inspiration from the innovators of European cinema. The impact of German expressionism and the work of animator Lotte Reiniger are apparent in the designs and themes. Ultimately, Inge argues, "Faithfulness to the art of filmmaking is more important than faithfulness to the text, and the principles of evaluation should be cinematic, not literary" (ibid.). Moreover, Zipes argues, "Filmmakers are so thoroughly conversant with so many different versions of oral and literary tales that they may not need to re-read and analyze texts" (2011, 83). Filmmakers often owe more to their own art than to source texts.

The makers of *SWTT* seem to have consciously avoided Disney's influence. While Engleman's recollection suggests that the Grimms' text was important, a range of cinematic inspiration is abundantly clear. Lighting, sound, interiors, exteriors, and artifacts borrow from Gothic horror. The Hoffman home external shots use the suitably dramatic fifteenth-century Kost Castle, Prague, and the medieval stone interiors become increasingly shadowy as the narrative progresses. The great magic mirror, encased in a cabinet adorned by an intricately carved midsection of a woman's body, has interlocking clasped hands holding the door closed. The castle's inhabitants become zombie-like as Claudia takes control of them to protect her from curious intruders. Haunting incorporeal voices speak to the characters, dense woodland holds terrors for the heroine, and expressionistic weather echoes the stepmother's vengeful rage. The dark and mature content with Oedipal overtones owes much to earlier adult-oriented screen fairy tales such as Neil Jordan's *The Company of Wolves* (1984), a treatment of Angela Carter's reworking of "Little Red Riding Hood." Cinematic influence also came from more unexpected sources. Of the Outcasts, the misfit band who replace the Grimms' and Disney's seven dwarves as Snow White's initially reluctant assistants, Engleman noted, "The main image we worked from with the Outcasts were the gang in *The Wild Bunch*" (Jones 1997a, 26).

Screen fairy tales offer a complex suturing of influences. The oral or literary tale may well be the foundation, but popular cultural imaginings and a range of artistic and historical inspirations contribute to the finished productions. Cinematic fairy tales must provide a simultaneously satisfactory and convincing interpretation of the fantasy space. Most spectators' knowledge of the genre is based on previous cinematic adaptations, some version of the written text, and the fairy-tale motifs broadly disseminated throughout popular culture. As Richard Allen suggests, genre cinema in particular relies on audience expectations. Because "the generic intertext already forms a part of the spectator's stock knowledge, the individual genre film simply taps into a reservoir of themes and images already possessed by the spectator" (1995, 15). It is the role of the screen designer, therefore, to meet and exceed these expectations and provide a cinematic reality that has texture, depth, and dimension but also fidelity to the genre. As a result, Zipes points out, "Just as we know—almost intuitively—that a particular narrative is a fairy tale when we read it, we seem to know immediately that a particular film is a fairy tale when we see it" (1997, 61).

The design choices made by producers of screen fantasies vary considerably. Quite liberal adaptation of and borrowing from different time periods and blending the loosely historical with the fantastical (see also Barzilai's, Nelson and Walton's, and Rudy's chapters) are common. The producers of *SWTT* worked to validate the Grimms' story by making particular decisions about setting and characters. Engleman commented,

I insisted that each image [i.e., the sections of the story] be analyzed for what lay behind it too. For example, Who is Prince Charming? Is it someone she already knows, or a stranger? Who her real Prince would be and who it actually is are two entirely different things. Also, the idea of Kings and Queens seemed outdated. In the late fifteenth century, when our story is set, powerful people tended to be barons or landowners. It was vitally important that we made specific what the Brothers Grimm left general; interpret the poetic images to reflect a more realistic, historic and accurate truth. (qtd. in Jones 1997a, 26)

This final claim is rather bold, especially when the finished film's design schemes are far more indistinct. The script sets the film's opening date as 1493, thus coinciding with the Renaissance in Northern Europe. This period marks the passing of European society from a religious orientation to a far more secular one, a move away from mysticism and unquestioning faith to belief in reason and scientific inquiry. Indeed, some signs of this period of change appear early in the film in Frederick's (Sam Neill) study/library; the background of the room reveals what appears to be a large scientific apparatus. Moreover, tensions between science and the supernatural manifest throughout the film. The costumes look like a combination of medieval and early Renaissance designs, also signaling a point of change. The film does, though, appear less firmly rooted in the Renaissance than another 1990s Grimm adaptation, Andy Tennant's *Ever After: A Cinderella Story* (1998; see Preston 2004; Williams 2010), which shoehorns Leonardo da Vinci into the Cinderella story.

The historical setting's uncertainty, despite the script's precise date, is emphasized by other elements of costuming and style. For example, actor Weaver enthusiastically describes the design for stepmother Claudia's old hag disguise: "We concocted this person from 'The Canterbury Tales'; hunched over, slightly drunk, with big ears, horrendous teeth and a Breugel face" (Jones 1997b, 31). *The Canterbury Tales* reference is probably to "The Wife of Bath's Tale," the old woman the knight describes as "a fouler wight ther may no man devyse" (Fisher and Allen 2011, 128). Combined with mention of mid-1500s painter Breugel, the reference further demonstrates the vagueness of the film's historical setting.

Moreover, the clothing for the two central women, Claudia (when she is not in disguise) and Lilli (Monica Keena), is more in keeping with Pre-Raphaelite romantic medievalism than with the alleged date. For example, when she first arrives at the Hoffman home, Claudia's clothing and hairstyle, particularly her overgown of rich ivory silk with a bold yellow print, is reminiscent of Dante Gabriel Rossetti's 1867 painting *Monna Rosa*. Weaver's own physical appearance further accentuates the link; her strong and angular jawline and full hair suggest a look Rossetti seems to have favored. Lilli also looks like a Pre-Raphaelite woman, especially when she wears her mother's gown at a party. Her costume recalls the delicate-featured maids found in the work of artists like John William Waterhouse.

Through a combination of design and representation decisions, *SWTT* appears to be what Zipes terms an "experimental film." Such works, "while often commercial as well, question the essentialist notion of representation and the arbitrary authority of the male mirror. The traditional Grimms' tale is often fractured to provide multiple and alternative perspectives about the story" (2011, 123). The representation of gender, in particular, makes this film unconventional. The complex gender and gender role depictions are available to numerous readings and interpretations that may unsettle existing approaches to the story.

Feminists in particular have commented on the mirror's function and importance placed on beauty within the "Snow White" story. Sandra M. Gilbert and Susan Gubar discuss how the mirror functions to uphold patriarchy and its evaluation of feminine beauty. They suggest that it is the king who makes the choice as to who is the fairest of them all. But eventually he himself becomes unnecessary because his is the mirror's voice and the internal voice perpetually evaluating the women. The queen, they argue, is not threatened simply by the youth and burgeoning sexuality of Snow White and her competition for the king's affections. Snow White actually represents the part of the queen that she wishes to destroy within herself—the submissive, pure angel—an ideal that the queen finds abhorrent (2000, 39). Her desire to reject the role of obedient and submissive woman makes her dangerous to patriarchy, and therefore she cannot be permitted to exist. While numerous adaptations of the Snow White story enunciate the masculine appraisal of feminine beauty and polarity between the good and passive princess and her evil and active stepmother, it is difficult to read *SWTT* as adhering to these conventions. The film complicates the representation of, and the conflict between, masculine and feminine and between women.

The film's sinister opening sees Lilliana Hoffman (Joanna Roth) beg her husband to save her child by cutting it from her dying body after a coach accident in the woods. The scene is presented in muted colors as daylight fades. The Hoffmans' carriage travels with urgency as Lilliana's labor pains become more frequent. On the perilous snow-covered track the carriage veers dangerously close to the edge and wolves begin to close in on the travelers. An ominous black crow settles in the trees above and squawks loudly, signaling the impending tragedy. When the carriage leaves the road and careers down the steep hillside, the mortally wounded Lilliana insists that her child be saved. A mother sacrificing herself in childbirth, historically not uncommon, is represented particularly violently in a combination of white, black, and red. As John Stephens and Robyn McCallum observe, "Thus Lil[l]i's life begins not only in violence and death, but at a moment when the uncanny, in the shape of sentient ravens and wolves with glowing eyes, irrupts into the world. There thus appears to be some inherently evil force in the forest that causes the accident that mortally injures the older Lil[l]iana, and this in turn points towards the conflict between the privileged civilized world and what lies beyond" (2002, 204; see also Tiffin 2009, 205).

This opening makes Lilliana the idealized, good, even angelic mother; later the audience sees her grave marked by an angel and a portrait in the Hoffman home showing her dressed in white. Bruno Bettelheim contends that the fairy tale distinguishes between the good pre-Oedipal mother and the evil Oedipal stepmother. The female child's wish to enjoy an uninterrupted relationship with the father but to still experience a mother's loving care sets up a conflict, resulting in a "benevolent female in the past or background of the fairy tale, whose happy memory is kept intact, although she has become inoperative" (1976, 112). Vanessa Joosen argues Bettelheim's influence on contemporary criticism, retellings, and popular understandings of fairy tales: "Retellings and criticism participate in a continuous and dynamic dialogue about the traditional fairy tale" (2011, 3). Such exchange makes unsurprising the appearance of Bettelheimian ideas in new retellings like *SWTT.*

After the opening credits, the film skips forward in time. The child, named Lilli for her mother, is introduced as mischievous and willful. However, unlike numerous "Snow White" adaptations, such as those of Disney (1937), Shelley Duvall's *Faerie Tale Theatre* "Snow White and the Seven Dwarfs" (1984), and the Cannon Movie Tales *Snow White* (1987), the difficult relationship between Lilli and Claudia is instigated by not a vain stepmother but a jealous daughter. When Claudia first arrives at the Hoffman home, she attempts to win her new stepdaughter's favor by presenting her with a puppy. The older woman shows no malice toward the child, but the girl perceives her as an intruder who comes between herself and her father. The first time any tension is caused by Claudia's actions is when Lilli observes Claudia and her father embrace. Claudia clearly notices the girl hidden in the shadows; she stares directly at her and lifts a possessive hand to her soon-to-be husband's head. This gesture signals that he is now hers. Soon afterward, at Claudia and Frederick's wedding, the envious child attempts to ruin the ceremony. While a priest prays and anoints the bed with holy water, the guests and household queue up to pour a small cup of wine onto the covers. Lilli reluctantly steps forward and, after a moment's hesitation, throws the red liquid over Claudia. The child's action, while appearing simply petulant, signals the couple's misfortune.

At the two women's next encounter, some years later, Lilli is sixteen and Claudia is heavily pregnant. This time Claudia's unwillingness to acknowledge that the child is now a woman causes tension between them. Reluctant to put on the simple gown that Claudia chooses for her to wear at a party, Lilli searches for her dead mother's belongings and discovers a white, fur-trimmed dress. She then makes an entrance late at the party. Her stepmother literally occupies center stage with a vocal performance while the guests and her husband listen in silence and watch in rapt admiration. Claudia is dressed in heavy gold fabrics accentuated with fine embroidery and precious metal. Her radiance and beautiful singing voice make her a mesmerizing spectacle. Slowly the crowd parts and heads turn as Lilli makes her way through the room; eventually she attracts her father's attention and her stepmother abruptly discontinues her song. Lilli basks in the admiration and her father's approval. When the two dance, Claudia becomes visibly agitated. The camera spins with the carefree musical rhythm and whirling as father and daughter laugh together. Claudia becomes dizzy and disoriented. She calls her husband's name to no avail and eventually collapses and loses the child. Once again, childbirth is displayed as violent and dangerous. Claudia's anguished cries echo in the castle hallways, and servants carry away blood-soaked sheets. When the audience sees Claudia again she sits in the birthing chair with one leg raised, covered in blood. Outside the room, for the first time, Lilli seems upset and frightened.

From this point, Claudia becomes the recognizably malevolent stepmother. But, as Weaver notes, "The key to Claudia is that she starts out as normal as the rest of us, she isn't evil" (Jones 1997c, 28). Arriving in a new household, eager to be a good wife and bear a child for her husband, she not only has his jealous daughter to contend with but also difficultly conceiving. When she loses her child, in her mind the stillbirth is linked explicitly to Lilli, and she descends into madness and seeks revenge.

Fundamentally, Claudia's failure to be the perfect wife and mother drives her to psychosis and murder. Weaver confirms that the child's death and the realization that she will never bear another is Claudia's turning point: "I always felt the problem with the Snow White story was that you knew nothing about the Frederick character and you could never understand why this nice guy would pick someone so obviously horrible for his new wife. It was vitally important to me to make it clear that Claudia and Frederick are madly in love at the beginning and that's what Lilli resents. Then when she changes from the perfect wife into the worthless mother of a stillborn child, that's when she looks hideous in the mirror and blames Lilli for everything" (Jones 1997b, 28). Although the mirror's destructive influence has already been indicated to the audience—when the curious nanny opens the cabinet, she collapses and dies in front of Lilli—its power is not fully revealed until Claudia unfastens it after the stillbirth. It is precisely Claudia's predicament that complicates the reading of this particular fairy tale.

From a feminist perspective, Marcia Lieberman argues that fairy stories tend to offer somewhat narrow options for their characters and too often link satisfactory closure to heterosexual roles. These narratives often repeat circumstances in which beauty and obedience are rewarded or imply that happiness is only attainable through submission and marriage. Lieberman's fundamental concern is that fairy tales' presence and popularity gives them the power to impart cogent instruction to their readers ([1972] 1998, 187). Karen E. Rowe echoes this perspective, arguing that traditional fairy tales provide readers with limited and restrained roles and choices and, as romantic fiction, offer up marriage and maternal responsibility as social and cultural ideals (1993, 210). These scholars agree that the fairy tale perpetuates myths of femininity and feminine roles, producing almost inescapable patterns that women are encouraged to emulate from a very early age. Fairy tales consign women to wishing that their own lives will follow a similar course. As Joosen asserts, Lieberman's critique continues to resonate with writers of contemporary retellings: "The negative impact of traditional fairy tales on gender construction that troubles Lieberman is further addressed in metatextual references within the fairy-tale retellings themselves. In particular, the suspicion that children harbor toward stepmothers and stepsisters is frequently blamed on Perrault's, the Grimms', and Disney's exclusively negative representations of stepparents and stepsiblings" (2011, 60).

Knowledge of traditional fairy-tale conventions, and influential criticism of them, provides storytellers and filmmakers with an opportunity to confront and subvert customary representations and narrative patterns. However, recent feminist studies re-view the fairy tale and its tellers, revealing that the genre is more complex and ambivalent than earlier criticism of its patriarchal values might indicate. Donald Haase highlights the ways that fairy tales can be reclaimed and reinterpreted to give new insights and understandings. He argues, "Complex cultural conversations, coding, and personal voices embedded in the language and structures of the fairy tale" need to be acknowledged (2004b, 30).

SWTT appears to respond to the dominant understanding of fairy tales as patriarchal, but it also delivers a more progressive reading of "Snow White." The film offers a scenario whereby a woman's life crumbles because she *cannot* fulfill society's expectations, not because she *wants* to reject them. Claudia, from the outset, desires to be the perfect wife and mother. When she first arrives at the Hoffman home she is greeted by her betrothed, his reluctant daughter, and the staff. Welcomed inside, she turns to a circular mirror on the hallway wall. This brief moment potentially has multiple meanings. It is the first indication of the relationship between the woman and the reflective surface and assures the audience that they are watching a retelling of the "Snow White" story. The mirror's curved surface also distorts Claudia's appearance, perhaps indicating that this woman is not all that she seems. But more likely, it reflects Claudia's ambition to become pregnant, as her image is distinctly fuller from the chest down and her face shows contentment and satisfaction. In this instance, the mirror is linked explicitly to Claudia's desires, and indeed this theme continues throughout the film.

Claudia's willingness to submit to marriage and motherhood, a path deemed by some feminist critics to constrict women's ambitions, is underlined by her behavior and some of her dialogue before the stillbirth. As she is installed into her new home, Claudia, partly to herself and partly to her brother, Gustav (Miroslav Táborský), says, "Tomorrow I will be a wife. A Hoffman. What would mother say if she could see me now? Here? Would she be happy for me? Would she smile? Would she be angry knowing that the world that despised her has embraced me? I do love him, Gustav. And he will love me." From this exchange, it appears that Claudia's mother resisted her societally designated maternal and matrimonial role. By contrast, her daughter is eager to take up hers. When the story shifts to nine years later, Claudia looks in the mirror and speaks to her child. In a soft, wistful voice she tells her unborn infant, "And now you move inside of me. Your blood mingles with mine. You grow stronger with every beat of my heart. And I seem to grow more beautiful with each beat of yours." This speech seems to negate the stepmother's traditional desires in "Snow White" stories. Claudia is not simply vain, yearning to be the fairest of them all. Her beauty, and indeed the hold that she has over her husband, are because of her pregnancy. When she loses the child she loses everything. When Frederick learns that his son was stillborn and that his wife will not bear any more children, he walks away and does not enter the room to comfort his wife.

In her despair, Claudia looks in the ornate magic mirror—which seems to open by itself—and sees a tired, disheveled woman who appears much older than she did previously. In horror, she reaches for face cream and applies it liberally. Seeing that the beauty product makes no difference to her appearance, she smears the greasy substance on the mirror, thus further warping her reflection. This distortion seems a cruel inversion of the reflection in the hallway mirror. "Why is this happening to me?" she pleads. The mirror seems to answer her; a disembodied voice calls her name softly and the glass's image transforms Claudia into her previously radiant self. The reflection offers reassurance.

> Reflection: There, you are beautiful.
> Claudia: Yes.
> Reflection: Your face is perfection.
> Claudia: Is it?
> Reflection: I will always tell you the truth.
> Claudia: Yes.
> Reflection: There is so much to envy. They have always envied you.
> Claudia: They?
> Reflection: Your enemies.

At this point in the film, it does appear that vanity is, to a certain degree, responsible for her actions, but the sequence also encourages empathy with a desperate woman.

Despite this sympathetic treatment of the stepmother, the text is ambivalent in its approach to gender and gender roles. Male and female, as represented by Claudia and Frederick, regularly work in distinct opposition. The contrast is highlighted when Claudia speaks to her unborn child and blesses it with what seems to be a pagan or magic ritual. She burns what appears to be a bird's wing or a bunch of feathers and then strokes her enlarged, pregnant form with them. She also speaks of casting the runes for nine long years in order to conceive. The shot then cuts to a pious Frederick praying for a son at a church altar. Later, when Claudia plans to murder her husband, she drags him, bound, back to the church. In the pews, the bewitched servants mindlessly rock backward and forward in a hypnotic state. Blasphemously she addresses the crucified Christ statue, "I brought someone to keep you company." When the narrative cuts back to the chapel, Claudia is winching a now inverted cross back into place above the altar with Frederick tied to its reverse side. As the catatonic servants chant, she begins a black magic ritual.

Claudia as woman is linked to mysterious, ancient arts, while Frederick as man is attached to orthodox religion. Additionally, as Stephens and McCallum suggest, Claudia embodies a "split between the civilized (her exquisite singing, as of the Middle English poem "Lullay, Lullay") and the dark otherworld of magic and evil witchcraft" (2002, 204). Weaver notes that the script made explicit reference to Claudia's mother's connection to witchcraft, but this material was omitted. Nevertheless, the suggestion remains and the implication that the feminine is dangerous and unpredictable is propagated by the mirror and its female voice. Director Cohn noted, "As she [Weaver] plays it, the mirror could be a fragment of her own psyche, her id, or even some vestige of her own mother. There are implications that the Vanity is a talisman willed to her so that the spirit of her mother can always be close by" (Jones 1997c, 29). The notion that the mirror is Claudia's internal expression is supported by the fact that Weaver also provides its voice. Shuli Barzilai also explores the possibility that the mirror's vocal expression is the queen's. She contends, "The mirror images the mother's wound. This is not the general 'genital deficiency' Freud finds in all women; rather, this is the wound inflicted by the mother's experience of separation. The child of her making finds completion without her" (1990, 530). The notion that the queen's experiences of loss and separation could trigger regression to the fragmentation associated with the mirror phase could apply to Claudia. Not only is she unable to form a maternal connection with Lilli, but she also fails to experience the completeness of giving birth to and nurturing her own living child.

For what is essentially the film's second act, Claudia causes mayhem, and a conventional representation of the nefarious and vengeful woman dominates. She instructs her brother to kill Lilli, but the girl escapes to the woods and finds some unlikely allies in a group of outlaws. Gustav, hoping to appease his sister, slaughters a pig and delivers a heart wrapped in leather and a small sack of remains to her. Claudia, elated, rewards her brother with a lingering, incestuous kiss. She keeps the heart and instructs Gustav to take what is left and put it in the stew by the fire. The filmmakers present this cannibalistic act with zeal, and the scene cuts to a close-up of an appetizing meal being served from the pot. Claudia eats the stew with relish, but, grief-stricken over his missing daughter, Frederick does not touch the food.[1]

Claudia's victory over Lilli is short-lived and her psychosis deepens as she realizes that the girl is not dead. She wills her terrified brother to kill himself and attempts to murder Lilli herself. First, she brings about a collapse in the mine where the outlaws work, and one dies. Second, she initiates a storm in the woods that brings down trees and kills another of the outlaw band. Finally, she disguises herself as an old woman and offers the young girl an apple. Even though this scenario has been played out in countless adaptations, Cohen makes the scene memorable and original. The forest is vibrant with autumn colors and the ground is carpeted with golden and orange fallen leaves. Lilli washes her face in a pool and stops to gaze on her reflection. The water's surface ripples and the image changes to a hideous old woman's. Lilli is perhaps given a glimpse of herself when her youth and beauty have faded; she is not immune to the aging process. Conventionally, the queen looks into her magic mirror and sees Snow White, and "in typical fairy-tale style the mirror simply externalizes the natural process of life and aging" (Bacchilega 1997, 33). By reversing the mirroring, this sequence is more overtly pessimistic, offering not an older woman jealously gazing at the youth and beauty she has lost but a young woman given a foretaste of her own future.

A voice behind her says, "Boo" and she turns to see a woman who, as described earlier, epitomizes physical ugliness. Lilli does not seem to fear the repugnant woman and they converse. As she settles on a tree stump beside the water, the woman takes a bright red apple from the folds of her dress. She hums an indistinct tune and polishes its surface. The rosy fresh fruit contrasts with the woman's gnarled, age-spotted hands. Lilli observes hungrily as the crone bites into the apple and declares it "delicious." Reaching into her dress again, the old woman offers Lilli a second apple and dismisses the need for payment, saying that they are "two ladies on the road together." This short dialogue, like the reflection in the pool, may further emphasize that, as women, Lilli and the crone (Claudia) are on the same journey—one that will unavoidably involve aging and disappointment.

Claudia's malice and the extreme steps she takes to either control or destroy those around her are ultimately tied to her child's death. After the birth, the midwives roughly wrap the dead boy in a sheet and remove the body. Claudia begs her brother, "Don't let them throw him away. He's mine."

Outside, the women toss the small bundle on a fire and hurry off, but Gustav retrieves it and extinguishes the flames. Claudia keeps the dead infant in a shrine in the forest and later brings him back to life in her chamber, now filled with mirrors that seem to amplify her power. The tenderness she shows the child and the lengths to which she is prepared to go to have him live make her a tragic figure.

In the scene at the film's end when Lilli confronts her stepmother in her chambers, Claudia cradles a bundle in her arms and a small, blackened, claw-like hand emerges from the folds. It is also because of the baby that she dies. In their final confrontation, Claudia is about to kill Lilli, but her child's cry distracts her as fire threatens to consume the bed where he lies. The reflection in the magic mirror, for the first time in front of Lilli, speaks out to warn Claudia that the younger woman has a dagger, drawing attention to its uncanny connection with the living woman. Lilli spins around and plunges the blade into the image, wounding Claudia. In homage to the Grimm tale, wherein the queen must dance herself to death in red-hot iron shoes, the injured Claudia steps into the flames that rapidly engulf the room and staggers and whirls in a ghastly dance before collapsing.[2]

Despite Claudia's rather predictable death at the end, the film consistently problematizes conventional representations and readings of "Snow White." Numerous interpretations "tend to agree that its basic themes are female development and female jealousy" (Bacchilega 1997, 31). This version avoids such a narrow emphasis and shifts focus to the damage caused by society's rigid imperatives; fundamentally, Claudia cannot live up to patriarchy's expectations. Her motives for wanting to kill her stepdaughter complicate the usual conflict between women based on vanity and founded on the envy experienced by the aging woman. Susan Cahill, writing about *Stardust* (2007) and *The Brothers Grimm* (2005) argues, "The repetition of this trope in the films points to particular unease concerning, among other things, the maintenance of beauty through artificial means and the position of the older woman within such a beauty economy. The films also often echo a conservative impulse to erase and destroy the older, often more powerful, woman in favor of youth and beauty" (2010, 59). In *SWTT*, Claudia knows that she has become worthless but not merely within a beauty economy. In this respect, perhaps the film criticizes the treatment of older women, particularly those who can no longer bear children. Or, it highlights women's insecurities and the possible consequences for those who fail or are unable, through no fault of their own, to perform their expected maternal roles within society. The film thus aligns with feminist retellings that critique the idealization of virginity and the importance that society places on beauty, in particular, Anne Sexton's poem "Snow White and the Seven Dwarfs" ([1971] 2001).

Lilli's character is also quite unconventional; she does not adhere to the customary representations of a princess waiting to be rescued. As noted earlier, she is willful, is disobedient, deliberately attempts to ruin her father's marriage, and obstructs her own potential for a relationship with her new stepmother. She certainly looks beautiful and innocent, but her angelic exterior is somewhat misleading. When living with the Outcasts, although she is initially frightened, she challenges them and asserts herself. Yet she never becomes masculinized, even when she takes the lead in confronting Claudia at the film's end. Recent adaptations of the same tale, like *Mirror, Mirror* (2012) and *Snow White and the Huntsman* (2012), make the princess into warrior, supplanting the notion of a helpless female protagonist. Lilli is bold and courageous, but she does not change; nor, unlike her recent counterparts, does she take up and use a sword. She fights off a demonic dog, resists the attack of one of Claudia's zombies, realizes the power of the mirrors in her stepmother's chambers and methodically smashes them, and inflicts the knife wound that causes Claudia's demise. But maintaining her feminine demeanor and without incorporating masculine traits or appearance, she avoids the potentially problematic representations of women found in some action cinema. The muscular or masculinized female body may be "disconcerting" and "threatening" because it upsets the conventional balance of male/active, female/passive (Holmlund 2002, 19). Lilli still challenges this balance but remains feminine throughout. She also defies the princess's traditional fairy-tale trajectory and chooses one of the Outcasts over the young, respectable doctor who had previously asked for her hand.

This is a film about women; the male characters occupy the periphery of a narrative about female experience. Lilli and Claudia, but also their physically absent yet ubiquitous mothers, dominate the film's story and visual spectacle alike. Alison Lurie claims that fairy tales are "among the most subversive texts in children's literature. Often, though usually in disguised form, they support the rights of disadvantaged members of the population—children, women, and the poor—against the establishment" (1990, 16). Lurie sees fairy-tale women and girls as, on every level, their male counterparts' equal (1990, 18). In *SWTT,* the male characters are easily manipulated, damaged, and often ineffectual. They are also forgettable when compared to Claudia and her struggle. Although the well-known and popular New

Zealand actor Sam Neill plays Frederick Hoffman, he is a character acted upon rather than one who instigates the action. At the film's beginning he cannot save his wife and it is she who, despite her injuries, thinks decisively and instructs him to save the child. The women around him control him; he indulges Lilli, and Claudia easily beguiles him. When Lilli disappears, Frederick attempts to find his daughter but falls from his horse and returns, in a state close to death, to the castle. The implication is that his wife is responsible. As the search goes on, Claudia lies on the bed and smears the blood from what she believes is Lilli's heart down her bare neck. She gets up and spins wildly around the room as a storm rages outside and her husband is thrown from his terrified horse. Frederick's injury emasculates him; he is physically unable to resist his wife's growing authority. The film also strongly implies that Claudia hinders her husband's recovery through poisoning. When Claudia learns that after three attempts upon her life, Lilli is not dead, angry and desperate she returns to the mirror. It tells her to kill the girl, take her husband's seed, and bathe the infant's body in his blood to bring her son back to life. Frederick is helpless against the powerfully seductive Claudia, and his facial expressions and moans show that their sexual encounter is a mixture of pleasure and agony.

Three of the remaining male roles within the film could be significant characters, but ultimately none have the impact of the story's women. Claudia's brother Gustav, the outlaw Will (Gil Bellows), and Doctor Peter Gutenburg (David Conrad), added to the story by screenwriters Thomas E. Szollosi and Deborah Serra, are, like Frederick, largely acted upon rather than being instigators of action. Gustav is a somewhat sinister and unsettling presence, often in the background, silently observing. He can skillfully perform magic tricks but is mute and seems to be present largely to attend his sister. He approximates the Grimm story's huntsman; although the audience does not witness the command, he has obviously been charged with killing Lilli. Gustav waits for her in the woodland near her home and approaches her with a knife. He shows no mercy and a violent struggle ensues. Lilli breaks free and runs through the trees but slips down a steep bank into a deep hole. Hearing her cries fall silent, Gustav ends his pursuit and retreats to the castle to kill a pig in her place. Bloodied, beaded with perspiration, and accompanied by lightning, he visits his sister and presents a neatly wrapped heart to her.

Later, Gustav drinks heavily in a tavern. He looks afraid. The mirror tells Claudia that he is a turncoat, and her voice whispering "traitor" echoes in his head. As he becomes more agitated, he looks down at a cut on his hand from which a spider emerges. Director Cohn comments that with this scene and other horrific moments, he wanted "to deal in surrealist dream images that have a basis in nature" (Jones 1997c, 29). Outside the tavern, still plagued by his sister's voice, an unseen force makes him pick up a knife and stab himself. He can do nothing to resist the powerful and malicious female's will.

Will is the leader of the mismatched outlaw band whom Lilli stumbles upon in the forest. When the men are first introduced, all, except Will who is restraining Lilli, are filmed in close-up as they huddle around the frightened girl. Their framing as each leans in to speak to Lilli makes them appear grotesque, enhancing their varying disfigurements, poor teeth, dirty skin, and lank hair. By contrast, Will has a neatly cropped beard, short hair, and a smooth complexion. His branding as one of the Outcasts is an angry red scar across his right eye and cheek. His behavior also sets him apart from the others' more vulgar and aggressive conduct; he steps in when Rolf (Anthony Brophy) threatens to rape Lilli. Lingering glances and a crude gentleness signal that Will is attracted to the young woman. However, instead of transforming him into a heroic male, the filmmakers reveal that he is emotionally as well as physically damaged. Lilli is awoken one night by Will crying out in his sleep, and Lars (Brian Glover) tells her that he dreams of fire. Will's family was burned and his face was branded because he declined to fight for crusaders. His refusal to take up the church's cause makes him a rebel and doubly unsuitable for a nobleman's daughter. This fundamental rejection of Christian underpinnings differs from the Grimms' fairy tales.

However, Will dislodges the piece of apple from Lilli's throat. Stricken with grief, he breaks open the unusual stained glass coffin and shakes her, demanding repeatedly that she breathe. However, his potential status as hero is ultimately compromised. He willingly offers to aid Lilli when she returns to the castle to save her father, but overcome by fear, he flees the shadowy zombie-like figures of the former household servants. He forfeits his right to be a hero because of his cowardice. Usually in films of the 1990s that incorporate fallible masculinity and the so-called New Man, "the male hero falls only to ascend, and narrative closure is achieved when the male hero recuperates the power privileges of masculinity" (Stukator 1997, 214). No such restoration of the normative male/active female/passive dichotomy occurs in *SWTT*. As noted earlier, Lilli's agency drives the narrative in a way denied to the film's male characters. As such, it shares some similarities with action movies that elevate women from subordinate positions and disrupt "the equation of men with strength and women with weakness that underpins gender roles and power relations, that has by now come to seem familiar and comforting (though perhaps in differing ways) to both women and men" (Holmlund 2002, 19).

This "comforting" division is further disrupted by the representation of Peter. The young doctor is a rather foppish character with shoulder-length wavy hair and fine clothes. He seems to be a long-term family friend, with Lilli destined to be his wife. He is present at the stillbirth and initially joins the hunt for Lilli when she goes missing. However, he returns to the Hoffman home alone when it is deserted and Frederick is incapacitated by his injury and Claudia's poisoning. In a darkened corridor, Claudia greets the doctor. As she bemoans her loneliness and the misfortune that has struck down her household, she leans in and seductively kisses the young man on the lips. He attends Lilli when she has bitten the cursed apple, but he fails to help her and admits that there is nothing that he can do.

On this occasion and at the stillbirth, Peter shows the inadequacies of science against more mysterious arts. When Will takes the girl from her glass coffin, Peter dolefully tells the outlaw to leave her in peace. Perhaps the doctor is under Claudia's spell after their kiss, but his defeatist attitude supports her evil intention to eliminate the younger woman. When she is revived, Peter takes Lilli back to her father's home, but his manner further undermines the possibility that he is the fairy-tale prince. Peter, with an air of superiority, throws a bag of money at Will for saving his betrothed, rather oddly juxtaposed with the next scene in which he and Lilli ride through the sun-dappled forest on horseback. It mocks the notion that a dashing prince will ride into the sunset with his true love whom he has rescued, especially as Will follows them and offers to help Lilli take on her stepmother. Peter is eliminated unceremoniously in the closing minutes; Claudia pushes him from a window.

Despite having a fairly low-key release on television in North America and straight to video sell-through in Europe, *SWTT* offers a thematically and visually fascinating version of a well-known and often adapted story. Although the film does not appear to be a self-consciously feminist retelling, it certainly disrupts conventional readings of "Snow White" and offers unorthodox representations of both masculinity and femininity. The narratives of both central women unsettle the regularly portrayed conflict between women in adaptations of the fairy tale, and the notion that persecution of youth and beauty is precipitated by vanity is challenged throughout. Unusually, the roles of protagonist and antagonist are problematized, and the anticipated heroes fail to emerge. This is a dark and complex adaptation, even, as Stephens and McCallum argue, "an apocalyptic narrative about which the most positive comment possible is that some of the main characters more or less survive" (2002, 204). *SWTT* reconnects with the Grimm story's sinister nature, but at the same time, it is an innovative and unconventional film.

Notes

1. Compare with the representation of motherhood, murder, incest, and paternal cannibalism in "The Juniper Tree," including director Nietzchka Keene's (1990) *The Juniper Tree* (see Greenhill and Brydon 2010).
2. Contrast Tiffin's understanding of the mirror's relation to Claudia: "Lady Claudia's interactions with her ideal self in the mirror provide an effective visual metaphor for female beauty as power in fairy tale's patriarchal system. In the final scenes of the film, Lady Claudia's existence is seen to be intrinsically and narcissistically bound up with her beauty—when Lily [*sic*] stabs the image in the mirror, Claudia dies (2009, 206).

12

Catherine Breillat's Rescripting
of Charles Perrault's "Bluebeard"

Shuli Barzilai

To Begin at the End

French filmmaker Catherine Breillat's made-for-television movie *Blue-beard* (2009) concludes with a highly stylized scene.[1] Composed of an almost unmoving image, shot at medium range, it shows Bluebeard's last wife, the lucky one, and the decapitated head of her husband on the table before her (Figure 12.1). The scene eludes definition as a *tableau vivant*, a "living picture" used to reconstruct paintings on a theatrical stage, only because of the woman's minimal hand and eye movements. The shot is sustained for about two minutes with the prayer "Kyrie Eleison" (Lord Have Mercy), chanted by an offscreen choir, briefly breaking the silence.

This final scene encapsulates the climax of Charles Perrault's "Blue-beard" (1697; ATU 312), a grisly fairy tale about a serial killer who murders his wives shortly after they transgress his prohibition against using a magic key to open his secret chamber. "Open everything," he intones, "and go everywhere except into that little room, which I forbid you to enter. . . . If you should dare to open the door, my anger will exceed anything you have ever experienced" (2001a, 732). The chamber is a kind of collector's cabinet or gallery in which the bodies of Bluebeard's previous wives hang on the walls.

FIGURE 12.1 Catherine Breillat, still from *Bluebeard* (2009).

In her fright, each wife drops the key into the pool of blood on the floor and cannot remove the stain from it. With proof of disobedience in his expect-ant hand, Bluebeard carries out the punishment he promised, and she joins the other women in his bloody chamber. The last wife, no less subject to the temptations of female curiosity than her predecessors, is saved from their fate only by her brothers' timely intervention: "With swords drawn they ran straight at Bluebeard" (ibid., 735). Breillat's conclusion presents the after-math of this rescue: he who would have added her to his gallery is now put on display.

In this chapter, the tableau-like image of the woman with the trophy head provides me with a mode of access (I hesitate to use "key" here) to Breillat's adaptation and appropriation of the fairy tale.[2] After further discussing the image, I examine several earlier scenes in chronological cinematic order. This approach in reverse enables me to explore the significance these scenes acquire *après coup*—as a result of re-viewing and rearranging cer-tain moments in the light or, perhaps more accurately, in the shadow cast by Breillat's parting shot. After beginning again at the end, my discussion returns to the beginning. But the end cannot be kept from coming back.

To Rebegin at the End

If the final scene of *Bluebeard* were a tabloid headline, it might blare, "Months After Their Fairy-Tale Wedding, Avenging Wife Shows Off Decapitated Husband!" Despite this potentially sensationalist content, Breillat's camera presents a strangely idyllic picture to her viewers. Initially, it seems as if we are looking at a Renaissance painting such as those commissioned by royalty or wealthy patrons. Hanging on the wall behind Marie-Catherine (Lola Créton) is a rich damask and before her, a table covered in green cloth. (I will return to that damask and tablecloth later.) Her shoulders are draped in a red cloak atop which she wears an elaborate chain necklace. Her black dress, appropriate for a widow—but which she wore formerly as a bride—is embellished by a gold brocade panel on the bodice and gold brocade cuffs. Both her attire and placement at the scene center emblematize her newly elevated position as the successor to Bluebeard's (Dominique Thomas) fortune. Similarly, Perrault's tale ends with good news: "It was found that Bluebeard had no heirs, and so his widow inherited all his wealth" (2001a, 735).

There is one odd note, however, in Marie-Catherine's representations as a lady of great means in a bygone era. Her uncoiffed hair falls plainly to her shoulders, indistinguishable from a contemporary teenager's. It would seem to be an anachronism or lapse on the director's part and, as it turns out, was a subject of contestation. As Breillat disclosed in a roundtable talk at *Bluebeard*'s 2009 Berlin Film Festival world premiere: "I had a big discussion with my producer [Sylvette Frydman] because she wanted to have the girls' hair styled in a certain way, but I said no. They had to look exactly how they imagine themselves in the fairy tale, dressed as though they are in the Middle Ages" (Jahn 2010).

To put this statement in context, I would differentiate between two pairs of girls. Those referred to in "the girls' hair" are not coextensive with those in "how they imagine themselves." Breillat's screenplay consists of parallel narratives: one based on Perrault's "Bluebeard," set in the far past, tells of adolescent sisters, Marie-Catherine and Anne (Daphné Baiwir), impoverished by the sudden death of their father; the other, set in the 1950s, takes place inside an attic where a pair of much younger sisters find a storybook titled "*CONTES DES FÉES par Charles Perrault.*" The little sister, Catherine (Marilou Lopes-Benites), an intrepid five-year-old, reads the "Bluebeard" tale with great relish to her sensitive, easily intimidated older sister Marie-Anne (Lola Giovannetti).

This doubling of names—Marie-Catherine and Anne in the fairy-tale world and Catherine and Marie-Anne in the 1950s—points to the distinct yet interconnected story lines of Breillat's script. These names also bring into play a personal history. "My sister's name is Marie-Hélène," Breillat explained during the roundtable, "and in the film she's called Marie-Anne [and Anne], and the little sisters are called Catherine and Marie-Catherine." Moreover, she recalled, "When I read the fairy tale to my [older] sister at the age of five, I did so because I knew she was going to cry and break down before me, and at that point I felt stronger than her. I could have shouted 'I have no fear, I have no fear,' like the little one in the film" (Jahn 2010). Not just two, then, but three pairs of sister rivals with similar or identical names feature in this story. Supplemented by Breillat's extratextual interventions on several occasions, her *Bluebeard* points to a sibling rivalry not prominent in Perrault's tale.[3]

However, for the purposes of my analysis, the film's temporal rhetoric has greater relevance. Set in the vague far past of "Once upon a time," which is how Perrault opens his "Bluebeard," Breillat's adaptation may be understood, at least in part, as the projective fantasy of the little children sharing a literary fairy tale in the near past. As the words read aloud resonate in the dusty air, they take shape and acquire substance for the sisters. Breillat elaborates: "In stories or fairy tales or fiction in general, people usually like to project themselves onto the story," and these children are no different in "projecting their own feelings onto ancient times" (Jahn 2010). Likewise, when discussing projection's significant role in the reading experience, she observes, "For the first time—via the 26 letters of the alphabet—it's all there, and that's what fascinates me about books. . . . You transport yourself into a world of thought, fantasy and image" (Jenkins 2010). The projective processes integral to the pleasures and seductions of reading help to explicate the "untimely" aspects of Breillat's mise-en-scène—her arrangement of the elements placed in front of the camera—that have puzzled and even provoked some viewers.

To (Re)turn to the Beginning

Breillat's *Bluebeard* begins, and similarly ends, with the musical motif of "Kyrie Eleison" and the close-up of a painting or sculptural relief whose theme is decapitation. Against a sky-blue background decorated with golden fleurs-de-lis, an enthroned woman is flanked on both sides by a fallen headless warrior in full armor, and yet beneath her, only one head lies above what appears to be an inverted arch. The soundtrack music augments the religious concept transmitted through the conjunction of colors and forms: the victorious Virgin Mary has defeated Christianity's enemies, as prefigured by the apocryphal Judith's slaying of Holofernes.[4] But it is possible to see something else in the composition. "As the film opens," Catherine Wheatley writes, "we are confronted with a painting of the murdered John the Baptist, his head resting on a platter before the woman who has demanded it" (2010, 41). Only on subsequent viewings can the spectator begin to take in this opening image's implications for the closing scene.

The camera cuts from the painted image to a choir of adolescent girls singing the liturgical "Kyrie" inside an austere convent school, and the fairy-tale plot is set in motion. If the late seventeenth century when Perrault published his *Histoires ou contes du temps passé* is the time frame for this narrative level, these girls' costuming is totally inappropriate. Their uniform dresses end just below the knee and their legs are exposed, sans stockings. They wear white ankle socks with their black shoes. Their unfitting feet in this scene, like Marie-Catherine's uncoiffed hair in the last, belong to the twentieth century.

Analogously, throughout the film's fairy-tale segments, an assortment of clothing and props appear in disregard of any coherent historical style. Thus, sometime after Marie-Catherine and Anne are dismissed from the convent school because their widowed mother cannot afford the tuition—the film's critique of Christian "charity" goes beyond any particularized institutional instance—they accept an invitation from Bluebeard and join a group of young guests dancing on the lawn beneath his feudal castle. Like the ball in "Cinderella" (ATU 510), this scene is a bride show, for one of the attending girls will be chosen as Bluebeard's next wife.[5] The men and women at the party wear a conspicuous mishmash of period costumes. One viewer complained, "I spent about 20 minutes trying to figure out when it is supposed to be set. . . . the party guests [are] dressed like 18th-century musketeers, together with 16th-century dresses" (dosgatosazules 2012). The sartorial anomalies of this scene and others correspond to the incongruent sets and dialogues in which actors utter lines that stretch credulity. Picture, for example, the dreaded Bluebeard, a massive man sitting on the ground beneath a tree, attired in a sixteenth-century garment copied from the state portrait of a king, telling the wide-eyed teenage Marie-Catherine, while she stands gazing down at him with open curiosity: "Everyone sees me as a monster. I take it in. In effect, I become a monster. A sort of ogre, do you understand?" He has a beautiful, gentle, melancholy voice. Sympathy is what he seeks. "Yes," she says.

All of this may be even more baffling when compared to Breillat's previous film, *The Last Mistress* (2007). Paying careful attention to details of period authenticity, she adapted a novel by Jules-Amédée Barbey d'Aurevilly, *Une Vieille Maîtresse* (1851). One critic appreciatively observed, "Swiftly and deftly immersing us in the fashions—not just the clothes and decor, but also the changing sexual and social ethics—of the 1830s, Breillat's meticulous, eloquent script and direction succeed . . . in providing an insightful commentary on the mores and literary concerns of the time" (Andrew 2008). So why the lack of consistency in her 2009 film? Why does her *Bluebeard* elude attempts to situate the tale in a specific period and seem to cultivate temporal ambiguity?

In addressing this question, I stress that from beginning to end, from the bare-legged choir girls in the first scene to the bare-headed widow in the last, the anachronisms are found exclusively in the fairy-tale narrative. Realism prevails in the cluttered 1950s attic: "The little girls are naturals," as Manohla Dargis notes, "and the dusty attic in which they read and play looks genuine enough to sneeze at" (2010). So there is a consistency to this inconsistency, something controlled and methodical in the midst of recurrent confusion, that invites viewers to seek out a function, meaning, or consequence.

One corollary of Breillat's "unruly" re-creation is to generate a sense of timelessness. Although Perrault's seventeenth-century *Histoires,* like the Grimm brothers' nineteenth-century *Hausmärchen,* are rooted in the reality of the times in which they appeared,[6] the classic fairy tales also transcend time-bound categories. This tension between historicity and ahistoricity may be resolved by recognizing that "Bluebeard," "Cinderella," "Little Red Riding Hood" (ATU 333), and "Sleeping Beauty" (ATU 410), among others, constitute memetic narratives: "cultural units of information," transmitted and transformed over time, which remain identifiable as members of the same tale type (Zipes 2012, 18–19).[7] In this sense, the "Bluebeard" story is "ageless" or, at least, transgenerational. It may be traced back to the oral traditions of late antiquity as well as forward to the diversely mediated forms of our postmodern era.[8] Fairy tales such as "Bluebeard" are indeed for all ages (in both implications of this phrase) as Breillat shows by rejecting that hobgoblin of little minds—consistency. Particularly after her 2007 film, she seems to play with audience expectations and confound demands for "authenticity," or the illusion of realism, in period television shows and movies.[9]

Another significant function of *Bluebeard*'s anachronisms is to signal the space left open for fantasy. In interviews and forums, Breillat reiterates that the fairy-tale narrative is engendered by the projective fantasies of the little sisters (and, particularly, of the five-year-old she was) in the 1950s. However, even without such commentary, it becomes clear on re-viewing the film that Breillat's mises-en-scène are designed to reify the imaginative dimension involved in experiencing fairy tales. Marie-Anne and Catherine may be said to enter into the tale of Bluebeard, to inhabit and furnish it as they best know how given their ages and cultural background. They have yet to be hemmed in by the rigors of historical regularity. Above all, the creative child who revels in reading a scary story to her sister may be counted a strong presence in the fairy-tale world, although she literally, physically, appears in it only once at a crucial point discussed in the next section.

To Dwell in (on) the Middle

In narratological terms, then, another complication arises. In addition to the question of "when?" prompted by the fairy-tale setting's equivocal temporality, the question of "who sees?" is occasionally difficult to resolve. Is it the child Catherine who reads from an open book or the adult Catherine who looks over her shoulder, as it were, and oversees the parallel narratives? Both Catherines—two *conteuses* who are nonetheless one and the same—seem to determine how Perrault's "Bluebeard" is reconstructed on-screen. Breillat creates something, call it a mirror or a movie, that reflects her younger self but does not, and indeed cannot, eliminate the adult perspective she brings to the tale.

Nevertheless, while in many instances the child and the adult may be designated "codirectors," in others one takes over as the focalizing agent. Two episodes exemplify this distinction: the first is the bridal bed scene in which Bluebeard and Marie-Catherine seal their marriage pact; the second, the bloody chamber scene in which that pact is broken, and the marriage irrevocably terminated.

On the night Marie-Catherine enters Bluebeard's bedroom as his newly wedded wife, she is displeased at once by what she sees. "Ah no," she says. At the foot of his large four-poster bed, he has prepared a pretty little bed for his bride. "I'm not a dog," she says looking around her, and then tells her husband, "You must snore like an ogre." That is not all: "If I don't have a room in such a castle, I'll return to live with my mother until I'm twenty.

I want a room of my own size." The bridegroom is successively taken aback ("What did I do wrong?") and apologetic ("I thought it was the right thing to do")—and always attentive to his wife.

Thus a solemn *and* comic procession begins as manservants carry the bride's bed along the corridor, while the couple follows side by side. She is all the more diminutive and slight when seen beside him. She is also whimsical, fearless, even dictatorial, and he obliges at every turn of the bed. "There," she announces at last. "This shelf is unworthy of you, Madame," he tries to reason, genuinely appalled by her choice, "You're sure that it suits you?" Marie-Catherine insists, "This will be my room. I want no other." And so it is. The bed is placed inside the little room, and she happily takes possession: "Here, this will be my secret place," and she adds, "No one will have the right to enter. Never." Bluebeard stands at the doorway looking in: "I'm too big to enter," he says. "My husband will always be too big for me," she laughs. He sighs and begins to retreat. "Did I upset you?" she asks, concerned, for they are quite fond of each other. "No," Bluebeard says, "as long as you tell me the truth, nothing will upset me. Goodnight. Sweet dreams."

The episode in its entirety may be read as seen through the eyes of a fanciful five-year-old. Dressed in a pink gingham pinafore of far more innocent times than our own information age, little Catherine is this scene's external focalizer; she is positioned at an observation point outside or above the objects she perceives. So when Bluebeard says, "I'm too big to enter" ("*trop gros,*" meaning also too fat or huge) and indeed appears blocked at the pint-sized room's threshold, his statement means exactly what it says. But the episode may also be read, and with equal cogency, as the focally externalized construction of a sophisticated French feminist filmmaker. Bearing in mind that Breillat has not previously hesitated to portray sexually explicit scenes— scenes so graphic they have elicited the opprobrium of general viewers and movie reviewers alike—"I'm too big to enter" suggests more than it says. Moreover, the camera placed inside the bedroom, looking out and framing Bluebeard's body in the narrow doorway, cannot but add to the suggestiveness. Breillat thus negotiates the disparity between the selves who construe these events. The scene masterfully manipulates dual perspectives.

This wedding night receives no mention in Breillat's source text. It is her own (and the child Catherine's) invention. Perrault writes, "Immediately upon their return to town the marriage took place. At the end of a month Bluebeard told his wife that he was obliged to take a journey" (2001a, 732). The movie fills in the gap between the end of one sentence and the beginning of the next. By doing so, Breillat creates a counterpart to the bloody chamber scene in Perrault's tale, for after Marie-Catherine orders her bed conveyed into the little room, she calls it her "secret place" and prohibits her husband's access. Bluebeard respects the prohibition: he does not violate her private space; he leaves it (or her) intact. There is no transgression of the limits set on the eve of their marriage. The first scene provides a foil to the second through inversion and contrast: *she* forbids; *he* obeys.

Before proceeding to the bloody chamber, let us recall the prohibition pronounced in the fairy tale as the husband hands over his keys just before allegedly departing on a journey. Bluebeard too, of course, has a secret place, a room of his own: "As for this small key, it is for the little room at the end of the long corridor. . . . Go everywhere except into that little room"; and, "She promised to carry out all his instructions" (Perrault 2001a, 732–33). Perrault's and Breillat's plots equally hinge on an act of transgression. Yet, although both stories require the forbidden door be opened, the pattern of Bluebeard's behavior in the movie points to an alternative course.[10] Marie-Catherine could have refrained from sealing his fate, and hers, by not breaking (her promise) and entering (his room). In Breillat's feminist revision, a form of affirmative action takes place. The implicit contrast of the invented bridal bed scene with the prescripted bloody chamber scene demonstrates the screenwriter's contemporary sensibilities.

Unlike the bridal bed scene, Breillat's staging of the transgression repeats her source text almost verbatim. The camera cross-cuts between extreme close-ups of Catherine's face as she reads and long shots of the chamber in which the characters (dead and alive) are shown from head to toes. However, despite Breillat's marked fidelity to Perrault at this juncture, several borders are simultaneously trespassed. Just as Marie-Catherine violates the order of the law within the diegesis, so concurrently the filmmaker replicates her transgression at the metadiegetic level above the diegesis. That is, while until now *Bluebeard*'s narrative levels were kept strictly separate, with no intermingling of the protagonists belonging to each world, suddenly five-year-old Catherine appears hastily descending the stairs of Bluebeard's castle. In the attic she has just uttered the words: "Her curiosity increased to such a degree that . . . she ran down a back staircase." The adult Catherine stands back, as it were, for so vivid is the child's imaginative composition of the scene that her perceptions take over.

Little Catherine slowly opens the door and enters the dimly lit room chanting, as she did earlier in the attic, "I'm not scared, I'm not scared." Her singsong voice further conflates narrative levels as screen–story boundaries collapse: the fictional world of the far past and the "real" world of the near past interpenetrate. The child reads, "The floor was all covered with clotted blood" and puts herself inside the chamber of horrors. Her bare feet slip and slide in a shiny viscous red pool like an oil spill, staining the hem of her white nightgown. She wanders among the suspended corpses of three women in white. The setting is ghoulish, gothic, dreamlike, and somehow innocuous—even when Catherine picks the key up from the slimy floor. The camera swiftly cuts to Marie-Catherine, also wearing a white nightgown and trying desperately to clean the key and, then, back to a close-up of Catherine's face in the attic. "She wiped it two or three times," she reads, "but the blood would not come off" (Perrault 2001a, 733).

Breillat enables these multiple transgressions with postmodern panache: while the child Catherine crisscrosses between fantasy and reality, and while Marie-Catherine breaches her promise by failing to stay on the other side of the door, the adult Catherine closely tracks these illicit movements with her intrusively curious camera. Only Bluebeard observes the rules and codes dictated by circumstance—be it the conventions of an old plot or the exigencies of a new wife—and stays well within storybook limits. He occupies no liminal zones and is fated to be what he is: a gentleman and a murderer.

To Re-rebegin at the End

On the table lies the bearded head, as if asleep and reposeful. All would appear to be in abeyance, static and still, were it not for the woman's hand slowly stroking the head and her eyes, which alternate between gazing out and looking downward. Or perhaps she is looking inward. Unlike her eyes, her head remains motionless, held at a slant. Despite the signs of her recent victory, her expression is neither triumphant nor elated but, on the contrary, pensive and sad. She feels that head beneath her hand.

The scene's subdued, elegiac mood represents a double departure on Breillat's part. In *Bluebeard,* she swerves away not only from the traditional tale but also from her own filmography. Having surveyed the varieties of sexual experience in such controversial movies as *Romance X* (1999) and *Anatomy of Hell* (2004)—in both she cast porn star Rocco Siffredi as a male principal[11]—and *The Last Mistress,* to mention only a few, Breillat sets out now to explore a filmic place she has not visited before: celibacy. Her adaptation gives visual and affective articulation to a celibate, companionate relationship. However improbably, Bluebeard and Marie-Catherine are visibly bonded, help to lighten each other's loneliness, and find solace, tenderness, and interest in being together. Hence the widow is not merry at the end. Breillat departs from both Perrault's *histoire* and her own film history in representing this oddly yet happily matched couple. It is only because he must give her the telltale key, only because a bride test is integral to their story that things fall apart.

Yet the picture needs adjustments. Breillat's final long cut—the shot's "deceleration" or relatively lengthy duration—is dialogically layered. Its composition calls attention not only to specific texts, to stories familiar through scriptural tradition, but also to a broader participation in the discursive spaces of Judeo–Christian culture. The image of a young woman and a decapitated head comprises multiple, sometimes conflicting, literary and pictorial references. This *intersection of textual surfaces*, to use Julia Kristeva's (1980, 65) phrase, is allusive and elusive, plain to see and still difficult to pin down. In yet other words, Breillat superimposes pictures borrowed from different exhibitions onto one wall screen. What follows could therefore be called a "gallery talk" in three parts about some pre-texts or prequels for her composition.

1. Judith and Holofernes

A primary source for the final scene appears in the Book of Judith. The apocryphal story describes how Holofernes, an Assyrian general, lays siege to the town of Bethulia (which guards the routes to Jerusalem) for over a month, cutting off its water supplies.[12] Judith, a chaste and beautiful widow, steps forward to prevent her town's surrender to the pagan invaders. Imploring God for strength to fell the enemy of the people of Israel, Judith puts on her best finery "to entice the eyes of all the men who might see her" and goes with a maid to the Assyrian camp (Jdt 10:4).[13] Dazzled by her dignity and beauty, soldiers escort Judith to their general's tent. After four uneventful days pass in the camp, Holofernes, who "had been waiting for an opportunity to seduce her" (12:16), invites Judith to a banquet in his tent. God directs the wine goblet frequently to Holofernes's lips, and he drinks "much more than he had ever drunk in any one day since he was born" (12:20). Holofernes falls into a stupor upon his bed. Judith prays again, "Strengthen me, O Lord God of Israel," and then wielding his own sword, "she smote twice upon his neck with all her might, and she took away his head from him" (Jdt 13:7–8). Judith gives the head to her maid, who puts it inside a "bag of meat," and returns to her people: "Behold the head of Holofernes, the chief captain of the army of Assur, and behold the canopy, wherein he did lie in his drunkenness; and the Lord hath smitten him by the hand of a woman" (13:10, 13:15). Judith is celebrated as a woman of valor *and* virtue, for no defilement took place during her stay in Holofernes's camp.

Numerous artists depict Judith's triumph in varied paintings and sculptures. However, an iconographic pattern, a kind of visual shorthand, has emerged over the ages: Judith often holds the head up by the hair or carries it on a plate, or it appears on a table before her. During the northern Renaissance, Lucas Cranach the Elder (1472–1553) and his workshop painted the topos at least a dozen times. One canvas, circa 1530, expressly served as a template for *Bluebeard*'s closing scene (Figure 12.2). Breillat interrupted an interview question to emphasize her appropriation of this picture: "It's *Judith with the Head of Holofernes* by Cranach. He painted several versions, but the one I chose to model the shot on is the most beautiful. . . . All my images are composed to the inch, and in this case I wanted his head tilted at exactly the same angle as in the painting and I wanted her to strike exactly the same pose. It's the incredible precision in positioning the bodies that transmits the emotion (Taubin 2010, 43).[14] Cranach's and Breillat's precisely rendered images are classic portrait studies, or, in filmic terms, medium shots showing an individual from the waist up. Her appropriative replication almost constitutes a *tableau vivant,* as well as an homage, to his pictorial text.

But there are two salient differences. First, Cranach's Judith holds up a sword in her right hand, signifying an inverted cross that points heavenward; by contrast, Breillat's Marie-Catherine rests her weaponless right hand on the table. Unlike the divinely inspired Judith, she did not behead the "enemy" herself, and so one could say Breillat got it right. Her knowledge of both literary sources, of Perrault's "Bluebeard" and the Book of Judith, led her to eliminate the sword, even though she modeled the final shot on Cranach's painting. Second, Holofernes's head lies directly on a flat surface; Bluebeard's lies on what appears to be a silver charger. So Cranach definitely got it right, for as Erwin Panofsky observes, "The charger would not agree with the Judith theme because the text explicitly states that the head of Holofernes was put into a sack" (1939, 12).

The question of the dish thus arises: why is Breillat interpolating an extraneous object? Why does she infringe on the integrity of her illustrious model, *Judith with the Head of Holofernes,* which she faithfully reproduces in other respects? One possible answer is that she deliberately introduced

FIGURE 12.2 Lucas Cranach the Elder, *Judith with the Head of Holofernes*. Oil and tempera on limewood. Courtesy of Museumslandschaft Hessen Kassel, Gemäldegalerie Alte Meister.

iconographic ambiguity into the scene, making identities and identifications problematic. Another approach is to suggest that she had been looking at (too) many paintings and confused her subject's symbolic markers.

2. Salome and John the Baptist

It is after all the voluptuous Salome, and not the virtuous Judith, who demands, and receives, a head on a platter in the Gospels of Matthew and Mark:

> When Herod's birthday was kept, the daughter of Herodias danced before them, and pleased Herod. Whereupon he promised with an oath to give her whatsoever she would ask. And she, being before instructed of her mother, said, Give me here John Baptist's head in a charger. And the king was sorry: nevertheless for the oath's sake, and them which sat with him at meat, he commanded it to be given her. . . . And his head was brought in a charger, and given to the damsel.[15] (Matt. 14:6–11; see also Mark 6:21–29)

The image of Salome with *her* trophy head has constituted a popular icon for centuries as part of the femme fatale paradigm in literature and the arts.[16]

Consequently, like the adversaries in medieval morality plays, no coupled figures seem more diametrically opposite than Judith (virtue)–Holofernes (vice) and Salome (vice)–John (virtue). However, as their stories' iconography stabilized over time, the women grew closer together, both visually and thematically. In Giorgione's Italian Renaissance *Judith* (ca. 1505), "the emblem of Virtue is flawed, for the one bare leg appearing through a special slit in the dress evokes eroticism, indicates ambiguity and is thus a first allusion to Judith's future reversals from Mary to Eve, from warrior to *femme fatale*" (Peters 2001, 117). Indeed, Judith's demure face and downcast eyes are incompatible with the lovely naked leg that rests on Holofernes's head, lying like a footstool on the ground beneath her (Figure 12.3).[17] The figurative uses of "browbeaten" and "downtrodden" are literalized in Giorgione's painting.

A generation later, the Flemish Vincent Sellaer's *Judith with the Head of Holofernes* (ca. 1540) is far more revealing and ambiguous.[18] In keeping with scriptural and pictorial traditions, Sellaer's Judith typically grasps the severed head by the hair with one hand, while the maid at her side holds

FIGURE 12.3 Giorgione (Giorgio Barbarelli da Castelfranco), *Judith*. Oil on canvas. Courtesy of The State Hermitage Museum, St. Petersburg. Photograph © State Hermitage Museum. Photo by Vladimir Terebenin.

a sack to receive it. Her other hand rests on the hilt of an upright sword that symbolically forms a cross. But this painting's most arresting feature is the contrast between the somewhat prudish expressional quality of Judith's face, with its pure high forehead, and her voluptuous, bare-breasted body displayed almost to her sex by an open cape. The figure of Salome has visibly encroached on the iconography of Judith. In fact, sometimes the only way to tell the women apart is by an artwork's title.

In Titian's exquisite *Salome with the Head of John the Baptist* (ca. 1515), for example, Salome is shown holding the head on a dish.[19] It is once again a visual representation of scripture: "his head was brought in a charger, and given to the damsel" (Matt. 14:11). The girl's head is positioned at a slant as in Cranach's *Judith*. Moreover, her eyes are cast downward, and her shoulders modestly covered with a reddish cape. Not just her attire but her whole expression denotes chastity and innocence. Even more complexly, Titian has transferred the motif of the maid—but *not* Judith's sword—to Salome.[20] Because a maid stands at Salome's side, a feature that generally distinguishes Judith, an ambiguity accrues to Titian's painting. Unsurprisingly, the work has also been identified as *Judith with the Head of Holofernes*.

An analogous difficulty awaits the spectator invited to attend the results of a beheading in Breillat's film: should the woman be correlated with Salome or Judith? Titian's equivocal depiction of Salome/Judith, I propose, offers another model for interpreting Breillat's arrangement. Marie-Catherine alone is not the entire problem. Not so much reversing as subverting Bluebeard's public image as a monster, Breillat presents him as a solitary and lonely man, who generously shares his vast erudition with his unlearned bride and who, at her behest, does not consummate their marriage but, nonetheless, gives her power over his heart and castle until he also gives her (as the story mandates he must) the fatal key. The iconographic ambiguity of Breillat's last mise-en-scène, with its conflicting cultural allusions, is inseparable from the moral ambiguity surrounding the male and female principals in her appropriation of the "Bluebeard" story.

3. François the First and Ivan the Terrible

The eighteenth- and nineteenth-century European vogue for the Orient and Orientalism, and for the exotically dangerous Other, often led to representations of Bluebeard as a Turk with scimitar, turban, and various outlandish accoutrements. Breillat briefly alludes to this tradition in a scene just before his execution, when Bluebeard brandishes a scimitar while reluctantly but resolutely preparing to put Marie-Catherine to death. In general, however, his outer show takes other geopolitical directions. Insofar as clothes or style make the man, Breillat dresses him in robes borrowed from two divergent sources. This hybridity, yet another costuming inconsistency, has repercussions for the issue of gender.

Breillat's conceptualization of Bluebeard differs from that of the other characters in the fairy-tale world. Because they are conceptualized as projections, including Marie-Catherine and Anne, Breillat has them correspond in appearance and behavior to the way the 1950s sisters imagine them. Bluebeard, belonging to a different ontological dimension, stands as a creature (and creation) apart from his first apparition in the party scene. Breillat specifies, "All the characters are themselves"—an extension of the girls reading the story—"with the exception of Bluebeard, who is dressed half way between François I by Clouet and Ivan the Terrible because he is a ghost and therefore is dressed like in a dream" (Jahn 2010).

"Ghost" and "dream" may seem cryptic here, for there is nothing supernatural or fantastic about the film's Bluebeard. On the contrary, he has a tangible, fleshy, "real" presence as seen, for instance, when Marie-Catherine places her slender bare hand atop his sizeable ringed fingers while he sleeps. However, he is ghostly and dreamlike in the sense that Bluebeard had "obsessed" (haunted) the adult Catherine for years prior to making the movie. When asked "Of all fairy tales, what is it that fascinated you so much about the story of Bluebeard?" she responded, "If you look at my films, you will see that I am somewhat obsessed by the relationship between victims and their executioner, but as if the relationship was a rational thing in a physical sense, a relationship between two different forces that measure themselves. And therefore I've always wanted to make a movie about Bluebeard" (Jahn 2010). There is a difficulty again in deciding who's who: who is the victim and who the executioner in her *Bluebeard*? Is the decapitated head supposed to recall the martyrdom of John the Baptist or the justified murder of Holofernes? This uncertainty is intensified by the two powerful monarchs, François I of France (1494–1547) and Ivan IV of Russia (1533–1584), who provide the basis for Bluebeard's wardrobe in the film.

Particularly enhancing Bluebeard's substantial dimensions is the gold and black striped satin doublet he wears on several occasions, a garment inspired by Jean Clouet's *Portrait of François I, King of France* (1525–1530; Figure 12.4).[21] Breillat thereby proposes an affinity between Bluebeard and

FIGURE 12.4 Jean Clouet, *François Ier, roi de France*. Oil on oak panel. Courtesy of musée du Louvre, Paris. © RMN—Grand Palais (musée du Louvre).

the highly cultivated François I, Renaissance patron of the arts and man of letters. In other scenes, however, this image is adulterated, if not fully invalidated, by Bluebeard's sartorial resemblance to Ivan IV, the formidable, despotic, and possibly mentally unbalanced "Tsar of All Russia," also known by his sobriquet "the Terrible" (*grozny*, "fearsome, dangerous, or threatening").

By way of visual allusion, the fur-trimmed cap and embossed gold cloak that Bluebeard wears when he carries his bride off to his castle seems indebted to Viktor Vasnetsov's 1897 painting *Tsar Ivan the Terrible.*[22]

Another motive for introducing the Russian Ivan into Breillat's French picture could be his matrimonial record. Whereas King Henry of England notoriously married six times ("King Henry the Eighth, to six wives he was wedded. / One died, one survived, / two divorced, two beheaded"), Ivan the Terrible notched the number up by two. Although the Orthodox Church permitted only three marriages, the Tsar wedded eight wives; each one died or disappeared in turn, due to illness or some mysterious cause or relegation to a convent. Analogies are sometimes drawn between King Henry and Bluebeard. But if historical truth be told, Tsar Ivan resembles the fairy-tale villain more closely.

The hybrid costuming of Bluebeard, "half way between François I by Clouet and Ivan the Terrible," thus serves the filmmaker's study in moral dualities. Moreover, in perspectival terms, *how* he looks on-screen also defines *who* sees him. On one hand, through Bluebeard's sartorial disposition, Breillat links him to the *civilité* and intellectual attainments that denote the majestic figure in Clouet's painting; on the other, he also assumes a mantel of deadly male authority, visually and historically linked to another sovereign power. Viewed thus, Bluebeard is an oxymoron—an *homme fatale sympathique:* a very nice man, albeit inclined to serial marriages that end badly. This ambiguation of Bluebeard, partly by means of an artful collusion or collage of historical models, comes through the focalizing auspices of Catherine the adult. And yet, I would not exclude the child who, to recast a Wordsworthian phrase, is mother of this woman. In the very scene in which Bluebeard conveys Marie-Catherine to his fortress castle, while looking like Ivan the Terrible with fur-trimmed cap and cloak, he rides a white horse.

This object is of course a consummate twentieth-century signifier that heralds the arrival of Prince Charming. Recall the daydream of the girl with ebony hair at the wishing well in Walt Disney's popular and pervasive first animated feature film, *Snow White and the Seven Dwarfs* (1937). There is no reason to suppose little girls (or grown-up women) in the 1950s in France would be exempt from this cultural icon's effects. That the fantasy continues to feed the imagination is amply demonstrated by the "Disney Deluxe Snow White Prince Charming Doll and Horse," also known as "The Prince Horse," currently available online. The product description reads, "This handsome Prince fashion doll from Snow White and the Seven Dwarfs looks dashing in his royal blue tunic and comes with a full-sized steed to carry Snow White away to their castle-in-the-clouds. He has but one song in his heart—only for Walt Disney's original princess. . . . Prince comes with deluxe costume, satin cape, boots and faux-fur trimmed hat. Horse has long mane to comb, plus royal reins and saddle. . . . The perfect match for our Deluxe Snow White Doll, sold separately." The prince, appropriately enough, is the height of a ruler, twelve inches, and his white horse, one inch shorter. Recommended for ages three and up, the toy's description nevertheless cautions in capital letters: "WARNING: CHOKING HAZARD."

Ending up at the End

To return to the end (which we never really left) one more time, let us look to the portrait of François I, rather than to images of Judith or Salome, as a model for Marie-Catherine in the final shot. This combination—another marriage of cinematography and Renaissance painting—yields some interesting results. As indicated earlier, Breillat herself specifies she copied the opulent doublet of François for Bluebeard's initial appearances in the film. I now examine other details from Clouet's painting that (in)formed her last tableau.

Both the king of France's formal portrait and Marie-Catherine's are half-length frontal depictions of their subjects. Moreover, certain features of Clouet's mise-en-scène have been closely observed and reproduced: like the king, Marie-Catherine poses against a damask background; and like the king, her right hand rests on a table covered by a green cloth. Her left hand is on the severed head instead of the sword hilt held by the king. The head with bloodied beard in this intricately coded discourse subsumes the sword. Both objects, however, are emblems signifying power and sovereignty. Summarily stated, in Breillat's ultimate scene, Marie-Catherine occupies a masculine subject position.

The sustained duration of this picture, *Marie-Catherine with the Head of Bluebeard,* provides an interval, a space within which to consider Breillat's challenge to conventional gender arrangements. In over a century of more than thirty "Bluebeard" screen adaptations, dating back to Georges Méliès's *Bluebeard* (1901), Breillat is the first woman to direct a full-length feature film (Zipes 2011, 408–9).[23] Her incursion into the male field of "Bluebeard" moviemakers—not just her decision to adapt Perrault's tale—extends into the fine arts, for all of the painters whose works she appropriates are male as well. Given Breillat's well-earned credentials as "the most willful feminist *provocatrice* in cinema today" (Anderson 2012), it is not surprising that her transformation of "Bluebeard" presents a montage of value-laden intertexts, a weave of cultural resources, that unsettle the symbolic paternal order and traditional hegemonic oppositions.

In particular, the influential Freudian association of decapitation with castration needs mention among the sources that contribute to the final composition's meanings. "Decapitation is," Freud expounds, "a well-known symbolic substitute for castration; so Judith is a woman who castrates [a] man" ([1918] 1957, 207). And so it would seem that Marie-Catherine, like Judith, has acquired the privilege of the phallus, although—putting it all too plainly—she holds no sword in hand. As Elena Ciletti and Henrike Lähnemann aptly observe, "Freud could make the decapitation of Holofernes a symbol of castration because Judith was already the product of many centuries of animated cultural appropriation in which her 'coup de grace' has acquired emblematic diversity—as divine act, as triumph of virtue over vice, as fatal blow to carnal lust, as severing of the chains of tyranny, as *female act of liberation*" (2010, 64, emphasis added).

But Breillat presents no straightforward reversal of feminine/masculine subjectivities. Marie-Catherine does not simply put on Bluebeard's power with his possessions; we see her, at the same time, stroking him gently, tenderly. He still makes her feel *like* a natural woman. She still performs her scripted part.

So what or who exactly is she? Villainous seductress, virtuous heroine, or virgin ruler of vast estates? Moreover, if she be construed as king, what does that make of her former consort? The scene's staging ground builds on so many precursor texts in different genres that it merits description as a polymorphously diverse intertext, a "polytext." By means of this polytext, Breillat calls into question in the early twenty-first century, as French feminists did in the previous one, the binary opposition between the sexes. Although it is possible to argue that at the end of her *Bluebeard,* the second sex becomes first—as in "François the First"—and acquires primacy, since a male subject no longer takes precedence—as in *"le roi et moi"* (the king and I)—such a claim needs to be qualified, bracketed, or, in Derridean terms, put under erasure. Bluebeard dies by the sword in the film, just as Holofernes dies in the Book of Judith. But two cavaliers, and *not* Marie-Catherine, "took away his head from him" (Jdt 13:7–8). It was a man's job, rightly performed by men. Then again, the woman actually rescued herself by the stratagem of delay, by using the feminine arts of persuasion to postpone her execution until the cavalrymen arrived to do the messy work. Hence in the moments before the film credits appear and reality returns, Marie-Catherine occupies neither a feminine nor a masculine position.

In this rereading, Breillat "complexifies" an already complicated story by refusing to allow her last mise-en-scène and, retroactively, her film in its entirety, to represent a clear case of either this or that: womanly/manly, victim/executioner, Christian/pagan, virtue/vice, and so forth. Just as Bluebeard is neither a Holofernes nor a John the Baptist, so Marie-Catherine is not reducible to the categories of a Judith or a Salome. In the final analysis, Breillat's protagonists exceed such binary oppositions through her transformative configuration of their twenty-first-century roles.

Notes

1. Breillat filmed *Bluebeard* for the Franco–German television channel ARTE. However, aside from the running time (eighty minutes) and low budget (approximately $2,400,000), it does not seem to have been conceived for television's small scale. Breillat's painterly scenes suit a large screen and, in fact, discussions of the film rarely mention its original format.
2. For informative discussions of prior filmic renditions of "Bluebeard," see especially Hermansson (2009, 151–58); Tatar (2004, 89–107); and Zipes (2011, 158–71).
3. *Bluebeard* harks back to Breillat's *Fat Girl* (2001), focusing on the rivalry between two sisters entangled in a love/hate dynamic. Both films end with the older sister's death: in *Fat Girl*, a stranger murders the sister as well as the girls' mother; in *Bluebeard*, she accidentally falls to her death through a trapdoor, while backing away from her little sister, who is relentlessly reading the story's finale. The younger girl's wish fulfillment is manifest in both cases.
4. See Ciletti and Lähnemann's analysis of Judith's assimilation into Christianity: "As a type of both Mary and the Church, her core identity as instrument of divine will and savior of her people expanded to encompass victory over the devil and sin itself" (2010, 46). See also Ciletti (2010, especially 355–60).
5. "Bride show" designates an ancient custom whereby sovereigns wishing to select a consort would call for maidens to be assembled. This historically rooted practice "left its trace on popular imagination" and passed into the realms of folklore (Bourboulis [1982] 1988, 99). As Lee's chapter discusses, reality TV shows display a similar format/structure.
6. See, for example, Bottigheimer (1987), Davies (2001), and Warner (1994). Warner pertinently writes, "I began investigating the meanings of the tales themselves, but I soon found that it was essential to look at the context in which they were told, at who was telling them, to whom and why" (xvi).
7. See Zipes (2006b, 2008a) for expanded articulations of the concept of memes and of memetic narratives.

8. See the chapter on *Genesis Rabbah* in Barzilai (2009, 1–21).

9. As Nelson and Walton's chapter discusses, *Merlin* similarly uses deliberate temporal ambiguity in an apparent period piece.

10. Russell-Watts argues against the tendency to focus on female subjectivity and sexuality in Breillat's works and persuasively demonstrates that her representation of masculinity is far more complex than generally thought: "What Breillat's films—and Breillat's men—allow us [is] . . . a reconfiguration of masculine subjectivity" (2010, 82). Although Russell-Watts does not refer to *Bluebeard*, Breillat's portrayal of the character substantiates this reading.

11. Angelo (2010) insightfully discusses Siffredi's role as a dubious icon of virility and sexual relationships as a "territory" (de)forming female subjectivities in Breillat's works.

12. "Bethulia" derives from the Hebrew *betula* denoting a "virgin" and therefore is congruent with Judith's portrayal as a virtuous widow.

13. I reference scriptural works with their abbreviated titles. For an incisive discussion of the authorship, date, and reception history of the Book of Judith, see Gera (2010, 23–39).

14. The version she selected is probably the wood panel at the Museumslandschaft Hessen in Kassel, Germany. I would like to thank the museum staff members, and especially Ingrid Knauf, for their kind assistance in reproducing this image.

15. Salome is not named in the Gospels; however, her name and family details appear in Josephus's *The Antiquities of the Jews* (ca. 94 CE), Bk. XVIII, ch. 5, sec. 4. Its account of John the Baptist's death, unlike the Gospels', does not implicate her: "Herod, who feared lest the great influence John had over the people might put it into his power and inclination to raise a rebellion, [for they seemed ready to do any thing he should advise,] thought it best by putting him to death, to prevent any mischief he might cause" (Bk. XVIII, ch. 5, sec. 2).

16. See Lurie (2006) for a survey of depictions of Salome.

17. Giorgione's *Judith* is accessible at the Hermitage Museum's "Collection Highlights": www.hermitagemuseum.org/html_En/03/hm3_3_1c.html.

18. According to Lurie (2006, n. 17), Sellaer's *Judith* is in a private collection in Canada. The painting appears on the Hebrew cover of the dual-language catalog for the Tel Aviv Museum of Art exhibition above the title *Femme Fatale—Ha'isha Ha'horeset.* Although the Hebrew adjective *horeset* literally means "destructive," in contemporary slang it has laudatory connotations: roughly, a drop-dead gorgeous woman. The English cover, simply titled *Femme Fatale*, shows Beardsley's *The Climax* (*Salome with the Head of John the Baptist*, 1893), thus counterposing these emblematic figures of lethal women. Of Sellaer's several portrayals of Judith, I refer to the image accessible at http://bjws.blogspot.com/2011/08/judith-holofernes-1500s.html.

19. Titian's painting is in the Galleria Doria Pamphilj in Rome (www.doriapamphilj.it/uksalome.asp).

20. Artists transferred the charger to Judith but not the sword to Salome, because "the sword was an established and honorific attribute of Judith, of many martyrs, and of such virtues as Justice, Fortitude etc.; thus it could not be transferred with propriety to a lascivious girl." By contrast, the charger with John the Baptist's head evolved into "an isolated devotional image . . . singled out from a representation of the Salome

story," and therefore it "could more easily be substituted for the motif of a sack in an image of Judith" (Panofsky 1939, 13–14).

21. For a curatorial gloss and views of Clouet's *Portrait of François I*, now at the Louvre in Paris, see www.louvre.fr/en/node/36515.

22. See Vasnetsov's portrait of *Tsar Ivan* at http://russiapedia.rt.com/prominent-russians/the-ryurikovich-dynasty/ivan-iv-the-terrible.

23. Jessica Fox directed a fifteen-minute silent *Bluebeard* in 2008 (Zipes 2011, 409).

PART IV

Fairy Tales Are Real!
Reality TV, Fairy-Tale Reality,
Commerce, and Discourse

13

UGLY STEPSISTERS AND UNKIND GIRLS

Reality TV's Repurposed Fairy Tales

Linda J. Lee

Though many recognize reality TV as a dominant aspect of television today, it has been part of North American culture since *Candid Camera* debuted in 1948. The turn of the millennium, however, witnessed a dramatic increase in reality TV thanks to the hugely popular *Survivor* and *American Idol*. The genre comprises programs that present supposedly unscripted dramatic, humorous, or otherwise out-of-the-ordinary situations. During the past decade, reality TV has splintered to cover myriad interests, from the documentary-style *COPS* (embedded camera crews shadow on duty law enforcement officials) and *Ghost Hunters* (a paranormal investigation team searches for evidence of the supernatural) to competitions like *Dancing with the Stars* (celebrities are paired with professionals in a dance off) and *Iron Chef America* (celebrity chefs create dishes from themed ingredients). Although media critics like Jennifer Pozner (2010) decry the genre's increasing popularity, suggesting it comes at the expense of more costly, high-quality, scripted television dramas, the phenomenon is too popular to ignore.

Reality TV relies on mixing, "recombinantly drawing conventions and assumptions from a range of genres in both innovative and derivative fashions" (Mittell 2004, 197). Many hybrids result. For instance, combining game shows like *Jeopardy!* with cooking shows like Julia Child's *The French Chef* produces competition cooking shows like *Iron Chef America* and *The Next Food Network Star*. Successful innovations spawn ever increasing fragmentation and recombination. For example, elimination game shows include dating and romance competitions like *The Bachelor* and its gender reversal spin-off, *The Bachelorette*. Beginning in 2010, eliminated contestants and fans from these programs have competed for money on a spin-off elimination show, *The Bachelor Pad*. These immensely popular programs have inspired both imitations like *Who Wants to Marry a Multi-Millionaire?* and innovations including the prankster dating competition *Joe Millionaire*, in which the supposed wealthy bachelor turned out to be a working-class construction worker.

This genre mixing draws on many different sources, including traditional fairy tales. *Who Wants to Marry a Multi-Millionaire?* and the long-running *The Bachelor* (its seventeenth season aired in 2013); "social experiments" like *Beauty and the Geek;* and makeover programs like *Extreme Makeover* and *The Swan* all consciously incorporate narrative structures, motifs, and conventions of "Cinderella" (ATU 510A), "Beauty and the Beast" (ATU 425C), and Hans Christian Andersen's "The Ugly Duckling," respectively. This chapter considers how traditional fairy-tale conventions, narrative expectations, and motifs—beyond the fantasy of becoming "a real-life Cinderella"—are repurposed in reality TV.

Evoking fairy-tale tropes and structures, these programs highlight television's potential to offer a vehicle for wish fulfillment and fantasy. As the key for attaining fully actualized, adult status, transformation serves as a central theme of both fairy tales and reality TV. This connection has not gone unnoticed by media, popular culture, and cultural studies scholars (Bratich 2007; Orosan-Weine 2007; Pozner 2010). Unfortunately, though critics from various disciplines have long been interested in reality TV's fairy-tale aspects, few discussions go beyond what Mikel Koven disparagingly calls "motif spotting" (2008, 3–15; see, e.g., Albright 2007; Heyes 2007; Palmer 2007; Gray 2009; Pozner 2010). In this chapter, I suggest that the relationship between fairy tales and reality television is more complicated than previous literature suggests. In their efforts to transform into a "swan" or to marry a "real-life Prince Charming," participants enact fairy tales through, on, and with their bodies.[1] None of these programs recreates the source fairy tale whole cloth. Rather, they are postmodern fairy tales or fairy-tale pastiches (Jorgensen 2007). Specifically, I consider *Extreme Makeover: Home Edition* (2003–2012), a spin-off of ABC's personal makeover show of the same name, and *The Bachelor* franchise. I focus on *The Bachelor* (2002–), though other franchise shows, including *The Bachelorette* (2003–2005, 2008–) and the short-lived *More to Love* (2009), also demonstrate concerns and preoccupations with fairy tales. I examine how these shows reproduce and transform "Cinderella," "The Ugly Duckling," and "The Kind and the Unkind Girls" (ATU 480) for ideological and economic purposes, often resulting in damaging gender portrayals.

Fairy Tales and Reality TV

Alan Dundes affirms, "Folklorists [must] study the popular versions of Cinderella. . . . For it is those changes, some subtle, some not, that provide invaluable clues to understanding the world of today" ([1982] 1988, 295; see Sawin's and Barber's chapters). Though reality television is a significant vector for transmitting contemporary versions of folktales and fairy tales, it has been largely ignored by folklorists and fairy-tale scholars. Exceptions include Cathy Lynn Preston, who discusses Fox's 2000 special *Who Wants to Marry a Multi-Millionaire?* as a postmodern fairy-tale text. She reports that most of her students "readily identified the show as a contemporary literalization of a Cinderella script, one that disclosed, openly reproduced, and sanctioned the gendered economic relations of the older tale" (2004, 206). More recently, Koven (2008, 153–74) examined the convergence of folklore, belief, and popular media to consider whether a program like the British *Most Haunted* can be a form of ostension. His folkloristic concerns center on the show's relationship to legends rather than fairy tales, however.

In contrast, television, popular culture, and cultural studies scholars have long been interested in reality TV's fairy-tale aspects. The title of Fox's short-lived makeover program *The Swan* (2004) is an intertextual reference to Andersen's literary fairy tale "The Ugly Duckling." ABC's *Extreme Makeover* (2002–2007) promised participants a "Cinderella-like" makeover. Dating competition contestants affirm that they are looking for their "real-life Prince Charming" and frequently refer to their experiences as "a fairy tale." The remote castle-like settings reinforce this interpretation. Yet few scholars examining these shows look beyond the iconic and stereotypic fairy-tale characters, settings, and plots. Some suggest that these programs innovate on fairy-tale formulas through competitions, challenges, and other narrative twists. I argue instead that many supposed innovations actually repurpose less well-known traditional fairy-tale elements, such as tests that the heroine must undergo and/or tasks she must complete.

Jack Z. Bratich offers a nuanced consideration of fairy tales' relationship to reality TV. Fairy tales themselves are "transformative narratives on transformations" (Vaz da Silva 2008, 982) and Bratich sees reality TV "as a performative phenomenon that captures, modifies, reorganizes, and distributes" what he calls "powers of transformation" (2007, 8). He suggests, "Regardless of the explicit goals of a programme (money, victory, romance, an entertainment industry contract), the informal processes include a demand for learning about oneself, for 'getting out of the comfort zone,' for assessing character flaws in oneself, and ultimately, committing to a metamorphosis based on these processes" (ibid., 10). He connects the "instructional and transformative component of traditional fairy tales" with reality TV, which "makes over its audience as much as its protagonists," commenting, "Fairy tales are the code for reality software." He suggests that the "whole of reality itself has become *programmable*" and the reality television is a "televisual mechanism for conducting powers of transformation" (ibid., 20) in an effort to create "malleable subjects adequate to new economic and social conditions" (ibid., 7). While I disagree with Bratich's larger argument about the intentionality behind efforts to remake society through reality TV, I agree that reality TV preserves the "transformative potential" of fairy tales. Transformation—or at least the potential for transformation—is one of the essential links between fairy tales and reality TV programs.

Transformation is a central motif of the fairy tales most often explicitly referenced in reality TV programs: "Cinderella," arguably the world's best-known fairy tale, and Andersen's "The Ugly Duckling." In "Cinderella," the female protagonist, abused and debased by her stepmother, escapes her circumstances with a donor figure's (often magical) assistance, which enables her to attend a ball where the prince searches for a bride. This help comes with a specific condition; she must return by midnight, when the magical transformation ends. The heroine attracts the prince; he marries her and lifts her from an impoverished condition. The Grimms' version is marked by the extreme measures that Cinderella's stepsisters use to try to win the prince's affections: they mutilate their feet to fit into the golden slipper, the recognition token that proves Cinderella's identity.[2] Though often conflated with "Cinderella," Andersen's tale notably differs, focusing on personal—rather than magical or matrimonial—transformation. "The Ugly Duckling" features a young bird, abused by the other animals because of his ugliness, who grows up to become a beautiful swan.

Some programs also invoke—unintentionally, I suspect—a fairy tale less well known to contemporary American audiences: "The Kind and the

Unkind Girls." Found across Europe, Asia, and parts of Africa, it dates to the fifteenth century and is often joined with "Cinderella" (Roberts 1958; Uther 2004). Two girls—one kind and one not, often stepsisters—undergo a similar quest or set of tasks (sometimes domestic, sometimes impossible) and are either rewarded or punished accordingly. The kind girl falls down a well (in many versions, her stepmother pushes her), where she encounters an old woman (often an ogress) who assigns her various tasks, such as milking a cow or carrying water in a sieve. Her benefactor rewards her helpfulness and hard work with beauty, wealth, or jewels falling from her mouth when she speaks. When the heroine returns home, her jealous stepmother sends her own daughter on the same quest. The unkind girl refuses to help or disobeys instructions, which the old woman punishes with ugliness, disfigurement, or pitch or frogs falling from her mouth when she speaks.

Beyond the central themes of transformation, these stories share a concern with relationships—in particular, those among women. "Cinderella" prioritizes competition among women for a man's affection. The circumstances are explicitly zero-sum; only one woman can end up with the prince. "The Kind and the Unkind Girls" similarly focuses on competitive relationships. Its central theme, jealousy, motivates the stepmother to send her own daughter to follow the kind girl's path. Competition between the stepsisters is emphasized, as the kind girl's successes and reward contrast with the unkind girl's failures and punishment.

Extreme Makeover: Home Edition as Fairy Tale

Extreme Makeover: Home Edition, henceforth *EM:HE,* premiered on ABC in 2003, as a spin-off from its personal transformation sibling reality program, *Extreme Makeover.*[3] Throughout its nine-season run, *EM:HE* aired 200 regular episodes from December 3, 2003, until January 13, 2012, and more than a dozen special episodes innovating on the basic formula, all providing home renovations for "deserving" families facing specific hardships, often related to disease or disability. Each episode follows a specific template. In a single week, star contractor/builder Ty Pennington's crew, aided by a local builder and community volunteers, designs and implements a complete home renovation. After the first few seasons homes were generally demolished and rebuilt. All improvements—including landscaping and interior furnishing—take just seven days while the family is away on vacation. This around-the-clock effort is edited and compressed into one or two hour-long episodes.

On the surface, *EM:HE* seems an odd choice to argue as a "Cinderella" story. After all, there is no persecuted heroine, no evil stepmother and stepsisters, no prince, no glass slipper—indeed, it lacks elements that would make even motif-spotting possible. If "in postmodernity the 'stuff' of fairy tales exists in fragments . . . in the nebulous realm that we might most simply identify as cultural knowledge" (Preston 2004, 210), then an obvious question to ask is "Where is the fairy tale stuff?" To consider how *EM:HE* may function as a fairy tale, I turn to Jessica Tiffin's suggestion that fairy tale–ness is communicated through "*texture* rather than simple form and pattern" (2009, 5). Noting the impossibility of defining "fairy tale through any single factor," she points to "a constellation of central characteristics" that create "an overall, instantly recognizable *effect*" (ibid., 6). Although referring primarily to fictions like those by Angela Carter, her idea of a recognizable effect helpfully fosters thinking about the ways reality TV uses, invokes, rescripts, and re-presents fairy tales.

In *EM:HE,* the "instantly recognizable *effect*" that suggests "fairy tale" comes from the magical worldview underlining the renovation process. Magical donors and helpers appear in contemporary media genres that use fairy tales to promise a "quick magical fix or solution" (Jorgensen 2007, 216). Pennington—the host of *EM:HE*—functions as the fairy godmother here. Metaphorically speaking, he waves his magic wand and—rather than going *to* a ball—the family gets to *have* a ball on vacation, usually at Disney World. During the family's absence, their home becomes a site of frenzied, nonstop activity. Hundreds—sometimes thousands—of volunteers descend on the worksite like helpful animals in a Disney film. When the family returns a week later, they find a new home in place of the old. From the family's perspective this transformation happens instantaneously and effortlessly. The audience, of course, sees some of this process, so viewers know that it is neither magical nor easy. Rather, it is an incredibly coordinated, Herculean effort that under other circumstances would take months to achieve.

Any hint of cost is hidden from the audience—and presumably from the family as well. The deserving families are chosen to receive renovations because they cannot afford to pay for them on their own. The show's success depends on volunteer effort and donated time and materials from local contractors, builders, and other workers. Volunteers generally work on the house around the clock, regardless of weather conditions, to meet the deadline. The show's producers provide the family's vacation, but multinational companies like Sears and local businesses donate most other expenses.

The invisibility of specific costs reinforces the magical worldview presented through the transformation.

In contrast to the fairy-tale hero or heroine, often isolated from family and home (Lüthi 1984, 134–44), kin and dwellings play a central role in *EM:HE*. I see the nuclear family functioning collectively in the tale role of (female) protagonist and the house as an exterior manifestation of the family's unified identity. Further, families must demonstrate heroic or admirable traits. Supervising casting director Kelly Mooney, in an August 2011 call for nominations, indicated the program searches for "deserving people and inspiring families that Americans can really root for" ("Extreme Makeover: Home Edition Needs Your Help" 2011). The producers sought families whose homes were "in desperate need of being rebuilt," wanting to help people "whose homes are making it difficult, or even impossible, to cope with challenges that face them" (ibid.). Of course, the more desperate, the better; abject need makes for compelling television drama. Need alone is not enough, though. Nominations require an explanation of why the nominated family "is deserving, heroic, and/or a great role model for their community" (ibid.).

This program may initially seem to show the stereotypical "rags-to-riches" story, as Cinderella appears in North America's popular imagination. However, "'Cinderella' is *not* a story of rags to riches but rather riches recovered; *not* poor girl into princess but rather rich girl (or princess) rescued from improper or wicked enslavement" (Yolen 1982, 296). *EM:HE*'s fairy tale is similar. The families eligible for home makeovers must already have a home—specifically, a single-family home. With rare exceptions, this limits the population of "deserving families" to those who have already achieved the "American dream" of home ownership.[4]

Those who comprise "deserving families" are limited in other ways, too. By emphasizing nuclear families tied by blood and marriage, *EM:HE* implicitly comments on who does and who does not deserve help. Not many nontraditional families appear on this show—with the exception of those nuclear families who have "extra" children, usually blood relations. For example, "Hill Family" (7, 143)[5] features William and Catherine Hill, who took in seven nieces and nephews (in addition to their own four children) after their mother was declared unfit. Thus, a nontraditional family situation (a single mother with seven children) becomes a problem to be solved through a traditional, heteronormative family. *EM:HE*'s focus on traditional, heterosexual nuclear families serves to present them as the idealized American family, implicitly excluding other choices and lifestyles.[6] Doing so privileges a version of American families that aligns with a conservative ideology but is also becoming less common in modern American society.[7]

If *EM:HE* presents a Cinderella story for idealized American families, then it ends with the assumption that everyone featured on the program will live "happily ever after." Of course, that is not true. Fairy godmothers have only limited powers; they cannot magically change someone's essential circumstances, only alleviate a curse's most negative effects (Opie and Opie 1974, 12–14). Even in "Cinderella," the fairy godmother's magic effects only a temporary transformation from low to high status for the female protagonist. Permanent transformation depends on marriage to a prince: "The fairy godmother . . . can make Cinderella's plight less painful, and she can prepare her for the social recognition of her natural qualities . . . [but the fairy godmother] is incapable of permanently altering Cinderella's position in society" (Pace 1982, 255–56). Similarly, in *EM:HE*, a home renovation cannot be a cure-all for what ails the family. They are arguably better off than they were before: they have a comfortable house far exceeding their needs and substantially more wealth, thanks to a higher home value. In some cases, families have had mortgages paid off, or their children receive scholarships to local colleges.[8] Despite these markers of elevated social status, the family's disease, disability, or tragedy remains.

The homes Pennington and his team rebuild and furnish undoubtedly become showpieces, customized to solve specific problems for the family. For example, an episode centered on another Hill family (9, 7, November 4, 2011) highlights the mental health problems experienced by retired National Guard member Allen Hill, an Iraq war vet who suffered a traumatic brain injury from a roadside bombing and has severe posttraumatic stress disorder (PTSD). Because the family's Ottawa, Kansas, residence was near both a rock quarry and a train, the noise triggered his PTSD, making it impossible to return home; Allen was staying in a treatment facility in California until he could return. The *EM:HE* team relocated the family to a quieter location on a donated three-acre plot. The house—with triple-paned windows, sufficient soundproofing, a special "quiet room," and numerous technological devices to help manage Allen's condition—provided a safe environment for him and his family. These environmental remedies, however, do not eliminate Allen's PTSD or the very real problems that come along with his mental illness.

Though the house for Allen Hill and his family was intended to accommodate his physical and psychological problems, many reconstructions go far beyond what is necessary to meet a family's needs. This excess embeds an ideology of conspicuous consumption within the overall narrative. The new houses are often significantly larger—often 4,000 square feet or more—and consequently valued at and taxed more than others in their areas. Inside the minicastles, large-screen televisions, swimming pools, exercise equipment, and other luxury amenities increase the cost of living. Excessive overheads sometimes become a hardship, and the show recommends that families consult with a financial planner to understand their new home's expenses. While the show's producers disclaim any responsibility for a family's individual financial decisions, the design team chooses the amenities that drive up utility and tax costs. Sometimes community members step in to donate or raise money for anticipated increased expenses. For example, a fundraiser for Allen and Gina Hill totaled more than $40,000, and Operation Finally Home—which helps place wounded veterans in new accommodations—donated $10,000 and offered to cover their property taxes and insurance costs for two years.

But this financial assistance depends on the community and in all cases is temporary. Consequently, there is no guarantee of lasting happiness for these families. Indeed, many families encounter problems due to construction quality issues or unanticipated higher upkeep and utility costs. For example, the Okvaths' renovated home in Gilbert, Arizona, quadrupled in size to 5,300 square feet and included such luxury amenities as a carousel and a home theater. Though they had no mortgage, and builder Taylor Woodrow covered the property taxes and $500 toward monthly utilities for the first year, the family's actual costs far exceeded this assistance, with monthly electric bills sometimes reaching $1,800 ("Contents" 2012). The Okvath family took out a home equity loan to help cover these costs as well as higher tax payments, landscaping costs, and unexpected repairs (ibid.). They quickly realized they could not afford to live there and would need to sell ("'Extreme Makeover' left Gilbert family" 2009). Some recipients ultimately lost their new homes to foreclosure; the series' first known example was the Hebert family of Sandpoint, Idaho (Wotapka 2010a). Concerns like these prompted the show to scale back on the new homes' size and amenities as well as to include green design features like solar panels (Wotapka 2010b).

Living the Fairy Tale on *The Bachelor*

Competitive dating shows like ABC's *The Bachelor* and *The Bachelorette*—both hosted by Chris Harrison—present a different "Cinderella" story line.

This category of reality TV program remains very popular—the sixteenth season of *The Bachelor* and the eighth of *The Bachelorette* aired in 2012—even though twenty-four televised seasons have resulted in only three marriages.[9] Both programs are produced and directed by Mike Fleiss, who was also responsible for *More to Love,* which appeared on Fox during summer 2009. A verbal play on the idea that love is more than skin deep and on the participants' physical size, *More to Love* uses the same basic premise and format as *The Bachelor,* with plus-size participants. *The Bachelor*'s sixteenth season ran weekly from January 2 to March 12, 2012, comprising ten regular two-hour episodes, two special episodes, a "The Women Tell All" episode, and an "After the Final Rose" reunion show that aired immediately after the season finale. It featured Sonoma winemaker Ben Flajnik, the runner-up on *The Bachelorette* season 7, featuring Ashley Hebert; model Courtney Robertson won the competition.

The shows' format is similar: a bachelor (or bachelorette) searches for a potential wife (or husband) from a predetermined set of participants. Everyone resides in a mansion, largely separated from friends, family, and work for the program's duration. During each one- or two-hour episode, the bachelor/bachelorette goes out on a series of individual and group dates, and everyone participates in other events, such as cocktail parties. Consequently, the competing women (or men) spend more time with each other than with the bachelor (or bachelorette). *The Bachelor* uses a competition–elimination format. Each episode ends with a "rose ceremony" during which some participants are invited to remain in the competition; those who do not receive a rose must leave immediately. A few roses are given out (or denied) in advance of the rose ceremony, including a "first impression" rose on the first night and roses for group and individual dates. Elimination from the competition seems to be solely at the bachelor's (or bachelorette's) discretion. Stellar performance does not guarantee that a contestant will remain. One by one, contestants are expelled from the competition like Cinderella's unwanted ugly stepsisters and the "unkind girls" who cannot successfully complete the tasks before them. As the season progresses and the number of competing women (or men) decreases, the dates become more exotic, featuring locations like Puerto Rico, Panama, and Belize. When four contestants remain, the bachelor (or bachelorette) travels to each contestant's hometown to meet the family; in the finale, the final two contestants meet the bachelor's (or bachelorette's) family. The final rose ceremony ends, ideally, with a marriage proposal and acceptance.

Though presented as an authentic search for love, the narratives that unfold on-screen are fictions created through the editing process. Participants on *The Bachelor* and its sibling programs are constantly under surveillance. Taping includes hidden or handheld cameras apparently capturing everything that happens. In the "Bachelor Industry" (Dubrofsky 2011), the private confession is among the devices most frequently used to construct narratives. Though it appears that participants declare their private thoughts to the camera, they are often responding to production staff questions and prompts. Confession is strategically embedded into the program's structure—usually interspersed with scenes from interactions—to communicate the participants' motives to the audience (ibid., 17–19). Further, by allegedly revealing the women's innermost thoughts, these confessions add an air of legitimacy and authenticity to the narrative unfolding on-screen (ibid., 19–26). Noticeably awkward for some women, this constant surveillance seems calculated to catch them in the middle of emotional breakdowns. Crashes most frequently occur after elimination ceremonies. For example, eliminated Amber Tierney (16, 1), crying, turns her back on the camera, presumably for some privacy, yet the microphone clearly catches her tearful question, "What did I do wrong?" Borrowing the language of pornography, Rachel Dubrofsky refers to such moments of excessive emotion caught on camera as the "money shot" of reality TV (ibid., 65–71). Confessionals often feature the women's strong feelings for the bachelor and their fear of never finding love.

Competitive dating programs may not be deliberately constructed as fairy tales, but their fairy-tale "effect" (Tiffin 2009, 6) results in many participants viewing them as an opportunity to live one. Indeed, during the season 16 finale, after Courtney accepts the final rose and they exchange expressions of love, Ben says to the camera, "It's hard for me to believe in fairy tales, so to actually experience a fairy tale . . . we found a fairy tale, and we found each other, and that's all that really matters." Notably, Ben repeats the phrase "fairy tale" several times. His statement suggest that—at least in the moment—he experienced his participation in *The Bachelor* as filling the role of the fairy-tale prince on a quest to find a bride. Such sentiments are common on dating elimination shows, and other contestants read their respective experiences similarly. For example, during *The Bachelor,* episode 2, Jennifer Fritsch confesses, "I would love for this to be the beginning of my fairy tale." Pozner documents seventeen contestants on *Joe Millionaire* comparing their experience to a fairy tale (2010, 39–44). Similarly, in *More to Love,* Kristian extends this comparison, explicitly casting bachelor Luke as the archetypal fairy-tale prince: "Growing up as a little girl, you dream about this knight in shining armor, this prince that's going to take you away from all the bad things that you face as a kid. And that's how I look at Luke. I look at him as that amazing man, who I've dreamt of since I could think about princesses and princes" (1, 3). Little information had been revealed about Luke by this point—just his name, age, occupation, and that he thinks this show will help him find love. Through this lack, Luke becomes a blank slate on which the women project their dreams and ideals. And Kristian's statement clearly shows that fairy-tale motifs influence those imaginings.

Despite broad agreement on the experience's fairy tale–ness, few markers directly indicate "Cinderella." As with *EM:HE,* these dating competition shows lack explicit reference to specific fairy-tale types and motifs. Certainly, *The Bachelor,* wherein one man searches for love from a predetermined set of potential brides, suggests the ball where the prince falls in love with Cinderella. The women's formal attire at this first meeting reinforces this impression. One of the few direct "Cinderella" references appears in *The Bachelorette* (8, 1), when single father Tony Pieper arrives holding a pillow with a glass shoe on top, introducing himself to bachelorette Emily Maynard saying, "The name's Charming. Prince Charming. And I'm looking for my princess. I believe in fairy tales. I believe in love. And I believe that if the shoe fits, me and my princess will live happily ever after. So would you mind if I try to see if this fits?" He prompts her to try on the shoe, which conveniently fits. Bringing the iconic glass slipper confirms that he wants to be Cinderella's Prince Charming, rather than Snow White's or Sleeping Beauty's. Tony's gimmick serves two purposes. First, he explicitly claims the role of active male protagonist rather than that of passive participant.[10] The former role has more power and authority than the latter. Second, through this ploy, he captures Emily's attention, increasing the chance that he will survive the first elimination ceremony.

Through its core identity as a competition–elimination show, *The Bachelor* and its spin-offs make explicit what is implicit in "Cinderella": the thematic importance of competition between women. Many contestants attempt—as Tony did—to do something memorable that catches the bachelor's or bachelorette's attention. The introduction is the first competition. For example, in *The Bachelor* (16, 1), Brittney Schreiner arrives with her grandmother, Sheryl, to emphasize that family is important to her, and Lindzi Cox (who receives the first impression rose) arrives on a horse. Though these women may have made a strong positive first impression on Ben, they make a correspondingly negative one on the other women who are their competition. These women never forget that they are actively engaged in a competition and frequently make disparaging comments about one another. For example, during a confessional on the first night, Shawn Reynolds gives two women nicknames referencing how they introduced themselves to Ben, implicitly acknowledging the necessity of standing out from the group: "So we have Sammy Sash and Holly Hat, and competition's looking pretty tough. You've got to do what you've got to do." "Sammy Sash" refers to Samantha Levey's wearing of her beauty pageant sash, and "Holly Hat" refers to Holly Johnson's Kentucky Derby hat. Immediately afterward, Shawn takes Ben outside with a soccer ball to show that she can—and will—play soccer in a ball gown and heels. These women directly compete for a man they do not yet know, much like Cinderella's stepsisters. Though they have not (yet) resorted to cutting off heel and toe, as do their fairy-tale counterparts in the Grimms' version, they deliberately and knowingly engage in an ongoing game of one-upmanship.

These programs' fairy tale–ness is emphasized in other ways, too. A kiss is a key motif, associated primarily with the Disney versions of "Snow White" (ATU 709; see Wright's chapter) and "Sleeping Beauty" (ATU 410) stories (see Jorgensen and Warman's chapter). In Euro–North American understandings, a fairy-tale kiss is more powerful than almost anything else in the world—it can transform beasts into men and revive comatose (or dead) princesses. This transformative power is critical during Ben and Emily O'Brien's date in episode 3, when the couple climbs to the top of San Francisco's Bay Bridge. Midway up, Emily becomes paralyzed by acrophobia. Narrative tension is strengthened by cutting to the other women discussing her fear of heights, serving to legitimize her emotional response. Though Ben is momentarily stumped by Emily's paralysis, he overcomes it with a kiss that jolts her out of her panic attack, emotionally freeing her to continue the climb. Not only a romantic moment between the two, this action undeniably invokes the fairy-tale kiss's transformative potential. The producers go to great lengths to make the couple's second kiss just as memorable, setting off fireworks above their heads. And Emily obligingly responds as expected: after discussing both the figurative and real-world fireworks of kissing, she acknowledges the day as the "first step in the path of falling in love with Ben."

A common criticism levied against reality TV is that it is not real. That is, despite its purported unscripted quality, its narrative is a fiction constructed during editing, often following specific direction to the contestants by producers and directors designed to make for more drama. One such mode is the creation of "good" characters and "villainous" ones. Among the most villainously constructed characters is Courtney Robinson, season 16 winner of *The Bachelor,* who is arguably one of the most divisive in the program's history. Her behavior both during on screen interactions with other women and in private confessions is often appalling. As early as her introduction video, she seems more interested in competing with the other women than in Ben:

> I'm not really too concerned about the other girls. Girls are competitive with me, but I can't be bothered. I don't let it slow me down. So I'm okay with competition. It's something I've had a lot of experience with. I'm sure there will be some girls intimidated by me, and they probably should be. [laugh] I've been a fake bride so many times modeling. I might be a real bride soon. It's exciting. I think wedding rings look pretty amazing on me, actually. I can see a big rock on there. I know what I want, and I think two carats is you know . . . I deserve it. I'm worth it." (16, 1)

Rather than emphasizing her interest in the bachelor as the other women do in their introduction videos, Courtney discusses competing with other "girls" and her desire for marriage's expensive material accessories like the ring. From this initial introduction on, her story line is motivated by this competition. Her ambiguous motives suggest the show's central paradox: the goal is simultaneously to win *by any means necessary* and to win Ben's affection.[11]

The show relentlessly and negatively presents Courtney as someone who disregards social conventions. Most of her screen time in the second episode develops this villainous persona. She repeatedly expresses her twin desires to win and to be rid of the competition—wishes reminiscent of the stepsisters who seek to usurp Cinderella's rightful place as the prince's bride. For example, Courtney says in a confessional, "I would like Lindzi to go home. Ben gave the first impression rose to the one person I had the worst first impression of. . . . But I think the *horse* got the first impression rose." She is no less dismissive when speaking directly to the other women. She diminishes Lindzi's first impression rose, attributing it to the gimmick, saying, "The first impression. . . . Or is it like, you rode in on a horse?" Though Courtney may vocalize what other women think, their surprised reactions suggest that, in doing so, she violated social norms. She disparages

Lindzi's sense of connection with Ben, promoting her own sexual chemistry with him: "I can see the way he looks at me, and there's something there. It's undeniable. It's *there*. I felt something, and I could see that he felt something. It's either there or it's not. You know. You can't force it. So, I'm not going to beat a dead horse." Courtney routinely revisits this presumed sexual connection throughout the episode. For example, when Kacie Boguskie reads aloud a date card inviting Courtney to "spin the bottle" with Ben, she proclaims, "He wants to kiss me!" then immediately asks, "How'd that taste coming out of your mouth?" Courtney's shocking follow-up question is at once mean-spirited and juvenile, suggesting a lack of knowledge about or respect for social norms and appropriate behavior.

Throughout the season Courtney makes similarly divisive comments and acts in ways the other women condemn as inappropriate. In doing so, she presents herself as an "unkind girl" unwilling or unable to perform beyond her own immediate self-interest. After receiving a rose on her individual date with Ben in episode 2, she taunts her competitors by repeatedly saying, "Winning!" Courtney presents herself—and the other women perceive her—as someone who will do whatever is necessary to achieve her goal. She frequently pushes the boundaries of appropriate behavior, often through sexuality.[12] For example, in Puerto Rico (16, 5), Courtney ambushes Ben to invite him skinny-dipping. Though he willingly participates, in a confessional, he expresses ambivalence about her "breaking the rules" and admits feeling "kind of crappy about what happened." Additionally, Courtney rejects social overtures that norms dictate she should accept. For example, in episode 6, when Emily apologizes for making a "rash judgment" about her, Courtney refuses to accept, saying, "I don't forgive and forget. And we will never be friends. I don't respect you." When Jamie Otis mediates, Courtney again rejects Emily's apology, asking, "Do you want me to bend over and take it up the tailpipe?" Her vulgarity contributes to her presentation as a polarizing and divisive figure. The other women routinely criticize her behavior. For example, during "The Women Tell All," Erika Uhlig says, "For as worldly as [Courtney] claims to be, you'd think [she] would have encountered enough people to know how to be respectful, and to know that's what people around the world expect of you. And I don't know how she's going to learn from this if she hasn't [yet], how to be nice to other people, and how to play nice." Erika's statement emphasizes the expectation that social conventions trump the competition.

Courtney's self-presentation as a mean or "unkind girl" contrasts with Brittney's as a "kind girl" within the show. While Courtney prizes winning over all else—this is, after all, an elimination game—Brittney quits the competition in episode 3 after she realizes that she is not attracted to Ben; her individual date went to Lindzi instead. During "The Women Tell All" episode, Brittney explains, "There was no attraction towards Ben whatsoever. So I felt that there were a few girls who had that attraction. Lindzi being one of them. I just felt that was such a unique date in San Francisco, that it should go to a girl that deserves it. I'm so happy with my decision because she rode it out to the end; she's in the final two." Audience applause reinforces the correctness of Brittney's apparently altruistic decision. Minutes later, however, she proves just as catty as other women when she insults Samantha, "First of all, you are like the Chihuahua of the house. You just don't stop talking. You don't stop talking! So shut up! God, she's so annoying. Just shut up." This episode underlines discrepancies between how women are presented in the edited show and their personalities outside it.

The other women question both the legitimacy of Courtney's motives and the authenticity of her presentation of self. They recognize a difference in how she behaves toward them and how she acts with Ben. Within ATU 480, such an inconsistency would suggest that the character is not the heroine but rather her unkind stepsister who ends up being punished for failing to behave appropriately. *The Bachelor,* however, has no such result—at least not during the program's filming. Rather, the women who bring these conflicts to Ben's attention are punished for doing so. Emily's warning to Ben about Courtney's behavior results in his cautioning Emily to "tread lightly" where Courtney is concerned (16, 5); Emily believes that this warning led to her elimination in week 7. Courtney's "punishment" came later; when the season was broadcast, Ben saw the difference between the self that Courtney presented to him and the edited version of the one she showed her competitors. This incongruity contributed to the couple's temporary breakup in February and March 2012. Ben addresses the issue in the "After the Final Rose" episode, admitting that he wishes Courtney had been "more gracious." He also acknowledges that viewers never saw "the whole story" and insists that he "hadn't been tricked by a temptress." He recommits to Courtney during the episode, but the couple eventually parted ways permanently in October 2012.

In several ways, the "Cinderella" metaphor breaks down. As both contestants and viewers, women are invited to participate in the show's fantasy romantic and life-changing premise. However, with a flock of women competing to become Cinderella, dating shows like *The Bachelor* and *More to Love* depart significantly from traditional fairy tales by denying the audience a central female protagonist with whom to identify. Editing compresses days or even weeks into a single one- or two-hour episode. During the initial episodes there are too many women for the audience to know and care about individually. In contrast to *EM:HE*, wherein a family's backstory is central to its choice, dating competition viewers know little about the women.

What is emphasized, however, is the competition among them. Such competition is a necessary structural element of the shows but also a key thematic connection to fairy tales. Women may be directly (as in "Cinderella") or indirectly (as in "The Kind and the Unkind Girls") set as rivals vying for a prince's affection or other reward. As in their fairy-tale counterparts, viewers see few moments of congeniality and friendship; editors instead dwell on the women's occasionally ridiculous attempts to catch the bachelor's attention. Sometimes they receive tasks directly pitting them against each other, as in episode 5 when they play baseball. Episode 4 of *More to Love* intensifies this tactic. The women must openly rate each other as a "good wife" or "bad wife" for Luke. The "good wife" is rewarded with an idyllic candlelit dinner in a fairy tale–like setting, while the "bad wife" eats Moroccan food and is humiliated by being coerced into belly dancing in public.[13]

So what is accomplished through repurposing "Cinderella" and other fairy tales in reality television? As discussed previously, both serve as a means for communicating cultural values. When both vehicles combine in a single venue, the message is intensified and naturalized. Thus, reinforcing the idea of the heteronormative nuclear family composed of one man and one woman remains the dominant ideological message of shows as diverse as *EM:HE* and *The Bachelor* and its spin-offs. Reality TV also functions as a site for audience response to the actions and attitudes they see on-screen. Annette Hill observes that audiences do not watch reality TV passively: "When audiences watch reality TV they are not only watching programmes for entertainment, they are also engaged in critical viewing of the attitudes and behavior of ordinary people in the programmes, and the ideas and practices of the producers of the programmes. . . . Audiences of reality programmings are involved in exactly the type of debates about cultural and social values that critics note are missing from the programmes themselves" (2005, 9). Programs like *EM:HE* and dating shows like *The Bachelor, The Bachelorette,* and *More to Love* have the potential to effect positive social change by encouraging volunteerism and presenting positive images of plus-size women and the process of falling in love. However, they have just as much potential to do harm, especially when they exploit weak and vulnerable members of society in pursuit of good drama. This dramatizing of disadvantage is particularly true for the contestants on *More to Love,* many of whom were young and had never been on a date or been kissed. While this inexperience sets up conditions for great television drama, there is little consideration about psychological damage to competitors. The women who compete for the bachelor's affections often appear strongly invested in the show as a possible route to find love. While some, like Courtney, seem focused on winning for its own sake, many others—like Amber T.—take their expulsion from the program as a sign of personal failure.

These programs—especially those in the Bachelor Industry—also naturalize ideas about who deserves the opportunity to fall in love. Like *EM:HE,* which provides renovations specifically for those who have already achieved the American dream of home ownership, the Bachelor Industry attracts only participants who have the financial security to leave their jobs and participate in this live-in program—apparently the homeless are not welcome here, either. Further, the vast majority of the participants on these programs are white, suggesting that people of color have little place in this kind of romantic fantasy.

Notes

An earlier version of this chapter was presented at the 2009 American Folklore Society meeting in a double session on "repurposing folktales" sponsored by the Folk Narrative Section.

1. In fact, reality TV plays with the idea that it is unscripted; it is in fact extensively structured and edited (see, e.g., Bignell 2013, 136–39). Most have writers; for example, IMDb lists Rob Cohen, Trace Slobotkin, and David Wollock as writers for *Beauty and the Geek.*
2. The prince falls in love with Cinderella's "enchanted state," but her escape from subservience depends on his recognition and acceptance of her "humble state" (Opie and Opie 1974, 121).
3. Created by Howard Schultz, *Extreme Makeover* provided contestants with "Cinderella-like makeovers": plastic surgery, dentistry, exercise, clothing, and hairstyles. The show's four seasons ran from 2002 to 2007. In 2010, it spawned a second spin-off, *Extreme Makeover: Weight Loss Edition,* following extremely obese contestants through

a year-long attempt to lose 50 percent of their body weight. The third season, with the name shortened to *Extreme Weight Loss*, aired during summer 2013.

4. Rare episodes feature renovations of other dwellings. "Friends Helping Friends" (1, 10) featured the day-long renovation of an apartment shared by New York City firefighters Pete Wasserman and Joe Liselli. Other specials renovated a firehouse and a church.

5. (Season, episode).

6. The "Friends Helping Friends" special (see note 4) emphasizes Wasserman and Liselli as long-time heterosexual friends—not gay romantic partners—as does the show's collateral material, like *Extreme Makeover: Home Edition: The Official Companion Book* (2005).

7. Gareth Palmer (2007) argues that *EM:HE* promotes a right-wing ideology privileging both traditional families and business interests, with the community rather than the state providing necessary assistance to needy families.

8. The five children in "Dickinson Family" (8, 20) received full-tuition scholarships to the College of Charleston.

9. Season 1 bachelorette Trista Rehn (runner-up of the first *The Bachelor*) married competition winner Ryan Sutter on December 3, 2003. During the "After the Final Rose" episodes, season 13 bachelor Jason Mesnick broke his engagement with winner Melissa Rycroft and resumed a relationship with runner-up Molly Malaney; the two married on February 27, 2010. Season 7 bachelorette Ashley Hebert married competition winner J. P. Rosenbaum on December 1, 2012; the marriage aired on December 16, 2012, as *The Bachelorette: Ashley and J. P.'s Wedding*.

10. Tony continued to be an active guide in his own decision making; he withdrew from the competition during episode 3 because he missed his son.

11. Some contestants with suspect motives are asked to leave *The Bachelor* and *The Bachelorette*. For example, Chris Harrison confronted Casey Shteamer when her ex-boyfriend reported that they were still involved; she was sent home (16, 6).

12. During a confessional in episode 6, Courtney says, "The girls here are very slow moving. And they're not very sexual. They're making it easy on me. And they are so naïve that they don't even see it happening." Minutes later, she uses her physical attractiveness to distract Ben's attention from Jamie, whom he eliminates from the competition that week.

13. While Moroccan food and belly dancing as punishment seems an odd choice, competitive dating programs are overwhelmingly white; hardly any people of color survive beyond the first few episodes. See Dubrofsky (2011) and Pozner (2010) for more about race in *The Bachelor*. Ethnic food, thus, marks difference and contrasts with romance and candlelight. Given many contestants' body image issues, public belly dancing seems intended to humiliate.

14

GETTING REAL WITH FAIRY TALES

Magic Realism in *Grimm* and *Once Upon a Time*

Claudia Schwabe

Ever since the Harry Potter phenomenon engaged and inspired millions of readers all over the globe, the fantasy genre has gained new acceptance and appreciation among different age groups. However, the phenomenon stirred up an old question, raised time and time again, about the relationship between fantasy and reality. Many critics and reviewers, from British novelist Amanda Craig (2007) to horror writer Stephen King (2000), praise J. K. Rowling's novels for their highly imaginative originality. One crucial aspect is their dynamic interplay between the magical world of wizardry and apparently mundane reality. Supernatural characters and creatures coexist with ordinary humans in the modern world. Rowling places enchanted objects in "muggle" (nonmagical) contexts and implants wondrous locations into realistic settings. For example, even if the reader has never been to King's Cross railway station in London, as Rowling describes it in the Harry Potter books, it evokes familiar images. However, tension with its everyday associations arises when Harry runs through a brick wall barrier between platforms 9 and 10 to enter the secret platform 9¾, the hidden starting point of the Hogwarts Express.[1] This precise juxtaposition of the supernatural and the natural, and the fact that they cross paths multiple times throughout the story lines, creates an intriguing tension between the familiar and the unfamiliar as well as between the apparent and what lies hidden beneath the surface.

In this chapter, I argue that current televisual fairy-tale reinventions are based on the rapprochement of the dichotomy between the familiar, visible, nonmagical, ordinary, and rational (the everyday) and the unfamiliar, invisible, magical, extraordinary, and nonrational (the magical). Realistic narratives are set in the everyday—the first reality. Many fantasy stories display an alternative magical place—Narnia, Middle Earth, and so on—that exists in the narrative as its own, second reality. However, contemporary fairy-tale reinventions synthesize quotidian reality with supernatural/magical reality, forming a new reality with magical influences. This continuous amalgamation and blending of the fantastic with an everyday setting constitutes a sphere I call a "third reality." In it, real magic exists in today's world, which fuses the magical with the everyday—a literal magic realism.[2] Based on the extent and nature of convergence between the supernatural and nonmagical dimensions, the third reality's magic realism varies between and even within current TV fairy tales. I differentiate between three relevant forms of magic realism: the *one-world fairy tale* (my term), the *reality fairy tale* (so-called *Wirklichkeitsmärchen,* coined by Germanist Richard Benz in 1908 and taken up by Paul-Wolfgang Wührl [2003] almost a century later), and *neomagical realism* (coined by Tracie D. Lukasiewicz in 2010; see Charts 14.1 and 14.2).

The concept of magic realism also evokes the aesthetic style of low fantasy, usually set in the rational, physically familiar world. Low fantasy "takes place wholly in the primary world and introduces elements of magic into it" (Nikolajeva 2008, 333)—similar to my third reality. Maria Nikolajeva sets magic realism and low fantasy apart from epic or high fantasy, which takes place only in a secondary (dream, fairy-tale, fantasy) world. J. R. R. Tolkien delineates the concept of the secondary world and stresses its cohesiveness: "What really happens is that the story-maker proves a successful 'sub-creator.' He makes a Secondary World which your mind can enter. Inside it, what he relates is 'true': it accords to the laws of that world. You therefore believe it, while you are, as it were, inside. The moment of disbelief arises, the spell is broken; the magic, or rather art, has failed. You are then out in the Primary World again, looking at the little abortive Secondary World from outside" (1964, 36). High or epic fantasy[3] incorporates elements of Tolkien's secondary world, the created "otherworld" (1964, 39–40). Nikki Gamble and Sally Yates (2008, 102–3) distinguish three subtypes of high fantasy: a setting in which the primary world does not exist (e.g., *The Lord of The Rings,* J. R .R. Tolkien 1954–1955; *A Song of Ice and Fire,* George R. R. Martin 1996–); a secondary/parallel world(s) that is/are entered through a portal from the

Chart 14.1

Different Forms of Magic Realism

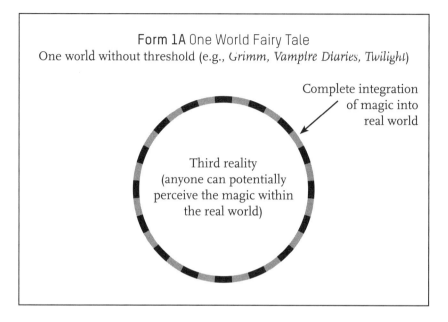

Form 1A One World Fairy Tale
One world without threshold (e.g., *Grimm*, *Vampire Diaries*, *Twilight*)

Complete integration
of magic into
real world

Third reality
(anyone can potentially
perceive the magic within
the real world)

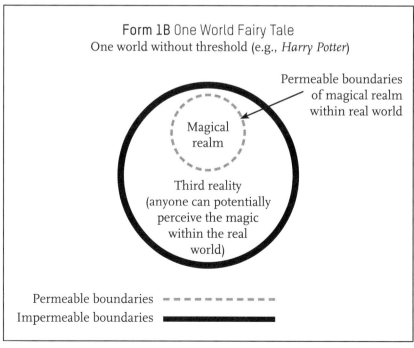

Form 1B One World Fairy Tale
One world without threshold (e.g., *Harry Potter*)

Permeable boundaries
of magical realm
within real world

Magical
realm

Third reality
(anyone can potentially
perceive the magic
within the real
world)

Permeable boundaries ---------
Impermeable boundaries ▬▬▬▬▬▬

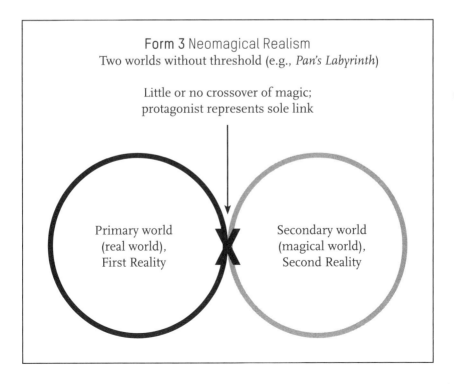

Form 2 Reality Fairy Tale
Two worlds with threshold (e.g., *Once upon a Time, The Golden Pot*)

Magic crosses over into the real world

Primary world
(real world),
First Reality

Third
reality
(perceived by
protagonist)

Secondary world
(magical world),
Second Reality

Form 3 Neomagical Realism
Two worlds without threshold (e.g., *Pan's Labyrinth*)

Little or no crossover of magic;
protagonist represents sole link

Primary world
(real world),
First Reality

Secondary world
(magical world),
Second Reality

Chart 14.2

MAGIC REALISM	WORLDS	SPACE	CROSSOVER FROM MAGIC INTO REAL WORLD	
Form 1a One-world fairy tale without threshold	One world	No boundaries	Magic is completely integrated into the real world	
Form 1b One world with threshold	One world with integrated magical realm	Permeable boundaries	Magic permanently crosses over into the real world.	
Form 2 Reality fairy tale with threshold	Primary and secondary world	Permeable boundaries	Magic crosses over into the real world but might be confined to a certain space within that world.	
Form 3 Neomagical Realism without threshold	Primary and secondary world	Impermeable boundaries	No magic crosses over into the real world or only to a minimal degree.	

primary world (e.g., *Alice's Adventures in Wonderland,* Lewis Carroll 1865; *The Chronicles of Narnia,* C. S. Lewis 1950–1956); and a distinct world-within-a-world as part of the primary world (e.g., the *Harry Potter,* J. K. Rowling 1997–2007). Contemporary fantasy is set in the modern world.[4] Incorporating some but not all of Gamble's distinctions, I categorize *Harry Potter,* for example, within magic realism, as a one-world fairy tale with a threshold, since magic exists not only in a confined space within the real world (Hogwarts) but also in modern-day England and throughout the world (as implied in *Harry Potter and the Goblet of Fire,* Rowling 2000).

While many scholars (e.g., Zamora and Faris 1995; Bowers 2004) explain the complex term "magic realism" in literature, few have applied

	PERCEPTION OF THIRD REALITY	EXAMPLES
	More than one person perceives the Third Reality. While anyone can potentially perceive the Third Reality, most humans do not perceive the fantastic entering the real world (only under special circumstances)	*Grimm, Vampire Diaries, Twilight*
	More than one person perceives the Third Reality. While anyone can potentially perceive the Third Reality, most humans do not perceive the fantastic entering the real world (only under special circumstances)	*Harry Potter*
	Only the protagonist perceives the Third Reality.	*Once upon a Time, The Golden Pot*
	Only the protagonist perceives the Third Reality.	*Pan's Labyrinth*

the idea to fairy-tale television. My typology of one-world fairy tale, reality fairy tale, and neomagical realism widens understandings of how magic realism relates to the fairy-tale genre and provides a framework to shed light on contemporary televisual fairy-tale reinventions. I contend that two American fairy tale–inspired television series, *Grimm* (2011–) and *Once Upon a Time* (2011–), creatively employ various forms of magic realism. Such stories suggest that the real world is nuanced with multiple layers of detail and meaning and with connections that are sometimes difficult to uncover given our limited perception.

To begin, I explore the distinctions between the three forms of magic realism in their historical literary contexts. I then examine differences between the genres of one-world fairy tales, reality fairy tales, and neomagical realism as they appear in *Grimm* (see Willsey's chapter) and *Once Upon a Time* (see Hay and Baxter's chapter). I consider how recognition of these concepts as employed in the two series visualizes the third reality, which emerges from the coalescence of the two apparently opposite epistemological concepts of magic and realism. I compare the depiction of fairy-tale characters within their different narrative contexts; I also examine the series' approaches to the third reality and magic realism. Finally, I speculate upon the significance of this form in the context of contemporary American television.

Magic Realism in Literary Context

Many scholars (e.g., Ocasio 2004; Williams 2007) associate magic realism or its Spanish equivalent *realismo mágico* primarily with the emergence of the twentieth-century movement of literary expression and artistic style by Latin American writers and artists, such as Colombian author Gabriel García Márquez, Mexican author Elena Garro, Colombian figurative artist Fernando Botero Angulo, and Mexican painter Frida Kahlo. However, the term's history stretches back to the early 1920s, when German historian and art critic Franz Roh championed a new direction in painting during the Weimar Republic that tried to capture the mystery of life behind the surface reality. Roh (1925) invented the phrase "magic realism" to characterize "a form of painting that differs greatly from its predecessor (expressionist art) in its attention to accurate detail, a smooth photograph-like clarity of picture and the representation of the mystical nonmaterial aspects of reality" (Bowers 2004, 8).[5] In this new style, Roh saw ordinary, identifiable, real objects depicted with an aura of mystery or magic.

Magic realism's foremost characteristic is that the magic must appear integral to reality. Roh states, "With the word 'magic,' as opposed to 'mystic' I wish to indicate that the mystery [of magic realism] does not descend to the represented world, but rather hides and palpitates behind it" (1925, 16). Magic realism thus illustrated the real world's mysterious aspects. Specifically, "whereas the old Realists merely painted the exteriors of objects, magic realism shows the object from its inner essence, or spirit, to its outer surface" (H. Martin 2011, 25). Only two years after Roh coined the term, the concept became prevalent in literature. In 1927, Roh's book was translated into Spanish and published in Madrid, and Italian writer and critic Massimo Bontempelli extended magic realism to literature in his cosmopolitan avant-garde periodical *"900": Cahiers d'Italie et d'Europe* (Notebooks of Italy and Europe; H. Martin 2011, 26).

Although it gained popularity throughout the twentieth century, the concept already existed in literature. For several scholars (e.g., Flores 1995; Schroeder 2004), Franz Kafka's novella *Die Verwandlung* (The Metamorphosis, 1915) serves as an early example. Preceding even Kafka, German Romantic writer E. T. A. Hoffmann embedded the trope in a variety of his *Kunstmärchen* (literary fairy tales), including *Der goldne Topf* (The Golden Pot, 1814), *"Nußknacker und Mausekönig"* ("The Nutcracker and the Mouse King," 1816), *"Der Sandmann"* ("The Sandman," 1816), *"Klein Zaches, genannt Zinnober"*[5] ("Little Zaches, Called Cinnabar," 1819), and *"Meister Floh"* ("Master Flea," 1822). Renowned fairy-tale scholars Benz (1908) and Wührl (2003) used the oxymoron *Wirklichkeitsmärchen* (reality fairy tale) to describe narratives using magical elements and events in otherwise ordinary realistic situations.

Hoffmann's *Der goldne Topf,* subtitled *Ein Märchen aus der neuen Zeit* (A Fairy Tale from the New Time), represents one of the earliest reality fairy tales. Scholars (e.g., Benz 1908; Brunken 2002; Neuhaus 2003; Wührl 2003) therefore generally consider Hoffman the reality fairy tale's inventor. In the poetic process leading up to writing *Der goldne Topf,* Hoffmann explained in a letter, dated August 19, 1813, to his friend and publisher Carl Friedrich Kunz: "The whole thing is to be endowed with a fairy tale and a fantastical quality but stepping boldly into ordinary life and seizing its forms" (1905, my translation). Inspired by the stories and the narrative style of *Les Mille et une nuit, contes Arabes* (One Thousand and One Nights: Arab Stories, Galland 1704–1717) in which ordinary people experience wondrous adventures while walking the streets of Baghdad or Basra, Hoffmann intended to portray his characters in everyday life.

Hoffman's character Anselmus has multiple magical encounters in the primary world: animals sing and talk; a doorknob turns into the visage of an old woman; a bell rope becomes a gigantic transparent white serpent; and a man changes into a large bird that flies away. Furthermore, Anselmus's life in the German city Dresden is punctuated by flights of fantasy that release him into the magical world of Atlantis. The reader wonders whether Anselmus has found his happily ever after in another realm, fallen victim to his imagination, become insane, or died. Finally, the narrator attests to the existence of magic and the fantasy world of Atlantis. Validating supernatural experiences in the primary world, the novella closes with his personal encounter with one of the fairy tale's characters. Yet "the conflict between

everyday reality and a poetic world of the mind produces a radical polarization of the self. Anselmus can live mentally in Atlantis, yet physically
he remains moored in Dresden" (Tatar 1978, 141). His mental oscillation
between the opposed dimensions of reality and fantasy invites the reader to
question Anselmus's underlying reason for choosing a fictional existence
over his Biedermeierianlife in Dresden.[7] Some conclude that his real life is
unbearable: "He is alienated in a state of crisis, so that he has to exercise the
dream functions of his mind as an escape from his real predicament" (Gallagher 2009, 290).

That Hoffmann's fantasy world of Atlantis impinges on reality exclusively through one character evokes Ofelia (Ivana Baquero) in Guillermo del
Toro's fantasy film *El laberinto del fauno* (Pan's Labyrinth, 2006) and Lukasiewicz's concept of neomagical realism. Like Hoffmann's hero Anselmus, Ofelia sees two worlds: post–Civil War, Fascist Spain in 1944 and the fantastical
underworld kingdom. This unique power of "*real* double vision," as Jack
Zipes aptly puts it, enables the young girl to navigate both realms, which
exist separately (2008b, 236). Since del Toro's work draws simultaneously
on magic realism and fairy tales, Lukasiewicz sees a hybrid genre she terms
"neomagical realism." Her concept distinguishes *Pan's Labyrinth* from the
conventional fairy tale's acceptance of magic within its fantasy world and
magic realism's incorporation of magic into the real world: "Neomagical
realism prevents the fantastical from crossing over into the real, at least as
given conscious validation by other real-world characters. Conversely, some
Pan's Labyrinth's fairy tale–world characters seem quite aware of what's going
on in both locations and can move between them. Others, like the creepy
and dangerous Pale Man,[8] cannot cross the border" (Lukasiewicz 2010, 70).
Whereas in one-world fairy tales and reality fairy tales the fantastical and
real dimensions converge to a third reality that incorporates the supernatural into the ordinary world, no such rapprochement occurs within the film.
Ofelia represents the sole link between them. The fantastic's traces appear in
the real world (e.g., a mandrake root, magic chalk), but no other characters
validate their efficacy or see the inhabitants (e.g., the gigantic faun).[9]

Magic Realism in *Once Upon a Time* and *Grimm*

Related to Lukasiewicz's neomagical realism as a hybrid genre based on
magic realism and fairy tales, yet very different in constructing a third reality, are *Grimm* and *Once Upon a Time*. The reality fairy tale *Once Upon a*

Time differs from neomagical realism as the fantastical characters and magic navigate between the fantasy and today's world. Due to permeable boundaries between the primary and the secondary worlds, in *Once Upon a Time,* the fantastical and the real partially converge. However, that third reality's space (where magic enters reality) is bound to a specific place within the diegetical real world, the (fictional) town of Storybrooke. *Pan's Labyrinth, Once Upon a Time,* and Hoffmann's *Der goldne Topf* present fantastical elements primarily from one or a few main protagonists' points of view. In contrast, *Grimm* introduces fairy-tale characters and fantastical events not as a personal escape from reality or a limited group's experiences in a specific place but as real people's verifiable actions, occurrences existing independent of any protagonists' perspectives.

Magic realism is the foundation for the third reality depicted in *Grimm* and *Once Upon a Time,* but the two series offer a different layout of the relation between the natural and the supernatural. The magical in *Grimm* not only coexists with the nonmagical but also originates in the human world (the primary world). Hence, all fairy-tale characters are natives of this single world and, the story line reveals, have always been integral to its history. Therefore, *Grimm* is what I call a "one-world fairy tale." In *Once Upon a Time,* on the other hand, a fairy-tale realm (the secondary world) exists parallel to the human world. Every fantastical figure in Storybrooke originally derives from this otherworldly place (and does not exist simultaneously in both worlds)—a reality fairy tale. I offer a clear distinction between magic realism's forms that feature only one world—*Grimm,* L. J. Smith's *Vampire Diaries* (1991–2012) series, and Stephenie Meyer's *Twilight* (2005–2008) series—and those that also incorporate a parallel realm of fantasy—*Once Upon a Time, Pan's Labyrinth, Der goldne Topf,* Michael Ende's children's novel *Die unendliche Geschichte* (The Neverending Story, 1979), Disney's *Enchanted* (2007), and J. M. Barrie's *Peter and Wendy* (later named *Peter Pan,* 1911).

As Chart 14.1 illustrates, the number of worlds and the permeability of the boundaries linking magical with nonmagical spheres determine the third reality. In the one-world fairy tale without threshold, the third reality represents the only world, with magic fully integrated into it (Form 1A). In the one-world fairy tale with threshold, a confined space of magic with permeable boundaries exists within the real world's third reality (Form 1B). Reality fairy tales incorporate permeable boundaries between the primary and secondary worlds; magical elements and/or characters can enter reality and vice versa (Form 2). In neomagical realism, the real and fantasy worlds remain (for the most part) separate. The narrative's main character represents the sole link between both. Consequently, for the most part there is no third reality; little or no magic transfers into the primary world (Form 3).

Along with the primary and secondary worlds, the magic realist genre also crucially differs depending on whether perception of the fantastic is limited to one character. If magic exists in the primary world only from the main protagonist's point of view, the audience remains in doubt whether the fantastic is solely in the character's imagination or actually in the diegetic reality. In *Grimm*, for example, the majority of humans do not perceive the fantastical layer of the third reality. At first, this special ability appears to be reserved for the main protagonist, who sees fantastical creatures, so-called Wesen (beings), in everyday life—and, of course, for the Wesen themselves. Later on, however, the show reveals that all humans could perceive the fairy-tale beings and do so when the Wesen want to be seen, confirming that the magic is integral to the mundane world. In stark contrast to this one-world fairy tale, where anyone can potentially perceive the fantastic, are neomagical realism and the reality fairy tale (see Chart 14.2). Although similar, they are not synonymous. In neomagical realism only one character (commonly the main protagonist) witnesses the fantastic and its influence on the real world, whereas in the reality fairy tale, magic is part of everyone's ordinary world. Thus, the distinction between forms of magic realism is based on three criteria: number of worlds, who perceives the marvelous and under what circumstances, and whether or not magic crosses from the (second) supernatural world into the (first) natural world (see Charts 14.1 and 14.2).

Grimm, Once Upon a Time, and Fairy Tales

Based *loosely* on legends and folktales collected by the brothers Jacob and Wilhelm Grimm, the two structurally diverse television series *Grimm* and *Once Upon a Time*—the former mixing horror, mystery, fantasy, drama, and police procedural,[10] the latter combining fantasy and drama—interweave fairy tales with today's reality. While the coalescence of magic and realism is their fundamental concept, they employ different characters, themes, styles, and stories.

While NBC's *Grimm* draws inspiration from popular Grimm fairy tales, such as "Cinderella" (ATU 510, 510A), "Sleeping Beauty" (ATU 410), "Hansel and Gretel" (ATU 327A), and "Rapunzel" (ATU 310), many episodes and characters have other sources. They include early French folktales (e.g.,

"Bluebeard" [ATU 312]); English fables (e.g., "Three Little Pigs," "The Story of the Three Bears"); Cornish folklore (e.g., "Jack the Giant Killer"); Japanese stories (e.g., "The Goblin Spider"); and medieval German legends (e.g., "Pied Piper of Hamelin"). ABC's *Once Upon a Time* takes similar liberties. The show makes multiple allusions to Disney fairy-tale films, such as the names of Snow White's dwarves (unnamed in the Grimms' "Snow White" [ATU 709]) and Sleeping Beauty's wicked fairy godmother "Maleficent," as well as references to songs like "Heigh-Ho" and "With a Smile and a Song" from *Snow White and the Seven Dwarfs* (1937).[11] *Once Upon a Time* also features non-Grimm figures: Pinocchio, Geppetto, Jiminy Cricket, and the Blue Fairy (from Disney's version of Carlo Collodi's Italian fairy-tale novel *Le avventure di Pinocchio* [The Adventures of Pinocchio], 1883); Belle (from the French fairy tale "Beauty and the Beast" [ATU 425C], 1740); the Mad Hatter (from Lewis Carroll's novel *Alice's Adventures in Wonderland,* 1865); and the Genie (from the folktales compiled in *One Thousand and One Nights*).

In *Grimm,* horror, fantasy, and mystery are inherent to the third reality—a world needing protection from frightening fairy-tale monsters. The series centers on Nick Burkhardt (David Giuntoli), a homicide detective in his late twenties to early thirties, who, according to his police partner Hank Griffin (Russell Hornsby), is a "happily-ever-after guy." Shortly before his aunt Marie Kessler (Kate Burton) dies of cancer, Nick learns that he has inherited supernatural powers, having descended from a long line of human warrior guardians called "Grimms." In the pilot episode, Marie describes the secret Grimm ancestry as the "misfortune of the family" since it ultimately leads to a life in danger and isolation, with no room for romantic relationships. Marie avers further, "This is no fairy tale—the stories are real" and assures her nephew that what the Brothers Grimm wrote about "really happened," thereby establishing authenticity of a nonfictitious reality including uncanny, flesh-and-blood fairy-tale characters. Indeed, Nick can see the animalistic and/or monstrous faces of the Wesen, who not only masquerade as humans but also live and work undetected among them. With his newly inherited powers, however, comes the responsibility of keeping balance between humanity and the supernatural beings of today's world.

Fairy-tale characters who live among humans and the continuous blending of fantastical elements with a realist setting tie *Grimm* stylistically to magic realism. Set and filmed in Portland, Oregon, the wild, rural landscape of the outskirts evokes a mystical, enchanted atmosphere, which contrasts sharply with shots of the busy city life and quiet, peaceful suburbs that are home to humans and Wesen alike. The fantastic and the real coexist, accentuated by fairy-tale creatures residing effectively next door, such as the "Eisbibers" (ice beavers), a small community of meek, shy, buck-toothed people who live in Nick's own neighborhood. Throughout the series Nick establishes friendships with them and some other gentler Wesen, including a reformed "Blutbad" (bloodbath; vulgarized by the show as Big Bad Wolf), or rather "Wider-Blutbad" (against bloodbath), Eddie Monroe (Silas Weir Mitchell). This wolf man, who abstains from killing humans through a self-described "strict regimen of diet, drugs, and Pilates," enjoys a quiet life in his suburban bachelor pad. Several Wesen are based on classic Grimms' *Kinder-und Hausmärchen* (Children's and Household Tales, 1812) albeit with considerable artistic license. Blutbad Monroe comes from "Little Red Cap" (ATU 333) and "Wildermann" Larry Mackenzie (Kenneth Mitchell) from "Hans My Hedgehog" (ATU 441).

A closer examination of *Grimm*'s supernatural creatures reveals that they bear resemblance neither to Grimms' fairy-tale characters nor to Disneyfied beings familiar to the series' North American viewership. The series counteracts most audience expectations by alienating the traditional fairy-tale characters in sometimes radical and uncanny ways. The transformations create a dramatic tension and can evoke feelings ranging from amusement and excitement to irritation, surprise, and shock. For example, an online fan review states, "The portrayals of the 'monsters' is a great blend between scary and amusing that brings back the nostalgic Buffy fan in me" (Jecreath-235–941347 2011). Another notes, "When we see the CG [computer graphics] of seemingly normal humans flashing into glimpses of their true monster nature, it looks creepy and amazing" (Grimm: Season 1).

On more than one level, *Grimm*'s fairy-tale characters are not what they seem. First comes a visual deception; if only for a brief moment, Nick sees people who otherwise appear human in their true identity as Wesen. Second comes a twist of character; a fairy-tale figure commonly fearsome, threatening, ominous, or dangerous may be quite the opposite. Blutbad Monroe becomes Nick's charmingly humorous sidekick and unofficial deputy detective, whose expertise in fantastical matters helps solve cases. In contrast, those characters generally friendly, harmless, or cute become aggressive, ugly, and bloodthirsty. Cinderella turns into a *"murciélago,"* a monstrous bat with glowing red eyes and vicious rows of teeth. The Three Little Pigs transmute into murderous, wild boars with giant tusks jutting up from their lower jaws. The Three Bears become ferocious hunters and human slayers.

Third, the Wesen's German names are linguistically contorted. The German compounds do not exist in the Grimms' stories or in spoken or written German (e.g., "Hexenbiest" [witch beast], "Bauerschwein" [farmer pig], "Hundjäger" [dog hunter], "Jägerbär" [hunter bear], "Lausenschlange" [louse snake], "Seltenvogel" [rare bird], "Spinnetod" [spider death], "Ziegevolk" [goat people]). The German-sounding words appear as a tongue-in-cheek reference to the language's common use of long compound nouns.

At first glance, *Once Upon a Time*'s third reality seems a lot more ordinary than magical. But in contrast to *Grimm,* its quotidian world comes across as a dreadful prison. Indeed, the fairy-tale realm's evil queen Regina (Lana Parrilla) has cursed all its creatures, casting them out of the Enchanted Forest to the disenchanted human world, which she describes in the pilot episode as "Somewhere horrible. Absolutely horrible." The dark curse condemns the fairy-tale characters, including Snow White (Ginnifer Goodwin) and her wedded Prince Charming (Josh Dallas), to a life without memory of their past identities. As mayor, Regina maintains power over the fairy-tale characters, trapped not only physically (unable to leave the town limits) but also in time (at the beginning of the pilot episode the town clock is stuck at 8:15). In flashbacks, viewers learn that Snow White and Prince Charming saved their newborn child Emma from the curse by sending her through a magic wardrobe into the modern world. Twenty-eight years later, Emma Swan's (Jennifer Morrison) life drastically changes when Henry (Jared Gilmore), the now ten-year-old son she gave up for adoption at birth, finds her and asks for help. He has discovered that only Emma can save the fairy-tale people and break the magic spell. Henry also tells his disbelieving mother of her royal parentage and her destiny.

Once Upon a Time thus conforms to a reality fairy tale: the primary world, reflecting contemporary reality, is paralleled by a secondary magic world; fantasy characters and magic cross into the primary world and converge with reality; and the main protagonist experiences the fantastic within an ordinary, realistic setting. As Benz outlines,

> At first, we are introduced to the life of the hero, who reveals himself, and we descend with him to the first area of the marvelous, which appears to exist in his imagination for the time being. Suddenly the grand world of faerie emerges in front of us, and its links influence all aspects of life, as becomes evident along with the growing sense of the supernatural. A venerable man shows him the wonders of the

realm, . . . tells him about the curse and the myth of salvation, and shows him the role he is destined to play in the process. (1908, 145, my translation)

Storybrooke is a typical small waterfront town in Maine with a jagged, mostly rocky coastline. Multiple clues reinforce the notion of a place frozen in time: the sleepy, provincial atmosphere; the 1980s vintage cars; the spider webs on the front desk of Granny's Bed and Breakfast. Yet anachronistically, technology such as the internet and current TV broadcasts are available. The fairy-tale characters' modern world is a secluded, bubble-like space of reality, a cursed place "with no happy endings." Unaware of their true selves, the characters' ordinary lives reflect new identities and normal jobs: Snow White, Mary Margaret Blanchard, is an elementary school teacher and lay sister; Red Riding Hood, Ruby (Meghan Ory), is a waitress; Rumpelstiltskin, Mr. Gold (Robert Carlyle), is a pawnbroker and dealer of antiquities; Jiminy Cricket, Archie Hopper (Raphael Sbarge), is a child therapist; and so forth. Emma, a former bail bonds collector, literally becomes the new sheriff in town.

The chief protagonists of *Grimm* and *Once Upon a Time,* Nick and Emma, share the same occupation: law enforcement. This is no coincidence, I argue, since they embody the archetypal hero figure, commonly a warrior, rescuer, protector, defender, and savior—white America's view of the police. Nick and Emma, both modern-day knights in shining armor, protect the people of their respective towns using their profession's power and authority. While Nick fights evil supernatural forces to defend innocent humans and fairy-tale creatures alike, Emma personifies the ultimate savior who can break the dark curse. Further, she defends the banished fairy-tale characters against the oppression and corruption of the mayor's established power structure.[12]

Even though Nick and Emma are both guardians of the law working in criminal investigation, they differ in family background, physical appearance, gender, family status, and, especially, their relationship to the fantastic. Nick, a man from the middle class, has short, dark hair and lives with his long-term girlfriend Juliette Silverton (Bitsie Tulloch). As a distant descendant of the Brothers Grimm, he uses his special ability to see, identify, and expose fairy-tale characters disguised as human beings. In sharp contrast, Emma is a fairy-tale princess (although she grew up as an orphan in the modern world) with long, blonde hair and the biological mother of a son. Initially, unaware of her origin, she also refuses to believe in anything fantastical and therefore cannot recognize the fairy-tale figures trapped in Storybrooke.

Whereas Nick has sightings of magical transformations before he believes in their reality, Emma can only see the fairy-tale magic once she is convinced of its existence.[13]

Third Reality: *Once Upon a Time* and *Grimm*

Not only do the main protagonists of *Once Upon a Time* and *Grimm* diverge, but the shows also approach the third reality and magic realism very differently. *Once Upon a Time* features a nonlinear plotline incorporating character-centered episodes with flashbacks to fairy-tale land to complement the central story occurring in present-day Storybrooke. While the viewer gains insight into the secondary world, existing parallel to the real world, for most of season 1 Emma does not. Though the show makes viewers aware that the fantastic and its objects (e.g., a magic hat, a magic ring, a poisoned apple, a potion of true love), characters, and powers have crossed into the primary world, Emma at first has no knowledge of this influence. Yet as soon as she enters Storybrooke, the enchanted town begins to change as the dark curse weakens. Time moves forward, clocks start ticking, and the hitherto oblivious fairy-tale characters slowly regain their former memories and discover their true identities.

Storybrooke is infused with magic. The curse makes it so. But despite plenty of signs of magic, Emma is at first either unaware or chooses not to believe. For example, in the pilot episode Henry tells her that the dark curse prevents anyone from leaving Storybrooke. Whenever someone tries to go, Henry explains, "bad things happen." When Emma ignores his warning and attempts to return to Boston, a wolf appears in the middle of the road and she wrecks her car on the Storybrooke sign. In "True North" (1, 9),[14] Emma again attempts to depart, this time with Hansel and Gretel (Ava and Nicholas Zimmer [Karley Scott Collins and Quinn Lord]). Her vehicle breaks down as they reach the town limits. Similar mysterious fates befall other inhabitants who try to leave. Yet she sees these as mere accidents, failing to recognize the supernatural barrier that turns Storybrooke into a magical prison.

Emma's denial prevents her from seeing the truth even when directly faced with it. In "The Stranger" (1, 20), August Booth (Pinocchio [Eion Bailey]) shows her his wooden leg. Though visible to the viewer, a camera shot from Emma's perspective portrays a normal human leg. Clearly, some characters perceive their fairy-tale backgrounds. "The Heart Is a Lonely Hunter"

(I, 7) reveals that the mayor possesses magical powers and knowledge of her fairy-tale past. At its closing, Regina walks into her secret vault, opens a storage box, clutches the stolen heart of the huntsman (Sheriff Graham [Jaime Dornan]), and crushes it to dust, killing him. But it is not until the first season's finale that Emma believes in magic and the fantastical elements become visible to her. In previous episodes the magical blended with the nonmagical only sporadically, but magic realism fully unfolds at the first season's end.

The penultimate episode, "An Apple Red as Blood" (I, 21), focuses on Snow White's poisoned fruit and imports the fantastic into the real. Whereas in neomagical realism the two juxtapose but remain in separate spaces, in reality fairy tales they converge. Regina uses the Mad Hatter's (Jefferson [Sebastian Stan]) magical hat to create a portal within the primary world that links directly to the secondary world to retrieve Snow White's poisoned apple from Fairy Tale Land. In the final episode, "A Land without Magic" (I, 22), Henry falls into a coma after taking a bite of Regina's poisoned apple turnover that was intended for Emma. At that point she begins to believe in the curse and realizes the truth. Now possessing the ability to see the wondrous influences around her, she accepts the fairy tales in Henry's book *Once Upon a Time* as indeed true, pervading reality, and representing chapters of her own life story.

Yet Emma at first doubts her role as the savior of all fairy-tale characters. When she finds August lying in bed, his human body turns slowly into wood before her eyes as he becomes Pinocchio. She expresses her self-doubt: "This is all too much. I just talked to the evil queen and Rumpelstiltskin about a quest to find magic. I can't do it, August. I can't. No normal person can." August reminds Emma of her magical origin before he turns completely into a wooden puppet: "Luckily for us, you're not normal." Accepting her destiny, Emma seeks a powerful potion of true love to save Henry's life. Below the Storybrooke town library lies a secret cavern where Emma must fight the dragon Maleficent to retrieve the bottle of true love in the creature's belly. When Mr. Gold steals the potion, Emma's kiss wakes Henry and breaks the curse, allowing all residents to remember their true identities. However, the residents of Storybrooke witness a gigantic purple cloud of smoke engulfing the town, which brings abundant magical powers to the real world.

In contrast to the reality fairy tale *Once Upon a Time,* the fantastic in *Grimm* originates in the primary world. There is no secondary world of fairy tales and fantasy. Moreover, the marvelous is not bound to a secluded space within the real world but exists throughout Portland, Oregon and the entire world. The marvelous always has been an integral part of the human world and its history, as the books of Nick's ancestor Grimms confirm. From the outset, the third reality is a magic realist space. Animal-like fantasy creatures walk among humans, and magical objects (such as seven mysterious keys[15] and the magical Coins of Zakynthos[16]) become instruments of power struggles that are highly sought after by humans and Wesen alike. In the pilot episode, the audience learns that the fantastic is not limited to the protagonist's perception; descendants of the Grimm bloodline in every generation inherit the ability to recognize the true nature of fairy-tale creatures in the real world. Moreover, the Grimms inherit the unparalleled power to fight rogue Wesen to maintain harmony in society.

Setting the one-world fairy tale *Grimm* apart from neomagical realism as defined by Lukasiewicz is the fact that real-world characters validate the fantastic's existence. In "Big Feet" (1, 21), for example, Monroe's Wildermann friend Larry Mackenzie is stuck in "woge" (wave), the hormones that change Wesen into creature form. Those who see Larry partly morphed believe they have encountered Bigfoot. In the same episode, Nick's police partner Hank is terrified after catching a glimpse of Blutbad Monroe and distraught after watching a dying Wesen's face regain its human features. Further, in "Bad Moon Rising" (2, 3), he witnesses the fantastical transformation when a young "Coyotl" (a coyote-like creature) unthinkingly reveals her appearance due to her fear of Nick and again when a killer shifts into a Coyotl before attacking Hank.

The story line eventually reveals that there are two ways to see Wesen. First, mature Grimms can see through their disguise whenever the creatures are startled, afraid, upset, or otherwise emotional. In return, the Wesen in morphed form can perceive a Grimm. Second, Wesen can intentionally drop their disguise or shift their shape to make their true form visible to other humans. In "Organ Grinder" (1, 10), Monroe indicates that though Wesen can allow themselves to be seen, "The vast majority of humans just can't process that kind of information. They can believe in all kinds of stuff, you know. Gods, for example. Angels, demons, and dinosaurs and the Big Bang Theory, and E = mc squared, man. But that's only because it's not right in front of them. They're not looking directly into the boiling core of the raw universe. So, you know, confronted with that kind of reality, a lot of brains just turn to mush."

This episode establishes *Grimm*'s relationship to magic realism, locating the fantastic within the mundane world but also addressing how perceiving magic affects humans. Indeed, Hank's encounters with the fantastic leave him on the verge of a nervous breakdown. In the season finale, "Woman in Black" (1, 22), Monroe and Nick discuss the situation:

> Monroe: Hank's got to be shook up about this in some way. You know, I mean whether he's talking about it or not, when I saw him looking up at me, he was freaked. . . . This is not, like, your ordinary nightmare, okay? He knows he was awake. And his brain is trying to process the unprocessable. I mean, what did you think when you first saw one woge?
>
> Nick: I thought I was going crazy.

Initially, Nick leads Hank to believe that his visions are a product of his imagination. Later Nick has no choice but to share his Grimm identity for the sake of Hank's mental state and to prevent his confused friend from shooting his own Coyotl goddaughter in "Bad Moon Rising."

While *Grimm* visualizes the third reality as a space where various fairy-tale species coexist with humans, it foregrounds the fantastical figures' portrayals and character developments. It shows their emotional depth and ties them to a historicized narrative, which makes them appear real and authentic. As one review noted, "Silas (Monroe) gives Grimm its emotional core and more humanity than most humans could ever hope to possess" (Stailey 2012). Another concurs: "Monroe is the only recurring character with sufficient depth, while Nick and his girlfriend Juliette . . . still seem relatively flat" (*Crimespree Magazine* 2012). The personalities of Nick's police partner Hank, co-worker Sergeant Wu (Reggie Lee), and girlfriend Juliette fade next to that of Monroe. One fan commented, "Bitsy (Juliette), though, has always made this character feel so hollow to me, like a cardboard cut out rather than an actual person to whom I could relate . . . frankly I don't think she brings any depth or cerebral qualities to her role at all" (MsTaken 2012).

While in "Love Sick" (1, 17) Detective Hank and Sergeant Wu fall victim to poisoned cookies and become critically ill, fans express sympathy for the perpetrator, the beautiful but cunningly evil Hexenbiest Adalind Schade (Claire Coffee). She loses her magic powers by ingesting Grimm blood: "The end of the episode, starting where Nick forces her to drink his blood, is so chilling and haunting; it left me with such sympathy for a character who was doing some pretty vile things. I hope we continue to see her" (*Grimmophilia* 2012). A devastated shell of her former self, Adalind goes to her mother for comfort but finds revulsion and disdain instead. Another fan noted, "Claire Coffee did such a great job of making you feel for Adalind even when she's so evil. My heart just broke for her at the end of Love Sick, she was like a little girl, totally lost and alone" (ibid.).

Similarly, insight into the villains' background stories, feelings, and personal motivations in *Once Upon a Time* explains why the evil queen and Rumpelstiltskin became malicious. For both, the loss of a loved one plays a pivotal role and can evoke in the viewer a strong sense of compassion for these miscreants: "Yes, I do feel sorry for Regina. As it is stated many times 'Evil is not born. It's made.' She wasn't evil until she lost her love. Snow White made that evil spark to life within Regina when she betrayed her secret and created that metaphorical snowball that ruined EQ's [evil queen's] life" (Adevilishdiva 2012). Another fan posted, "Both of them were never evil to begin with and they have reasons for doing what they did. I sympathize with both Rumpel and Regina" (fallingparachutes 2012).

It may initially appear that these viewers' reactions resist the shows' manifest structures. Conventional fairy tales and fairy-tale readings suggest that audiences should root for the princesses and rejoice at the downfall of their adversaries. But it cannot be entirely coincidental that both *Grimm* and *Once Upon a Time* offer sympathetic villains like Regina, monstrous creatures with soft hearts like Monroe, somewhat tedious apparent heroes like Nick, and usually positive characters with murderous proclivities like Ruby/Red. When magic deploys in these shows' (fictional) real worlds, the third reality they display ironically offers more nuance than the rhetoric of most contemporary news reports in the media.

There are plenty of rotten apples and black sheep in our society who may indeed, like Rumpelstiltskin/Mr. Gold, have backstories that explain their apparent malevolence; they may have positive qualities, like Regina's fierce and protective mothering. While thriving on sensationalism and the magnification of negative events, American news coverage tends to paint the world as the grim battleground of good versus evil forces—of heroes versus villains—and it thus propagates a worldview that is as black-and-white as Grimms' fairy-tale versions. At the same time, when we think of monstrous crimes in the recent past committed, for instance, by single shooters (e.g., the 2012 Sandy Hook Elementary School massacre in Connecticut with the death toll of twenty-six children and adults; the 2011 Norwegian attacks by Anders Behring Breivik, who killed seventy-seven people; the Virginia Tech massacre that left thirty-three people dead in 2007), the Wesen's banal human forms masking potentially dangerous interiors seem metaphorically plausible. However, the view of reality shifts when threats reported in the media prove fictional or simply blown out of proportion, such as Iraq's alleged hidden weapons of mass destruction or the dangers of an H1N1 virus outbreak, and those exaggerated hazards enter the public consciousness the way the purple smoke of magic engulfs Storybrooke.

Magic realist stories such as *Once Upon a Time* and *Grimm* indicate that the real world does not follow a black-and-white pattern reminiscent of the interior design in Regina's office. They rather urge the viewer to never stop questioning what might lie hidden beneath the façade of a certain object, person, or place. In other words, if we choose to simplify, generalize, and polarize, we lose out on the richness that is this life. When reality television uses fairy-tale structures to narrate transformation, when news is fiction, when good and evil become difficult to distinguish, the one-world fairy tale's and the reality fairy tale's infusions of magic into everyday life offer a compelling perspective of truth: everything has two or more sides, nothing in this world is only what it seems, and magic always comes with a price.

Notes

1. Although Hogwarts is a magic place located in the modern world, Harry crosses a threshold from the muggle world into the wizarding world at platform 9¾. The brick wall represents both a figurative and a literal frontier. Tale heroes or heroines commonly traverse a distinctive threshold before entering into an otherworldly realm, e.g., a looking glass, a trapdoor, a secret tunnel, a well (compare Steven Jones 2002, 15; Matrix 2010, 194; H. Martin 2011, 23).

2. Most critics and theorists use the terms "magic" and "magical" realism interchangeably. The term "magic realism" was introduced in the 1920s for visual art that "attempts to produce a clear depiction of reality that includes a presentation of the mysterious elements of everyday life," and "magical realism" is "a term introduced in the 1940s [for] referring to narrative art that presents extraordinary occurrences as an ordinary part of reality" (Bowers 2004, 131). I use the term "magic realism" throughout this chapter.

3. High fantasy traditionally presents the ongoing, epic battle of good versus evil within the construct of a mythic, folkloric, or feudal world (Saltman 2004, 192).

4. Both contemporary and low fantasy are set in the real world. However, low fantasy is not necessarily located in the current, modern age (Gamble and Yates 2008, 102–3).

5. Also called "*neue Sachlichkeit*" (the new objectivity), this new painterly style was "related to, but distinctive from, surrealism due to magic realism's focus on the material object and the actual existence of things in the world," unlike the more cerebral,

psychological and subconscious reality that the surrealists explored (Bowers 2004, 10).

6. *Zinnober* is a German colloquial expression meaning "nonsense, rubbish, worthless."

7. *Biedermeier* derives from the fictitious naïve and unintentionally comic poet Gottlieb Biedermaier, lampooned in the Munich humorous weekly *Fliegende Blätter* (Flying Sheets) as early as 1855. *Biedermeier* ("e" replacing the "a") compounds *bieder* (worthy, honest, respectable) and *Meier*, a common German surname (forms include Meyer, Maier, and Mayer [Garland and Garland 1976, 85]). It defines a person who loves the idyll, the comfort of domesticity, and living in quiet humility and self-sufficiency (Neubuhr 1974, 8).

8. The Pale Man, a child- (and fairy-)eating monster who sits silently before a large feast, may refer to Lamia, a Greek mythological female creature with a serpent's tail below the waist. In ancient classical mythology, this beautiful queen of Libya became a child-eating demon.

9. The faun gives Ofelia a mandrake root, which instantly begins to cure her mother's illness. However, soon after her mother discovers the root and throws it in the fireplace, she dies in childbirth. The faun also presents Ofelia with a piece of magical chalk, which she uses to draw a door on a wall to enter the Pale Man's lair and to escape her guarded bedroom.

10. Police procedurals concern a crime that must be solved by the episode's end, usually employing a generic structure: crime, investigation, arrest, and sometimes trial.

11. The Walt Disney Company owns the television network American Broadcasting Company (ABC), a link further discussed in Hay and Baxter's chapter.

12. The trend of portraying the hero as a law enforcement officer in fairy tale–inspired television series continues. In CW's *Beauty and the Beast*, which premiered fall 2012, protagonist Catherine Chandler (Kristin Kreuk) is a New York Police Department homicide detective. The show remakes the 1980s *Beauty and the Beast* created by Ron Koslow, in which Catherine Chandler (Linda Hamilton) was an assistant district attorney.

13. Actor Giuntoli states that the journey of his character Nick Burkhardt "is one that goes from total bewilderment to full acceptance" (Farinordin 2012).

14. (Season, episode).

15. The keys, each held by a Grimm (Nick has one), together form a map that leads to a secret treasure trove containing a hidden source of power that can control the world.

16. The three coins inspire megalomaniac behavior in humans and Wesen alike. Grimms are more immune to their influence than most, but the coins leave other owners obsessed, driving them to madness, e.g., Nero, Liu Bang, and Hitler.

15

HAPPILY NEVER AFTER

The Commodification and Critique of Fairy Tale in ABC's *Once Upon a Time*

Rebecca Hay and Christa Baxter

reator Edward Kitsis, asked why he and Adam Horowitz wanted to develop a television show about fairy-tale characters, answered that they "just wanted to write about something hopeful that for one hour a week allows one to put everything aside and have that feeling that your dreams just may come true" (2011). His statement tellingly mirrors the Disney corporation's perspective that fairy tales offer simple, happy, escapist narratives for children and their families, with wholesome morals entirely free of political implications and only coincidentally capitalist ventures. Commercially, Kitsis and Horowitz's ABC/Disney show *Once Upon a Time* (*OUAT*) has succeeded; it was one of the most popular debut dramas among adults eighteen to forty-nine years old in 2011 ("ABC Wins" 2012). Yet the show diverts not only from its creators' stated aims but also from some expectations that go along with any Disney production. Specifically, it delays the conventional happy ending by transplanting fairy-tale characters to contemporary Maine, where they struggle with their love lives, family relationships, and making ends meet.

By relocating familiar protagonists to a modern locale, *OUAT* defers and complicates the possibility of happily ever after—and sells the idea of fairy tale as an everyday story that ordinary viewers can relate to. To keep the show popular and viable for as long as possible—thus continuing to generate direct revenue through commercial spots and DVD sales—*OUAT* adapts classic stories to the ambitiously lengthy plotline of a television long-arc serial, a format whose basic story line extends across multiple episodes and seasons (Gillan 2011, 6). With the series' plot based on fairy tales, the creators of *OUAT* take advantage of a serial structure that provides time and space for developing innovative, complex, and realistic characters with whom the audience may empathize and relate. But as we explore, *OUAT*'s mixing of reality and fantasy also helps bolster its economic interests, through fan identification and participation in the Disneyfication of everyday life.[1]

Because of the financial advantages of resisting the final denouement as long as possible, *OUAT* thrives on the unrest within its narrative—which may unsettle viewers accustomed to a happy ending delivered in a bedtime story or a ninety-minute children's movie. But the lack of narrative closure also adds complexity to well-known figures. The backstories create characters who resemble everyday people and offer characterizations viewers may identify with. As we explore, fan involvement continues as ABC's new media platforms deliberately invite audiences to insert themselves into the show's main roles. Indeed, audience identification forms the crux of *OUAT*'s commercial appeal—and the resulting commodification of fairy tales—because viewers who identify with the cast are more likely to become loyal and lucrative fans.[2] To that end, *OUAT* not only offers likable, nuanced, and relatable characters but also literally asks viewers, via new media platforms, to see themselves in those figures. Viewer identification, however fleeting or superficial, encourages further watching to see how characters cope with challenges both quotidian and fantastic that may mirror their own. But even more, the cycle of presentation, identification, and commodification in *OUAT* moves a Disney corporate strategy from films like *Enchanted* (2007; see, e.g., Bacchilega and Rieder 2010; Pershing and Gablehouse 2010) into television. This chapter explores how *OUAT*'s complex and relatable characters, and viewers' actual identification with them in new media contexts, not only serve corporate capitalism but also affect how audiences view fairy tales in their own lives.

Traditionally, television offered a scheduled transfer of content from network creators to viewers at home. However, in the age of new media, this top-down arrangement becomes a web of cyberinfused interactions. Television scholar Derek Kompare says, "As the internet, and not the television set, is increasingly the cultural hub of the global cosmopolitan household, more and more television viewing and contextualizing is occurring online" (2011,

98). Originally, fans created and ran their own online forums. But now, networks colonize these digital spaces by creating sponsored websites with message boards, interactive content, and news updates (Jenkins 2006, 25–92). Because long-arc serials must maintain fans' interest over several episodes and seasons, these marketing platforms keep the show fresh in the viewers' minds before and after each episode and between seasons (Gillan 2011, 27). Many new media digital platforms, including Twitter and Facebook, endeavor to both attract and create fans for a show. ABC began marketing *OUAT* online before the series even began, using their own network website, Twitter accounts, and a Facebook page to give plot teasers and casting news.

These online marketing platforms demonstrate ABC's commercial logic, positing that viewers with a personal connection with Snow White (Ginnifer Goodwin) or Emma Swan (Jennifer Morrison) are more likely to become loyal fans. Fan forums, the show's official Facebook page, and ABC's website underline how *OUAT* depicts real-life problems, commodifying these challenges for fans who may be eager to see their own lives and concerns as tidily resolved as they are on the screen. The show's marketing team drives the point home by inviting viewers on Facebook to literally imagine themselves as fairy-tale characters in a real-life setting, as we demonstrate below. While many networks and series use social media–based marketing, we argue that *OUAT* succeeds because those media invite the viewership not only to watch the tales unfold but also to insert themselves into the story. The show's commodification, seen blatantly in its serialized deferment of a happily ever after, expands through this use of social media and audience identification. *OUAT* invites viewers not to rewrite the classic tales but rather to inscribe their own stories within the show's structure. In that act of personalizing and internalizing, the show suggests that fairy tales are more reality than fantasy. And by linking their own lives to the show's cast, viewers become loyal fans willing to invest in the long-arc serial of *OUAT*—and in the hope for the everyday fairy-tale ending it purveys.

Entering the World of *Once Upon a Time*: The Fairy Tales We Think We Know

To quickly attract and resonate with American viewers, *OUAT* draws upon the fairy-tale retellings most familiar to its audience: Disney movies. Because these versions are so widely known, *OUAT* makes a smart commercial move by remaining generally faithful to their premises but adding narrative depth.[3]

Given that ABC Television Network belongs to the Disney/ABC Television Group, it's no coincidence that most tales allude to Disney versions (Disney/ABC Television Group 2012). Online viewer comments suggest that fans are willing and anxious to see what surprises lie in store for this cast they have recognized as Disney characters, as we discuss below. Of course, the surprises—through plot twists and embellishments—humanize these characters in ways that invite those viewers to identify with them.

OUAT deliberately capitalizes on this tension between the Disney canon and the show's innovative retellings. Indeed, the 2011 pilot episode opens with this text on the screen: "Once Upon a Time, There was an enchanted forest filled with all the classic characters we know. Or think we know." Promotional material aired during the episode also promises, "The real story behind all your favorite fables will be told." Because *OUAT* has multiple episodes to explore and thus humanize these Disney fairy-tale characters, the show dives into their relationships, revealing romantic ties deeper than love at first sight and explaining classic antipathies as more than an aging stepmother's jealousy of her younger, fairer stepdaughter. The marketing theory behind these plot developments suggests that it's much easier to relate to an evil stepmother with a complex resentment of her stepdaughter and to a prince who wasn't always royal than to simply polarized or socially remote characters. If viewers identify with nuanced protagonists, they may faithfully watch until happily ever after does indeed arrive. Of course, audience fidelity translates into higher ratings, commercial revenues, and the show's longevity.

In addition to humanizing Disney characters, *OUAT* makes them more relatable by depicting them participating and interacting in the contemporary United States. The basic framework of *OUAT* spans two worlds: one magical, set in a wooded, Disneyesque land with castles and peasants' huts, containing magical objects and creatures; and one realistic, set in present-day Storybrooke, Maine. The two worlds feature the same cast, but the familiar characters of "Fairy Tale Land"—the originating location—have been cursed by the great dame of wicked witches, Snow White's stepmother. Her curse transports Snow White and the Prince (Josh Dallas), but also Red Riding Hood (Meghan Ory), Rumpelstiltskin (Robert Carlyle), and many more, to the initially unchanging world of Storybrooke, where time has stopped and the characters can neither remember their past identities nor find true happiness. *OUAT* employs flashbacks and visual hints to connect the worlds of magical past and dreary present (see Schwabe's chapter).

The pilot episode features a fairy-tale ending—or rather, what happens after Snow White and Prince Charming's apparently happy ending. The evil queen sends the couple and the other fairy-tale characters to a world where, as she states, "Everything you love will be ripped from you while you suffer for all eternity. No more happy endings." In Fairy Tale Land, to combat the curse, Snow and Charming employ Geppetto (Tony Amendola) and the fairies to help send Snow's newborn, the prophesied savior who can break the curse, to safety. The baby, who grows up to become Emma Swan, escapes just before Queen Regina's (Lana Parilla) curse goes into effect. The banished Snow White becomes a chaste and lonely schoolteacher named Mary Margaret; Prince Charming, gravely wounded just before the curse takes effect, becomes a coma patient named David; the evil queen becomes Regina, Storybrooke's controlling mayor; Rumpelstiltskin becomes its wealthy landlord; and so on. Indeed, much of season 1 revolves around identifying other fairy-tale characters in their new environs. While Emma grows up in the world outside Storybrooke, Snow, Charming, and the rest of the Fairy Tale Land characters, as well as Henry (Jared Gilmore)—Emma's relinquished biological child, adopted by Regina—are trapped in a stagnant life where time has stopped and nothing changes.

Assuming a basic familiarity with Disney fairy-tale structure, the writers turn their creative energies in season 1 to the ever expanding middle of the story: what happens after Snow White and Prince Charming's happily ever after but before Emma's final confrontation with the queen. The pilot establishes this beginning-at-the-end through multiple scenes, opening with Charming's race to Snow, dead in a casket without true love's first kiss. Upon his arrival, one of the seven dwarves tells Charming, "You're too late." The prince asks to kiss Snow one last time, and that embrace revives her. She awakens and gasps, "You found me." The scene shifts to their wedding, implying that happily ever after is where this show's tale starts.

Horowitz and Kitsis's long-arc serial structure propels the story line ever closer to a denouement without arriving too soon at a resolution. Characters as diverse as the Mad Hatter (Sebastian Stan), Hansel and Gretel (Quinn Lord and Karley Scott Collins), Cinderella (Jessy Schram), and Pinocchio (Eion Bailey) inhabit Storybrooke—and sometimes Fairy Tale Land—while dealing with custody battles, parental abandonment, financial hardships, unwed motherhood, and tense father–son relationships. The fairy-tale characters' contemporary counterparts grapple with problems typical of the white American middle class—not coincidentally, the show's key intended viewership. Kitsis and Horowitz defer happily ever after to humanize and flesh out the show's characters—in both Storybrooke and Fairy Tale Land.

Although the show alludes to Disney fairy-tale lore, it does more than merely reference known clichés. As actor Ginnifer Goodwin explained, "The thing about the script was that . . . [the writers] were fleshing out these characters and they were showing us their flaws. It's not that we were aiming to replicate the performances of others. . . . We weren't trying to bring the Disney animated feature to life or something. I feel that we justify all of those stories. You can say, like, 'Oh, I can see how Disney's Snow White is kind of loosely based on the real Snow White,' which we hope that everyone feels this [*OUAT*] is the real Snow White" ("A Conversation" 2012). By promising "the real Snow White," the show nods to the Disney canon while creating new fairy-tale variations—and therein lies part of its appeal. Viewers may be pleased to recognize Belle's (Emilie de Ravin) golden ball gown or Snow White's gift with bluebirds, but many fans watch to find out what—or who— will be different from the Disney retellings they already know. For example, while anticipating a season 2 appearance by Hook, fan Cynthia Richards wrote, "I hope you do bring in Peter Pan. OH PLEASE remember that Peter was always played by a woman. OH PLEASE don't ruin him, like the movies have done and let a boy be the lead role. PLEASE OH PLEASE find a girl to play Peter make it right" (*Once Upon a Time* Facebook page).[5]

OUAT brings these fairy-tale characters to the television screen by enacting the process Pierre Bourdieu describes as "position-taking," in which "[the] meaning of a work . . . changes automatically with each change in the field within which it is situated for the spectator or reader" (1993, 30). As *OUAT* resituates fairy tales in the narrative structure of the long-arc serial and in a setting that combines the fantastical with the contemporary, their meaning shifts. The characters have new life not just as beloved figures from cherished stories but also as relatable people traversing a world just as complex as the viewer's own.

Commodifying the Characters

TV comedies and dramas, like *Seinfeld* and *Grey's Anatomy*, hitherto used loosely related but self-contained episodes. In recent years, however, networks have experimented with the long-arc serial (Gillan 2011, 6). With story lines and character arcs spanning multiple seasons, long-arc serials ask for a large time investment from audiences—and risk losing them for that reason (ibid., 136). Yet because *OUAT* follows that commercially risky yet potentially

profitable format, the series has the freedom to humanize fairy-tale characters—and attract viewers curious to see those characters in a real-life setting.
Creators Kitsis and Horowitz, veterans of other well-known serials, dreamed
for nearly a decade of bringing a fairy-tale show to television (Littleton 2012).

In many ways, fairy tales offer ideal subject matter for the long-arc serial
because to be profitable, it must quickly captivate a viewership. Given the
familiarity of Disney fairy tales, *OUAT*'s large cast of characters (and potential characters) already resonates with American audiences. But long-arc
serials must also attract a loyal fan base willing to watch conflicts develop
over entire seasons. Its narrative arc affords *OUAT* the scope to develop
characters more complex than the archetypal sketches in most fairy tales or
their Disney film versions. Thus, within Fairy Tale Land, *OUAT* fleshes out
familiar plots with more elaborate backstories. In Storybrooke, however, the
cast's lives are much more open ended than their traditional precursors',
prompting curious viewers to tune in and see whether their favorite characters will get their happy ending in the contemporary setting.[6] Indeed, the
mystery of who the Storybrooke characters are and how they relate to their
fairy-tale selves fostered the first-season popularity, as evidenced by fan spec-
ulation. For example, Erin Furches commented, "Hey but maybe whale [the
doctor played by David Anders] is Gaston from Beauty an[d] the Beast. Just a
thought!" (*Once Upon a Time* Facebook page 2011–2012). Viewers ask, Which
classic storybook character does each figure represent? How will they deal
with real-life problems? *OUAT* commercially depends on viewers' empathy
with fairy-tale characters who must face the same challenges they do.

While *OUAT* embellishes Disney stories within Fairy Tale Land, the Storybrooke setting allows for origin and originality to interplay, resulting in a
pull between the apparently simple Disney character and her or his modern-
day version. Creative writing instructor Robert McKee addresses the importance of implementing dynamic characters in screenwriting: "Story is about
originality, not duplication. . . . A story is not only what you have to say but
how you say it. . . . We shape the telling to fit the substance, rework the substance to support the design" (1997, 8). As the *OUAT* producers depict the
substance of fairy-tale narratives within a modern setting, they play on the
tension between characterization and what McKee calls "True Character."
Characterization is "the sum of all observable qualities of a human being,
everything knowable through careful scrutiny: age, and IQ, sex and sexuality; style of speech and gesture; choices of home, car and dress; etc." (ibid.,
100). True Character, in contrast, "waits behind the mask. . . . Despite his

[*sic*] characterization, at heart who is this person?" Any given character falls among a nexus of attributes: "Loyal or disloyal? Honest or a liar? Loving or cruel? Courageous or cowardly? Generous or selfish? Willful or weak?" (ibid., 375).

In *OUAT,* characterization occurs through allusions to Disney figures via visual cues (such as hair color and wardrobe) and basic background stories. Using such familiar figures gives access to ideas, plots, and themes without spending time establishing their foundations. But beyond the familiar Disney characterization, what are a person's enduring characteristics and attributes? True Character is based on desire; what is it the person wants? Thus the show's originality thrives on exploring and exploiting True Character, both in Fairy Tale Land and in Storybrooke. Each episode sets up a familiar characterization that is then mimicked, explored, and sometimes countered in both worlds. This paralleling process offers a more nuanced view of the show's mode of commodification; it is about not just connecting dual worlds but also developing True Characters in a world of familiar Disney characterizations.

These multifaceted characters have become both a key attraction for viewers (as we discuss below) and an engaging method to drive the plot forward. Actor Josh Dallas commented, "I think in all the incarnations that we've seen Prince Charming, we don't know much about him. We knew he comes in and saves the day, kisses the girl and that's kind of it. Which is not a bad gig, but that's what is so great about Eddie Kitsis and Adam Horowitz, the creators, is that they have created characters that have levels to them" (Vogt 2011). The idea of characters' levels plays a central role in the continuation of each episode and the series as a whole. *OUAT*'s pilot text, quoted above, invites viewers to discover who these familiar fairy-tale characters become without their happy endings, after them, or when they're like the average Americans that Storybrooke's characters are supposed to represent. Using McKee's terminology, exploration of True Character occurs in both worlds. In Fairy Tale Land, this examination leads to further elaboration on already familiar tales: Snow White becomes a rebel bandit in the woods, Prince Charming rises from working on a humble farm to a royal position, and young Regina's bitter enmity comes from her youthful broken heart. On the other hand, when True Character is explored in Storybrooke, even as each fairy-tale character's personality begins to emerge, the figures we know (or think we know) are given a twist because of the contemporary world they inhabit. Just as in the viewers' lives, the question of happily ever after remains undefined in Storybrooke. *OUAT* does promise that true love will conquer all, but because happily ever after is continually deferred, the series questions and explores how a perfect ending can come from imperfect people.

The character Regina is a good example of this tension—and its potential for audience identification. The show's evil queen, who is Snow White's stepmother and her biological grandson Henry's adopted mother (and step-great-grandmother), when cast as mayor, develops into a far more complex villain than fairy-tale conventions often allow. *OUAT* sells a new tale with a dynamic, empathic Regina. Indeed, it goes to great lengths to humanize her in Fairy Tale Land by explaining why she comes to loathe Snow White. In episode 17, a flashback to Regina as a kind, aristocratic young woman who loves her stable boy, Daniel (Noah Bean), shows her ridiculed by Cora (Barbara Hershey), her conniving, social-climbing mother, as a masculine and unwanted old maid. Regina's likability is bolstered by her rescuing the child Snow White (Bailee Madison) from a runaway horse. She hardly seems capable of becoming an evil queen.

But Snow White's betrayal of Regina is complex and undeniable. In the same episode Snow White's father wants to marry Regina because he sees her as a suitable mother for his young daughter. When Snow White sees her soon-to-be-stepmother kissing the stable boy, she is heartbroken at the thought that Regina is betraying King Leopold (Richard Schiff). Regina chases the tearful Snow and explains, eliciting a vow of silence from her. But the young girl accidentally reveals the secret. Cora's wrath is unleashed, and she kills Daniel before Regina can elope with him. Witnessing her fiancé's murder and sentenced to a loveless marriage in which she is valued only as a stepmother, never as a wife, Regina's bitterness festers and grows. Her backstory questions the fairy-tale conventions of good and evil. Could the apparently loveless queen have loved someone so much that his loss numbed her heart? And if Regina truly deserves sympathy, how can audiences cheer on her impending demise, even if it is necessary to a traditional happily ever after? When even traditional villains become relatable, how can traditional endings become similarly realistic?

Even in Storybrooke, the site for Regina's bitter revenge, the queen-turned-mayor reveals her humanity. Her villain role crosses into Storybrooke; she is authoritative and monstrous in positions of domesticity (adoptive mother to Henry) and political power (the evil queen and mayor) alike. Yet the evil queen and ironfisted mayor adopted Henry and loves him.

The juxtaposition of both sides—the humanized traditional fairy-tale characters against their Storybrooke counterparts—makes this show compelling. In the pilot, modern-day Regina sneers to Emma, "And in the last decade while you've been . . . well, who knows what you've been doing . . . I've changed every diaper, soothed every fever, endured every tantrum. You may have given birth to [Henry] but he is my son!" Emma asks, "Do you love him?"; Regina immediately responds, "Of course I love him," prompting viewers to question previous assumptions about her coldheartedness. This evil queen has a mother's tender, loving feelings. *OUAT* relies on the tension between Storybrooke and Fairy Tale Land to heighten viewers' empathy. It humanizes the queen/mayor in ways viewers can relate to—familiar betrayal, a broken heart, and a struggle to connect with her son. By showing Regina's development from adolescent to adult to mother, *OUAT* creates a dynamic and understandable character.

Fan comments online show viewers relating to her. Fan "Utter solitude" commented, "I like Regina too. I'm really loving the humanity that's being brought to these traditionally evil characters. And I can't wait to find out more of EQ's [evil queen's] back story" (Utter solitude 2012). If the villain is a pitiable former princess betrayed by her mother and robbed of true love, her structural counterpart's wickedness and flat, foundational role move into complex character development. Season 1 establishes Regina as the figure whom savior Emma must face. But fans identify with Regina as more than an evil queen; they see her as a person.

Writing Themselves into the Story: New Media Platforms and Audience Identification with *OUAT*

While *OUAT*'s long-arc serial structure provides time to humanize fairy-tale characters, the show deliberately seeks audience identification through its online marketing platforms. On both ABC-sponsored and fan-run websites, *OUAT* viewers combine the fictional worlds of Fairy Tale Land and Storybrooke with their own life stories. This amalgamation not only alters *OUAT*'s narrative implications but also subtly reframes how audience members view their own lives and how they see fairy tales. Official ABC platforms invite fans to identify their connections with characters—and they do, albeit not in great detail. Within fan-based communities, that identification reaches new horizons, as participants not only identify more deeply with characters but also write themselves and their own social concerns into *OUAT* fan fiction. Identifying with and writing as show characters, fans collapse the distinction between fairy tales and their own lives.

As already indicated, before the series premiere, the *OUAT* producers used new media platforms to interpolate potential viewers as characters within the stories. On the show's official Facebook page, for example, viewers were asked several weeks before the series premiere, "If you were really a fairytale character and didn't know it, who do you think you'd be?" (*Once Upon a Time* Facebook page 2011–2012). Judging by the 818 "likes" or thumbs up that Facebook users gave and the 1,348 responses, asking followers to identify so directly with the show resonated with potential fans (ibid.). Most respondents simply named a favorite character, but several reacted more thoughtfully, with answers ranging from sarcastic to playful to painfully serious. Olivia Knight said, "sleeping beauty. I'd rather sleep than go to class anyhow," while Keisha Burke replied, "idk [I don't know] is there a rocker princess?" More serious responses included Mamie Patton's comment, "gretel . . . getting lost and shoved in the ove[n]" and Chelsea Botticelli's remark, "Cinderella or Snow White, easily. I've had bad problems with my mom before, I've always been poor or worked to death in some ways, but I'm extremely hopeful and don't let it get to me. and also, I'm pretty sure someone either wants me dead or I have a fairy godmother." The *OUAT* Facebook page asked a nearly identical question just after the series started ("What fairytale character are you most like?"), generating many similar responses.

Whether in response to these questions or to the show's humanized characters, fans on the *OUAT* Facebook page continue to identify with the show's characters as media for exploring and explaining their own lives. After the wrap of the first season, the Facebook page regularly posted stills of favorite characters with their iconic one-liners. This practice continues the show's narrative through references to previous episodes, while again allowing the viewership to write their own tale. For example, on July 20, 2012, a shot of Prince Charming included the quotation "I will always find you" emblazoned across it. A mere four days later, this post had more than 5,000 page shares, more than 49,000 likes, and 1,356 comments. While the sentiments vary, many fans show a degree of self-identification with Snow White, hoping a prince will come and find them. Some comments were confident, such as Shaina Milagros's "I know you will," Ana Havea's "you will find me dont worry:)," and Lux Hurtado's "i will always find you . . . .;)." Other comments expressed playful frustration, as when Maureen Hewitt quipped,

"How long before you find me then? Lol," Rosalyne J. Ireland commented, "I'm right here . . . waiting!" and Lynn Hudson complained, "Where are you then I've been wa[i]ting awhile. Did something happen to your GPS?" Joan E. Birch took a more general approach, responding with "Isn't that what we all want to hear from our loved ones?! LOVE LOVE LOVE this show!!!!" These fans use a character and line from *OUAT* to express their own emotions of frustration, hope, and/or confidence. Thus, the show's depiction of Snow White and Prince Charming becomes one more narrative through which these viewers process their own lives.

Even Regina inspires identification. When her image was posted with the trademark phrase "I will destroy your happiness if it's the last thing I do," several fans related her character to their own interpersonal struggles. This post had far fewer comments than Prince Charming's one-liner, and a majority compared Regina to others in their lives—mothers, exes, girlfriends, mothers-in-law, and even teachers—rather than to themselves. Some empathized with Regina's victims: Dalton Albrecht replied, "lol its all ready destroyed" and Gwendolyn Rose said, "I got out of that bad fairy tale marriage, lol." Donna Budd-Foley-Scheffel even expressed jealousy, saying, "I wish I had that power over my frenemy!" *OUAT* thus becomes "an enactment of a personal identity" (Bryan et al. 2011, 12656). When viewers make that shift, they're more likely not only to self-identify as a loyal fan but also to approach watching the show as part of who they are (Ciotti 2012).

ABC's official *OUAT* website includes the same interactive content that many series use to include viewers as loyal fans by fictively offering them authorship within the narrative. For example, under a list of "extras," a link to the discussion boards is offered with the phrase "Tell Your Story." Even more significant, the ABC site features an interactive magic mirror that communicates to viewers as both characters and fans of *OUAT*: "The Magic Mirror serves The Evil Queen as her vaporous visage, his curse: to always be truthful. He has the freedom to advise, disagree, or even scold those under his auspices. If you request his guidance, be forewarned: only ask questions that you seek to know the true answers to. For those of you who wish to delve deeper, allow him to show you your true reflection" ("Ask the Magic Mirror" 2011). The website's lack of self-conscious irony conveys how seriously ABC endeavors to embrace viewers as fairy-tale characters. By directing visitors to consult the magic mirror with their most serious questions, the site prompts fans to act like the characters they see in *OUAT*. Where the show depicts fairy-tale characters coming into the real world, the mirror allows fans to insert themselves into Fairy Tale Land. This shift happens quite literally when the site prompts users to allow access to their Facebook profiles; the magic mirror site grabs photos of users and their relatives and friends and places them within the mirror's frame while discussing their futures in terms sufficiently vague to apply to anyone. Displaying the user's image, the voice says,

> Once upon a time there was you. You've had so many adventures, almost as harrowing as those citizens of Storybrooke. Almost. . . . I believe that maybe your story mirrors our fairytale in OUAT. In fact, I believe you could exist there as well. Who are you? Let's take a look. You are inquisitive and you seek knowledge. And although you seem to live in the real world, I suspect you are a dreamer, and that is a wonderful place to inhabit. All great stories must come to an end, and now I leave you to your happily ever after. ("Ask the Magic Mirror" 2011)

The open-ended predictions parallel the lack of closure in the show's long-arc serial narrative. By identifying viewers as fairy-tale characters—rather than asking them to make their own connections—this website augments the link between fans and *OUAT* characters that will ideally translate into more constant and loyal viewers and higher ratings.

Significantly, viewers do identify with the show's characters even when not explicitly asked to do so, revealing the familiarity of loyal fans who tune in regularly and boost ratings. On the unofficial, fan-run *OUAT* Wiki, viewers often discuss their favorite characters, scenes, and episodes. A few write in-depth responses relating the show to their personal lives. Escaily connects her relation with her own mother to Emma's on-screen devotion for her son. Discussing Emma's kiss of the comatose young Henry that breaks the curse, Escaily says,

> of course this is my favorite scene in the whole finale, as if there was any doubt in this, i think it was so surprising, but obvious at the same time, how emma's "true love" was the one she had for henry, because what love is stronger than that of a parent towards it's child?, i personally could relate to it because my mother is the kind of woman who is always making sure we know how much she loves us, so watching emma break henry's curse with a kiss in the

forehead, got me thinking about my own mom, and how she's my best friend and how much she loves me *(no offense to those people out there whos[e] mom is either diseased or neglectfull, it's not my intention to make you uncomfortable)*. so yeah the beauty of the finale was how henry woke up, basically the sleeping curse broke, because his mom loved him, loved him so much, so much she fought a dragon, and started to beleive in fairytales, not because somebody convinced her, but because she realized beleiving was the only way to save him, and in the process, Henry saved her . . . i loved this part, and i will always love it, that's why this scene is my number one. (Escaily 2012)

Just as the characters' dynamism comes from both their Fairy Tale Land and Storybrooke settings, the viewers use *OUAT* to inform their lives and conversely use their lives as a basis for understanding the show. The Wiki's forum provides a place for such an interaction of worlds to occur and "story worlds spill over into interfaces that allow for more direct modes of audience engagement and community interaction" (Stein 2011, 129). Comments like Escaily's suggest that the lines between reality and fiction are not as clean as many would assume. In the equation of her mother's love for her with Emma's for Henry, Escaily's reality changes from her mother's love being strong enough to overcome earthly forces to metaphorically being sufficient to defeat those that are unearthly and even fantastical. While Escaily's comment does not suggest she believes in magic, she uses the show, magic included, to explain and make a parallel to her reality—which is exactly what the show and its paratexts invite viewers to do within its televisual parallel worlds.

Fan-based forums often function subversively. Yet even positing a romantic affair between Regina and Emma, as some fan fiction does, though contrary to Disney's patriarchal, heteronormative princess–industrial complex (see Pershing and Gablehouse 2010), may encourage viewers to keep watching. Whether in the hope of seeing Swan–Queen sexual tension, imagining themselves as a new series character, or identifying with the persecuted Snow White, fans' creative meanings funnel into loyal viewership. But because the show is so heavily Disney based, any character depiction simultaneously functions as a product placement. A sizable portion of the corporation focuses on princess products, fairy-tale adaptations, and Disney World and Disneyland vacations; interest in these characters translates to profit (Gillan 2011, 15).

Television pitching fiction as reality is nothing new (see Lee's chapter). For the show's predominant viewership (adults eighteen–forty-nine, based on the show's ratings), the trend of happily ever after is metaphorically written in their dreams and literally written on their wedding napkins (Gorman 2012; see also Greenhill and Matrix 2006). In a culture so obsessed with making every girl a princess and every wedding a fairy tale, the concept of bringing fantasy into contemporary settings is already manifest. *OUAT* simply takes that premise and places it in a fictional story. Because of the corporate relationships between ABC and Disney, *OUAT* as an enterprise makes inherently commercial links between story and consumption. Like other recent Disney productions, for example the film *Enchanted,* the series uses "iconic, self-referential humor and imagery to reinforce Disney products and values" (Pershing and Gablehouse 2010, 143). Similarly, "the ball, the wedding, and the other make-believe scenarios naturalize the appeal of fantasy and display the power of magic for sale in the contemporary world" (Bacchilega and Rieder 2010, 29–30). *OUAT* thus functions as a response to the myriad ways contemporary culture reappropriates fairy tales. In particular, its relationship between and combining of worlds mirrors how Disney commercializes the genre by ensuring retellings are simultaneously a commodity and a product placement for Disney experiences and consumable objects (Gillan 2011, 15).

OUAT's attention to characters of various ages and stages of life reflects its parent corporation's commercial expansion beyond child consumers. Take for example Disney's Fairy Tale Weddings & Honeymoons, whose website advertises, "Whether you envision a grand affair or an intimate gathering, your wedding can be anything your heart desires" (2012). Princess wedding dresses (e.g., the Ariel dress is "inspired by the gentle movement of the ocean's tides [and] features cascading ruffles and self-made flowers that softly sway and dance as if under the sea"); movie-themed honeymoon packages (e.g., where you too can live the dream, spending your honeymoon exploring Cinderella's Castle in Disney World); and even Oral-B's princess toothpaste reflect a Disney-saturated culture fixated on the idea of an alternate reality becoming one's own.

Disney's push for profits results in products and experiences that seek to sell happy endings as commercial commodities. From the above examples to the theme parks in Tokyo, Hong Kong, and Paris that promise they're "Where Memories Begin," Disney's reach is undoubtedly international. Arguably, Disney fairy tales specifically sell a particular ending: the Disney

2009 theme "Where Dreams Come True" and European fairy tales' "They lived happily ever after." *OUAT* is a game changer by specifically using television to rethink tales as old as the Grimms' (or older) to sell Disney's commercialized presentations of happily ever after. Yet because *OUAT* has been conceived of as a long-arc serial and will defer happily ever after as long as possible, it cuts against the commercialization of happy endings. Jack Zipes has accused Disney of betraying fairy tales and using happy endings to sell products, exploiting the willing self-identification of young children (primarily girls) with princesses and fairy-tale characters: "Disney sought to replace all versions with his animated version" (1995, 343). He argues that these films are "an attack on the literary tradition of a fairy tale. [Disney] robs the literary tale of its voice and changes its form and meaning" (ibid., 344). Richard Schikel echoes the sentiment: "[Disney] could make something his own, all right, but that process nearly always robbed the work at hand of its uniqueness, of its soul, if you will. In its place he put jokes and songs and fright effects, but he always seemed to diminish what he touched. He came always as a conqueror, never as a servant" (1968, 277).

By using Disney fairy-tale markers to sell their show while also complicating the notion of happily ever after, *OUAT*'s first season is poised between an idealistic, shallow happy ending and a difficult, sometimes drab, but always dynamic progressing story. As the episodes work through escalating tensions and brief narrative reprieves, the series seems to continually ask and yet never quite answer the question "Can there be a happily ever after in real life?" *OUAT*'s continual deferment may speak to its audience's hope, but television's episodic nature positions any ending as a temporary state rather than a conclusive finish. It is not the ending that is happy; it is tender kisses, brief smiles, temporary resolutions to never ending problems, the small moments that leave lasting impressions. Indeed, in the pilot episode when Emma asks, "How's the book supposed to help [Henry]?" Mary Margaret responds, "Well what do you think stories are for? These stories, they're classics. There's a reason we all know them. They're a way for us to deal with our world for when it doesn't always make sense." Her voice is that of the creators and consumers of *OUAT*.

Fairy Tales, Imagination, and the Combining of Worlds

As the first season progresses and more and more Storybrooke characters realize their past life in Fairy Tale Land, the separation between worlds begins collapsing. In the finale when Emma breaks the curse, the worlds combine as the rest remember their lives in Fairy Tale Land and magic enters Storybrooke. *OUAT* thus asks viewers once again to rethink the relationship between fairy tale and real life. Clearly, the first season revolves around the tension of a dual reality—Storybrooke is beyond and yet originated in Fairy Tale Land (see Schwabe's chapter). Regina's curse affects everyone from Fairy Tale Land. But for those who believe—characters who see past the contemporary world and into the reality of the storybook—the synthesis of the worlds is possible. The first character who believes in both is Henry, the only child protagonist. Several other cast members (Jiminy Cricket's psychologist counterpart Archie Hopper, for one) explain away Henry's obsession with fairy tales as a way to cope with his emotions. But what happens now that Henry's persistence has paid off, Emma believes, the magic is rediscovered, and the curse is broken? What happens when Storybrooke and Fairy Tale Land combine into only one fairy tale? Actor Josh Dallas commented, "The nature of the curse is that no one can have their happy ending, so . . . the saga continues" ("A Conversation" 2012). The only solution is another season.

The season 1 finale pivotally reconstructs viewers' notions of the two worlds. Although many characters have already remembered their lives in Fairy Tale Land, the two worlds' integration comes to a climax in "A Land without Magic" (1, 22).[7] The first breakthrough happens after Henry takes a bite of Regina's poisonous apple turnover, meant for Emma. He falls into a Snow White–like coma; it's his way of proving the curse's reality to his biological mother. When Emma rushes Henry to the hospital, Dr. Whale assures her the boy shows no traces of poison, saying, "I understand your frustration Ms. Swan, I do. But I need something to treat and right now there is no explanation. It's like . . ." As Emma empties Henry's backpack on the bed and picks up his storybook, she finishes the doctor's sentence: ". . . like magic." The book glows red as she touches it, and Emma perceives the last few moments of her life as a newborn in the magic world. By the end of this dramatic flashback, Emma believes. She accepts the dual worlds and, hoping to save her son, embarks on a journey to break the curse and unite each character with the entirety of their lived experience.

Emma and Regina, sharing the need to save Henry, approach Mr. Gold ("Actually, he goes by Rumpelstiltskin," Regina wryly comments) and demand a cure. Gold sends Emma on a quest for the last vial of magic but cons it from her and escapes. Emma, broken and resigned to Henry's death, returns to the hospital to keep vigil by her son's apparently lifeless form. As she sees him lying there, she leans down, whispers she loves him, and kisses his forehead. In that moment, the curse is broken. "True love's kiss" is not the romantic kiss between two lovers but one given by a mother to her son. The two worlds combine; magic is not some mystical power alien to Storybrooke but a kiss that belongs to both the characters' and the viewers' lived reality. Within that ordinary, familial embrace lies the power to break even the most otherworldly of curses and connect the most disparate of worlds. Just as viewers online use *OUAT* to process their own lives, Emma views her fairy-tale past to make sense of her Storybrooke present. The televisual melding of fairy tale and reality echoes the links that corporate and fan sites foster.

But true to the long-arc serial's structure, no complete resolution comes through the season finale. In the final moments, Mr. Gold brings magic to Storybrooke. The last scene cuts to Regina's smirking face watching what appears to be an oncoming cloud of smoke. The season's climax could only occur in Storybrooke, signifying to the audience that their world is more crucial than Fairy Tale Land. As the curse is broken, Snow and Charming recognize and remember their love for each other, Emma realizes she is Snow and Charming's daughter, and the evil queen must run for her life from the townsfolk. The deferral of happily ever after that occurred in previous episodes seems resolved. The curse no longer weighs down the town with ignorance. The characters in Storybrooke are no longer torn between dual worlds; they become one: both Snow White and Mary Margaret, Prince Charming and David, the evil queen and Regina. But breaking the curse simultaneously resolves and complicates the show's premise. The presumption that ending the spell would bring happily ever after refigures into a question: Will breaking the curse bring happily ever after? Clearly, the answer is no. But what happens when fairy tales are no longer a fictional means to help understand the present reality? What happens when fairy tale becomes reality?

Mr. Gold's phrase "And I'm bringing it. Magic is coming" suggests a different type of fairy tale for season 2. It may contain the same basic elements: magic, a smorgasbord of Disney characters, good/evil binaries, and so on. Yet by showing a contemporary world in conflict, the producers open a realm of vision hitherto unexplored in *OUAT*. If the magic world is the real world, what world is marketed for consumption: their own world or a fairy tale? In one pivotal move the focus on the premise that "there once lived a beautiful princess and handsome prince" shifts to "there once lived a person like you and me"—as long as we live in white, middle-class America. The fairy tale becomes real, and reality is the fairy tale.

This move harks back to fairy tales' folkloric origins—born in and of a culture contingent on that society's time and place. As Marina Warner states, "Fairy tales are stories which, in the earliest mentions of their existence, include that circle of listeners, the audience; as they point to possible destinies, possible happy outcomes, they successfully involve their hearers or readers in identifying with the protagonists, their misfortunes, their triumphs. *Schematic characterization leaves a gap into which the listener may step*" (1994, 316). While the overarching moral may remain ("good will always triumph over evil"), the stories told to convey such messages are updated to the society in which they are being taught. *OUAT*'s creators recognize the potential they offer viewers. Kitsis comments, "For us, that's what a fairytale is. It's that ability to think your life will get better. It's why you buy a lottery ticket—because if you win you get to tell your boss that you're quitting and you get to move to Paris or wherever and be who you always wanted to be. And that's Cinderella, right? One day she's sweeping up and the next she's going to the ball" (2011). *OUAT*'s viewers openly admit that they find themselves pulled into a story that resonates with many phases of their lives: childhood Disney fairy-tale tropes, adult hardships, real-world complexities, and, finally, the show's redefinition of true love's kiss. *OUAT*'s characters, dilemmas, and solutions speak to a human need for answers to difficult questions of love and finding peace in life. The show provides engaging entertainment by twisting classic fairy tales. But perhaps more importantly, it offers a message of hope—of perseverance—of each society's potential to shape, construct, and leave a tale of its very own happily ever after.

Notes

1. See also Bacchilega and Rieder's chapter on interactions of the aesthetic and the commercial.
2. A Stanford University sociology study of voting motivations and behaviors found that participants were more invested in an action perceived as an "enactment of personal identity" (Bryan et al. 2011, 126–53). The results have been applied by marketing teams seeking to build fan loyalty. Marketer Gregory Ciotti asserts, "People like being labeled," claiming that to create a cult fandom, "you need to define your ideal customer and just what sets them apart from 'the rest,' then you need [to] create the kind of content that affirms their acceptance into your select group" (2012).
3. Edward Kitsis stated that Disney has been "very supportive" of their adaptation: Obviously at first when they heard there's eight dwarves and we've killed one, they wanted us to talk to them . . . but they've been really great, and they've been very supportive. Even from the beginning. I think our pilot was the first time we show Snow White

giving birth or wielding a sword on TV. This is the beloved franchise of Disney. Snow White. And they've said, "Okay. Go have fun" (qtd. in Byrne 2012).

4. The name is capitalized on ABC's *OUAT* website "About the Show" (Kitsis 2011).

5. We copied fan comments verbatim from websites, preserving original spelling and grammar.

6. Fan Jamie Evangelista commented, "Upset seeing Sneezy not remember [his true fairy-tale past]. :(Hope to see more of Archie soon. Love the Pinocchio characters. Tony, Raphael, and Eion are three of my favorites on the show. Can't really choose between them and the lovely dwarfs. Always hoping to see more. . . . Just not in these circumstances! Ouch my heart!" (*Once Upon a Time* Facebook page 2011–2012).

7. (Season, episode).

16

Cristina Bacchilega and John Rieder

One outstanding feature of television's typical assemblage of narrative genres is that it resembles the set that emerged in late nineteenth-century print—romance as love story, adventure tale, detective fiction, Western, and so on—in tandem with mass culture itself. Most generic forms and distinctions one associates with Western canonical literary and dramatic tradition, such as epic, tragedy, lyric, essay, and novel, seem almost entirely irrelevant in television. Even those that retain some importance, such as comedy, satire, and quest romance, only remain pertinent by adaptation to and assimilation into modern mass culture's forms. Linda Dégh may be grasping the same generic history when she argues, "Television, which terminated the occasions for traditional storytelling, now helps the *Märchen* to survive on the basis of entirely new traditions" (1994, 43).

For Dégh, the wonder tale negotiates the treacherous passage from more traditional face-to-face practices to television by its assimilation into the most crucial and ubiquitous of all mass cultural genres, the advertisement. This assimilation's price is the disintegration of fairy-tale plots into atomized fragments—the "giants, dwarves, fairies, witches, mermaids, anthropomorphic objects, and personified principles" that give televised commercials "a magical–animistic worldview, parodistic and anachronistic" (1994, 36–37).

Perhaps, anticipating our discussion below, for Dégh the fairy tale is always already fractured by its traumatic transition into televisual mass culture.[1]

In this chapter we raise questions of the fairy tale's adaptation in and to the context of the commercial advertising in the milieu of television circa 1960 by analyzing, first, *Carosello,* the dramatized commercial series that ran on Italian TV from 1957 to 1977 and shaped the consumer and narrative habitus of the Italian baby boom generation, and, second, *Fractured Fairy Tales,* which aired as part of *Rocky and His Friends* and later *The Bullwinkle Show* from 1959 to 1964 on the American ABC and NBC networks. Our questions concern generic form: What can the collision or collusion of the commercial and the wonder tale in *Carosello* and *Fractured Fairy Tales* tell us about mass cultural narrative forms' coalescence around the nexus of marketing strategies? (see also Hay and Baxter's chapter). How are the narrative possibilities of fairy-tale material foreshortened or expanded by their adaptation to the commercialized mass cultural context? What are the ideological effects of its assimilation into a commercial function, and what modes of resistance and rebellion emerge in response? In short, what are the narratological and ideological consequences of the fairy tale's generic recontextualization?

For if the title of *Fractured Fairy Tales* (henceforth *FFT*) announces a collision of forms as its premise, *Carosello* antithetically invites viewers to board a merry-go-round of short narratives entirely centered on advertising; each narrative leads to a closing commercial. Thus the topic of marketing strategies raises questions about belief or ideology (belief from the nonbeliever's perspective) concerning, for instance, the "magical–animistic worldview" Dégh discerns in commercials employing fairy-tale elements. And the topic of belief raises the further issue of the televised texts' relation to their audiences, not only in terms of assumptions about shared identities and everyday, common sense realities that inform *Carosello* and *FFT* but also in terms of their very different institutional contexts of production.

Mass Culture and Advertising

Richard Ohmann defines mass culture as "voluntary experiences, produced by a relatively small number of specialists, for millions across the nation to share, in similar or identical form, either simultaneously or nearly so; with dependable frequency; mass culture shapes habitual audiences, around common needs or interests, and it is made for profit" (1996, 14). He traces the rise of the "homogeneous national experience" that makes mass culture possible to the displacement of local news by the national news, wire services, and the rise of syndicated columns in the latter decades of the nineteenth century. The decisive moment came in the 1890s, when a few newspapers and magazines pioneered a new business model in which their income mainly depended on advertising rather than sales. Their product became not the news, journalistic features, or fiction they provided but rather the public's attention, which they sold to advertisers. From 1880 to 1930, Raymond Williams sees "the full development of an organized system of commercial information and persuasion, as part of the modern distributive system in conditions of large-scale capitalism" ([1980] 1997, 179). This shift of corporate resources from production to sales "located advertising . . . in the center of American cultural production, [where] it has remained [ever] since" (Ohmann 1996, 362).

Advertising's centrality to mass culture has without question had profound ideological effects. By 1960, advertising "in the last forty years . . . passed the frontier of the selling of goods and services and has become involved with the teaching of social and personal values; . . . [it is] the official art of modern capitalist society" (Williams [1980] 1997, 184). Crucial demands made on the form in World War I led to the subsequent introduction into commercial practices of "the methods of psychological warfare" developed in wartime propaganda: "The need to control nominally free men, like the need to control nominally free customers, lay very deep in the new kind of society" (ibid., 180). The citizen becomes the consumer, and the act of consumption attains the aura of both a utopian avenue to fulfill all desires and an ethical duty uniting private choices with the public good. But modern advertising's "crucial quality" is an all-abiding dissatisfaction or lack that the commodity never completely overcomes: "the material object being sold is never enough . . . but must be validated, if only in fantasy, by associations with social and personal meanings which in a different cultural formation might be more directly available" (ibid., 185). Thus the act of consumption itself takes on a magical quality.

Any rational expectation of the good that would result from using the commodities is overshadowed by a fantasy of satisfaction that advertising discourse associates with merely owning them: "The fundamental choice that emerges, in the problems set to us by modern industrial production, is between man as consumer and man as user. The system of organized magic which is modern advertising is primarily important as a functional obscuring of this choice" (Williams [1980] 1997, 186). Advertising bolsters consumption's mystique by calling into service fairy tales' ability to invoke a suspension of disbelief and to entertain ideas of magical satisfaction, which becomes a symptom of the systematic irrationality of producing for individual profit rather than in response to social needs and in turn reduces fairy tales' capacity for imagining social and developmental transformations to fetishistic wish fulfillment. The intersection of ideologies in television advertising and fairy tales leads us to ask how *Carosello* and *FFT* register and respond to this co-opting and repurposing of fairy-tale conventions.

A key question in assessing advertising's ideological effects regards what kind of belief it seeks to inspire in its audience. Sut Jhally's (1989) argument that advertising resembles a fetishistic, polytheistic religion resonates with Dégh's later suggestion that the resulting worldview is "anachronistic" and "magical–animistic." But the key term "parodistic" connects her to a line of commentary running from Williams to Northrop Frye, Erving Goffman, and Michael Schudson, who link advertising rhetoric with propaganda techniques and the ideological posture that Slavoj Žižek (1989, 2009, 65–69) calls cynicism, a disavowal of belief in "the system" coupled with a continued practice of drawing energy and profit from it. Williams cites, "The development of a knowing, humorous advertising, which . . . made claims either casual and offhand or so ludicrously exaggerated as to include the critical response. . . . Thus it became possible to 'know all the arguments' against advertising, and yet accept or write pieces of charming or amusing copy" ([1980] 1997, 181). So for Frye, "Advertising can be taken as a kind of ironic game. Like other forms of irony, it says what it does not wholly mean, but nobody is obliged to believe its statements literally. Hence it creates an illusion of detachment and mental superiority even when one is obeying its exhortations" (qtd. in Schudson 1984, 225–26).

Schudson, working from Goffman's insight into how advertising exaggerates the semiotics of gender coding to metonymically invest the advertised commodities with fantasies of sexual fulfillment, expands its scope from the aim of "characterizing the conventions of commercial art" to "link[ing] them to their cultural role in advanced capitalist societies" (Schudson 2000). He moves from the question of belief in the "small sense" of whether "people put faith in the explicit claims" of ads to the "larger sense—do the assumptions and attitudes implicit in advertising become the assumptions and attitudes of the people surrounded by ads" (ibid.) He concludes that advertising achieves this larger effect precisely "because it does not make the mistake of *asking* for belief"; instead it lulls people into "get[ting] used to, or get[ting] used to not getting used to, the institutional structures that govern their lives" (ibid.).

To explain how advertising achieves this effect, Schudson calls attention to the similarity of its aims and methods to those of Soviet era "socialist realism," primarily its presentation of a simplified, typified, and eternally optimistic version of reality. One might thus connect advertising's "capitalist realism" with fairy-tale conventions. Peopled by types rather than individuals, offering magical solutions to real problems and overwhelmingly inclined toward happy endings, commercials clearly have a certain formal affinity with fairy tales—or, rather, with those elements of the wonder tale that are most easily and prolifically associated with its conventional and formulaic retellings in mass culture.

The analyses of Williams, Ohmann, and Schudson can be summed up by invoking a distinction Antonio Gramsci (e.g., 1971) famously applied to intellectuals: advertising is the "organic" genre of corporate capitalism and therefore of mass culture, while the fairy tale, in contrast, comes as a "traditional" genre to mass culture where it is stripped of some qualities and functions while others are appropriated to new purposes and ideologies. Those appropriated qualities include simple plots, typical rather than individualized characters and settings, and a propensity for happy endings, all of which metonymically transfer a set of more or less complicated and disparate desires—and conflicts—on to the representation of the commodity that the commercial is trying to sell.

The larger problem that hovers over this rhetorical activity, then, is belief. To say that both commercials and fairy tales depend on a suspension of disbelief is not to say that they do the same thing or for the same reasons. Nor does the suspension of disbelief simply detach the storyworlds of commercials or fairy tales from time, place, and the vicissitudes of national, gendered, and racial identification. *Carosello* and *FFT* offer two quite different examples of articulating commercial and narrative strategies. How much difference does this difference make? What separates *Carosello*'s disarming embrace from the comic "fracturing" of traditional tales in the American serial? Does the suspension of disbelief enable a politics of wonder or act as an alibi for cynicism?

Carosello

Cristina: Our family ate dinner in the kitchen at eight on the dot, and as I recall the television would be on in the living room and, when he was done, my father would go and watch the news. On weeknights, my younger sister and I would join him but (up until we were deemed old enough to watch the evening programs) we'd have to go to bed right after *Carosello*, that is at 9 p.m., in what unbeknownst to us had become the national ritual: "and after *Carosello* all off to bed!" I know that when we were too young to be interested in the news, the tarantella-like tune announcing *Carosello* would have us rushing to the living room to watch, hoping our favorite characters and stories would be on that night: Calimero for sure, Topo Gigio (but that character would also be featured weekly in the afternoon one-hour program for children), Susanna Tutta Panna. The children would jump up and down on their parents' bed to the catchy "Bidi Bodi Bù" song in the advertisement for Permaflex mattresses. I don't recall my parents being there with us, but they must have been as we all quoted lines from *Carosello* at the appropriate times and drew on it for some family words too. It was many years later, in Honolulu, when some Italian friends and I by chance at some dinner started singing tunes from *Carosello* and reciting its jingles, that I realized how this show had left its mark on many other families and my generation. Maybe they had a television in their kitchen and their experience was therefore somewhat different, but we'd grown up in totally different parts of Italy and we could all sing and recite lines that made no sense to anyone else. *Carosello* had been a national ritual, and in performing its highlights we were—ridiculous as it seemed while we were doing it—nostalgically reaching for our childhood and our shared experience of it. And yes, I have since consciously played this game again with different groups of Italians of my generation and never been disappointed so far in how much we remember and how we responded intensely but variedly to *Carosello*. It was, after all, our bedtime storytelling.

When television made its Italian debut in 1954, it had one channel, which was run by the national state-regulated corporation RAI and financed by subscribers via a tax or license fee. Advertisements appeared only in February 1957, specifically with *Carosello*. This show, sandwiched between the news and the evening programming, consisted of four shorts, each lasting two and a quarter minutes and including no more than thirty seconds devoted to publicity. Setting up commercials as a separate show within the framework of television as public service, *Carosello* constituted a stark contrast to the US formula of interruptions and sponsors. *Carosello*'s viewing ratings soared in the first year, and the show remained an everyday feature of Italian life for twenty years. *Carosello*'s influence was momentous not only as it somewhat perversely shaped the national imaginary of several generations, especially of those who, like Cristina, grew up with it, but also because the show ushered millions of Italians into consumerism as *the* sign of modernity. We discuss here the role the magic tale (*fiaba* or *favola*) plays in *Carosello*'s commercial and ideological project.

Carosello featured famous Italian actors, directors, singers, dancers, and even painters as well as some international celebrities like Frank Sinatra and Jerry Lewis. Several taglines entered everyday speech as authoritative or ironic quotations.[2] Jingles became ingrained in the minds of children and adults. Some puppets, like Carmencita and Caballero (advertising Paulista coffee) and Pippo l'Ippopotamo (Pippo the Hippo for Lines diapers), and animated characters, like pseudo-Native American Unca Dunca and the persecuted-by-injustice baby chick Calimero, became cultural icons. Calimero became so popular that it brought about the neologism *un Calimero,* about which Umberto Eco famously wrote, "When a character generates a common noun, that character has shattered the barrier of immortality and entered myth: one is a Calimero the way one is a Don Giovanni, a Casanova, a Don Quixote, a Cinderella, a Judas" ([1976] 1996).[3] Eco associated *Carosello* with the *fiaba* and referred to Calimero as having become "something like Red Riding Hood" in the Italian popular imaginary. What justifies his and our bringing the *Carosello*–fairy tale connection to public attention when there were literally no classic magic tales in the show?[4]

Let's take a brief look at the show's institutional parameters. While the *Carosello* shorts varied in form (featuring animation, live action, and puppets) and genre (slapstick comedy, detective story, dream, adventure tale), their formulaic physiognomy depended in part on specific norms that a board associated with the RAI, the Sacis, watched over. Its brevity was mandated to the second. Each Carosello short had to be a complete story in and of itself. No reference within it could be made to the advertised product; nor could the product be mentioned more than five times in the advertisement. In contrast to the endlessly repeatable spot, each short could be aired no more than twice. These prescriptions were designed to ensure that viewers' right to public service television programming would not be compromised by intrusive publicity. The televised "flash fictions" of *Carosello* also had to

FIGURE 16.1 Portal to *Carosello*, 1962.

conform to propriety norms censoring, for example, any sexual, antifamily, vulgar, terrifying, excessively luxurious, or so-called indecent contents.

For many years, *Carosello*'s creators, somewhat like folktale and fairy-tale tellers, made the best of these rules by grounding viewers' pleasure in narrative brevity and simplicity as well as in their enjoyment of variation and creativity within iteration, "the comfort of ritual combined with the piquancy of surprise" (Hutcheon 2006, 4). Two other aspects of *Carosello*'s storytelling connected it with the wonder tale: the expectation of a happy ending and the understanding that children were an important target audience.

To represent and naturalize a happy "possible world"—one of advertising's premises and promises—*Carosello* drew on the fairy-tale genre in distinctive ways that capitalized on its viewers' suspension of disbelief. Three structural features of *Carosello* elicited and facilitated this approach: coming right after the news positioned it as a welcome relief from real-life problems; the children's theater (later a bucolic portal) and signature tune framing the show signaled entry into a wholesome (if not innocent) and uplifting world; and the formulaic storytelling moved toward a comforting and expected happy ending (Figure 16.1).

Within the *Carosello* miniature theater, live-action shorts naturalized happy endings in the everyday—thanks to modernity's magic help in the guise of appliances, packaged and canned goods, and hygiene and comfort items—and blended other mass culture genres with the fairy-tale's optimism and focus on the individual or family in small-scale struggles. In "Penne Rosse" (a 1958 spoof on John Ford's classic Western *Stagecoach,* which bore the Italian title *Ombre rosse*), a passenger's smile brightened by Colgate puts an end to the "Red Indian's" violent attack. In "Matrimonio misto" (1960) newlyweds quarrelling over their regional accents and differences make peace in the end over their shared tradition: a passion for *formaggino mio,* a packaged soft cheese marketed by Locatelli.

The animated shorts, where catering to realism was not an issue and children were assumed to be the privileged audience, used a Proppian-like formula rewarding the unpromising hero with magic help and success. Nino Pagot, cocreator with his brother, discussed the birth of Calimero:

> They told us: what would you do for this laundry detergent? This is how we thought about it. To sell we must interest women: what attracts the attention of women? Children and animals. Good, the prototype for a defenseless child is a baby chick. If we make him sad and ill-fated, he'll draw even more sympathy. If we make him black, we introduce from the start the idea that he must be cleaned up. If we have him protesting, we can humor one of the Italians' oldest quirks. If we have him getting into trouble a lot, we avoid making him too pathetic or too sweet, which could be annoying. There is in any case the commercial happy ending that fixes everything. (qtd. in Ballio and Zanacchi 2000, 101)[5]

Calimero's most famous line—spoken as he transits from the storyworld of his misfortunes to the commercial spot—is "What a way to behave! Everyone here picks on me because they are big and I am small and black. But it's not fair!" (Figure 16.2). Whether at the farm, at school, or visiting neighbors, the hapless, goodhearted, and naïve Calimero has no idea how he got into trouble or how to get out of it. Defenseless in a world of crooks and deviousness, he feels victimized, but rather than succumbing to the events, he protests—albeit in a somewhat whining voice. We all want to rescue him, and a prim, clean young woman in a "Dutch" outfit saves him in motherly fashion, pointing out that he is not black, only dirty and then immersing him in a

FIGURE 16.2 "Everyone here picks on me because they are big and I am small and black."

laundry tub filled with bubbles (Figure 16.3). When he reemerges, white and reborn, he gives thanks to Ava, the Mira Lanza laundry detergent. As with the fairy tale's Cinderella and Jack, Calimero's very nature as the unpromising hero is rewarded in the end and prevails over life's trials.

If our examples suggest *how Carosello* instrumentalized the fairy tale as powerful formula on Italian television, to what ideological effects did its confluence with commerce work? For sociologist Vanni Codeluppi, *Carosello* "was most of all a fairy-tale world, where happiness and well-being reigned, a very fascinating world for the Italian people who were emerging from a long period of poverty and social malaise. It was thus an oneiric space . . . that justified abandoning the culture of sacrifice and savings that characterized the peasant world in favor of new values proposed by urban culture and consumerism" (2000, 22). Eco visualizes Codeluppi's diagnosis: *Carosello* "has created an autonomous make-believe world, a fairy tale of commodities, realizing Marx's theoretical fancy: 'If commodities could speak. . . .' In *Carosello* commodities would often speak" ([1976] 1996, 3). *Carosello* enlisted specific generic aspects—the upside-down world and wish fulfillment—while

FIGURE 16.3 "Calimero, you're not black, you're just dirty."

keeping existing fairy tales out. It sought to replace living Italian traditions with new characters and values. It worked to produce the modern Italian fairy tale as a fetishized commodity to enchant the young and indulge adults' hopes for the so-called economic boom. To do this, *Carosello*'s creators chose *not* to adapt tales that continued to circulate in oral settings, regional dialects, and emplaced traditions, perhaps because such a move could have generated discussion, disbelief, even protest. For the fairy tale to be the ground on which to build *Carosello*'s capitalist fantasy world, living tales had to be excluded while their happily-ever-after aura was put to new purposes.

Not coincidentally, Italo Calvino published *Le fiabe italiane* (translated as *Italian Folktales* in 1980) in 1956, the year before *Carosello*'s advent. Gathering magic tales from various regions, Calvino sought to identify and valorize the genre's distinctively Italian characteristics. Earning the honorific title of "the Italian Grimm," he thus made a landmark intervention in the humanistic project of post–WWII nation building. Documenting the Italian people's resourcefulness, hard work, and diverse histories, Calvino's collection of archival and previously published tales from the late 1800s and early 1900s showcased a prevalently peasant Italy on whose unofficial knowledge and values the nation could draw for strength. Furthermore, by translating the tales from their regional vernaculars and often combining different versions for narrative effect, Calvino artfully pulled specific located traditions together to render a national Italian literature. Both *Carosello* and *Fiabe italiane* deployed the folktale and fairy tale, but they constructed very different relationships to modernity for ordinary people, positioning them differently within the project of nation (re)building in the aftermath of a devastating war and in the frenzy of capitalist Americanization. Thanks to its fairy-tale mystique, *Carosello* projected a spectacular transformation of Italians' lifestyle and value system that depended on the magic of consumerism and foreign capital, while *Fiabe italiane* established transformation as an ongoing resource from within Italians' cultural habitus (even among the peasants, usually labeled as conservative forces).

While cumulatively *Carosello* stripped the fairy tale of all but its aura and happy endings, it did not always do so—due to the creativity that sustaining its formula required of so many different artists—nor did it always have the same degree of success over its twenty years of production. Furthermore, as with storytelling in any media, there was no guarantee that its commercial project's encoding would match the audience's actual practices of decoding (Hall 1980). First, several discussions of televised publicity in Italy note that people frequently remembered the comedy or characters of a *Carosello* short but forgot the product they advertised. Second, an episode's or character's popularity did not necessarily correspond to its impact on sales. For instance, while Calimero was and remains a cultural icon, sales of the Mira Lanza detergent as a result of that *Carosello* campaign increased—but not spectacularly. Third, beloved characters and catchy jingles survived the advertising for which they had been created. Calimero went on to enjoy several afterlives in popular culture: nationally in short films and books of *fiabe* for children since the mid-1970s and internationally as anime in Japan in the 1970s and 1990s that also aired in other countries. In 2013 he made a comeback in a CGI (computer-generated imagery) series on French and Italian television thanks to his creator's son Pagot (see Zahed 2012).

Post-*Carosello* adaptations are beyond this chapter's scope, but they speak to Calimero's complex legacy; as his fairy-tale association became more explicit, he continues to strike a chord with children internationally. In Japan the famous baby chick is not dirty but simply black, living up to or naturalizing the epithet "Calimero, the black baby chick" that the commercials disproved. Most images of Calimero indeed present him as black. This led us to think further about Calimero's blackness in the *Carosello* series and its role in his popularity as the hero of a "new" fairy tale.

In his 1963 origin story, Calimero clumsily breaks free from his egg and falls into a puddle of mud: he is black *because* he gets dirty, and this fits his advertising function for Ava beautifully. But Calimero's blackness signified an excess of what Pagot intended ("If we make him black, we introduce from the start the idea that he must be cleaned up"), pointing to some unconscious shame that detergents could not erase as well as to submerged and emerging meanings. In a post–WWII Italy that sought to associate itself with the whiteness and cleanliness of Western (and in the European context, Northern) modernity, Calimero was a blotch that needed blotting. Was Calimero mistreated because he was black? Was he blaming his persecutors for being prejudiced? Was that blame misplaced when he was in the end proven not to be black? Or was it confirmed since he was still small and defenseless?

As new generations encounter Calimero, these questions continue to be debated on blogs and in comments to *Caroselli* on YouTube. Regardless, Calimero's misfortunes on *Carosello* have over time evoked the specter of racism and its associated shame, speaking in the 1960s to the experiences of "darker" Southern Italians migrating to Northern Italy to participate in the economic boom that excluded the South; those of blacks from the former colonies of Ethiopia and Eritrea living in Rome; and, more recently, those of so many "colored" immigrants from Africa and Asia. And yet, as Donatella Izzo (personal communication 2012) pointed out, in post–WWII Italy, the cleansing of Calimero "the little black chick" could *also* evoke shame and disavowal of the nation's recent Fascist experience, very much alive in collective memory; "blacks" referred in everyday speech to the Fascists, and many wanted it forgotten that they had been "black shirts."

"Go away, you little black blotch!" Calimero's unexpected popularity and power may, then, lie in the very ambiguity and multivalence of what constitutes his blackness. For those who never saw or forgot the episode recounting his birth (shown twice at the most), Calimero might as well have been black. The Dutch woman says he is not, as she lowers him into a washtub or, later, a washing machine, but this statement does not wash over the fact that he *is* black in his storyworld as he is ill treated one time after another (in a way, adding to the magical properties of the Ava detergent). As Calimero's plot became routine on Italian television, no one cause of his pariah status emerged; what mattered was that he was always undeservedly mistreated and yet not silenced.

Take *Calimero da Papero Piero* (Calimero at Piero Duck's, 1969). Calimero and his parents are invited to his father's boss's home. Calimero is polite and well behaved, but the boss's spoiled son Duck Piero smashes his own train set and then accuses Calimero of the misdeed. Calimero's father, a simple gofer, is instantly fired, and the family is expelled as the boss's snobbish wife comments what a bad idea it was to invite "certain kinds of people." Calimero's family is clearly represented as experiencing classist behavior, but, adding insult to injury, Calimero's father does not want to hear his son's side of the story and shouts, "Go away; you'll be the end of me!" There is no mention of Calimero's blackness until *he* miserably brings it up as one marker of his mistreatment. We read his assertion and consistent response to his many misadventures as symptomatic of how Calimero calls out against prejudice and injustice that do not exclude racism but are not limited to it. Whether he is black, dirty, or misbehaved, Calimero is innocent and knows it. "What a way to behave! Everyone here picks on me because they are big and I am small and black. But it's not fair!" Calimero's signature line affirms the simplicity of an alternative morality that Jack Zipes (2012) associates with fairy tales' subversive power and their working to undo prejudice. Thus the Calimero *Caroselli* may have, intentionally or not but in fairy-tale guise, educated several generations of Italian children to recognize everyday inequities and speak against them.

Fractured Fairy Tales

John: My memories of watching *The Bullwinkle Show* on Saturday afternoons are of a crowded room with lots of laughter and jocular commentary. Unlike some other cartoon shows which I, a ten-year-old, watched by myself because none of my older siblings could be interested in joining me (e.g., Hanna-Barbera's *Huckleberry Hound* and *Quick-Draw McGraw*), my college-age brothers and their friends were more than happy to join me watching Moose and Squirrel versus Boris and Natasha fighting out their parody of the Cold War, Doctor Peabody the dog genius and his pet boy Sherman cruising the past in their WABAC machine, or Edward Everett Horton narrating his "fractured" retellings of well-known fairy tales. I now find that quite a good gauge of how much and how fondly I remember my childhood cartoon shows is whether I remember watching them accompanied by the laughter and wisecracking commentary of my elder siblings.

In retrospect, these memories corroborate Jason Mittel's analysis of the early 1960s transformation of the American animated short. Mittel argues that the cartoon, which had functioned as a mass audience genre in the 1940s, when its most typical venue was as a preliminary to films in cinemas, was transformed by the industrial practices of the major TV networks in the late 1950s and early 1960s into a kids-only genre. In concert with the decision to target children in the advertisements they sold for cartoon shows, the networks moved cartoons out of prime time, eventually settling predominantly on Saturday morning. Reruns of older cinematic short features were common, partly because the networks discovered that young children preferred watching something familiar to watching a new show (see Brodie and McDavid's chapter). Production values were drastically reduced compared to the older made-for-cinema short features, not just because the networks wanted to cut costs but also because they assumed that children did not care about high-quality animation or sophisticated story lines. Mittel concludes, "The Saturday morning era represents the nadir of the animation genre, as innovations were foreclosed by the factory-style lowest common denominator approach and kid-only stigma offered by the networks" (2004, 91). Furthermore, these shows collectively participated in a "politicized construction of childhood" that hypocritically "protected" children from content such as racial tensions "but not from other messages, like ads for candy, violent toys, or commercialism itself" (ibid., 93).

If John's memories can be trusted, *Rocky and His Friends* and, later, *The Bullwinkle Show* ran counter to this trend, at least at the production end. Indeed, Mittel comments that the two series "form the primary exception to today's critical disdain for early television animation" (2004, 70). Zipes includes *FFT* in the honorific category of "carnivalesque" adaptations, as opposed to the "non-reflective, standard, and conservative" work of Disney and his imitators (2011, 53). But, as Zipes notes, *FFT* deliver neither the sexual suggestiveness of Max Fleischer's Depression era Betty Boop nor the raucousness of Tex Avery's World War II era work, and the animation offers none of those earlier artists' shape-shifting, surreal energy. While they do treat their audience to a heavy dose of the self-referential humor typical of Avery, *FFT* follow more closely the more subtly ironic, minimalist work of the McCarthy era renegades from the Disney studio, the UPA (United

FIGURE 16.4 Self-parodying serial repetition in the title frame of *Fractured Fairy Tales*.

Productions of America), in such films as the 1954 feature *The Fifty-First Dragon* (ibid., 63–67). The emphasis is not on chases or burlesque routines but on the storytelling's inventiveness and wry humor. For Zipes, the key is the way "the ideological twists in the plots tend to explore the contradictions in contemporary social relations" (ibid., 67).

Zipes takes those ideological twists to constitute the "fracturing" of the fairy tale in *FFT*, but, as we observed above, Dégh implies that another fracturing has already taken place in the genre's passage from traditional storytelling venues into the milieu of mass culture. Our reading of *FFT* does not begin with how the series alters the tales' traditional content, therefore, but rather how, in retelling them, it responds to the shaping force of its "organic" commercial context, to some extent by parodying television commercials but even more by making commercial practices and ideologies its subject matter. *FFT*'s "fracturing" is a recuperative gesture that responds to and comments on what a strange place the world has become and how the fairy tale can still fit into it (Figure 16.4).

We begin with one of the most obvious features of commercial television, as of mass culture in general, its seriality. *FFT* is a series within a series, and it echoes this embeddedness with its assigned time slot within each episode and its opening ditty and credits. But the external seriality of *The Bullwinkle Show* within network television and of *FFT* within it has more complex and substantial echoes within the episodes. This internal seriality includes the way some retellings generate sequels: "Rumpelstiltskin" is followed by "Rumpelstiltskin Returns," "Cinderella" by "Cinderella Returns." Similarly, in addition to "Sleeping Beauty" we have "Leaping Beauty," along with "Snow White" we have "Red White," and with "Red's Riding Hood" we have "Riding Hoods Anonymous." This self-referential repetition also enters some episodes' content. "Sleeping Beauty" starts with the narrator announcing, "We all know" how Sleeping Beauty was cursed, she fell asleep, the castle was surrounded by thorns, and so on. In "Leaping Beauty," an offended witch threatens the heroine with a curse only to have her reply, "We all know" there's a happy ending, so go ahead and do your worst. The witch responds by delivering a different curse that responds with all the force of poetic justice to the heroine's been-there-done-that attitude: the curse of boredom. Rather than going to sleep herself, this beauty bores everyone else to sleep because she can't stop looking in her portable mirror and exclaiming how beautiful she is. This is more than just a clever plot reversal. Since the audience's attention is itself the primary product the mass entertainment industry sells its clients, and seriality is an industrial strategy for making that attention habitual, perhaps Leaping Beauty's curse playfully but pointedly suggests that commanding routine attention—or, for the audience's part, being a little too sure about what "we all know"—can turn into a different way to put people to sleep.

Another thematic meditation on seriality in *FFT* is its satirical reflection on the way formulaic mass culture tries to fend off the curse of boredom by fetishizing superficial change in the form of fads. Consider "The Ugly Duckling." This hero, like many others in *FFT,* wants to be a movie star. He has loads of talent, but agent after agent rejects him because he is too ugly. Discouraged, he returns to his native swamp, where his magic helper—his own reflection in a pond—advises him to have plastic surgery. Yet when the now handsome duck returns to the talent agencies he is rejected because he is too handsome. The trend now is horror pictures; the agents' offices have posters for *It Ducked from Outer Space* and *Ugly Duck Meets Wolfman.* Our hapless hero ends up at a carnival sticking his head through a bull's eye, where he pronounces the final lines: "I figure in a week I'll be ugly enough to please anybody. Meanwhile, I'm still in show business."

While the plot twists of "The Ugly Duckling" mock the ephemerality of mass cultural fads, its ending stresses the hero's persistence and determination despite the fact that his quasimagical transformation from ugly to handsome fails to solve his problem. The plot twist and ending distance themselves not only from the familiar fairy-tale solution of becoming beautiful and the happily-ever-after ending but also from the simplicity and eternal optimism that Schudson sees as keys to commercial rhetoric. In contrast to these rhetorical staples, *FFT* sometimes pack absurdly convoluted plots into their five-minute span, and they tend to end neither happily ever after nor with a neat moral—but with a joke.

In "Aladdin's Friendly Lamp-o-Rama," for instance, young Aladdin runs a lamp shop, without lamps because it is a front for a card game held in the back room. When the king enters the shop and demands a lamp, Aladdin must look for one. He immediately falls into a large hole. At the bottom he finds a lamp with a sign on it saying, "Rub me and get a surprise." When he rubs it, out pops a genie, or rather a Jeannie with light brown hair, who proclaims herself "just an ordinary girl who was brought up in a lamp." She advises Aladdin that he has three wishes. He uses the first to get them out of the hole. Meanwhile back at the palace, the king returns to find his throne is missing and the grand vizier has taken over. He goes to the lamp shop only to find it crowded with young women, all recent inhabitants of the lamp. He grabs the lamp and rubs it—and out pops the vizier. As the two prepare to fight for the kingdom, the backroom card game breaks up, and three men dressed only in barrels walk out, followed by Aladdin counting his take. Seeing the situation, he thinks to use one wish to make himself king but discovers that he has unwittingly already used them up while playing cards. At this point Aladdin and the grand vizier struggle over the lamp, both rub it, and both disappear. The king is left to pronounce the moral: "Never try to jump a king, except in checkers."

The force of turning the Aladdin story into this series of nonsensical detours has less to do with *The Arabian Nights* (in fact almost nothing to do with it) than with parodying the illogical but calculated way that commercials link commodities—here, the lamp—to desires wholly unrelated to them, in order to proffer the quasimagical promise that owning the commodity will fulfill those desires. Even more important is this story's response to another staple of commercial rhetoric, the preference for the typical over the individual, in its parodic rendering of Aladdin's "friendly" shop. The shop is important,

FIGURE 16.5 Magic mirror as vending machine.

not because it is Aladdin's but simply because it is a shop. The plot's motor is a customer's request for a certain item—consumer demand, in the language of retail or advertising. Exactly the same set of shop, fairy-tale proprietor, and consumer demand appears in "Red's Riding Hood," where Red runs a clothing shop. The story begins because a rich older woman enters and requests a wolfskin fur coat. One of the key ways *FFT* responds to formal affinities between the fairy tale and the commercial advertisement is by its satirical typification of commercial settings and motifs that it imports into its modernized fairy-tale domain. The overlapping and interpenetration of fairy tale and commercial worlds in *FFT* bring about a mixture of different versions of magic and different versions of disbelief that constitutes the show's most complex set of responses to the fairy tale's fracturing in the mass cultural milieu.

The effect of turning magic devices into commercial ones often undermines fairy-tale magic altogether. In "Snow White," for example, the queen consults a coin-operated mirror that keeps telling her Snow White is more beautiful but suggests that she consult the seven dwarves for help (Figure 16.5). At the Seven Dwarves Health Club she is assured she can become the fairest if she signs their contract and pays their price. When the mirror tells the pumped-up queen she is still not as beautiful as Snow White, she returns to the dwarves, who sign her up for dance lessons, charm school, and their health food plan in succession. She keeps asking, by the way, why there are only six dwarves. Finally a decidedly plain Snow White shows up, puts her coin in the mirror, and is assured that she is the most beautiful in the land and can stay that way with help from the dwarves. The tale ends with the revelation that the seventh dwarf has been inside the not-so-magic mirror. As a commentary on the selling of beauty products, this is quite direct and unequivocal. "Fairy tale" here takes on its unfortunate colloquial meaning of a false promise, and the fracturing exposes the beauty industry as a con game played against its gullible customers.

On other occasions the commercialized magical device turns into a burlesque negotiation of the terms of a contract. The two Rumpelstiltskin retellings both turn on finding and enforcing the contract's fine print, and both Cinderellas involve rather complicated rental agreements.[7] In "Cinderella," the fairy godmother agrees to supply Cinderella with a ball gown, carriage, jewelry, and so on, but the contract's terms stipulate that she must sell a large set of cookware for $39.95 by midnight. Meanwhile the prince, who is broke, is looking to marry a rich heiress to stave off the creditors besieging his castle. Mistaking Cinderella for a real princess, he praises her for having "such grace, such beauty, such real cash value," to which Cinderella replies, brandishing a saucepan: "There's no vitamin waste, see? And these scour clean in a jiffy." This comic courtship gets nowhere, Cinderella returns home at midnight, and the creditors descend on the prince. In the final scene he shows up at her door, not to fit her with a slipper but because he is now a Fuller brush salesman employed by the fairy godmother.

"Cinderella Returns" carries this final motif a step further. Again the fairy godmother has sold Cinderella a contract. This time the prince looks to escape his boring life in the castle by marrying a commoner. Again their courtship goes nowhere, but this time Cinderella leaves behind one of her (comically huge) rented shoes. When the prince shows up at her door, he is calling to collect the other shoe for the rental agency, of which he is now an employee, having achieved his goal of escaping the castle by marrying the fairy godmother. The episode concludes with her delivering a commercial for "Good Fairy Rentals."

All this wrangling over contracts humorously accentuates the distance between the world of legal and commercial transactions and the world, not of traditional fairy tales but of the idealized class hierarchies and gender roles that the conventionalized retellings "we all know" try to sell. Far from showing antipathy to the wonder tale's magical world, *FFT* are often extravagantly fanciful, with the genre's suspension of disbelief absolutely required and taken for granted. But disbelief about the power and goodness of being beautiful, the beneficence and nobility of the rich and handsome prince, and the magic solution of marriage are definitely in place. *FFT* are not antimagical but rather antinostalgic. They direct their demystifying energy against the fantasy world of the stable, rural, patriarchal, and morally black-and-white but luxuriantly drawn and lavishly colored fairy tales that dominated American mass culture from Disney's *Snow White and the Seven Dwarfs* (1937) through the 1960s. And a large share of that energy lodges in the trickster characters who act on the same type of motives that "we all know" underlie the calculating magic of Disney-type narratives in their alliance with the beauty industry and with commercial con artistry in general.

Making fun of commercialization comes closest to explicit criticism of Disney enterprises in our final *FFT* exhibit, "Sleeping Beauty." It begins by saying we all remember how the story starts and how the princess falls asleep and the castle is surrounded by thorns. The typical *FFT* prince shows up, pointing to his costume and presenting an ID card to prove that he is really a prince. After unsuccessfully brandishing the "traditional" ("i.e., Disney version) broadsword against the thorns, he successfully breaches the barrier on a riding lawn mower. Once he enters Sleeping Beauty's chamber and is about to kiss her, he has second thoughts. Wouldn't people pay to see this sleeping princess?

He sets up "Sleeping-Beauty Land," where hordes of customers are shepherded through a series of gates, each time paying another fee, in order to finally reach Sleeping Beauty's chamber. Trade headlines proclaim the prince's success, and we see him counting bushels of money. A young woman calling herself the wicked fairy, and sporting a pair of wings to prove it, shows up and demands half the take for her contribution to the enterprise. The prince, smiling all the while, tries to get rid of her. He locks her in a dungeon, drops her in the moat, and sends her on a rocket to the moon, but each time she comes back, politely asking for her share. But along the way the novelty has worn off their star attraction; business is bad, so they decide maybe it is time to wake Sleeping Beauty. When the prince suggests that the wicked fairy revoke her curse, however, she sheds her fake wings and declares that she is not a fairy, just wicked. When she suggests he wake Sleeping Beauty with a kiss, he confesses that he is not a prince but a hog-flogger in disguise.

FIGURE 16.6 Fairy tale as theme park.

Yet the story ends happily as Sleeping Beauty rises from her bed and declares she never really was asleep: "I just wanted to see if I could make it in show biz" (Figure 16.6).

Sleeping Beauty's disenchantedness points to what these tales most emphatically do not believe in: the magical power that advertising's condensations of desire attribute to the commodity itself. But of course, as the unmasking of the phony prince and the wicked fairy makes clear, neither do the ads (or theme parks) that promote them. *FFT* on the whole attributes to its commercial tricksters precisely the attitude of cynicism: disavowal of belief in the self-justifying claims of a system they continue to operate for personal profit. Nonetheless *FFT* do not withhold sympathy from their tricksters, and even more they embrace the disarming optimism of characters like the ugly duckling and Sleeping Beauty who just want to make it in show biz. This sympathy and optimism complement the bemused, understated, gentle style of Edward Everett Horton's narration, which firmly steers these retellings away from the Disney style's visually oriented prettiness. The result is a series that does not share the cynicism it comically portrays. *FFT*'s tone is joyful rather than disillusioned, sympathetic rather than disengaged, vulnerable rather than callous; and finally, after all is said and done, these fairy tales remain optimistic about the extravagant wishes of ordinary people.

Beyond Fairy-Tale Commodity Fetishism

Our readings of *Carosello* and *FFT* explore two contemporaneous episodes in the ongoing, century-long process of generic recontextualization of the wonder tale within the mass cultural genre system in general and, more specifically, within the context of televised narratives and advertisements. These analyses might serve, first, as a caution against any too hasty generalizations about that process. For although our reading of *FFT* supports the notion that the fairy tale enters the context of American television in a state that is always already fractured, we also argued that, in the Calimero episodes of the Italian *Carosello,* the wonder tale regenerates itself precisely as a result of the alliance of narrative entertainment and advertisement. Such regeneration is anything but the whole story of *Carosello,* of course, but it reminds us that cultural production, as a field of positions within which generic choices take on value and significance, is never merely a given but always presents a shifting, historically and geographically sensitive target for analysis. Thus we hope that our analyses perform the same service that Mittel proposes for his theory of television genres as cultural constructions: to situate "genre distinctions and categories as active processes embedded within and constitutive of cultural politics" (2004, xii). The positioning of the traditional fairy-tale genre within mass culture and in relation to mass culture's organic genre, the advertisement, is far from being unilaterally determined by the cultural politics of promoting consumption per se as the avenue to individual happiness and collective well-being. On the contrary, our analysis shows that the active process of connecting genres to values and of reconstructing genres in the spaces and with the means afforded by mass culture both offers paths of least resistance and generates strategies that respond critically and eccentrically to the homogenizing pressures endemic to the television milieu.

Recognizing and responding to the generic component of a text or performance involves being aware of the traces of past texts and performances in the present one. As we have tried to broach the difficult relation between narrative suspension of disbelief and the drastically different cultural functions it opens to fantasy, our readings have perhaps inevitably encountered the problem of nostalgia, in which the form of memory gives itself over to an amnesiac forgetfulness and concomitant complacency about history and our place in it. The boundaries separating and connecting naïveté, wonder, and nostalgia seem to us crucially at stake in the cultural politics surrounding the fairy tale, and they comprise a matrix of possibilities that is if anything more fraught and contentious today than in the 1960s. At least since the Grimms, the fairy tale has been recruited into the service of tendentious reconstructions of the past and the permanent, and that particular fairy-tale tradition shows no sign of weakening in recent television adaptations, for example, *Once Upon a Time*. We hope that our readings run counter to it, however, so that any temptation to say what "we all know" about the fairy tale—instead of being allowed to pass under the guises of humanistic universality or formal essentialism or fidelity to gender and class stability—will be moved to confront its own historical, geographical, and institutional contingency.

Notes

1. We use "wonder tale" and "magic tale" interchangeably with "fairy tale" given their links in popular cultural memory. We use "folktale and fairy tale" to acknowledge strong ties between traditional tales of magic (ATU 300–749) and literary fairy tales.
2. For example, the expert inspector Rock always takes off his hat in the publicity coda to his successful detective story. Showing he is bald, he confesses to his one error—not having used the Linetti hair pomade. The first part of his statement—"I too have committed an error" or "I too have made a mistake"—pronounced in his tone, became a lighthearted way to own up to something in everyday interactions.
3. This and all other translations from Italian are Bacchilega's.
4. See also Nelson and Walton's chapter. Most of Cristina's watching took place 1960–1970. In Rome in 1997, we viewed the exhibit commemorating *Carosello*'s fortieth anniversary. More recently, we watched extensive selections from *Carosello . . . e poi a letto* 4 DVDs (totaling some 350 minutes), the fifty Caroselli in the DVD accompanying *Carosello Story*, the *Tutto il meglio di Carosello* DVD, and many YouTube videos. We thank our friends, scholars Donatella Izzo and Pier Carlo Bontempelli for supporting us in this (anti)nostalgic research project.
5. Assumptions about gender play a pernicious role in *Carosello* but not in the same way they do in fairy tales. *Carosello*'s prevalent female type is the good mother, a figure often absent in fairy tales.
6. But Calimero spoke in a Northern accent, specific to the Padua countryside near Venice, so his blackness has nothing to do with race, some will argue. Yet Northern Italians met with prejudice in Northern European and more developed capitalist nations. Thus, the Italian North was not immune to internalized shame.
7. A third Cinderella version takes a different tack unrelated to commercial motifs.

PART V

Fairy-Tale Teleography

17

A CRITICAL INTRODUCTION TO
THE FAIRY-TALE TELEOGRAPHY

Kendra Magnus-Johnston

> Given its ephemeral nature, television is still largely viewed
> as disposable culture, and what is saved is in large part
> based on what happens to be recorded, what happens to be
> in someone's basement, a thrift store, flea market, some-
> one else's flight of fancy. . . . With the advent of the VCR
> and the new digital TV systems, much of what remains of
> the TV past is really just what someone else recorded.
>
> Lynn Spigel 2005, 92

As Lynn Spigel explains, the underestimation of television's historic, aesthetic, and cultural value results in some rather inconvenient conditions for archival work. Spigel uses the Library of Congress's description of its own collections to outline why early television records are often difficult to procure: "The Library simply underestimated the social and historical significance of the full range of television programming. There was no appreciation of television's future research value. So before the mid-1960s, few TV programs were acquired for the Library collections" (2005, 68). Others call television a "dirty" medium because it is "recalcitrant when it comes to identifying where the text should stop" (Hartley 1992, 22). For John Hartley, "Television cannot be reduced," and that makes it "resistant to classification" (ibid., 27). Indeed, the flow[1] of television, its instantaneous-ness—its ability to convey a dynamic perpetual present—Spigel terms "TV's aesthetic of liveness," a quality she uses to explain its resistance to documentation (2005, 91). As an inherently ephemeral medium (see Worsley 1970), television presents obvious practical and theoretical complications when compiling a thematic archive. Given our current project[2]—to compile a fairy tale teleography—it is fitting (or just my luck) that the tensions between the ephemeral and the artifactual are infused in both television and fairy tales.

Kay Stone, folklorist and storyteller, describes the intangible quality of her storytelling as "ephemeral as writing in air" (2004, 127). While the transient and ever changing qualities of oral storytelling create moral imperatives to preserve them,[3] their very ephemerality presents an ethical drawback; the very act of recording violates their transcendent nature. A storyteller cannot tell the same story twice; unlike television, in oral traditions there is no syndication. Television programs can be reproduced ad nauseam and they frequently are. The very inundation of televisual texts sustains television's status as ephemeral.

By contrast, when folktales and fairy tales are adapted in different media, the resulting plethora of texts is attributed to the malleability of supposedly singular tales, reflecting their timeless essence and illuminating new interpretive possibilities. New retellings reveal new frameworks for understanding folk texts, folklore studies, and contemporary mediation. New retellings also suggest that attempts to contain and catalog folk texts will always be frustrated by their incomplete and fragmentary nature. Thus, their perpetual resurrection and transformation challenges folklorists to find theoretical frameworks and organizing principles as dynamic as the subject matter. Re-mediation has inspired reconfigurations of folklore studies' foundational principles and moved scholars to reject the notion of an "original" text and embrace intertextual and multivocal models.

The fairy-tale teleography comprises fairy-tale retellings[4] of many genres and sizes—some as short as a *Saturday Night Live* comedy sketch and others as long as ABC's *Bewitched* (1964–1972). Whether they are live-action ballets, televised operas, made-for-television movies, animated series, miniseries, serialized dramas, variety shows, or anthology series, we have endeavored to include them. In 1961, Newton Minow, chair of the US Federal Communications Commission, famously described TV content's impermanence and its endless processional flow—the airtime that now straddles every minute of the broadcast day—as a "vast wasteland" (qtd. in Minow and Lamay 1995, 188). If Minow thought that the immensity of TV land could be perceived by "sit[ing] down in front of your television set . . . and keep[ing] your eyes glued to that set until the station signs off" (ibid.), I wonder how he might portray the experience of creating a teleography such as this!

I describe attempting to compile a fairy tale–themed television archive as an arduous, quixotic endeavor. It is arduous because the task is both interminable and limitless; new texts continue—to this day—to surface, forcing us to return and add more entries at each revision. Such arduousness is anticipated in Jacques Derrida's emphasis on the interminability of all archival works: "For while an archive may not be an end, it is only a beginning" (1996, 109). The project is quixotic because despite the many, many problems of crafting it, I retain the excessively romantic position that a fairy-tale teleography is a wondrous idea.

Imagining an archive of televised adaptations of ATU 327A, "Hansel and Gretel," may help to explain the fairy-tale teleography's value and why I think it is so marvelous. Television has produced many works under the title "Hansel and Gretel." To sample those in the teleography, *Kraft Television Theatre* produced an episode in 1948; ten years later, Paul Bogart directed a TV movie for NBC; *Live from the Metropolitan Opera* produced an adaptation in 1982; in the same year, Tim Burton directed a TV special for Disney[5]; the BBC produced a TV musical starring Muriel Pavlow in 1937 and aired the Royal Opera House Covent Garden's opera production in 2008; even Tom Davenport's TV movie series included "Hansel and Gretel" (1975). And we cannot omit individual episodes like *Buffy the Vampire Slayer*'s "Gingerbread" (3, 11, 1999)[6] and *The Simpsons* "Treehouse of Horror 'Scary Tales Can Come True'" (24, 2, 2012; see Tresca's chapter). Acknowledging the diversity of televised fairy-tale retellings helps to emphasize their undeniable multifariousness. It reminds us to read across production eras and surf across channels. Too often, textual analyses focus only on individual programs, as if their mediation ever existed in an isolated form in the first place.

The teleography, like *Channeling Wonder* itself, includes animated and live-action works, scripted fictions and so-called reality television. Regrettably, the almost exclusive proclivity for English-language titles has resulted in a rather Anglocentric compilation. Culture and language substantially curtailed the entry samples' international diversity. The ease of access to web-based television archives in Canada, the United States, and the United Kingdom has engendered a greater density of representation from these regions. Moreover, because many entries came as recommendations from colleagues, I am indebted to them and so cannot take full credit for the final tally's eclecticism. I hope that this project will eventually expand into an online interactive format, integrating international collaboration from other archivists, professional or recreational. This is not a venture for one human being. But despite its limitations, just as television and fairy tales should be shared and not hoarded, so too should this teleography. Part courtesy for the collection's readers and part professional curiosity, the teleography amassed here may assist those who seek to navigate the expansive landscape of fairy-tale television. This short introduction aims to illustrate some limiting factors and distinctive qualities.

The entries are divided into four categories: individual episodes; TV specials and live performances (including ballets, teleplays, musicals, operas, and ice capades); TV series, miniseries, and educational TV; and TV movies. It focuses on fictional works produced for mainstream entertainment; thus, commercial advertisements (see Bacchilega and Rieder's chapter), news media, documentary works, infomercials, and music videos are excluded—despite the use of fairy-tale themes in all these genres.[7] My initial reason for exclusion was that the segments were too short to count; I soon revised this rationalization, however, given the theoretical context of television studies.

Describing television's "distinctive aesthetic form," John Ellis explains broadcast television's composition "as a programmed series of meaningful segments" (1982, 148). For Ellis, segmentation is the medium's definitive feature (whereas it is flow for Williams), with discrete segments remaining "relatively self-contained" and sequencing lasting a "maximum duration [of] about five minutes" (ibid., 112, 148). He further observes, "These segments are organized into groups which are either simply cumulative, like news broadcast items and advertisements, or have some kind of repetitive or sequential connection, like the groups of segments that make up the serial or series"; accordingly, "broadcast TV narration takes place across these segments" (ibid., 112). Considering Ellis's vision of self-contained, fragmentary segments as television's building blocks, excluding material lasting less than five minutes appears problematic. However, including segments that are not feature length[8] would result in an insurmountable (or even more insurmountable!) project. A teleography of fairy tale–themed advertisements alone would generate volumes.[9]

Respecting television's fragmentary nature and *not* excluding segments based on duration, we eventually found sound justification for excluding ads, infomercials, news, documentaries, and music videos. Eliminating nonfiction boiled down to honoring *Channeling Wonder*'s project—fairy-tale retellings, not just *any and all* fairy-tale content. Moreover, Spigel's "aesthetic of liveness" is especially pertinent to news media. The chance that a station would retain *all* its daily news reports in a way that was user-friendly for our purposes is unlikely, if not unheard of, in corporate broadcasting. I was unable to find an analytically sound reason for excluding music videos and advertisements, except for the simple reality that including them would be impractical, given limited resources of time and funding. Their brevity is matched by their disengagement from other programming, which makes them especially difficult to locate in formal records. This lack is especially disappointing since "music video clips tend to defy the familiar regimes of narrative structure," so the genre likely produces innovative and experimental retellings (Goodwin 1993, 72). Nevertheless, I feel some disappointment with our failure to include everything.

Originally, we envisioned the teleography as a reference for *every* fairytale text to appear on international broadcast television. That enterprise's sheer size is not just ambitious but insurmountable in print.[10] Setting the obstacle of language aside for a moment, the Central Intelligence Agency lists more than 200 countries with television broadcast stations ("Field Listing" 2013). An overview of broadcast television per country is instructive: in 1998, Russia had 7,306 different stations; in 1997, China had 3,240; in 1995, the European Union had 2,700; in 2006, the United States had 2,218; in 2009, India had 1,400.[11] The dates listed emphasize the already outdated nature of these figures; the estimates are likely conservative.

Public records and copyright laws present another difficulty limiting accurate citation. Take, for example, *Looney Toons*. It has aired on more than fifty different networks in more than twenty-five countries. Through its licensing/copyright history, it has shuffled between Warner Bros., Turner Broadcasting System, and Time Warner, with episodes repackaged into multiple different programs. For the multiple fairy tale–themed segments, it is difficult to ascertain which originally aired in which order and with which accompanying segments. In the filmography, we've listed the "Looney Toon" and "Merry Melodies" shorts into one section, offering each episode's original broadcast year and director. Many have been reproduced, sometimes appearing in color or edited for content and duration. Some might argue that each reproduction is an altogether new text.

Despite television's ubiquity, public records for broadcast television are paradoxically insubstantial. The growth of TV programming over the past few decades, not to mention the proliferation of stations internationally, poses contradictory conditions for an archivist; whereas there are *too few* records of historical broadcasts, today, there are *too many* to count. Jonathan Bignell concurs. Although "writing a history of television over the last twenty years or so looks easy . . . there is simply too much that could be investigated" (2008, 39). By contrast, those historical records that *were* kept by broadcasting companies were retained not for preservation but for commercial purposes, such as training staff, syndicating programs, and international export. As Bignell explains, "The copies of programmes that can be found in broadcasters' archives represent a fragmentary patchwork that was not intended as an objective record" (ibid.). His claims offer some consolation for our decision to limit the teleography. However, as above, we acknowledge a certain homogeneity in the result. I have been unable to reflect international diversity to the extent that the project warrants, so I have no alternative but to humbly present it as the beginning of a much longer, larger journey.

Getting Lost in the Archive: From Loop Holes to Loose Ends

The entries in this teleography are static in the properties of their given era of production. Although televised works can be edited, recut, and reproduced into new syndicated programming, the fact of their original broadcast remains.[12] Encapsulating programming into succinct citations cataloging year(s) of production and the creative teams who produced them emphasizes the entries' historic and productive continuity, especially in relation to each other. In this format, the intersections and repetitious nature of fairy-tale programming is apparent. It is obvious when reviewing the teleography, for example, that many musicals are redone with similar cast and crew. I sometimes struggled to distinguish whether versions were in fact new when they shared the same title, the same score, even the same lead performer. The TV special *Cinderella* with music by Richard Rodgers and lyrics by Oscar Hammerstein, for example, aired on CBS in 1957, 1964, and 1997. It was easy to distinguish them because the first version stars Julie Andrews, the second, Lesley Ann Warren, and the third, Brandy Norwood (see Sawin's chapter). *Once Upon a Mattress* is more confusing because it was remade in 1964, 1972, and 2005 always featuring Carol Burnett. CBS telecast the Broadway show *Peter Pan* three times. The first two productions featured the *same* cast in the anthology series *Producers' Showcase* (for 1955 and 1956). Distinctions between the productions are just as significant as the common ground, so it is important to read carefully.

To be sure, the diversity of television formats creates unique demands for generating a thematic archive. Compiling this teleography necessitated constant negotiation of the guidelines for what had to be included. Kevin Paul Smith's literary model of fairy-tale intertexts directed us. Each entry employs fairy-tale intertexts in ways that are authorized (explicit in the title); writerly (implicit in the title); incorporated (explicit in text); an allusion (implicit in text); a re-vision (giving an old tale a new spin); a fabulation (creating a new tale); metafictional (overtly discussing fairy tales); and architextual/chronotopic (referential in setting/environment; 2007, 10). Whenever I had a moment of doubt, such as when I wondered if Showcase's *Lost Girl* qualified, I would refer to Smith's outline and decide whether or not it fit in any of the categories.[13]

Television plots can accommodate imaginative substitutions; for example, when viewers are familiar enough with characters, they can be slotted into new and unusual contexts without disrupting the narrative coherence.[14] Such series are hardly the standard though; anthology TV series that feature original plots and a new cast of characters are just as common. Anthology series provide ample evidence for the diversity of fairy-tale retellings, including Shelley Duvall's *Faerie Tale Theatre; Happily Ever After: Fairy Tales for Every Child;* and Jim Henson's *The StoryTeller* (see Rudy's chapter).

Some anthology series and even miniseries are not so explicitly fairy-tale themed but include fairy-tale episodes or segments. In Bruce D. Johnson's miniseries *Adventures from the Book of Virtues* (1996), for example, six 25-minute episodes are titled "Work," "Honesty," "Responsibility," "Compassion," "Courage," and "Self-discipline." Although these titles do not imply fairy-tale content, the tales included within the individual didactic episodes do. Each is conveyed through multiple stories. Despite the inclusion of "George Washington and the Cherry Tree" in the second episode, "Honesty," the presence of both "The Frog Prince" (ATU 440, "The Frog King or Iron Henry") and "The Algonquin Cinderella" justifies its inclusion in the teleography. Because the majority of stories in the episodes are not fairy tales (e.g., "King Alfred and the Burnt Cakes" and "How Genghis Khan Loses His Anger and Kills His Friend the Hawk"), we've referenced the series but also listed individual episodes with fairy-tale content.

As with *Adventures from the Book of Virtues,* it is often difficult to assess how developed a retelling should be to warrant inclusion. Should it be based on how much the fairy tale is elaborated or developed narratively? What about variety programs that feature segments lasting less than five minutes or those that are segmented into ten-minute features? What about situation comedies, like *Family Guy* and *The Simpsons*, that feature hypothetical asides? Drawing lines is difficult given broadcast TV's fragmented nature as a medium. Analysis of genre is incredibly difficult too, if not simply impracticable given the intertextual dynamism of television content. TV theorist Mimi White aptly writes, "Familiar categories are combined in such a manner that no single genre can adequately account for the narrative and dramatic practices" of many programs (1985, 43). What White calls the "overlap and mixing" of genre codes in contemporary television programs undermines its generic unity. John Fiske describes the discontinuity of television formats as a fracturing force: "The movement of the television text is discontinuous, interrupted, and segmented. Its attempts at closure, at a unitary meaning, or a unified viewing subject, are constantly subjected to fracturing forces" (2011, 105). The fracturing forces confound any desire for a clean and contained bibliographic account. Indeed, the discontinuity, interruptions, and segmentation of so many popular programs at once frustrate this project while simultaneously encouraging us to marvel at the broadcast medium's complexly intertextually reinforced nature. Allow me to explain.

Parodies: Sketch Comedy and Intertextuality

One good example is the episode of Seth McFarlane's *Family Guy* "Road to the Multiverse" (8, 1). While it parodies Disney and is *not* a fairy-tale retelling, Donald Haase provides compelling reasons to consider it. He explains that for many viewers, "the normative influences of Disney's animated fairy tales has been so enormous, that the Disney spirit—already once removed from the originals—tends to become the standard against which fairy-tale films are created *and* received" (1988, 196). Although he refers here to film adaptations, the observation also applies in the context of television. Given the hurried nature of TV texts, produced in relatively short periods of time, employing visual cues from Disney is sometimes just easier (if not also somewhat unimaginative).

Programs may resort to Disney tropes as a cut-rate time-saver to assist audiences in establishing the traditional fairy-tale source. A piecemeal Disney reference used as a savvy mediated storytelling technique does not render the text any less of a fairy-tale retelling. The reality is that the visual cues for fairy tales are often associated with Walt Disney's major motion pictures.[15] Laden in many of these texts is a layered critique of the traditional fairy tale(s) and the Disney adaptation(s) alike.[16]

However, I will show how "Road to the Multiverse" offers a compelling example of a parodic segment aimed at Disney but not at fairy tales and thus is not included in the teleography. "Road to the Multiverse" features the infant genius Stewie traveling to various parallel universes with the family dog Brian. When arriving in the Disneyfied dimension, Stewie remarks, "It seems we're in a universe where everything is drawn by Disney." Soon after, *Family Guy*'s cast emerges in the form of Disney film caricatures. After less than two minutes in this universe, Stewie and Brian use their remote control to depart.[17] The teleography seeks to present televised works that reference specific tales, not generic intertextual commentary on mainstream producers like Disney. While I draw a distinction between fairy-tale intertexts and parodies of mainstream creative productions, namely the "Disney spirit," the question remains of whether or not there is a discernable difference (Haase 1988, 196). While the two may be hard to differentiate in some circumstances, MacFarlane's segment in this instance does not re-create a fairy tale; it mocks Disney as a franchise and Walt Disney as a human being, in particular.[18]

Contrast the *Family Guy*'s token gesture to *Saturday Night Live*'s (*SNL*'s) sketch "The Real Housewives of Disney" (March 3, 2012). The actors in *SNL*'s sketch don costumes and reference the Magic Kingdom and characters like Iago, but the humor's crux is the "new spin," wherein fairy-tale princesses become belligerent contemporary reality TV divas.[19] Despite the diversity of characters referenced (Belle, Jasmine, Cinderella, Snow White, and Rapunzel are featured), its poignant critique of fairy-tale story lines is itself presented in a developed self-contained plot. The scene from *Family Guy*'s "Road to the Multiverse" does not focus on a single tale either, but its critique is not about fairy tales. Had the segment from *Family Guy* focused on Snow White, an argument might be made for it as a retelling; however, it uses visual cues from multiple films without developing those cues in any depth. Moreover, the segment from *Family Guy* is a scene, rather than a stand-alone sketch, which explains its lack of narrative development. It also must be considered in light of the other "universes" presented in the episode—the Flintstones and Robot Chicken also appear. *Family Guy*'s pastiche method and its fragmentary, but often complexly intertextual one-liners that interrupt the primary narrative do not merit inclusion in the teleography.[20]

Family Guy is certainly not the only nonlinear comedy show or parodic segment-based program to feature fairy tales. Sketch comedy programs like *SNL, MadTV,* and *Robot Chicken,* among many others, refer to fairy tales in single segments. Although I mention some examples briefly here, which are included in the teleography, the integration of every broadcast segment presented issues. Due to their titular ambiguity (often titles do not identify fairy-tale content), locating the sketches required personally sifting through episodes on record.[21] In most circumstances, such records are not readily available. Fortuitously, *SNL*'s online archive is extensive; but it is an exceptional case.

As *SNL* is one of the longest running variety shows in American broadcast history, with more than 700 individual episodes, mining the archive would be a project in itself. Admittedly, exploring the website for just a few hours uncovered a surprising number of fairy-tale segments; a more thorough exploration would probably uncover a great deal more. I found an animated short titled "Up Close with Geppetto" (April 15, 2000); I also learned that Ellen Page was featured as Peter Pan in a sketch titled "Hook's Revenge" (March 1, 2008); Steve Buscemi guest starred in an Alice in Wonderland–inspired sketch titled "The Mad Tea Party" (April 4, 1998); the Little Mermaid was portrayed by Tina Fey ("Below the Waves," May 7, 2011) and Reece Witherspoon ("The Little Mermaid," September 29, 2001); I discovered two sketches referencing ATU 425C. The first featured Demi Moore ("Beauty and the Beast: The Double Date," November 12, 1988), and the second starred Gerard Butler ("Beauty and the Beast," October 17, 2009). In addition, I found two sketches inspired by the *Wizard of Oz*—the first featuring Elliot Gould as a flying monkey ("The Incredible Man," February 16, 1980) and a more recent one with Anne Hathaway as Dorothy ("The Essentials," November 20, 2010).

During a brief supplementary online search for *Wizard of Oz* sketch comedy, I discovered segments from the short-lived *Dana Carvey Show* ("If I Only Had an Ass," April 30, 1996) and two from *MadTV* (the first, a two-part sketch exploring an alternative ending [March 20, 2004] and the second, a deleted scene from the Hollywood picture, titled "The Runaway Slave" [May 16, 2009]). Obviously, plenty of sketch comedy routines parody fairy tales. My reluctance to include them here reflects the limitations of time and resources available to complete such an exhaustive search. The fact additionally remains that a written entry cannot convey each sketch routine's unique features—nor is the referenced fairy tale readily apparent from the citation.

That we couldn't devote more time, energy, and resources to variety television segments was disappointing given the critical nature of parody-centered programs. One *Robot Chicken* segment, for example, features a nightgown-donning wolf preening before a mirror. When a female wolf inquires, "How long are you going to keep dressing like that?" the cross-dressed wolf emphatically retorts, "As long as it makes me happy!" *The Simpsons* also often features fairy-tale themes. In "Four Great Women and a Manicure" (20, 20, 2009), the segmented episode includes Queen Elizabeth I, Snow White, Lady Macbeth, and Maggie Roark (from Ayn Rand's *The Fountainhead*). Lisa explains, "Snow White" centers on a "dangerous obsession with female beauty." Although a lawyer interrupts to inform her that the tale is copyrighted "property of the Walt Disney Corporation," Lisa is quick to explain, "'Snow White' is a fairy tale from hundreds of years ago," and "no one owns that." This "Snow White" segment is more than twice the length of *Family Guy*'s two-minute segment but still only one quarter of the full episode. Yet Lisa's comment on the proprietary rights of fairy tales evidences how such references can at once critique the corporation and the fairy-tale tradition generally.

For more developed fairy-tale retellings, *The Simpsons* also annually features "Treehouse of Horror" Halloween specials. The segment, "Scary Tales Can Come True" (12, 1; see Tresca's chapter), which uses the plot of "Hansel and Gretel," also features fairy-tale tropes such as trolls and the Three Bears from "Goldilocks." A stellar adaptation of "Hansel and Gretel," the segment amounts to only one third of the episode. As Jonathan Gray points out, programs like *The Simpsons* operate within "a network of other programs," using humor that is "deeply transitive" signaling to "other genres, texts, and discourses" (2006, 10). Shows like *The Simpsons* have no more interest in fairy tales than in any other cultural referent. Although this teleography privileges sustained engagements with fairy-tale fabulations over token references, since both segments from *The Simpsons* offer developed narrative arcs and align with several of Smith's tenets, they are included.

More obvious titles to include within the variety television genre are those with recurring supporting segments with fairy-tale themes. *The Adventures of Rocky and Bullwinkle* regularly featured *Fractured Fairy Tales*, comprising classics retold for comic effect (see Bacchilega and Rieder's chapter). With more than ninety retellings, *Fractured Fairy Tales* presents a valuable collection of fairy-tale adaptations from the late 1950s to the early 1960s. Even though some segments last less than five minutes, their profusion necessitates inclusion. Assessed cumulatively, they amount to more than seven hours of fairy-tale television! In the interest of space, however, the teleography acknowledges the *Adventures of Rocky and Bullwinkle* with *Fractured Fairy Tales* in the years 1959–1964 as a list of undated segments. Although it would have been preferable to catalog each segment individually, differentiating between retellings drawn from fairy tales, nursery rhymes, fables, and adventure stories and crediting individual titles, creators, voice actors, and so on, the teleography's space limitations did not permit it. Additionally, the format did not permit the inclusion of supplementary contextual information; however, I gladly embrace the opportunity to expand here.[22]

Drawing More Distinctions: Straw into Gold and Wheat from Chaff

While most televised series do not typically include fairy-tale themes, they may occasionally feature themed episodes. Undeniably, the choice to include these creates a collection that is both sprawling and incomplete. The task of amassing *every* fairy-tale themed episode from programming that is *not* fairy-tale themed overall means that every fictional televised program qualifies as a potential entry. The choice to include such examples substantiates the fairy tale's applicability to almost all genres. Using popular fairy tales, television producers secure a guaranteed audience—or at least anticipate the expectations of its viewers (see Hay and Baxter's chapter).

Some genres, for example nonrealist productions such as fantasy and especially animated features, are more likely to make the crossover to fairy-tale content. Similarly, some programs are structured in ways that enable flexibility with each episode's narrative context. *Alvin and the Chipmunks,* for example, is not a prototypical fairy-tale series, but featuring its protagonists in unique circumstances in each episode means that the characters can be recontextualized within well-known plots.[23] Occasionally, episodes parody familiar films, television programs, literary texts, and idioms. Titles like "The Incredible Shrinking Dave," "The Prize Isn't Right," "Swiss Family Chipmunks," and "Theodore and Juliette" signal which text is being parodied. That time never elapses between episodes is not unlike the format of other sitcoms or animated series. Typically, two segments appear during each episode with differing titles and plotlines; there are more than 150 distinct segments in total. The popularity of the episodes devoted to cinema prompted the program's creators to devote its eighth and final season to film, with the revised title *The Chipmunks Go to the Movies*. The fairy tale–themed episodes included in the teleography are "Snow Wrong," "The Legend of Sleeping Brittany," "The Princess and the Pig," and "Cinderella? Cinderella!"[24] Literary fairy tales, such as "Alvin in Neverland," were also featured; and the final season included the episode "Sploosh," an adaptation of the film *Splash* (1984), riffing on Hans Christian Andersen's "The Little Mermaid." I also note another episode, "Once Upon a Crime," which also employed titular fairy-tale themes. The program's flexibility as a nonlinear animated series made it ideally suited for fairy tale–themed episodes. Its fan base made the research significantly easier. Indeed, ease of access was often the constituting factor that decided whether an entry was included or a potential entry never found at all.

Made-for-TV movies (discussed in Barzilai's, Greenhill and Kohm's, and Wright's chapters) and some individual episodes from anthology series occasionally had to be distinguished between direct-to-video releases and major motion pictures with histories on television. For example, *Muppet Classic Theater* was released direct-to-video on September 27, 1994. It consists of six stories: "Three Little Pigs," "King Midas," "The Boy Who Cried Wolf," "Rumpelstiltskin," "The Emperor's New Clothes," and "The Elves and the Shoemaker." Although we struggled to locate the individual segments and when they aired, they likely first appeared on *The Muppet Show* televised series.

Special telecasts of classic films like Metro-Goldwyn-Mayer's *The Wizard of Oz* (1939) and Disney's *Alice in Wonderland* (1951) were experienced by a great many viewers *first* as televised specials (premiering on television on CBS in 1956 and on ABC in 1954, respectively). Although we did not ultimately include such films, we acknowledge the reality that television often subsumes cinematic forms into its folds. Film series we *did* include, however, were those produced by Tom Davenport. Initially, Davenport's adaptations—such as *Ashpet; Hansel and Gretel, an Appalachian Version;* and *The Frog King*—were excluded because we understood them to be cinematic, not televisual. We eventually changed our minds. The justification for including *Tales from the Brothers Grimm* is a compelling example of cinematic/television crossover. Several sources referred to Davenport's films as "television" (see "Movies & TV: Tom Davenport" 2013). We were persuaded when we discovered that the series aired on TV as "three programs based on classic stories by the Brothers Grimm" (*Turner Classic Movies* 2013). Indeed, the films' implementation in an educational context is what inspired funding from organizations like the Corporation for Public Broadcasting. Davenport describes the nuances of funding such projects:

> In 1981, Mimi and I wrote a successful proposal to the Corporation for Public Broadcasting, and received money to do four more folktale adaptations for release to schools via instructional television. We proposed that our series would appeal to all age groups from kindergarten through senior high and submitted *The Frog King* as our pilot. . . . We called the CPB series 'From the Brothers Grimm' and continued to follow faithfully the Grimm tales in our production of *Bristlelip* (1982), *Bearskin* (1982), and *The Goose Girl* (1983). (Davenport, 2013)

In correspondence with Pauline Greenhill, he explains, "The series was broadcast for many years on Educational TV and is still used in schools and libraries" (Davenport, personal communication). The films' presence on "education television" is also underscored by Tina L. Hanlon (2008, 255).

Another film series we included was *Hallmark Hall of Fame*. For an anthology film series (not a prototypical television series), the number of fairy-tale adaptations included was impressive. *Hallmark Hall of Fame*'s historically long run began in 1951 and continues today. Its fairy-tale productions include *Alice in Wonderland* (1955), *Pinocchio* (1968), *Beauty and the Beast* (1976), *Peter Pan* (1976), *Arabian Nights* (2000), and *Snow Queen* (2002).

Value and Meaning in Re-mediation: Concluding Thoughts

Although the mass consumption of fairy tales on a popular medium like TV in forms like musicals, sitcoms, and holiday specials can be construed to confirm a campy aesthetic for fairy tales, the cyclical resurrection through syndication and other transformative re-mediations confirm the extraordinary memetic quality of fairy-tale content. As a primary vehicle of entertainment, fairy-tale television is variously featured as a special occasion—something for the holidays, a made-for-TV movie or miniseries—but also a theme that can persist over multiple seasons, spanning years. The flexibility of fairy-tale content to accommodate so many formats speaks to the pliability of the form to appeal to variable demographics. As Haase contends, "In its conventional form, television is a commercial medium offering mass entertainment, so it is no surprise that many of television's fairy-tale broadcasts have been familiar, predictable, and consistent with the viewers' expectations. Like cheaply produced picture-book versions of fairy tales, television relies on the fairy tale's readily available plots and popularity" (2008, 947). The resulting teleography (and its defects) offers compelling evidence substantiating the recirculation of fairy tales in contemporary culture. We hope that it offers a valuable resource to provide scholars with inspiration and fuel for further research in the cultural mediation of fairy tales.

Notes

1. Raymond Williams concluded that television's "real character" consists in not "a pro-gramme of discrete units with particular insertions, but a planned flow" that includes commercials as well as primary programs. He saw "flow" as the "defining character-istic of broadcasting" (1974, 86). Williams's flow must not be confused with Mihaly Csikszentmihalyi's concept of the "holistic sensation that people feel when they act with total involvement" (1997, 36). Csikszentmihaly specifies that "very rarely do people report flow in passive leisure activities, such as watching television or relax-ing" (ibid., 34).

2. For personal reflections I use "I"; however, I occasionally invoke "we" to acknowledge Pauline Greenhill and Jill Rudy, who helped shape this contribution from its outset.

3. This push is usually inspired by fear that new technologies will supplant old ones—that oral tradition will be replaced by written texts, which will be replaced by audiovi-sual and/or digital forms, and so on. Haase writes that while "television was perceived as a threat to oral and literary culture," these concerns are "similar to those that were expressed in the late eighteenth and early nineteenth centuries about the effects that literacy and book production were allegedly having on oral tradition" (2008, 947).

4. Joosen chooses "fairy-tale retelling" from the mass (or "mess" in her words) of alter-native namesakes: "reversion, revision, reworking, parody, transformation, anti–fairy tale, postmodern fairy tale, fractured fairy tale, and recycled fairy tale" (2011, 9).

5. Tim Burton's *Hansel and Gretel* (1982) is rumored to have aired only once.

6. (Series, episode, year).

7. A brief search for "Alice in Wonderland"–themed music videos yielded work that included that of Tom Petty and the Heartbreakers, Gwen Stefani, and the Estonian recording artist Kerli.

8. We *already* made an exception by opting to include fairy tale–themed segments from variety television shows and sketch comedy programs.

9. Considering the problems I faced locating and garnering accurate information about feature-length fairy-tale television (original airdates, networks, directors, and pro-duction companies), I imagine documenting something like commercials—often amounting to less than thirty seconds of air time—would be cruel and unusual punishment.

10. Linear bibliographic formatting (ordering alphabetically, chronologically, categorically) does not accommodate the cross-listing that would prove beneficial for users. Moreover, given the sheer volume of potential entries internationally, finding a user-friendly interactive platform would be ideal. We are currently developing an online format for such an interactive, collaborative database.

11. Though updated weekly, the CIA's online World Factbook estimates and projections are subject to "factors including data availability, assessment, and methods and protocols"; in other words, the data are time sensitive and subject to human error (2013).

12. Entire networks devoted to timeworn broadcasting include Teletoon Retro and Nickelodeon's "TV Land."

13. I classified *Lost Girl* as a "fabulation"; the protagonist is "one of the fae," a succubus—other characters include shape shifters, sirens, a "wish-granting, tree-dwelling crone," brownies, and a genie (Showcase 2013). Even if we did not consider it a fairy tale–themed series, the episode "Mirror, Mirror" (2, 4) would be included (see Tresca's chapter).

14. This habitually occurs on loosely structured parody programs, variety television, and animated sitcoms but also in fantasy, sci-fi, and supernatural genres.

15. Most chapters discuss, at least in passing, Disney's influence.

16. While one could bemoan the sacrilege that any corporate body could signify a given fairy tale, the teleography demonstrates the wealth of alternatives (many not offering so much as a nod to Disney!).

17. Stewie and Brian's use of a *remote control* as their tool for mobility is fitting. This choice emphasizes the series' constant metatextual in-jokes. Stewie and Brian *do* exist on TV; it makes sense for other "universes" to be other programs on different "channels."

18. The segment concludes when the Jewish neighbor appears, only to be menacingly identified as a "Jew" and beaten to death by the parallel universe's Griffith family and friends—a disturbing commentary on Walt Disney's purported anti-Semitism.

19. The segment also revises Prince Charming as a flamboyant, shoe-loving, "Evil Queen."

20. How could we justify including one-liners when we've excluded so many more complex fairy-tale adaptations, like Suzy Boguss's 1993 music video "Hey Cinderella?"

21. Admittedly, this was not an altogether unpleasant experience.

22. *Fractured Fairy Tales* was briefly replaced by a supposedly less satirically biting, more "audience-friendly" segment, *Aesop and Sons* (Peterson 2008, 373). Only thirty-nine fables were adapted before audience response prompted returning to the popular, critically potent fractured fairy-tale format. Perhaps fables channel less wonder than fairy tales?

23. The American animated television series was developed from *The Alvin Show* (1960–1961). It aired from 1983 to 1990 on NBC and continues in syndication. The franchise expanded to include a major motion picture, made-for-television movies, and the computer-animated/live-action films *Alvin and the Chipmunks* (2007), *The Squeaquel* (2009), and *Chipwrecked* (2011).

24. These episodes feature the Chipettes, rather than the male protagonists Alvin, Simon, and Theodore.

FAIRY-TALE TELEOGRAPHY

Individual Episodes

ABC Afterschool Special. 1972–1995. Children's anthology series. Created by Guy Fraumeni. USA: ABC.

    "Cindy Eller: A Modern Fairy Tale." 1985. [Season] 14, [Episode] 2. Directed by Lee Grant. USA: AIMS Media.

Adventures from the Book of Virtues. 1996–2000. TV series. Created by Bruce D. Johnson. USA: KCET.

    "Courage." 1998. 3, 8. [Jack and the Beanstalk].

    "Honesty." 1996. 1, 2. [The Frog Prince and the Algonquin Cinderella].

    "Honesty." 1998. 3, 9. [The Pied Piper].

    "Humility." 1997. 2, 2. [The Emperor's New Clothes].

    "Moderation." 1998. 3, 6. [The Goose That Laid the Golden Egg].

    "Self-Discipline." 1996. 1, 6. [King Midas and the "Golden Touch"].

Alvin and the Chipmunks. 1983–1990. Animated TV series. Written by Ross Bagdasarian. USA: Ruby-Spears Productions.

    "Alvin in Neverland." 1989. 7, 9.

    "Cinderella? Cinderella!" 1986. 4, 5. Directed by Charles A. Nichols.

    "The Incredible Shrinking Dave." 1983. 1, 8. Directed by John Kimball, Rudy Larriva, and Charles A. Nichols.

    "The Legend of Sleeping Brittany." 1989. 7, 9.

    "Once Upon a Crime." 1988. 6, 9.

    "The Princess and the Pig." 1989. 7, 11.

    "The Prize Isn't Right." 1985. 3, 9. Directed by Charles A. Nichols.

    "Snow Wrong." 1984. 2, 13. Directed by Charles A. Nichols.

    "Sploosh." 1990. 8, 12. Directed by Don Spencer.

    "Swiss Family Chipmunks." 1983. 1, 11. Directed by John Kimball, Rudy Larriva, and Charles A. Nichols.

    "Theodore and Juliet." 1988. 6, 14.

American Playhouse. 1982–1993. Anthology TV series. Directors various. USA: PBS.

    "Into the Woods." 1991. 10, 1. Directed by James Lapine.

Animaniacs. 1993–1998. Directed by Audu Paden. USA: ABC Studios.

    Unspecified episodes.

The Bachelor. 2002–. Reality TV game show. Created by Mike Fleiss. USA: Next Entertainment.

"After the Final Rose, part 1." 2009. 13, 10. Directed by Mike Fleiss.
"After the Final Rose, part 2." 2009. 13, 11. Directed by Mike Fleiss.
"After the Final Rose." 2012. 16, 12. Directed by Mike Fleiss.
"Week 1." 2012. 16, 1. Directed by Mike Fleiss.
"Week 2." 2012. 16, 2. Directed by Mike Fleiss.
"Week 3." 2012. 16, 3. Directed by Mike Fleiss.
"Week 4." 2012. 16, 4. Directed by Mike Fleiss.
"Week 5." 2012. 16, 5. Directed by Mike Fleiss.
"Week 6." 2012. 16, 6. Directed by Mike Fleiss.
"Week 7." 2012. 16, 7. Directed by Mike Fleiss.
"Week 8 (Finale)." 2009. 13, 9. Directed by Mike Fleiss.
"Week 8." 2012. 16, 8. Directed by Mike Fleiss.
"Week 9." 2012. 16, 9. Directed by Mike Fleiss.
"Week 10 (Finale)." 2012. 16, 11. Directed by Mike Fleiss.
"The Women Tell All." 2012. 16, 10. Directed by Mike Fleiss.

The Bachelor Pad. 2010–. Reality TV game show. Created by Mike Fleiss. USA: Next Entertainment.
Unspecified episodes.

The Bachelorette. 2003–2005, 2008–. Reality TV game show. Created by Mike Fleiss. USA: Next Entertainment.
"Week 1." 2012. 8, 1. Directed by Mike Fleiss.
"Week 3." 2012. 8, 3. Directed by Mike Fleiss.

Batfink. 1966–1967. Animated TV series. Directed and produced by Hal Seeger. USA: Screen Gems.
"Beanstalk Jack." 1967.
"Cinderobber." 1967.
"Goldyunlocks and the Three Bears." 1967.
"The Thief from Baghdad." 1967.

Beetlejuice. 1989–1991. Animated TV series. Created by Tim Burton. Canada, USA: Warner Bros. Television, ABC.
"Beauty and the Beetle." 1991. 4, 12.
"A Very Grimm Fairy Tale." 1992. 4, 59.
"Wizard of Ooze." 1991. 4, 40.

B.J. and the Bear. 1978–1981. TV series. Created by Christopher Crowe and Glen A. Larson. USA: Universal TV.
"Snow White and the Seven Lady Truckers: Part 1." 1979. 2, 1.
"Snow White and the Seven Lady Truckers: Part 2." 1979. 2, 2.

Black Lagoon. 2006–. Anime TV series. UK: Funimation Entertainment, Madhouse Inc.
"Snow White's Payback." 2006.

Blue's Clues. 1996–2006. Children's animated and live-action series. Created by Traci Paige Johnson, Angela Santomero, and Todd Kessler. USA: Nickelodeon Productions.
"The Fairy Tale Ball." 6, 7. 2004. Directed by Alan Zdinak.

Bones. 2005–. TV series. Created by Hart Hanson. USA: Far Field Productions.
"The Cinderella in the Cardboard." 2009. 4, 19. Directed by Steven DePaul.
"The Pinocchio in the Planter." 2011. 6, 20. Directed by Francois Velle.
"The Princess and the Pear." 2009. 4, 14. Directed by Steve DePaul.

The Brady Bunch. 1969–1974. TV series. Created by Sherwood Shwartz. USA: Paramount Television, ABC.

"Snow White and the Seven Bradys." 1973. 5, 3.

Buffy the Vampire Slayer. 1997–2003. TV series. Created by Joss Whedon. USA: Mutant Enemy.
"Band Candy." 1998. 3, 6. Directed by Michael Lange.
"Fear Itself." 1999. 4, 4. Directed by Tucker Gates.
"Gingerbread." 1999. 3, 11. Directed by James Whitmore Jr.
"Halloween." 1997. 2, 6. Directed by Bruce Seth Green.
"Hush." 1999. 4, 10. Directed by Joss Whedon.

The Bullwinkle Show. 1961–1964. Animated TV series. USA: Jay Ward Productions (NBC). (See *The Rocky and Bullwinkle Show*).

The Carol Burnett Show. 1967–1978. Variety TV series. Directed by Dave Powers. USA: CBS.
"Cinderella Gets It On." 1975. 9, 6.
"La Caperucita Roja." 1974. 8, 17.
"Sleeping Beauty." 1967. 1, 2.
"Snow White 15 Years Later." 1973. 6, 16.

Cartoon Teletales. 1948–1950. Animated TV series. Starring Jack Luchsinger and Charles Luchsinger. USA: ABC.
Unspecified episodes.

Castle. 2009–. TV series. Created by Andrew W. Marlowe. USA: ABC Studios.
"Once Upon a Crime." 2012. 4, 17. Directed by Jeff Bleckner.

The Cleaner. 2008–2009. TV series. Created by Robert Munic and Jonathan Prince. USA: CBS Paramount Network Television.
"Cinderella." 2009. 2, 10. Directed by Steve Boyum.

Criminal Minds. 2005–present. TV series. Created by Jeff Davis. USA: Paramount Network Television.
"The Boogeyman." 2005. 2, 6.

Crossing Jordan. 2001–2007. TV series. Created by Tim Kring. USA: Tailwind Productions, NBC.
"Sleeping Beauty." 2007. 6, 12. Directed by Bethany Rooney.

CSI: Crime Scene Investigation. 2000–present. TV series. Created by Ann Donahue and Anthony E. Zuiker. USA: Paramount Network Television.
"Gum Drops." 2005. 6, 5.

Cupid. 1998–1999. TV series. Created by Rob Thomas. USA: Columbia Tristar Entertainment.
"A Truly Fractured Fairy Tale." 1998. 1, 4. Directed by Elodie Keene.

The Dana Carvey Show. 1996. Variety TV series. Produced by Robert Smigel, Bernie Brillstein, Charles Dalaklis, and Brad Grey. USA: Tristar Entertainment.
"If I Only Had an Ass." 1996. 1, 7.

Dancing with the Stars. 2005–. TV series. Created by BBC Worldwide. USA: BBC Worldwide Americas.
"Round 7." 2011. 13, 16. Directed by Alex Rudzinski.

Dawson's Creek. 1998–2003. TV series. Created by Kevin Williamson. USA: Columbia Tri-Star Entertainment.
"Cinderella Story." 2000. 3, 17. Directed by Janice Cooke.
"Good Bye, Yellow Brick Road." 2003. 6, 21. Directed by Peter B. Kowalski.
"Neverland." 2000. 3, 18. Directed by Patrick R. Norris.

Dead Like Me. 2003–2004. TV series. Created by Bryan Fuller. USA: John Masius Productions.
    "Ghost Story." 2004. 2, 3. Directed by Milam Cheylov.

Desperate Housewives. 2004–2012. TV series. Created by Marc Cherry. USA: Touchstone Television.
    "Running to Stand Still." 2004. 1, 6. Directed by Fred Gerber.

Dora the Explorer. 2000–. Children's animated series. Created by Chris Gifford, Eric Weiner, and Valerie Walsh. Canada, USA: Nickelodeon Studios.
    "Dora's Fairytale Adventure." 2004. 4, 3.
    "What Happens Next?" 2003. 3, 18.

Ducktales. 1987–1990. Animated TV series. Directors various, including Bob Hathcock, James T. Walker, and Steve Clark. USA: Walt Disney Television Animation.
    "The Golden Goose." 1990. 3, 6. Directed by Rick Leon and Alan Zaslove.

The Dupont Show of the Month. 1957–1961. Anthology TV series. Directors various, including Sidney Lumet, Ralph Nelson, and Robert Mulligan. USA: CBS.
    "Aladdin." 1958. 1, 6. Directed by Ralph Nelson.

Eight Is Enough. TV series. 1977–1981. USA: Lorimar Productions.
    "Cinderella's Understudy." 1978. 3, 4. Directed by Marc Daniels.
    "If the Glass Slipper Fits." 1981. 5, 15. Directed by Stan Lathan.

Engrenages (Spiral). 2005–2012. TV series. Created by Alexandra Clert and Guy-Patrick Sainderichin. France: Canal+.
    Season 1. 2005–2006.

Extreme Makeover. 2002–2007. Reality TV series. Created by Howard Schultz. USA: Lighthearted Entertainment.

Extreme Makeover: Home Edition. 2003–2012. Reality TV series. Created by Tom Forman. USA: Endemol.
    "The Dickinson Family." 2011. 8, 20.
    "Friends Helping Friends." 2004. 1, 10.
    "The Hebert Family." 2006. 3, 15.
    "The Hill Family." 2009. 7, 3.
    "The Hill Family." 2011. 9, 7.
    "The Okvath Family." 2005. 2, 31.

Extreme Makeover: Weight Loss Edition. 2011–. Reality TV series. Created by Tom Forman. USA: 3 Ball Productions. [Renamed *Extreme Weight Loss*, summer 2013.]
    Unspecified episodes.

The Famous Adventures of Mr. Magoo. 1965. Animated TV series. Directed by Abe Levitow. USA: NBC.
    "Mr. Magoo's Little Snow White: Part 1." 1965. 1, 14.
    "Mr. Magoo's Little Snow White: Part 2." 1965. 1, 15.

Festival of Family Classics. 1972–1976. Animated anthology series. Produced by Arthur Rankin Jr., Jules Bass, and Mary Alice Dwyer. USA: Rankin–Bass Productions, Mushi Studios.
    "Alice in Wonderland." 1973.
    "Arabian Knights." 1973.
    "Cinderella." 1972.
    "Puss in Boots." 1972.
    "The Sleeping Beauty." 1973.
    "Snow White and the Seven Dwarfs." 1973.

The Finder. 2011–. TV series. Created by Hart Hanson. USA: Josephson Entertainment.

"A Cinderella Story." 2012. 1, 3. Directed by Adam Arkin.

The Flintstones. 1960–1966. Animated TV series. Written by Joseph Barbera and Ralph Goodman. USA: Hanna-Barbera Productions, Screen Gems Television.
 "Cinderella Stone." 1964. 5, 6.
 "Once Upon a Coward. 1963. 4, 15.

Ford Startime—TV's Finest Hour. 1959–1960. Anthology TV series. Directors various. USA: NBC-TV.
 "Cindy's Fella." 1959. Directed by Gower Champion.

The Goodies. 1970–1981. TV series. Created by Tim Brooke-Taylor, Graeme Garden, and Bill Oddie. UK: BBC, London Weekend Television.
 "The Goodies and the Beanstalk." 1973. 4, 4. Directed by Jim Franklin.
 "Snow White 2." 1981.

Goodyear Television Playhouse. 1951–1957. Anthology live telecast series. USA: Showcase Productions, NBC.
 "Backwoods Cinderella." 1957. 6, 14.
 "Her Prince Charming." 1953. 2, 16. Directed by Delbert Mann.

The Hanna-Barbera New Cartoon Series. 1962–1963. Animated TV series. USA: Hanna-Barbera Productions.
 "Aladdin's Lampoon." 1963.
 "Aliblabber and the Forty Thieves." 1963.
 "Little Red Riding Gator." 1962.
 "Red Riding Hoodlum." 1963.
 "A Thousand and One Frights." 1962.

The Harveytoons Show. 1950–1962. Animated anthology series. USA: Famous Studios.
 The proper bibliographic documentation for *Harveytoons* is difficult because the program consisted of various shorts sourced from a number of Harvey comics' characters, which have been syndicated and reaired on various networks and rereleased in recombined sets since. Characters included Little Audrey, Casper the Friendly Ghost, Tommy Tortoise and Moe Hare, Baby Huey, Herman and Katnip, and Modern Madcaps. The series also contained "toontakes," which were literally spliced from full episodes of other shows, such as those appearing on *The New Casper Show* (1963–1969).
 "Little Audrey Riding Hood."
 "Once Upon a Rhyme."
 "Puss 'n Boos."
 "Red Robbing Hood."

Hey Dude. 1989–1991. TV series. Written by David A. Litteral and Stephen Land. USA: Cinetel Productions.
 "Goldilocks." 1989. 1, 3. Directed by Frederick King Keller.
 "Hey Cinderella." 3, 2. Directed by Ross K. Bagwell, Jr.

The Jetsons. 1985–1987. Animated TV series. Produced by William Hanna and Joseph Barbera. USA: Hanna-Barbera Productions, World Vision Enterprises.
 "Elroy in Wonderland." 1985. 2, 21. Directed by Arthur Davis, Oscar Dufau, Carl Urbano, Rudy Zamora, Alan Zaslove, and Ray Patterson.

Joe Millionaire. 2003. Reality TV series. Produced by Chris Cowan and Jean-Michel Michenaud. USA: Rocket Science Laboratories.
 Unspecified episodes.

Keeping Up with the Kardashians. 2007–. Reality TV series. Created by Ryan Seacrest and Eliot Goldberg. USA: Bunim-Murray Productions.
    "Cinderella Story." 2009. 3, 6. Directed by Chris Ray.
    "Kim's Fairy Tale Wedding: A Kardashian Event—Part 1." 2011. 6, 14.
    "Kim's Fairy Tale Wedding: A Kardashian Event—Part 2." 2011. 6, 15.

The Kids in the Hall. 1988–1994. Variety TV series. Various directors. Canada: CBC. Unspecified episodes.

Kingswood Country. 1980–1984. TV series. Created by Gary Reilly and Tony Sattler. Australia: 7 Network, RS Productions.
    "Snow White and the Seven Jockies." 1984. 6, 7.

Kraft Television Theatre. 1947–1958. Anthology TV series. Directors various, including George Roy Hill, Fielder Cook, and Sidney Lumet. USA: J. Walter Thompson Agency, NBC.
    "Alice in Wonderland." 1954. 7, 36. Directed by Maury Holland.
    "Hansel and Gretel." 1948. 2, 14. Conducted by Sam Morgenstern.
    "A Kiss for Cinderella." 1952. 6, 3.
    "The Tale of the Wolf." 1951. 5, 1. Adapted by Hans Barstch.

Johnny Bravo. 1997–2004. Animated TV series. Created by Van Partible. USA: Cartoon Network.
    "Dental Hijinks/Little Red Riding Johnny/Pouch Potato." 2000. 3, 7. Directed by Kirk Tingblad.
    "The Hansel and Gretel Witch Project/I. Q. Johnny/Get Stinky." 2002. 3, 18. Directed by Kirk Tingblad.
    "Karma Krisis/A Star Is Bruised/The Prince and the Pinhead." 1999. 2, 3. Directed by Kirk Tingblad.

L.A. Law. 1986–1994. TV series. Created by Steven Bochco and Terry Louise Fisher. USA: 20th Century Fox, NBC.
    "Beauty and the Breast." 1992. 6, 20. Directed by Tom Moore.
    "Beauty and Obese." 1987. 2, 13. Directed by Sam Weisman.
    "The Brothers Grimm." 1987. 2, 5. Directed by Michael Zinberg.
    "Goldilocks and the Three Barristers." 1987. 2, 8. Directed by Rick Wallace.
    "The Princess and the Pee." 1988. 3, 5. Directed by Sam Weisman.
    "The Princess and the Wiener King." 1986. 1, 4. Directed by Shannon Miller.

Life Goes On. 1989–1993. TV series. Created by Michael Braverman. USA: ABC.
    "The Fairy Tale." 1992. 3, 17. Directed by Michael Lange.

Live from Lincoln Center. 1976–. Live telecast. USA: Lincoln Center for the Performing Arts.
    "American Ballet Theatre: The Sleeping Beauty." 1979. 4, 6.
    "New York City Opera: Cinderella." 1980. 6, 3.
    "New York City Opera: The Magic Flute." 1987. 12, 5. Directed by Kirk Browning.

Live from the Metropolitan Opera. 1977–. Live telecast. USA: WNET, PBS.
    "Arabella." 1994. Directed by Brian Large.
    "Hansel and Gretel." 1982. Directed by Kirk Browning.
    "La Cenerentola." 1997. Directed by Brian Large.

Looney Toons. 1930–1969 (original), 1987–present (revival). Animated TV series. Directors various, including Tex Avery, Friz Freleng, Ub Iwerks, and Alex Lovy. USA: Warner Bros. Production.
    "A Bear for Punishment." 1951. Directed by Charles M. Jones.
    "A Gander at Mother Goose." 1940. Directed by Tex Avery.
    "A-Lad-in Baghdad." 1938. Directed by Cal Howard and Cal Dalton.

"A-Lad-in His Lamp." 1948. Directed by Robert McKimson.
"Ali Baba Bound." 1940. Directed by Bob Clampett.
"Ali Baba Bunny." 1957. Directed by Chuck Jones.
"Beanstalk Bunny." 1955. Directed by Charles M. Jones.
"The Bear's Tale." 1940. Directed by Tex Avery.
"Beauty and the Beast." 1934. Directed by Friz Freleng.
"Bewitched Bunny." 1954. Directed by Chuck Jones.
"Birdy and the Beast." 1944. Directed by Bob Clampett.
"Bugs Bunny and the Three Bears." 1944. Directed by Chuck Jones.
"Bye, Bye, Bluebeard." 1949. Directed by Arthur Davis.
"Cinderella Meets Fella." 1938. Directed by Tex Avery.
"Coal Black and de Sebben Dwarfs." 1943. Directed by Bob Clampett.
"Foney Fables." 1942. Directed by Friz Freleng.
"The Foxy Duckling." 1947. Directed by Arthur Davis.
"Goldilocks and the Jivin' Bears." 1944. Directed by Friz Freleng.
"Goldimouse and the Three Cats." 1960. Directed by Friz Freleng.
"Harabian Nights." 1959. Directed by Ken Harris.
"Jack Wabbit and the Beanstalk." 1943. Directed by Friz Freleng.
"Little Red Riding Rabbit." 1944. Directed by Friz Freleng.
"Little Red Rodent Hood." 1952. Directed by Friz Freleng.
"Little Red Walking Hood." 1937. Directed by Friz Freleng.
"Lumber Jack-Rabbit." 1953. Directed by Charles M. Jones.
"Paying the Piper." 1949. Directed by Robert McKimson.
"Pied Piper Porky." 1939. Directed by Bob Clampett.
"Porky the Giant Killer." 1939. Directed by Cal Dalton and Ben Hardaway.
"Puss 'n Booty." 1943. Directed by Frank Tashlin.
"Red Riding Hoodwinked." 1955. Directed by Friz Freleng.
"Señorella and the Glass Huarache." 1964. Directed by Hawley Pratt.
"Three Little Bops." 1957. Directed by Friz Freleng.
"Tom Thumb in Trouble." 1940. Directed by Chuck Jones.
"The Trial of Mr. Wolf." 1941. Directed by Friz Freleng.
"The Turn-Tale Wolf." 1952. Directed by Robert McKimson.
"Tweety and the Beanstalk." 1957. Directed by Friz Freleng.

MadTV. 1995–2009. Variety TV series. Created by Fax Bahr and Adam Small. USA: Quincy Jones–David Salzman Entertainment Inc.
"Wizard of Oz Deleted Scene: The Runaway Slave." 13, 1.

Magic Mansion. 1965–1967. TV series. Created by Captain Warren Chaney, Sgt. James Mortensen, and Sgt. David Castle. USA: Armed Forces Radio and Television Broadcast.
"The Lamp of Aladdin." 1967. 2, 16.
"The Magic Genii." 1966. 1, 19.
"Over the Rainbow." 1967. 2, 18.
"Snow White." 1967. 3, 3.
"The Wicked Witch of the East." 1966. 1, 38.

Make Room for Daddy. 1953–1965. TV series. Created by Melville Shavelson. USA: Marterto Productions.
Unspecified episodes.

Martin. 1992–1997. TV series. Created by Martin Lawrence, John Bowman, and Topper Carew. USA: HBO.
"Snow White." 1996. 5, 8.

Medium. 2005–2011. TV series. Created by Glenn Gordon Caron. USA: Picture Maker Productions.

> "The Night of the Wolf." 2005. 1, 4. Directed by Artie Mandelberg.

Merlin. 2008–2013. TV series. Created by Julian Jones, Jake Michie, Johnny Capps, and Julian Murphy. UK: BBC Worldwide.

> "Beauty and the Beast (Part 1)." 2009. 2, 5. Directed by David Moore.
> "Beauty and the Beast (Part 2)." 2009. 2, 6. Directed by Metin Huseyin.
> "The Beginning of the End." 2008. 1, 8. Directed by Jeremy Webb.
> "Behind the Magic." 2009. DVD. 1, Special Features.
> "Commentary." 2009. DVD. 1, 1.
> "The Dragon's Call." 2008. 1, 1. Directed by James Hawes.
> "Excalibur." 2008. 1, 9. Directed by Jeremy Webb.
> "The Gates of Avalon." 2008. 1, 7. Directed by Jeremy Webb.
> "Lancelot and Guinevere." 2009. 2, 4. Directed by David Moore.
> "Le Morte d'Arthur." 2008. 1, 10. Directed by David Moore.
> "The Making of Merlin." 2011. DVD. 2, Special Features.
> "The Moment of Truth." 2008. 1, 10. Directed by David Moore.
> "The Poisoned Chalice." 2008. 1, 4. Directed by Ed Fraiman.
> "Queen of Hearts." 2010. 3, 10. Directed by Ashley Way.
> "The Sword in The Stone." 2012. 4, episodes 12 and 13. Directed by Alice Troughton.
> "Valiant." 2008. 1, 2. Directed by James Hawes.
> "The Wicked Day." 2012. 4, 3. Directed by Alice Troughton.

Millionaire Matchmaker. 2007–. Reality TV series. USA: Intuitive Entertainment, Bayonne Entertainment.

> "Cinderella and Moondoggie Walk into a Bar." 2010. 4, 6.

More to Love. 2009. Reality TV series. Created by Mike Fleiss. USA: Next Entertainment.

> 1, 1. 2009. Directed by Mike Fleiss.
> 1, 3. 2009. Directed by Mike Fleiss.
> 1, 4. 2009. Directed by Mike Fleiss.

Muppet Babies. 1984–1991. Animated TV series. USA: Marvel Productions, Jim Henson Company.

> "Beauty and the Schnoz." 1988. 5, 2.
> "Kermit Pan." 1990. 7, 12."
> "Muppet Goose." 1986. 3, 13.
> "Once Upon an Egg Timer." 1985. 2, 1.
> "The Pig Who Would Be Queen." 1988. 5, 5.
> "Pigerella." 1986. 3, 1.
> "Puss 'n Boots 'n Babies." 1990. 7, 5.
> "Slipping Beauty." 1988. 5, 4.
> "Snow White and the Seven Muppets." 1985. 2, 6.
> "When You Wish upon a Muppet." 1985. 2, 13.

The Muppet Show. 1976–1981. TV series. Created by Jim Henson. USA, UK: ATV, ITC Entertainment, Disney–ABC Domestic Television.

> Unspecified episodes.

Murder, She Wrote. 1984–1996. TV series. Created by Peter S. Fischer, Richard Levinson, and William Link. USA: Corymore Productions, Universal TV.

> "Ever After." 1992. 6, 16. Directed by Anthony Pullen Shaw.
> "Mirror, Mirror on the Wall: Part 1." 1989. 5, 21. Directed by Walter Grauman.

"Mirror, Mirror on the Wall: Part 2." 1989. 5, 22. Directed by Walter Grauman.
"Murder through the Looking Glass." 1988. 4, 16. Directed by Seymour Robbie.
"Night of the Headless Horseman." 1987. 3, 11. Directed by Walter Grauman.
"Snow White, Blood Red." 1988. 5, 4. Directed by Vincent McEveety.
"We're off to Kill the Wizard." 1984. 1, 8. Directed by Walter Grauman.

The Nanny. 1993–1999. TV series. Created by Peter Marc Jacobson and Fran Drescher. USA: CBS.
Unspecified episodes.

Night Heat. 1985–1989. TV series. Created by Don Flynn. Canada, USA: Alliance Entertainment.
"Snow White." 1985. 1, 18. Directed by Mario Azzopardi.

Northern Exposure. 1990–1995. TV series. Created by Joshua Brand and John Falsey. USA: Cine-Nevada Productions, Universal Television.
"Aurora Borealis: A Fairy Tale for Big People." 1990. 1, 8. Directed by Peter O'Fallon.

The O.C. 2003–2007. TV series. Created by Josh Schwartz. USA: Wonderland Sound and Vision.
"The Brothers Grim." 2005. 2, 17. Directed by Michael Lange.
"The Sleeping Beauty." 2006. 3, 4. Directed by Ian Toynton.

Oh Baby. 1998–2000. TV series. Created by Susan Beavers. USA: Columbia TriStar Television.
"Cinderella." 2000. 2, 15.

One Tree Hill. 2003–. TV series. Created by Mark Schwahn. USA: Mastermind Laboratories.
"Even Fairy Tale Characters Would Be Jealous." 2008. 6, 10. Directed by Janice Cooke.

Out of the Inkwell. 1962–1963. Animated anthology series. Directed and produced by Hal Seeger. USA: Seven Arts Associated.
"Bluebeard's Treasure." 1962.
"Mean Moe's Fairy Tale." 1963.
"The Sleeping Beauty." 1963.

The Paper Chase. 1978–1979, 1983–1986. TV series. Directed by Joseph Pevney. USA: CBS.
"Cinderella." 1983. 2, 4.

Popeye the Sailor. 1960–1963. Animated TV series. Produced by Al Brodax. USA: King Features Syndicate.
"Little Olive Riding Hood." 1960. 1, 71. Directed by Jack Kinney.

Producers' Showcase. 1954–1957. Anthology live telecast series. Various directors. USA: Showcase Productions, NBC.
"Cinderella." 1957. 3, 10. Directed by Clark Jones.
"Jack and the Beanstalk." 1956. 3, 3. Directed by Clark Jones.
"Peter Pan." 1955. 1, 7. Directed by Clark Jones.
"Peter Pan." 1956. 2, 5. Directed by Clark Jones.
"The Sleeping Beauty." 1956. 2, 4. Directed by Clark Jones.

Rainbow. 1972–1992. Children's TV series. Created by Pamela Lonsdale. UK: Teddington Studios, Thames Television, Tetra Films, ITV Network.
"Jack and the Beanstalk." 9, 65.
"Rumpelstiltskin." 16, 46.
"Traditional Tales: Babes in the Wood." 9, 67.
"Traditional Tales: Cinderella." 9, 68.
"Traditional Tales: Goldilocks." 9, 66.

"Traditional Tales: Little Red Riding Hood." 9, 69.

The Riches. 2007–2008. TV series. Created by Dmitry Lipkin. USA: Maverick Television. "Cinderella." 2007. 1, 8. Directed by Matt Shakman.

Robot Chicken. 2005–. Animated TV series. Created by Seth Green, Matthew Senrei, and Mike Fasolo. USA: Stoopid Buddy Stoodios.

The Rocky and Bullwinkle Show. 1959–1964. Animated TV series. Created by Jay Ward, Alex Anderson, and Bill Scott. USA: Jay Ward Productions, ABC, NBC.

> As an anthology series where the "main storyline of each episode . . . was intersected by brief (usually 3½ minutes) mini-episodes of six component series," we have opted to list the titles *without* the individual airdates of the individual segments, except when they are cited in a chapter (Steinle 2001, 122).

Fractured Fairy Tales:

"The Absent-Minded King."

"Aladdin."

"Aladdin and His Lamp."

"Aladdin's Friendly Lamp-o-Rama." 1961. 2, 25.

"Beauty and the Beast."

"Booty and the Beast."

"The Brave Little Tailor."

"Cinderella." 1960. 1, 15.

"Cinderella; Elves and Shoemaker."

"Cinderella Returns." 1960. 2, 8.

"Cutie and the Bird."

"Dancing Cinderella."

"Dick Whittington's Cat."

"Enchanted Fish."

"The Enchanted Fly Felicia and the Pot of Pinks."

"The Enchanted Frog."

"The Enchanted Gnat."

"Fee Fi Fo Fum."

"The Fisherman and His Wife."

"The Frog Prince."

"The Giant and the Beanstalk."

"The Golden Goose."

"Goldilocks."

"Goldilocks and the Three Bears."

"The Goose That Laid a Golden Egg."

"Hans Clinker."

"Hansel and Gretel."

"Jack and the Beanstalk."

"Jack B. Nimble."

"John's Ogre Wife."

"The King and the Witch."

"Leaping Beauty." 1961. 2, 19.

"The Little Man in the Boat."

"The Little Princess."

"Little Red Riding Hood."

"The Little Tinker."

"The Magic Chicken."

"The Magic Lichee Nut."

"The Magical Fish."
"The Mysterious Castle."
"Pied Piper 1."
"Pied Piper 2."
"Pinocchio."
"Potter's Luck."
"The Prince and the Popper."
"Prince Darling."
"Prince Hyacinth and Dear Princess."
"The Princess and the Pea."
"The Princess of Goblins."
"Puss and Boots 1."
"Puss and Boots 2."
"Rapunzel."
"Red White." 1962. 4, 1.
"Red's Riding Hood." 1960. 1, 26.
"Riding Hoods Anonymous." 1960. 2, 5.
"Rumpelstiltskin." 1960. 1, 8.
"Rumpelstiltskin Returns." 1961. 2, 18.
"The Seven Chickens."
"Sir Galahad or the Tomorrow Night."
"Sleeping Beauty." 1960. 1, 24.
"Slipping Beauty."
"Slow White and Nose Red."
"Snow White." 1960. 1, 22.
"Snow White, Inc."
"Snow White Meets Rapunzel."
"Son of Beauty and the Beast."
"Son of King Midas."
"Son of Rumpelstiltskin."
"Son of Snow White."
"Speeding Beauty."
"Sweeping Beauty 1."
"Sweeping Beauty 2."
"Sweet Little Beat."
"The Tale of a King Peter and the Three Pennies."
"The Teeth of Baghdad."
"The Thirteen Helmets."
"Thom Tum."
"The Three Bears."
"The Three Little Pigs 1."
"Tom Thumb 1."
"Tom Thumb 2."
"The Ugly Almond Duckling."
"The Ugly Duckling." 1960. 2, 6.
"The Wishing Hat."
"The Witch's Broom."

Rocky and His Friends. 1959–1961. Animated TV series. USA: Jay Ward Productions (ABC) (see The Rocky and Bullwinkle Show).

The Rosemary Clooney Show. 1956–1957. Variety TV series. USA: Michigan TV.

"The Little Red Riding Hood." 1957. 1, 29.

Rugrats. 1991–2004. Animated TV series. Created by Gabor Csupo, Paul Germain, and Arlene Klasky. USA: Nickelodeon.
"Rugrats Tales from the Crib: Snow White." 2006. 10, 1.
"Rugrats Tales from the Crib: Three Jacks and a Beanstalk." 2006. 10, 2.

The Runaways. 1978–1979. TV series. Directed by Kenneth Gilbert and Jeffrey Hayden. USA: Quinn Martin Productions.
"No Prince for My Cinderella." 1978. 1, 1. Directed by William Wiard.

Salute Your Shorts. 1991–1992. TV series. Created by Steve Slavkin. USA: Propaganda Films.
"Cinderella Play." 1991. 1, 10. Directed by Jay Dubin.

Saturday Night Live. 1975–. Variety TV series. Created by Lorne Michaels. USA: NBC.
"Beauty and the Beast." October 17, 2009. Guest starring Gerard Butler.
"Beauty and the Beast: The Double Date." November 12, 1988. Guest starring Demi Moore.
"Below the Waves." May 7, 2011. Guest starring Tina Fey.
"The Essentials." November 20, 2010. Guest starring Anne Hathaway.
"Hook's Revenge." March 1, 2008. Guest starring Ellen Page.
"The Incredible Man." February 16, 1980. Guest starring Elliott Gould.
"The Little Mermaid." September 29, 2001. Guest starring Reece Witherspoon.
"The Mad Tea Party." April 4, 1998. Guest starring Steve Buscemi.
"The Real Housewives of Disney." March 3, 2012. Guest starring Lindsay Lohan.
"Up Close with Geppetto." April 15, 2000. Guest starring Tobey Maguire.

Saved by the Bell. 1989–1993. TV series. Created by Sam Bobrick. USA: NBC, Peter Engel Productions.
"Snow White and the Seven Dorks." 1992. 4, 20.

Sesame Street. 1969–present. Educational TV series. Created by Joan Ganz Cooney. USA: CTW, PBS.
There are more to list here, but many instances are individual segments embedded within entire episodes. See, for example, the direct-to-video release of *Silly Storytime* (2011). The show's daily "newsflash" segments (which often feature fairy-tale characters) are spliced throughout the film. With a history that spans forty years of broadcasting, a more thorough examination of the series is necessary.
"Big Bad Wolf Huffs and Puffs Slimey." 2011. 42, 10.
"Cinderella's Fairy Godmother's Mistake." 2004. 35, 5.
"Elmo in Numberland." 1990. 21, 118.
"Fairy Tale Emergencies." 2007. 38, 11.
"Jack Grows His Own Beanstalk." 2010. 40, 25.
"The Prince and the Penguin." 2010. 40, 26.
"A Prince of a Frog." 2011. 42, 17.
"Sesame Street Fairy Tale Science Fair." 41, 21.
"Snow White's Meltdown." 2006. 37, 6.
"Who'll Replace the Big Bad Wolf?" 2005. 36, 13.

Sherlock. 2010–. TV series. Created by Mark Gatiss and Steven Moffat. UK: BBC Wales.
"The Reichenbach Fall." 2012. 2, 3.

The Simpsons. 1989–. Animated TV series. Created by Matt Groening. USA: Gracie Films.
"Four Great Women and a Manicure." 2009. 20, 20. Directed by Raymond S. Persi.
"Once Upon a Time in Springfield." 2010. 21, 10. Directed by Matthew Nastuk.

"Treehouse of Horror XI: Scary Tales Can Come True." 2012. 12, 1. Directed by Matthew Nastuk.

"When You Wish upon a Star." 1998. 10, 5. Directed by Pete Michels.

Smash. 2012. TV series. Created by Theresa Rebeck. USA: Madwoman in the Attic, Inc.

"Publicity." 1, 12. Directed by Michael Mayer.

Strong Medicine. 2000–2006. TV series. Created by Tammy Ader. USA: Sony Pictures Television.

"Cinderella in Scrubs." 2004. 5, 12. Directed by John Perrin Flynn.

Studio 57. 1954–1956. Anthology TV series. Directors various. USA: DuMont Television Network, Revue Productions.

"Mr. Cinderella." 1956. 3, 11.

Superboy. 1988–1992. TV series. Created by Jerry Siegel and Joe Shuster. USA: DC Comics, CBS.

"The Beast and Beauty." 1988. 1, 7. Directed by Jackie Cooper.

Supernatural. 2005–. TV series. Created by Eric Kripke. USA: Wonderland Sound and Vision.

"Bedtime Stories." 2007. 3, 5. Directed by Mike Rohl.

Taking the Stage. 2009–. Reality TV series. Created by Nick Lachey and Colton Gramm. USA: MTV.

"A Cinderella Story." 2009. 1, 6. Directed by Rob Bruce and Morgan J. Freeman.

Tales from the Crypt. 1989–1996. TV series. Created by William Gaines. USA: HBO.

"The Third Pig." 1996. 7, 13. Directed by Bill Kopp.

Tales from the Cryptkeeper. 1994–1999. Animated TV series. Created by Libby Hinson and Ben Joseph. Canada, USA: Nelvana, ABC, CBS.

"The Brothers Gruff." 1994. 2, 22.

"Sleeping Beauty." 1993. 1, 6.

Thirtysomething. 1987–1991. TV series. Created by Edward Zwick and Marshall Herskovitz. USA: Bedford Falls Productions, MGM Television.

"Chuck (and Melvin) and the Beanstalker." 2, 25.

"Melissa in Wonderland." 1991. 4, 22. Directed by Ellen S. Pressman.

"Once a Mermaid." 1990. 3, 14. Directed by Ellen S. Pressman.

Tiny Toon Adventures. 1990–1995. Animated TV series. Created by Tom Ruegger. USA: Amblin Entertainment.

"Buster and the Wolverine." 1990. 1, 25. [Peter and the Wolf]

"Fairy Tales for the 90's." 1990. 1, 49. [Pinocchio and Goldilocks]

"Toon Physics." 1991. 2, 6. ["Once Upon a Star"]

Too Close for Comfort. 1980–1986. TV series. Created by Brian Cooke. USA: D. L. Taffner Productions.

"Cinderella Update." 1984. 4, 22. Directed by Lee Lochhead.

"The Prince and the Frog." 1981. 2, 4. Directed by Lee Lochhead.

"Who's Afraid of the Big Bad Wolfe." 1980. 1, 7. Directed by Howard Storm.

True Blood. 2008–. TV series. Created by Alan Ball. USA: HBO.

"And When I Die." 2011. 4, 12. Directed by Scott Winant.

Walt Disney's Wonderful World of Color. 1954–1990. Anthology TV series. Directors various. USA: ABC.

"Alice in Wonderland." 1954. 1, 2. Directed by Bill Walsh.

"From Aesop to Hans Christian Andersen." 1955. 1, 19.

"The Truth about Mother Goose." 1963. 10, 7.

The Wednesday Play. 1964–1970. Anthology teleplay series. Created by Sidney Newman. UK: BBC.
> "The Wednesday Play." 1965. Directed by Gareth Davies.

Who Wants to Marry a Multi-Millionaire? 2000. Reality TV game show. Directed by Don Weiner. USA: Twentieth Century Fox.
> Unspecified episodes.

Wildfire. 2005–2008. TV series. Created by Michael Piller and Christopher Teague. USA: Lions Gate Television.
> "Fairy Tale Endings." 2007. 3, 1. Directed by Bradford May.

Wonder Woman. 1976–1979. TV series. Created by William M. Marston. USA: Warner Bros. Television, ABC, CBS.
> "The Pied Piper." 1977. 2, 6. Directed by Alan Crosland.

The Wonder Years. 1988–1993. TV series. Created by Neal Marlens and Carol Black. USA: New World Television, ABC.
> "Alice in Autoland." 6, 12. 1993. Directed by Arthur Albert.

The Worst Witch. 1998–2001. TV series. Directed by Andrew Morgan and Alex Kirby. Canada: Canada Television and Cable Production Fund License Program.
> "Cinderella in Boots." 2000. 3, 8. Directed by Andrew Morgan.

Xena: Warrior Princess. 1995–2001. TV series. Created by John Schulian and Robert G. Tapert. USA: MCA Television.
> "If the Shoe Still Fits. . . ." 1999. 4, 12. Directed by Josh Becker.

TV Specials, Live Performances

Aladdin. 1967. TV special. Directed by Bill Hitchcock. USA: CBS.

Aladdin. 2000. Teleplay. Directed by Geoff Posner. UK: Independent Television.

Alice. 1946. TV short. Directed by George O'Ferrall. UK: BBC.

Alice at the Palace. 1982. Teleplay. Directed by Emile Ardolino. USA: New York Shakespeare Festival Company.

Alice in Wonderland. 1937. TV short. Directed by George O'Ferrall. UK: BBC.

Alice in Wonderland. 1982. Teleplay. Directed by John Clark Donahue and John Driver. USA: Children's Theatre Company.

Alice in Wonderland. 1983. Live Broadway telecast. Directed by Kirk Browning. USA: PBS Great Performances.

The Bachelorette: Ashley and J. P.'s Wedding. 2012. Reality TV special. Created by Mike Fleiss. USA: Next Entertainment.

Beauty. 2004. Teleplay. Directed by Ben Bolt. UK: Thames Television.

Cinderella. 1957. TV special. Directed by Ralph Nelson. Performed by Julie Andrews. USA: CBS.

Cinderella. 1965. TV special. Directed by Charles S. Dubin. Performed by Lesley Ann Warren. USA: CBS.

Cinderella. 1997. TV special. Directed by Robert Iscove. Performed by Brandy Norwood. USA: Brownhouse Productions.

Cinderella. 2000. Teleplay. Directed by Liddy Oldroyd. UK: Wishbone Productions.

Cinderella: A Ballet by Sergei Prokofiev. 1989. Live ballet telecast. Directed by Maguy Marin. France: RM Arts Associated, Lyon Opera Ballet.

Cinderella Frozen in Time. 1994. Ice Capades TV special. Directed by Sterling Johnson. USA: Dorothy Hamill International, ABC.

Cinderelmo. 1999. TV special. Directed by Bruce Leddy. USA: CTW.

A Dream Is a Wish Your Heart Makes: The Annette Funicello Story. 1995. Teleplay. Directed by Bill Corcoran. USA: CBS.

A Dream of Alice. 1982. TV special. Produced by Yvonne Littlewood. UK: BBC.

The Emperor's New Clothes. 1972. TV special. Directed by Jules Bass. USA: ABC, Rankin–Bass Productions.

Goldilocks. 1970. TV special. Directed by Marc Breaux. USA: DePatie-Freleng Enterprises, NBC.

Hansel and Gretel. 1937. TV musical. Produced by Stephen Thomas. UK: BBC.

Hansel and Gretel. 1982. TV special. Directed by Tim Burton. USA: Walt Disney Studios.

Hansel and Gretel. 2008. TV opera. Directed by Sue Judd. UK: Royal Opera House Covent Garden, BBC.

Hey Cinderella! 1969. TV special. Directed by Jim Henson. USA: CBS.

Jack and the Beanstalk. 1966. TV special. Directed by Nick Havinga. USA: CBS, Prince Street Productions.

Little Claus & Big Claus. 2005. TV special. Directed by James Ricker. Canada: Portara Pictures.

Maurice Bejart's The Nutcracker. 2000. TV ballet special. Directed by Ross MacGibbon. Bolivia, France: Theatre Musical de Paris.

The Muppets' Wizard of Oz. 2005. TV special. Directed by Kirk R. Thatcher. USA: Jim Henson Company, ABC.

The Nightingale. 1987. Directed by Rick Morrison. Canada, China: Atkinson Film Arts.

The Nutcracker. 1968. TV ballet special. Directed by John Vernon. UK: Covent Garden Pioneer FSP, the Royal Ballet, and Kultur Video.

Once Upon a Mattress. 1964. TV special. Directed by Joe Layton and Dave Geisel. Performed by Carol Burnett, Jack Gilford, and Joe Bova. USA: CBS.

Once Upon a Mattress. 1972. TV special. Directed by Ron Field and Dave Powers. Performed by Carol Burnett, Jack Gilford, Jane White, Bernadette Peters, Ken Berry, and Wally Cox. USA: CBS.

Once Upon a Mattress. 2005. TV special. Directed by Kathleen Marshall. Performed by Carol Burnett, Denis O'Hare, Tom Smothers, Tracy Ellman, Zooey Deschanel, and Matthew Morrison. USA: ABC, Disney, Touchstone Television.

Peter Pan. 1960. Live musical telecast. Directed and choreographed by Jerome Robbins. USA: NBC.

Peter Pan. 1976. TV special. Directed by Dwight Hemlon. USA: NBC.

The Pied Piper of Hamelin. 1957. TV special. Directed by Bretaigne Windust. USA: NBC.

Pinocchio. 1957. TV special. Directed by Hanya Holm. USA: NBC.

Pinocchio's Christmas. 1980. Animated TV special. Directed by Jules Bass and Arthur Rankin Jr. USA: NBC.

Prokofiev's Cinderella. 1957. TV ballet special. Directed by Clark Jones. USA: NBC, Sadler's Wells Company.

Return to Oz. 1964. Animated TV special. Directed by F. R. Crawley, Thomas Glynn, and Larry Roemer. USA: Rankin–Bass Productions, Crawley Films.

Rudolph's Shiny New Year. 1976. Animated TV special. Directed by Jules Bass and Arthur Rankin Jr. USA: Rankin–Bass Productions.

Rumpelstiltskin. 1985. Animated TV special. Directed by Pino Van Lamsweerde. Canada: Atkinson Film Arts.

Scooby-Doo! in Arabian Nights. 1994. Animated TV special. Directed by Jun Falkenstein and Joanna Romersa. USA: Hanna-Barbera Productions.

The Tin Soldier. 1986. Directed by Chris Schouten. Canada: Atkinson Film Arts.

Who Wants to Marry a Multi-Millionaire? 2000. Reality TV game show special. Created by Mike Fleiss. Directed by Don Weiner. USA: Next Entertainment.

TV Series, Miniseries, and Educational TV Series

The 10th Kingdom. 2000. TV miniseries. Directed by David Carson and Herbert Wise. UK, USA, Germany: Babelsberg Film und Fernsehen, Carnival Films, Hallmark Entertainment.

Adventures in Wonderland. 1991–1995. TV series. Directed by Gary Halvorson. USA: Walt Disney Television.

The Adventures of Sinbad. 1996–1998. TV series. Created by Ed Naha. Canada: Alliance Atlantis.

Akazukin Chacha. 1994–1995. TV series. Directed by Tsuji Shoki. Japan: TV Tokyo, Nihon Ad Systems, Studio Gallop.

Alice. 2009. TV miniseries. Directed by Nick Willing. Canada, UK: Reunion Pictures, RHI Entertainment.

Alice in Wonderland. 1986. TV miniseries. Directed by Barry Letts. UK: BBC.

The Amazing Tales of Hans Christian Andersen. 1954. TV series. Directors various. UK: Scandinavian American Television.

Andersen Monogatari [Andersen Stories]. 1971. TV series. Directed by Hata Masami. Japan: Mushi Productions.

Arabela. 1979. TV series. Directed by Václav Vorlícek. Czechoslovakia: Ceskoslovenská Televize, Westdeutscher Rundfunk.

Arabian Nights. 2000. TV miniseries. Directed by Steve Barron. USA, Germany: RTL Television, Babelsberg International Filmproduktion, Hallmark Entertainment.

Arabian Nights: The Adventures of Sinbad. 1975–1976. Anime TV series. Directed by Fumio Kurokawa and Kunihiko Okazaki. Japan: Nippon Animation, Zweites Deutsches Fernsehen.

Beauty and the Beast. 1987–1990. TV series. Created by Ron Koslow. USA: Witt–Thomas Production, Republic Pictures.

Beauty and the Beast. 2012–. TV series. Directed by Gary Fleder. USA: CBS, CW Television Network.

Beauty and the Geek. 2005–2008. Reality TV game show. Created by Ashton Kutcher. USA: Twentieth Century Fox.

Bewitched. 1964–1972. TV series. Created by Sol Saks. USA: Ashmont Productions, Screen Gems Television, ABC.
> "Hansel and Gretel in Samanthaland." 1971. 8, 10. Directed by Richard Michaels.

Bishōjo Senshi Sailor Moon [Pretty Soldier Sailor Moon]. TV series. 1992–1997. Directed by Satō Jun'ichi et al. Japan: Toei Animation.
> "Mezame yo Nemureru Bishoujō! Mamoru no Kunoū." 2, 22. Directed by Satō Jun'ichi and Ikuhara Kunihiko.
> "Umino no Kesshin! Naru-chan wa Boku ga Mamoru." 1, 32. Directed by Satō Jun'ichi.
> "Waizuman no Mashu! Chibiusa Shōmetsu." 2, 37. Directed by Satō Jun'ichi and Ikuhara Kunihiko.

The Box of Delights. 1984. TV miniseries. Directed by Renny Rye. UK: BBC.

Camelot. 2011. Directed by Mikael Salomon, Stefan Schwartz, Ciaran Donnelly, and Jeremy Podeswa. Canada: CBC.

Captain Kangaroo: Fairy Tales and Funny Stories. 1985. Children's TV series. Created by Bob Keeshan. Chicago: CBS.

Carosello. 1957–1977. TV series. Italy: RAI.
> "Calimero da Papero Piero." 1969.

"Calimero, il pulcino nero." 1963.
"L'infallibile ispettore Rock." 1961.
"Matrimonio misto." 1960.
"Penne Rosse." 1958.

Charmed. 1998–2006. TV series. Created by Constance M. Burge. USA: Spelling Television.

    "Happily Ever After." 2003. 5, 3. Directed by John T. Tretchmer.
    "Malice in Wonderland." 2005. 8, 2. Directed by Mel Damski.
    "Once Upon a Time." 2000. 3, 3. Directed by Joel J. Feigenbaum.
    "Prince Charmed." 2004. 6, 12. Directed by David Jackson.
    "We're off to See the Wizard." 2002. 4, 19. Directed by Timothy J. Lonsdale.

The Charmings. 1987–1988. TV series. Created by Prudence Fraser and Robert Sternin. USA: Embassy Television, ABC.

Cinderella's Sister. 2010–. TV series. Directed by Kim Yeong-Jo. South Korea: Korean Broadcasting System.

Dollhouse. 2009–2010. TV series. Created by Joss Whedon. USA: Twentieth Century Fox Film Corporation.

    "Briar Rose." 2009. 1, 11. Directed by Joss Whedon.
    "Ghost." 2009. 1, 1. Directed by Joss Whedon.
    "Haunted." 2009. 1, 10. Directed by Elodie Keene.
    "Man on the Street." 2009. 1, 6. Directed by David Straiton.
    "Needs." 2009. 1, 8. Directed by Felix Alcalá.
    "The Target." 2009. 1, 2. Directed by Steven S. DeKnight.

Dragon Ball. 1986, 2001–2003. Animated TV series. Directed by Nishio Daisuke. Japan: Blue Water Studios.

Drawn Together. 2004–2008. Animated TV series. Created by Matthew Silverstein and Dave Jeser. USA: Comedy Central, MTV, Polybrand.

Faerie Tale Theatre. 1982–1987. TV series. Created by Shelley Duvall. USA: Gaylord Productions.

    "Little Red Riding Hood." 1983. 2, 5. Directed by Graeme Clifford.
    "Snow White and the Seven Dwarfs." 1984. 3, 5. Directed by Peter Medak.

Fairy Tale. 2003. TV series documentary. Directed and produced by Naomi and Jonathan Hiltz. Canada: Hiltz Squared Media Group, PrideVision.

Fairy Tales. 2008. TV miniseries. Directors various, including Catherine Morshead and Peter Lydon. UK: Hat Trick Productions, BBC Northern Ireland.

The Fisherman and His Wife: A Tale from the Brothers Grimm. 1985. Educational TV series. New Zealand: Curriculum Development Division, Minimal Produkter, Weston Woods Studios.

Garasu no Kutsu: Cinderella and the Glass Shoe. 1997. TV series. Directed by Amamiya Nozomu. Japan: NTV.

The Gingerbread Man. 1992. TV series. Created by David Wood. UK: FilmFair Production.

Grimm. 2011–. TV series. Created by Stephen Carpenter, David Greenwalt, and Jim Kouf. USA: GK Productions, NBC.

    "Bad Moon Rising." 2012. 2, 3. Directed by David Solomon.
    "Bears Will Be Bears." 2011. 1, 2. Directed by Norberto Barba.
    "BeeWare." 2011. 1, 3. Directed by Darnell Martin.
    "Big Feet." 2012. 1, 21. Directed by Omar Madha.
    "Happily Ever Aftermath." 2012. 1, 20. Directed by Terrance O'Hara.
    "Last Grimm Standing." 2012. 1, 12. Directed by Michael Watkins.
    "Leave It to Beavers." 2012. 1, 19. Directed by Holly Dale.

"Lonelyhearts." 2011. 1, 4. Directed by Michael Waxman.
"Love Sick." 2012. 1, 17. Directed by David Solomon.
"Of Mouse and Man." 2012. 1, 9. Directed by Omar Madha.
"Organ Grinder." 2012. 1, 10. Directed by Clark Mathis.
"Tarantella." 2012. 1, 11. Directed by Peter Werner.
"The Thing with Feathers." 2012. 1, 16. Directed by Darnell Martin.
"Three Coins in a Fuchsbau." 2012. 1, 13. Directed by Norberto Barba.
"Woman in Black." 2012. 1, 22. Directed by Norberto Barba.

Grimm's Fairy Tale Classics. See *Grimm Masterpiece Theatre.*

Grimm Masterpiece Theatre [Gurimu meisaku gekijō], aka, Grimm's Fairy Tale Classics. 1987–1989. TV series. Directed by Kerrigan Mahan and Saitō Hiroshi. Japan, USA: Nippon Animation–Saban Entertainment.
"Briar Rose." 1988. 1, 18. Directed by Saitō Hiroshi.

Happily Ever After: Fairy Tales for Every Child. 1995–2000. Animated anthology series. Directed by Bruce W. Smith, Anthony Bell, and Edward Bell. USA: HBO.

Hello Kitty's Furry Tale Theater. 1987. Animated TV series. Directed by Michael Maliani. USA, Japan: DiC Enterprises, MGM, UA Television, Sanrio Company, CBS.

I Dream of Jeannie. 1965–1970. TV series. Created by Sidney Sheldon. USA: Screen Gems Television.

James Marshall's Favorite Fairy Tales. 2005. Educational TV series. Created by James Marshall. USA: Weston Woods Studios, Maxwell's Collection, Scholastic Inc.

Jim Henson's Mother Goose Stories. 1997–1998. Anthology TV series. Directed by Brian Henson. USA: Jim Henson Company, Disney Channel.

Jim Henson's The StoryTeller. 1988–1991. Anthology TV series. Created by Jim Henson. UK, USA: Henson Associates, TVS Television.
"Fearnot." 1, 2. 1988. Directed by Steve Barron.
"Hans My Hedgehog." 1988. 1, 5. Directed by Steve Barron.
"The Heartless Giant." 1988. 1, 8. Directed by Jim Henson.
"Sapsorrow." 1988. 1, 7. Directed by Steve Barron.
"The Soldier and Death." 1988. 1, 1. Directed by Jim Henson.

Lost Girl. 2010–. TV series. Created by M. A. Lovretta. Canada: Prodigy Pictures.
"Mirror Mirror." 2011. 2, 4.

Lost Tales of the Brothers Grimm. 2006. TV series. Directed by Quinn Merkeley. Canada: Sunburst Productions.

The Magic Lady. 1951. TV Series. Created by Geraldine Larsen. USA: Telemount Pictures Inc.

Manda fra Momungao. 1987. TV miniseries. Directed by Dorte Laumann. Denmark: Denmark Radio.

Mia and Me. 2011–2012. Children's animated and live-action series. Directed by Andrea De Sica, Gerhard Hahn, Luca Morsella, and Larry Whitaker. Netherlands, Germany, Italy, Canada: Lucky Punch.

Mikhail Baryshnikov's Stories from My Childhood. 1998. TV series. Produced by Mikhail Baryshnikov. USA, Russia: Image Entertainment, Soyuzmultfilm Studios, PBS.
"Beauty and the Beast (A Tale of the Crimson Flower)."
"Cinderella and the House on Chicken Legs."
"The Golden Rooster."
"The Nutcracker."
"Pinocchio and the Golden Key."
"The Prince and the Swan."
"The Snow Queen."

"The Wild Swans."

Mother Goose Rock 'n' Rhyme. 1997. TV series. Created by Shelley Duvall, Dan Gilroy, Jean Stapleton, and Jeff Stein. USA: Lyrick Studios.

Neverland. 2011. TV miniseries. Directed by Nick Willing. UK: RHI Entertainment, SyFy Network.

The New Adventures of Pinocchio. 1961. Stop-motion animated TV series. Produced by Arthur Rankin and Jules Bass, Jr. USA: Rankin–Bass Productions, Videocraft International.

Off to See the Wizard. 1967–1968. Animated anthology series. Created by Chuck Jones and Abe Levitow. USA: Metro-Goldwyn-Mayer, ABC.

Once Upon a Classic. 1976–1979. TV series. Directors various, including Ben Bolt and Tristan DeVere Cole. USA: Metropolitan Pittsburgh.

Once Upon a Time. 2011–. TV series. Created by Edward Kitsis and Adam Horowitz. ABC: Disney, ABC Television Group.
> "An Apple Red as Blood." 2012. 1, 21. Directed by Milan Cheylov.
> "The Heart Is a Lonely Hunter." 2011. 1, 7. Directed by David Barrett.
> "A Land without Magic." 2012. 1, 22. Directed by Dean White.
> "Pilot." 2011. 1, 1. Directed by Mark Mylod.
> "The Stableboy." 2012. 1, 18. Directed by Dean White.
> "The Stranger." 2012. 1, 20. Directed by Gwyneth Horder-Payton.
> "True North." 2012. 1, 9. Directed by Dean White.

Once Upon a Tune. 1951. TV series. Directed by Barnaby Smith. USA: DuMont Television Network.

Revolutionary Girl Utena. 2011. TV series. (English version of *Shōjo Kakumei Utena.* 1997. Directed by Ikuhara Kunihiko. Japan: Be-Papas.) Directed by Ikuhara Kunihiko. USA: Nozomi Entertainment.
> "End of the World." 38. Directed by Ikuhara Kunihiko.
> "For Friendship's Sake, Perhaps." 12. Directed by Ikuhara Kunihiko.
> "For Whom the Rose Smiles." 2. Directed by Ikuhara Kunihiko.
> "Gracefully Cruel—The One Who Picks That Flower." 11. Directed by Ikuhara Kunihiko.
> "The Love That Blossomed in Wintertime." 35. Directed by Ikuhara Kunihiko.
> "The One to Bring the World Revolution." 37. Directed by Ikuhara Kunihiko.
> "The Prince Who Runs through the Night." 33. Directed by Ikuhara Kunihiko.
> "The Rose Bride." 1. Directed by Ikuhara Kunihiko.
> "The Rose Crest." 34. Directed by Ikuhara Kunihiko.
> "Someday, Together, We'll Shine." 39. Directed by Ikuhara Kunihiko.
> "Their Eternal Apocalypse." 25. Directed by Ikuhara Kunihiko.

Rich Man, Poor Woman [Ricchi man, pua ūman]. 2012. TV series. Directed by Nishiura Masaki and Tanaka Ryō. Japan: Fuji Television Network.
> "Jisan 250-oku no otoko to shūshoku nanmin onna no saitei saiaku no deai" [The Worst, Most Horrible Meeting between the Man with a 250 Billion Yen Fortune and the Woman Struggling to Find a Job]. 2012. 1. Directed by Nishiura Masaki.

Saban's Adventures of the Little Mermaid [Ningyo Hime Marina no Bōken]. 1991. Animated TV series. English version created by Jean Chalopin and Miyano Takehiro. Original created by Miyano Takehiro and Jean Chalopin. USA, Japan: Fuji Eight Company Ltd., Saban Entertainment.

Sailor Moon. 1995–2000. TV series. Directed by Satō Jun'ichi. Japan: Toei Animation.

Shari Lewis: Have I Got a Song for You. 1985. TV series pilot. Created by Shari Lewis. USA.

Shirley Temple's Storybook. 1958–1961. Anthology TV series. Hosted and produced by Shirley Temple. USA: Henry Jaffe Enterprises, NBC.

The Singing Lady. 1948–1954. TV series. Created by Ireene Wicker. USA: ABC.

The Snow Queen [Yuki no Joō]. 2005–2006. Anime TV series. Directed by Dezaki Osamu. Japan: NHK Network, TMS Entertainment.

The Snow Queen. 2006–2007. TV miniseries. Directed by Lee Hyung-min. South Korea: KMS2.

The Sorcerer's Apprentice, 1975. Educational TV series. Directed by Terry Bryan. New Zealand: Department of Education, Television New Zealand.

Story Theatre. 1971. TV series. Created by Paul Sills. Canada: Winters-Rosen.

The StoryTeller. See *Jim Henson's The StoryTeller.*

Super Why! 2007–. Educational TV series. Created by Angela C. Santomero. USA: Out of the Blue.

> "Cinderella." 2007. 1, 12. Directed by Aaron Linton.
> "The Gingerbread Boy." 2008. 1, 34. Directed by Aaron Linton.
> "Hansel and Gretel." 2007. 1, 2. Directed by Aaron Linton.
> "Hansel and Gretel: A Healthy Adventure." 2009. 1, 46. Directed by Aaron Linton.
> "Juan Bobo and the Pig." 2009. 1, 40. Directed by Aaron Linton.
> "The Magic Porridge Pot." 2008. 1, 31. Directed by Aaron Linton.
> "Momotarō the Peach Boy." 2008. 1, 33. Directed by Aaron Linton.
> "Rumpelstiltskin." 2008. 1, 26. Directed by Aaron Linton.
> "Sleeping Beauty." 2008. 1, 28. Directed by Aaron Linton.
> "The Three Feathers." 2008. 1, 37. Directed by Aaron Linton.
> "Tiddalick the Frog." 2008. 1, 27. Directed by Aaron Linton.

The Swan. 2004. Reality TV series. Created by Nely Galan. USA: Galan Entertainment.

Tales from the Brothers Grimm. 1990. TV movie series. Directed by Tom Davenport. USA: Davenport Films.

> "Ashpet: An American Cinderella." 1990.
> "Bearskin, the Man Who Didn't Wash for Seven Years." 1984.
> "Bristlelip." 1984.
> "The Frog King." 1984.
> "The Goose Girl." 1985.
> "Hansel and Gretel." 1975.
> "Jack and the Dentist's Daughter." 1984.
> "Mutzmag." 1992.
> "Rapunzel, Rapunzel." 1978.
> "Soldier Jack, an American Folktale." 1988.
> "Willa: An American Snow White." 1996.

Tin Man. 2007. TV miniseries. Directed by Nick Willing. USA: Sci Fi Channel.

Train Man [Densha otoko]. 2005. TV series. Directed by Takeuchi Hideki, Nishiura Masaki, and Kobayashi Kazuhiro. Japan: Fuji Television Network.

> "Hyakuman-nin ga mimamotta koi no yukue" [The Love Watched over by One Million People]. 2005. 1, 1. Directed by Takeuchi Hideki.

Tsubasa: RESERVoir CHRoNiCLE. 2005–2006. TV series. Created by CLAMP. Japan: Bee Train.

Werewolf. 1987–1988. TV series. Created by Frank Lupo. USA: Tristar Television.

Wizards and Warriors. 1983. TV series. Directed by Bill Bixby and Richard Colla. USA: Warner Bros. Television, CBS.

Wolves, Witches, and Giants. 1995–1999. TV series. Adapted by Ed Welch. UK: Honeycomb Animation, Wolfgang Cartoons.

The Wonderful Wizard of Oz [Oz no Mahōōtsukai]. 1986–1987. Anime TV series. Directed by Naisho Tonogawa. Tokyo: Panmedia, NHK, TV Tokyo.

Zoe & Charlie [Léa et Gaspard]. Children's animated series. 1994–. Directed by Gilles Gay and Alain Jaspard. Brazil: CineGroupe, TVE.

Made-for-TV Movies

Alice at the Palace. 1981. Directed by Emile Ardolino. USA: New York Shakespeare Festival, NBC.

Alice in Wonderland. 1955. Directed by George Schaefer. USA: Hallmark Hall of Fame Productions.

Alice in Wonderland. 1966. Directed by Jonathan Miller. UK: BBC.

Alice in Wonderland. 1985. Directed by Harry Harris. USA: Irwin Allen Productions, Columbia Pictures Television.

Alice in Wonderland. 1999. Directed by Nick Willing. USA, Germany: Hallmark Entertainment, Babelsberg International Filmproduktion.

Alice in Wonderland, or What's a Nice Kid Like You Doing in a Place Like This? 1966. Directed by Alex Lovy. USA: Screen Gems, Hanna-Barbera Productions.

Alice through the Looking Glass. 1966. Directed by Alan Handley. USA: Alwynn Productions, Dum and Dee Productions, NBC.

Alice through the Looking Glass. 1974. Directed by James MacTaggart. UK: BBC.

Alice through the Looking Glass. 1998. Directed by John Henderson. UK: Projector Productions, Channel 4 Television Corporation.

The Alphabet Conspiracy. 1959. Directed by Robert M. Sinclair. USA: Bell Telephone System, N. W. Ayer & Son, Warner Brothers Pictures.

Babes in Toyland. 1986. Directed by Clive Donner. USA, Germany: The Finnegan Company, Orion Television, Bavaria Film.

Beauty and the Beast. 1952. Produced by Joy Harington. UK: BBC.

Beauty and the Beast. 1976. Directed by Fielder Cook. USA, UK: Hallmark Hall of Fame Productions, Palm Films Ltd.

Beauty and the Beast. 2009. Directed by David Lister. USA, Australia: America World Pictures, Pacific Film and Television Commission.

Beauty and the Beast: A Concert on Ice. 1996. Directed by Steve Binder. USA: ABC.

Bluebeard [Barbe Bleue]. 2009. Directed by Catherine Breillat. France: Flach Film.

Cenerentola '80. 1984. Produced and directed by Roberto Malenotti. Italy: Compania Distribuzione Europea, RAI-TV Channel 2, TVC-Television Center, Strand Art.

Cinderella 2000. 1977. Directed by Beeban Kidron. UK: Isle of Man Film Commission, Projector Productions.

Cindy. 1978. Directed by Jim Vance. USA: ABC.

Confessions of an Ugly Stepsister. 2002. Directed by Gavin Millar. Canada, Luxembourg: Alliance Atlantis Communications, Luxembourg Film, ABC.

The Counterfeit Contessa. 1994. Directed by Ron Lagomarsino. USA: Fox West Pictures.

The Dancing Princesses. 1962. Directed by Gordon Murray. UK: BBC.

The Dancing Princesses. 1978. Directed by Ben Rea. UK: BBC.

The Dancing Princesses. 1978. Directed by Jon Scoffield. UK: PBS, Associated Television.

The Dangerous Christmas of Red Riding Hood. 1965. Directed by Sid Smith. USA: ABC.

Der Froschkönig [The Frog King]. 2008. Directed by Franziska Buch. Germany: Bavaria Filmverleih- und Produktions GmbH and Südwestrundfunk.

Dornröschen. 2009. Directed by Oliver Dieckmann. Germany: Bavaria Filmverleih- und Produktions GmbH und Südwestrundfunk.

The Enchanted Nutcracker. 1961. Directed by Jack Smight. USA: ABC, Westinghouse.

The Frog Prince. 1971. Directed by Jim Henson. USA: Jim Henson Productions, CBS.

Geppetto. 2000. Directed by Tom Moore. USA: Walt Disney Studios, ABC.

Goldilocks. 1971. Produced by David H. DePatie, Friz Freleng, Richard M. Sherman, Robert B. Sherman. USA: DePatie-Frelend Enterprises, NBC.

Hansel and Gretel. 1958. Directed by Paul Bogart. USA: NBC.

The Ice Princess: A Classic Tale on Ice. 1997. Directed by Danny Huston. USA: Wellspring Media.

If the Shoe Fits [aka *Stroke of Midnight*]. 1990. Directed by Tom Clegg. USA, France: Canal+, Centre National de la Cinématographie.

I Want to Be Cinderella! [Shinderera ni naritai!]. 2006. TV series. Directed by Takezono Hajime. Japan: Tokyo Broadcasting System.

Jack and the Beanstalk. 1956. Directed by Clark Jones. USA: NBC.

Jack and the Beanstalk. 1967. Directed by Gene Kelly. USA: Hanna-Barbera Productions.

Jack and the Beanstalk. 1998. Directed by John Henderson. UK: London Weekend Television, Wishbone Productions.

Jack and the Beanstalk: The Real Story. 2001. Directed by Brian Henson. USA: Hallmark Entertainment, The Jim Henson Company.

La Belle au bois dormant [Sleeping Beauty]. 2000. Directed by Pierre Cavassilas. France: Opera National de Paris, Telmondis.

La Belle endormie [Sleeping Beauty]. 2010. Directed by Catherine Breillat. France: Arte France, CB Films, Flach Film.

Mother Goose Rock 'n' Rhyme. 1990. Directed by Jeff Stein. USA: Lyrick Studio.

The Muppet Musicians of Bremen. 1972. Tales from Muppetland series. Directed by Jim Henson. USA: Jim Henson Productions.

My Life as a Fairytale: Hans Christian Andersen. 2001. Directed by Phillip Saville. USA, Germany: Hallmark Entertainment, Mat I Productions.

Neberte nám princeznú. 1981. Directed by Martin Hoffmeister. Czechoslovakia: Ceskoslovenská Televízia Bratislava.

The Nutcracker. 1977. Directed by Tony Charmoli. USA: Jodav Productions, CBS.

The Nutcracker. 1985. Directed by John Vernon. UK: BBC, NVC, the Royal Ballet.

Nutcracker! 2003. Directed by Ross MacFibbon. UK: Adventures in Motion Picture, Trio Network.

Once Upon a Brothers Grimm. 1977. Directed by Norman Campbell. USA: CBS.

Once Upon an Eastertime. 1954. Directed by Byron Paul. USA: CBS, DuMont Television Network.

Peter Pan. 1960. Directed by Vincent J. Donehue. USA: Vitagraph Studios.

Peter Pan. 2000. Directed by Glenn Casale and Gary Halvorson. USA: Arts and Entertainment Network.

Pinocchio. 1965. Directed by Nick Havinga. USA: CBS, Prince Street Productions.

Pinocchio. 1968. Directed by Sid Smith. USA: Hallmark Hall of Fame, NBC.

Pinocchio. 1976. Directed by Ron Field and Sid Smith. USA: NBC.

Prince Charming. 2001. Directed by Allan Arkush. USA: Hallmark Entertainment.

Pro Krasnuyu Shapochku. 1977. Directed by Leonid Nechayev. Soviet Union: Belarusfilm, Gosteleradio.

Puss in Boots. 1982. Directed by John Clark Donahue and John Driver. USA: MCA, Universal.

Rapunzel. 2009. Directed by Bodo Fürneisen. Germany: ANTAEUS Film- und TV-Produktion, Rundfunk Berlin-Brandenburg.

Red Riding Hood. 1995. Directed by Donald Sturrock. UK: EMI.

Red Riding. 2009. UK: Channel Four Film.

"In the Year of Our Lord 1974." Directed by Julian Jarrold.

"In the Year of Our Lord 1980." Directed by James Marsh.

"In the Year of Our Lord 1983." Directed by Anand Tucker.

Red: Werewolf Hunter. 2010. Directed by Sheldon Wilson. USA, Canada: Chelsier, Perlmutter Productions.

The Secret of the Nutcracker. 2007. Directed by Eric Till. Canada: Joe Media Group, CBC.

The Snow Queen. 1976. Directed by Andrew Gosling. UK: BBC.

Snow Queen. 2002. Directed by David Wu. USA, Germany, Canada: Hallmark Entertainment, Mat 1 Productions.

The Snow Queen. 2005. Directed by Julian Gibbs. UK, Canada: Amberwood Entertainment, SQ Productions.

Snow Queen. 2007. Directed by Yelena Rayskaya. Russia: Central Partnership.

Snow White: A Tale of Terror. 1997. Directed by Michael Cohn. USA: PolyGram Filmed Entertainment.

Snow White and the Seven Dwarfs. 1984. Directed by Peter Medak. USA: Gaylord Productions, Lions Gate Films, Platypus Productions.

Snow White: The Fairest of Them All. 2001. Directed by Caroline Thompson. Canada, Germany: Hallmark Entertainment.

A Tale of Cinderella. 1998. Directed by Patricia Di Benedetto Snyder and Tom Gliserman. USA: PBS.

Through the Looking Glass. 1973. Directed by James McTaggart. UK: BBC.

The Trial of Red Riding Hood. 1992. Directed by Eric Till. Canada: Bernard Rothman Productions, CBC.

Yeh-Shen: A Cinderella Story from China. 1985. Directed by Ray Patterson. USA: CBS.

Other Television References

American Idol. 2002–. Reality TV game show. Created by Simon Fuller. USA: Fremantle Media North America.

Angel. 1999–2004. TV series. Created by David Greenwalt and Joss Whedon. USA: Fox.

Candid Camera. 1948–1950. Reality TV series. Created by Allen Funt. USA: Allen Funt Productions.

The Cat in the Hat Knows a Lot about That. 2010–. Animated TV series. Directed by Tony Collingwood, Steve Neilsen, and Andrea Tran. Canada, USA, UK: Portfolio Entertainment.

COPS. 1989–. Reality TV series. Created by John Langley and Malcolm Barbour. USA: Barbour, Langley Productions.

Family Guy. 1999–. TV series. Created by Seth MacFarlane. USA: 20th Century Fox Television.

"Road to the Multiverse." 2009. 8, 1. Directed by Greg Colton.

Firefly. 2002–2003. TV series. Created by Joss Whedon. USA: Mutant Enemy.

The French Chef. 1963–1973. TV cooking series. Created by Julia Child. USA: WGBH.

General Hospital. 1963–present. TV series. Created by Doris Hursley, Frank Hursley, and Jim Hursley. USA: ABC.

Ghost Hunters. 2004–. TV series. Created by Tom Thayer and Craig Piligian. USA: Pilgrim Films & Television.

Gidget. 1965–1966. TV series. Created by Frederick Kohner. USA: ABC.

Gilligan's Island. 1964–1967. TV series. Created by Sherwood Schwartz. USA: CBS.

Iron Chef America. 2005–. TV cooking series. Created by the Food Network. USA: Food Network.

Jeeves and Wooster. 1990–1993. TV series. Created by Clive Exton. UK: Independent Television Authority.

Kasimasi: Girl Meets Girl. 2006. TV series. Directed by Ruben Arvizu. Japan: Bandai Visual Company.

Law and Order. 1990–2010. TV series. Created by Dick Wolf. USA: NBC Studios.

Lost. 2004–2010. TV series. Created by J. J. Abrams, Jeffrey Lieber, and Damon Lindelof. USA: ABC Studios.

The Man from U.N.C.L.E. 1964–1968. TV series. Developed by Sam Rolfe. USA: NBC.

Most Haunted. 2002–2011. TV series. Created by Yvette Fielding and Karl Beattie. UK: Antix Productions.

The Next Food Network Star. 2005–. TV cooking series. Created by Food Network. USA: Food Network.

The Odd Couple. 1970–1975. TV series. Created by Garry Marshall, Jerry Belson, Jerry Paris, Harvey Miller, Bob Brunner, Mark Rothman, and Lowell Ganz. USA: Paramount Television.

The Patty Duke Show. 1963–1966. TV series. Created by William Asher and Sidney Sheldon. USA: Chrislaw Productions, Cottage Industries Inc., and United Artists Television.

Petticoat Junction. 1963–1970. TV series. Created by Paul Henning. USA: Filmways Television, McCadden Productions, and Wayfilms.

The Rose of Versailles. 1979–1980. TV series. Directors various. Japan: Tokyo Movie Shinsha.

Seinfeld. 1989–1998. TV series. Created by Larry David and Jerry Seinfeld. USA: Castle Rock Entertainment.

The Sopranos. 1999–2007. TV series. Created by David Chase. USA: HBO.

Survivor. 2000–. Reality TV series. Created by Charlie Parsons. USA: Mark Burnett Productions.

Walt Disney's Wonderful World of Color [aka Disneyland, Walt Disney Presents, The Wonderful World of Disney, Disney's Wonderful World, Walt Disney, The Disney Sunday Movie, The Magical World of Disney]. 1954–1990. Children's anthology series. Created by Walt Disney. USA: Walt Disney Productions and The Walt Disney Company.

What Not to Wear. 2003–. Reality TV series. Directors various. USA: BBC Productions USA.

The X Files. 1993–2002. TV series. Created by Chris Carter. USA: Fox.

Alice in Wonderland. 1951. Directed by Clyde Geronimi, Wilfred Jackson, and Hamilton Luske. USA: Walt Disney Productions.

Alvin and the Chipmunks. 2007. Directed by Tim Hill. USA: Fox 2000 Pictures.

Alvin and the Chipmunks: Chipwrecked. 2011. Directed by Mike Mitchell. USA: Fox 2000 Pictures.

Alvin and the Chipmunks: The Squeaquel. 2009. Directed by Betty Thomas. USA: Fox 2000 Pictures.

Anatomy of Hell [Anatomie de l'enfer]. 2004. Directed by Catherine Breillat. France: CB Films, Canal+.

Basic Instinct. 1992. Directed by Peter Verhoeven. USA: TriStar Pictures.

Beastly. 2011. Directed by Daniel Barnz. USA: CBS Films.

Beauty and the Beast. 1946. Directed by Jean Cocteau. France: Lopert Pictures.

Beauty and the Beast. 1991. Directed by Gary Trousdale and Kirk Wise. USA: Walt Disney Pictures.

Bluebeard [Barbe-bleue]. 1901. Directed by Georges Méliès. France: Star Film.

Bluebeard. 2008. Directed by Jessica Fox. USA: Mythic Image Studios.

The Bourne Ultimatum. 2007. Directed by Paul Greengrass. USA: Universal Studios.

Brave. 2012. Directed by Mark Andrews, Brenda Chapman, and Steve Purcell. USA: Walt Disney Pictures and Pixar Animation Studios.

The Brothers Grimm. 2005. Directed by Terry Gilliam. UK, Czech Republic, USA: Dimension Films, MGM.

Camelot. 1967. Directed by Joshua Logan. USA: Warner Brothers, Seven Arts.

Capturing the Friedmans. 2003. Directed by Andrew Jarecki. USA: HBO.

Cinderella. 1950. Directed by Clyde Geronimi, Wilfred Jackson, and Hamilton Luske. USA: Walt Disney Pictures.

Cinderfella. 1960. Directed by Frank Tashlin. USA: Paramount Pictures.

The Company of Wolves. 1984. Directed by Neil Jordan. UK: ITC, Palace Pictures.

Diva. 1981. Directed by Jean-Jacques Beineix. France: United Artists.

Dracula. 1931. Directed by Tod Browning. USA: Universal Pictures.

Dragon Ball: Sleeping Beauty in the Magic Castle. 1987. Directed by Nishion Daisuke. Japan: Toei Animation.

Donkey Skin [Peau d'âne]. 1970. Directed by Jacques Demy. France: Marianne Productions.

Dr. Jekyll and Mr. Hyde. 1931. Directed by Rouben Mamoulian. USA: Paramount Pictures.

Enchanted. 2007. Directed by Kevin Lima. USA: Walt Disney Pictures.

Ever After: A Cinderella Story. 1998. Directed by Andy Tennant. USA: Fox.

Excalibur. 1981. Directed by John Boorman. USA: Orion Pictures Corporation.

The Fall. 2006. Directed by Tarsem Singh. USA, India: Googly Films.

Fantasia, "The Sorcerer's Apprentice." 1940. Directed by James Algar. USA: Walt Disney Productions.

Fat Girl [À ma soeur!]. 2001. Directed by Catherine Breillat. France: CB Films and Canal+.

The Fifty-First Dragon. 1954. Directed by Pete Burness. USA: United Productions of America.

Freeway. 1996. Directed by Matthew Bright. USA: Kushner, Locke Company.

Freeway 2: Confessions of a Trick Baby. 1999. Directed by Matthew Bright. USA: Kushner-Locke Company.

Hanna. 2011. Directed by Joe Wright. USA, UK, Germany: Focus Features.

Hansel and Gretel: Witch Hunters. 2013. Directed by Tommy Wirkola. USA, Germany: Siebzehnte Babelsberg, MGM, Paramount.

Hard Candy. 2005. Directed by David Slade. USA: Vulcan Productions.

Henjel gwa Geuretel [Hansel and Gretel]. 2007. Directed by Pil-Sung Yim. South Korea: Barunson Film Division.

Jack the Giant-Slayer. 2013. Directed by Bryan Singer. USA: New Line Cinema.

The Juniper Tree. 1990. Directed by Nietzchka Keene. USA: Keene Productions.

The Last Mistress [Une Vieille Maîtresse]. 2007. Directed by Catherine Breillat. France, Italy: Studio Canal.

Little Erin Merryweather. 2003. Directed by David Morwick. USA: Three Stone Pictures Inc.

The Little Mermaid. 1989. Directed by Ron Clements and John Musker. USA: Walt Disney Pictures and Silver Screen Partners IV.

Little Red Riding Hood. 1997. Directed by David Kaplan. USA: Little Red Movie Productions, JV.

Mirror Mirror. 2012. Directed by Tarsem Singh. USA: Relativity Media, Yuk Films.

Mulan. 1998. Directed by Tony Bancroft and Barry Cook. USA: Walt Disney Pictures.

Mulholland Drive. 2001. Directed by David Lynch. USA, France: Universal Pictures.

Muppet Classic Theater. 1994. Directed by David Grossman. USA: Henson Associates.

My Fair Lady. 1964. Directed by George Cukor. USA: Warner Bros.

The Odd Couple. 1968. Directed by Gene Saks. USA: Paramount Pictures.

Pan's Labyrinth. 2006. Directed by Guillermo del Toro. Mexico, Japan, USA: Tequila Gang.

Pocahontas. 1995. Directed by Mike Gabriel and Eric Goldberg. USA: Walt Disney Pictures.

Pretty Woman. 1990. Directed by Garry Marshall. USA: Touchstone Pictures.

The Princess and the Frog. 2009. Directed by Ron Clements and John Musker. USA: Walt Disney Pictures.

Promenons-nous dans les bois/Deep in the Woods. 2000. Directed by Lionel Delplanque. France: Centre National de la Cinématographie.

Queen Bee. 1955. Directed by Ranald MacDougall. USA: Columbia Pictures.

Raiders of the Lost Ark. 1981. Directed by Steven Spielberg. USA: Paramount Pictures.

Red Riding Hood. 2003. Directed by Giacomo Cimini. Italy: KOA Films Entertainment.

Red Riding Hood. 2011. Directed by Catherine Hardwicke. USA: Warner Brothers.

Revolutionary Girl Utena: Adolescence of Utena. 2011 [Shōjo Kakumei Utena: Adure-sensu Mokushiroku, Be-Papas], 1999. Directed by Ikuhara Kunihiko. USA: Nozomi Entertainment.

Romance X [Romance]. 1999. Directed by Catherine Breillat. France: Flach Film, CB Films.

The Secret of My Succe$s. 1987. Directed by Herbert Ross. USA: Universal Pictures.

Seven Samurai. 1954. Directed by Kurosawa Akira. Japan: Toho Co., Ltd.

Sleeping Beauty. 1959. Directed by Clyde Geronimi. USA: Walt Disney Productions.

The Sleeping Beauty. 1990. Directed by Kawamoto Kirachirō. Czechoslovakia: Kawamoto Productions Ltd.

Snow White. 1987. Directed by Michael Berz. USA: Golen-Globus Productions.

Snow White and the Huntsman. 2012. Directed by Rupert Sanders. USA: Universal Pictures.

Snow White and the Seven Dwarfs. 1937. Directed by David Hand et al. USA: Walt Disney Productions.

Stagecoach. 1939. Directed by John Ford. USA: Walter Wanger Productions.

Stardust. 2007. Directed by Matthew Vaughn. UK, USA, Iceland: Paramount Pictures, Marv Films.

The Sword in the Stone. 1963. Directed by Wolfgang Reitherman. USA: Walt Disney Productions.

Tangled. 2010. Directed by Nathan Greno and Byron Howard. USA: Walt Disney Pictures.

The Terminator. 1984. Directed by James Cameron. USA: Orion Pictures.

Whoever Slew Auntie Roo? 1972. Directed by Curtis Harrington. UK: American International.

The Wild Bunch. 1969. Directed by Sam Peckinpah. USA: Warner Brothers/Seven Arts.

The Wizard of Oz. 1939. Directed by Victor Fleming. United States: Warner Bros.

The Wolves of Kromer. 1998. Directed by Will Gould. UK: Discodog Productions.

The Woodsman. 2004. Directed by Nicole Kassell. USA: Dash Films.

Working Girl. 1988. Directed by Mike Nichols. USA: Twentieth Century Fox.

REFERENCES

"ABC Wins Its 4th Straight Sunday, as Finales of 'Once Upon a Time' and 'Housewives' Surge." 2012. *The Futon Critic*. May 14. www.thefutoncritic.com/ratings/2012/05/14/abc-wins-itss4th-straight-sunday-as-finales-of-once-upon-a-time-and-housewives-surge-392200/20120514abc02/#IgB1WyyR1sFPRgFO.99.

Abjørnsen, Peter Christen, and Jørgen Engebretsen Møe. [1843–1844] 1970. *East o' the Sun and West o' the Moon*. Translated by George Webbe Dasent. New York: Dover.

Adevilishdiva. 2012. *Once Upon a Time* Podcast Forums. April 19. http://oncepodcast.com/forums/viewtopic.php?f=29&t=503&start=20.

Agnew, Robert. 1998. "The Causes of Animal Abuse: A Social–Psychological Analysis." *Theoretical Criminology* 2(2): 177–209.

Albright, Julie M. 2007. "Impossible Bodies: TV Viewing Habits, Body Image, and Plastic Surgery Attitudes among College Students in Los Angeles and Buffalo, New York." *Configurations* 15: 103–23.

Aldred, B. Grantham. 2008. "Henson, Jim (1936–1990)." In *The Greenwood Encyclopedia of Folktales and Fairy Tales*, edited by Donald Haase, 449–51. Westport, CT: Greenwood Press.

Allen, Jessica, Sonia Livingstone, and Robert Reiner. 1997. "The Changing Generic Location of Crime in Film: A Content Analysis of Film Synopses, 1945–1991." *Journal of Communication* 47(4): 89–101.

Allen, Richard. 1995. *Projecting Illusion: Film Spectatorship and the Impression of Reality*. Cambridge: Cambridge University Press.

Allen, Robert C. 1992. "Audience-Oriented Criticism and Television." In *Channels of Discourse, Reassembled: Television and Contemporary Criticism*, edited by Allen, 77–103. 2nd ed. London: Routledge.

Allison, Brent. 2007. "Anime: Comparing Macro and Micro Analyses." *Mechademia* 2: 287–98.

Andersen, Hans Christian. [1843] 2012. *The Nightingale*. Translated by H. B. Paull [1872]. N.p.: The Planet Books.

Anderson, Melissa. 2012. "Q&A with *Bluebeard*'s Catherine Breillat." *The Village Voice*, March 2. www.villagevoice.com/2010–03–02/film/q-a-with-bluebeard-s-catherine-breillat.

Anderson, Tami. 2010. "Whose Story Is This, Anyway?" In *Inside Joss' Dollhouse: From Alpha to Rossum*, edited by Jane Espenson, 161–73. Dallas, TX: Smart Pop.

Andrew, Geoff. 2008. "The Last Mistress (2007)." *Time Out London*, April 10–16. www.timeout.com/film/reviews/84676/the-last-mistress.html.

Angelo, Adrienne. 2010. "Sexual Cartographies: Mapping Subjectivity in the Cinema of Catherine Breillat." *Journal for Cultural Research* 14(1): 43–55.

Arkoff, Vicki. 2009. "How Disney Princess Works." *HowStuffWorks.* May 31. entertainment.howstuffworks.com.

Artús. Opera. 1895. Composed by Amadeu Vives.

Ashliman, D. L. 1996–2012. *Folklore and Mythology Electronic Texts.* www.pitt.edu/~dash/folktexts.html.

———. 2005. "Grimm 050: Little Brier-Rose." www.pitt.edu/~dash/grimm050.html.

———. 2008. "Princess." In *The Greenwood Encyclopedia of Folktales and Fairy Tales,* edited by Donald Haase, 771–73. Westport, CN: Greenwood Press.

"Ask the Magic Mirror." *Ask the Magic Mirror.* 2011–2012. www.askthemagicmirror.com.

Attwood, Feona. 1999. "Who's Afraid of Little Red Riding Hood?: Male Desire Phantasy and Impersonation in the Telling of a Fairytale." *Thamyris* 6(1): 95–105.

Auden, W. H. 1962. *The Dyer's Hand and Other Essays.* New York: Random House.

Babu, Jennifer. 2012. "We All Need a Little Escape: A Look at Modern Fairy Tales." *Like Owl Vision,* December 3. http://likeowlvision.wordpress.com/category/fairy-talesdisney.

Bacchilega, Cristina. 1993. "An Introduction to the 'Innocent Persecuted Heroine' Fairy Tale." *Western Folklore* 52(1): 1–12.

———. 1997. *Postmodern Fairy Tales: Gender and Narrative Strategies.* Philadelphia: University of Pennsylvania Press.

———. 2013. *Fairy Tales Transformed?: Twenty-First-Century Adaptations and the Politics of Wonder.* Detroit: Wayne State University Press.

Bacchilega, Cristina and John Rieder. 2010. "Mixing It Up: Generic Complexity and Gender Ideology in Early Twenty-First Century Fairy Tale Films." In *Fairy Tale Films: Visions of Ambiguity,* edited by Pauline Greenhill and Sidney Eve Matrix, 23–41. Logan: Utah State University Press.

Bakhtin, M. M. 1981. *The Dialogic Imagination: Four Essays.* Edited by Michael Holquist, translated by Caryl Emerson and Michael Holquist. Austin: University of Texas Press.

Ballio, Laura, and Adriano Zanacchi. 2000. *Carosello Story. La via italiane alla pubblicità televisiva.* 2nd ed. [with DVD]. Rome: Rai Radiotelevisione Italiana.

Barr, Marleen S. 2000. "Biology Is Not Destiny; Biology Is Fantasy: *Cinderella,* or the Dream Disney's 'Impossible'/Possible Race Relations Dream." In *Fantasy Girls: Gender in the New Universe of Science Fiction and Fantasy Television,* edited by Elyce Rae Helford, 187–99. Lanham, MD: Rowman & Littlefield.

Barretta, Manuela. 2008. "The 'Noir' in David Peace's Shadow." *Other Modernities* 1(3): 95–102.

Barrie, J. M. 1911. *Peter and Wendy.* London: Hodder & Stoughton.

Barzilai, Shuli. 1990. "Reading 'Snow White': The Mother's Story." *Signs: Journal of Women in Culture and Society* 15(3): 515–34.

———. 2009. *Tales of Bluebeard and His Wives from Late Antiquity to Postmodern Times.* New York: Routledge.

Bascom, William R. 1954. "Four Functions of Folklore." *Journal of American Folklore* 67(266): 333–49.

———. 1965. "The Forms of Folklore: Prose Narratives." *Journal of American Folklore* 78(307): 3–20.

Basile, Giambattista. 2001. "Sun, Moon, and Talia." In *The Great Fairy Tale Tradition: From Straparola and Basile to the Brothers Grimm,* edited by Jack Zipes, 685–88. New York: Norton.

Baum, L. Frank. 1900. *The Wonderful Wizard of Oz.* Chicago: George M. Hill Company.

Bauman, Richard, and Charles L. Briggs. 2003. *Voices of Modernity: Language Ideologies and the Politics of Inequality.* Cambridge: Cambridge University Press.

Bausinger, Hermann. 1987. "Concerning the Content and Meaning of Fairy Tales." *Germanic Review* 62: 75–82.

Beauchamp, Fay. 2010. "Asian Origins of Cinderella: The Zhuang Storyteller of Guangxi." *Oral Tradition* 25(2): 447–96.

Beirne, Piers. 2007. "Animal Rights, Animal Abuse and Green Criminology." In *Issues in Green Criminology: Confronting Harms against Environments, Humanity and Other Animals,* edited by Piers Beirne and Nigel South, 55–83. Cullompton, UK: Willan Publishing.

Beirne, Piers, and Nigel South. 2007. "Introduction: Approaching Green Criminology." In *Issues in Green Criminology: Confronting Harms against Environments, Humanity and Other Animals,* edited by Piers Beirne and Nigel South, xiii–xxii. Cullompton, UK: Willan Publishing.

Bell, Elizabeth, Lynda Haas, and Laura Sells, eds. 1995. *From Mouse to Mermaid: The Politics of Film, Gender, and Culture.* Bloomington: Indiana University Press.

Ben-Amos, Dan. 1971. "Toward a Definition of Folklore in Context." *Journal of American Folklore* 84(331): 3–15.

———. 2010. "Introduction: The European Fairy-Tale Tradition between Orality and Literacy." *Journal of American Folklore* 123(490): 373–76.

Bendix, Regina. 1992. "Diverging Paths in the Scientific Search for Authenticity." *Journal of Folklore Research* 29(2): 103–132.

———. 1993. "Seashell Bra and Happy End: Disney's Transformations of 'The Little Mermaid.'" *Fabula* 34: 280–90.

———. 1997. *In Search of Authenticity: The Formation of Folklore Studies.* Madison: University of Wisconsin Press.

Bennett, R. E. 1938. "Arthur and Gorlagon, the Dutch Lancelot, and St. Kentigern." *Speculum* 13: 68–75.

Benson, Stephen. 2003. *Cycles of Influence: Fiction, Folktale, Theory.* Detroit: Wayne State University Press.

Benz, Richard. 1908. *Märchen-Dichtung der Romantiker: Mit einer Vorgeschichte.* Gotha, Germany: Perthes.

Benzon, William. 2007. "Godzilla's Children: Murakami Takes Manhattan." *Mechademia* 2: 283–87.

Bernheimer, Kate, ed. 1998. *Mirror, Mirror, on the Wall: Women Writers Explore Their Favorite Fairy Tales.* New York: Vintage/Anchor.

Bettelheim, Bruno. 1976. *The Uses of Enchantment: The Meaning and Importance of Fairy Tales.* New York: Knopf.

Bianchi, Diana, and Catia Nannoni. 2011. "Back to the Future: The Journey of *The Bloody Chamber* in Italy and France." *Marvels & Tales* 25(1): 51–69.

Bignell, Jonathan. 2008. *An Introduction to Television Studies.* 2nd ed. London: Routledge.

———. 2013. *An Introduction to Television Studies.* 3rd ed. London: Routledge.

Blank, Trevor J., ed. 2009. *Folklore and the Internet: Vernacular Expression in a Digital World.* Logan: Utah State University Press.

———, ed. 2012. *Folk Culture in the Digital Age: The Emergent Dynamics of Human Interaction.* Logan: Utah State University Press.

Block, Geoffrey. 2003. *Richard Rodgers.* New Haven: Yale University Press.

Bordwell, David. 1988. "ApPropriations and ImProprieties: Problems in the Morphology of Film Narrative." *Cinema Journal* 27(3): 5–20.

Bottigheimer, Ruth B. 1987. *Grimms' Bad Girls and Bold Boys: The Moral and Social Vision of the Tales.* New Haven: Yale University Press.

Bourboulis, Photeine P. [1982] 1988. "The Bride-Show Custom and the Fairy-Story of Cinderella." In *Cinderella: A Casebook,* edited by Alan Dundes, 98–109. New York: Wildman Press.

Bourdieu, Pierre. 1993. *The Field of Cultural Production: Essays on Art and Literature.* New York: Columbia University Press.

Bowers, Maggie Ann. 2004. *Magic(al) Realism: The New Critical Idiom*. New York: Routledge.

Bratich, Jack Z. 2007. "Programming Reality: Control Societies, New Subjects and the Powers of Transformation." In *Makeover Television: Realities Remodelled,* edited by Dana A. Heller, 6–22. London: I. B. Tauris.

Bridges, Elizabeth. 2009. "Grimm Realities: *Buffy* and the Uses of Folklore." In *Buffy Meets the Academy: Essays on the Episodes and Scripts as Text,* edited by Kevin K. Durand, 91–113. Jefferson, NC: McFarland.

Briggs, Charles. 1993. "Metadiscursive Practices and Scholarly Authority in Folkloristics." *Journal of American Folklore* 106(422): 387–434.

Briggs, K. M. 1968. "The Transmission of Folk-Tales in Britain." *Folklore* 79(2): 81–91.

Brisman, Avi. 2008. "Crime-Environment Relationships and Environmental Justice." *Seattle Journal for Social Justice* 6(2): 727–817.

———. 2010. "The Indiscriminate Criminalisation of Environmentally Beneficial Activities." In *Global Environmental Harm: Criminological Perspectives,* edited by Rob White, 161–92. Portland, OR: Willan Publishing.

Brook, Vincent. 2000. "The Fallacy of Falsity: Un-'Dresch'ing Masquerade, Fashion, and Postfeminist Jewish Princess in *The Nanny*." *Television and New Media* 1(3): 279–305.

Brownmiller, Susan. 1975. *Against Our Will: Men, Women and Rape*. New York: Fawcett Columbine.

Brunken, Otto. 2002. *Geschichte der deutschen Kinder- und Jugendliteratur*. Stuttgart, Germany: Metzler.

Bryan, Christopher J., Gregory M. Walton, Todd Rogers, and Carol S. Dweck. 2011. "Motivating Voter Turnout by Invoking the Self." *Proceedings of the National Academy of the Science of the United States* 108(31): 12653–56.

Buchan, David. 1972. *The Ballad and the Folk*. London: Routledge and Kegan Paul.

Buell, Lawrence. 1998. "Toxic Discourse." *Critical Inquiry* 24: 639–65.

Bui, Tran Quynh Ngoc. 2009. "Structure and Motif in the 'Innocent Persecuted Heroine' Tale in Vietnam and Other Southeast Asian Countries." *International Research in Children's Literature* 2(1): 36–48.

Bunia, Remigius. 2010. "Diegesis and Representation: Beyond the Fictional World, on the Margins of Story and Narrative." *Poetics Today* 31(4): 679–720.

Burns, Tom. 1969. "Folklore in the Mass Media: Television." *Folklore Forum* 2(4): 90–106.

Butler, Judith. 1993. *Bodies That Matter: On the Discursive Limits of Sex*. New York: Routledge.

Byers, Michelle, ed. 2005. *Growing Up Degrassi: Television, Identity and Youth Cultures*. Toronto, ON: Sumach Press.

Byrne, Craig. 2012. "*Once Upon a Time*'s Kitsis & Horowitz Talk Dark Sides, A Happy Evil Queen, & More." *KSITE TV*. www.ksitetv.com/once-upon-a-time/once-upon-a-times-kitsis-horowitz-talk-dark-sides-a-happy-evil-queen-more/12794.

Cahill, Susan. 2010. "Through the Looking Glass: Fairy-Tale Cinema and the Spectacle of Femininity in *Stardust* and *The Brothers Grimm*." *Marvels & Tales* 24(1): 57–67.

Calvino, Italo. 1956. *Fiabe italiane*. Torino, Italy: Einaudi. Translated by George Martin as *Italian Folktales* (New York: Pantheon, 1980).

Camelot. Broadway musical, 1960–1963. Created by Alan Jay Lerner (book and lyrics) and Frederick Loewe (music), directed by Moss Hart.

Carroll, Lewis. 1865. *Alice's Adventures in Wonderland*. London: Macmillan.

Carter, Angela. 1979. *The Bloody Chamber*. New York: Harper & Row.

Cavallaro, Dani. 2010. *Anime and the Art of Adaptation: Eight Famous Works from Page to Screen*. Jefferson, NC: McFarland.

———. 2011. *The Fairy Tale and Anime: Traditional Themes, Images, and Symbols at Play on Screen*. Jefferson, NC: McFarland.

Chalmers, Sharon. 2002. *Emerging Lesbian Voices from Japan*. New York: RoutledgeCurzon.

Choo, Kukhee. 2008. "Girls Return Home: Portrayal of Femininity in Popular Japanese Girls' Manga and Anime Texts during the 1990s in Hana yori Dango and Fruits Basket." *Women: A Cultural Review* 19(3): 275–96.

Ciletti, Elena. 2010. "Judith Imagery as Catholic Orthodoxy in Counter-Reformation Italy." In *The Sword of Judith: Judith Studies across the Disciplines,* edited by Kevin E. Brine, Elena Ciletti, and Henrike Lähnemann, 345–68. Cambridge, UK: Open Book Publishers.

Ciletti, Elena, and Henrike Lähnemann. 2010. "Judith in the Christian Tradition." In *The Sword of Judith: Judith Studies across the Disciplines,* edited by Kevin E. Brine, Elena Ciletti, and Henrike Lähnemann, 41–65. Cambridge, UK: Open Book Publishers.

"Cinderella (Musical)." N.d. *Wikipedia.* http://en.wikipedia.org/wiki/Cinderella_%28 musical%29.

Ciotti, Gregory. 2012. "The Marketer's Guide to Cult Addiction: How Loyal Are Your Customers?" *Unbounce.* http://unbounce.com/online-marketing/marketers-guide-to -cult-addiction.

Cixous, Helene. 1981. "Castration or Decapitation?" Translated by Annette Kuhn. *Signs* 7(1): 41–55.

Clapp-Intyre, Alisa. 2010. "Help! I'm a Feminist but My Daughter Is a 'Princess Fanatic'! Disney's Transformation of Twenty-First-Century Girls." *Children's Folklore Review* 32: 7–22.

Clements, Jonathan, and Helen McCarthy. 2006. *The Anime Encyclopedia: Revised and Expanded Edition: A Guide to Japanese Animation Since 1917.* Berkeley, CA: Stone Bridge Press.

Codeluppi, Vanni. 2000. *Pubblicità.* Bologna: Zanichelli.

Cohn, Angel. 2011. "*Once Upon a Time* versus *Grimm*: Will Either Fairy Tale Series Live Happily Ever After?" *Television Without Pity,* October 29. www.televisionwithoutpity. com/telefile/2011/10/once-upon-a-time-vs-grimm-will.php.

Coker, Catherine. 2010. "Exploitation of Bodies and Minds in Season One of Dollhouse." In *Sexual Rhetoric in the Works of Joss Whedon: New Essays,* edited by Erin B. Waggoner, 226–38. Jefferson, NC: McFarland.

Cole, Babette. 1987. *Prince Cinders.* London: Hamilton.

Collodi, Carlo. 1883. *Le avventure di Pinocchio.* Florence, Italy: Flice Paggi Libraio-Editore.

Connell, R. W. 2000. *The Men and the Boys.* Cambridge, UK: Polity.

———. 2005. "Globalization, Imperialism, and Masculinities." In *Handbook of Studies on Men and Masculinities,* edited by Michael S. Kimmel, Jeff Hearn, and R. W. Connell, 71–89. Thousand Oaks, CA: Sage.

Conrad, JoAnn. 2008. "Wonder Tale." In *The Greenwood Encyclopedia of Folktales and Fairy Tales,* edited by Donald Haase, 1041–42. Westport, CN: Greenwood Press.

"Contents of 'Extreme Makeover' house in Gilbert to be sold." 2012. *azcentral.com.* October 31. www.azcentral.com/community/gilbert/articles/20121030gilbert-extreme-makeover -house-auction.html.

"A Conversation with the Stars and Creators of *Once Upon a Time*." 2012. *The Paley Center for Media.* www.hulu.com/watch/338438#i1,p0,d2.

Cookson, Steven. 2010. "Red Dwarf, Red Riding, Ripping Yarns and Rising Damp." *Suite101. com.* April 29. www.suite101.com/content/red-dwarf-red-riding-ripping-yarns-and-ris ing-damp-a231593#ixzz1MpWmGg97.

Cope, Jim. 1998. "Why I Teach, Promote, and Love Adolescent Literature: Confessions of a College English Professor." *Voices from the Middle* 5(2): 7–9.

Corporation for Public Broadcasting. 2011. *Findings from Ready to Learn 2005–2010.* www. cpb.org/rtl/FindingsFromReadyToLearn2005–2010.pdf.

Corrigan, John Michael and Maria Corrigan. 2012. "Disrupting Flow: Seinfeld, Sopranos Series Finale and the Aesthetic of Anxiety." *Television and New Media* 13(2): 91–102.

Craig, Amanda. 2007. "Harry Potter and the Deathly Hallows." *Sunday Times*, UK. July 28. https://acs.thetimes.co.uk/?gotoUrl=http%3A%2F%2Fwww.thetimes.co.uk%2Ftto%2Farts%2Fbooks%2F.

Crowley, Karlyn, and John Pennington. 2010. "Feminist Frauds on the Fairies?: Didacticism and Liberation in Recent Retellings of 'Cinderella.'" *Marvels & Tales* 24(2): 297–313.

Csikszentmihalyi, Mihaly. 1997. *Finding Flow: The Psychology of Engagement with Everyday Life*. New York: HarperCollins.

D'Acci, Julie. 2002. "Gender, Representation and Television." In *Television Studies*, edited by Toby Miller, 91–94. London: British Film Institute.

———. 2004. "Cultural Studies, Television Studies, and the Crisis in the Humanities." In *Television after TV: Essays on a Medium in Transition*, edited by Lynn Spigel and Jan Olsson, 418–45. Durham: Duke University Press.

Dargis, Manohla. 2010. "False Security of Wealth: A Tale Turns Cautionary." *New York Times*, March 25. http://movies.nytimes.com/2010/03/26/movies/26bluebeard.html.

Darnton, Robert. 1984. *The Great Cat Massacre and Other Episodes in French Cultural History*. New York: Basic Books.

Dasgupta, Romit. 2000. "Performing Masculinities?: The 'Salaryman' at Work and Play." *Japanese Studies* 20(2): 189–200.

———. 2003. "Creating Corporate Warriors: The 'Salaryman' and Masculinity in Japan." In *Asian Masculinities: The Meaning and Practice of Manhood in China and Japan*, edited by Kam Louie and Morris Low, 118–34. London: Routledge Curzon.

———. 2005. "Salarymen Doing Straight: Heterosexual Men and the Dynamics of Gender Conformity." In *Genders, Transgenders and Sexualities in Japan*, edited by Mark McLelland and Romit Dasgupta, 168–82. London: Routledge.

Davenport, Tom. 2013. "Behind the Scenes." *Davenport Films & From the Brothers Grimm*. www.davenportfilms.com/pages/main_behindthescenespage.html.

Davies, Mererid Puw. 2001. *The Tale of Bluebeard in German Literature: From the Eighteenth Century to the Present*. Oxford, UK: Clarendon.

De Lauretis, Teresa. 1987. *Technologies of Gender: Essays on Theory, Film, and Fiction*. Bloomington: Indiana University Press.

De Vito, John, and Frank Tropea. 2010. *Epic Television Miniseries: A Critical History*. Jefferson, NC: McFarland.

Dégh, Linda. 1979. "Grimm's 'Household Tales' and Its Place in the Household: The Social Relevance of a Controversial Classic." *Western Folklore* 38(2): 83–103.

———. 1994. *American Folklore and the Mass Media*. Bloomington: Indiana University Press.

Dégh, Linda, and Andrew Vázsonyi. 1979. "Magic for Sale: Märchen and Legend in TV Advertising." *Fabula* 20(1): 47–68.

Dennis, Jeffrey P. 2003. "The Same Thing We Do Every Night: Signifying Same-Sex Desire in Television Cartoons." *Journal of Popular Film and Television* 32(3): 132–40.

Denzin, Norman K. 2006. "Pedagogy, Performance, and Autoethnography." *Text and Performance Quarterly* 26(4): 333–38.

Deritter, Lillian. 2010. "We're Not Men." In *Inside Joss' Dollhouse: From Alpha to Rossum*, edited by Jane Espenson, 189–203. Dallas, TX: Smart Pop.

Derrida, Jacques. 1996. *Archive Fever: A Freudian Impression*. Translated by Eric Prenowitz. Chicago: University of Chicago Press.

Dickens, Charles. 1852. *A Child's History of England: Volume I. England from the Ancient Times, to the Death of King John*. London: Bradbury and Evans.

Dickinson, Emily. 1990. *Selected Poems*, edited by Stanley Appelbaum. New York: Dover.

Disney/ABC Television Group. 2012. "Fact Sheet." *Disney/ABC Television Group*. www.disneyabctv.com/division/index_facts.shtml.

"Disney Renaissance." N.d. *Wikipedia*. http://en.wikipedia.org/wiki/Disney_Renaissance.

"Disney's Fairy Tale Weddings & Honeymoons." 2012. *Disney's Fairy Tale Weddings & Honeymoons*. http://disneyweddings.disney.go.com.

Do Rozario, Rebecca-Anne C. 2004. "The Princess and the Magic Kingdom: Beyond Nostalgia, the Function of the Disney Princess." *Women's Studies in Communication* 27(1): 34–59.

Doig, Alan. 1996. "From Lynskey to Nolan: The Corruption of British Politics and Public Service." *Journal of Law and Society* 23(1): 36–56.

Dollase, Hiromi Tsuchiya. 2003. "Early Twentieth Century Japanese Girls' Magazine Stories: Examining Shoujo Voice in *Hanamonogatari* (Flower Tales)." *The Journal of Popular Culture* 36(4): 724–55.

Donoghue, Emma. 1997. *Kissing the Witch: Old Tales in New Skins*. New York: Joanna Cotler Books.

dosgatosazules. 2012. "Why All of the Costuming Anachronisms?" *IMDb Bluebeard Discussion Board*. May 21. www.imdb.com/title/tt1355623/board/nest/199384187.

Douglas, Mary. 1995. "Red Riding Hood: An Interpretation from Anthropology." *Folklore* 106: 1–7.

Du Brow, Rick. 1965. "Television in Review." *Chicago Daily Defender,* March 3: 18.

Dubrofsky, Rachel E. 2011. *The Surveillance of Women on Reality Television: Watching the Bachelor and the Bachelorette*. Lanham, MD: Lexington Books.

Dundes, Alan. 1969. "The Devolutionary Premise in Folklore Theory." *Journal of the Folklore Institute* 6(1): 5–19.

———, ed. [1982] 1988. *Cinderella, a Casebook*. New York: Garland.

———, ed. 1989. *Little Red Riding Hood: A Casebook*. Madison: University of Wisconsin Press.

———. 1991. "Bruno Bettelheim's Uses of Enchantment and Abuses of Scholarship." *Journal of American Folklore* 104(411): 74–83.

Dworkin, Andrea. 1974. *Women-Hating*. New York: Dutton.

Eberly, Susan Schoon. 1988. "Fairies and the Folklore of Disability: Changelings, Hybrids and the Solitary Fairy." *Folklore* 99(1): 58–77.

Eco, Umberto. [1976] 1996. "Così la merce è diventata fiaba e racconto." *L'Unità*. December 4. http://archiviostorico.unita.it/cgi-bin/highlightPdf.cgi?t=ebook&file=/golpdf/uni_1996_12.pdf/04DUE02A.pdf.

Elliott, Kamilla. 2003. *Rethinking the Film/Novel Debate*. Cambridge: Cambridge University Press.

Elliott, Stuart. 2011. "In TV Pilots, Paranormal Is the New Normal." *New York Times,* May 22.

Ellis, Bill. 2008a. "Japanese Popular Culture." In *The Greenwood Encyclopedia of Folktales and Fairy Tales*, edited by Donald Haase, 513. Westport, CN: Greenwood Press.

———. 2008b. "Sleeping Beauty Awakens Herself: Folklore and Inversion in Cardcaptor Sakura." In *The Japanification of Children's Popular Culture: From Godzilla to Miyazaki*, edited by Mark I. West, 249–66. Lanham, MD: Scarecrow Press.

Ellis, Carolyn. 2004. *The Ethnographic I: A Methodological Novel about Autoethnography*. New York: Altamira.

Ellis, Carolyn, Tony E. Adams, and Arthur P. Bochner. 2011. "Autoethnography: An Overview." *Forum Qualitative Sozialforschung/Forum: Qualitative Social Research* 12(1): article 10. www.qualitative-research.net/index.php/fqs/article/view/1589/3095.

Ellis, Carolyn, and Arthur Bochner. [1994] 2000. "Autoethnography, Personal Narrative, Reflexivity: Research as Subject." In *Handbook of Qualitative Research*, edited by Norman K. Denzin and Yvonna S. Lincoln, 733–68. 2nd ed. Thousand Oaks, CA: Sage.

Ellis, John. 1982. *Visible Fictions: Cinema, Television, Video*. London: Routledge and Kegan Paul.

Ellis, John M. 1985. *One Fairy Story Too Many: The Brothers Grimm and Their Tales*. Chicago: University of Chicago Press.

Ellis, Sigrid. 2011. "The Ages of *Dollhouse* Autobiography through Whedon." In *Whedonistas! A Celebration of the Worlds of Joss Whedon by the Women Who Love Them*, edited by Lynne M. Thomas and Deborah Stanish, 42–48. Des Moines, IA: Mad Norwegian Press.

Empty Movement. 2000. "Kunihiko Ikuhara IRC Chat Interview." http://ohtori.nu/creators/a_nyaf.html.

———. 2002. "Empty Movement: Revolutionary Girl Utena." www.ohtori.nu.

Ende, Michael. 1979. *Die unendliche Geschichte*. Stuttgart, Germany: Thienemann.

Escaily. "my ten favorite scenes in the finale." 2012. *Once Upon a Time Wiki*. May 20. http://onceuponatime.wikia.com/wiki/User_blog:Escaily/my_ten_favorite_scenes _in_the_finale.

Espenson, Jane, ed. 2010. *Inside Joss' Dollhouse: From Alpha to Rossum*. Dallas, TX: Smart Pop.

Eubanks, Charlotte. 2008. "Japanese Tales." In *The Greenwood Encyclopedia of Folktales and Fairy Tales*, edited by Donald Haase, 513–18. Westport, CN: Greenwood Press.

Ewers, Hans-Heino. 2003. "Male Adolescence in German Fairy-Tale Novellas of the Enlightenment, Romanticism, and Biedermeier." *Marvels & Tales* 17(1): 75–85.

"Extreme Makeover: Home Edition Needs Your Help." 2011. *ABC13.com*. August 9. http://abclocal.go.com/ktrk/story?section=news/entertainment&id=8296732.

Extreme Makeover: Home Edition: The Official Companion Book. 2005. New York: Hyperion.

"'Extreme Makeover' left Gilbert family with unforeseen expenses." 2009. *Azcentral.com*. October 3. www.azcentral.com/style/hfe/decor/articles/2009/10/03/20091003extre mehome.html.

Facebook. 2012a. "Merlin—Official." www.facebook.com/MerlinOfficial/posts/337213052 964986.

Facebook. 2012b. "Merlin the Game." www.facebook.com/MerlinGame.

Falassi, Alessandro. 1980. *Folklore by the Fireside: Text and Context of the Tuscan Veglia*. Austin: University of Texas Press.

fallingparachutes. 2012. *Once Upon a Time Fan Site Forums*. September 30. http://forums. onceuponatimefansite.com/viewtopic.php?f=3&t=461&start=160.

Farinordin, Faridul Anwar. 2012. "When Two Worlds Collide." *New Straits Times*, March 23. www.nst.com.my/life-times/showbiz/when-two-worlds-collide-1.64521.

Fay, Carolyn. 2008. "Sleeping Beauty Must Die: The Plots of Perrault's 'La Belle au bois dormant.'" *Marvels & Tales* 22(2): 259–76.

Fell, John L. 1977. "Vladimir Propp in Hollywood." *Film Quarterly* 30(3): 19–28.

Fennell, Philip W. H. 1994. "Mentally Disordered Suspects in the Criminal Justice System." *Journal of Law and Society* 21(1): 57–71.

"Field Listing: Television Broadcast Stations." 2013. *The World Factbook*. www.cia.gov/library/publications/the-world-factbook/fields/2015.html.

Fish, Cheryl J. 2008. "Environmental Justice Issues in Literature and Film: From the Toxic to the Sustainable." In *Teaching North American Environmental Literature*, edited by Laird Christensen, Mark C. Long, and Fred Waage, 294–305. New York: The Modern Language Association of America.

Fisher, John H., and Mark Allen, eds. 2011. *The Complete Poetry and Prose of Geoffrey Chaucer*. 3rd ed. Wandsworth, UK: Cengage Learning.

Fisher, Mark. 2009. "The Red Riding Trilogy." *Frieze*. March 1. www.frieze.com/comment/article/the_red_riding_trilogy.

Fisherkeller, Jo Ann. 1997. "Everyday Learning about Identities among Young Adolescents in Television Culture." *Anthropology and Education Quarterly* 28(4): 467–92.

Fiske, John. 2011. *Television Culture*. New York: Routledge.

Flavius Josephus, Titus. 2009. *The Antiquities of the Jews*. Translated by William Whiston. www.gutenberg.org/files/2848/2848-h/2848-h.htm.

Flitterman, Sandy. 1983. "The *Real* Soap Operas: TV Commercials." In *Regarding Television: Critical Approaches—An Anthology*, edited by E. Ann Kaplan, 84–96. Los Angeles: American Film Institute.

Flores, Ángel. 1995. "Magical Realism in Spanish American Fiction (1955)." In *Magical Realism: Theory, History, Community*, edited by Lois P. Zamora and Wendy B. Faris, 109–18. Durham: Duke University Press.

Foreign Press Center Japan. 2007. "22: Women." http://fpcj.jp/old/e/mres/publication/ff/pdf_07/22_women.pdf.

Foucault, Michel. 1980. *The History of Sexuality*. Vol. 1. Translated by Robert Hurley. New York: Random House.

Frank, Arthur. 2010. *Letting Stories Breathe: A Socio-Narratology*. Chicago: University of Chicago Press.

Frankel, Valerie Estelle. 2010. "All Dolled Up: Twisted Princes and Fairytale Heroines." In *Inside Joss' Dollhouse: From Alpha to Rossum*, edited by Jane Espenson, 63–77. Dallas, TX: Smart Pop.

Freedman, Alisa. 2009. "*Train Man* and the Gender Politics of Japanese '*Otaku*' Culture: The Rise of New Media, Nerd Heroes and Consumer Communities." *Intersections: Gender and Sexuality in Asia and the Pacific* 20. http://intersections.anu.edu.au/issue20/freedman.htm.

Freud, Sigmund. 1957. "The Taboo of Virginity (Contributions to the Psychology of Love, Part 3)." *The Standard Edition of the Complete Psychological Works of Sigmund Freud*, edited and translated by James Strachey, 191–208. Vol. 11. London: The Hogarth Press and the Institute of Psycho-Analysis.

Friedan, Betty. 1963. *The Feminine Mystique*. New York: Norton.

Friedenthal, Andrew J. 2012. "The Lost Sister: Lesbian Eroticism and Female Empowerment in 'Snow White and Rose Red.'" In *Transgressive Tales: Queering the Grimms*, edited by Kay Turner and Pauline Greenhill, 161–80. Detroit: Wayne State University Press.

Frye, Northrop. 1967. *The Modern Century*. Toronto, ON: Oxford University Press.

Fukao, Kyoji. 2010. "The Structural Causes of Japan's 'Two Lost Decades.'" *RIETI Research Digest*. www.rieti.go.jp/en/about/Highlight_32/chap6.pdf.

Fuller, Graham. 2012. "Hollywood Fairy Tale Feeding Frenzy: 'Mirror, Mirror,' 'Snow White and the Huntsman.'" *Blouin Art Info*. March 7. http://artinfo.com/news/story/762270/hollywoods-fairy-tale-feeding-frenzy-continues-with-mirror-mirror-and-snow-white-and-the-huntsman.

Gallagher, David. 2009. *Metamorphosis: Transformations of the Body and the Influence of Ovid's Metamorphoses on Germanic Literature of the Nineteenth and Twentieth Centuries*. New York: Rodopi.

Galland, Antoine. 1704–1717. *Les Mille et une nuit, contes Arabes Traduites en François*. 12 vols. Paris: n.p.

Gamble, Nikki and Sally Yates. 2008. *Exploring Children's Literature*. London: Sage.

Garber, Marjorie. 1992. *Vested Interests: Cross-Dressing and Cultural Anxiety*. New York: Routledge.

Garland, Henry Burnand and Mary Garland. 1976. *The Oxford Companion to German Literature*. Oxford, UK: Clarendon.

Garrard, Greg. 2004. *Ecocriticism*. New York: Routledge.

Gates, Anita. 2012. "Celeste Holm, Witty Character Actress, Is Dead at 95." *New York Times*, July 15. www.nytimes.com/2012/07/16/theater/celeste-holm-witty-character-actress-dies-at-95.html?pagewanted=all.

Genette, Gérard. 1997. *Paratexts: Thresholds of Interpretation*. Translated by Jane E. Lewin. Cambridge: Cambridge University Press.

Georges, Robert A. 1969. "Toward an Understanding of Storytelling Events." *Journal of American Folklore* 82(326): 313–28.

Gera, Deborah Levine. 2010. "The Jewish Textual Traditions." In *The Sword of Judith: Judith Studies across the Disciplines*, edited by Kevin R. Brine, Elena Ciletti, and Henrike Lähnemann, 29–39. Cambridge, UK: Open Book Publishers.

Ghesquiere, Rita. 2006. "Little Red Riding Hood Where Are You Going?" In *Toplore: Stories and Songs*, edited by Paul Catteeuw, Marc Jacobs, Sigrid Rieuwerts, Eddy Tielemans, and Katrien Van Effelterre, 84–99. Trier, Germany: Wissenschaftlicher Verlag.

Gilbert, Sandra M., and Susan Gubar. 2000. *The Madwoman in the Attic: The Woman Writer and the Nineteenth Century Literary Imagination*. 2nd rev. ed. New Haven: Yale University Press.

Gillan, Jennifer. 2011. *Television and New Media: Must-Click TV*. New York: Routledge.

Gillespie, Marie. 2002. "Television and Race in Britain (from Comic Asians to Asian Comics)." In *Television Studies*, edited by Toby Miller, 116–19. London: British Film Institute.

"Ginger Rogers." n.d. In *Wikiquotes*. http://en.wikiquote.org/wiki/Ginger_Rogers.

Ginsberg, Faye and Lorna Roth. 2002. "First Peoples' Television (Aboriginal Peoples Television Network)." In *Television Studies*, edited by Toby Miller, 130–32. London: British Film Institute.

Goffman, Erving. 1974. *Frame Analysis: An Essay on the Organization of Human Experience*. Boston: Northeastern University Press.

Gombeaud, Adrien. 2009. "The Red Riding Trilogy." *Positif* 586: 42.

Goodwin, Andrew. 1993. *Dancing in the Distraction Factory: Music Television and Popular Culture*. London: Routledge.

Gorbman, Claudia. 1987. *Unheard Melodies: Narrative Film Music*. Bloomington: Indiana University Press.

Gorman, Bill. 2012. "'Once Upon a Time' Draws Its Top Audience in 11 Weeks." *TV by the Numbers*. January 30. http://tvbythenumbers.zap2it.com/2012/01/30/once-upon-a-time-draws-its-top-audience-in-11-weeks/117990.

Gössmann, Hilaria, Ilse Lenz, Kerstin Katherina Vogel, and Ulrike Wohr. 2004. "Gender." In *Modern Japanese Society*, edited by Josef Kreiner, Ulrich Möhwald, and Hans-Dieter Ölschleger, 181–218. Leiden: Brill.

Grady, D. B. 2011. "How Young Adult Fiction Came of Age." *The Atlantic*, August 1. www.theatlantic.com/entertainment/archive/2011/08/how-young-adult-fiction-came-of-age/242671.

Gramsci, Antonio. 1971. *Selections from the Prison Notebooks of Antonio Gramsci*. Edited and translated by Quintin Hoare and Geoffrey Nowell Smith. New York: International Publishers.

Gravett, Paul. 2004. *Manga: 60 Years of Japanese Comics*. London: Laurence King Publishing.

Gray, Jonathan. 2006. *Watching with the Simpsons: Television, Parody, and Intertextuality*. New York: Routledge.

———. 2009. "Cinderella Burps: Gender, Performativity, and the Dating Show." In *Reality TV: Remaking Television Culture*, edited by Susan Murray and Laurie Ouellette, 260–77. 2nd ed. New York: New York University Press.

———. 2011. "The Reviews Are in: TV Critics and the (Pre) Creation of Meaning." In *Flow TV: Television in the Age of Media Convergence*, edited by Michael Kackman, Marnie Binfield, Matthew Thomas Payne, Allison Perlman, and Bryan Sebok, 114–27. New York: Routledge.

Gray, William S., William H. Elson, Marion Monroe, and Zerna Sharp. 1930–1970. *The Dick and Jane Readers.* Chicago: Scott Foresman.

Greenhill, Pauline. 1989. *True Poetry: Traditional and Popular Verse in Ontario.* Montreal: McGill-Queen's University Press.

———. 1995. "'Neither a Man nor a Maid': Sexualities and Gendered Meanings in Cross-Dressing Ballads." *Journal of American Folklore* 108(428): 156–77.

Greenhill, Pauline, Anita Best, and Emilie Anderson-Grégoire. 2012. "Queering Gender: Transformations in 'Peg Bearskin,' 'La Poiluse,' and Related Tales." In *Transgressive Tales: Queering the Grimms,* edited by Kay Turner and Pauline Greenhill, 181–205. Detroit: Wayne State University Press.

Greenhill, Pauline, and Anne Brydon. 2010. "Mourning Mothers and Seeing Siblings: Feminism and Place in The Juniper Tree." In *Fairy Tale Films: Visions of Ambiguity,* edited by Pauline Greenhill and Sidney Eve Matrix, 116–36. Logan: Utah State University Press.

Greenhill, Pauline, and Steven Kohm. 2009. "Little Red Riding Hood and Pedophile in Film: Freeway, Hard Candy, and The Woodsman." *Jeunesse: Young People, Texts, Cultures* 1(2): 35–65.

———. 2013. "*Hoodwinked!* and *Jin-Roh: The Wolf Brigade*: Animated 'Little Red Riding Hood' Films and the Rashômon Effect." *Marvels & Tales* 27(1): 89-108.

Greenhill, Pauline, and Sidney Eve Matrix, eds. 2006. "Special Issue: Wedding Realities: Les noces en vrai." *Ethnologies* 28(2).

———. 2010a. "Envisioning Ambiguity: Fairy Tale Films." In *Fairy Tale Films: Visions of Ambiguity,* edited by Greenhill and Matrix, 1–22. Logan: Utah State University Press.

———, eds. 2010b. *Fairy Tale Films: Visions of Ambiguity.* Logan: Utah State University Press.

Greenwalt, David, and Jim Kouf. 2011a. Interview with Andre Dellamort. *Collider.com.* October 28. http://collider.com/jim-kouf-david-greenwalt-grimm-interview/123236.

———. 2011b. "Q&A with GRIMM EPs/Writers David Greenwalt and Jim Kouf." *No(Re) Runs.net.* October 28. http://noreruns.net/2011/10/28/qa-with-grimm-epswriters-david-greenwalt-jim-kouf.

———. 2011c. "We Preview the Fairytale World of GRIMM with Executive Producers David Greenwalt and Jim Kouf." *The TV Addict.com.* October 26. www.thetvaddict.com/2011/10/26/we-preview-the-fairytale-world-of-grimm-with-executive-producers-david-greenwalt-and-jim-fouf.

———. 2012. "Grimm and Bear It: Q & A with Grimm's David Greenwalt and Jim Kouf." *The Morton Report.* February 1. www.themortonreport.com/entertainment/television/grimm-and-bear-it-q-a-with-grimms-david-greenwalt-and-jim-kouf.

Greydanus, Steven D. N.d. "Quo Vadis Disney?: Notes on the End of the Disney Renaissance, circa 2001." *Decent Films Guide: Film Appreciation and Criticism Informed by Christian Faith.* www.decentfilms.com/articles/quovadisdisney.

Grieveson, Lee, and Haidee Wasson, eds. 2008. *Inventing Film Studies.* Durham: Duke University Press.

Grigsby, Mary. 1998. "*Sailormoon: Manga (Comics)* and *Anime (Cartoon)* Superheroine Meets Barbie: Global Entertainment Commodity Comes to the United States." *Journal of Popular Culture* 32(1): 59–80.

———. 1999. "The Social Production of Gender as Reflected in Two Japanese Culture Industry Products: *Sailormoon* and *Crayon Shin-Chan.*" In *Themes and Issues in Asian Cartooning: Cute, Cheap, Mad and Sexy,* edited by John A. Lent, 183–201. Bowling Green, OH: Bowling Green State University Popular Press.

"GRIMM: A Midseason Review by Kristen Micek." 2012. *Crimespree Magazine,* February 26. http://crimespreemag.com/blog/2012/02/grimm-a-midseason-review-by-kristen-micek.html.

Grimm, Jacob, and Wilhelm Grimm. 1998. *Kinder- und Hausmärchen*. Berlin: Realschul-buchhandlung. Translated by D. L. Ashliman (*Folklore and Mythology Electronic Texts*. www.pitt.edu/~dash/grimm021.html).

———. 1812–1815. *Kinder- und Hausmärchen* [Children's and Household Tales]. 2 vols. Berlin: Realschulbuchhandlung.

———. [1982] 1988. "Ash Girl (Aschenputtel)." In *Cinderella: A Casebook*, edited by Alan Dundes, 23–29. Madison: University of Wisconsin Press.

———. 1998. "Little Brier-Rose: Version of 1812." *Folktexts*—"Sleeping Beauty." Translated by D. L. Ashliman (www.pitt.edu/~dash/type0410.html).

———. 2001. "Brier Rose." In *The Great Fairy Tale Tradition: From Straparola and Basile to the Brothers Grimm*, edited by Jack Zipes, 696–98. New York: W.W. Norton and Company.

Grimm: Season 1. 2011. "IceMetalPunk." November 2. www.metacritic.com/tv/grimm/ user-reviews.

Grimmophilia. 2012. "Emphasisismine and Grimmophilia." June 6. http://grimmophilia. tumblr.com/post/24541851309/emphasismine-grimmophilia-replied-to-your-post.

Grishakova, Marina and Marie-Laure Ryan eds. 2010. *Intermediality and Storytelling*. Berlin: Walter de Gruyter.

Grosz, Elizabeth. 1994. *Volatile Bodies: Toward a Corporeal Feminism*. Bloomington: Indiana University Press.

Gunning, Tom. 2009. "Preface to the English-Language Edition." In *From Plato to Lumiere: Narration and Monstration in Literature and Cinema*, by Andre Gaudreault. Translated by Timothy Barnard, xvii–xxvi. Toronto, ON: University of Toronto Press.

Gutierrez, Anna Katrina. 2013. "Metamorphosis: The Emergence of Glocal Subjectivities in the Blend of Global, Local, East and West." In *Subjectivity in Asian Children's Literature and Film: Global Theories and Implications*, edited by John Stephens, 19–42. New York: Routledge.

Haase, Donald. 1988. "Gold into Straw: Fairy Tale Movies for Children and the Culture Industry." *The Lion and the Unicorn* 12(2): 193–207.

———. 1993. "Response and Responsibility in Reading Grimms' Fairy Tales." In *Reception of the Grimms' Fairy Tales: Responses, Reactions, Revisions*, edited by Donald Haase, 230–49. Detroit: Wayne State University Press.

———. 2000a. "Children, War, and the Imaginative Space of Fairy Tales." *The Lion and the Unicorn: A Critical Journal of Children's Literature* 24: 360–77.

———. 2000b. "Television and Fairy Tales." In *The Oxford Companion to Fairy Tales: The Western Fairy Tale Tradition from Medieval to Modern*, edited by Jack Zipes, 513–18. New York: Oxford University Press.

———, ed. 2004a. *Fairy Tales and Feminism: New Approaches*. Detroit: Wayne State University Press.

———. 2004b. "Feminist Fairy-Tale Scholarship." In *Fairy Tales and Feminism: New Approaches*, edited by Donald Haase, 1–36. Detroit: Wayne State University Press.

———. 2008. "Television." In *The Greenwood Encyclopedia of Folktales and Fairy Tales*, edited by Donald Haase, 947–51. Westport, CT: Greenwood Press.

Hale, Shannon. 2003. *The Goose Girl*. New York: Bloomsbury Publishing.

———. 2007. *Book of a Thousand Days*. New York: Bloomsbury Publishing.

———. 2012. "In Which I Gamely Stick Out My Tongue." *Squeetus Blog*. January 16. http:// oinks.squeetus.com/2012/01/in-which-i-gamely-stick-out-my-tongue.html.

Hall, Stuart. 1980. "Encoding/Decoding." In *Culture, Media, Language*, edited by Stuart Hall, Dorothy Hobson, Andrew Love, and Paul Willis, 128–38. London: Hutchinson.

Handler, Richard, and Jocelyn Linnekin. 1984. "Tradition, Genuine or Spurious?" *The Journal of American Folklore* 97(385): 273–90.

Haney, Jack V. 1999. *An Introduction to the Russian Folktale*. Armonk, NY: M.E. Sharpe.

Hanlon, Tina L. 2008. "Davenport, Tom (1939–)." In *The Greenwood Encyclopedia of Folktales and Fairy Tales,* edited by Donald Haase, 253–55. Westport, CT: Greenwood Press.

Harries, Elizabeth Wanning. 2004. "The Mirror Broken: Women's Autobiography and Fairy Tales." In *Fairy Tales and Feminism: New Approaches,* edited by Donald Haase, 99–111. Detroit: Wayne State University Press.

———. 2008. "Literary Fairy Tale." In *The Greenwood Encyclopedia of Folktales and Fairy Tales,* edited by Donald Haase, 578–83. Westport, CN: Greenwood Press.

Harris, Trudier. 1995. "Genre." *Journal of American Folklore* 108(430): 509–27.

Harriss, Chandler. 2008. "Policing Propp: Toward a Textualist Definition of the Procedural Drama." *Journal of Film and Video* 60(1): 43–59.

Hartley, John. 1992. *Tele-ology Studies in Television.* London: Routledge.

———. 2002. "The Constructed Viewer." In *Television Studies,* edited by Toby Miller, 60–63. London: British Film Institute.

Havens, Thomas R. H. 1975. "Women and War in Japan, 1937–45." *American Historical Review* 80(4): 913–34.

Hayward, Eva. 2008. "Lessons from a Starfish." In *Queering the Non/Human,* edited by Noreen Giffney and Myra J. Hird, 249–64. Aldershot, UK: Ashgate.

Hearn, Lafcadio. 1931. *Japanese Fairy Tale, The Goblin Spider.* Tokyo: Takejiro Hasegawa.

Hearne, Betsy. 1997. "Disney Revisited, or, Jiminy Cricket, It's Musty Down Here!" *The Horn Book* 73(2): 137–46.

Heiner, Heidi Anne, ed. 2010. *Sleeping Beauties: Sleeping Beauty and Snow White Tales from around the World.* Nashville, TN: SurLaLune Press.

———. 2012. "*Sherlock* and Hansel and Gretel." *SurLaLune Fairy Tales.* http://surlalune-fairytales.blogspot.com/2012/01/sherlock-and-hansel-and-gretel.html.

Hendershot, Heather. 2002. "Children and Education (*Sesame Street*)." In *Television Studies,* edited by Toby Miller, 80–83. London: British Film Institute.

Henry, Gordon D., Jr. 2009. "Allegories of Engagement: Stories/Theories—A Few Remarks." In *North American Indian Writing, Storytelling, and Critique,* edited by Gordon D. Henry, Jr., Nieves Pascual Soler, and Silvia Martinez-Falquina, 1–24. East Lansing: Michigan State University Press.

Herman, David. 1997. "Scripts, Sequences, and Stories: Elements of a Postclassical Narratology." *PMLA* 112(5): 1046–59.

Hermansson, Casie E. 2009. *Bluebeard: A Reader's Guide to the English Tradition.* Jackson: University Press of Mississippi.

Heuscher, Julius. 1974. *A Psychiatric Study of Myths and Fairy Tales: Their Origin, Meaning, and Usefulness.* Springfield, IL: Thomas Books.

Heyes, Cressida J. 2007. "Cosmetic Surgery and the Televisual Makeover." *Feminist Media Studies* 7(1): 17–32.

Higham, N. J. 2002. *King Arthur: Myth-Making and History.* London: Routledge.

Hill, Annette. 2005. *Reality TV: Audiences and Popular Factual Television.* New York: Routledge.

Hill, Rodney. 2005–2006. "Donkey Skin (Peau d'âne)." *Film Quarterly* 59(2): 40–44.

Hine, Thomas. 2000. *The Rise and Fall of the American Teenager: A New History of the American Adolescent Experience.* New York: HarperCollins.

Hoffer, Tom W., and Richard Alan Nelson. 1978. "Docudrama on American Television." *Journal of the University Film Association* 30(2): 21–27.

Hoffmann, Ernst Theodor Amadeus. 1905. *Sämtliche Werke.* Edited by Eduard Grisebach. Vol. 1. Leipzig, Germany: Hess & Becker.

———. 2004. *Der goldne Topf. Ein Märchen aus der neuen Zeit.* Stuttgart, Germany: Reclam.

Holbek, Bengt. 1989. "The Language of Fairy Tales." In *Nordic Folklore: Recent Studies,* edited by Reimund Kvideland and Henning K. Sehmsdorf, 40–62. Bloomington: Indiana University Press.

Holdsworth, Amy, and Barbara Sadler. 2010. "Northern Views: A Report from the Northern Television Studies Research Group." *Visual Culture in Britain* 11(1): 137–41.

Holmlund, Chris. 2002. *Impossible Bodies: Femininity and Masculinity at the Movies.* New York: Routledge.

Horkheimer, Max, and Theodor W. Adorno. 2002. "The Culture Industry: Enlightenment as Mass Deception." In *Dialectic of Enlightenment,* edited by Gunzelin Schmid Noerr, translated by Edmund Jephcott, 94–136. Stanford: Stanford University Press.

Horsley, Lee. 2010. "From Sherlock Holmes to the Present." In *A Companion to Crime Fiction,* edited by Charles J. Rzepka and Lee Horsley, 28–42. Chichester, UK: Blackwell.

Howkins, Tom. 2010. "The Red Riding Trilogy: A Review." *Suite101.com.* April 20. www.suite101.com/content/the-red-riding-trilogy-a-review-a227765.

Hurford, Emily M. 2009. "Gender and Sexuality in Shoujo Manga: Undoing Heteronormative Expectations in *Utena, Pet Shop of Horrors,* and *Angel Sanctuary.*" MA thesis, Bowling Green State University.

Hutcheon, Linda. 1985. *A Theory of Parody: The Teachings of Twentieth-Century Art Forms.* New York: Methuen.

———. 1988. *A Poetics of Postmodernism.* New York: Routledge.

———. 2006. *A Theory of Adaptation.* New York: Routledge.

Iacuone, David. 2005. "'Real Men Are Tough Guys': Hegemonic Masculinity and Safety in the Construction Industry." *Journal of Men's Studies* 13(2): 247–66.

Ikuhara, Kunihiko. 2011a. "Director Kunihiko Ikuhara's Episode Commentary: Part 3." In *Revolutionary Girl Utena: The Apocalypse Saga,* by Ikuhara, translated by Sarah Alys Lindhom, 5–11. n.p.: Nozomi Entertainment.

———. 2011b. "Kunihiko Ikuhara Director Interview." In *Revolutionary Girl Utena: The Apocalypse Saga,* by Ikuhara, translated by Sarah Alys Lindhom, 12–17. N.p.: Nozomi Entertainment.

Inge, M. Thomas. 2004. "Walt Disney's *Snow White and the Seven Dwarfs*: Art Adaptation and Ideology." *Journal of Popular Film and Television* 32(3): 132–42.

Ishii-Kuntz, Masako. 2003. "Balancing Fatherhood and Work: Emergence of Diverse Masculinities in Contemporary Japan." In *Men and Masculinities in Contemporary Japan: Dislocating the Salaryman Doxa,* edited by James E. Roberson and Nobue Suzuki, 198–216. London: Routledge.

Ito, Kimio. 1996. *Danseigaku nyūmon* [Introduction to Men's Studies]. Tokyo: Sakuhinsha.

Jacobs, Linda. 2011. "Resurrecting the Buried Self: Fairy Tales and the Analytic Encounter." *Psychoanalytic Review* 98(6): 871–90.

Jahn, Pamela. 2010. "Bluebeard: Interview with Catherine Breillat." *Electric Sheep: A Deviant View of Cinema.* July 16. www.electricsheepmagazine.co.uk/features/2010/07/16/bluebeard-interview-with-catherine-breillat.

Jecreath-235-941347. 2011. "Not Your Momma's Fairy Tale." Reviews and Ratings for *Grimm.* December 10. www.imdb.com/title/tt1830617/reviews.

Jenkins, David. 2010. "Catherine Breillat on *Bluebeard.*" *Time Out London.* July 13. www.timeout.com/film/features/show-feature/10295/catherine-breillat-on-bluebeard.html.

Jenkins, Henry. 1991. "'It's Not a Fairy Tale Anymore': Gender, Genre, *Beauty and the Beast.*" *Journal of Film and Video* 43(1/2): 90–110.

———. 1992. *Textual Poachers: Television Fans & Participatory Culture.* New York: Routledge.

———. 2006. *Convergence Culture: Where Old and New Media Collide.* New York: New York University Press.

Jenkins, Philip. 1988. "Serial Murder in England 1940–1985." *Journal of Criminal Justice* 16(1): 1–15.

Jennings, Tom. 2009. "Parcel of Rogues." *Variant* 35. www.variant.org.uk/35texts/Rogues.html.

Jhally, Sut. 1989. "Advertising as Religion: The Dialectic of Technology and Magic." In *Cultural Politics in Contemporary America*, edited by Ian Angus and Sut Jhally, 217–29. London: Routledge.

Jones, Alan. 1997a. "Snow White in the Black Forest: The Fairy Tale Returns to Its Roots in Showtime's Gothic Chiller." *Cinefantastique* 29(3): 24–26.

———. 1997b. "Snow White Makeup & Effects: The Visual Tricks Behind-the-Scenes, Plus Linda Devetta on Prosthetics." *Cinefantastique* 29(3): 30–31.

———. 1997c. "Weaver on Her Wicked Star Turn as the Evil Queen." *Cinefantasique* 29(3): 27–30.

Jones, Sara Gwenllian. 2002. "Gender and Queerness (*Xena: Warrior Princess*)." In *Television Studies*, edited by Toby Miller, 109–12. London: British Film Institute.

Jones, Steven Swann. 1987. "On Analyzing Fairy Tales: 'Little Red Riding Hood' Revisited." *Western Folklore* 46(2): 97–114.

———. 2002. *The Fairy Tale: The Magic Mirror of the Imagination*. London: Routledge.

Joosen, Vanessa. 2011. *Critical and Creative Perspectives on Fairy Tales: An Intertextual Dialogue between Fairy-Tale Scholarship and Postmodern Retellings*. Detroit: Wayne State University Press.

Jorgensen, Jeana. 2007. "A Wave of the Magic Wand: Fairy Godmothers in Contemporary American Media." *Marvels & Tales* 21(2): 216–27.

———. 2010. "Political and Theoretical Feminisms in American Folkloristics: Definition Debates, Publication Histories, and the *Folklore Feminists Communication*." *The Folklore Historian* 27: 43–73.

Judith. 1995. In *The Holy Bible (Apocrypha)*, King James Version. Electronic Text Center. Charlottesville: University of Virginia Library. http://etext.lib.virginia.edu/toc/modeng/public/KjvJudi.html.

Just, Julie. 2010. "The Parent Problem in Young Adult Lit." *New York Times*, April 1. www.nytimes.com/2010/04/04/books/review/Just-t.html?pagewanted=all&_r=0.

Kafka, Franz. 1915. *Die Verwandlung*. Leipzig: K. Wolff.

Kamenetsky, Christa. 1972. "Folklore as a Political Tool in Nazi Germany." *Journal of American Folklore* 85(337): 221–35.

———. 1977. "Folktale and Ideology in the Third Reich." *Journal of American Folklore* 90(356): 168–78.

———. 1984. *Children's Literature in Hitler's Germany: The Cultural Policy of National Socialism*. Athens: Ohio University Press.

Kaplan, E. Ann, ed. 1983. *Regarding Television: Critical Approaches—An Anthology*. Los Angeles: American Film Institute.

Kerridge, Richard, and Neil Sammells, eds. 1998. *Writing the Environment: Ecocriticism and Literature*. London: Zed Books.

Kimmel, Michael S. 2001. "Masculinity as Homophobia: Fear, Shame, and Silence in the Construction of Gender Identity." In *The Masculinities Reader*, edited by Stephen M. Whitehead and Frank J. Barrett, 266–87. Cambridge: Polity Press.

King Arthur. Opera. 1691. Composed by Henry Purcell, libretto by John Dryden.

King, Stephen. 2000. "Wild about Harry." *New York Times*, July 23. www.nytimes.com/books/00/07/23/reviews/000723.23kinglt.html.

Kinsella, Sharon. 1998. "Japanese Subculture in the 1990s: Otaku and the Amateur Manga Movement." *The Journal of Japanese Studies* 24(2): 289–316.

Kitsis, Edward. 2011. "About the Show." *Once Upon a Time*. http://beta.abc.go.com/shows/once-upon-a-time/about-the-show.

Kohm, Steven, and Pauline Greenhill. 2010. "'Little Red Riding Hood' Crime Films: Criminal Themes and Critical Variations." *The Annual Review of Interdisciplinary Justice Research* 1: 77–93.

———. 2011a. "'Little Red Riding Hood' Crime Films: Critical Variations on Criminal Themes." *Law, Culture and the Humanities.* September 12. Online First. doi:10.1177/1743872111416328. http://lch.sagepub.com/content/early/2011/07/19/17 43872111416328.full.pdf+html.

———. 2011b. "Pedophile Crime Films as Popular Criminology: A Problem of Justice?" *Theoretical Criminology* 15(2): 195–216.

———. 2013. "'This Is the North, Where We Do What We Want:' Popular Green Criminology and 'Little Red Riding Hood' Films." In *Routledge International Handbook of Green Criminology,* edited by Nigel South and Avi Brisman, 365–78. London: Routledge.

Kokorski, Karin. 2011. "I Want More!: Insatiable Villains in Children's Literature and Young Adults' Fiction." In *Villains: Global Perspectives on Villains and Villainy Today,* edited by Burcu Genc and Corinna Lenhardt, 147–54. Oxford, UK: Inter-Disciplinary Press.

Kompare, Derek. 2011. "More 'Moments of Television': Online Cult Television Authorship." In *Flow TV: Television in the Age of Media Convergence,* edited by Michael Kackman, Marnie Binfield, Matthew Thomas, Allison Perlman, and Bryan Sebok, 95–113. New York: Routledge.

Kotani, Mari. 2006. "Metamorphosis of the Japanese Girl: The Girl, the Hyper-Girl, and the Battling Beauty." *Mechademia* 1: 162–69.

Kousaleos, Nicole. 1999. "Feminist Theory and Folklore." *Folklore Forum* 30(1/2): 19–34.

Koven, Mikel J. 2003. "Folklore Studies and Popular Film and Television: A Necessary Critical Survey." *Journal of American Folklore* 116(460): 176–95.

———. 2008. *Film, Folklore, and Urban Legends.* Lanham, MD: Scarecrow.

Kozloff, Sarah. 1992. "Narrative Theory and Television." In *Channels of Discourse, Reassembled: Television and Contemporary Criticism,* edited by Robert C. Allan, 67–100. 2nd ed. Chapel Hill: University of North Carolina Press.

Kristeva, Julia. 1980. *Desire in Language: A Semiotic Approach to Literature and Art,* edited by Leon S. Roudiez and Alice Jardine, translated by Thomas Gora. New York: Columbia University Press.

Kuwada, Brian. 2009. "How Blue *Is* His Beard?: An Examination of the 1862 Hawaiian-Language Translation of 'Bluebeard.'" *Marvels & Tales* 23(1): 17–39.

Kuykendal, Leslee Farish, and Brian W. Sturm. 2007. "We Said Feminist Fairy Tales, Not Fractured Fairy Tales! The Construction of the Feminist Fairy Tale: Female Agency over Role Reversal." *Children and Libraries* 5(3): 38–41.

Labrie, Vivan. 1997. "Help! Me, S/he, and the Boss." In *Undisciplined Women: Tradition and Culture in Canada,* edited by Pauline Greenhill and Diane Tye, 151–66. Montreal: McGill-Queen's University Press.

Lamarre, Thomas. 2007. "Platonic Sex: Perversion and Shôjo Anime (Part Two)." *Animation* 2(1): 9–25.

———. 2009. *The Anime Machine: A Media Theory of Animation.* Minneapolis: University of Minnesota Press.

Lang, Andrew. 1889. *The Blue Fairy Book.* London: Longmans, Green, and Co.

Lanham, Betty B., and Masao Shimura. 1967. "Folktales Commonly Told American and Japanese Children." *Journal of American Folklore* 80: 33–48.

Lau, Kimberly J. 2012. "A Desire for Death: The Grimms' Sleeping Beauty in *The Bloody Chamber.*" In *Transgressive Tales: Queering the Grimms,* edited by Kay Turner and Pauline Greenhill, 121–40. Detroit: Wayne State University Press.

Lee, Jeffrey. 2000. *Crown of Venus: A Guide to Royal Women around the World.* Lincoln: Writers Club Press.

Lee, Sung-Ae. 2009. "Re-visioning Gendered Folktales in Novels by Mia Kun and Nora Okja Keller." *Asian Ethnology* 68(1): 131–50.

———. 2011. "Lures and Horrors of Alterity: Adapting Korean Tales of Fox Spirits." *International Research in Children's Literature* 4(2): 135–50.

Leung, Helen Hok-Sze. 2006. "Unsung Heroes: Reading Transgender Subjectivities in Hong Kong Action Cinema." In *The Transgender Studies Reader,* edited by Susan Stryker and Stephen Whittle, 685–97. New York: Routledge.

Leupp, Gary P. 1995. *Male Colors: The Construction of Homosexuality in Tokugawa Japan.* Berkeley: University of California Press.

Levine, Elana. 2005. "Fractured Fairy Tales and Fragmented Markets: Disney's Weddings of a Lifetime and the Cultural Politics of Media Conglomeration." *Television & New Media* 6(1): 71–88.

Lewis, C. S. 1950. *The Lion, the Witch and the Wardrobe.* London: Geoffrey Bles.

———. 1951. *Prince Caspian.* London: Geoffrey Bles.

———. 1952. *The Voyage of the Dawn Treader.* London: Geoffrey Bles.

———. 1953. *The Silver Chair.* London: Geoffrey Bles.

———. 1954. *The Horse and His Boy.* London: Harper Trophy.

———. 1955. *The Magician's Nephew.* London: The Bodley Head.

———. 1956. *The Last Battle.* London: The Bodley Head.

Lieberman, Marcia R. 1972. "'Some Day My Prince Will Come': Female Acculturation through the Fairy Tale." *College English* 34(3): 383–95 (reprinted in *Don't Bet on the Prince: Contemporary Feminist Fairy Tales in North America and England,* edited by Jack Zipes, 185–200. Aldershot, UK: Scholar Press, 1998).

Lin, Ming-Hsun. 2010. "Fitting the Glass Slipper: A Comparative Study of the Princess's Role in the Harry Potter Novels and Films." In *Fairy Tale Films: Visions of Ambiguity,* edited by Pauline Greenhill and Sidney Eve Matrix, 79–98. Logan: Utah State University Press.

Lindholm, Charles. 2008. *Culture and Authenticity.* Malden, MA: Blackwell.

Littleton, Cynthia. 2012. "Fairy Tale Comes True for 'Lost' Boys: ABC's 'Once Upon a Time' Successfully Tackles Unique Challenges." *Variety,* May 5. www.variety.com/article/VR1118053530?refCatId=14.

Long, Darlene. 2012. "Grimm: Turning the Page—An Interview with Creators David Greenwalt and Jim Kouf." *The Voice of TV.* February 1. http://thevoiceoftv.com/news-and-gossip/grimm-turning-the-page-%E2%80%93-an-interview-with-creators-david-greenwalt-and-jim-kouf.

Lord, Albert B. 2000. *The Singer of Tales.* Edited by Stephen Mitchell and Gregory Nagy. Cambridge: Harvard University Press.

Luckett, Moya. 1999. "Girl Watchers: Patty Duke and Teen TV." In *The Revolution Wasn't Televised: Sixties Television and Social Conflict,* edited by Lynn Spigel and Michael Curtin, 95–116. New York: Routledge.

Lukasiewicz, Tracie D. 2010. "The Parallelism of the Fantastic and the Real: Guillermo del Toro's *Pan's Labyrinth/El Laberinto del fauno* and Neomagical Realism." In *Fairy Tale Films: Visions of Ambiguity,* edited by Pauline Greenhill and Sidney Eve Matrix, 60–78. Logan: Utah State University Press.

Lupack, Alan. 2002. "Foreword." In *King Arthur in Popular Culture,* edited by Elizabeth S. Sklar and Donald L. Hoffman, 1–4. Jefferson, NC: McFarland.

Lurie, Alison. 1970. "Fairy Tale Liberation." *New York Review of Books.* December 17. www.nybooks.com/articles/archives/1970/dec/17/fairy-tale-liberation/?pagination=false.

———. 1971. "Witches and Fairies: Fitzgerald to Updike." *New York Review of Books.* December 2: 6.

———. 1990. *Don't Tell the Grown-ups: Subversive Children's Literature.* London: Bloomsbury.

Lurie, Doron J. 2006. *Femme Fatale.* Translated by Jerry Aviram. Tel Aviv, Israel: Tel Aviv Museum of Art.

Lüthi, Max. 1970. *Once Upon a Time: On the Nature of Fairy Tales*. New York: Frederick Ungar.

———. 1982. *The European Folktale: Form and Nature*, translated by John D. Niles. Bloomington: Indiana University Press.

———. 1984. *The Fairytale as Art Form and Portrait of Man*, translated by Jon Erickson. Bloomington: Indiana University Press.

Lyall, Sarah. 2010. "William and Kate: A Fairy Tale, Ending Unknown." *New York Times*, November 20. www.nytimes.com/2010/11/21/weekinreview/21lyall.html.

Lynch, Michael J., and Paul B. Stretsky. 2003. "The Meaning of Green: Contrasting Criminological Perspectives." *Theoretical Criminology* 7(2): 217–38.

MacDonald, George. 1999. *The Complete Fairy Tales*. New York: Penguin Books.

MagicalUnicorn22. 2010. "Merlin Fan Questionnaire." *YouTube.com*. August 27. www.youtube.com/watch?v=x5G_fW05pF0.

Magnus-Johnston, Kendra. 2013. "'Reeling In' Grimm Masculinities: Hucksters, Cross-Dressers, and Ninnies." *Marvels & Tales* 27(1): 65–88.

Mallan, Kerry M. 2000. "Witches, Bitches and Femme Fatales: Viewing the Female Grotesque in Children's Film." *Papers: Explorations into Children's Literature* 10(1): 26–35.

Malory, Sir Thomas. 1485. *Le Morte d'Arthur*. England: William Caxton.

Mankin, Nina, James Lapine, Tony Straiges, Ann Hould-Ward, Stephen Sondheim, Chip Zien, Tom Aldredge, Richard Nelson, Jonathan Tunick, Lar Lubovitch, Joanna Gleason, and Bernadette Peters. 1988. "The PAJ Casebook #2: Into the Woods." *Performing Arts Journal* 11(1): 46–66.

Martin, George R. R. 1996. *A Game of Thrones*. New York: Bantam.

———. 1999. *A Clash of Kings*. New York: Bantam.

———. 2000. *A Storm of Swords*. New York: Bantam.

———. 2005. *A Feast for Crows*. New York: Bantam.

———. 2011. *A Dance with Dragons*. New York: Bantam.

Martin, Holly E. 2011. *Writing between Cultures: A Study of Hybrid Narratives in Ethnic Literature of the United States*. Jefferson, NC: McFarland.

Mathews, Gordon. 2003. "Can 'a Real Man' Live for His Family?: *Ikigai* and Masculinity in Today's Japan." In *Men and Masculinities in Contemporary Japan: Dislocating the Salaryman Doxa*, edited by James E. Roberson and Nobue Suzuki, 109–25. London: Routledge.

Matrix, Sidney Eve. 2010. "A Secret Midnight Ball and a Magic Cloak of Invisibility." In *Fairy Tale Films: Visions of Ambiguity*, edited by Pauline Greenhill and Sidney Eve Matrix, 178–97. Logan: Utah State University Press.

Matthew. 1995. In *The Holy Bible*, King James Version. Electronic Text Center. Charlottesville: University of Virginia Library. http://etext.virginia.edu/toc/modeng/public/KjvMatt.html.

Mayer, Fanny Hagin. 1986. *The Yanagita Kunio Guide to the Japanese Folk Tale*. Bloomington: Indiana University Press.

McCallum, Robyn. 2002. "Masculinity as Social Semiotic: Identity Politics and Gender in Disney Animated Films." In *Ways of Being Male: Representing Masculinities in Children's Literature and Film*, edited by John Stephens, 116–32. New York: Routledge.

McDavid, Jodi, and Ian Brodie. 2005. "Vladimir Propp, Meet Happy Gilmore: Adam Sandler and Vernacular Cinema." *Culture & Tradition* 27: 7–23.

McGlathery, James M. 1991. *Fairy Tale Romance: The Grimms, Basile, and Perrault*. Urbana: University of Illinois Press.

McKee, Robert. 1997. *Story: Substance, Structure, Style, and the Principles of Screenwriting*. New York: Harper-Collins.

McLane, Maureen. 2008. *Balladeering, Minstrelsy, and the Making of British Romantic Poetry*. Cambridge: Cambridge University Press.

McLean, Adrienne L. 1998. "Media Effects: Marshall McLuhan, Television Culture, and 'The X-Files.'" *Film Quarterly* 51(4): 2–11.

McLelland, Mark J. 2000. *Male Homosexuality in Modern Japan: Cultural Myths and Social Realities.* Abingdon, Australia: RoutledgeCurzon.

———. 2005. *Queer Japan from the Pacific War to the Internet Age.* Lanham, NJ: Rowman & Littlefield.

McMillan, Graeme. 2012. "Another Bite of the Poisoned Apple: Why Does Pop Culture Love Fairy Tales Again?" *Time Entertainment.* May 30. http://entertainment.time.com/2012/05/30/another-bite-of-the-poisoned-apple-why-does-pop-culture-love-fairy-tales-again.

Meehan, Eileen R. 2002. "Targeting Women (Who Is Television's Audience?)." In *Television Studies,* edited by Toby Miller, 113–15. London: British Film Institute.

Merlin. Opera. 1886. Composed by Carl Goldmark.

Meslow, Scott. 2012. "Fairy Tales Started Dark, Got Cute, and Are Now Getting Dark Again." *The Atlantic,* May 31. www.theatlantic.com/entertainment/archive/2012/05/fairy-tales-started-dark-got-cute-and-are-now-getting-dark-again/257934.

Meyer, Stephenie. 2005. *Twilight.* New York: Little, Brown and Company.

———. 2006. *New Moon.* New York: Little, Brown and Company.

———. 2007. *Eclipse.* New York: Little, Brown and Company.

———. 2008. *Breaking Dawn.* New York: Little, Brown and Company.

Miller, Laura. 2006. *Beauty Up: Exploring Contemporary Japanese Body Aesthetics.* Berkeley: University of California Press.

———. 2008. "Japan's Cinderella Motif: Beauty Industry and Mass Culture Interpretations of a Popular Icon." *Asian Studies Review* 32(3): 393–409.

Miller, Scott. 2007. *Strike Up the Band: A New History of Musical Theater.* Portsmouth, NH: Heinemann.

Miller, Toby. 2002. *Television Studies.* London: British Film Institute.

———. 2010. *Television Studies: The Basics.* New York: Routledge.

Minow, Newton, and Craig LaMay. 1995. *Abandoned in the Wasteland: Children, Television, and the First Amendment.* New York: Hill and Wang.

Mittell, Jason. 2004. *Genre and Television: From Cop Shows to Cartoons in American Culture.* New York: Routledge.

Monmouth, Geoffrey of. 1136. *Historia Regum Britanniae.* N.p.

Mordden, Ethan. 1992. *Rodgers and Hammerstein.* New York: Harry N. Abrahams, Inc., Publishers.

"Movies & TV: Tom Davenport." 2013. *New York Times,* January 30. http://movies.nytimes.com/person/717945/Tom-Davenport/filmography.

MsTaken. 2012. "Grimm: It's Loaded with Wesenality!" *Television without Pity.* August 30. http://forums.televisionwithoutpity.com/index.php?showtopic=3205259&st=5790.

Mulhern, Chieko Irie. 1985. "Analysis of Cinderella Motifs, Italian and Japanese." *Asian Folklore Studies* 44(1): 1–37.

Munsch, Robert N. 1980. *The Paper Bag Princess.* Toronto, ON: Annick Press.

"Muppet Wiki: The StoryTeller." 2013. http://muppet.wikia.com/wiki/index.php?search=the+storyteller&fulltext=Search.

Mustich, Emma. 2011. "Are 'Dark' Fairy Tales More Authentic?" *Salon.com.* August 20. www.salon.com/2011/08/20/fairy_tale_movies.

Nakamura, Momoko. 2001. "Power Relations in Fairy-Tale Discourse: Invisible Power in a Japanese Cinderella." *Shizen Ningen Shakai: Kantō Gakuin Daigaku Keizaigakubu Kyōyō Gakkai* [Nature, People, Society: Joint Bulletin of Liberal Arts Kantō Gakuin University Economics Department] 31: 103–38.

Napier, Susan. 2001. *Anime: From Akira to Princess Mononoke Experiencing Contemporary Japanese Animation*. New York: Palgrave.

———. 2011. "Where Have All the Salarymen Gone?: Masculinity, Masochism, and Technomobility in *Densha Otoko*." In *Recreating Japanese Men*, edited by Sabine Frühstück and Anne Walthall, 154–76. Berkeley: University of California Press.

Napikoski, Linda. N.d.a. "Feminism in 1964." *About.com Women's History*. http://womenshistory.about.com/od/feminism-second-wave/a/Feminism-in-1964.htm.

———. N.d.b. "The Personal Is Political: Widespread Slogan of the Women's Movement." *About.com Women's History*. http://womenshistory.about.com/od/feminism/a/consciousness_raising.htm.

Nelson, Barbara Barney. 2008. "Predators in Literature." In *Teaching North American Environmental Literature*, edited by Laird Christensen, Mark C. Long, and Fred Waage, 256–68. New York: The Modern Language Association of America.

Nennius. 828–830. *Historia Brittonum*. N.p.

Neubuhr, Elfriede. 1974. *Begriffsbestimmung des literarischen Biedermeier*. Darmstadt, Germany: Wissenschaftliche Buchgesellschaft.

Neuhaus, Stefan. 2003. *Grundriss der Literaturwissenschaft*. Tübingen, Germany: A. Francke.

Nikolajeva, Maria. 1996. *Children's Literature Comes of Age: Toward a New Aesthetic*. New York: Garland.

———. 2008. "Fantasy." In *The Greenwood Encyclopedia of Folktales and Fairy Tales*, edited by Donald Haase, 329–34. Westport, CT: Greenwood.

Noone, Kristin. 2010. "No Place Like the O.Z.: Heroes and Hybridity in Sci-Fi's Tin Man." In *The Universe of Oz: Essays on Baum's Series and Its Progeny*, edited by Kevin K. Durand and Mary K. Leigh, 94–106. Jefferson, NC: McFarland.

Ocasio, Rafael. 2004. *Literature of Latin America*. Westport, CT: Greenwood.

O'Connor, John J. 1987. "TV Review: 'The StoryTeller,' with John Hurt." *New York Times*, October 26. www.nytimes.com/1987/10/26/arts/tv-review-the-storyteller-with-john-hurt.html.

Ogg, Kerin. 2010. "Lucid Dreams, False Awakenings: Figures of the Fan in Kon Satoshi." *Mechademia* 5: 157–74.

Ohmann, Richard. 1996. *Selling Culture: Magazines, Markets, and Class at the Turn of the Century*. London: Verso.

Oliver, Laura M. and Kae Reynolds. 2010. "Serving the Once and Future King: Using the TV Series *Merlin* to Teach Servant-Leadership and Leadership Ethics in Schools." *Journal of Leadership Education* 9(2): 122–34.

Once Upon a Time Faccbook page. 2011–2012. www.facebook.com/OnceABC.

Opie, Iona and Peter Opie. 1974. *The Classic Fairy Tales*. New York: Oxford University Press.

Orenstein, Catherine. 2002. *Little Red Riding Hood Uncloaked: Sex, Morality, and the Evolution of a Fairy Tale*. New York: Basic Books.

Orenstein, Peggy. 2011. *Cinderella Ate My Daughter: Dispatches from the Front Lines of the New Girlie-Girl Culture*. New York: Harper.

Oring, Elliott. 1986. "Folk Narratives." In *Folk Groups and Folklore Genres: An Introduction*, edited by Elliott Oring, 121–46. Logan: Utah State University Press.

Orme, Jennifer. 2012. "Happily Ever After . . . According to Our Tastes: Jeanette Winterson's 'Twelve Dancing Princesses' and Queer Possibility." In *Transgressive Tales: Queering the Grimms*, edited by Kay Turner and Pauline Greenhill, 141–60. Detroit: Wayne State University.

Orosan-Weine, Pamela. 2007. "The Swan: The Fantasy of Transformation versus the Reality of Growth." *Configurations* 15: 17–32.

Osborne, Joe. 2012. "How *Merlin* on Facebook Is Anything But 'A Marketing Exercise.'" *Games News Blog.* August 24. http://blog.games.com/2012/08/24/merlin-facebook -game-interview.

Out of the Blue Enterprises. 2007a. *Super Why!* PBS Kids. http://pbskids.org/superwhy.

———. 2007b. *Super Why!* PBS Parents. www.pbs.org/parents/superwhy/program.

Pace, David. 1982. "Beyond Morphology: Lévi-Strauss and the Analysis of Folktales." In *Cinderella, a Folklore Casebook,* edited by Alan Dundes, 245–58. New York: Garland.

Palma, Shannan. 2012. *Tales as Old as Time: Myth, Gender, and the Fairy Tale in Popular Culture.* PhD dissertation, Emory University.

Palmer, Gareth. 2007. *"Extreme Makeover: Home Edition:* An American Fairy Tale." In *Makeover Television: Realities Remodelled,* edited by Dana A. Heller, 165–76. London: I. B. Tauris.

Panofsky, Erwin. 1939. *Studies in Iconology: Humanist Themes in the Art of the Renaissance.* New York: Harper and Row.

Panttaja, Elisabeth. 1993. "Going Up in the World: Class in 'Cinderella.'" *Western Folklore* 52(1): 85–104.

Peace, David. 1999. *Nineteen Seventy-Four.* London: Serpent's Tail.

———. 2001. *Nineteen Eighty.* London: Serpent's Tail.

———. 2002. *Nineteen Eighty-Three.* London: Serpent's Tail.

Peppard, Murray B. 1971. *Paths through the Forest: A Biography of the Brothers Grimm.* New York: Holt, Rinehart, and Winston.

Perper, Timothy, and Martha Cornog. 2006. "In the Sound of the Bells: Freedom and Revolution in *Revolutionary Girl Utena.*" *Mechademia* 1: 183–86.

Perrault, Charles. 2001a. "Bluebeard (La barbe bleue)." In *The Great Fairy Tale Tradition: From Straparola and Basile to the Brothers Grimm,* edited by Jack Zipes, 732–35. New York: W.W. Norton.

———. 2001b. "Sleeping Beauty." In *The Great Fairy Tale Tradition: From Straparola and Basile to the Brothers Grimm,* edited by Jack Zipes, 688–95. New York: W.W. Norton.

Pershing, Linda. 2010. "Disney's *Enchanted:* Patriarchal Backlash and Nostalgia in a Fairy Tale Film." With Lisa Gablehouse. In *Fairy Tale Films: Visions of Ambiguity,* edited by Pauline Greenhill and Sidney Eve Matrix, 137–56. Logan: Utah State University Press.

Peters, Renate. 2001. "The Metamorphoses of Judith in Literature and Art: War by Other Means." In *Dressing Up for War: Transformations of Gender and Genre in the Discourse and Literature of War,* edited by Andrew Monnickendam and Aránzazu Usandizaga, 111–26. Amsterdam: Rodopi.

Peterson, D. K. 2008. *"Fractured Fairy Tales* (1959–1964)." In *The Greenwood Encyclopedia of Folktales and Fairy Tales,* edited by Donald Haase, 372–73. Westport, CN: Greenwood.

Petro, Patrice. 1986. "Mass Culture and the Feminine: The 'Place' of Television in Film Studies." *Cinema Journal* 25(3): 5–21.

Pflugfelder, Gregory M. 1999. *Cartographies of Desire: Male–Male Sexuality in Japanese Discourse, 1600–1950.* Berkeley: University of California Press.

Phelps, Ethel Johnston. 1981. *The Maid of the North: Feminist Folk Tales from around the World.* New York: Holt, Rinehart, and Winston.

Pickard, Anna. 2009. *"Dollhouse,* Season One, Episode 2: 'The Target.'" *The Guardian,* May 27. www.guardian.co.uk/culture/tvandradioblog/2009/may/27/whedon-dollhouse-epi sode-two.

Poulos, Christopher N. 2010. "Spirited Accidents: An Autoethnography of Possibility." *Qualitative Inquiry* 16: 49–56.

Pozner, Jennifer L. 2010. *Reality Bites Back: The Troubling Truth about Guilty Pleasure TV.* Berkeley, CA: Seal Press.

Preston, Cathy Lynn. 2004. "Disrupting the Boundaries of Genre and Gender: Postmodernism and the Fairy Tale." In *Fairy Tales and Feminism: New Approaches*, edited by Donald Haase, 197–212. Detroit: Wayne State University Press.

Propp, Vladimir. 1968. *Morphology of the Folktale*. Translated by Laurence Scott. Austin: University of Texas Press.

Purcelli, Marion. 1965. "Pidge: Picture of Health, Wealth, Happiness." *Chicago Tribune*, February 21: SC4.

Radner, Hilary. 2011. *Neo-Feminist Cinema: Girly Films, Chick Flicks and Consumer Culture*. New York: Routledge.

Radner, Joan N. 2009. "Coding." In *Encyclopedia of Women's Folklore and Folklife*, edited by Liz Locke, Theresa A. Vaughan, and Pauline Greenhill, 93–97. Westport, CT: Greenwood.

Radner, Joan N., and Susan S. Lanser. 1993. "Strategies of Coding in Women's Cultures." In *Feminist Messages: Coding in Women's Folk Culture*, edited by Joan Newlon Radner, 1–29. Urbana: University of Illinois Press.

Radway, Janice. 1984. *Reading the Romance: Women, Patriarchy, and Popular Literature*. Chapel Hill: University of North Carolina Press.

Rafferty, Terrence. 2012. "The Better to Entertain You with, My Dear." *New York Times*, March 21. http://www.nytimes.com/2012/03/25/movies/mirror-mirror-grimm-and-hollywood-love-for-fairy-tales.html?_r=0.

Rafter, Nicole. 2006. *Shots in the Mirror: Crime Films and Society*. 2nd ed. New York: Oxford University Press.

———. 2007. "Crime, Film and Criminology: Recent Sex-Crime Movies." *Theoretical Criminology* 11(3): 403–20.

Rankin, Walter. 2007. *Grimm Pictures: Fairy Tale Archetypes in Eight Horror and Suspense Films*. Jefferson, NC: McFarland.

Ransome, Arthur. 1920. *The Soldier and Death: A Russian Folk Tale Told in English*. New York: B. W. Huebsch.

Rauch, Eron, and Maranathan Wilson. 2007. "Bridges of the Unknown: Visual Desires and Small Apocalypses." *Mechademia* 2: 143–54.

Reed-Danahy, Deborah. 2009. "Anthropologists, Education, and Autoethnography." *Reviews in Anthropology* 38: 28–47.

Reider, Noriko T. 2011. "'Hanayo no hime,' or 'Blossom Princess': A Late-Medieval Japanese Stepdaughter Story and Provincial Customs." *Asian Ethnology* 70(1): 59–80.

Rich, Adrienne. 1972. "When We Dead Awaken: Writing as Re-Vision." *College English* 34(1): 18–30.

Richards, Patricia. 1999. "Don't Let a Good Scare Frighten You: Choosing and Using Quality Chillers to Promote Reading." *The Reading Teacher* 52: 833–40.

Roberson, James E., and Nobue Suzuki. 2003. "Introduction." In *Men and Masculinities in Contemporary Japan: Dislocating the Salaryman Doxa*, edited by James E. Roberson and Nobue Suzuki, 1–19. London: Routledge.

Roberts, Warren E. 1958. *The Tale of the Kind and Unkind Girls: AA-TH 480 and Related Tales*. Detroit: Wayne State University Press.

"Rodgers and Hammerstein: Our Shows." n.d. *Rodgers & Hammerstein*. www.rnh.com/show/22/Cinderella#shows-history.

Rodriguez, Carolina Fernandez. 2002. "The Deconstruction of the Male-Rescuer Archetype in Contemporary Feminist Revisions of 'The Sleeping Beauty.'" *Marvels & Tales* 16(1): 51–70.

Roh, Franz. 1925. *Nach-Expressionismus, Magischer Realismus: Probleme der neuesten europäischen Malerei*. Leipzig, Germany: Klinkhardt & Biermann.

Rosenblatt, Louise. 1938. *Literature as Exploration*. New York: Appleton-Century.

Rosenfeld, Gavriel David. 2002. "Why Do We Ask 'What If?' Reflections on the Function of Alternate History." *History and Theory* 41: 90–103.

Rossetti, Christina. 2001. *The Complete Poems*. New York: Penguin Classics.

Rowe, Karen E. 1986. "To Spin a Yarn: The Female Voice in Folklore and Fairy Tale." In *Fairy Tales and Society: Illusion, Allusion, and Paradigm*, edited by Ruth B. Bottigheimer, 53–74. Philadelphia: University of Pennsylvania Press.

———. 1993. "Feminism and Fairy Tales." In *Don't Bet on the Prince: Contemporary Feminist Fairy Tales in North America and England*, edited by Jack Zipes, 209–26. Aldershot, UK: Scholar Press.

Rowling, J. K. 1997. *Harry Potter and the Philosopher's Stone*. London: Bloomsbury.

———. 1998. *Harry Potter and the Chamber of Secrets*. London: Bloomsbury.

———. 1999. *Harry Potter and the Prisoner of Azkaban*. London: Bloomsbury.

———. 2000. *Harry Potter and the Goblet of Fire*. London: Bloomsbury.

———. 2003. *Harry Potter and the Order of the Phoenix*. London: Bloomsbury.

———. 2005. *Harry Potter and the Half-Blood Prince*. London: Bloomsbury.

———. 2007. *Harry Potter and the Deathly Hallows*. London: Bloomsbury.

Ruggiero, Vincenzo. 2002. "Moby Dick and the Crimes of the Economy." *British Journal of Criminology* 42: 96–108.

Russell-Watts, Lynsey. 2010. "Marginalized Males?: Men, Masculinity and Catherine Breillat." *Journal for Cultural Research* 14(1): 71–84.

Ryan, Erin L. 2010. "*Dora the Explorer*: Empowering Preschoolers, Girls, and Latinas." *Journal of Broadcasting & Electronic Media* 54(1): 54–68.

Ryan, Marie-Laure. 2004. *Narrative across Media: The Languages of Storytelling*. Lincoln: University of Nebraska Press.

"Sailor Moon Gets New Anime in Summer 2013." 2012. *Anime News Network*. July 6. www.animenewsnetwork.com/news/2012–07–06/sailor-moon-manga-gets-new-anime-in-summer-2013.

Saito, Chiho. 2001–2004. *Revolutionary Girl Utena*. 5 vols. San Francisco: VIZ Media.

———. 2004. *Revolutionary Girl Utena: The Adolescence of Utena*. San Francisco: VIZ Media.

Sale, Roger. 1979. *Fairy Tales and After: From Snow White to E. B. White*. Cambridge: Harvard University Press.

Saltman, Judith. 2004. "The Ordinary and the Fabulous: Canadian Fantasy Literature for Children." In *Worlds of Wonder: Readings in Canadian Science Fiction and Fantasy Literature*, edited by Jean-François Leroux and Camille R. La Bossière, 189–200. Ottawa: University of Ottawa Press.

Sanger, David E. 1993. "Tokyo Journal; Silent Empress, Irate Nation (and Contrite Press)." *New York Times*, December 24. www.nytimes.com/1993/12/24/world/tokyo-journal-silent-empress-irate-nation-and-contrite-press.html?pagewanted=all&src=pm.

Santomero, Angela. 2010. "Setting the Record Straight: Positive Media Can Teach Kids." *The Huffington Post*, March 15. www.huffingtonpost.com/angela-santomero/setting-the-record-straig_b_475721.html.

Schacker, Jennifer. 2005. *National Dreams: The Remaking of Fairy Tales in Nineteenth-Century England*. Philadelphia: University of Pennsylvania.

Schikel, Richard. 1968. *The Disney Version: The Life, Times, Art, and Commerce of Walt Disney*. New York: Simon and Schuster.

Schneider, Stephen J. 2002. "Thrice Told Tales: 'The Haunting,' from Novel to Film . . . to Film." *Journal of Popular Film and Television* 30(3): 166–76.

Schroeder, Shannin. 2004. *Rediscovering Magical Realism in the Americas*. Westport, CT: Greenwood.

Schudson, Michael. 1984. *Advertising, the Uneasy Persuasion: Its Dubious Impact on American Society.* New York: Basic Books.

———. 2000. "Advertising as Capitalist Realism." *Advertising & Society Review* 1(1). Project MUSE. http://muse.jhu.edu/login?auth=0&type=summary&url=/journals/asr/v001/1.1schudson.html.

Sconce, Jeffrey. 2004. "What If?: Charting Television's New Textual Boundaries." In *Television after TV: Essays on a Medium in Transition,* edited by Lynn Spigel and Jan Olsson, 93–112. Durham: Duke University Press.

Seki, Keigo. 1966. "Types of Japanese Folktales." *Asian Folklore Studies* 25: 1–220.

Sexton, Anne. [1971] 2001. *Transformations.* New York: Mariner Books.

Sharp, Gwen. 2011. "Whitewashing Princess Presto." *Sociological Images.* January 17. http://thesocietypages.org/socimages/2011/01/17/whitewashing-princess-presto.

Sheehan, Anna. 2011. *A Long, Long Sleep.* Somerville, MA: Candlewick Press.

Sherman, Sharon R. 1998. *Documenting Ourselves: Film, Video, and Culture.* Lexington: University of Kentucky Press.

———, ed. 2005. "Special Issue: An Expanded View of Film and Folklore." *Western Folklore* 64(3–4).

Sherman, Sharon R., and Mikel J. Koven, eds. 2007. *Folklore/Cinema: Popular Film as Vernacular Culture.* Logan: Utah State University Press.

Showcase. 2013. "*Lost Girl*: Episodes." www.showcase.ca/lostgirl/lostgirlepisodes.aspx.

Simons, Natasha. 2011. "Reconsidering the Feminism of Joss Whedon." *The Mary Sue: A Guide to Girl Geek Culture.* www.themarysue.com/reconsidering-the-feminism-of-joss-whedon.

Sipe, Lawrence R. 2002. "Talking Back and Taking Over: Young Children's Expressive Engagement during Storybook Read-Alouds." *The Reading Teacher* 55(5): 476–83.

Slater, David H., and Patrick W. Galbraith. 2011. "Re-Narrating Social Class and Masculinity in Neoliberal Japan: An Examination of the Media Coverage of the 'Akihabara Incident' of 2008." *Electronic Journal of Contemporary Japanese Studies.* www.japanesestudies.org.uk/articles/2011/SlaterGalbraith.html.

Smith, Anne Collins. 2010. "Memories Cloaked in Magic: Memory and Identity in *Tin Man.*" In *The Universe of Oz: Essays on Baum's Series and Its Progeny,* edited by Kevin K. Durand and Mary K. Leigh, 158–71. Jefferson, NC: McFarland.

Smith, Cecil. 1965. "Once Again, the Magic of 'Cinderella.'" *Los Angeles Times,* February 21: A1.

Smith, Kevin Paul. 2007. *The Postmodern Fairy Tale: Folkloric Intertexts in Contemporary Fiction.* New York: Palgrave Macmillan.

Smith, L. J. 1991a. *Vampire Diaries: The Awakening.* New York: HarperPaperbacks.

———. 1991b. *Vampire Diaries: The Fury.* New York: HarperPaperbacks.

———. 1991c. *Vampire Diaries: The Struggle.* New York: HarperPaperbacks.

———. 1992. *Vampire Diaries: Dark Reunion.* New York: HarperPaperbacks.

———. 2009. *Vampire Diaries: The Return: Nightfall.* New York: HarperPaperbacks.

———. 2010. *Vampire Diaries: The Return: Shadow Souls.* New York: HarperPaperbacks.

———. 2011a. *Vampire Diaries: Hunters: Phantom.* New York: HarperPaperbacks.

———. 2011b. *Vampire Diaries: The Return: Midnight.* New York: HarperPaperbacks.

———. 2012. *Vampire Diaries: Hunters: Moonsong.* New York: HarperPaperbacks.

Snowden, Kim. 2010. "Fairy Tale Film in the Classroom: Feminist Cultural Pedagogy, Angela Carter, and Neil Jordan's *The Company of Wolves.*" In *Fairy Tale Films: Visions of Ambiguity,* edited by Pauline Greenhill and Sidney Eve Matrix, 157–77. Logan: Utah State University.

Spigel, Lynn. 2004. "Introduction." In *Television after TV: Essays on a Medium in Transition,* edited by Lynn Spigel and Jan Olsson, 1–34. Durham: Duke University Press.

———. 2005. "Our TV Heritage: Television, the Archive, and the Reasons for Preservation." In *A Companion to Television,* edited by Janet Wasko, 67–102. Malden, MA: Blackwell Publishing.

St. Louis, Renee, and Miriam Riggs. 2010. "'A Painful, Bleeding Sleep': Sleeping Beauty in the Dollhouse." *Slayage: The Journal of the Whedon Studies Association* 8(2–3): 57–79.

Stailey, Michael. 2012. "Grimm: Season One." *Television without Pity DVD Verdict.* August 13. www.dvdverdict.com/reviews/grimmseason1bluray.php.

Statistics Bureau, Japan. 2013. "Chapter 16 Education and Culture." *Statistical Handbook of Japan 2013.* www.stat.go.jp/english/data/handbook/c0117.htm#c16.

Stefánsson, Halldór. 1998. "Media Stories of Bliss and Mixed Blessing." In *The World of Japanese Popular Culture,* edited by D. P. Martinez, 155–66. Cambridge: Cambridge University Press.

Stein, Louisa Ellen. 2011. "'Word of Mouth on Steroids': Hailing the Millennial Media Fan." In *Flow TV: Television in the Age of Media Convergence,* edited by Michael Kackman, Marnie Binfield, Matthew Thomas, Allison Perlman, and Bryan Sebok, 128–43. New York: Routledge.

Steinbeck, John. 1962. "Banquet Speech." *Nobelprize.org.* www.nobelprize.org/nobel_prizes/literature/laureates/1962/steinbeck-speech_en.html.

Steinle, Pam. 2001. "The Bullwinkle Show." In *The Guide to United States Popular Culture,* edited by Ray B. Browne and Pat Browne, 122. Bowling Green: Bowling Green State University Popular Press.

Stephens, John. 1992. *Language and Ideology in Children's Fiction.* New York: Longman.

———. 2000. "Myth/Mythology and Fairy Tales." In *The Oxford Companion to Fairy Tales,* edited by Jack Zipes, 330–34. New York: Oxford University Press.

———. 2011a. "Between Imagined Signs and Social Realities: Representing Others in Children's Fantasy and Folktale." *International Research in Children's Literature* 4(2): v–viii.

———. 2011b. "Schemas and Scripts: Cognitive Instruments and the Representation of Cultural Diversity in Children's Literature." In *Contemporary Children's Literature and Film: Engaging with Theory,* edited by Kerry Mallan and Clare Bradford, 12–35. London: Palgrave Macmillan.

Stephens, John, and Robyn McCallum. 1998. *Retelling Stories, Framing Culture: Traditional Story and Metanarratives in Children's Literature.* New York: Garland.

———. 2002. "Utopia, Dystopia, and Cultural Controversy in *Ever After* and *The Grimm Brothers' Snow White.*" *Marvels & Tales* 16(2): 201–13.

Stewart, Susan. 1991. *Crimes of Writing: Problems in the Containment of Representation.* New York: Oxford University Press.

———. 2007. "And They All Read Happily Ever After. Review of *Super Why!*" *New York Times,* September 10. www.nytimes.com/2007/09/10/arts/television/10supe.html.

Stone, Kay. 1975. "Things Walt Disney Never Told Us." *Journal of American Folklore* 88(347): 42–50.

———. 1985. "The Misuses of Enchantment: Controversies on the Significance of Fairy Tales." In *Women's Folklore, Women's Culture,* edited by Rosan A. Jordan and Susan J. Kalčik, 125–45. Philadelphia: University of Pennsylvania Press.

———. 1993. "Burning Brightly: New Light from an Old Tale." In *Feminist Messages: Coding in Women's Folk Culture,* edited by Joan Newlon Radner, 289–305. Urbana: University of Illinois Press.

———. 2004. "Fire and Water: A Journey into the Heart of a Story." In *Fairy Tales and Feminism: New Approaches,* edited by Donald Haase, 113–28. Detroit: Wayne State University Press.

Strong, Laura. 2001. "Baba Yaga's Hut: Initiatory Entrance to the Underworld." *Mythic Arts*. www.mythicarts.com/writing/Baba_Yaga.html.

Stryker, Susan. 2006. "(De)Subjugated Knowledges." In *The Transgender Studies Reader,* edited by Susan Stryker and Stephen Whittle, 1–17. New York: Routledge.

"Stuart Damon." N.d. *Wikipedia.* http://en.wikipedia.org/wiki/Stuart_Damon.

Stukator, Angela. 1997. "'Soft Males,' 'Flying Boys,' and 'White Knights': New Masculinity in *The Fisher King," Literature Film Quarterly* 25(3): 214–21.

Sugiyama, Michelle Scalise. 2004. "Predation, Narration, and Adaptation: 'Little Red Riding Hood' Revisited." *Interdisciplinary Literary Studies: A Journal of Criticism and Theory* 5(2): 110–29.

"*Super Why!*" 2007–2012. *Wikipedia.* http://en.wikipedia.org/wiki/Super_Why!

Sutton-Smith, Brian. 1981. *The Folkstories of Children.* Philadelphia: University of Pennsylvania Press.

Tabuchi, Hiroko. 2009. "When Consumers Cut Back: An Object Lesson from Japan." *New York Times,* February 21. www.nytimes.com/1993/12/24/world/tokyo-journal-silent-empress-irate-nation-and-contrite-press.html.

Taga, Futoshi. 2005. "Rethinking Japanese Masculinities: Recent Research Trends." In *Genders, Transgenders and Sexualities in Japan,* edited by Mark McLelland and Romit Dasgupta, 153–67. London: Routledge.

Takeuchi, Naoko. 1992. "Act 8: Sailor V." *Bishoujo Senshi Sailor Moon Volume 2.* Tokyo: Kodansha.

Talmadge, Eric. 2011. "Japanese Tabloids Make Hay of Royal Family Foibles." *CBS Newsworld.* February 4. www.cbsnews.com/2100-501712_162-7316856.html.

Tatar, Maria. 1978. *Spellbound: Studies on Mesmerism and Literature.* Princeton: Princeton University Press.

———, ed. 1999. *The Classic Fairy Tales.* New York: Norton.

———, ed. 2002. *The Annotated Classic Fairy Tales.* New York: Norton.

———. 2003. *The Hard Facts of the Grimms' Fairy Tales.* 2nd ed. Princeton: Princeton University Press.

———. 2004. *Secrets beyond the Door: The Story of Bluebeard and His Wives.* Princeton: Princeton University Press.

———. 2012. "Cinderfellas: The Long Lost Fairytales." *New Yorker,* March 16. www.newyorker.com/online/blogs/books/2012/03/long-lost-fairy-tales.html.

Taub, Lora. 2002. "Class." In *Television Studies,* edited by Toby Miller, 87–90. London: British Film Institute.

Taubin, Amy. 2010. "Blood Sisters." *Film Comment,* March–April: 41–44.

Taylor, Edgar, trans. 1985. *Grimms' Fairy Tales,* by Wilhelm and Jacob Grimm. Harmondsworth: Puffin Books.

Taylor, Victor E. and Charles E. Winquist, eds. 2001. *The Encyclopedia of Postmodernism.* New York: Routledge.

Tennyson, Lord Alfred. 1856–1885. *The Idylls of the King.* Great Britain: Self-published.

Thomson, David. 2010. "Murder in the North." *The New York Review of Books* 57(1): 32–34.

Thompson, Stith. [1946] 1977. *The Folktale.* Berkeley: University of California Press.

Thorn, Matt. 2001. "Shôjo Manga—Something for the Girls." *The Japan Quarterly* 48(3). www.matt-thorn.com/shoujo_manga/japan_quarterly/index.php.

Tibbetts, John C. 2001. "Mary Pickford and the American 'Growing Girl.'" *Journal of Popular Film and Television* 29(2): 50–62.

Tiffin, Jessica. 2009. *Marvelous Geometry: Narrative and Metafiction in Modern Fairy Tale.* Detroit: Wayne State University Press.

Todd, Drew. 2006. "The History of Crime Films." In *Shots in the Mirror: Crime Films and Society,* edited by Nicole Rafter, 21–59. 2nd ed. New York: Oxford.

Toelken, Barre. 1996. *The Dynamics of Folklore.* Rev ed. Logan: Utah State University Press.

Toku, Masami. 2007. "Shoujo Manga! Girls' Comics! A Mirror of Girls' Dreams." *Mechademia* 2: 19–32.

Tolkien, J. R. R. 1954a. *The Fellowship of the Ring.* London: George Allen and Unwin.

———. 1954b. *The Two Towers.* London: George Allen and Unwin.

———. 1955. *The Return of the King.* London: George Allen and Unwin.

———. 1964. "On Fairy-Stories." In *Tree and Leaf,* by Tolkien, 9–73. London: George Allen and Unwin.

Tosenberger, Catherine. 2008a. "'The Epic Love Story of Sam and Dean': Supernatural, Queer Readings, and the Romance of Incestuous Fan Fiction." *Transformative Works and Cultures* 1. http://journal.transformativeworks.org/index.php/twc/article/view /30/36.

———. 2008b. "Homosexuality at the Online Hogwarts: Harry Potter Online Fan Fiction." *Children's Literature* 36(1): 185–207.

———. 2010. "'Kinda Like the Folklore of Its Day': *Supernatural,* Fairy Tales, and Ostension." *Transformative Works and Culture.* http://journal.transformativeworks.org/index. php/twc/article/view/174.

Trites, Roberta Seelinger. 2012. "Growth in Adolescent Literature: Metaphors, Scripts, and Cognitive Narratology." *International Research in Children's Literature* 5(1): 64–80.

Tropiano, Stephen. 2009. "Playing It Straight: Reality Dating Shows and the Construction of Heterosexuality." *Journal of Popular Film and Culture* 37(2): 60–69.

Tsukioka, Izumi, and John Stephens. 2003. "Reading Development across Linked Stories: Anna Fienberg's Tashi Series and the Magnificent Nose and Other Marvels." *The Lion and the Unicorn* 27(2): 185–98.

Tucker, Elizabeth. 1980. "Concepts of Space in Children's Narratives." In *Folklore on Two Continents: Essays in Honor of Linda Dégh,* edited by Nikolai Burlakoff and Carl Lindahl, 19–25. Bloomington, IN: Trickster Press.

Turner Classic Movies. 2013. "Tales from the Brothers Grimm (1990)." www.tcmuk.tv/ movie_database_results.php?action=title&id=477311.

Turner, Kay. 2012. "Playing with Fire: Transgression as Truth in Grimms' 'Frau Trude.'" In *Transgressive Tales: Queering the Grimms,* edited by Kay Turner and Pauline Greenhill, 245–74. Detroit: Wayne State University Press.

Turner, Kay, and Pauline Greenhill, eds. 2012. *Transgressive Tales: Queering the Grimms.* Detroit: Wayne State University Press.

Undercover Blonde. 2007. "Shirley Polykoff, the Patron Saint of Blonde Marketing." www. undercoverblonde.com/2007/11/shirley-polykoff-patron-saint-of-blonde.html.

US Department of Education. 2011. "Ready to Learn Television." *ED.gov.* www2.ed.gov/ programs/rtltv.

"Utena." N.d. *The Manga Store.* http://buyanime.homestead.com/Utena.html.

Uther, Hans-Jörg. 2004. *The Types of International Folktales: A Classification and Bibliography.* Helsinki: Academia Scientiarum Fennica.

Utter solitude. 2012. *Once Upon a Time* Wiki. February 16. http://onceuponatime.wikia. com/wiki/User_blog:Totalsolitude/Favourite_Characters%3F.

Valdivia, Angharad. 2002. "Targeting Minorities (Rosie Perez)." In *Television Studies,* edited by Toby Miller, 127–30. London: British Film Institute.

Valverde, Mariana. 2006. *Law and Order: Images, Meanings, Myths.* New Brunswick: Rutgers University Press.

Vaz da Silva, Francisco. 2002. *Metamorphosis: The Dynamics of Symbolism in European Fairy Tales.* New York: Peter Lang.

———. 2008. "Transformation." In *The Greenwood Encyclopedia of Folktales and Fairy Tales,* edited by Donald Haase, 981–86. Westport, CN: Greenwood.

Velay-Vallantin, Catherine. 1998. "From 'Little Red Riding Hood' to the 'Beast of Gévaudan': The Tale in the Long Term Continuum." Translated by Binita Mehta. In *Telling Tales: Medieval Narratives and the Folk Tradition,* edited by Francesca Canadé Sautman, Diana Conchado, and Giuseppe Carlo di Scipio, 269–95. New York: St. Martin's Press.

Verdier, Yvonne. 1980. "Le Petit Chaperon Rouge dans la tradition orale." *Le Debat* 3: 31–56.

Vinci, Tony M. 2011. "'Not *an* Apocalypse, *the* Apocalypse': Existential Proletarisation and the Possibility of Soul in Joss Whedon's *Dollhouse." Science Fiction Film and Television* 4(2): 225–48.

Virtanen, Leea. 1986. "Modern Folklore: Problems of Comparative Research." *Journal of Folklore Research* 23(2–3): 221–32.

Vogt, Tiffany. 2011. "Get to Know the Enchanting Cast of ABC's *Once Upon a Time." The TV Addict.com.* October 23. www.thetvaddict.com/2011/10/23/once-upon-a-time-cast -interviews/#more-28304.

Von Franz, Marie-Louise. [1972] 1982. "The Beautiful Wassilissa." In *Cinderella: A Folklore Casebook,* edited by Alan Dundes, 200–218. New York: Garland.

Ware, Jim. 2003. *God of the Fairy Tale.* Colorado Springs, CO: WaterBrook Press.

Warner, Marina. 1994. *From the Beast to the Blonde: On Fairy Tales and Their Tellers.* London: Chatto & Windus.

Waterman, Patricia Panyity. 1987. *A Tale-Type Index of Australian Aboriginal Oral Narratives.* Helsinki: Suomalainen Tiedeakatemia.

Weber, Eugen. 1981. "Fairies and Hard Facts: The Reality of Folktales." *Journal of the History of Ideas* 42(1): 93–113.

Wells, Paul. 2003. "'Smarter Than the Average Art Form': Animation in the Television Era." In *Prime Time Animation: Television Animation and American Culture,* edited by Carol A. Stabile and Mark Harrison, 15–32. New York: Routledge.

Wells, Rosemary. 1991. "The Making of an Icon: The Tooth Fairy in North American Folklore and Popular Culture." In *The Good People: New Fairylore Essays,* edited by Peter Narváez, 426–53. Lexington: University Press of Kentucky.

Wheatley, Catherine. 2010. "Behind the Door." *Sight and Sound: The International Film Magazine,* August 10: 38–42.

White, Mimi. 1985. "Television Genres: Intertextuality." *Journal of Film and Video* 37(3): 41–47.

White, Rob. 2008. *Crimes against Nature: Environmental Criminology and Ecological Justice.* Portland, OR: Willan Publishing.

White, T. H. 1938. *The Sword in the Stone.* Glasgow, UK: William Collins, Sons.

———. 1958. *The Once and Future King.* Glasgow, UK: William Collins, Sons.

Wilcox, Rhonda V. 1999. "There Never Will Be a 'Very Special' *Buffy: Buffy* and the Monsters of Teen Life." *Journal of Popular Film and Television* 27(2): 16–23.

Willard, Tracy. 2002. "Tales at the Borders: Fairy Tales and Maternal Cannibalism." *Reconstruction.* http://reconstruction.eserver.org/022/cannibal/ cannibalismintro.html.

Williams, Christy. 2010. "The Shoe Still Fits: *Ever After* and the Pursuit of a Feminist Cinderella." In *Fairy Tale Films: Visions of Ambiguity,* edited by Pauline Greenhill and Sidney Eve Matrix, 99–115. Logan: Utah State University Press.

Williams, Clover, and Jean R. Freedman. 1995. "Shakespeare's Step-Sisters: Romance Novels and the Community of Women." In *Folklore, Literature, and Cultural Theory: Collected Essays,* edited by Cathy Lynn Preston, 135–68. New York: Garland.

Williams, Raymond. 1974. *TeleVision: Technology and Cultural Form.* London: Fontana/ Collins.

———. [1980] 1997. *Problems in Materialism and Culture.* London: Verso.

———. 2003. *Television: Technology and Cultural Form.* London: Taylor & Francis.

Williams, Raymond Leslie. 2007. *The Columbia Guide to the Latin American Novel Since 1945*. New York: Columbia University Press.

Willoquet-Maricondi, Paula, ed. 2010. *Framing the World: Explorations in Ecocriticism and Film*. Charlottesville: University of Virginia Press.

Wilson, William A. 2006. *The Marrow of Human Experience: Essays on Folklore*. Edited by Jill Terry Rudy. Logan: Utah State University Press.

Winters, Ben. 2010. "The Non-Diegetic Fallacy: Film, Music, and Narrative Space." *Music and Letters* 91(2): 224–44.

Wloszczyna, Susan. 2003. "Disney Princesses Wear Merchandising Crown." *USA Today*, September 17.

Wolf, Werner. 2011. "(Inter)Mediality and the Study of Literature." *CLCWeb: Comparative Literature and Culture* 13(3): Article 2. http://docs.lib.purdue.edu/clcweb/vol13/iss3/2.

Wolff, Patricia Rae. [1995] 2000. *The Toll Bridge Troll*. Singapore: First Voyager Books.

Wood, Graham. 2009. "Ten Minutes and Fifty (Two) Years Ago: The Three TV Versions of Rodgers and Hammerstein's *Cinderella*." *Studies in Musical Theater* 3(1): 109–16.

Wood, Juliette. 2006. "Filming Fairies: Popular Film, Audience Response and Meaning in Contemporary Fairy Lore." *Folklore* 117(3): 279–96.

World Factbook. 2013. "Field Listing: Television Broadcast Stations." www.cia.gov/library/publications/the-world-factbook/fields/2015.html

Worsley, Thomas Cuthbert. 1970. *Television: The Ephemeral Art*. London: Ross.

Wotapka, Dawn. 2010a. "Extreme Stories." *WSJ.com*. April 6. http://online.wsj.com/article/SB10001424052702304871704575160312975375930.html.

———. 2010b. "Realty Check: 'Extreme Makeover' Downsizes Its Dream Homes." *WSJ.com*. April 5. http://online.wsj.com/article/SB10001424052702304017404575165840903285032.html.

Wührl, Paul-Wolfgang. 2003. *Das deutsche Kunstmärchen: Geschichte, Botschaft und Erzählstrukturen*. Baltmannsweiler, Germany: Schneider.

Yolen, Jane. 1982. "America's Cinderella." In *Cinderella, a Folklore Casebook,* edited by Alan Dundes, 294–306. New York: Garland.

———. 1992. *Briar Rose*. New York: Tor Books.

Yoshimi, Shunya. 2001. "Japan: America in Japan/Japan in Disneyfication: The Disney Image and the Transformation of 'America' in Contemporary Japan." In *Dazzled by Disney?: The Global Disney Audiences Project*, edited by Janet Wasko, Mark Phillips, and Eileen R. Meehan, 160–81. London: Leicester University Press.

Young, Allison. 2008. "Culture, Critical Criminology and the Imagination of Crime." In *The Critical Criminology Companion*, edited by Thalia Anthony and Chris Cunneen, 18–29. Sydney, Australia: Hawkins Press.

———. 2010. *The Scene of Violence*. New York: Routledge-Cavendish.

Young, John. 2012. "Box Office Report: 'Snow White and the Huntsman' Is Victorious with 56.3 mil; 'The Avengers' Becomes Third Biggest Movie Ever." *Entertainment Weekly Inside Movies*. June 3. http://insidemovies.ew.com/2012/06/03/box-office-report-snow-white-huntsman.

Young, Katharine Galloway. 1987. *Taleworlds and Storyrealms: The Phenomenology of Narrative*. Dordrecht, The Netherlands: Martinus Nijhoff.

———. 1993. "Still Life with Corpse: Management of the Grotesque Body in Medicine." In *Bodylore*, edited by Katharine Young, 111–33. Knoxville: University of Tennessee.

Zahed, Ramin. 2012. "Alphanim's 'Calimero' to Hatch on Italy's RAI." *Animation Magazine*. June 6. www.animationmagazine.net/tv/alphanims-calimero-to-hatch-on-italys-rai.

Zamora, Lois P., and Wendy B. Faris. 1995. *Magical Realism: Theory, History, Community*. Durham: Duke University Press.

Zielenziger, Michael. 2006. *Shutting Out the Sun: How Japan Created Its Own Lost Generation.* New York: Vintage Books.

Zipes, Jack. [1983a] 1991. *Fairy Tales and the Art of Subversion: The Classical Genre for Children and the Process of Civilization.* New York: Wildman.

———, ed. 1983b. *The Trials and Tribulations of Little Red Riding Hood: Versions of the Tale in Sociocultural Perspective.* South Hadley, MA: J.F. Bergin Publishers.

———. 1984. "Folklore Research and Western Marxism: A Critical Replay." *Journal of American Folklore* 97(385): 329–37.

———, ed. 1987. *The Complete Fairy Tales of the Brothers Grimm.* New York: Bantam Books.

———, ed. [1988] 2002. *The Brothers Grimm: From Enchanted Forests to the Modern World.* New York: Routledge.

———. 1992. *Spells of Enchantment: The Wondrous Fairy Tales of Western Culture.* New York: Penguin.

———. 1994. *Fairy Tale as Myth: Myth as Fairy Tale.* Lexington: University Press of Kentucky.

———. 1995. "Breaking the Disney Spell." In *From Mouse to Mermaid: The Politics of Film, Gender, and Culture,* edited by Elizabeth Bell, Lynda Haas, and Laura Sells, 21–42. Bloomington: Indiana University Press.

———. 1997. *Happily Ever After: Fairy Tales, Children, and the Culture Industry.* New York: Routledge.

———. 2000. "Introduction: Towards a Definition of the Literary Fairy Tale." In *The Oxford Companion to Fairy Tales: The Western Fairy Tale Tradition from Medieval to Modern,* edited by Jack Zipes, xv–xxxii. New York: Oxford.

———. 2002a. *Breaking the Magic Spell: Radical Theories of Folk and Fairy Tales.* Rev. ed. Lexington: University Press of Kentucky.

———, ed. 2002b. *The Complete Fairy Tales of the Brothers Grimm.* 3rd ed. New York: Bantam.

———. 2006a. *Fairy Tales and the Art of Subversion.* 2nd ed. New York: Routledge.

———. 2006b. *Why Fairy Tales Stick: The Evolution and Relevance of a Genre.* New York: Routledge.

———. 2008a. "What Makes a Repulsive Frog So Appealing: Memetics and Fairy Tales." *Journal of Folklore Research* 45(2): 109–43.

———. 2008b. "Review of *Pan's Labyrinth.*" *Journal of American Folklore* 121(480): 236–40.

———. 2009. *Relentless Progress: The Reconfiguration of Children's Literature, Fairy Tales, and Storytelling.* New York: Routledge.

———. 2011. *The Enchanted Screen: The Unknown History of Fairy-Tale Films.* New York: Routledge.

———. 2012. *The Irresistible Fairy Tale: The Cultural and Social History of a Genre.* Princeton: Princeton University Press.

Zipes, Jack, Pauline Greenhill, and Kendra Magnus-Johnston, eds. forthcoming. *Fairy Tale Films beyond Disney: International Perspectives.* New York: Routledge.

Žižek, Slavoj. 1989. *The Sublime Object of Ideology.* London: Verso.

———. 2009. *First as Tragedy, Then as Farce.* London: Verso

CONTRIBUTORS

CRISTINA BACCHILEGA teaches fairy tales and adaptations, folklore and literature, and cultural studies at the University of Hawai'i at Mānoa. Co-editor of Marvels & Tales, she authored *Legendary Hawai'i and the Politics of Place: Tradition, Translation, and Tourism* (2007); and *Fairy Tales Transformed? Twenty-First-Century Adaptations and the Politics of Wonder* (2013).

CHRISTIE BARBER is a lecturer in Japanese studies at Macquarie University, Sydney, Australia. Her research focuses on representations of masculinity in Japanese popular media.

SHULI BARZILAI, Professor of English at the Hebrew University of Jerusalem, and author of *Lacan and the Matter of Origins* (1999) and *Tales of Bluebeard and His Wives from Late Antiquity to Postmodern Times* (2009) has articles in *Critique, Marvels & Tales, Signs,* and *Word & Image,* among other journals.

CHRISTA BAXTER earned her B.A. and M.A. in English at Brigham Young University. Her work focuses on fairy-tale scholarship, new media, and feminist studies.

IAN BRODIE is Associate Professor of Folklore at Cape Breton University. His research interests focus on the intersection of folk and popular culture. He is currently the editor of Contemporary Legend. His first book, *A Vulgar Art: A New Approach to Stand-Up Comedy,* will be published in 2014.

PAULINE GREENHILL is Professor of Women's and Gender Studies at the University of Winnipeg, Canada. Her recent books include *Make the Night Hideous: Four English-Canadian Charivaris* (2010); *Fairy Tale Films: Visions of*

Ambiguity (Sidney Eve Matrix, co-editor, 2010) and *Transgressive Tales: Queering the Grimms* (Kay Turner, co-editor, 2012).

REBECCA HAY, a graduate of Brigham Young University, earned her M.A. in American literature, focusing on nostalgia theory in contemporary American poetry. Her interests include fairy tale, folklore, trauma theory, and Western literature. In her spare time, Becca enjoys teaching fitness classes, swimming, and lying in the sun.

JEANA JORGENSEN completed her PhD at Indiana University. Her research focuses on gender and sexuality in fairy tales, feminist and queer theories, the body, and dance. She currently teaches at Butler University.

STEVEN KOHM is Associate Professor and Chair of Criminal Justice at the University of Winnipeg, Canada. His recent research on crime in popular culture appears in *Theoretical Criminology*, *Crime Media Culture*, and *Canadian Journal of Criminology and Criminal Justice*. He is editor of *The Annual Review of Interdisciplinary Justice Research*.

LINDA J. LEE holds advanced degrees in folklore from the University of California, Berkeley, and the University of Pennsylvania. She researches transformations of folk narratives in popular culture, and teaches humanities and folklore at Philadelphia-area universities. She co-curated "Grimms' Anatomy: Magic and Medicine 1812-2012" for the Mütter Museum, Philadelphia.

KIRSTIAN LEZUBSKI received her MA in Cultural Studies from the University of Winnipeg, where she focused her research in young peoples' texts and cultures. Her current research interests include youth culture and the internet and the intersecting representations of gender and adolescence in Japanese popular media.

KENDRA MAGNUS-JOHNSTON is a Ph.D. student at the University of Manitoba, and teaching/research assistant at the University of Winnipeg, where she completed her B.A. (Rhetoric and Communications) and M.A. (Cultural Studies). She has published in *Journal of Folklore Research*, *Children's Literature Quarterly*, *Marvels & Tales*, and *Young Scholars in Writing*.

JODI MCDAVID is a research administrator and instructor at Cape Breton University. She completed her Ph.D. in Folklore at Memorial University, and teaches and researches both in Folklore and in Gender and Women's Studies. She has published articles in *Culture & Tradition* and *Ethnologies*.

EMMA NELSON received an MA in American literature from Brigham Young University, where she focused on folklore and cultural studies, including Native American culture, folklore in literature, fairy tales, and the Western. Her publications can also be found in *The Sophie Journal*, *Brevity*, and *Gruff Variations*.

JOHN RIEDER is Professor of English at the University of Hawai'i at Mānoa and editor of *Extrapolation*. His publications include *Colonialism and the Emergence of Science Fiction* (2008), *Wordsworth's Counterrevolutionary Turn* (1997), and essays on genre theory, fairy-tale film, and other topics.

JILL TERRY RUDY, Associate Professor of English, Brigham Young University, researches the history of American folklore scholarship, fairy tale and folk narratives, family folklore, and foodways. She has published in *College English*, *Journal of American Folklore*, and other folklore journals. She edited *The Marrow of Human Experience: Essays on Folklore* by William A. Wilson.

PATRICIA SAWIN, Associate Professor and Coordinator of the Folklore Program, Department of American Studies, University of North Carolina, Chapel Hill, researches narrative performance of gender identity and the politics of recycling others' speech. She has written *Listening for a Life: A Dialogic Ethnography of Bessie Eldreth through Her Songs and Stories* (2004).

CLAUDIA SCHWABE, PhD in German studies (University of Florida) is Assistant Professor of German at Utah State University. She is currently working on an edited collection titled *New Approaches to Teaching Folk and Fairy Tales* (University Press of Colorado) and a book on romantic literary fairy tales.

DON TRESCA is an independent scholar with an M.A. in English from California State University, Sacramento. He has published on the works of Sylvia Plath and Joss Whedon, among others.

ASHLEY WALTON has a master's degree in English with an emphasis in contemporary American literature. She is currently the managing editor at a marketing firm in Salt Lake City, and she runs the pop culture blog Geek Appetite.

BRITTANY WARMAN is a PhD Student in English and folklore at The Ohio State University. Her work focuses on the intersection of folklore and literature, particularly fairy-tale retellings, and she is currently beginning the process of putting together her dissertation on fairy tales and the Gothic aesthetic.

KRISTIANA WILLSEY has a Ph.D. in folklore from Indiana University. She is a Lecturer at Otis College of Art and Design. Her research interests include narrative, performance, linguistic anthropology, children's folklore, and the relationship between orality, literacy, and new media.

ANDREA WRIGHT is a senior lecturer in Film Studies at Edge Hill University. Fantasy/fairy-tale cinema (particularly aesthetics, costume, set design, and location) and New Zealand cinema are central to her current research. Other research interests include film marketing and merchandising in the post-classical era and British cinema and television.

INDEX

Note: In this index, several different topics will have the same name. A name without quotation marks—like Little Red Riding Hood—is a character. A name inside quotation marks is a tale, story, or TV episode. A name in italics is a film or TV show. To avoid further confusion after that point, items have their original air or publication date and author, director, or owning corporation.